Praise for *The Emperor's Blades*

"Come for the intrigue, assassination, death priests, black-ops bird riders, and giant poisonous hive-lizards. Stay for Staveley's characters, his language, and his way-cool fantasy Zen."
—Max Gladstone, author of *Three Parts Dead*

"A richly layered world that melds together elements of ancient magic, religion, political intrigue, and battles large and small. The suspense is relentless and the moral compromises the protagonists confront, often accompanied by violence, are wrenching." —*Shelf Awareness*

"Takes a story of family, loss, conspiracy, and revenge and gives it new legs. It's epic fantasy with a sharp, jagged edge to it, a modern sensibility, prose as tight as the leather wrapped around a sword's hilt, and characters that you can relate to and give a damn about."
—R. S. Belcher, author of *The Six-Gun Tarot*

"Filled to the brim with history, lore, and potential . . . mixed in with a nice dose of Lovecraftian weirdness." —*io9*

"An exciting first salvo involving Machiavellian politics on multiple levels, an intriguing world of magic, and three protagonists whose personal journeys will keep the reader impatiently waiting for the next book!"
—Richard A. Knaak, *New York Times* bestselling author for *The Legend of Huma*

"This book kept me on the edge of my seat. This book gave me actual adrenaline rushes. This book was unputdownable. This book blew my fucking mind. Favorite fantasy book of the year . . . maybe even ever."
—*Litchick's Hit List*

THE EMPEROR'S BLADES

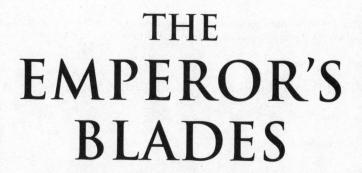

Chronicle of the Unhewn Throne, Book I

BRIAN STAVELEY

A TOM DOHERTY ASSOCIATES BOOK
NEW YORK

THE EMPEROR'S BLADES

Copyright © 2013 by Brian Staveley

Map by Isaac Stewart

A Tor Book
Published by Tom Doherty Associates, LLC
175 Fifth Avenue
New York, NY 10010

www.tor-forge.com

Tor® is a registered trademark of Tom Doherty Associates, LLC.

The Library of Congress has cataloged the hardcover edition as follows:

Staveley, Brian.
    The Emperor's Blades / Brian Staveley.—First Edition.
        p. cm.—(Chronicle of the Unhewn Throne ; Book 1)
    "A Tom Doherty Associates Book."
    ISBN 978-0-7653-3640-8 (hardcover)
    ISBN 978-1-4668-2843-8 (e-book)
    1. Fantasy fiction.   I. Title.
PS3619.T3856E47 2014
813'.6—dc23

                                          2013025451

ISBN 978-0-7653-3643-9 (trade paperback)

Tor books may be purchased for educational, business, or promotional use. For information on bulk purchases, please contact Macmillan Corporate and Premium Sales Department at 1-800-221-7945, extension 5442, or write specialmarkets@macmillan.com.

First Edition: January 2014
First Trade Paperback Edition: August 2014

Printed in the United States of America

0 9 8 7 6 5

For my parents, who read me stories

ACKNOWLEDGMENTS

I'm sure that some writers write books all by themselves, but I needed a lot of help. The following people read chapters, brainstormed names, ridiculed my bad ideas, encouraged my good ones, demanded cooler fights, lobbied for more dastardly villains, insisted on scarier monsters, complained about inaccuracies ranging from the military to the cartographical, made paintings of the Bone Mountains, and generally heckled and herded me into doing better. Writing without them would have been a bleak and lonely process: Suzanne Baker, Oliver Snider, Tom Leith, Patrick Noyes, Colin Woods, John Muckle, Leda Eizenberg, Heather Buckels, Kyle Weaver, Kenyon Weaver, Brook Detterman, Sarah Parkinson, Becca Heymann, Katherine Pattillo, Matt Holmes, John Norton, Mark Fidler, Andrika Donovan, Shelia Staveley, Skip Staveley, Kristin Nelson, Sara Megibow, Anita Mumm, Ryan Derby, Morgan Faust, Adrian Van Young, Wes Williams, Jean Klingler, Amanda Jones, Sharon Krauss, Susan Weaver, Bella Pagan, Robert Hardage, Bill Lewis.

Special thanks to my agent, Hannah Bowman, and my editor, Marco Palmieri, for having faith in the book, a keen eye for detail, and for reintroducing me to characters and places I thought I already knew.

Gavin Baker, an indefatigable reader and friend, has read every last word of every last draft. His critical insights have been invaluable, but even more important has been his unshakable belief that I could write the book, that I would write the book, and that it would be good. I borrowed from his storehouse of conviction more often than he knows.

Finally, Johanna Staveley. The Csestriim have no words for gratitude or love, but there is a phrase common in their writings: *ix alza—crucial to, of absolute necessity.* It captures perfectly Jo's relationship to both this book and the author. Without her, I would be living under a rock somewhere, lonely without knowing it, baffled by an unapprehended absence, eating my own toenails, probably still rewriting the prologue.

THE
EMPEROR'S
BLADES

PROLOGUE

Rot. It was the rot, Tan'is reflected as he stared down into his daughter's eyes, that had taken his child.

Screams and imprecations, pleading and sobbing shivered the air as the long lines of prisoners filled the valley. The scent of blood and urine thickened in the noon heat. Tan'is ignored it all, focusing instead on the face of this daughter of his who knelt, clutching at his knees. Faith was a woman grown now, thirty years and a month. At a casual glance she might have passed as healthy—bright gray eyes, lean shoulders, strong limbs—but the Csestriim no longer bore healthy children, not for centuries.

"Father," the woman begged, tears streaming down her cheeks.

Those tears, too—a symptom of the rot.

There were other words for it, of course. The children, in their ignorance or innocence, called the affliction *age,* but in this, as in so much else, they erred. Age was not decrepitude. Tan'is himself was old, hundreds of years old, and yet his sinews remained strong, his mind nimble—if needed, he could run all day, all night, and the better part of the next day. Most of the Csestriim were older still, thousands upon thousands of years, and yet they continued to walk the earth, those who had not fallen in the long wars with the Nevariim. No; time passed, stars swung through their silent arcs, seasons gave way one to the next, and yet none of these, in and of itself, brought harm. It was not age but rot that gnawed at the children, consuming their bowels and brains, sapping strength, eroding what meager intelligence they once possessed. Rot, and then death.

"Father," Faith pleaded, unable to proceed past that single word.

"Daughter," Tan'is replied.

"You don't . . . ," she gasped, glancing over her shoulder toward the ditch, toward where the *doran'se* went about their work, steel flashing in the sunlight. "You can't . . ."

Tan'is cocked his head to the side. He had tried to understand this daughter of his, tried to understand *all* the children. Though he was no healer, as a soldier he had learned long ago to tend shattered bones and ruptured skin, to treat the festering flesh that came from a soiled wound or the racking coughs of men too long in the field. And yet this . . . he could no more comprehend the nature of this decay than he could cure it.

"It has you, daughter. The rot has you."

He reached down and ran a finger along the creases in Faith's forehead, sketched the delicate tracery of lines beside her eyes, lifted a slender filament of silver hair from the brown locks. Just a few decades of sun and wind had already begun to roughen her smooth olive skin. He had wondered, when she first burst from between her mother's thighs, strong-lunged and screaming, if perhaps she might grow up unscathed. The question had intrigued him, and now it was answered.

"It touches you gently," he pointed out, "but its grip will grow stronger."

"And so you have to do *this*?" she exploded, jerking her head desperately toward the freshly turned earthen ditch. "*This* is what it comes to?"

Tan'is shook his head. "It was not my decision. The council voted."

"Why? Why do you *hate* us?"

"Hate?" he replied. "That is your word, child, not ours."

"It's not just a *word*. It describes a feeling, a *real thing*. A *truth* about the world."

Tan'is nodded. He had heard such arguments before. *Hate, courage, fear.* Those who thought the rot an affliction merely of the flesh understood nothing. It corroded the mind as well, rusting the very foundations of thought and reason.

"I grew from your seed," Faith continued, as though that followed logically from what came before. "You fed me when I was small!"

"This is the way of many creatures: wolves, eagles, horses. When they are young, dependent, all must rely on their progenitors."

"Wolves, eagles, and horses *protect* their children!" she protested, weeping openly now, clawing at the backs of his legs. "I've seen it! They guard and tend, feed and nurture. They *raise* their young." She reached a trembling, imploring hand toward her father's face. "Why will you not raise us?"

"Wolves," Tan'is replied, brushing away his daughter's hand, "raise their young to be wolves. Eagles, eagles. You—," he continued, frowning once more, "we have raised you, but you are broken. Polluted. Compromised. You can see it for yourself," he said, gesturing to the hunched, defeated forms that stood waiting at the rim of the pit—hundreds of them, just waiting. "Even without this, you would die on your own, and soon."

"But we're *people*. We are your *children*."

Tan'is shook his head wearily. It was no good reasoning with one whose reason had decayed.

"You can never be what we are," he said quietly, drawing his knife.

At the sight of the blade, Faith made a strangled sound deep in her throat and flinched away. Tan'is wondered if she would try to run. A few did. They never made it far. This daughter of his, however, did not run. Instead, she balled her hands into white, trembling fists, and then, with an obvious effort of will, straightened from her knees. Standing, she was able to look him directly in the eye, and though tears plastered her hair to her cheeks, she no longer wept. For once, however briefly, the disfiguring terror had left her. She looked almost whole, hale.

"And you cannot love us for what *we* are?" she asked, words slow, steady for the first time. "Even polluted, even broken? Even rotten, you cannot love us?"

"Love," Tan'is repeated, tasting the strange syllable, revolving it on his tongue as he drove the knife in and up, past the muscle, past the ribs, into her galloping heart, "like hate—it is your word, daughter, not ours."

1

The sun hung just over the peaks, a silent, furious ember drenching the granite cliffs in a bloody red, when Kaden found the shattered carcass of the goat.

He'd been dogging the creature over the tortuous mountain trails for hours, scanning for track where the ground was soft enough, making guesses when he came to bare rock, doubling back when he guessed wrong. It was slow work and tedious, the kind of task the older monks delighted in assigning to their pupils. As the sun sank and the eastern sky purpled to a vicious bruise, he started to wonder if he would be spending the night in the high peaks with only his roughspun robe for comfort. Spring had arrived weeks earlier according to the Annurian calendar, but the monks didn't pay any heed to the calendar and neither did the weather, which remained hard and grudging. Scraps of dirty snow lingered in the long shadows, cold seeped from the stones, and the needles of the few gnarled junipers were still more gray than green.

"Come on, you old bastard," he muttered, checking another track. "You don't want to sleep out here any more than I do."

The mountains comprised a maze of cuts and canyons, washed-out gullies and rubble-strewn ledges. Kaden had already crossed three streams gorged with snowmelt, frothing at the hard walls that hemmed them in, and his robe was damp with spray. It would freeze when the sun dropped. How the goat had made its way past the rushing water, he had no idea.

"If you drag me around these peaks much longer . . . ," he began, but the words died on his lips as he spotted his quarry at last—thirty paces distant, wedged in a narrow defile, only the hindquarters visible.

Although he couldn't get a good look at the thing—it seemed to have trapped itself between a large boulder and the canyon wall—he could tell at once that something was wrong. The creature was still, too still, and there was an unnaturalness to the angle of the haunches, the stiffness in the legs.

"Come on, goat," he murmured as he approached, hoping the animal hadn't managed to hurt itself too badly. The Shin monks were not rich, and they relied on their flocks for milk and meat. If Kaden returned with an animal that was injured, or worse, dead, his *umial* would impose a severe penance.

"Come on, old fellow," he said, working his way slowly up the canyon. The goat appeared stuck, but if it *could* run, he didn't want to end up chasing it all over the Bone Mountains. "Better grazing down below. We'll walk back together."

The evening shadows hid the blood until he was nearly standing in it, the pool wide and dark and still. Something had gutted the animal, hacked a savage slice across the haunch and into the stomach, cleaving muscle and driving into the viscera. As Kaden watched, the last lingering drops of blood trickled out, turning the soft belly hair into a sodden, ropy mess, running down the stiff legs like urine.

" 'Shael take it," he cursed, vaulting over the wedged boulder. It wasn't so unusual for a crag cat to take a goat, but now he'd have to carry the carcass back to the monastery across his shoulders. "You had to go wandering," he said. "You had . . ."

The words trailed off, and his spine stiffened as he got a good look at the animal for the first time. A quick cold fear blazed over his skin. He took a breath, then extinguished the emotion. Shin training wasn't good for much, but after eight years, he *had* managed to tame his feelings; fear, envy, anger, exuberance—he still felt them, but they did not penetrate so deeply as they once had. Even within the fortress of his calm, however, he couldn't help but stare.

Whatever had gutted the goat did not stop there. Some creature—Kaden struggled in vain to think of what—had hacked the animal's head from its shoulders, severing the strong sinew and muscle with sharp, brutal strokes until only the stump of the neck remained. Crag cats would take the occasional flagging member of a herd, but not like this. These wounds were vicious, unnecessary, lacking the quotidian economy of other kills he had seen in the wild. The animal had not simply been slaughtered; it had been destroyed.

Kaden cast about, searching for the rest of the carcass. Stones and branches had washed down with the early spring floods and lodged at the choke point of the defile in a weed-matted mess of silt and skeletal wooden fingers, sun-bleached and grasping. So much detritus clogged the canyon that it took him a while to locate the head, which lay tossed on its side a few paces distant. Much of the hair had been torn away and the bone split open. The brain was gone, scooped from the trencher of the skull as though with a spoon.

Kaden's first thought was to flee. Blood still dripped from the goat's gory coat, more black than red in the fading light, and whatever had mauled it could still be in the rocks, guarding its kill. None of the local predators would be likely to attack Kaden—he was tall for his seventeen years, lean and strong from half a lifetime of labor—but then, none of the local predators would have hacked the head from the goat and eaten its brain either.

He turned toward the canyon mouth. The sun had settled below the steppe, leaving just a burnt smudge above the grasslands to the west. Already night filled the canyon like oil seeping into a bowl. Even if he left immediately, even if he ran at his fastest lope, he'd be covering the last few miles to the monastery in full dark. Though he thought he had long outgrown his fear of night in the mountains, he didn't relish the idea of stumbling along the rock-strewn path, an unknown predator following in the darkness.

He took a step away from the shattered creature, then hesitated.

"Heng's going to want a painting of this," he muttered, forcing himself to turn back to the carnage.

Anyone with a brush and a scrap of parchment could make a painting, but the Shin expected rather more of their novices and acolytes. Painting was the product of seeing, and the monks had their own way of seeing. *Saama'an,* they called it: "the carved mind." It was only an exercise, of course, a step on the long path leading to the ultimate liberation of *vaniate,* but it had its meager uses. During his eight years in the mountains, Kaden had learned to see, to *really* see the world as it was: the track of a brindled bear, the serration of a forksleaf petal, the crenellations of a distant peak. He had spent countless hours, weeks, *years* looking, seeing, memorizing. He could paint any of a thousand plants or animals down to the last finial feather, and he could internalize a new scene in heartbeats.

He took two slow breaths, clearing a space in his head, a blank slate on which to carve each minute particular. The fear remained, but the fear was an impediment, and he pared it down, focusing on the task at hand.

With the slate prepared, he set to work. It took only a few breaths to etch the severed head, the pools of dark blood, the mangled carcass of the animal. The lines were sure and certain, finer than any brushstroke, and unlike normal memory, the process left him with a sharp, vivid image, durable as the stones on which he stood, one he would be able to recall and scrutinize at will. He finished the *saama'an* and let out a long, careful breath.

Fear is blindness, he muttered, repeating the old Shin aphorism. *Calmness, sight.*

The words provided cold comfort in the face of the bloody scene, but now that he had the carving, he could leave. He glanced once over his shoulder, searching the cliffs for some sign of the predator, then turned toward the opening of the defile. As the night's dark fog rolled over the peaks, he raced the darkness down the treacherous trails, sandaled feet darting past the downed limbs and ankle-breaking rocks. His legs, chill and stiff after so many hours creeping after the goat, warmed to the motion while his heart settled into a steady tempo.

You're not running away, he told himself, *just heading home.*

Still, he breathed a small sigh of relief a mile down the path when he rounded a tower of rock—the Talon, the monks called it—and could make out Ashk'lan in the distance. Thousands of feet below him, the scant stone buildings perched on a narrow ledge as though huddled away from the abyss. Warm lights glowed in some of the windows. There would be a fire in the refectory kitchen, lamps kindled in the meditation hall, the quiet hum of the Shin going about their evening ablutions and rituals. *Safe.* The word rose unbidden to his mind. It was safe down there, and despite his resolve, Kaden increased his pace, running toward those few, faint lights, fleeing whatever prowled the unknown darkness behind him.

2

Kaden crossed the ledges just outside Ashk'lan's central square at a run, then slowed as he entered the courtyard. His alarm, so sharp and palpable when he first saw the slaughtered goat, had faded as he descended from the high peaks and drew closer to the warmth and companionship of the monastery. Now, moving toward the main cluster of buildings, he felt foolish to have run so fast. Whatever killed the animal remained a mystery, to be sure, but the mountain trails posed their own dangers, especially to someone foolish enough to run them in the darkness. Kaden slowed to a walk, gathering his thoughts.

Bad enough I lost the goat. Heng would whip me bloody if I managed to break my own leg in the process.

The gravel of the monastery paths crunched beneath his feet, the only sound save for the keening of the wind as it gusted and fell, skirling through the gnarled branches and between the cold stones. The monks were all inside already, hunched over their bowls or seated cross-legged in the meditation hall, fasting, pursuing emptiness. When he reached the refectory, a long, low stone building weathered by storm and rain until it looked almost a part of the mountain itself, Kaden paused to scoop a handful of water from the wooden barrel outside the door. As the draft washed down his throat, he took a moment to steady his breathing and slow his heart. It wouldn't do to approach his *umial* in a state of mental disarray. Above all else, the Shin valued stillness, clarity. Kaden had been whipped by his masters for rushing, for shouting, for acting in haste, or moving without consideration. Besides, he was home now. Whatever killed the goat wasn't likely to come prowling among the stern buildings.

Up close, Ashk'lan didn't look like much, especially at night: three long, stone halls with wooden roofs—the dormitory, refectory, and meditation hall—forming three sides to a rough square, their pale granite walls washed as though with milk in the moonlight. The whole compound perched on the cliff's edge, and the fourth side of the square opened out onto cloud, sky, and an unobstructed view of the foothills and distant steppe to the west. Already the grasslands far below were vibrant with the spring froth of flowers: swaying blue chalenders, clusters of nun's blossom, riots of tiny white faith knots. At night, however, beneath the cold, inscrutable gaze of the stars, the steppe was invisible. Staring out past the ledges, Kaden found himself facing a vast emptiness, a great dark void. It felt as though Ashk'lan stood at the world's end, clinging to the cliffs, holding vigil against a nothingness that threatened to engulf creation. After a second swig of water, he turned away. The night had grown cold, and now that he had stopped running, gusts of wind off the Bone Mountains sliced through his sweaty robe like shards of ice.

With a rumble in his stomach, he turned toward the yellow glow and murmur of conversation emanating from the windows of the refectory. At this hour—just after sunset but before night prayer—most of the monks would be taking a modest evening meal of salted mutton, turnips, and hard, dark bread. Heng, Kaden's *umial,* would be inside with the rest, and with any luck, Kaden could report what he had seen, dash off a quick painting to show the scene, and sit down to a warm meal of his own. Shin fare was far more meager than the delicacies he remembered from his early years in the Dawn Palace, before his father sent him away, but the monks had a saying: *Hunger is flavor.*

They were great ones for sayings, the Shin, passing them down from one generation to the next as though trying to make up for the order's lack of liturgy and formal ritual. The Blank God cared nothing for the pomp and pageantry of the urban temples. While the young gods glutted themselves on music, prayer, and offerings laid upon elaborate altars, the Blank God demanded of the Shin one thing only: sacrifice, not of wine or wealth, but of the self. *The mind is a flame,* the monks said. *Blow it out.*

After eight years, Kaden still wasn't sure what that meant, and with his stomach rumbling impatiently, he couldn't be bothered to contemplate it. He pushed open the heavy refectory door, letting the gentle hum of conversation wash over him. Monks were scattered around the hall, some at rough tables, their heads bent over their bowls, others standing in front of a fire that crackled in the hearth at the far end of the room. Several sat playing stones, their eyes blank as they studied the lines of resistance and attack unfolding across the board.

The men were as varied as the lands from which they had come—tall, pale, blocky Edishmen from the far north, where the sea spent half the year as ice; wiry Hannans, hands and forearms inked with the patterns of the jungle tribes just north of the Waist; even a few Manjari, green-eyed, their brown skin a shade darker than Kaden's own. Despite their disparate appearances, however, the monks shared something, a hardness, a stillness born of a life lived in the hard, still mountains far from the comforts of the world where they had been raised.

The Shin were a small order, with barely two hundred monks at Ashk'lan. The young gods—Eira, Heqet, Orella, and the rest—drew adherents from three continents and enjoyed temples in almost every town and city, palatial spaces draped with silk and crusted with gold, some of which rivaled the dwellings of the richest ministers and atreps. Heqet alone must have commanded thousands of priests and ten times that number who came to worship at his altar when they felt the need of courage.

The less savory gods had their adherents as well. Stories abounded of the halls of Rassambur and the bloody servants of Ananshael, tales of chalices carved from skulls and dripping marrow, of infants strangled in their sleep, of dark orgies where sex and death were hideously mingled. Some claimed that only a tenth of those who entered the doors ever returned. *Taken by the Lord of Bones,* people whispered. *Taken by Death himself.*

The older gods, aloof from the world and indifferent to the affairs of humans, drew fewer adherents. Nonetheless, they had their names— Intarra and her consort, Hull the Bat, Pta and Astar'ren—and scattered throughout the three continents, thousands worshipped those names.

Only the Blank God remained nameless, faceless. The Shin held that he was the oldest, the most cryptic and powerful. Outside Ashk'lan, most people thought he was dead, or had never existed. Slaughtered by Ae, some said, when she made the world and the heavens and stars. That seemed perfectly plausible to Kaden. He had seen no sign of the god in his years running up and down the mountain passes.

He scanned the room for his fellow acolytes, and from a table over by the wall, Akiil caught his eye. He was seated on a long bench with Serkhan and fat Phirum Prumm—the only acolyte at Ashk'lan who maintained his girth despite the endless running, hauling, and building required by the older monks. Kaden nodded in response and was about to cross to them when he spotted Heng on the other side of the hall. He stifled a sigh—the *umial* would impose some sort of nasty penance if his pupil sat down to dinner without reporting back first. Hopefully it wouldn't take long to relate the tale of the slaughtered goat; then Kaden could join the others; then he could finally have a bowl of stew.

Huy Heng was hard to miss. In many ways, he seemed like he belonged in one of the fine wine halls of Annur rather than here, cloistered in a remote monastery a hundred leagues beyond the border of the empire. While the other monks went about their duties with quiet sobriety, Heng hummed as he tended the goats, sang as he lugged great sacks of clay up from the shallows, and kept up a steady stream of jests as he chopped turnips for the refectory pots. He could even tell jokes while he beat his pupils bloody. At the moment, he was regaling the brothers at his table with a tale involving elaborate hand gestures and some sort of birdcall. When he saw Kaden approach, however, the grin slipped from his face.

"I found the goat," Kaden began without preamble.

Heng extended both hands, as though to stop the words before they reached him.

"I'm not your *umial* any longer," he said.

Kaden blinked. Scial Nin, the abbot, reassigned acolytes and *umials* every year or so, but not usually by surprise. Not in the middle of dinner.

"What happened?" he asked, suddenly cautious.

"It's time for you to move on."

"Now?"

"The present is the present. Tomorrow will still be 'now.' "

Kaden swallowed an acerbic remark; even if Heng was no longer his *umial,* the monk could still whip him. "Who am I getting?" he asked instead.

"Rampuri Tan," Heng replied, his voice flat, devoid of its usual laughter.

Kaden stared. Rampuri Tan did not take pupils. Sometimes, despite his faded brown robe and shaved head, despite the days he spent sitting cross-legged, eyes fixed in his devotion to the Blank God, Tan didn't seem like a monk at all. There was nothing Kaden could put his finger on, but the novices felt it, too, had developed a hundred theories, attributing to the man a series of implausible pasts by turn both shadowy and glorious: he earned the scars on his face fighting wild animals in the arena at The Bend; he was a murderer and a thief, who had repented of his crimes and taken up a life of contemplation; he was the dispossessed brother of some lord or atrep, hiding at Ashk'lan only long enough to build his revenge. Kaden wasn't much inclined to believe any of the stories, but he had noticed the common thread: violence. Violence and danger. Whoever Rampuri Tan had been before arriving at Ashk'lan, Kaden wasn't eager to have the man for his *umial*.

"He is expecting you," Heng continued, something like pity tingeing his voice. "I promised to send you to his cell as soon as you arrived."

Kaden spared a glance over his shoulder for the table where his friends sat, slurping down their stew and enjoying the few unstructured minutes of conversation that were allowed them each day.

"Now," Heng said, breaking into his thoughts.

The walk from the refectory to the dormitory was not far—a hundred paces across the square, then up a short path between two lines of stunted junipers. Kaden covered the distance quickly, eager to be out of the wind, and pushed open the heavy wooden door. All the monks, even Scial Nin, the abbot, slept in identical chambers opening off the long, central hallway. The cells were small, barely large enough to fit a pallet, a rough woven mat, and a couple of shelves, but then, the Shin spent most of their time outdoors, in the workshops, or in meditation.

Inside the building and out of the slicing wind, Kaden slowed, readying himself for the encounter. It was hard to know what to expect—some masters liked to test a student immediately; some preferred to wait and watch, judging the aptitudes and weaknesses of the younger monk before deciding on a course of instruction.

He's just another new master, Kaden told himself. *Heng was new a year ago, and you got used to him.*

And yet, something about the situation felt odd, unsettling. First the slaughtered goat, then this unexpected transfer when he should have been seated on a long bench with a steaming bowl in front of him, arguing with Akiil and the rest of the acolytes. . . .

He filled his lungs slowly, then emptied them. Worry was doing no good.

Live now, he told himself, rehearsing one of the standard Shin aphorisms. *The future is a dream.* And yet, a part of his thoughts—a voice that refused to be stilled or settled—reminded him that not all dreams were pleasant, that sometimes, no matter how one thrashed or turned, it was impossible to awake.

3

Rampuri Tan sat on the floor inside his small cell, his back to the door, a broad sheet of blank parchment spread on the flagstones before him. He held a brush in his left hand, but however long he had been sitting, had not yet dipped it into the saucer of black ink at his side.

"Enter," the man said, beckoning with his free hand without turning toward the door.

Kaden crossed the threshold, then paused. The first few moments with a new *umial* could set the tone for the entire relationship. Most of the monks wanted to make an impression on their pupils early, and Kaden wasn't eager to earn himself some grueling penance because of a careless misstep or lapse in judgment. Tan, however, seemed content to contemplate his blank page in silence, and so Kaden schooled himself to patience, attending to his strange new master.

It wasn't hard to see where the novices had come up with the idea that the older monk had fought in the arena. Though well into his fifth decade, Tan was built like a boulder, thick in the shoulders and neck, and powerfully muscled. Furrowed scars, pale against his darker skin, ran through the stubble of his scalp, as though some clawed beast had raked at his head again and again, slicing the flesh right down to the skull. Whatever inflicted the wounds, they must have been excruciating. Kaden's mind jumped back to the carcass of the goat, and he shivered.

"You found the animal that Heng sent you for," the older monk began abruptly. It was not a question, and for a moment Kaden hesitated.

"Yes," he said finally.

"Have you returned it to its flock?"

"No."

"Why not?"

"It had been killed. Savagely killed."

Tan lowered the brush, rose fluidly to his feet, and turned to face his pupil for the first time. He was tall, almost as tall as Kaden, and suddenly it felt as though there was very little space in the small cell. His eyes, dark and hard as filed nails, fixed Kaden to the spot. Back in Annur, there were men from western Eridroa and the far south, animal handlers, who could bend bears and jaguars to their will, all with the power of their gaze. Kaden felt like one of those creatures now, and it was with an effort that he continued to meet the eyes of his new *umial*.

"Crag cat?" the older monk asked.

Kaden shook his head. "Something severed its neck—hacked straight through. Then consumed the brain."

Tan considered him, then gestured to the brush, bowl, and parchment lying on the floor. "Paint it."

Kaden took his seat with some relief. Whatever surprises were in store for him under Tan's tutelage, at least the older monk shared some habits with Heng—if he heard about something unusual, he wanted an image. Well, that was easy enough. Kaden took two breaths, composed his thoughts, then summoned the *saama'an*. The sight filled his mind in all its detail—the sopping hair, the gobbets of hanging flesh, the empty bowl of the skull cast aside like broken crockery. He dipped the tip of the brush into the bowl and began to paint.

The work went quickly—his study with the monks had provided plenty of time to hone his craft—and when he was finished, he set down the brush. The painting on the parchment could have been the image of his mind reflected in a pool of still water.

Silence filled the room behind him, silence huge and heavy as stone. Kaden was tempted to turn around, but he had been instructed to sit and to paint, nothing else, and so, the painting finished, he sat.

"This is what you saw?" Tan asked at last.

Kaden nodded.

"And you had the presence of mind to remain for the *saama'an*."

Satisfaction swelled in Kaden. Maybe training under Tan wouldn't be so bad after all.

"Anything else?" the monk asked.

"Nothing else."

The lash came down so hard and unexpectedly, Kaden bit into his tongue. Pain screamed across his back in a bright, bold line as his mouth filled with the coppery taste of blood. He started to reach back, to block the next blow, then forced the instinct down. Tan was his *umial* now, and it was the man's prerogative to dole out penance and punishment as he saw fit. The reason for the sudden assault remained a mystery, but Kaden knew how to deal with a whipping.

Eight years among the Shin had taught him that *pain* was far too general a term for the multitude of sensations it purported to describe. He had learned the brutal ache of feet submerged too long in icy water and the furious stinging and itching of those same feet as they warmed. He had studied the deep reluctant soreness of muscles worked past exhaustion and the blossoms of agony that bloomed the next day as he kneaded the tender flesh under his thumbs. There was the quick, bright pain of a clean wound after the knife slipped and the low, drumming throb of the headache after fasting for a week. The Shin were great believers in pain. It was a reminder, they said, of how tightly we are bound to our own flesh. A reminder of failure.

"Finish the painting," Tan said.

Kaden called the *saama'an* back to mind, then compared it with the parchment before him. He had transferred the details faithfully.

"It is finished," he replied reluctantly.

The lash came down again, although this time he was prepared. His mind absorbed the shock as his body swayed slightly with the blow.

"Finish the painting," Tan said again.

Kaden hesitated. Asking questions of one's *umial* was usually a fast route to penance, but since he was being beaten already, a little more clarity couldn't hurt.

"Is this a test?" he asked tentatively. The monks created all sorts of tests for their pupils, trials in which the novices and acolytes attempted to prove their understanding and competence.

The lash took him across the shoulders again. The first two blows had split open the robe, and Kaden could feel the switch tearing into his bare skin.

"This is what it is," Tan replied. "Call it a test if you like, but the name is not the thing."

Kaden suppressed a groan. Whatever eccentricities Tan might possess, he spoke in the same infuriating gnomic pronouncements as the rest of the Shin.

"I don't remember anything else," Kaden said. "That's the entire *saama'an.*"

"It's not enough," Tan said, but this time he withheld the lash.

"It's the entire thing," Kaden protested. "The goat, the head, the pools of blood, even a few stray hairs that were stuck on a rock. I copied everything there."

Tan *did* hit him for that. Twice.

"Any fool can see what's there," the monk responded dryly. "A child looking at the world can tell you what is in front of him. You need to see what is not there. You need to look at what is *not* in front of you."

Kaden struggled to make some kind of sense out of this. "Whatever killed the goat isn't there," he began slowly.

Another lash.

"Of course not. You scared it away. Or it left on its own. Either way, you wouldn't *expect* to find a wild animal hunkered over its prey if it heard or scented a man approaching."

"So I'm looking for something that should be there, but isn't."

"Think in your mind. Use your tongue when you have something to say."

Tan followed the words with three more sharp blows. The gashes wept blood. Kaden could feel it running down his back, hot, and wet, and sticky. He had had worse beatings before, but always for a major mistake, a serious penance, never in the course of a simple dialogue. It was becoming more difficult to ignore the lacerating pain, and he struggled to keep his mind on the subject at hand. Tan wasn't going to stop whipping him out of mercy; that much was clear.

You need to see what is not there.

It was typical Shin nonsense, but like much of that nonsense, would probably turn out to be true.

Kaden scanned the *saama'an*. Every part of the goat was accounted for, even the intestines, which lay piled in sloppy blue-white ropes beneath the creature's abdomen. The brain was gone, but he had painted the broken skull clearly, showed where it was scooped out. What *else* would he expect to see? He'd been tracking the goat, followed it to the canyon, and . . .

"Tracks," he said, realization coming with the word. "Where are the tracks of whatever killed it?"

"That," Tan said, "is a very good question. Were they present?"

Kaden tried to remember. "I'm not sure. They're not in the *saama'an* . . . but I was focused on the goat."

"It seems that those golden eyes of yours don't see any better than anyone else's."

Kaden blinked. He'd never had a *umial* mention his eyes before—that was too close to mentioning his father or his birthright. The Shin were profoundly egalitarian. Novices were novices; acolytes were acolytes; and full brothers were all equal before the Blank God. Kaden's eyes, however, *were* unique. Tan had called them "golden," but in fact, the irises blazed. As a child, Kaden had stared at his father's eyes—all Annurian Emperors shared them—marveling at the way the color seemed to shift and burn. Sometimes they raged bright as a fire caught in high wind; others, they smoldered with a dark, red heat. His sister, Adare, had the eyes, too, though hers seemed to spark and snap like a blaze of green twigs. As the oldest of the Emperor's children, Adare rarely focused her bright gaze on her younger brothers, and when she did, it was usually in a flash of irritation. According to the family, the burning eyes came from Intarra herself, the Lady of Light, who had taken human form centuries or millennia earlier—no one seemed quite sure—to seduce one of Kaden's forebears. Those eyes marked him as the true heir to the Unhewn Throne, to Annur itself, an empire that sprawled across two continents.

The Shin, of course, had no more interest in empires than they did in Intarra. The Lady of Light was one of the old gods, older than Meshkent and Maat, older even than Ananshael, Lord of Bones. Upon her depended the arc of the sun in the sky, the heat of the day, the numinous glow of the moon. And yet, according to the monks, she was a child, an infant playing with fire in the vast mansion of emptiness, the unending and eternal void that was home to the Blank God. One day Kaden would return to Annur to claim his place on the Unhewn Throne, but while he lived at Ashk'lan, he was just another monk, expected to work hard and obey. The eyes certainly weren't saving him from Tan's brutal interrogation.

"Maybe the tracks were there," Kaden concluded weakly. "I can't be sure."

For a while Tan said nothing, and Kaden wondered if the beating was about to resume.

"The monks have been too easy on you," Tan concluded finally, voice level but hard. "I will not make that mistake."

Only later, as Kaden lay awake in his bunk, breathing shallowly to try to ease the pain of his inflamed back, did he realize what his new *umial* had said: "the monks." As though Rampuri Tan were not one of them.

4

Even with the salt-sharp breeze gusting in off the sea, the bodies stank. Adaman Fane's Wing had found the ship on a routine patrol two days earlier, sails rent and luffing, dried blood on the rails, the crew cut to pieces and left to rot on the decks. By the time the cadets arrived, the searing springtime sun had started its work, bloating bellies and pulling skin tight over knuckles and skulls. Flies crawled in and out of dead sailors' ears, foraged between slack lips, and paused to rub their mandibles over desiccated eyeballs.

"Any theories?" Ha Lin asked, nudging the nearest body with her toe.

Valyn shrugged. "I think we can rule out a cavalry charge."

"Very helpful," she shot back, lips pursed, almond eyes skeptically narrowed.

"Whoever did this, they were good. Take a look here."

He squatted to peel back the crusted cloth from a nasty stab puncture just below the fourth rib. Lin knelt beside him, licked her little finger, then slid it into the wound up to the second knuckle.

A stranger meeting Ha Lin on the street might mistake her for a carefree merchant's daughter on the cusp of womanhood: buoyant and blithe, brown skin tanned from long hours in the sun, glossy black hair pulled back from her forehead and gathered in a leather thong. She had a soldier's eyes, though. For the past eight years, she'd been through the same training as Valyn, the same training as all the cadets on the deck of the doomed vessel, and the Kettral had long ago hardened her to the sight of death.

Still, Valyn couldn't help but see her for the attractive young woman she was. As a rule, the soldiers avoided romantic entanglements on the Islands. Whores of both sexes were cheap over on Hook, and no one wanted a lover's quarrel between men and women trained to kill in dozens of ways. Nonetheless, Valyn sometimes found his eyes straying from the exercise at hand to Ha Lin, to the quirk of her lip, the shape of her figure beneath her combat blacks. He tried to hide his glances—they were embarrassing and unprofessional—but he thought, from the wry grin that sometimes flickered across her face, that she had caught him looking on more than one occasion.

She didn't seem to mind. Sometimes she even looked back with that bold, disarming stare of hers. It was easy to wonder what might have evolved between them if they'd grown up somewhere different, somewhere that training didn't subsume an entire life. Of course, "somewhere different" for Valyn hui'Malkeenian meant the Dawn Palace, which had its own rules and taboos; as a member of the imperial family, he couldn't have loved her any more than he could as a soldier.

Forget it, he told himself angrily. He was there to focus on the exercise, not to spend the morning daydreaming about other lives.

"Professional," Lin said appreciatively, evidently unaware that his mind had drifted. She pulled her finger out and wiped the crusted gore on her blacks. "Deep enough to burst the kidney, but not so deep as to get the blade stuck."

Valyn nodded. "There are plenty more like that, more than you'd expect from amateurs."

He considered the purpling contusion a moment longer, then straightened up and stared out over the slapping chop of the Iron Sea. After all the blood, it felt good to look at the unblemished blue for a minute, the wide expanse of the meridian sky.

"Enough lounging!" Adaman Fane bellowed, cuffing Valyn across the back of the head as he strode the length of the deck, stepping over the sprawled bodies as though they were downed spars or coils of rope. "Get your asses aft!" The massive bald trainer had been with the Kettral better than twenty years and still swam across the sound to Hook and back every morning before dawn. He had little patience for cadets standing around during one of his exercises.

Valyn joined the rest. He knew them all, of course; the Kettral were as small a fighting force as they were elite—the enormous birds that they used to drop in behind enemy lines couldn't carry more than five or six soldiers at a time. The Empire relied on the Kettral when a mission had to be executed quickly and quietly—for everything else, the Annurian legions could usually get the job done, or the navy, or the marines.

Valyn's training group numbered twenty-six, seven of whom had flown out to the abandoned ship with Fane for the morning's exercise. They were a strange crew: Annick Frencha, slim as a boy, snow-pale, and silent as stone; Balendin with his cruel grin and the falcon perched on his shoulder; Talal, tall, serious, bright eyes set in a face dark as coal; Gwenna Sharpe, impossibly reckless and incurably hot-tempered; Sami Yurl, the arrogant blond son of one of the empire's most powerful atreps, bronze-skinned as a god and vicious as a viper with his blades. They didn't have much in common aside from the fact that someone in command believed that one day they could be very, very good at killing people. Provided nothing killed them first.

All the training, all the lessons, the eight years of language study, demolitions work, navigational practice, weapons sparring, the sleepless nights on watch, the never-ending physical abuse, abuse intended to harden both the body and the mind, all of it aimed at one goal: Hull's Trial. Valyn remembered his first day on the Islands as though it had been branded on his mind. The new recruits had stepped off the ship straight into a barrage of curses and insults, into the fierce, angry faces of the veterans who called this distant archipelago their home, who seemed to resent any incursion, even by those eager to follow in their footsteps. Before he'd taken two steps, someone cuffed him across the cheek, then drove his face into the wet, salty sand until he could barely breathe.

"Get this in your heads," someone—one of the commanders?—hollered. "Just because some incompetent bureaucrat has seen fit to ship you out here to our precious Qirin Islands, it does *not* mean you will *ever* become Kettral. Some of you will be begging for mercy before the week is out. Others we will break in the course of training. Many of you will die, falling from birds, drowned in the spring storms, sobbing pathetically to yourselves as you submit to fleshrot in some miserable Hannan backwater. And that's the easy part! That's the fucking *fun* part. Those of you lucky or stubborn enough to live through the training will still need to face Hull's Trial."

Hull's Trial. Despite eight years of whispered speculation, neither Valyn nor the other cadets knew what it was any more than they had when they first arrived on Qarsh. It always seemed so distant, invisible as a ship beyond the cusp of the horizon. No one forgot it, but it was possible to ignore it for a while; after all, no one reached Hull's Trial if he didn't survive the years of training leading up to it. And yet, after all those years, it had come at last, like a debt long due. In a little over a month, Valyn and the others would earn the rank of full Kettral or they would die.

"Maybe we can start this morning's parade of incompetence," Fane began, tugging Valyn's attention back to the present, "with Ha Lin's assessment." He gestured with a huge hand for her to begin. It was a standard exercise. The Kettral were always dragging cadets to fresh battlefields, the examination of which would both harden them to the sight of death and hone their tactical understanding.

"It was a night attack," Lin replied, voice crisp and confident. "Otherwise, the sailors on deck would have seen their assailants. The raiding party came from starboard—you can see the gouges left by the grapples on the rails. When the—"

"Sweet 'Shael on a stick," Fane interrupted, raising a hand to silence her. "A first-year could tell me all this. Will someone please explain something that's *not* obscenely obvious?" He cast about, eyes finally fixing on Valyn. "How about His Most Radiant Highness?"

Valyn hated the title. It wasn't even accurate, for one thing—despite the fact that his father was Emperor, *he* was never going to sit the Unhewn Throne—and for another, his high birth was irrelevant. There were no ranks on the Islands, no special perquisites or prerogatives. If anything, Valyn probably worked a little harder than most. Still, he'd learned long ago that complaining just landed you deeper in the shit, and he did not, at the moment, need to spend more time in the shit, so he took a deep breath and began.

"The crew barely even knew they were in trouble—"

Before he could finish the sentence, Fane cut him off with a snort and a curt chop of his hand.

"I give you ten minutes to look over this 'Kent-kissing goat fuck, and your only conclusion is that it was a surprise attack? What have you been doing? Pilfering rings and going through pockets?"

"I was just starting—"

"And now you're finished. How about you, Yurl?" Fane asked, pointing to the tall blond youth. "Maybe you can find some way to contribute to His Most Radiant Highness's exhaustive analysis."

"There's just so much to say," Sami Yurl began, shooting Valyn a satisfied smirk.

"That spit-licking son of a whore," Lin hissed, low enough that only Valyn could hear.

Though all the cadets endured the same privations and aimed at the same goal, there were rifts in the group. Most of the young soldiers enlisted out of a hybrid desire to defend the empire, see the world, and fly those enormous birds to which only the Kettral had access. For a peasant's son from the plains of Sia, the Kettral offered opportunities too fantastic to be believed. Others, however, came to the Islands for other reasons: the chance to fight, to inflict pain, to take life—these drew some as rotting flesh drew vultures. Despite Sami Yurl's smooth good looks, he was a brutal and nasty fighter. Unlike most of the other cadets, he seemed never to have put his past behind him, striding around the Islands as though expecting everyone to bow and scrape. It was tempting to dismiss him as the pampered, puffed-up son of a lord, an aristocratic fool who had lucked into the cadets through coin or family connections. The truth was more galling: Yurl was an effective, dangerous fighter, better with his blades than some full-rank Kettral. He'd beaten Valyn bloody dozens of times over the years, and if there was one thing he enjoyed more than winning, it was humiliating those he had defeated.

"The attack," Yurl continued, "happened three days ago, judging by the air temperature, the number of flies, and the rot on the bodies. As Lin said"—he shot her a sly glance—"it was a night assault; otherwise, more of the crew would have been armed. When the pirates hit—"

"Pirates?" the trainer asked sharply.

Yurl shrugged and turned to the nearest corpse, casually kicking the head aside to reveal a gash running from clavicle to chest. "Wounds are consistent with the weaponry that kind of trash tends to favor. The hold is ransacked. They hit the boat and took the goods. Bang the whore and get out the door—pretty standard."

Balendin chuckled at the crack. Lin bristled, and Valyn put a calming hand on her arm.

"Lucky for them," Yurl added, "there weren't any professionals on board." His tone suggested that if *he* had been manning the deck, the attackers would have encountered a very different reception.

Valyn wasn't so sure.

"Pirates didn't do this."

Fane cocked a bushy eyebrow. "The Light of the Empire speaks again! You wouldn't want to rest on your laurels after so astutely identifying the 'surprise attack.' Please, enlighten us."

Valyn ignored the goading. Kettral trainers could crawl under one's skin quicker than a sandfly. It was one of the reasons they made good trainers. A cadet who couldn't keep his cool wasn't likely to make much of a soldier when the arrows started flying, and Fane was nothing if not adept at making people lose their cool.

"This crew wasn't the usual mix of sailors with a few mercenary marines to guard the cargo," Valyn began. "These men were professionals."

Yurl smirked. "Professionals. Right. Which explains why they're scattered around the deck like chum."

"You've had a chance to run your mouth, Yurl," Fane said. "Now, shut it, and see if the golden boy over here can manage to do something other than embarrass himself."

Valyn suppressed a smile and nodded to the trainer before continuing. "The crew *looks* pretty standard. A dozen men—the kind you'd find running a sloop like this anywhere from Anthera to the Waist. But only two of the bunks have been used. That means ten men on the deck at all times. They were ready for an attack." He waited for that to sink in.

"And their weapons. They don't look like much." He lifted a standard deckblade from the hand of the nearest corpse and held it up to the light. "But this is Liran steel. What kind of merchant rig runs ten on the deck, every man carrying Liran steel?"

"I'm sure," Fane drawled, "that you're planning to make a point sometime before the sun sets." The man sounded bored, but Valyn could see the glint in his eye. He was onto something.

"All I'm saying is that if this lot were professionals, then the ones who boarded the ship and cut them down weren't your garden-variety pirates."

"Well, well," the trainer replied, looking around the cluster of cadets to see that everyone had followed the argument. "Even a blind horse finds the paddock once in a while."

By Eyrie standards, the backhand remark counted as high praise. Valyn nodded, hiding his satisfaction. Sami Yurl's lips tightened into a scowl.

"Ten minutes on deck," Fane continued, glaring, "and only the imperial mascot here has been able to tell me a single worthwhile thing about this 'Kent-kissing wreck. I didn't rope two birds into flying you out here just so you could spend the morning sticking your thumbs up one another's asses. Go over it again. Use your eyes. Find me something worth knowing."

Eight years earlier, the admonition would have shamed Valyn to his core. Such tongue-lashings, however, were standard fare on the Islands. He nodded crisply to Fane, then turned to Lin.

"Split up?" he asked. "You stay topside, I'll check belowdecks again?"

"Whatever you say, O Divine Light of the Empire," she responded with a smirk.

"Let me remind you," Valyn said, eyes narrowing, "that you're not as big as Fane."

She put a cupped hand to her ear. "What was that? It sounded like . . . was it a *threat*?"

"*And* you're just a girl."

It was a meaningless crack on the Qirins, where more than a third of the soldiers were women. Other imperial forces would have scoffed at the idea of a mixed-gender fighting unit, but the Kettral handled unusual situations, situations in which stealth, impersonation, deception, and surprise were as important as brute strength and speed. Still, if Lin was going to needle him about his parentage, Valyn intended to give as good as he got.

"I wouldn't want to have to turn you over my knee and paddle you," he added, wagging a finger at her.

"You know that Shaleel taught us how to crush testicles, right?" Lin replied. "It's pretty easy, actually, sort of like cracking a walnut." She demonstrated with one hand, a quick, twisting gesture that made Valyn wince.

"Why don't you stay up here," he said, taking a good step backwards, "and I'll make sure we didn't miss anything in the hold."

Lin squinted appraisingly. "It might be more like a chestnut, now that I think of it. . . ."

Valyn tossed back the hatch and dropped below before she could finish the sentence.

The ship's hold was low and dim. A few bars of sunlight lanced through the unchinked cracks in the decking above, but most of the space lay in deep, thick shadow. In a fight like this, there usually wasn't much to see belowdecks, and only a few of the other cadets had already been down there. Still, it paid to look places other people didn't.

Valyn waited for his eyes to adjust, then moved ahead, picking his way cautiously around stray barrels and bales as the vessel rocked gently beneath him, waves lapping at the hull. Whoever hit the ship *had* made off with most of the cargo, if there had been any cargo to begin with. According to the ink seals, the barrels that remained carried wine from Sia, although most of that trade tended to follow the shorter, overland route to the capital. A few crates were still lashed against the bulkhead, and Valyn pried one open with his belt knife: bales of cotton, also from Sia. It was good cargo, but not something professionals would usually go after. He was just starting to crack open the next crate when what sounded like a quiet moan caught his ear.

Without thinking, he drew one of the two standard short blades strapped across his back.

The sound was coming from the bow of the ship, all the way up by the foremost scuppers. Fane's Wing should have checked the vessel over already, should have made sure that everyone was either dead or tied up before Valyn and the rest of the cadets came anywhere close. Fane, however, was one of the Eyrie's more impulsive trainers, more interested in swinging a blade than skulking around belowdecks, checking pulses. He would have given the hold a glance, to be sure—but at a glance, a gravely wounded man could easily pass for dead.

Briefly Valyn considered calling someone else. If there *were* a sailor still alive, Fane would want to know immediately. On the other hand, he wasn't certain just what he'd heard, and he didn't relish the idea of hollering for the whole group only to find some untended livestock milling around in the bow. After a quick glance over his shoulder, Valyn glided silently ahead, belt knife held down by his waist, short blade in a tight guard before him—standard position for close-quarters fighting.

The man was tucked all the way forward against the curve of the keel itself, slumped in a puddle of his own blood. For a moment Valyn thought he *was* dead, that the sound had been the groaning of hawser against capstan, or the protestation of wood warping beneath the sun. Then the sailor opened his eyes.

They shone in the meager light, baffled and tormented by pain.

Valyn took half a step forward, then stopped. *Assume nothing.* That was the entire first chapter of *Hendran's Tactics,* a tome that virtually every Kettral had committed to memory. The man looked near death, but Valyn held back.

"Can you hear me?" he asked quietly. "How badly are you wounded?"

The sailor's eyes rolled in his head as though searching for the source of the sound before coming to rest, finally, on Valyn.

"You . . . ," he groaned, the word gravelly and weak.

Valyn stared. He had never seen the man before, certainly not in his years on the Islands, but recognition filled that feverish gaze and pinned him to the spot.

"You're delirious," he said carefully, edging closer. Unless the man was a professional masker, he wasn't faking. "Where are you wounded?"

"You have the eyes," the sailor responded weakly.

Valyn froze. Usually when people referred to "the eyes," they were talking about his father, Sanlitun, or his brother, Kaden, both of whom had been blessed with the famous burning gaze, flaming irises that marked them as the heirs to Intarra herself, as the rightful Emperors of Annur. Even his older sister, Adare, had that gaze—although as a woman, she would never sit the Unhewn Throne. Growing up, Valyn had been fiercely jealous of those eyes, had, in fact, almost blinded himself once with a burning twig while trying to light his own eyes ablaze. The truth was, though, that Valyn's stare was no less unsettling: black pupils set in irises brown as char. Kaden's eyes might be fire, Ha Lin said, but Valyn's were the remains after the fire had guttered out.

"We came . . . for you," the sailor insisted.

Valyn felt suddenly dizzy, disoriented, and the ship seemed to roll more treacherously with the swells.

"Why?" he asked. "Who is 'we'?"

"Aedolians," the man managed. "The Emperor sent us."

The Aedolian Guard. That explained both the professionalism and the Liran steel. The personal bodyguards of the Emperor were both well trained and well supplied; aside from the Kettral, they were the most fabled troops in the empire, iron-willed men whose loyalty to the Annurian throne was the stuff of legend. The founder of their order, Jarl Genner, had decreed that they take no wives, father no children, and own no property, all to ensure their unstinting allegiance to the Emperor and to the Guard.

None of which explained their presence *here,* on a clipper three full weeks' sail from the capital, all of them dying or already dead. Or who could board such a ship and kill these men, some of the finest troops in the world. Valyn glanced back over his shoulder into the murky gloom of the hold, but whoever had wreaked the havoc appeared to be long gone.

The soldier was panting at the effort and the pain of speech, but he clenched his jaw and continued. "A plot. There is a plot. We were to . . . take you . . . away . . . protect you."

Valyn tried to make sense of the claim. There were plenty of nefarious political currents in Annur, but the Kettral had chosen the Qirin Islands as their training ground and home because they were hundreds of leagues from anywhere. Besides, the Qirins were populated by the *Kettral.* The

Aedolian Guard was storied, but the Kettral were legend. Anyone who planned to attack the Islands would have to be mad.

"Wait here," Valyn began, although where the man would go he had no idea. "I have to tell someone. Fane. Eyrie command."

"No," the Aedolian managed, yanking a bloody hand from his jerkin and reaching toward Valyn, his voice surprisingly powerful. "Someone here . . . maybe someone important . . . is part of it. . . ."

The words landed like a slap. "Who?" Valyn demanded. "Who's a part of it?"

The soldier shook his head wearily. "Don't know . . ."

His head dropped to the side. Bright crimson blood hemorrhaged from somewhere beneath the jerkin, splattering Valyn and the surrounding deck in fading spurts. An arterial wound, Valyn realized . . . only, an arterial wound killed in minutes, not days. The man should have bled out onto the deck by the time his attackers slipped back over the gunwales. He stepped forward to part the soldier's jerkin carefully and stared at the long gash, then turned his attention to the gore-drenched hand that had dropped limp into the Aedolian's lap.

"There's no possible way . . . ," he muttered to himself. And yet, the evidence was clear.

The man had been holding his own artery, had forced his fingers in through the sagging rent in his flesh, found the slippery tube, and clamped it shut. It was possible—Ellen Finch had gone over the technique in medical training—but even Finch acknowledged that you'd be lucky to last a day in that state. The Aedolian had gone close to three, waiting for someone, praying to whatever god he had trusted in, a god who had fucked him over well and for good.

Valyn touched his fingers to the man's neck. The pulse fluttered, faltered, then failed. He reached out to shut the eyes when Fane's earsplitting roar yanked him upright.

"Cadets on deck! Bird incoming!"

Just as Valyn shoved open the hatch, an ear-rending screech split the morning air. He burned to tell someone what he'd just heard, but the soldier's warning echoed in his ears: *Someone here is part of it.* At the moment, he wasn't even sure he *could* have told anyone: all eyes were turned to the sky to see a kettral soar overhead, dark wings blotting the sun.

Even after eight years on the Islands, eight years learning to fly on, fight from, load up, and drop off of the massive birds, Valyn still wasn't fully at ease with them. If the annals were correct, the species was older than men, older even than the Csestriim and the Nevariim, a throwback to the days when gods and monsters strode the earth. Though the Kettral had found them, had ostensibly tamed them, nothing in the dark, liquid eyes of the birds had ever looked tame to Valyn, and now, standing on the open deck as the great creature winged overhead, he thought he understood the terror of a mouse caught in the middle of a freshly mown field as the falcon takes to the air.

"Looks like the Flea's bird," Fane said, shading his eyes with a hand. "Although what he's doing all the way out here I've got no 'Kent-kissing idea."

Normally Valyn would have been intrigued. Although the Flea took his turn training cadets, he was one of the most deadly soldiers in the Eyrie's very deadly collection, and spent most of his time flying missions in the northeast, into the savage Blood Cities, or against the Urghul, or to the south, where the jungle tribes constantly pressed up through the Waist. His arrival in the middle of a run-of-the-mill exercise was unusual, if not unprecedented. Such surprises helped to liven up the training, although, after Valyn's encounter with the Aedolian, the black bird struck him as an inauspicious portent, and he looked over to take new stock of the cadets on deck. If the man hadn't been lying, dark forces were in play on the Islands, and if Valyn had learned one thing with the Kettral, it was that surprises were safe only if you were on the delivering end.

Without warning, the bird tucked its wings, all seventy feet of them, tight against its body and, like a spear falling from the heavens, dropped toward the ship. Valyn and the rest of the cadets stared. All the Kettral could make flying mounts and dismounts; the creatures weren't much good if you couldn't get on and off them. But this? He'd never seen anyone come in so fast.

"There's no way . . . ," Lin breathed beside him, shaking her head in horror. "There's just no—"

The bird was upon them in a rush of wind and a maelstrom of kicked-up debris that almost knocked Valyn from his feet. Even as he shielded his eyes, he caught a glimpse of the creature's talons reaching for the deck, a figure in Kettral blacks slipping loose from his harnesses, dropping to the boards, rolling smoothly to his feet. Before the wash of wind had subsided, the bird was gone, winging low over the waves to the north, and the Flea was there.

He didn't look like much of a soldier. Where Adaman Fane was tall and built like a bull, the Flea was short and weathered, his tar-dark skin pockmarked from some childhood disease, a fuzz of gray hair hazing his head like smoke. The drop was a reminder, though, of what the man and his Wing were capable of. No one else made drops like that, not the other cadets, not the trainers, not Adaman Fane—and onto a moving ship! If Valyn had tried the same entry over water, he would have been lucky to walk away without shattering all his ribs. Over a pitching deck . . . forget it. He'd always thought the other Kettral were stretching the truth just a bit when they claimed that the Flea had flown more than a thousand successful missions, but that . . .

"That was uncharacteristically flamboyant," Fane said with a raised eyebrow.

The Flea grimaced. "Sorry. Command sent me."

"And in a 'Kent-kissing hurry."

The smaller man nodded. He glanced over the assembled cadets, seemed to pause on Valyn, then took in the rest of the group before returning his attention to Fane. "You and your Wing are to be airborne as soon as possible. Yesterday, if you can manage it. You'll follow me north. Sendra's Wing's already on the way."

"Three wings?" Fane asked, grinning. "Sounds exciting. Where we headed?"

"Annur," the Flea responded. He didn't seem to share Fane's enthusiasm. "The Emperor is dead."

5

The Emperor is dead.

The words lodged in Valyn's brain like a bone and even now, hours after the Flea had landed in a flurry of wind and wings, they gouged at him mercilessly. It seemed impossible, like hearing that the ocean had dried up, or the earth had split in two. Sanlitun's death was a tragedy for the empire, of course—he had provided decades of steady, measured rule—but during most of the flight back to the Qirins, all Valyn could think about were the tiny, seemingly inconsequential memories: his father holding the bridle as his son learned to ride his first horse, his father winking during a tedious state dinner when he thought no one else was looking, his father sparring with his sons left-handed to give them the passing illusion of success. There would be a solemn ceremony on the Qirins, as elsewhere, to mourn the passing of the Emperor, but Valyn had no one else with whom to mourn the passing of the man.

He wasn't even sure how his father had died. "Some sort of treachery," was all the Flea could, or would, tell him. It was the standard Kettral horseshit: the trainers insisted that their charges memorize everything about the empire from the price of wheat in Channary to the length of the Chief Priest's cock, but when it came to ongoing operations—then you couldn't *buy* a straight answer. Every now and again, one of the veterans would toss the cadets a scrap—a name, a location, a grisly detail—just enough to whet the appetite without satisfying it. "Mission security," the Eyrie called it, although what security you needed on a 'Kent-kissing island with a captive population Valyn had no idea. He'd more or less made his peace with the policy, but this was his own father's death, and his ignorance tore at him like a cruel thorn lodged beneath the skin. Did *treachery* mean poison? A knife in the back? An "accident" in the Dawn Palace? It seemed like being Sanlitun's son should count for something, but on the Islands, Valyn was not the son of the Emperor; he was a cadet, like the rest of the cadets. He learned what they learned and no more. He had thought, after the Flea first delivered his news, that the Wing may have come to sweep him up, to deliver him back to Annur in preparation for the funeral. Before he could even ask the question, however, Adaman Fane's voice cut through his confusion and horror.

"And you, O Light of the Empire," the trainer had growled, poking Valyn roughly in the shoulder, "don't think this means you'll be getting some sort of holiday. People die all the time. Best to get that through your obdurate skull. If you're going to have even a pathetic shot at surviving Hull's Trial, I'd recommend giving your father an hour of thought tonight and then getting on with the training."

And so, as the Flea, Fane, and a dozen other Kettral winged their way northwest, over the slapping chop toward Annur, Valyn found himself, along with a handful of his fellow cadets, strapped into the talons of a different bird, this one flying south, back toward the Islands. It was nearly impossible to talk with the wind in his face and the great wingbeats of the creature buffeting him from above, and Valyn was grateful for the semblance of solitude. The Flea had come and gone so quickly, delivered his words with so little preamble, that Valyn still didn't feel as though the import of those words had really hit home.

The Emperor is dead.

He tested them again, as though he could feel their veracity in his throat, taste it on his tongue. The Aedolian Guard should have kept his father safe, but the Guard couldn't be everywhere, couldn't defend against every threat.

The ablest swordsman, Hendran wrote, *the consummate tactician, the peerless general: All seem invulnerable until luck turns against them. Make no mistake—place a man in death's way enough times, and his luck will turn.*

Of course, Sanlitun hadn't died of bad fucking luck. The Flea had said "treachery," which meant that someone, probably a group of people, had conspired to betray and murder the Emperor. Which brought Valyn back to the Aedolian he had found in the ship's hold only hours earlier. It didn't take a spymaster or a military genius to see that the threat against Valyn's life was tied to the murder of the Emperor himself. In fact, it looked very much as though a quiet coup was in process, a systematic elimination of the entire Malkeenian line. Sanlitun must have discovered it before his death, must have dispatched the ship full of Aedolians to rescue and protect his son, but the ship had come to grief, and Sanlitun's knowledge had failed to save him. Someone wanted to eliminate the Malkeenian line, and terrifyingly, they were managing it. Someone would be coming for Valyn, and not just him, but for Kaden, too. Even Adare might be in danger—although as a woman, she couldn't sit the Unhewn Throne. That simple fact, so galling to her as a child, may have saved her life. He hoped.

Holy Hull, Valyn thought grimly. As frightening as he found the idea of hidden assassins hunting him over the Qirin Islands, Kaden's situation was far worse. Kaden, not Valyn, had the golden eyes. Kaden, not Valyn, was heir to the throne, was *Emperor* now. And Kaden, not Valyn, was alone in some distant monastery, untrained, unguarded, and unwarned.

Overhead, strapped in to the kettral's back with an elaborate harness, Laith, the flier, banked the bird into a steep turn. Valyn looked over to see Gwenna watching him from her perch on the other talon, red hair swept around her head like flame. Of all the cadets, Gwenna was maybe the least plausible. She looked like a brewer's daughter rather than an elite soldier—all freckles and pale skin given to sunburn, curly hair, and womanly curves that her standard-issue blacks did nothing to hide. She *looked* like a brewer's daughter, but she had just about the worst temper on the Islands.

Her lips were turned down in something that was either a scowl or a frown of commiseration—it was hard to tell with her. *Could she be part of it?* Valyn wondered. It seemed ludicrous to suppose a high-level conspiracy bent at overthrowing the most powerful family in the world would enlist a cadet who hadn't even passed the Trial. Still, there was an intensity in Gwenna's green eyes that was hard to comprehend. Valyn had no idea how long she had been watching him, but when he looked over she pointed to the buckle linking his harness to the bird's thick, scaly leg. He glanced down and discovered to his alarm that he hadn't clinched the safety properly. If the bird stooped hard, he could have been ripped right off the talons, tossed a thousand paces to his death on the waves below.

You 'Kent-kissing idiot, he muttered to himself, yanking the leather tight, then nodding curtly to Gwenna. *No one's going to* need *to kill you if you take care of it for them.* With an effort, he forced his apprehensions down. Whatever plots were afoot, he couldn't foil them while dangling from his harness. There was nothing to do while strapped in to the bird but rest, and he tried to settle back into the rigging, to let his weary muscles slacken for a while, to find some of the calm he usually felt while soaring over the waves.

At sea level, it would be hot and humid already, the kind of day that plastered your shirt to your back and slicked your sword grip with sweat, but Laith was holding the bird a thousand paces up, where the sun warmed without scorching while the kettral's enormous wingspan provided plenty of shade for Valyn, Gwenna, and the two other cadets strapped in and balancing on the huge talons. He tried closing his eyes, but it was no good. Visions of his father's face filled his mind. Or was it Kaden's? All he could see were those golden irises, flaming high, then quenched as blood rose in the sockets.

He shook his head to clear away the visions, opened his eyes, then checked over his belt knife, short blades, and buckle once more, running through the standard flight list over and over. Gwenna had continued watching him, he realized, and he stilled his hands, redirecting his attention to the land and sea inching by below.

He could see most of the Qirins by now, the slender chain stretching across the waves like a necklace of islands. Qarsh, the largest of the group, lay just a little to the south, and Valyn could see the sandy beaches, dense stands of mangroves, dusty limestone bluffs, and the various buildings of Eyrie command—barracks, mess hall, training arenas, storehouses—as clearly as if they were lines inked on a map. A few ships, a merchant ketch and a couple of sloops by the look of them, lolled at anchor in the harbor, and almost directly beneath him, a sleek-hulled cutter sliced through the surf, making for the port.

Qarsh was his home—not just the long, low barracks that he'd shared with twenty-five other cadets for the past eight years or the mess hall where he took his meals, exhausted and numb after a long day of training, but the whole island, from the rocky headlands to the winding waterways between the mangroves. It was familiar, even comforting, in a way the Dawn Palace had never been. The Islands were *his*. Until now.

After the Aedolian's warning and the death of his father, the small archipelago looked different somehow, strange, treacherous, gravid with menace. One of the ships in the harbor might carry the men who had boarded the Aedolian vessel and slaughtered the crew. Someone in the barracks or mess hall, someone he had passed a thousand times in the training ring or labored beside in the storeroom, could be plotting to kill him. Those winding rocky trails offered too much seclusion, too many twists and turns

where a man could disappear without anyone the wiser, and Kettral training afforded a thousand opportunities for "accidents"—botched drops,
rigged munitions, sharp bits of steel just about everywhere you looked. In
the space of a single morning, his home had become a trap.

The bird skimmed above the wide landing field just to the west of the
harbor, and Valyn leapt from the talons. A small cluster of his peers
waited at the edge of the field, some awkwardly fingering their belt knives,
some openly studying him as he approached. Word traveled fast among
the Kettral.

Gent Herren stepped forward first, shaking his massive head. "Hard
luck," he growled, extending a hand like a mallet. The huge cadet stood at
least a foot taller than Valyn and had shoulders to match. He looked like a
bear—curly brown hair on his arms and chest hiding the pale skin
beneath—and generally seemed about as tame as one, although now his
manner was subdued. "Your father ran a tight ship," he went on, as though
unsure quite what to say.

"A loss for the empire," Talal added. Talal was a leach, and like all
leaches, he kept mostly to himself. Still, he and Valyn had cooperated on a
few training exercises over the years, and Valyn had developed a wary
trust for him, despite his strange and tainted powers. In addition to his
blacks, Talal wore an array of glittering bracelets, bands, and rings, and
his ears were pierced with hoops and studs. On another man, such adorn-
ment would have been a mark of vanity and frivolity; on Talal, the glints
and glimmers of metal were as lighthearted as the flash of an assassin's
blade. "Do they have any idea what happened?" he asked quietly.

"No," Valyn replied. "I don't know. Treachery. That was all they
told me."

Gent ground his knuckles into a meaty palm. "Fane and the Flea will
find the 'Kent-kissing bastards. They'll find 'em and sort 'em right out."

Valyn nodded halfheartedly. It was a tempting vision—Wings of Kettral
dragging the conspirators out into the light, beating the truth from them,
and then executing them in the middle of the Annurian Godsway. It
wouldn't bring his father back, but justice carried its own cold satisfaction,
and Valyn would breathe easier once the killers were hanged. *Provided it
proves that simple,* he thought to himself grimly. A hard, realistic voice inside himself told him it would not.

"You'd better keep a closer watch on your 'Kent-kissing buckles,"
Gwenna said, shouldering into the conversation. Her green eyes flashed

with rage, and she planted a finger right in the middle of Valyn's chest, driving her nail into his sternum. "You almost ended up in the drink back there."

"I know," Valyn replied, refusing to step back.

"He just found out his father was murdered," Gent protested.

"Oh, the poor *thing,*" Gwenna snapped back. "Maybe we should keep him on bed rest and spoon-feed him warm milk for a week."

"Gwenna," Talal began, holding out a hand to placate her, "there's no need—"

"There's *every* fucking need," she replied acidly. "He makes a mistake because his head's in the clouds, he could get himself killed. He could get someone else killed."

"Give it a rest, Gwenna," Gent rumbled, his voice menacing as a distant avalanche.

She ignored both the other cadets and fixed her green eyes on Valyn. "I catch you doing something like that again, I'm reporting it. I'll report it straight to Rallen. You understand?"

Valyn met her gaze squarely. "I appreciate the fact that you noticed the buckle. Could have saved my life. But I left my mother eight years ago when I set sail for the Islands, and I don't need you stepping in to play the role."

She pursed her lips as though she intended to argue the point. He took half a step backwards, shifting his weight and freeing his hand from his belt. The Kettral were a prickly bunch, and arguments, even small arguments, often came to blows. He had no idea why Gwenna was so mad, but he'd seen her take a swing at other cadets before, and he wasn't about to be caught wrong-footed. Back on the mainland, there were plenty of fools who would have scoffed at the threat of a woman's punch—but back on the mainland, the women weren't trained to crush your trachea or gouge out an eye. After a tense moment, however, Gwenna shook her head, snarled something about "fucking incompetence," and stalked off toward the barracks.

Silence reigned until Gent broke in, voice like a sack of rocks rolling downhill. "I think she's sweet on you."

Valyn coughed out a laugh. "I'll tell you one thing. If she's assigned to my Wing after the Trial, you both have permission to strangle me in my sleep."

"Might be better to strangle *her,*" Ha Lin chimed in. She had landed on the next bird and must have joined them just as Gwenna made her dramatic exit. "That's the usual idea, you know, Val. Enemy dead. You alive. That sort of thing? Maybe you haven't been following along too closely the last few years."

"Gwenna's not the enemy," Talal demurred.

"Oh no," Lin said, "she's a fucking peach."

Valyn found himself grinning. "I'm fine as long as she doesn't try to shove one of her flickwicks somewhere uncomfortable and light the fuse."

"A man wants to die with his limbs and his dignity intact," Gent agreed. "Stabbed. Poisoned. Drowned. Those are fine . . ." He trailed off, realizing what he was saying. "I'm sorry, Val. I'm a horse's ass. . . ."

Valyn waved the apology aside. "Don't worry. You don't have to stop talking shop because my father's dead."

"What about your brother?" Talal asked. "Is *he* safe?"

Valyn looked over sharply at the leach. It was a sensible question, given the circumstances, but it struck too close to Valyn's own worries for comfort. Was the leach prying for information?

"Of course he's safe," Gent responded, "out there at the ass end of the known world. Who's going to kill him? Another monk?"

Talal shook his head. "Someone betrayed Sanlitun. If they could kill one Emperor, they could kill another."

"It'd take anyone the better part of a season to get to the Bone Mountains if they left yesterday on a fast horse," Lin broke in, setting a hand on Valyn's shoulder. "Kaden—the *Emperor,* I should say—will be fine."

"Unless someone got on that fast horse a few months ago," Valyn interjected. It was maddening, not knowing what, exactly, had happened to his father. He was clenching his fist, he realized, and with an effort he loosened the fingers.

"Val," Lin replied, "you're making the whole thing sound like some grand plot."

"Probably just a disgruntled idiot with a death wish," Gent added.

A grand plot. That was precisely what the Aedolian had suggested.

"I've got to talk to Rallen," Valyn said.

Lin arched an eyebrow. "That sack of shit?"

"He's the Master of Cadets."

"Don't remind me," she snorted.

"That means he decides who leaves the Islands. And when. And for what purpose."

"You taking a vacation?"

"I could be in the Bone Mountains in under a week. Someone has to let Kaden know."

Lin stared at him incredulously, then pursed her lips. "Good luck with that."

✝

For all the myths and fables surrounding the place, the central command building of the Kettral—the Eyrie—didn't look like much. For one thing, despite the name, it was not perched on a dramatic cliffside—in fact, it squatted in the middle of a flat patch of ground a few hundred paces from the harbor. It wasn't even a fortress. When you lived on an island hundreds of miles from the nearest coast guarded by the only airborne fighting force in the world, you didn't need much in the way of fortresses. Instead, a few steps led up to a long, low, stone building facing the square. It might have served as a stable for some country gentleman, or a storehouse for a reasonably prosperous merchant. And yet, that nondescript building was where the men and women of the Eyrie made the decisions and gave the orders that toppled kings and subverted empires.

Valyn took the few steps without even noticing them, knocked the door open with a fist, and plowed down the stone hallway, his boots striking on the flags. Identical teak doors lined the hall; there were no names, no signs to direct a newcomer. If you didn't know where to find the person you were looking for, you didn't belong in the building. Valyn pulled up before the office of Jakob Rallen, the Master of Cadets. It was customary to knock, but Valyn was in no mood for custom.

Rallen was one of the few people on the Islands lacking the deadly look of the Kettral. In fact, the man didn't look like much of a soldier at all. His sharp beady eyes and sweating bald pate seemed more suited to a menial clerk than a warrior, and aside from the short knife all Kettral wore at their belts, Valyn thought he probably hadn't picked up a weapon in fifteen years. He wore blacks like the rest, of course, but he was fat to the point of obesity, and his belly slumped obscenely over his belt when he stood. *Probably why he doesn't stand,* Valyn thought as he waited at attention, forcing himself to remain silent until the man looked up from the parchment in front of him.

Rallen raised a single fat finger. "You're interrupting crucial business," he droned, his eyes on the figures in front of him, "and so you will have to wait."

The business didn't look all that crucial—a few grease-smeared papers next to a half-cleaned plate of chicken—but Rallen liked to make people wait. The exercise of power seemed to bring him almost as much pleasure as stuffing his face with food.

Valyn took a deep breath. For the thousandth time, he tried to muster some sympathy. After all, it wasn't as though Rallen had *chosen* to become a useless invalid. The man had actually passed Hull's Trial somehow, had flown missions once—or one mission, at least. He'd shattered his leg on a nighttime drop and hadn't been able to walk without the support of a cane ever since. It was a tough card to draw for someone who'd spent eight years training, and the man did not handle it well. He seemed to resent anyone more fortunate than him, and that put Valyn, with his royal name and luxurious childhood, just about at the top of the list.

Valyn couldn't count the number of times he'd drawn latrine duty or third watch or stable mop for barely discernible violations of minor regulations. It would have been a whole lot easier to feel pity for Rallen if someone hadn't made him Master of Cadets. The choice had baffled Valyn at first—why would anyone put an inept, undisciplined wash-up in charge, especially one with no combat experience? After a few years on the Islands, however, he thought he was starting to understand. Kettral training wasn't all about fighting. It was about dealing with people, about keeping calm in difficult situations. No one ever said as much, of course, but Valyn had started to suspect that Rallen was all part of the training. He took another breath and waited.

"Ah," the man said, shifting his gaze from the parchment at last. "Valyn. I'm sorry for your loss."

He sounded about as sorry as a butcher hawking his meat, but Valyn nodded. "Thank you."

"I hope, however," the man continued, pursing his lips, "that you're not here to beg for any sort of . . . leniency in your training as a result. Kettral remain Kettral, even when tragedy strikes."

"No begging, sir," Valyn replied, trying to keep his temper in check. "A request."

"Oh, of *course*! How foolish of me. The great Valyn hui'Malkeenian would never *beg*. You probably have slaves to do your begging for you, eh?"

"No more than you do, sir."

Rallen's eyes narrowed. "What's that now? I won't tolerate insouciance in my office, regardless of your *situation*—"

"No insouciance, sir. Just a request."

"Well?" the man asked, waving his hand as though he'd been waiting all along for Valyn to voice it. "Are you going to make it, then, or are you going to continue to waste my time and yours?"

Valyn hesitated, then plunged ahead. "I want to take a bird north. Off the Islands. To Ashk'lan. Kaden won't know about our father's death. He might be in danger."

For a moment Rallen just stared, eyes wide in his fleshy face. Then he doubled over with laughter—rolling, mirthless, sardonic laughter.

"You want . . . ," he managed in between wheezes, "to take a bird. That's wonderful. Truly wonderful. Every other cadet on the Islands is training for Hull's Trial, training to become true Kettral, and you want . . . to just *skip* it! You truly are the son of an Emperor!"

"It's not for me, sir," Valyn ground out. "I'm concerned about my brother."

"Oh, of *course* you are. And of course *you're* the man for the job, eh? The Emperor has the entire Aedolian Guard, men trained for one purpose only—to watch over him—but you think a raw cadet who hasn't even passed the Trial is going to take care of everything, eh? Probably the men in charge back in Annur haven't even *considered* this, is that it? They don't even *realize* just how *good* you really are!"

Valyn hadn't truly expected to be allowed the bird, but there was nothing to be lost in trying. At least it set him up for his real request. "Not me, then, but an established Wing. A Wing of veterans. The Flea, maybe—"

Rallen was already waving him to silence. "The Flea is north with Fane and half a dozen other Wings, trying to sort out what in 'Shael's name went wrong. Besides, this isn't Kettral work. As I just got done telling you, the Emperor, bright be the days of his life, has the Aedolian Guard to protect him. Here on the Islands, you're learning—those of you who can be taught—how to kill people, not how to keep them alive. The Emperor will be fine. This isn't your concern—or mine, for that matter."

"But, sir," Valyn began.

"No," Rallen said.

"Maybe if I spoke with Daveen Shaleel—"

"Shaleel won't speak with you."

"Perhaps if you intervened on my behalf—"

"I have other things to do than run errands for a pampered son of an Emperor."

"I see," Valyn replied, eyeing the chicken carcass. "Lunch *is* a priority."

Rallen heaved his bulk half out of his chair and loomed over his desk, face florid with anger. "You will stand down, cadet!"

Valyn had overstepped. He knew it the moment the words left his mouth, and yet he couldn't bring himself to swallow them.

"You think," Rallen continued, puffing so hard, Valyn thought he might collapse, "that just because you're the son of the Emperor you have the right to strut in here and *demand* things? Do you think that?"

"No, sir," Valyn said, trying to change course.

"It is not your place, not your place to judge. Not your place to question. *Obedience,* cadet. That is what is required of you."

Valyn gritted his teeth and nodded. If there were any choice, he would have taken his request directly to Shaleel. She was the commander of all field operations in northeastern Vash, which meant she coordinated everything the Kettral did in one of the stickiest parts of the world. She was also one of the hardest and smartest soldiers on the Islands. Unfortunately, whatever oddities the Kettral allowed, their command hierarchy was as inviolate as that of any other Annurian military order. If Valyn tried to bypass the Master of Cadets and barge directly into Shaleel's chart room, he'd find himself back scrubbing latrines quicker than he could recite the Soldier's Creed. And then, there were the words of the dead Aedolian echoing in his ears: *Someone here . . . maybe someone important . . . is part of it.*

"I'm sorry, sir," he said, trying out his very best conciliatory voice. "My place is to serve and to obey. I stepped out of line, and for that, I would like to volunteer myself for third watch every second night this week."

Rallen leaned back in his chair and squinted at him for a long time before nodding slowly. "You did. You did step out of line. You've got to get it through that dense head of yours that you're not in charge here. You. Are. Not. In. Charge." He smiled. "Third watch for a *month,* I think, should be adequate to convey the lesson."

6

W e're going to regret this in the morning," Valyn said, peering into the depths of his tankard.

"We've been drunk before," Lin replied, waving over Salia, the serving girl, with a free hand, "and with less cause. Your father just died. No one expects you to be swimming circuits of the Islands."

Your father just died. Even a week later, the words still landed like a sharp fist to the gut. Lin wasn't being cruel; she, like the rest of the Kettral, had long ago been trained to speak in the clear, crisp periods appropriate to combat. Talking round and round a point was like wearing lace into battle.

"I think Rallen would be happy to see me doing just that," Valyn said, settling his elbow on the table and his forehead against the heel of his hand.

Lin frowned, tossed back the remainder of her ale, then frowned again. "Rallen's a shit-sucking turd. It was bad form, giving you third watch at a time like this."

"I volunteered. It was the only way to get out of his office without something worse."

"Aside from avoiding his office in the first place."

"I had to try," Valyn snapped. "It'll take an imperial delegation at least two months to get to Kaden: a few weeks at sea and then twice that riding north from the Bend. They should have sent a Kettral Wing."

There was more venom in his voice than he'd intended. After a week of third watch, days training for the Trial, nights watching his own back, mourning his father silently, and the constant, nagging worry about Kaden, he'd taken the first free hour to catch the boat across the sound to Hook, made the short walk along the alley to Manker's, and polished off five tankards of ale before Lin even walked in the door. It was just as all the Kettral said: You went to Hook to escape your problems and came back with a dozen more.

While the Eyrie kept a close eye on Hook, they didn't control it in the same way as they did the other islands. In fact, sometimes it seemed as though *no one* controlled the place. There was no mayor or town guard, no merchant council, and no local aristocracy. Lin described it as a "hive of 'Shael-spawned pirates," and Valyn supposed she wasn't far wrong. Those who ended up on the island were all desperate—people hiding from mountains of debt, or death warrants, or some other kind of pain. He always got the impression they would have run farther, but there was no place farther to run.

Like most of the buildings on the island, Manker's was built out over Buzzard's Bay, the entire thing held up by tarred timbers sunk in the silt of the harbor bottom. On the outside, the tavern was painted a garish red to compete with the yellow and bilious green buildings flanking it; inside, however, it was low, and dark, and sagging, the kind of place where people held their purses close, kept their voices down, and sat with their backs to the wall. It suited Valyn's mood just fine.

"Kaden will be all right," Lin said, extending a tentative hand and resting it on Valyn's.

"There's no reason to believe that," he growled. "According to the Flea, my father was murdered. Score upon score of Aedolians plus the 'Shael-spawned Palace Guard, and someone *still* managed to kill him. Kaden's in some 'Kent-kissing monastery. What's to keep someone from getting to *him*?"

"The fact that he *is* in that monastery," Lin replied, her voice level. "He's safer tucked away there than he would be anywhere inside the empire. It's probably why he was sent there in the first place. No one even knows where it *is*."

Valyn took a swig of his ale, then hesitated. For the past week he'd been wrestling with himself over whether to tell Lin about the murdered Aedolian, about the plot the man had revealed. He had no question about her loyalty—of all the cadets on the Islands, he knew Lin the best. She'd covered his back in scores of training missions, saving him a dozen broken bones at the least, and he'd hauled her out of some tight spots as well. If there was anyone he could trust, it was Ha Lin, but then, according to Hendran, secrecy admitted no half measures. The fewer people who knew a thing, the safer it was.

"What?" she asked, tilting her head to the side.

"Nothing."

"You can lie to me if you want, but you're gnawing on something."

"Everyone's gnawing on something."

"Well, why don't you give me a bite?"

Valyn tapped absently at the side of his glass. Lin's eyes were warm and urgent, frank enough in their concern that he had to look away. Secrecy was all well and good, but there was always the possibility that the plot against him would *succeed*. If he were the only one to know about it, and someone killed him, the knowledge would die, too. And, if he was being honest with himself, it would feel good to tell someone. He leaned forward over the table.

"You remember that ship . . . ," he began.

The tale didn't take long to relate, and at the end of it, Lin sat back, took a long pull on her ale, and let out a low whistle.

"Meshkent, Ananshael, and a bucket of pickled shit," she swore quietly. "You believe him?"

Valyn shrugged. "Men don't tend to spend their last breath lying."

"But who?" she asked.

He sucked a breath slowly between his teeth. "No way to know. I've been over all the names a dozen times. It could be anyone."

"Rallen's high up at command. He doesn't like you," she pointed out.

"Rallen's too 'Kent-kissing lazy to hoist his fat ass out of his chair, let alone to put together a plot to topple the empire."

She took another swig of ale, then pursed her lips. "Let's go back to your father's murder. If you can figure out who killed him, it might give you a clue who to look out for here on the Islands."

Valyn shook his head. "I've been thinking about that whenever one of the trainers gives me half a breath to myself. The Flea didn't reveal much before he left, and no one else has told me shit since."

"Who were your father's enemies?"

Valyn spread his hands. "Take your pick. He was respected as Emperor, but even good emperors piss people off. Every time he passed judgment on some taxation issue, some disputed border, some stolen inheritance, he alienated at least half the people involved. None of the nobility appreciated the military draft—wanted to let the peasants do the fighting. None of the peasants liked forced labor, even when they got a stipend. The Black Shore Shipping Guild is always angry about something, despite the fact that they basically have an imperial monopoly. And then there's the constant unrest at the borders: Antherans, Urghul, Hannans—all of them with these blood cults that are springing up, all of them pressing back against the 'foreign oppressors,' never mind that our oppression is what brings law courts and foreign trade, military protection and technological advancement. Even the Manjari seem to be getting restless recently, if you can judge from the Wings we've sent. There are plenty of people who'd want to see an Annurian Emperor dead. Shit, we might as well throw the Csestriim into the mix along with everyone else—maybe they *weren't* all killed off three thousand years ago."

"All right, I take your point. It's a long list."

"It's *endless*. Until the Flea or Fane or *someone* gets back from Annur, it's impossible to know where to start. I have to distrust everyone."

Lin tilted her head to one side. "So why did you trust me?" she asked.

Valyn hesitated, suddenly conscious of the weight of her hand on top of his own, of the delicate, salty scent of her hair. She held his gaze with those wide, almond eyes of hers, her lips slightly parted.

Valyn took a deep breath. "I don't know." It was a lie, of course. He *did* know, but what was he going to say? He was a soldier. She was a soldier. If he suggested anything more, she'd be likely to laugh him off the Islands or put a blade in his gut. "I needed another pair of eyes," he finished lamely.

An inscrutable glint flashed in her eyes—gone so quickly he couldn't be sure he had even seen it. "So what are we going to do?" she asked.

In spite of himself, Valyn grinned. It felt good to have someone on his side. "I figured I'd have you guard my back every waking moment and take a dagger for me if the shit gets thick. How's that sound?"

"I signed up for the Kettral, not the Aedolian Guard," she shot back.

"Are you saying you wouldn't gladly throw down your life to keep me from harm?"

He had meant it as a joke, but the remark sobered Ha Lin. "You've got to be careful," she said.

"What I've got to be," Valyn replied, his mood souring with hers, "is off this 'Shael-spawned island. I could be at Ashk'lan in less than a week, and instead I'm here, drinking ale at Manker's."

"Just a month more," Lin replied. "We'll pass the Trial and become full Kettral. A month after that, you'll be flying your own missions, commanding your own Wing. You said it yourself—it'll take anyone traveling by land at least that long to get to Kaden anyway. Two months, Val, that's all."

Valyn shook his head. "I'm already too late."

"Meaning?"

Valyn exhaled heavily, pulling himself back to the table, searching in his cup for the words. "We've spent half our lives here, Lin, learning to fly, to fight, to kill people dozens of different ways, all to defend the empire." He shrugged. "Then, when the empire needed defending, when the *Emperor* needed defending, I wasn't there to do a 'Kent-kissing thing about it."

She shook her head. "It's not your fault, Valyn."

"I know," he replied, reaching for his ale.

She stopped his hand with her own, forcing him to look at her. "It's not your fault. You couldn't have protected him."

"I know," he said again, trying to believe the words. "I know, but maybe I can protect Kaden."

"Two months," she said once more, leaning in as though to will her patience upon him. "Just hold on."

Valyn freed his hand, took a deep swig from his tankard, then nodded.

Before he could otherwise respond, however, the door clattered open and Sami Yurl stepped in. The youth scanned the low room with an expression of amused distaste. He had left his father's gilded halls nearly ten years ago, but he still seemed to regard the workmanlike buildings of Hook and the other Islands as beneath his dignity, and he crossed under the lintel as though condescending to enter.

"Wench," he said, snapping his fingers at Salia. "Wine. Whatever's not watered down too horribly. And a clean glass this time, or I'll introduce you to my displeasure."

Salia cringed and bowed her way toward the kitchens, nodding obsequiously.

Lin growled deep in her throat, and Yurl, as though he heard the sound, turned to the corner table where she and Valyn sat. Salia came hurrying back with the full glass of wine, and he took it without looking at her, then raised it toward Valyn with a smirk.

"Congratulations! One step closer to the throne!"

Valyn moved his tankard to the side slowly, then reached down for the handle of his belt knife. Lin caught his wrist beneath the table, her grip surprisingly strong.

"Not now," she hissed.

Blood hammered in Valyn's ears, behind his eyes. It was partly the ale—he understood that dimly—but only Lin's hand kept him from drawing the knife.

"Not now," she said again. "You fight him, and you'll end up in the brig for the Trial. Is that what you want?"

Yurl watched the whole scene from a few paces away, sipping at his wine with an amused smile. Like Valyn and Ha Lin, he had left his swords behind, relying on his belt knife and Kettral blacks to keep Hook's more enterprising criminals at bay. Valyn flexed his hand beneath the table. Yurl's knifework was good, better than good, but nothing like his swordplay. Knife against knife, Valyn would have a chance. Not to kill the bastard—he'd end up hanged for that—but to cut him down a peg or two . . . but then, as Lin had already pointed out, he'd miss his chance at the Trial. He put his hands back on top of the table deliberately.

Yurl smiled even wider. "Don't tell me you don't *want* the Unhewn Throne," he mused, grinning.

"My brother has Intarra's eyes," Valyn grated. "My brother will sit the throne."

"How filial." Yurl turned his attention to Ha Lin. "And what about you? You figure if you fuck His Most Radiant Highness here enough times, you can ride his gilded cock to wealth and glory?"

It was a groundless gibe. Despite Valyn's confusing feelings for Lin, they had never so much as kissed. If they shared a blanket sometimes on a miserable patrol exercise, all the Kettral did as much—it was just to stay alive, shivering against each other beneath the woolen fabric, trying to save a little warmth from the hard ground below and the chill air above. The truth was, Valyn went out of his way to avoid such situations, wary, lest she realize he thought of her as more than a fellow soldier. Yurl, however, had never bothered much with the truth.

"Don't be hard on yourself," Lin sneered, "just because you don't measure up."

The youth chuckled as though amused, but Valyn could see the jest had hit home. Of all the people on the Islands, only Yurl seemed to harbor any lust for Valyn's position.

He sneered, then turned toward the bar.

"This wine is swill," he said to Salia, dropping the glass, letting it shatter, the shards bright in the flickering lamplight. "You can pay for it out of your earnings."

He cast a cool glance at Juren, the hulking thug Manker employed to keep something resembling order. Juren wasn't too bright, but he wasn't about to go toe to toe with a Kettral over a broken glass of wine. The man scowled at the floor, but made no move as Salia scurried to pick up the shattered vessel. Yurl chuckled in disgust, then turned toward the door and left.

Valyn slowly unclenched his hand, and as he did, Lin released his wrist.

"Someday," she said, her voice tight and hard. "But not today."

Valyn nodded, hoisted his tankard, and took a long pull. "Not today," he agreed.

A few paces away, Salia was weeping quietly as she swept the broken glass into a pan.

"Salia," he said, beckoning her over.

The girl rose unsteadily and approached.

"How much was the wine?"

"Eight flames," she snuffled. "I gave him Manker's own stock."

Eight flames. It was probably as much as the poor girl earned in a week. At least, if you didn't count the money she made on her back upstairs.

"Here," Valyn said, shelling out enough coin to cover his ale plus the spilled wine and broken glass. The Eyrie didn't pay soldiers much, especially not cadets, but he could afford it more than she could. Besides, the desire to drink had gone out of him.

"I couldn't," she began, though she eyed the coin hungrily.

"Take it," Valyn replied. "Someone has to clean up Yurl's mess."

"Thank you, sir," Salia said, ducking her head as she scooped up the coppers. "Thank you so much. You're always welcome here at Manker's, sir, and if you ever need . . . anything else—" She batted her eyes, suddenly bold. "—you just let me know."

"That was gallant," Lin said with a tight smile after the girl had left.

"She has a hard life."

"Who doesn't?"

Valyn snorted. "Good point. Speaking of hard lives, I'm heading back to the barracks—we're supposed to be running the perimeter before dawn tomorrow, and all this ale isn't going to be doing my head any favors."

Lin chuckled. Then, in her best imitation of Adaman Fane's gravelly voice, she began, "*Real* Kettral *embrace* adverse circumstances. Real Kettral *lust* for *suffering.*"

Valyn nodded ruefully. "Six tankards on an empty stomach—all part of the training."

As they stepped out of Manker's, he stopped to watch the sun setting over the sound to the west. In that direction, more than a thousand leagues distant, past the wind-lashed waves of Iron Sea, past the karst peaks of the Broken Bay, past dozens of islands, some too small for names, Annur glittered, tiled roofs, grand palaces, shit-reeking hovels all clustered around Intarra's Spear, the enormous glowing tower at the heart of the Dawn Palace. Sailors could make out the Spear when they were still two days distant—used it to navigate toward the heart of the empire. It was supposed to be impregnable, that tower, one of the final fortresses of the Csestriim, and yet, it had not protected the Emperor.

My father is dead, Valyn thought to himself, and for the first time, the words felt real. He turned to Lin, wanting to say something, to thank her for being there, for sharing the ale and the grief, for holding him back when his own anger drove him to strike out. She watched him with those bright, careful eyes, lips pursed as though she were about to speak. Before either of them could break the silence, however, a terrible crack shattered the still evening air.

Valyn turned, dropping his hand to his belt knife while Lin pivoted to put her back to his, settling into the low ready guard the Kettral used as their standard defensive position. His eyes flicked over the street, the alleys, the rooftops in quick succession, reading terrain and evaluating threat. The garish façades of the rickety structures stared back at him, red, and green, and blue, windows and open doors gaping like missing teeth. A dozen yards away, a dog perked up its ears at the strange sound, its bone momentarily forgotten. A few scraps of dingy curtain blew in the light breeze. An alley gate creaked idly on its hinges. Aside from that—nothing. The noise had probably come from the harbor—some drunken idiot who forgot to throw the catch on a winch and let his load go tumbling to the deck. *Jumping at shadows,* Valyn thought to himself. All the talk of plots and murders must have put them both on edge.

Then, just as he was about to straighten up, Manker's gave a low, horrible groan. The crack of splintering timber sent the dog bolting away as the alehouse's roof sagged in on itself, crumpling like wet paper, shedding slate tiles that fell in a deadly rain onto the street. The whole thing lurched toward the bay, then teetered horribly on its stilts. The people inside began to scream.

"The door!" Lin yelled, but Valyn was already moving. The two of them had spent enough time studying demolitions to know what happened to anyone trapped inside a building when it collapsed. People would be crushed or worse, drowned when the structure finally sloughed into the bay, dragging those pinned inside beneath the waves.

The whole building had peeled away from the alley, leaving a gap of several feet between the crumbling dirt of the lane and the listing doorway. Valyn glanced down—twenty-five feet or so to the water—a trivial distance, except for the jagged ends of the shattered stilts thrusting up like pikes. Anyone who tumbled into the space risked getting impaled on those splintered ends or ground into the murky water when the building finally collapsed. A hand appeared on the doorframe, groping desperately from the darkness within. Valyn swore once and vaulted the gap.

He caught the low lintel of the door with one hand, steadied himself, then reached through the door with his other to catch the wrist. He hauled, and Juren emerged, coughing and swearing. Blood poured from a nasty gash across his bald scalp and his ankle twisted sickeningly as he put weight on it, but other than that, the man appeared to be unharmed.

"Stay there," Valyn said. "I'll hand the others out to you. You can steady them before they jump over to Lin." He jerked his chin to indicate his companion, who waited warily on the bank a few paces away.

The man flicked his eyes toward the interior of the tavern. Something had arrested the slow, inevitable collapse, but over the screams of the injured, Valyn could still hear the cracking of posts and beams warped past their tolerance.

"Fuck that," Juren spat, his lips curled into a desperate rictus. He gathered his weight on his good leg, then leapt for the far bank.

"You shit-licking coward . . . ," Lin began, yanking the man painfully to his feet by the ear as soon as he hit the bank.

"Leave it, Lin," Valyn bellowed. "I need you over here."

Ha Lin snarled, backhanded Juren across the face, measured the gap at a glance, then leapt, alighting on the opposite side of the doorframe from Valyn.

"You or me?" she asked, peering in through the door.

"I'm stronger," Valyn said. "I'll drag them to you. You get them across."

Lin eyed the gap. "Right." She caught Valyn's gaze, hesitated, then waved him ahead. "Work fast."

He nodded, then stepped inside.

It was even worse than he had anticipated. Manker's had been a gloomy den before the collapse, and the buckling ceiling and slumping walls had

almost entirely blocked the few windows. Wreckage lay everywhere—
ceiling timbers, busted tables, chunks of lath, and plaster cracked from the
crumbling walls. Half a dozen small fires—kindled, no doubt, when the
lanterns smashed against the dry timber—licked at the jumble of broken
beams, illuminating a thousand scattered shards of glass. Valyn paused,
trying to get his bearings, trying to get his 'Kent-kissed *footing* on the
floor, which sloped as precipitously as the deck of a clipper under full sail.
People were shouting, moaning, crying for help, but at first he couldn't
even see them in the fitful gloom.

"'Shael take it," he swore, shoving a board out of his way with one
hand, trying to shield his eyes from the dust and debris.

He almost tripped over the first body—a thin, sallow man, his chest
staved in by one of the collapsing timbers. Valyn dropped to a knee and
put his fingers to the man's neck, checking for a pulse, though he knew
what he would find. As he rose, he heard a woman's voice sobbing nearby.
Salia—the serving girl.

She was trapped beneath a fallen rafter, but seemed alert and unin-
jured, if terrified. He took a step toward her, and the entire structure
shrieked, pitching another few feet toward the bay.

"Val," Lin shouted from the door. "Time to get out. The whole thing's
going down!"

He ignored the warning and crossed the few remaining steps to the
trapped girl.

"Are you hurt?" he asked, dropping to one knee and running his hands
along the beam, trying to discover what held her down.

Salia looked up at him, her dark eyes terrified, reflecting the fires that
raged all around them now, singeing his face and her dress.

"My leg," she gasped. "Don't leave me."

"*Valyn,*" Lin bellowed. "Extract *now.* You've got *no* time."

"I'm coming," he shouted back, looping a hand beneath the girl's armpit and pulling. She screamed at the pain, the piercing howl of a trapped
animal, bit down on her lip, and fainted.

"Son of a whore," Valyn swore. She was held up somehow, but in the
dusty murk, he couldn't see where. Somewhere to his left, a beam crashed
down from the ceiling and the whole tavern listed a few more degrees. He
ran his hands around Salia again, searching for the obstruction. "Slowly,"
he told himself. "Slowly." If there was one thing he'd learned as a cadet, it

was to act deliberately, even when the stakes were high. "Especially when the stakes are high, you fool," he muttered.

As his fingers brushed past her waist, he found the problem—her dress had snagged on a wide splinter of wood. He yanked at it, but it held firm.

"Valyn, you stupid son of a bitch!" Lin shouted. There was fear in her voice now, fear and anger. "Get the *fuck out!*"

"I'm moving!" he called back, slipping his belt knife from the sheath and hacking away the snagged portion of the dress.

The girl came free all in a lurch. He dropped the knife, grabbed her by the dress and the hair, and dragged her across the floor toward the dim outline of the door, where Ha Lin was gesturing furiously.

"Go," he shouted. "Get across! I'll throw her to you!"

Lin snarled, froze in an anguish of indecision, then nodded and disappeared.

When Valyn pulled the unconscious girl through the doorway, he found, to his horror, that the gap had grown to almost a dozen feet. He could jump it, but Salia was still unconscious, draped limply over his shoulder.

Lin read the situation instantly, shook her head, then stepped right to the edge of the yawning crevasse.

"Throw her," she said, gesturing.

Valyn stared at the gap, aghast. Salia couldn't have been three quarters of his weight, but there was no way he could toss her the full distance. He glanced down. The jagged pilings bristled like spikes.

"I can't," he shouted back.

"You have to! Now, fucking *throw* her! I'll catch her wrists."

It was impossible. Lin knew it as well as he did. *Which is why she wants me to do it,* Valyn realized in a rush. Salia was dead weight. He could make the jump alone, but just barely. As long as he held on to the unconscious girl, he was trapped on the wrong side of the gap, pinned to a burning, teetering shell that would drag him to his death. He saw it all clear as day, but what could he do? Drop the unconscious girl and leave her to die? It was the right choice, the mission-responsible choice, but this wasn't a 'Kent-kissing mission. He couldn't just . . .

"I'll jump with her," he shouted, preparing to sling Salia across his back. "I think I can make it."

Lin's eyes widened with horror. Then they hardened.

Before Valyn understood what was happening, she had her belt knife out, was cocking her arm, then throwing. Valyn watched, stunned, as the bright blade flashed end over end in the sun, then buried itself in Salia's neck with a sudden gush of hot, bright blood. The girl's lips parted in something that might have been a cry or a moan, but more blood choked it off.

"She's dead," Lin shouted. "You can't save her now, Valyn! She's fucking *dead*. Now, *jump!*"

Valyn stared at Salia, at the hilt of the knife pressed up against her neck. *She's dead.* Beneath him, the building shuddered and groaned. He let out a roar of rage, dropped the corpse, and leapt. His feet hit the crumbling verge, and Lin caught him by the wrists, dragging him to safety.

He shrugged her off and spun back toward the tavern. Salia was gone, tumbled down into the gap. Flames licked up through the open door. Inside, people were still screaming, trapped as fire consumed the tarry timbers. A hand appeared on the sill, bloody and burned. It flailed, trying to find purchase, then fell away. Finally, the entire building trembled, sloughed away from the shore, and then, as though exhausted, crushed beneath its own weight, collapsed inward and sank into the bay.

7

Adare hui'Malkeenian tried to keep her face still as the soldiers, resplendent in their full plate, dragged open the thick cedar doors to the tomb of her murdered father.

If you hope to play a part in this empire, Sanlitun had told her time and time again, *you must learn to divorce your feelings from your face. The world sees what you allow it to see, judges you according to what you reveal.*

"The world" seemed an apposite term for those who observed her now—tens of thousands of Annur's citizens gathered in the Valley of Eternal Repose to see a great man laid to his rest in this narrow, treeless vale lined with the tombs of her ancestors. It would not do to weep before them, regardless of her grief. She already looked out of place, a young woman seated amidst the clutch of aging High Ministers, all of them men.

The position on the raised podium was rightfully hers twice over—once by dint of her royal birth and, most recently, as a result of her elevation to Minister of Finance, an elevation spelled out in her father's testament. It was an important post, nearly as important as the *kenarang* or Mizran Councillor, and one for which she had been preparing for the better part of her life. *I'm ready for this,* she told herself, thinking back over the thousands of pages she had read, the countless delegations she had welcomed for her father, the ledgers she had studied late into the night. She understood Annur's finances better than the outgoing minister, and yet she was certain that, to those assembled in the valley, she did not look ready.

She would look, to many of the thousands of eyes that rested upon her, like a woman too long without a husband and children, attractive enough to invite marriage (even without her imperial titles), if perhaps too thin, tall, and honey-skinned in a city where the fashion ran to voluptuous, small women with darker complexions. Adare knew well enough that her straight hair emphasized the angularity of her face, making her look slightly severe. As a child, she had experimented with other styles. Now the severity suited her purposes; when the assembled throng looked up at her podium, she wanted people to see a minister, not a simpering girl.

Of course, those who stood close enough were unlikely to remember anything but her eyes, irises that burned like coals. Everyone used to say that Adare's eyes blazed even more brightly than Kaden's, not that it mattered. Despite the fact that she was two years older, despite her father's careful tutelage, despite her familiarity with the policies and politics of the Annurian Empire, Adare would never sit the Unhewn Throne. As a child, she had once been innocent enough to ask her mother why. *It is a man's seat,* the woman replied, ending the conversation before it began.

Adare had not felt the full heft of that statement until now, seated among these men, waiting for the bier carrying her father to make its progress up the long valley. Though she, like they, wore dark ministerial robes cinched around the waist with a black sash, though the golden chain of office hung around her neck as it did around theirs, though she sat shoulder to shoulder with these few who, beneath the Emperor himself, ruled the civilized world, she was not one of them, and she could feel their invisible doubts, their decorous resentment cold and silent as snow.

"This is a place heavy with history," Baxter Pane observed. Pane served as Chief Censor and Minister of Custom. Though, or perhaps because, his post was less significant than Adare's, he was among those who had questioned her ascension most openly. "History and tradition." That last word sounded like an accusation in his mouth, but gazing out over the Valley of Eternal Repose, Adare could not disagree. From Alial the Great's stone lions to her own father's façade, a rising sun in bas-relief above the doorway into darkness, she could trace the sure hand of the Malkeenian line.

"The problem with tradition," observed Ran il Tornja, "is that it takes so much 'Kent-kissing *time.*" Il Tornja was the *kenarang,* the empire's commanding general, and evidently some sort of military genius. The Ministerial Council, at any rate, had respected him enough to raise him to regent while Annur waited for Kaden's return.

"Surely you bury your soldiers when they are killed in battle?" she responded pointedly. Il Tornja was, after Adare, the youngest person on the podium, perhaps somewhere in his mid-thirties. More important, he had been the only one who seemed to accept her appointment to Finance. He might make a natural ally, but she couldn't help bristling at his tone. "Surely a general looks after his fallen men."

He shrugged off the note of challenge in her voice. "If there's opportunity. I'd rather be running down the ones who killed them."

Adare took a deep breath. "There will be time enough for that, and soon. Uinian should be dead within the month—within the week, if I have my way."

"I'm all for summary execution, but don't you need some sort of trial? The man *is* the Chief Priest of Intarra. I imagine his congregation might take it amiss if you just hanged him from the highest tree."

"My father went to the Temple of Light," Adare said, enumerating the facts on her fingers. "He met with Uinian the Fourth in secret. He was murdered during that secret meeting." She would have paid dearly to know *why* her father was meeting with the priest, why he had left behind the protection of his Aedolian Guard, but the outlines of his assassination were nonetheless clear. "Uinian will have his trial, and then he will die."

A deep bass tolling of drums halted the conversation. Again those drums came, and again, stately and solemn, as though the earth itself were reverberating. The funeral procession remained out of sight beyond a bend in the canyon, but it approached.

"Five hundred white bulls were sacrificed at the funeral of Santun the Second," Bilkun Hellel observed. The Azran Councillor was pink, oily, and grossly fat. His robes, cut of the finest cloth, fit him poorly. His small, shrewd eyes missed little, however, especially in the political realm. "It's a shame we could not have made a similar show for your father."

Adare waved the suggestion aside. "Five hundred bulls at ten suns apiece—five thousand suns. The coin is needed elsewhere."

A smile creased the corner of the councillor's mouth. "While I admire your mathematics, I'm not sure you realize the effect of such spectacle on the minds of the people. It glorifies your father and by extension your house."

"My father would have hated this. The ostentation, the frippery."

"It was your father," Baxter Pane observed archly, "who ordered it in the first place."

Adare opened her mouth to reply, then shut it firmly. She was here to mourn, not to trade barbs with old men who would never really listen to her anyway.

A hush fell over the valley as the first columns of Annurian foot marched into view, rank upon rank upon rank of soldiers, spears held at the same sharp angle, flashing points reflecting in the afternoon sun. A standard-bearer marched at the center of each line, flying the bold, rising sun of Annur on white silk cloth while to either side of him drummers beat out the procession on huge skins drawn taut over wooden drums.

Aside from their standards the legions were identical: the same steel armor, the same half helms, the same long spear in every right hand, the same short sword hanging from each hip. Only the pennants streaming in the wind identified them: the Twenty-seventh, called the Jackals; and the Rock (the Fifty-first) from the northern Ancaz; the Long Eye from the Rift Wall; the Red Eagle and the Black; the Thirty-second, who called themselves the Bastards of Night; even the legendary Fourth Legion—the Dead—from deep in the Waist, where the fight to subdue the jungle tribes had never really ended.

Next came the regional militias—militarily insignificant, but more varied and colorful: The Raaltans carried ludicrously long broadblades and must have worn their own weight in gleaming steel plate, their standard, a windmill with whirling swords in place of vanes. *Storms, Our Strength,* read the words emblazoned beneath the emblem. Then a contingent of four-score men in boiled black leather, each carrying a pitchfork.

"Fools," Pane snorted. "Upjumped peasants with their farm implements."

"Two hundred and twelve years ago," Adare pointed out, "Maarten Henke carved out an independent kingdom with one of those farm implements. For fifty-four years, he defied Annurian rule effectively enough with his pitchfork."

"Good weapon, a pitchfork," il Tornja observed idly. "Reach. Penetrating power."

"Henke was crushed," Hellel said. "Another failed rebellion."

"And yet, the man was hardly a fool," she insisted, irritated that they seemed to be missing her point.

As the next group marched into view, her stomach seized.

"The Sons of Flame," she muttered, grimacing. "After what Uinian did, they should not be here. They should not *be.*"

"While I happen to agree," Hellel replied, passing a hand over his thinning hair, "what is to be done? The people love Intarra. Our esteemed regent," he continued, nodding toward il Tornja, "has already imprisoned their Chief Priest. Take away their legion, and you might well have a riot."

"It is a *complex* matter, Adare," Pane added, raising his palms as though to placate her. "A *subtle* matter."

"I understand the complexity," she shot back, "but complexity is no excuse for inaction. Uinian's trial may give us leverage in the weeks to come, leverage to disband their militia."

Most imperial historians considered it a wise move to allow the provinces their small local armies—those armies provided an outlet for local pride and offered no real threat to the unity of the empire. Those same historians, however, had an entirely different opinion of Santun the Third's edict allowing for the formation of *religious* military orders. "Ill-considered and unwise," Alther wrote. Hethen went a step further, claiming the decision was "altogether lacking in common sense or historical perspective." "Just plain stupid," said Jerrick the Elder. Raaltans would never make common political cause with Si'ites, but both atrepies had citizens who worshipped Heqet and Meshkent, Ae and Intarra. It seemed never to have occurred to Santun that those citizens might very well join together for *religious* reasons and, in so doing, come to rival the strength of the Unhewn Throne. Miraculously, the worst had not come to pass. Most of the religious orders *did* maintain simple citizen groups to guard their temples and altars.

Uinian IV, however, the Chief Priest of Intarra, had been gradually building his forces for more than a decade. It was difficult to come up with an accurate estimate, but Adare reckoned they numbered in the tens of thousands spread across two continents. Worse, Intarra was the patron goddess of the Malkeenian line itself—the royal family with their blazing eyes claimed legitimacy precisely because of her divine favor. The growing power of the Temple of Intarra and its Chief Priest could only undermine the imperial mandate. Anyone wondering why Uinian would want to murder the Emperor need not have looked very far.

These troops were almost as neatly dressed as the Annurian legions, and like the legions, they eschewed martial pomp for serviceable weapons and armor. The first regiment carried flatbows while those behind bore a forest of short spears, the butts of which struck in cadence with their march. Also like the Annurians, these bore a sun standard, but unlike the symbol of imperial troops, it was not a rising sun, but a round orb in all its glory.

Only at the end of the long river of martial splendor did Sanlitun's bier arrive. Twelve Aedolians bore it on their shoulders—the same twelve who had been charged with guarding the Emperor the day Uinian had plunged the blade into his back. As they drew closer, Adare could make out the neat bandages binding the end of each man's wrist. Micijah Ut, the Aedolian First Shield since the death of Crenchan Xaw, had personally severed their sword hands. *Why do you need swords,* he had growled at them, rage rumbling beneath the words, *when not a single one of you drew a blade to defend the Emperor?*

Adare knew all twelve of the men—even the youngest had served in the Dawn Palace for the better part of five years. Anger and sorrow filled her at the sight of them. They had failed in their duty, and her father was dead because of that failure. And yet, her father had left them behind on his visit to the temple. It was difficult to protect a man who refused protection.

If the Aedolians felt the pain of their missing hands, they didn't show it any more than they did the strain of bearing the Emperor's bier. Each man's face might have been chipped from stone for all the emotion he showed, and despite the sweat beading on their brows, the soldiers marched in precise lockstep.

When the bier reached the entrance to the tomb, the entire column halted abruptly. Soldiers stood at attention and the drums fell silent as Adare and the others descended the wooden steps from their platform.

The words spoken before the tomb were as long-winded as they were meaningless, and Adare let them wash over her like a frigid rain: *duty, honor, power, vision.* They were applied to all Emperors in all imperial funerals. They failed utterly to capture the father she had known. When it was finished, a huge Kreshkan tolled on his wide gong, and then she was following the bier into the darkness of the tomb itself.

The crypt smelled of stone and damp, and despite the torches blazing from the sconces, her eyes took a long time to adjust. When they did, she couldn't help but smile through the welter of emotions. For all the severe grandeur of the tomb's exterior, the inside was small, little more than a natural cave scooped out of darkness with a raised stone platform at its center. There were no carvings, no hangings on the wall, no piles of treasure.

"I had expected a little more . . . ," Ran il Tornja began, waving a hand as he searched for the right word. "I don't know . . . more *stuff.*"

Adare bit off a sharp retort. The other High Ministers had accompanied her into the tomb to pay their final respects. Crass though he might have been, il Tornja was now the highest-ranking man in the empire.

It would not do to tangle with him before the others, especially given the fact that he seemed disposed to accept her recent appointment.

"Not from my father," Adare replied simply. "He gave the people the show they required out there, but in here . . . the stone is enough. He would not have wanted to waste anything on the dead that could be of use to the living."

The Aedolians lowered the bier into place, straightened from their burden, saluted the Emperor with their bandaged stumps, then filed silently from the chamber. The various ministers said a few words, and then they, too, took their leave until only Adare and il Tornja remained. *Say what you have to say,* she thought to herself, *and give me a few final moments with my father.* But il Tornja did not go, nor did he address the corpse.

Instead, he turned to Adare. "I liked your father," he said, nodding casually toward the bier. "Good soldier. Knew his tactics."

She bristled at the offhand tone. "He was *more* than a simple *soldier.*"

The *kenarang* shrugged. Il Tornja had held the post of *kenarang* barely more than a couple of years and was, of course, utterly new to the regency, and yet he didn't seem to feel any of the awe that was so typical of newcomers to the capital. He didn't seem to have much awe for *her* either. Most people quailed before Adare's fiery gaze; he didn't appear even to notice it. The man spoke as if he were seated in a tavern with his boots up, and she were the tavern wench. Come to think of it, he had more or less *dressed* for a tavern as well.

He was clean enough, but unlike the ministers in their somber robes or the soldiers in their crisp uniforms, il Tornja's garb wasn't the slightest bit funereal. He wore a blue cloak with a golden clasp over a blue doublet, the whole ensemble sumptuously tailored. A golden sash hung from his right shoulder, the metal inlaid with sparkling gems that might have been diamonds. If Adare didn't know that the man had won dozens of battles, several of them against daunting odds, she might well have mistaken him for a masker who had stumbled into the tomb while looking for his stage.

The *kenarang*'s uniform was expensive, but the cloth itself was clearly just an excuse to show off the physique beneath. The tailor had known his work, cutting the fabric to pull tight over the muscles, especially when il Tornja moved. Although he stood just barely taller than she, he was built like one of the statues lining the Godsway. She tried ignoring him, focusing her attention on her father's body.

"I'm sorry if I offended," he replied, sweeping a little bow. "I'm sure your father was great at the whole lot of it—the taxes and road-building and sacrifices and the rest of the tedium an Emperor has to attend to. Still, he liked a good horse and a good sword."

He delivered the last line as though it were the ultimate compliment.

"If only an empire could be governed with a sword from horseback," Adare replied, careful to keep her voice cold.

"Men have managed it. That Urghul—what was his name? Fenner. He had an empire, and people say the man hardly ever dismounted."

"*Fannar* had a bloodbath that lasted twenty years. Within weeks of his death, the tribes had dissolved back to their age-old rivalries and his 'empire' was gone."

Il Tornja frowned. "Didn't he have a son?"

"Three. The two eldest were thrown on the funeral pyre with their father, and the youngest, as far as anyone knows, was gelded and sold to slavers from east of the Bone Mountains. He died in chains in Anthera."

"Not such a good empire," il Tornja agreed with a shrug. Fannar's failure didn't seem to trouble him in the slightest. "I'll have to remember that, at least until your brother gets back." He fixed her with a level stare. "I didn't want it, you know. The regent thing."

The regent thing. As though his ascension to the most powerful post in the empire were nothing more than an irritating chore that kept him from drinking or whoring or whatever it was he did when he wasn't leading armies.

"Then why did you take it?"

His insouciance stung, in part because, though she had known Annur would never accept a woman in the post, she had hoped secretly that the Council of Ministers might appoint her nonetheless, at least for the short months until Kaden returned. Whatever battles he had won, il Tornja struck her as ill-suited to political rule.

"Why did they choose you in the first place?"

If the man took offense at the question, he didn't show it. "Well, they had to pick someone."

"They could have picked someone *else.*"

"Truth is," he said with a wink, "I think they tried. There were votes and votes and votes. You know they lock you into that 'Shael-spawned hall until you come up with a name?" He blew out a long, irritated breath. "And there's no ale. I'll tell you that. Wouldn't be so bad if there was ale."

This man, the one who complains about a lack of ale during the conclave, is the one the ministers chose as regent?

"At any rate," the *kenarang* continued, heedless of her dismay, "I don't think many of them much *wanted* me. In the end, I think they picked me because I *don't* have any plans for the governance of this fine empire." He frowned apologetically. "I'm not saying I'm going to shirk my duty. I'll see to what needs doing, but I know my limits. I'm a soldier, and a soldier shouldn't overstep himself when he's not on the battlefield." ·

Adare nodded slowly. There was a certain perverse logic to the decision. The various ministries were always jockeying for position: Finance with Ethics, Agriculture with Trade. No regent would actually try to seize power for himself, but the months during which Kaden was away would provide plenty of time to tip some very delicate scales. Il Tornja, on the other hand—the man was affable, a war hero, and perhaps most crucially, indifferent to political maneuvering.

"Well," she replied, "the delegation left for Kaden just after my father's death. If they have good winds to the Bend, they could be back in a matter of months."

"Months," il Tornja groaned. "At least it's not years. What's Kaden like?"

"I barely know my brother. He's been in Ashk'lan for half his life."

"Learning to run all this?" il Tornja asked, gesturing vaguely, presumably at the vast empire stretching away outside the walls of the tomb.

"I certainly hope so. The boy I knew liked to run around the palace waving a wooden stick in place of a sword. Hopefully he will shine as brightly as my father."

Il Tornja nodded, looked over at the body of Sanlitun, then back at Adare. "So," he said, spreading his hands. "Uinian. You plan to hold the knife yourself?"

Adare raised an eyebrow. "Excuse me?"

"The priest murdered your father. Once you go through the show of the trial, he'll be condemned. What I wonder is, will you kill him yourself?"

She shook her head. "I hadn't considered the question. There is an executioner—"

"You ever kill a man?" he asked, cutting her off.

"I haven't had much occasion."

He nodded, then gestured to the bier. "Well, it's *your* grief, and I don't mean to tell you how to handle it. Ananshael has your father now, and

Ananshael won't give him back. Still, when the time comes, you may find it helps if you execute the bastard yourself." He held her gaze a moment longer, as though to be sure she had understood, then turned on his heel and left.

Only then, when she was finally alone, did Adare allow herself to turn to her father's bier. Sanlitun hui'Malkeenian's body had been scrubbed, dried, and dressed by the Sisters of Ananshael, his mouth and nose stuffed with sweet-smelling herbs to keep off the stench of the rot. *Even Intarra's favor can't hold off the Lord of Bones.* The Emperor was dressed in his finest robes of state, his strong hands folded across his chest, fingers interlaced. Despite his pallor, he looked almost like the father she had known. If he had cried out or struggled in his final moments, the Sisters had smoothed his features until they were as stoic and somber in death as they had once been in life.

His eyes, however, those fiery eyes were closed. *I never saw him sleep,* she realized. She must have, surely, maybe when she was only a small child, but if so, those memories had dissolved. Every recollection she had of him involved that blazing gaze. Without it, he seemed smaller somehow, quieter.

Tears streamed down her cheeks as she took his hand. She had hoped for some message when his testament was read the week prior, some final note of love or comfort. But then, Sanlitun was never effusive. His only bequest to her was Yenten's *History of the Atmani,* "that she might better appreciate our history." It was a fine book, but just a book nonetheless. His true gift had been her appointment to the head of the Ministry of Finance, his belief that she was capable of the job.

"Thank you, Father," she murmured. "You will be proud. If Valyn and Kaden are equal to their fate, then so am I."

Then, anger welling inside her, she pulled the knife from the belt at his side.

"And, when the time comes for Uinian to die, I *will* wield the knife myself."

8

I think Tan's trying to kill me," Kaden said, straightening up from the bundle of tiles he had just hoisted up onto the dormitory roof and wiping the sweat from his brow.

Down below, Phirum Prumm was huffing with the effort of muscling the next load into place and hitching it to the rope. Kaden's back and hands ached from the repetitive labor, but compared with the rigors of Rampuri Tan's training, retiling the roof after the winter ice damage felt like a holiday. At least he could find the occasional moment to straighten from his task and knuckle the sore muscles without getting whipped.

"Quit whining," Akiil retorted, hunkering down to get a good grip on the tiles, then hauling the whole crate up with a grunt. Kaden had no idea how his friend could work with the mop of black curls hanging down over his eyes—by tradition he should have cropped his scalp like the rest of the monks, but a tradition wasn't exactly a rule, and Akiil was extremely adept at balancing on the fine line between the two. "The first month with a new *umial* is always the worst. Remember when Robert made me carry those stones for the new goat shed down from the Circuit of Ravens?" He groaned at the memory.

"I don't think this is so bad," Pater protested as Akiil dropped the bundle at his feet. The boy perched on the roof's apex, like a small gargoyle set against the austere background of the snowy peaks beyond. He was barely eight, a novice still, and had yet to experience a truly brutal *umial*.

"Of *course* you don't," Akiil responded, pointing an admonitory finger at the boy. "While the rest of us are lugging and lifting, all you have to do is sit there!"

"I'm *placing* them," Pater protested, his brown eyes round and aggrieved. He held up a loose tile by way of demonstration.

"Oh, *placing*," Akiil replied, rolling his eyes. "How demanding. My apologies."

"This is just work," Kaden pointed out as he wrapped his hands around the thick rope and began to haul. "Since I started with Tan, I haven't gone a single day without a beating. He's running out of unbroken skin."

"Just work?" Akiil demanded, fixing him with an incredulous glare. "*Just* work? Work is an affliction, my friend, a potentially *fatal* affliction."

Despite the pain of his wounds, Kaden suppressed a smile. Carrying rocks and hefting tiles probably *did* feel like murder to Akiil. The young acolyte had been at Ashk'lan as long as Kaden, but the Shin ethic and way of life weren't rubbing off on him as quickly as many of the older brothers would have liked. Scial Nin, the abbot, and some of the *umials* held out hope for the youth, but in most ways, he was little changed from the nine-year-old thief who had arrived from the gritty Perfumed Quarter of Annur so many years before.

Kaden had been at Ashk'lan for only a few months when Blerim Panno—the Footsore Monk, they called him—trudged into the main yard, brown robe ripped around the hem but otherwise looking no worse for the long walk from the Bend. The three boys who trailed behind him, however, the three boys who would soon be novices, appeared battered and uncertain. All limped on badly blistered feet, all slumped beneath the weight of the canvas sacks they carried on their backs, and of the three, only Akiil bothered to look around him, those brown eyes of his assessing the cold stone buildings of Ashk'lan with a shrewd gaze that had reminded Kaden of Edur Uriarte, his father's Minister of Finance. When that gaze landed on *him,* however, the new boy stiffened, as though pricked by the point of an invisible dagger.

"Who's he?" Akiil had asked Panno suspiciously, his vowels long and broad, almost incomprehensible to Kaden, who had grown up around the mellifluous, aristocratic accent of the imperial court.

"His name is Kaden," Panno replied. "He is also a novice."

Akiil had shaken his head. "I know them eyes. He's some kind of prince or lord or something. Nobody told me there'd be no princes or lords here." He spat the titles venomously, as though they were curses.

Panno had laid a calm hand on his shoulder. "That's because there *are* no princes or lords here. Only Shin. Kaden may have come from the Malkeenian line and one day he may return to it, but now, here, he is a novice, just like you."

Akiil measured Panno with his eyes, as though testing the truth of his words. "Meaning he don't get to boss me around none?"

Kaden had bristled at the suggestion. He wanted to object that he didn't boss people around even when he *wasn't* in a monastery, but Panno replied before he could fashion a retort.

"Here he is learning to obey, not to command." He turned to Kaden, as if by way of illustration. "Kaden, please run down to the White Pool and fetch some cold fresh water for our brothers. They have walked a good distance since dawn, and must be thirsty." Kaden had scowled at the injustice of the command, and Akiil, seeing the scowl, smiled his wide, dirty smile. It was not an auspicious start to their friendship.

After eight years, however, an unlikely camaraderie had grown up between the son of the Emperor and the thief from the Perfumed Quarter. As Blerim Panno had promised, the Shin ignored all differences in rank and rearing, and over time it became possible to forget that the parents Akiil had never known were hanged by the law of Kaden's father, that someday, if they went back to their former lives, Akiil might be put to death at the order of a scroll carrying Kaden's own sigil.

"Anyway," Akiil continued, stretching his neck and rubbing a sore forearm, "your sob stories are a heap of pickled pig shit. I don't see Tan hounding you now."

"The benefits of group labor," Kaden replied, passing the next crate of tiles to his friend. "As long as I'm stuck doing monastery work, Tan lets me off from my training."

"Well," Akiil said, shoving the load toward Pater and sitting down on the roof with a contented sigh. "I guess we want to stretch this job out as long as we can."

Kaden looked down into the courtyard. Late afternoon sun illuminated the stone buildings and stunted trees, warm in spite of the patches of dirty snow squirreled away in the corners. A few monks trod the gravel paths, their heads bowed in contemplation, and a pair of stray goats cropped the meager spring shoots in the shadow of the meditation hall, but Scial Nin, who had assigned them to the roofing project, was nowhere to be seen.

"That's the last of them," Phirum shouted up from below. "You want me to come up?"

"We'll take care of it," Akiil shouted back. "We're almost done."

"We are?" Kaden asked, eyeing the remaining crates skeptically, then glancing back down into the courtyard. The Shin provided severe penance for shirkers, although Akiil never seemed to learn that lesson, and Pater was picking up on the older youth's bad habits.

"Quit looking over your shoulder," Akiil said, settling back against the dark tiles. "No one's going to come hunting for us up here."

"You confident enough about that to risk a whipping?"

"Of course!" the youth replied, lacing his fingers behind his head and closing his eyes. "It was one of the first things I learned back in the Quarter—people never look up."

Pater scampered down from the crest of the roof, the bundle of tiles forgotten. "Is that Thieves' Wisdom?" he demanded. "*Is* it, Akiil?"

Kaden groaned. "Pater, I've told you before that 'Thieves' Wisdom' is just a fancy name Akiil gives to his pronouncements. Which are usually wrong, by the way."

Akiil fixed Kaden with a glare through one half-open eye. "It *is* Thieves' Wisdom, Pater. Kaden has just never heard of it because he spent his young life being pampered in a palace. Be thankful you have someone here who is willing to look after your education. Besides," he added, rushing on before Kaden could protest, "Tan's been keeping Kaden so busy, we haven't had a chance to talk to him about the goat he lost."

Akiil's words brought the *saama'an* of the slaughtered goat unbidden to Kaden's mind, and with it the chill, creeping fear pricking the skin between his shoulder blades. It was sloppy thinking, letting someone else's words dictate the contents of his thought, and he dismissed both the image and the emotion. Still, the afternoon sun was warm, the breeze carried the sharp scent of the junipers, and it wouldn't hurt to rest for just a few minutes before searching out his *umial* once more. After a final glance out over the monastery, he settled down onto the tiles beside his friends.

"What do you want to know?" he asked.

"You tell *me*," Akiil responded, rolling onto one elbow. "I know the goat was slaughtered. I know you didn't find any tracks—"

"And the *brain*," Pater burst in. "Something ate the brain."

Kaden nodded. He'd been over the events more times than he cared to admit, but couldn't add much more to the scene. "That's about it."

"A leach," Pater said, shoving between the two youths to gesture with a small but insistent hand. "A leach could have done it!"

Akiil dismissed the absurd suggestion with a lazy wave. "Pater, what would a leach be doing wandering around the Bone Mountains at the ass end of winter?"

"Maybe he's in hiding. Maybe his neighbors discovered what he was and he had to run away in the night. Maybe he put a kenning on someone," the boy went on, his expression rapt. "Something really evil, and—"

Akiil chuckled. "And then he came up here to kill a few goats?"

"They *do* things like that," the boy insisted. "Eat brains and drink blood and stuff."

Kaden shook his head. "They do not, Pater. They're men and women, just the way we are, only . . . twisted somehow."

"They're *evil*!" the small boy exclaimed. "That's why they have to get hanged or beheaded."

"They are evil," Kaden agreed. "And we do have to hang them. But not because they drink blood."

"They *might* drink blood," Akiil suggested unhelpfully, knuckling Pater in the ribs to goad him on.

Again, Kaden shook his head. "We have to hang leaches because they have too much power. No one should be able to twist the fabric of reality to their own ends." Hundreds of years earlier, the Atmani leach-lords had gone insane and nearly destroyed the world. Whenever Kaden wondered if leaches deserved the loathing and opprobrium heaped upon them, he had only to remember his history. "Only the gods should have that kind of power."

"Too much power!" Akiil crowed. "Too much *power*! And this from the person who's going to be the 'Kent-kissing Annurian *Emperor* someday."

Kaden snorted. "According to Tan, I don't have enough wit in my head to make it as a simple monk."

"You don't *have* to make it as a monk. You're going to rule half the known world."

"Maybe," Kaden responded, doubtfully. The Dawn Palace and the Unhewn Throne felt impossibly far away, a hazily remembered dream from his childhood. For all he knew, his father would rule another thirty years, years Kaden would spend at Ashk'lan hauling water, retiling roofs, and, oh yes, getting beaten by his *umial*. "I don't mind the work and the whippings when I feel like it's all part of some bigger plan. Tan, though . . . I might as well be some sort of insect, for all he cares."

"You should be happy," Akiil responded, rolling onto his back and staring up at the scudding clouds. "I've worked my ass off my whole life precisely in order to keep the expectations for me low. Low expectations are the key to success." He started to turn to Pater, but Kaden cut him off.

"That is *not* more Thieves' Wisdom," he said to the boy. Then, turning back to Akiil, "You know what Tan's had me doing for the past week? Counting. Counting all the stones in all the buildings at Ashk'lan."

"*That's* what you're complaining about?" Akiil demanded, stabbing a finger at him. "I was getting harder tasks when I was ten."

Kaden rolled his eyes. "You always were precocious."

"No need to show off the big words. Not all of us grew up with a Manjari tutor."

"Aren't you the one who claims the only schooling a man needs he can get from a butcher, a sailor, and a whore?"

Akiil shrugged. "The butcher and the sailor are optional."

Pater had been trying to follow the exchange, head swiveling back and forth with the conversation.

"What's a whore?" he asked. Then, distracted by his earlier reasoning, "If a leach didn't kill the goat, what did?"

Kaden saw it all again, the shattered skull, scooped clean.

"I told you, I don't know." He looked out across the courtyard, past the stone buildings and the granite ledges to where the sun was sinking toward the endless grasslands of the steppe. "But it's going to be dark soon, and if I don't get cleaned up and find Tan before dinner, I'm going to find myself envying that goat."

┼

Umber's Pool wasn't a proper pool so much as a pocket of rocks half a mile from the monastery where the White River paused, gathering itself in deep, still silence before spilling over a shelf in a dizzying waterfall, tumbling hundreds of feet into a deep ravine before snaking lazily into the steppe far below. After a childhood spent bathing in copper tubs filled with steaming water by the palace servants, Kaden had been shocked to realize that any washing at Ashk'lan would take place outside, in Umber's. Over the years, however, he had grown accustomed to it. The water was viciously cold, even in summer; anyone stoic enough to brave it in the winter had to hack a hole in the ice with the rusty, long-handled axe that was left between the rocks for just that purpose. Still, after a long day lugging tile beneath the glare of the mountain sun, the water would feel good.

He lingered before entering the pool. It was nice to have a few moments to himself, away from Tan's discipline, away from Pater's questions and Akiil's goading. He stooped to scoop up a clear handful of water, then straightened, allowing the icy drink to trickle down the back of his throat while he peered down the vertiginous trail that descended to the foothills and steppe below.

He had last walked that trail eight years ago, craning his skinny neck for a glimpse of his new home, a home that seemed to be perched in mountains so high that their peaks etched the clouds. He had been frightened; frightened of this cold, stone place, and frightened to show his fear.

"Why?" he had pleaded with his father before leaving Annur. "Why can't *you* teach me about ruling the empire?" Sanlitun's stern face softened as he replied. "Someday I will, Kaden. I will teach you, as my father taught me, to tell justice from cruelty, boldness from folly, friends from fawning sycophants. When you return, I will teach you to make the hard decisions through which a boy becomes a man. But there are other lessons you must learn first, lessons of the greatest importance, and these I cannot teach you. These, you must learn from the Shin."

"But why?" Kaden had begged. "They don't rule an empire. They don't even rule a kingdom. They rule nothing!"

His father smiled cryptically, as though the boy had made some kind of clever joke. Then the smile was gone and he was taking his son's wrist in the strong handshake men called the soldier's clasp. Kaden did his best to return the gesture, although his fingers were too small to gain any real purchase around his father's muscled forearm.

"Ten years," the man said, exchanging the face of a parent for that of the Emperor. "It is not long, in the life of a man."

Eight years gone, Kaden thought as he leaned back against the sloping boulder. Eight years gone, and the things he'd learned were as few as they were useless. He could craft pots, cups, urns, vases, and mugs from the clay of the river shallows, and he could sit still as a stone or run uphill for hours on end. He could mind goats. He could draw any plant, animal, or bird perfectly from memory—at least as long as someone wasn't beating him bloody, he amended wryly. Although he had grown fond of Ashk'lan, he couldn't stay there forever, and his accomplishments seemed a sad showing for eight years, nothing that would help him to run an empire. And now Tan had him counting rocks. *I hope Valyn's making better use of his time,* he thought. *I'll bet he's passing his tests, at the very least.*

The thought of tests conjured up the pain in his back where the willow switch had broken open his flesh. *Better to wash them out now,* he thought, eyeing the cold water. *Won't do any good to let them fester.* He pulled his robe over his head, wincing as the rough fabric scraped over the bloody gashes, and tossed it in a rough heap. The pool wasn't deep or wide enough to accommodate a dive, but at the upstream end one could step off a narrow ledge and drop in to the chest all at once. It was easier that way—like ripping off a scab. Kaden took three breaths, stilling his heartbeat and calming himself for the shock, then plunged.

As usual, the icy chill stabbed into him like a knife. He'd been bathing in the pool since he was ten, however, and had long ago learned to shepherd his body's heat. He forced himself to take a deep, calm breath; hold it; then drive the meager warmth out through his trembling limbs. It was a trick the monks had. Scial Nin, the abbot, could spend whole hours sitting quietly in the winter snow, his shoulders bare to the elements, flakes dissolving in little puffs of steam when they struck his skin. Kaden couldn't manage that yet, but he could keep himself from biting his tongue in two as he reached over his shoulders to wash the dried blood out of the gashes. After a minute of vigorous scrubbing, he turned to the bank. Before he could hoist himself out, however, a voice broke the stillness.

"Stay in the water."

Kaden froze and sucked in his breath. Rampuri Tan. He turned, searching for his *umial,* only to find the man seated in the shadow of an overhanging flake of granite just a few paces away, legs crossed, back erect. Tan looked like a statue hewn from the mountain itself rather than a figure of flesh and blood. He must have been sitting there the whole time, observing, judging.

"No wonder you can't paint," Tan said. "You're blind."

Kaden clamped his teeth together grimly, forced down the creeping cold, and kept silent.

Tan didn't move. He looked, in fact, as though he might *never* move, but he scrutinized Kaden with the attention one might bring to a vexing problem on the stones board.

"Why didn't you see me?" he asked finally.

"You blended with the rocks."

"Blended," Tan chuckled. The sound held none of Heng's mirth. "I blended with the rocks. I wonder what that might mean." He glanced up toward the darkening sky, as though the answer were scrawled in the flight of the peregrines wheeling far above. "A man blends water with tea. A baker blends flour with egg. But blending flesh with stone?" He shook his head as though the concept were beyond him.

Kaden had started to tremble beneath the icy water. The heat he had built up hauling tiles all afternoon was little more than a memory now, swept over the ledge with the chill current.

"Do you know why you are here?" the monk asked after an interminable pause.

"To learn discipline," Kaden replied, trying not to catch his tongue between his chattering teeth. "Obedience."

Tan shrugged. "Important, both of them, but you could learn discipline and obedience from a farmer, a bricklayer. The Shin can teach you more."

"Concentration," Kaden managed.

"Concentration? What does the Blank God want with your concentration? What does it matter to him if an acolyte in a dim stone building is able to recall the shape of a leaf?" Tan spread his hands as though waiting for Kaden's response, then continued. "Your concentration is an affront to your god. Your presence, your *self,* is an affront to your god."

"But the training—"

"—is a tool. A hammer is not a house. A knife is not death. You muddle the method with the goal."

"The *vaniate,*" Kaden said, trying desperately to control his shivering.

"The *vaniate,*" Tan agreed, repeating the strange syllables as though he were tasting them. "Do you know what it means?"

"Emptiness," Kaden stammered. "Nothingness."

Everything the monks studied, all the exercises the *umials* set their pupils, the endless hours painting, and running, and digging, and fasting, were aimed at that one constant goal: the emptiness of the *vaniate*. Two years earlier, in a frustrated moment, Kaden had been foolish enough to question the value of that emptiness. Heng had laughed out loud at the challenge, and then, smiling genially, replaced his pupil's bowl and mug with two stones. Each day Kaden stood in the refectory line only to have the monk serving the food ladle his soup over the shapeless lump of granite. Sometimes a chunk of lamb or carrot balanced miraculously on top. More often, he was forced to watch in famished agony as the thick broth ran off the stone and back into the serving pot. When the monks filled their own mugs with deep drafts of cold water, Kaden could only splash the stone and then lick it off, the quartz rough against his tongue.

After two weeks, Heng brought out Kaden's bowl and cup with a smile. Before he returned them, however, he hefted the rock Kaden had been trying to drink from. "Your mind is like this rock: full, solid. Nothing else can fit inside. You pack it with thoughts and emotions and claim that this fullness is something to be proud of!" He laughed at the absurdity of the notion. "How much you must have missed your empty old bowl!"

Over the following years, Kaden had worked diligently at the skill, learning how to hollow a space out of himself, out of his own mind. He hadn't mastered it, of course—most monks didn't reach the *vaniate* until their third or fourth decades—but he had made progress. Memorization and recall, the *saama'an,* played a central role in the practice; they were the picks and levers with which the Shin pried away the self. Heng taught him that a packed mind resisted new impressions; it tended to force itself onto the surrounding world, rather than filling itself with that world. The inability to recall the shape of a thrush's wing, for instance, indicated a mind transfixed with its own irrelevant ephemera.

And mind was not the only obstacle. The body, too, came packed with aches, itches, pains, and petty pleasures. When a monk emptied his mind of thought and emotion, the voice of the body proved all too ready to fill the void. To silence that voice, the Shin stood naked in the baking sun, ran barefoot in the snow, sat in the same cross-legged position for days on end as the muscles cramped and the stomach twisted itself into knots. As long as the body impinged on the mind, *vaniate* was impossible. So, one by one, the Shin confronted the demands of the body, faced them down, and discarded them.

The practice was not easy. Earlier in the year, Kaden had helped to carry the body of one of the acolytes from the bottom of a gorge. The boy, only eleven years old, had fallen to his death while trying to run away in the night. Such tragedies were rare, however. The *umials* knew the limits of their students, and the monk whose acolyte had fallen was subjected to severe penance. Still, the testers considered sliced feet, frostbitten hands, and broken bones an inevitable portion of a boy's first five years at the monastery.

The quest for the *vaniate* never ended, of course, and even the oldest monks admitted to difficulties. The mind was a clay pot set out in the rain. A monk could empty it daily and still the old hopes and worries, the body's meager strengths and perennial pains pattered against the bottom, trickled down the sides, filling it once more. The life of the Shin was a life of constant vigilance.

The monks were not cruel, exactly, but they made no allowances for

the vagaries of human emotion. Love or hate, sadness or joy, these were
cords that bound one to the illusion of self, and self, in the Shin lexicon,
was a curse. It spread everywhere, obscuring the mind, muddying the world's
clarity. As the monks struggled to achieve emptiness, the self always
seeped in, cold water in the bottom of a deep well.

Kaden's limbs felt like lead. The frigid snowmelt in Umber's Pool had
numbed his fingers and toes, chilled his core until it was an effort to lug
each breath into his heavy lungs. He had never stayed in the pool so long
so early in the season, and yet Tan showed no signs of relenting.

"Emptiness," the monk mused. "You could translate the word that way,
but our language doesn't map well onto such a foreign concept. Do you
know where the word comes from?"

Kaden shook his head helplessly. At the moment, there was nothing he
could have cared about less than the etymology of some strange Shin ob-
session. Two winters prior, one of the younger monks, Fallon Jorgun, had
died of cold when he broke his leg running the Circuit of Ravens, and
water chilled a body far more quickly than air.

"The Csestriim," Tan replied at last. "It is a Csestriim word."

At any other point, Kaden would have pricked up his ears and paid attention. The Csestriim were nursery stories—a vicious, vanished race,
who had walked the world when it was young, who had ruled that world
before the arrival of humans and then fought ruthlessly to exterminate
those same humans. Kaden had never heard them mentioned in conjunc-
tion with the *vaniate*. Why the Shin would want to master some skill of a
long-dead, evil race, he had no idea, and with the heat inside of him leaking away, he couldn't bring himself to care. The Csestriim were millennia
gone, if they had ever lived at all, and if Tan didn't let him out of the water,
he was going to follow them shortly.

"For the Csestriim," the older monk continued, "the *vaniate* was not an
arcane skill to be mastered. They *lived* in the *vaniate*. Emotion was as
alien to their minds as emptiness is to ours."

"Why do you want me to learn it?" Kaden managed weakly. Breathing
was difficult, and speaking felt nearly impossible.

"Learning," Tan said. "You care too much about learning. Studies.
Progress. Growth." He spat the words. "Self. Maybe if you stopped thinking about your learning, you might notice the world around you. You
would have noticed me sitting in the shadows."

Kaden kept silent. He wasn't sure he could have spoken anyway, not without biting off the end of his tongue. *He's made his point,* he thought to himself, *and now I can get out of this 'Shael-spawned water.* He wasn't at all sure his arms would be able to hoist him from the pool, but surely Tan would help to drag him out. The older monk, however, made no move to rise.

"Are you cold?" he asked, as though the thought had just struck him.

Kaden nodded vigorously.

Tan watched with the detached curiosity a monk might reserve for the study of a wounded animal. "What feels cold?"

"L-l-legs," Kaden managed. "Ar-arms."

Tan frowned. "But are *you* cold?"

There was some change in the inflection, but Kaden couldn't make sense of it. The world seemed to be getting darker. Had the sun set so quickly? He tried to remember how late it was when he'd started down to the pool, but he couldn't think of anything beyond the heavy stillness of his limbs. He forced himself to take a breath. There was a question. Tan had asked him a question.

"Are *you* cold?" the monk said again.

Kaden stared at him helplessly. He couldn't feel his feet anymore. Couldn't feel much of anything. The cold was gone, somehow. The cold was gone and he had stopped shivering. The water felt like . . . nothing, like air, like space. Maybe if he just closed his eyes for a moment . . .

"Are you cold?" Tan said again.

Kaden shook his head wearily. The cold had gone. He let his eyes slip shut. Nothingness surrounded him in a gentle embrace.

Then someone was behind him, dragging him by the armpits out of the water. He wanted to protest that he was too tired to move, that he just wanted to go to sleep, but the person kept tugging until he was sprawled out on the ground. Strong hands bundled him in what must have been a robe or blanket; his skin was too numb to feel the texture. A blow struck his face, jarring him from his stupor. He opened his eyes to protest, and Tan slapped him again across the cheek, hard.

"Hurts," Kaden mumbled blearily.

Tan paused. "What hurts?"

"Cheek."

"Do *you* hurt?"

Kaden tried to focus on the question, but it made no sense. The world was fog. The pain was a red line scribbled on nothingness.

"Cheek."

"And you?" Tan pressed.

Kaden opened his mouth, but for a long time words eluded him. "I don't . . . ," he managed at last. What did the monk *want*? There was pain and there was darkness. That was all. "I'm not . . . ," he began, then let the words go.

His *umial* paused, dark eyes bright and intense. "Good," he said finally. "That's a start."

9

The shrine to Hull, Lord of the Darkness, patron god of all those who moved in the shadows, wasn't a shrine at all, but a massive tenebral oak, gnarled black limbs stretching over a full quarter acre like arthritic fingers scratching at the sky. Hanging from every branch and twig—packed in so close that when Valyn first saw the tree, he took them for heavy black leaves—dangled bats, tens of thousands of bats, folded tight in their wings, waiting silently for night. When darkness fell, they would take to the air together, a wheeling, darting, silent swarm harrying the sky, leaving the branches bare as bones. Even in summer, the tenebral had no leaves—the bats *were* its leaves. When they returned to roost just before dawn, the blood dripping from their fangs would soak the heavy earth around the roots, feeding the tree. Unlike its brethren, the tenebral had no need of the sun.

Valyn had seen other tenebrals in the course of his training—they were rare, but grew scattered all over the continent of Eridroa. This tree, however, perching on a low hillside overlooking the Eyrie compound, was by far the largest he had ever come across. Down below, among the storage barns, bunkhouses, and training arenas, the Kettral had erected small shrines to several of the young gods: Heqet, God of Courage; Meshkent, Lord of Pain; even a tiny stone sanctuary dedicated to Kaveraa, in the hope that the Mistress of Fear might leave her worshippers untouched. It was here, however, at the foot of the ancient tenebral, that the Kettral worshipped most devoutly. Courage and pain were all well and good, but it was darkness that covered the soldiers as they winged in beneath their birds, darkness that cloaked them as they killed, and darkness that hung over their retreat like a cloak as they melted away into the night.

Before and after every mission, the soldiers would leave an offering.

There were no coins or gemstones littered among the roots, no candles or expensive silks. The Kettral knew how the tree survived. Valyn had spent years watching them wind their way up the narrow trail ground into the hillside, had watched them as they knelt and drew their blades, watched as they dragged the steel across warm flesh, squeezing blood onto the hungry roots. Whether Hull knew, or cared, was anyone's guess. The old gods were inscrutable.

When Valyn first arrived on the Islands, he had found the tree and the sodden ground beneath it unsettling, to say the least. Valyn's line, the Malkeenian line, claimed descent from Intarra, and the Dawn Palace where he had passed his childhood was filled with light and air. Now, however, the dark, brooding tree suited his mood just fine. Though Manker's had collapsed into the bay nearly a week earlier, he hadn't been able to shake the image of Salia's bloodied face from his mind. When he fell asleep, he found himself in the burning tavern all over again, heard her begging him not to leave her. When he woke, he expected to find her blood still spattered on his skin.

He was furious with Ha Lin, and felt foolish for his fury. She had made the right call in a difficult situation. As Hendran wrote, *Your ideals die, or you do.* If Valyn had tried to make the jump with Salia draped unconscious across his back, he would have ended skewered on one of the jagged pilings. *But it should have been my decision to make,* he thought, balling his hand into a fist. In addition to the basic instruction, each Kettral cadet trained for a specialty: sniper, demolitions, flier, leach. Someone in command had decided early on that Valyn might have the skills to actually lead a Wing; if he passed the Trial, he would find himself in command of his own soldiers, and command required decision.

Blood misted down from above. He ignored it. He hadn't spoken with Lin since Manker's, and he didn't know what to say. Here, at least, in the gloomy shadow of the tenebral oak, he had time to think, to work through his feelings without saying or doing something that he could not take back. Except, as he gazed down the hill in the direction of the compound, he could see a slender shape moving up the track toward him.

Ha Lin stopped just outside the reach of the tree's branches, glancing up at the quiescent bats with a look of disgust. Valyn had no doubt that when the time came, she would pay homage to the god like everyone else, but she had never overcome her revulsion of the place. It was one of the reasons Valyn had chosen it—he thought the dark limbs and quiet susurrations of the shifting bats might keep her away. No such luck.

Lin's lips were pursed, and her eyes, normally so open and warm, were hooded as she looked at him. She must have come directly from a training rotation; mud coated her blacks while a small cut wept blood on her left cheek. Somehow, even battered and dirty, she managed to look poised, beautiful even. *Which is part of the 'Shael-spawned problem,* Valyn thought sourly to himself. He wouldn't have had nearly so much trouble thinking what to say to Laith, or Gent, or even Talal.

"How long are you going to sulk?" Lin asked finally, raising an eyebrow.

Valyn gritted his teeth. "It was wrong to kill her."

"Valyn," Lin said, "right and wrong are luxuries."

"They are *necessities.*"

"Maybe for other people. Not for us."

"*Especially* for us," Valyn insisted. "If we don't have some sense of right and wrong, we're no better than Skullsworn, killing for the sake of killing, murdering to please Ananshael."

"We're not Skullsworn," Lin replied, "but we're not knights of Heqet either. We don't ride around on white steeds, waving idiotically heavy swords and delivering noble challenges to our foes. Or maybe you hadn't noticed. We're Kettral, Valyn. We kill people. If we have our way, we poison them, or we stab them in the back. Maybe we shoot them when they aren't looking, and if at all possible, we do it at night. It might not be noble, but it's necessary. It's what we trained for."

"Not serving girls," he said stubbornly. "Not civilians."

"Yes, serving girls. Yes, civilians. If we have to. If they get in the way of the mission."

"There *was* no 'Kent-kissing mission. We were trying to get people out of that place alive."

"Maybe that's what you were doing, but I was trying to keep *you* alive," she spat back, her eyes bright and angry. "The girl was deadweight. She was killing you. I did what I had to do."

"There might have been another way." He'd been over it a hundred times already. Maybe he could have forced his way out one of the other windows. Maybe he could have leapt to one of the adjacent buildings. It was academic now. Manker's was gone, and Salia with it.

"Of course there might have been another way. And you might have been killed. It's all about odds, Valyn. You know that as well as I do." Lin sighed deeply and slumped, as though the anger had gone out of her in a rush, leaving her weak and unsteady. "I always thought it would happen in battle," she said after a long pause. "In a fight at least."

Valyn hesitated, suddenly wrong-footed. "Thought what would happen?"

Lin met his eyes. "Salia was my first. My first kill."

On the Islands, most men and women celebrated their first kill the way civilians might celebrate an engagement or a birthday. As much as passing Hull's Trial or flying a first mission, killing was a rite of passage, a necessary step. Regardless of the training and the study, until you killed, you weren't really Kettral. Lin was right, though. You didn't expect your first to be an unconscious serving girl. You didn't want that.

Valyn blew out a long, slow breath. In his anger and guilt, he hadn't even thought about how Salia's death might have affected his friend. Although he'd held the girl as she died, Lin had thrown the knife. She had accepted the burden, and not for her own sake, but to protect him. From some forgotten corner of his mind, his father's words came back to him, firm and uncompromising: *You and Kaden will both be leaders someday, and when you are, remember this: Leadership isn't just about giving orders. A fool can give orders. A leader listens. He changes his mind. He acknowledges mistakes.* Valyn gritted his teeth.

"Thank you," he said. The words came out rougher than he had intended, but he said them.

Lin raised her eyes, her face guarded, as though she expected some sort of trap.

"You were right," Valyn said, forcing the syllables out. "I was wrong."

"Oh, for Ananshael's sake, Valyn!" Lin groaned. "You are so unbelievably *proud*. I have no idea why I—" She cut herself off. "I didn't come up here so that you could tell me I was right. I came because I'm worried."

"Worried?"

"Manker's," she said, gesturing across the bay toward Hook. "It didn't just fall down on its own."

Valyn frowned. He'd been gnawing at the same idea, but couldn't be sure if his misgivings were the result of paranoia or healthy concern.

"Buildings fall down," he replied. "Especially old ones. Especially on Hook."

"An Aedolian warns you about a conspiracy, and then, a week later, a building that's stood for decades just happens to collapse barely a minute after you step outside?"

Valyn shrugged, trying to put down the disquiet festering inside him. "You squint hard enough, and everything starts to look suspicious."

"Suspicion keeps people alive," Lin insisted.

"Suspicion drives people insane," Valyn countered. "If someone wanted me dead, there are more elegant ways to manage it than bringing down an entire building."

"Are there?" Lin asked, eyebrows raised. "Seems pretty elegant to me. An accident—one more hovel on Hook falls over, killing a dozen people. Nothing too unusual. Nothing to suggest an attack on the imperial family. It's sure to Hull more elegant than cutting your throat."

Valyn grimaced. She was right. Again. He knew she was right, and yet, there were accidents to go around on the Islands. Just a week earlier, Lem Hellen had had his leg crushed beneath a huge boulder during a training rotation out on Qarn. If Valyn started looking over his shoulder at every turn, he'd never get a wink of sleep, never trust anyone.

"There's just no way to know," he said, staring out over the sound. Hook's colorful riot of tenements and huts was clear across the narrow strip of water. "I could spend a week poking through the wreckage and still have no idea."

"Maybe," Lin began cautiously, "you're not the one who should poke through the wreckage. You've been training to lead a Wing the past eight years, and I've been studying the fine art of the bow. Half a dozen of our brothers and sisters, however, have been learning to knock down bridges and blow up buildings."

"Demolitions," Valyn replied, nodding.

"One of them ought to be able to tell you if Manker's was rigged."

Valyn considered the idea. "It would mean tipping my hand. I'd have to let on I was suspicious."

"Is that so bad? Might make whoever's trying to kill you think twice."

"I don't *want* them to think twice," Valyn said, rolling his eyes. "I want them to think once and, if at all possible, drunkenly."

"Point is, it's not likely to make anything worse."

That seemed like the truth. Valyn stared down at the neat grid of buildings below—storehouses and mess hall, bunkrooms and command center. Which one of them would come down on him next? Which was harboring the traitor or traitors? He could wait, looking over his shoulder every other heartbeat, for the next attack, or he could do something. "Does seem like I'm at a pretty low ebb," he admitted. "Who did you have in mind?"

"I'll give you two guesses," Lin replied with a smirk, "but you're only going to need one."

"Gwenna." He sighed heavily. "Hull help us."

Lin didn't seem pleased by the prospect either, but before she could respond, a dark shadow passed overhead, silent and swift. Valyn looked up to find a kettral, wings spread wide, swooping in for a drop on the field below.

"Bird in," Lin said, tracing the backflight over the island, toward the low bluffs to the northwest. "Looks like it's coming from . . ."

"Annur," Valyn concluded. "Fane's back."

┼

The Kettral mess hall, a low, one-story building packed with benches and long wooden tables, was a far cry from Manker's, or any of the Hook alehouses. For one thing, it didn't serve ale—if you wanted a drink stiffer than black tea, you had to cross the sound. For another, there were no whores, no civilians of any kind, just Kettral, same as everywhere else on Qarsh—men and women loading up on hard tack and dried fruit before flying out on a mission, or shoveling down a bowl of hot stew after they returned. The slaves in the kitchen worked all day and all night as well— soldiers needed food at odd hours. Usually everyone was so intent on their meals that any conversation was low and intermittent. When Valyn and Lin burst through the door, however, the place might as well have been a tavern, and doing good business at that.

It seemed as though half of Qarsh was shoved into the hall, packed in so tight around the tables, Valyn wondered if he'd been the last one to notice the bird winging in from the north. People clustered in small knots—a couple of Wings here, a few cadets there—but everyone was talking all at the same time.

Somewhere in the press he lost Lin, but Valyn had eyes only for the man in the far corner of the room. Adaman Fane sat near the door to the kitchens. He looked more intent on tearing apart a side of beef than he did on talking, but Valyn could see that, in between bites, he was responding to the questions of the veterans seated around him. It was a hard group—Gird the Axe, Plenchen Zee, Werren of Raalte—and Valyn hesitated before shoving into the inner circle, impatient though he was.

"Hold on, Val," someone said, catching his sleeve. "I wouldn't break into that little chat unless you want a busted head."

Valyn turned to find Laith, an easy smile on his face, gesturing back the way he had just come. The flier was a hand shorter than Valyn, and lean to go with it, but he had a loose, casual swagger and quick tongue that earned him a role in any conversation and made him seem larger than he really was. Most of the cadets on the Islands were a little cocky—you had to have a high opinion of yourself to think you could make a place for yourself among the most deadly women and men in the empire. Laith, despite the fact that he was a cadet just like Valyn, took self-confidence to a new level. He pushed his bird faster than some of the veteran fliers, executed maneuvers that made Valyn's stomach twist just watching from the ground, and never failed to brag about it all when he was finished. He infuriated half the trainers and amused the other half, who insisted he'd be dead before he even reached the Trial. For all his bravado, however, he was cheerful and easygoing—more than could be said for some of the other cadets—and he and Valyn were on pleasant terms.

"Come on," he said, catching Valyn around the shoulders to steer him away from the press. "We've got a table over in the corner."

"Fane's got news of my father."

"And you've got a strong grip on the obvious," Laith replied, "along with eight dozen other people here. The man's been flying all night and the better part of a day. He's not going to want to talk to you."

"I don't care what he wants . . . ," Valyn began, but then he saw Lin gesturing from across the room. She was at the table Laith had indicated, along with a few other cadets.

"Come on," Laith said again, not unkindly. "We've been here over an hour. We'll fill you in."

The five of them crunched into the low benches, Laith and Ha Lin, Gent, Talal, and a quiet youth named Ferron, whom no one thought would pass the Trial. The unexpected arrival of Fane had scrubbed the weariness from Valyn's mind, and he shouldered in among the group impatiently.

"So?" he asked, scanning the faces for some clue.

"Clergy," Gent replied abruptly. "Some 'Kent-kissing priest scraping for a little more power."

"Uinian the Fourth," Laith added, making room for Valyn on the bench. "I doubt that any future priests, if there *are* any future priests, will be too eager to style themselves Uinian the Fifth."

"Priest of *what*?" Valyn asked, shaking his head in disbelief. Killed in battle, he could have believed, or slain at the hand of a foreign assassin, but for Sanlitun to be murdered by some pasty prelate?

"Intarra," Laith replied.

Valyn nodded dumbly. *Not even one of the Skullsworn.* "How?"

"The old-fashioned way," Gent said. Then, miming the action, "Quick knife to the back."

"Gent," Talal interjected quietly, nodding over at Valyn.

"What?" Gent demanded. Then the realization set in. "Oh, I'm sorry, Val. As usual, I'm about as graceful as a bull's swollen cock."

"Considerably less so," Laith said, clapping a hand on Valyn's shoulder in sympathy. "The point is, looks like the whole thing was pretty simple. Overweening pride. Greed for power. The usual horrible day-to-day bullshit."

Valyn exchanged a quick glance with Lin. One disgruntled priest with a knife didn't sound much like a grand conspiracy, but then, the Church of Intarra was one of the largest in the empire. If Uinian was part of a larger plot, who knew where it might lead?

"How'd he get close enough?" Valyn asked. "My father had half a dozen Aedolians around him anytime he was outside his personal chambers."

"Sounds like he picked the wrong half dozen," Laith replied, spreading his hands.

"Mistakes *do* happen," Lin added. "We heard something about your father maybe leaving his guard behind."

Valyn tried to square the suggestion with what he remembered of his childhood, but the idea of his father abandoning his guard made less than no sense.

"Command still seems pretty stirred up," Talal said, absently fingering one of the iron bracelets on his arm. "There've been Wings coming and going day and night since we learned about the murder. Maybe someone thinks there's more to it." It was just like the leach to be thoughtful, deliberate, reserved in his judgment. Leaches learned early to keep their own secrets close; they learned or they ended up dangling by the neck from a rope. Talal was no exception, and approached the world more warily than Laith or Gent.

"What more do you need?" Gent asked with a shrug. "Uinian will face trial and then he'll die."

"It's like Hendran says," Laith agreed, " 'Death is a great clarifier.' "

"And my sister?" Valyn asked. "She's all right? Who's running the empire now?"

"Slow down," Laith replied. "Slow down. Adare's fine. She's been raised to the head of the Finance Ministry. Ran il Tornja was appointed regent."

"And a good thing, too," Gent added. "Can you imagine some bureaucrat trying to keep the military in order?"

Valyn shook his head. His father's death had clarified nothing, and this further information about Uinian and his priesthood, a *kenarang* appointed to the regency, about impending trials, only muddied the matter.

All of a sudden the room seemed too small. The press of people, the noise, the stench of grilling meat and lard turned Valyn's stomach and made his mind spin. The other cadets were just trying to help, just giving him the information he'd asked for, but there was something about the casual way they discussed his father's death that made him want to hit someone.

"Thanks," Valyn said, struggling up from his seat. "Thanks for the news. I've only got an hour to crash before second bell—I'd better make use of it."

"You trying to starve yourself?" Gent demanded, shoving a bowl of clotted curds across the table.

"I'm not hungry," he replied, shouldering his way toward the door.

He didn't notice until he was outside and halfway to his barracks that Ha Lin had followed him. He wasn't sure whether he was frustrated or glad.

"That must have been tough in there," she said quietly, catching up in a few quick steps and falling in next to him. "I'm sorry."

"Not your fault. Not anyone's fault. Death is normal. Isn't that what they've spent the last eight years teaching us? Ananshael comes for us all."

"Death is normal," she agreed. "Murder is not."

Valyn forced himself to shrug. "Lots of ways to die—gangrene, old age, a knife in the back—it all lands you in the same place."

10

The demolitions shed was just that: a shed tacked up from scrap lumber with a roof that looked like it wouldn't keep out a decent rain. There wasn't much point in building something more substantial, considering the place was blown up or burned down about every other year. Valyn approached with some trepidation. He'd spent a training rotation here, learning to craft and deploy the powerful munitions—starshatters, flickwicks, moles, lances—to which only the Kettral had access, but the place made most people a little uneasy. The low basin in which it was set looked like some sort of shattered desert, or the floor of a parched lake: a few charred remnants of plants stuck up from the broken soil, limestone chunks blasted from their bed bleached silently in the baking sun, while the sharp smell of nitre hung over everything. Aside from those cadets and Kettral whose training focused on demolitions, most people tended to avoid the entire area.

Valyn glanced over at Ha Lin, shrugged, then pushed open the rickety door. It groaned on its hinges as he stepped inside. The interior was dim but not dark. Daylight poured through cracks in the walls in a dozen places, and the thin sailcloth covering the windows admitted even more illumination. A row of battered workbenches ran down the center of the room, cleared off in some places, piled high with tools and instruments in others: alembics, retorts, vials, and tightly stoppered jars. As usual with the Kettral, nothing was standardized; the demolitions master for each Wing crafted his or her own munitions to fit his or her own needs and desires. There were basic recipes, of course, but most of them preferred to improvise, innovate, tinker. Valyn had seen starshatters that exploded in violet flame and moles that could rip a hole the size of a barn foundation out of the rock. Of course, such experimentation was not without risk.

During his own rotation in the shed, Valyn had watched a younger cadet, Halter Fremmen, light what looked like an innocuous candle. An errant gust of wind tugged at the flame until it caught the boy's blacks, burning quickly through the fabric and then biting into his skin. Several of Halter's friends had dragged him to one of the massive wooden tubs standing close by and forced him down into the water, but even beneath the surface, the flame continued to eat at the boy's flesh with a bright, savage glow. Valyn had stood transfixed. He was trained to respond quickly and decisively to emergencies, but this . . . No one had spoken a word to him about how to handle a flame that could not be quenched. In the end, Newt, the demolitions master everyone called the Aphorist, had dragged the screaming boy outside and buried him in the sand. The sand extinguished the unnatural blaze, but not before it had taken the skin off half Halter's body and melted one of his eyes in his face. He died three days later.

At first Valyn thought the shed was empty, but then he noticed Gwenna down at the far end, red hair obscuring her face, leaning over stock-still as she inserted something into a long tube with what looked like a pair of very narrow tongs. She didn't greet them or look up. Not that he had expected her to, really. He hadn't spoken to her since the day he learned of his father's death, since the day she had practically bitten his head off about his unbuckled harness, and he had no idea if she still harbored the grudge. Knowing Gwenna, she probably did.

It wasn't that Gwenna Sharpe was a bad soldier. In fact, she probably knew more about demolitions than any other cadet on the Islands. The problem was her temper. From time to time, one of the swaggering gallants over on Hook would find himself tempted by the bright green eyes and flaming red hair, by the supple, curvaceous body that she did her best to hide under her Kettral blacks. It never turned out well for him; Gwenna had tied her last would-be suitor to a dock piling and left him there for the tide. When his friends finally found him, he was sobbing like a baby as the waves washed over his face. Even Gwenna's trainers joked that with a temper like that, she didn't *need* any 'Kent-kissing munitions.

"Sorry to interrupt," Valyn began as he reached the end of the table opposite Gwenna.

"Then don't," she replied, her eyes fixed on her work as she slid the slender tongs down the inside of the hollow cylinder. He stifled a sharp retort, clasped his hands behind his back, and schooled himself to patience.

He wasn't sure Gwenna would agree to help in the first place, and he didn't want to make it any more difficult by irritating her right off the mark. Instead, he focused on the object of her attention, something that looked like a modified starshatter.

The tube was hollowed-out steel, twice the width of his thumb. Coated around the inside was some pitchlike substance he didn't recognize. Gwenna withdrew the tongs, picked up a small shard of stone, and started to insert it. Ha Lin gasped.

"Don't. Do. That," Gwenna said, pausing, then sliding the tongs deeper.

"That's claranth, isn't it?" Lin asked, her voice tight. "Claranth and nitre?"

"Sure is," Gwenna replied curtly.

Valyn stared. One of the first things that the Aphorist had taught his class of cadets was to always, always, *always* keep the two separate. "We like explosions here," the man had joked, "but we like to *control* those explosions." Unless Valyn had badly misunderstood something, if Gwenna so much as touched the content of the tongs to the side of the tube, someone would be sorting body parts out of the rubble. He started to reply, then thought better of it and held his breath instead.

"This is why," Gwenna grated, sliding the tongs deeper, releasing the stone, then withdrawing them with a smooth, measured motion, "you shouldn't interrupt."

"Is it done?" Lin asked.

Gwenna snorted. "No, it's not done. If I move it by half an inch, it'll take the roof off this shed. Now, stop talking."

Lin stopped talking, and the two of them watched in tense fascination as Gwenna reached for a vial of bubbling wax, grasped it with two gloved fingers, and upended it into the tube. There was a faint hissing, a whiff of acrid steam, and then a long pause.

"There," Gwenna said finally, laying the tube down on the workbench and straightening up. "*Now* it's done."

"What is it?" Valyn asked, eyeing the thing warily.

"Starshatter," she replied with a shrug.

"Doesn't look like a normal starshatter."

"I didn't realize you'd become a demolitions master when I wasn't around."

Valyn bit his tongue. He was here to ask Gwenna for a favor, after all. Lin, remarkably, had kept her mouth shut, and if she could be civil, so could Valyn. "Isn't it a little bit longer and thinner than the normal tube?" he asked, trying to sound interested.

"Marginally," Gwenna said, scrutinizing the weapon, then scratching away an errant drop of wax with her fingernail.

"Why?"

"Bigger. Louder. Hotter." She was trying to sound casual, but there was something in her voice, something Valyn had not expected to hear. It took him a moment to place it: pride. Gwenna was often so venomous, so closed off, that it was hard for him to imagine her feeling anything but rage or bile. The sudden revelation that she might actually take joy in some aspect of the world disarmed him, but just as he was starting to reassess his opinion of her, she rounded on him with a scowl. "You going to tell me what you want, or what?"

Now that it had come down to it, Valyn felt strangely hesitant. His fears, which Lin had done her best to fan, seemed bizarre and paranoid when he had to state them aloud.

Gwenna spread her hands impatiently.

"I assume you heard about Manker's," Valyn began tentatively. "The tavern over on Hook?"

"I know what Manker's is," Gwenna snapped. "I've given that bastard about half my pay for the watered-down swill he calls ale."

"Well, then I assume you know it collapsed," Valyn replied, trying to keep his own temper in check. "I was there, drinking, and it collapsed just after I stepped out the door."

"How lucky for you."

"Most of the people inside were killed. Crushed."

"How sad for them."

Lin pushed past Valyn, her own patience evidently nearing its end. "It might not have been an accident."

That gave Gwenna pause. Her eyes flicked from Valyn to Lin, then back. He waited for her to laugh, to make some crack about the self-involved son of the Emperor thinking the whole world turned around him. Everyone else on the Islands needled him about his birth, even his friends, and Gwenna had never been one of his friends. She didn't laugh.

"And you think it's tied up with the death of your father." Gwenna could be a bitch, but she wasn't stupid.

Valyn nodded.

"Doesn't do much good to stab the Emperor if his son plonks his own ass down on the throne a few days later."

"I'm not the heir—"

"Spare me the fucking politics," Gwenna replied, waving his objection aside. "I get the general idea."

"And Manker's . . . ," Lin pressed.

"You want me to look at it," Gwenna said, wiping her hands on her blacks. "You want me to check it out."

Valyn nodded carefully. "I don't understand the munitions as well as you. I'm not sure if you could use them to bring down a building like that."

"Of course you could knock over a building. That's the whole *point* of the 'Kent-kissing things."

"I know, but slowly like that? Without a visible explosion?"

Gwenna rolled her eyes. "You're expected to lead a Wing someday and you don't even understand the basics of munitions?"

"Look," Ha Lin interjected, her lips tight. "We don't spend all day in this little shed tinkering with matches and minerals—"

"You know more about this than we do," Valyn said, cutting his friend off before the whole thing turned into a verbal sparring match. "You're better than I am. You're better than Lin is. You're better than most of the 'Shael-spawned Kettral on the Islands. We could look, but maybe we'd miss something crucial." If Gwenna wanted to be stroked, Valyn could grind out some compliments, although the fact that the words were true didn't make them any easier to utter.

She scowled, then looked away, studying the wall of the shed. Valyn wondered if his strategy had backfired. Who knew how Gwenna's mind worked? "Do you think you'd have time to do it?" he pressed. "I'd be happy to give you—"

"Money?" Gwenna snapped, her green eyes ablaze. "Your imperial favor?" she sneered.

Valyn started to reply but she cut him off.

"I don't need anything from you. I'll do it because I'm interested, because I want to know. Got it?"

Valyn nodded slowly. "Got it."

11

Gwenna spent half the morning diving into the jumbled wreckage of Manker's. She must have been half fish, the way she could hold her breath, and a couple of times she stayed under so long, Valyn thought she'd gotten herself stuck in the treacherous underwater maze of collapsed beams and joists. Once, he even stripped his tunic to dive in after her, but just as he was approaching the water, she broke the surface, twenty paces from where she went down, scowling and shaking the salt water from her hair.

A few passersby, men and women going about whatever dubious activity passed for their business, stopped to watch the scene with sullen curiosity. One old man in a battered sailor's coat went so far as to ask if Valyn and Gwenna were checking over the corpses for jewelry, then cackled at his own suggestion, exposing a mouthful of rotting teeth. Valyn felt exposed. He'd suggested coming at night, but Gwenna had pointed out acerbically that it was hard enough to see anything in the murk of the bay at high noon. If Manker's *had* been rigged, and if whoever rigged it just happened to walk by, it would be more than obvious that Valyn had his suspicions. Still, there wasn't much to do but grit his teeth while Gwenna worked. It took all morning, and by the time she finally hauled herself out of the water, her lips were blue and she was trembling.

"Well," she said, tilting her head to one side and wringing the water from her hair as though twisting the head off a chicken, "if someone rigged the 'Shael-spawned place, they used some kind of explosive I've never heard of."

"How likely is that?" Valyn asked carefully.

"How likely are you to mistake your cock for your balls tomorrow morning?"

Valyn stared down into the murky water. A few charred beams thrust up from the surface while a skim of detritus sloshed around between the posts, jetsam from the ruined tavern that the tide had not yet managed to flush out to sea. None of the local residents had made any effort to clear away the wreckage, but that was the way on Hook. Several years earlier, fire had gutted an entire row of houses a few streets over. After scavenging the burned-out husks for anything valuable, the citizens of the island had left the places to rot.

"What'd you find down there?" Valyn asked.

"Bodies," Gwenna replied curtly. "More than a dozen."

Valyn watched the shifting waves, imagining the terror of people trapped between burning beams, dragged down below the surface and drowned. "Bad way to go."

She shrugged. "They were bad people."

Valyn paused. The inhabitants of Hook were a rough lot, no doubt about that: cutpurses who had pushed their luck too far on the mainland, pirates too tired or broken to haul anchor or reef sail, gamblers running from debts, whores and swindlers looking to mop up what little coin anyone had left. They were desperate and dangerous, almost to a man, but desperate didn't seem quite the same thing as bad.

"Did you check over the corpses?" he asked.

"Just one." Gwenna shrugged. "He owed me money. Wasn't doing *him* any good."

"What about the structure?" he asked, taking a step closer and lowering his voice. The dirt street was empty for the moment, but too many shutters hung loose around them. Too many doors creaked open on their hinges in the sea breeze.

"Nothing."

"You're sure?"

She glared at him. "The building was held up by forty-eight pilings. I checked every single one. No singeing, no impact scars, no explosive remnants. If someone rigged this building, I want to find the bastard and beat his secrets out of him."

Valyn wasn't sure whether to be relieved or not. On the one hand, the fact that the alehouse had collapsed under its own decrepit weight meant that no one had tried to kill him, at least not yet. On the other, there had been something strangely comforting about believing an attack had already taken place. He'd been trained to deal with real threats and concrete dangers; bringing a roof down on someone's head was about as real as it got. He could handle munitions and rigged demolitions almost as well as blades or barefisted fighting. Nebulous schemes, however, inchoate plots and faceless assassins—it was impossible to come to grips with those. Given the choice, he would have fought his assailants straight out, toe to toe, blade to blade. But he wasn't given the 'Kent-kissing choice. There wasn't much to do but grit his teeth and watch his back as he tried to focus on his training once more.

†

While he'd been lamenting his father and chasing phantoms, Hull's Trial had drawn steadily closer, and as the bleak list of names engraved on the Stone of the Fallen outside the barracks reminded him, a cadet could die on the Islands easily enough without the need of a shadowy conspiracy. He resumed his long, predawn swims, redoubled his evening runs around the coast, and returned to his study of tactics and strategy with a vengeance. The bright days of early spring gave way to heavy rains that soaked his blacks the moment he stepped out the door. After eight years of training, time felt suddenly, precariously short. There were maps to learn, languages to practice, diagrams of fleets and fortresses to pore over, and, of course, there was always fighting to be had.

Qarsh had a number of training rings where cadets and veterans alike could work up a good sweat running through forms or hammering each other into the dust with blunted blades. The simplest were just squares of earth vaguely delineated by a few pounded stakes strung with ropes. Past the west end of the compound, however, not far from the Eyrie's main landing field, overlooking a rocky expanse that swept down toward the sea, was the only true arena on the Islands—a shallow, wide circle a pace or so deep set into the earth and ringed with stones.

Valyn arrived just before seventh bell, stripped to the waist and sweating like a bull from his run around the perimeter of the island. It was a full week since Gwenna's investigation of Manker's, and though he had not forgotten the Aedolian's warning or his grief over his father's murder, the imperatives of training provided some kind of distraction from the looming threat—*time to shut up and buckle down,* as the Kettral liked to say—and there was nothing to focus the mind like three feet of steel whistling toward your forehead.

Late each afternoon, from seventh to eighth bell, was set aside for a session the Eyrie referred to as "Individual Close Combat." The cadets dubbed it, simply, Blood Time. If you somehow managed to make it through the morning without the proper complement of bruises and lacerations, Blood Time would make sure you went to bed sore. The setup was simple: two cadets in a wide, low ring just to the west of the armory and forge. Whoever asked for mercy first, lost. Sometimes the fights took place with blunted blades, sometimes with knives or cudgels, sometimes with bare fists. One of the trainers was always there, in theory to make sure everyone followed the few rules. In practice, however, the older soldiers tended to heap fuel on the fire, hurling insults and gibes from the edge of the ring. Sometimes there was betting.

Forty or fifty Kettral surrounded the ring, vets and cadets alike, some stretching out sore muscles, others windmilling the blood into their arms in great looping circles, others chatting quietly in small knots. Valyn spotted Ha Lin, Gent, Laith, and Talal on the far side, and circled over to them, taking the time to catch his breath.

"My point is," Laith was saying, hands spread as he tried to reason with Gent, "that the hammer is a ridiculous weapon. *Useless.*"

"It's useless if you can't lift it," Gent argued, eyeing the flier's thin arms skeptically.

"It's a *carpenter's* tool, for 'Shael's sake. There's a reason every Kettral carries two *swords* strapped across his back and not two hammers. Val," he said, turning to appeal to the new arrival. "Talk some sense into this ox."

"Don't bother," Lin interjected, raising a hand in warning. "They've been at it since sixth bell and left sense behind a long time ago."

"We're fighting with hammers today?" Valyn asked, glancing toward the arena apprehensively. The trainers loved nothing more than throwing unexpected twists into daily training, and a hammer was a dangerous weapon to spar with.

"Not that I know of," Lin replied, eyes flashing. "But don't worry. If we are, I'll be gentle with you."

"That's what the whores on Hook always tell me," Laith cut in with a wink. "Don't believe her, Val. Or," he added, considering the two of them, eyes narrowed in sly appraisal, "a pretty girl like Ha Lin, maybe you don't *want* her to go easy on you. . . ."

Lin took a casual swipe at the flier with her belt knife, but Valyn could see the flush rising to her cheeks. He wanted to think of something to say, something quick and clever that would catch her eye and make her laugh, but Laith was the one with the lines, and before Valyn could find the right words, a round of raucous laughter cut through the air from across the ring. Lin turned toward the sound, her face twisting into a scowl.

Sami Yurl, along with his small cabal. Plenty of the cadets were nasty and strong—you had to be both, to some degree, to survive on the Islands—but Yurl's lot was the worst, a handful of brutal young men who had signed on to become Kettral, not out of any great love for the empire, but because it satisfied some itch, a cruel glee derived from pain, and power, and killing. Meshkent's Minions, they called themselves, though most of Meshkent's most ardent worshippers lay beyond the boundaries of Annur. Regardless, the name suited them well enough; Valyn had little doubt that if they were promoted to full Kettral, they would inflict enough misery to make the Lord of Pain proud. He was also sure that most of them would sell the others to Manjari slavers for a handful of coin, but you needed someone to watch your back on the Islands, and over the years, the cadets had fallen into loose alliances.

Valyn frowned and turned back to Lin. "Try to stay away from Yurl today. We're just three weeks from the Trial, and if something goes wrong—"

"Nothing's going to go wrong," she snapped.

The blond youth caught them staring, and nudged one of his companions in the ribs. The two shared a rough laugh, and then Yurl returned his gaze to Lin and licked his lips ostentatiously.

"Keep laughing, you bastard," Lin murmured in a voice almost too low for Valyn to hear. "You just keep laughing."

The first fight of the afternoon was an ugly brawl between two of the younger cadets. It went right to the dirt and ended with the larger of the boys holding his eye and crawling for the edge of the ring. After that, a tedious, probing dance between a pair of kids with blades took up what seemed like half the afternoon. Most of the older youths and the trainers jeered and coached from the sidelines while Valyn waited impatiently for the fights that mattered, for the ones he needed to study. Finally one of the kids landed a lucky blow, the other collapsed in a heap, and Jordan Arbert, the senior trainer, decided it was time for some real combat.

"Somebody get that 'Shael-spawned idiot out of my ring," he growled. "Take him to the infirmary. There's a batch of would-be soldiers here who think they're ready to stand for Hull's Trial. I want to see a few matchups before I place my bets about who survives. Now, who do I want?" he mused, looking over the crowd.

Valyn reached over his shoulder to ease his training blades in their scabbards, twisted his head to one side to stretch out a knot in his neck.

"So many options! How about we mix things up a little today? Two on two—see if you murderous bastards can actually manage to cooperate." The trainer smiled a sinister smile. "I'm going to go with Yurl and Ainhoa on one side. That's a nasty little pair."

Valyn had to agree. Although Balendin Ainhoa was a part of Yurl's circle, they could not have looked more different. Where Yurl was well-muscled and handsome, the very image of well-heeled Annurian nobility, Ainhoa looked like a savage straight out of the Hannan jungles. The feathers of seabirds hung among his long, dark braids, rings of ivory and iron pierced his ears, and blue ink snaked up his arms. Rumor had it that Balendin had ended up on the Islands after the people in his town—some tiny settlement on the western coast of Basc—discovered that he was a leach. When they came for him, he killed half the mob and fled, stealing and murdering the whole way, until the Kettral were called in to deal with the problem. They dealt with it by recruiting him.

Anywhere else in the Annurian Empire, a leach would have been strung up, stabbed, or strangled on sight. Valyn had grown up believing such men and women were abominations, that their powers were unholy and evil. He remembered old Crenchan Xaw, commander of the Aedolian Guard, waggling his knife as he made the point: *They steal from the world around them, leach the power right out of the earth. No man should be able to twist and tangle the laws of nature to suit his will.* Xaw was not alone in his convictions. Everyone hated leaches. Everyone hunted them. Everyone except the Kettral.

The Eyrie was always looking for an edge. It wasn't enough that they had the birds, not enough that they controlled the few mines from which the fabled Kettral munitions were made. It wasn't enough that their soldiers were better trained and better equipped than any fighting force in the world. Eyrie Command wanted leaches, too, even killers like Balendin. Especially killers.

Valyn had been appalled when he first arrived on the Qirins to discover he would be fighting alongside such perversions of nature. It had taken months to overcome the most basic revulsion and years to grow comfortable around the strange breed of men and women. As it turned out, reports of both their power and their evil were greatly overblown. They didn't mutter incantations, for one thing, or drink the blood of infants. More important from a tactical standpoint, every leach had a different well, a different source from which he drew his power—granite, water, blood, anything—the secret of which he guarded as closely as his life. Without the presence of his well, he was no more powerful than the next man, a fact that could even the scales considerably. The problem was, if you didn't know a leach's well, you didn't know when you had to be careful.

Balendin motioned his twin wolfhounds—freakish slavering creatures that followed him everywhere—to stillness as he stepped into the ring. They sat like sentinels just outside the stones, jaws gaping, panting audibly in the afternoon heat. The leach glanced skyward, where his tamed hawk circled overhead. The bird let out a piercing shriek, as though aware of his gaze.

"'Kent-kissing thing reminds me of a vulture," Lin said.

"It's just a bird," Valyn replied.

"Maybe," Laith said, turning to Talal. "I don't suppose you've managed to figure out the bastard's well."

Talal shook his head somberly.

"You train with him at least twice a week. How hard can it be? There's only so much stuff in the world!"

"Harder than you think," Talal replied. "We're even more wary of each other than we are of the rest of you. Everyone has their disguises," he said, gesturing to the bracelets encircling his own dark wrists.

"You're telling me your well's not copper or gold?" the flier asked.

"I'm not telling you anything—but look at Balendin. The feathers, the rings, the ink . . . And that's just what he has on him. It could be something all around us—moisture or salt. Stone or sand."

"It could be those 'Kent-kissing beasts," Valyn added, eyeing the wolf-hounds warily. "He brings them with him everywhere."

"Could be," Talal acknowledged. "Leaches have had animal wells in the past. Rennon Pierce, the raven leach, had an entire flock that perched on his eaves and soared above him when he moved."

"And you wonder why everyone wants to string you bastards up," Gent grumbled. "No offense meant, Talal, but the whole thing is sick, filthy."

Talal eyed the larger cadet, his eyes hooded and inscrutable. Then he turned back to Valyn. "People have been speculating about Balendin's hawk and his hounds since the day he arrived. Maybe they're on to something. And maybe he's playing us. It's almost impossible to know."

"Besides," Laith said wryly, "it's not like it should matter in the arena anyway."

According to the rules, while in the ring, Balendin was restricted to the use of his body and blades, just like anyone else; the Eyrie believed in developing "the whole soldier," and had no interest in training a group of men and women who would be useless on the battlefield the moment their wells ran dry. The reality, however, was slightly different. As long as a leach could work subtly, could twist the world around him without anyone noticing, his intervention was permitted. Kettral commanders could ferret out this kind of meddling if they tried, but they never tried—cadets needed to learn to fight in all circumstances, needed to grow comfortable fighting any foe.

"That's one pair," Arbert mused. "Any thoughts about who I ought to pit against them?"

The cadets erupted in a chorus of suggestions. Between the rigors of training and the exhaustive study, there wasn't much leisure for entertainment on the Islands, and most of the assembled soldiers waited each day for Blood Time the way men and women back in Annur looked forward to a well-laid table at dinner.

Arbert held up a hand for silence, but before he could speak, Lin stepped into the ring.

" 'Shael on a stick," Valyn muttered beneath his breath.

"I'll fight them," she said flatly, not taking her eyes from the two.

Sami Yurl smirked.

Arbert chuckled. "All by yourself? Hardly seems fair." He turned to the crowd. "Anyone want to join her?"

The group shifted uncomfortably, some gazing off toward the barracks, others out toward the open ocean. Sami Yurl was a self-involved bastard, but he was also quick with his blades, and brutal in the ring. And then there was the leach to consider.

"Unnatural," Gent grumbled, eyeing Balendin warily. The huge cadet wasn't afraid of much, but he held a fear of leaches matched only by his loathing of them.

"I'd step up," Laith said, grinning at Valyn, "but I don't want to deprive you of an opportunity for gallantry."

Valyn sighed. It looked as though his return to the ring was going to be a little more exciting than he'd expected. He couldn't leave Lin on her own, and he'd been aching to put a fist in Sami Yurl's face since the scene over in Manker's. One-on-one he'd have little chance, but Balendin's bladework was mediocre. If they were able to take the leach out of the arrangement quickly, they could both concentrate on Yurl. *And besides,* he thought ruefully, *no one else is volunteering.*

"I'll do it," he said, stepping over the low rope.

The fight began poorly. Valyn would have preferred to square off against Yurl while Lin faced Balendin, but the leach managed to engage him first, leaving Lin to defend herself. She was a full head shorter than her opponent, and certainly weaker as well, but she was savvy. As Yurl's blades snaked in and out, slicing, probing, she fought elbow to elbow with Valyn, refusing to be drawn off her guard by a series of clever gambits.

When Valyn first arrived on the Islands, he had thought bladework was all about strength, technique, and courage. The reality was far more pedestrian. Although those qualities all mattered, they paled before the necessity of discipline, the ability to wait, to watch, and to avoid mistakes. *The first step in winning,* Hendran wrote, *is to avoid losing.* While Valyn battered back the leach's attacks, Lin held her own at his side, playing a tight, cautious game, her breathing heavy but steady. Valyn felt himself smile. If Lin could just hold Yurl off for a while longer, he would find an opening, and then they could both press Yurl.

Then the leach started talking.

"I never understood," he began in a laconic voice that belied the sweat dripping from his forehead, "why the Kettral let women fight."

Valyn swatted aside a thrust and forced him back a couple of paces, but the youth kept up his taunts.

"I know all the stated justifications, of course: women can pass unnoticed where a man would draw attention, they're often underestimated by a foe, but it just doesn't add up. For one thing," he observed, "they're small and weak. For another, they're a distraction. Here I am in the ring. I should be focusing on my bladework, and all I can think about is ripping the pants off this bitch."

Lin growled at Valyn's side as she parried a sweeping overhand slice.

"Ignore him," Valyn said. "He's just trying to get in your head."

"Actually," Balendin countered with a leer, "I'd be more interested in getting inside something else. What do you say, bitch?" he demanded. "I'll go easy on you here, as long as I can make you moan later. . . ."

Sami Yurl chuckled—a low, nasty sound—and took a step back, flamboyantly dropping his guard.

"Leave it . . . ," Valyn started to say, but Lin wasn't going after Yurl. Instead, she used the opening to drive at Balendin, cutting across Valyn's line of attack and breaking formation to drive the leach back.

For a second Valyn thought she was going to batter him straight into the ground, so great was the fury of her blows, but as she forced her way forward, her foot twisted on the packed sand beneath her, and she went down with a scream of rage and frustration.

Balendin grinned and, with a feline grace, leapt over her crumpled body to engage Valyn once again. The leach wasn't the strongest blade, but he knew how to tie up an opponent, and Valyn found himself pushing forward but unable to drive his enemy back.

Behind the screen, Sami Yurl took a step toward Lin. She swung at him with one of her swords, but he parried the blow easily. Then, in a rush, he was on top of her, driving her face into the dirt while she screamed. Valyn tried to keep his mind on his own fight—he couldn't help Lin if he, too, ended up sprawled out on the ground, but it was hard not to hear her shrieks of rage, and he felt his own anger rising, hot and bloody. Yurl had straddled her, and instead of ending the struggle with a blow to the back of the neck, he was reaching down between her legs, trying to force her thighs apart as she thrashed and writhed.

It's a trap, Valyn realized grimly. *Yurl wants you to rush.* The knowledge was as clear as it was irrelevant. He couldn't just trade ineffectual blows with Balendin while Lin was screaming. *'Shael take it,* he spat. Then, with a roar, he launched himself forward, hammering the leach back with a flurry of savage attacks. For a moment he thought it was going to work. Balendin gave ground, falling back with a look of alarm on his face, opening a path to Sami Yurl. Valyn stepped into the gap, but somehow, in his haste, he tripped, stumbled over what had seemed flat ground, and then he was falling. He had time to twist, to try to raise his guard, but the leach was too fast. The blunted blade came down on his forehead like midnight.

†

"That son of a *whore,*" Lin cursed as she savagely scrubbed the blood from her cheek. Instead of reporting to the infirmary as protocol dictated, she and Valyn had made the walk down to the harbor, away from the chatter and stares of the central compound, in order to clean their wounds. "That 'Shael-spawned, 'Kent-kissing *bastard.*"

"It was Balendin," Valyn said, probing the gash on his forehead. It would leave a scar, but then, he had plenty of those already.

"I *know* it was Balendin," Lin snapped. "When I went for him, my ankle twisted as though I'd stepped in mud. *Mud.* We haven't had rain in days."

Valyn nodded. "Same for me. Something tangled my feet. I went down before I even realized what was happening."

"Gent's right," Lin muttered. "Somebody *ought* to string them up. Every 'Kent-kissing leach on the two continents."

Valyn eyed her carefully. "Even Talal?"

"'Shael can *have* Talal," she spat back. "Oh, he's nice enough," she rushed on before he could interrupt, "but how can you trust him? How can you trust any of them? I don't care if the Eyrie wants another edge."

Valyn wasn't quite sure he agreed with her, but after the afternoon's ordeal, he wasn't about to argue further.

"The bitch of it is," Lin went on, "to anyone watching that fight, it looked like they actually won."

"They *did* win," Valyn observed.

"They *cheated*."

"It doesn't matter. We're the ones who ended up facedown in the dirt. I want to smash out a few of Yurl's teeth as badly as you do, but we've got to look at the thing straight on. There aren't going to be any rules to hide behind when we start flying missions."

"Spare me the 'Kent-kissing lecture," she said, spitting a bolus of blood into the waves, then checking a tooth with her tongue. "It's bad enough to lose to Yurl and Ainhoa without you scouring the wound with sanctimony."

Valyn had been about to put a hand on her shoulder, but he leaned back now, stung by Lin's bitterness.

"Don't bark at me. I'm not the one who broke formation."

She glared at him, then groaned in frustration. "I'm sorry, Val. I'm just burned because I'm sure that from the side of the ring, it looked like I slipped, like I just collapsed. People are probably still laughing about it back there."

Something about the words bothered Valyn, and he looked out to sea, running them over again. His head still ached from the blow, and it took him a while to collect his thoughts. "What did you just say?" he asked.

"It looked like I just *collapsed*!" Lin said. "Nobody realized what really happened."

Collapsed.

"Like Manker's," he said quietly.

"I like to think I'm a little more graceful than a termite-ridden alehouse."

"I'm not talking about you *or* the alehouse. I'm talking about what brought you both down."

Lin's head shot up, and she stared at him, eyes bright and angry. "Holy Hull," she breathed. "A fucking leach."

12

"C ome on, Kaden!" Pater said, tugging at Kaden's belt in an effort to hurry him along the trail. "They're going to be starting already. Hurry *up*!"

"Starting what?" Kaden asked for the third time.

Sometimes it seemed like the boy was all bright blue eyes and bony elbows. Normally Pater's enthusiasm made Kaden smile, but today he was hot and frustrated and in no mood for the small child tugging and pawing at his robe.

He had spent half the morning taking apart a small stone hut, and his Shin composure was beginning to fray. Under the best of circumstances, the work would be laborious and time-consuming; the rough blocks of granite had a way of shredding his palms and pinching his fingers until they turned black and blue. And these were not the best of circumstances. After all, he had just finished *building* the 'Shael-spawned thing only a day earlier. It was all part of Tan's "instruction," of course. For almost two weeks, ever since the incident at the pool, the monk had had Kaden lugging stones from all over the mountain, laying them into place, checking to see that the walls were true and plumb, then hauling more rocks. Tan never told him what the building was for, but Kaden had assumed it was for *something*. No sooner had he finished it, however, straightening from the placement of the final piece, than Tan nodded impassively.

"Good," the monk had said. "Now, take it down." He turned away as if to depart, then looked back over his shoulder. "And I don't want to see a pile of rubble here. Each of these stones is to go back exactly where you found it."

Kaden had just about reconciled himself to spending the next week and a half lugging the stones back up the steep paths and replacing them in their earthen divots when Pater arrived, breathing hard and waving him away from the work with a small hand. Tan had sent him, evidently—something about a meeting in the refectory, a meeting of all the monks. The abbot rarely called such an assembly, and Kaden felt his curiosity quicken.

"Why does Nin want the meeting?" he asked patiently.

Pater rolled his eyes. "I don't know. They don't tell me *anything*. Something about that goat you found."

Kaden's stomach twisted uncomfortably. It was almost a month since he'd come across the mangled carcass, and he'd done his best to put it out of his mind. After notifying Nin and the others, there wasn't much else to do, and Tan had kept him busy. Sometimes, however, as he was lugging a rock down from high in the mountain passes, he would feel the skin on his neck prickle and look back. There was never anything to be seen. Now, however, if Nin was calling a meeting . . .

"Has something happened?" he asked.

Pater just pulled harder. "I don't *know*. Come on!"

Clearly he wasn't going to get anything else out of the small boy, and so Kaden slowed his breathing and stilled his impatience. It wasn't far back to the main buildings of the monastery.

On a normal morning, the rough square would be quietly busy with monks going about their labors: novices hauling water in heavy iron pots for the afternoon meal, acolytes hurrying on errands for their *umials,* older monks strolling the paths or seated beneath the junipers, shaved heads bent beneath their cowls as they followed their own private devotions to the Blank God. On a normal morning, the low drone of chanting from the meditation hall would hang on the breeze, a bass rumble beneath the percussive striking of axe against block as acolytes split wood for the fires. While the monastery was rarely lively, it always felt alive. Today, however, Ashk'lan lay empty and silent beneath the harsh glare of the spring sun.

The inside of the refectory was another matter. Nearly two hundred bodies were crammed into the space, the oldest and most respected monks seated on benches near the front of the hall, novices standing on tiptoe in the back. The scent of wool, smoke, and sweat hung heavy in the air. Shin discipline obviated any real commotion—monks who had trained to sit silent and cross-legged in the snow for hours weren't likely to get rowdy—but the group was as animated as Kaden could remember. Dozens of quiet conversations buzzed at the same time, and everyone seemed curious and alert. He and Pater squeezed in at the rear of the hall and nudged the wooden doors shut behind them.

Akiil stood a few paces away, and Kaden caught his friend's eye as he sidled through the crowd with Pater in tow.

"How's that palace you're building coming along?" Akiil asked.

"Glorious," Kaden replied. "I might move my capital here when I finally ascend the throne."

"And give up that glitzy tower back in Annur that your family is so fond of?"

"Nothing wrong with a little honest stonework," Kaden replied, then gestured toward the front of the hall. "What's going on?"

Akiil shrugged. "Not sure. Altaf found something."

"Something?"

"Spare me a lecture on the importance of specificity. No one tells me anything. All I know is Altaf, Tan, and Nin have been locked up in the abbot's study for most of the morning."

"Tan?" Kaden raised an eyebrow. That explained why his *umial* hadn't been around to berate him. "What's he doing with them?"

Akiil fixed him with a long-suffering glare. "As I just explained, no one tells me shit."

Kaden was about to press harder when Scial Nin had stepped out in front of the assembled monks.

"I can't *see*," Pater whispered.

Kaden hefted the boy up onto his shoulders.

"Three weeks ago," the abbot began without preamble, "Kaden came across something . . . unusual."

He paused, allowing a silence to settle over the refectory. Scial Nin was around sixty, thin as a post, brown as a juniper trunk, and lean as old mutton. He no longer had to shave his head, which had gone naturally bald, and the corners of his eyes were deeply creased from squinting at objects in the distance. When Kaden first arrived at the monastery, he had thought the abbot elderly, even frail. Hours of laboring up steep trails in the man's wake, however, had disabused him of that notion. Nin's age and slight frame belied a vigor that appeared in his step when he ran, and resonated in his voice when he spoke, carrying clear and strong to the back of the hall.

"He found a goat slaughtered by an unknown creature. Two brothers and I investigated, but we were able to come to no conclusions. Since then, three more of our goats have gone missing. Rampuri and Altaf have found two of these, each far from its normal grazing range, each beheaded. Each with the skull split open and the brain missing. Recently, they found a crag cat in the same condition."

No one spoke, but the air hissed with a collective intake of breath. This was news to Kaden, and from the looks on the faces of the rest of the monks, it was the first they were hearing about it as well. Kaden glanced over at his friend. Akiil grimaced and shook his head. It was one thing to take down a goat, even brutally, but crag cats were natural predators. Even a brindled bear would have trouble bringing one to ground.

"The first animal was killed eight miles from here, but each successive carcass has been found closer. We had hoped, initially, that whatever found the goats was a migratory predator, killing then moving on. It seems, however, that this thing has come to stay."

Nin let that thought sink in, then continued. "It's not hard to see why. The Bone Mountains don't offer much in the way of game, especially in the winter. Our flock makes comparatively easy prey. Unfortunately, we need those goats to survive. The best solution open to us seems to be to hunt down this predator and kill it."

Akiil raised an eyebrow at that. Hunting might be something the monks could manage, but killing wasn't part of the Shin discipline. They knocked down a few dozen goats each year for the refectory pots, of course, but that was hardly preparation for whatever was tearing apart the monastery's livestock. Kaden wasn't even sure what Nin expected them to kill the creature *with*. Each of the monks carried a simple knife hanging from the belt of his robe—a short-bladed, all-purpose tool that one could use to trim back bruiseberries or skewer a chunk of mutton in the evening stew—but it wasn't likely to be much good against any kind of predator. Kaden tried to imagine attacking a crag cat with the pathetic blade and shuddered.

"The first step," Nin went on, "is finding the thing. It took us the better part of two weeks to come across a track—evidently the creature prefers to stick to the rocks—but Rampuri found one finally. He has painted several copies."

"So there *weren't* any tracks to memorize," Kaden said under his breath, thinking back to that first, brutal session with his *umial,* feeling resentful and vindicated at the same time.

"You're not a complete failure after all," Akiil replied with a smirk.

"Shhh," Pater hissed from atop Kaden's shoulders, batting him on the head with a small, imperious hand.

Nin was passing a few scrolls to the monks sitting in the front row. "I'd like to know, first, if anyone has seen these tracks before."

He waited patiently for the scrolls to circulate slowly toward the back of the room. Kaden watched as each monk took the paper, memorized it, then passed it on to his neighbor. The novices required more time, careful to make sure they etched the correct details on their memories, and a few minutes passed before the paintings reached the back. Someone handed a parchment to Akiil, who held it out where those around him could consider it.

Kaden wasn't sure what he'd been expecting: a variant on a crag cat print maybe, or something with the broad paws and deep claws of a bear. What he found himself staring at, however, was unlike any animal track he'd encountered. It wasn't made by a paw or pad—that much was clear. He couldn't even tell how many *feet* the thing had.

"What in 'Shael's name is *that*?" Akiil asked, turning the parchment in an effort to make sense of it.

The painting showed a dozen indentations, the kind of marks a medium-sized stick might make if driven repeatedly into the ground—a *sharp* stick. None of them measured more than two inches across, but the spacing suggested a creature the size of a large dog. Kaden looked closer. Half those marks appeared to be divided in two by a thin line, as though the foot, or whatever it was, was split.

"Cloven," Akiil observed. "Maybe some sort of hoof."

Kaden shook his head. A cleft would be wider, separating the two toes—the whole point of a cloven hoof was to offer the animal stability; it was what allowed the goats to keep their footing on the uneven terrain. Besides, the shape of the prints was wrong. They didn't look so much like hooves as they did like claws with the pincers squeezed shut. Reluctantly, he called to mind the *saama'an* of the goat's mutilated carcass, studying the severed neck, the shattered skull. Claws could inflict those sorts of wounds—big claws, at least. An uneasy chill tickled his spine. What kind of creature the size of a goat had twelve pincered legs?

"Now that you've had a chance to see the paintings," Nin said, "has anyone come across tracks like these before?"

"I'm not convinced that they *are* tracks," Serkhan Kundashi said, stepping forward from the wall. "Looks like the scratching of a stick on the ground."

"There was no stick," the abbot replied.

"I've lived in these mountains for thirty years," said Rebbin, the overseer of the refectory. "I've cooked everything there is to cook, and I've never seen anything like it."

The abbot nodded grimly, as though he had been expecting as much. He opened his mouth to continue when someone near the front spoke up.

Kaden couldn't see over the crowd, but from the slow, gentle voice, it had to be Yerrin, the hermit. Although Yerrin wore Shin robes and followed the Shin discipline, he kept himself apart from the rest, sleeping in a cave halfway to the Circuit of Ravens, appearing unexpectedly two or three times a month to scrounge food from the refectory or a scrap of thread from the storeroom. The man was dirty but kind. He had named every tree and half the animals in the high mountains, and sometimes Kaden would run into him on a ledge or in a narrow defile checking on "his friends" as he called them, splinting branches broken in a hailstorm, or gathering fallen leaves for his bedding. Kaden hadn't expected to see him here.

"I know these tracks," Yerrin said. The hall fell to absolute silence as everyone strained to hear the quiet voice. "Or tracks much like them." He paused, as though gathering his thoughts, then went on. "My friends leave these tracks around my cave."

"Who are your friends?" Nin asked, voice patient but firm.

"Why, the frost spiders, of course," Yerrin replied. "They come for the ants, who live in their great dirt mound."

Kaden tried to make sense of this. He had studied spiders, of course, all kinds of spiders, including the frost spider. He hadn't been aware that they left tracks.

"These aren't quite like the footprints my friends leave," Yerrin added genially. "There are more legs."

"And the thing is the size of a large dog," Serkhan interjected, pointing out what Kaden thought was the obvious objection. "Spiders don't grow to that size."

"True," the hermit agreed. "True. Still, the world is wide. I have many friends, but there are many more to make."

Kaden glanced over at Rampuri Tan. The man was standing in the shadows at the far end of the hall. It was hard to see the look on his face, but his eyes shone bright in the dimness.

"Well," Scial Nin concluded, once it was clear that Yerrin had nothing more to say. "We cannot let the creature destroy our flocks. We have little chance of following it. That means we will have to lure it to us. Rampuri has suggested that we stake out goats a half mile from the monastery. Several monks will wait in the rocks to watch for some sign of this creature. As for the rest of you, no one is to leave the central square alone. Novices and acolytes are forbidden to leave the monastery at *all* without an accompanying *umial.*"

That got a response. Chalmer Oleki, Kaden's old teacher, rose from his bench in the first row. He was the oldest of the Shin, half again as old as the abbot, and his voice was reed-thin when he spoke. "This thing has killed goats, yes. It is a problem for us, yes. But do you believe it would come against grown men?"

Scial Nin opened his mouth, but it was Tan who answered, stepping forward from the shadows. Kaden had always found his *umial* menacing, even before being forced to study under the man. In the past, however, something had held that menace in check. Tan had reminded him of a vast, silent slope of snow high on a peak, poised to break loose in avalanche at the first peal of thunder, or like a sword, still and suspended at the height of its arc, held indefinitely by some mysterious power. There was nothing strange in Tan's movement now, nothing more than a simple step forward, and yet Kaden shivered, as though the small movement marked a change, a tip in a balance long held.

"When you know nothing about a creature," the monk ground out, his voice hard as a rockslide, "expect it has come to kill you."

13

Once he was actually standing in front of the ruined tavern again, Valyn wasn't sure what he had hoped to see. Most of the place had disappeared beneath the murky water in a tumble of broken beams and waterlogged walls, and even if there *had* been something to look at, the sun was already dipping toward the horizon—a sullen, red orb—and the light was too poor to see much beyond the skeletal outlines.

The certainty he had felt immediately following his fight in the ring had faded like the afternoon light. It was possible that a leach had been behind the destruction of Manker's—there were probably more leaches on the Islands than anywhere else in the empire. It was possible that the whole thing had been part of a plot directed at him, at his family, part of an ongoing coup. The shit part of it was that just about anything was *possible.* He needed something concrete, something solid to explore, and a leach's kenning would leave even less trace than Kettral explosives. That meant turning to people, people who might have noticed something unusual, seen something they didn't expect.

"Only four made it out," he said, frowning. Juren, of course, and three others who had clawed their way clear of the wreckage.

"Four out of twelve," Lin replied with a shrug. "Not bad, considering the whole thing dropped straight into the bay. Better odds than you'd get on the losing side of most battles." The gash on her cheek had scabbed over, but the indignity of their defeat in the ring still seemed raw and ragged. The Kettral devoted countless hours to tourniquets, splints, medicinal herbs, and bandages. No one said much, however, about the humiliation of having your face ground in the dirt while a fellow soldier thrust a rough hand up between your legs and a few dozen others looked on.

"It wasn't a battle," he said, his mind jumping back to the image of

Salia, hot, bright blood leaking from the wound in her neck. "The people in there were just drinking. They didn't sign on."

"No one ever signs on to get killed."

"You know what I mean."

Lin fixed him with a hard stare. "You mean you feel guilty."

Valyn shrugged. "Sure. Someone comes after me and these poor bastards get crushed? I thought we were supposed to be *protecting* the citizens of Annur."

Lin spread her hands. "I'd hardly call the scum from Manker's 'citizens.' Most of them would be strung up or cut down within a day if they showed their faces back on the mainland."

"It doesn't mean they deserved to die."

"Spare me the guilt, Valyn. It's self-indulgent. It's a waste of time. You didn't kill them. You tried to save them. You're noble. Is that what you want to hear? You're a fucking prince."

Lin's cheeks were flushed, her eyes ablaze. Valyn swallowed a sharp retort and began to put a hand on her shoulder instead. She jerked back.

"Let's find the bastards who did this," she said curtly, refusing to meet his eyes. "Let's just find them."

Valyn started to respond, then, trying to cool his own anger, turned away. Dilapidated buildings hung over the muddy street, paint peeling, roofs sagging, thresholds rotting into the dirt beneath uneven doors. Despite the bright colors, they all looked about ready to give up and tumble into the harbor alongside Manker's. Maybe he and Lin were imagining the whole thing. *Everything falls apart eventually,* he thought, glancing over once more at his friend. *Maybe the tavern just gave up.*

On the other hand, his father had been killed. It was possible the plot went no further than a single disgruntled priest, but Valyn wasn't ready to believe that just yet. If there were people on the Islands responsible, he wanted them found. He wanted them *dead.*

"Juren was one of the ones who made it," he said, breaking the silence. "Laith says he's holed up at the Black Boat, drinking himself straight to 'Shael while he waits for his leg to heal."

"Who's Juren?"

"That thug Manker used to pay to watch over the place."

Lin's face hardened. "The first one to jump clear. The one who refused to help."

Valyn nodded. "He's not much good to anyone else now, not with a busted leg."

"Then he should have plenty of time to talk."

The common room of the Black Boat was poorly lit and cavernous, far too large for the number of chairs and tables scattered haphazardly around the floor. When Valyn had first arrived on the Islands, the Boat was the most prosperous alehouse on Hook, with wine all the way from Sia, blowsy whores hanging from the balconies, and music every night. In the intervening years, however, the owner had died, one of his sons had stabbed the other in a dispute over the property, and the place had fallen into gradual decline. Only half a dozen or so people were at the tables now, and after looking up, eyes heavy with drink and boredom, they returned to their muttered conversations and games of dice.

Juren sat by the bar, his splinted leg propped on a chair, a half-empty glass of wine beside him, and a half-full jug beside that.

"Mind if we join you?" Valyn asked, pulling up a chair.

The man darted them a bloodshot glare. He opened his mouth as though to suggest that he *did* mind, then took another look at their blacks and the Kettral-issue blades at their belts and thought better of it. He scowled. "Suit yourself."

"Juren, right?" Lin asked brightly, settling herself on the chair with a grim smile.

The man grunted.

"You used to work for Manker, didn't you?" she went on. "You were there the day the place collapsed."

"S'how I got this busted leg," he replied, waving a hand at the limb. "Manker bit it along with his shithole. Bastard owed me two weeks of pay."

Valyn shook his head in commiseration. "Bad luck, friend. Bad luck. Listen, we just got paid—why don't you let us top off that jug for you?"

Juren brightened momentarily, then narrowed his eyes. "What d'you want to drink with me for? I seen you often enough. I even seen you over at Manker's the day it dropped. You Kettral are usually too good to rub elbows with the likes of me."

Valyn suppressed a grimace. "Not our decision, friend. Command's got regulations. Security and all that."

Juren snorted. "Right. Security 'n' all that." Despite having served as Manker's hired muscle, he didn't look like he thought all that much of security.

Lin took the newly filled wine jug and topped off the man's glass before filling two more.

"I remember you now," she said, nodding as though at the memory.
"You made it to the doorway first."

The man edged back on his stool, putting a little more space between
them.

"You made it to the doorway," she continued, voice deceptively level,
"and then, instead of helping get anyone else out . . . you jumped."

"What are you, the town constables?" he asked, licking his lips furtively. "I came to Hook t'get away from this shit."

"By 'this shit,'" Valyn said, leaning in until he could smell the sour
wine on the man's breath, "I can only assume you mean things like courage and human decency."

"Don't lecture me," Juren snarled, pushing him back with a meaty
hand. "I don't get paid no tall stacks of gold to risk *my* life. I did what I
had to do. That's why I'm alive."

"Oh no," Lin said, airily. "We're not going to lecture you. We're just
going to ask you a few questions."

"Fuck your questions."

She pursed her lips and looked over at Valyn.

Valyn was rapidly tiring of the man's attitude. There were faster ways
to get answers out of a drunken brawler than plying him with wine, and
he and Lin had spent years mastering just about all of them.

"Look, *friend*," he began, tapping conspicuously at his belt knife.
"The questions are going to be easy. Don't make them complicated."

"Actually," Lin went on with a vicious smile, "I don't mind if you make
them complicated."

Juren scowled, then spat over his shoulder onto the floor. "What
questions?"

"Did you see any other Kettral in the tavern that day?" Valyn asked.
"Maybe in the morning, or just before we got there?"

"It was just you two," Juren grumbled. "You two and that slick, gold-
haired bastard. The one that broke the wineglass."

Valyn considered the claim. Sami Yurl was perfectly capable of plotting, of murder, and he *had* been in the alehouse. On the other hand, Yurl
was no leach. Maybe he was wrapped up in the thing somehow, but it
didn't seem possible that he'd brought down Manker's all on his own.

"No one in the morning?" Lin pressed. "No other Kettral?"

The thug wrinkled his brow as though fighting through a haze of wine. "Yeah. Yeah, there was someone else—short, crop-haired girl. Wore the same blacks as the rest of you lot. Eyes like nails. She didn't stay long."

"Looked about fifteen years old?"

"How'n Hull's name should I know?" the man snapped. "She barely talked."

"Annick," Valyn said, glancing over at Lin.

She grimaced and nodded. Annick Frencha was the best sniper among the cadets, one of the best snipers on the Islands, despite the fact that she had yet to pass Hull's Trial. The girl was a mystery. She seemed to have no need or desire for human contact, and despite her size, she was every bit as brutal as Yurl or Balendin. Valyn had watched her working with her bow once in the fields to the north of the compound. She had shot a rabbit through the foot at a hundred paces, and the creature was shrieking—a terrified, unearthly sound—as it tried to drag itself to safety. Annick cocked her head to the side before loosing a second arrow. This one transfixed the rabbit's back leg. Hitting the creature at all at that distance was impressive, but Valyn started to suspect that she was missing its heart on purpose. "Why don't you kill it?" he'd asked. Annick had looked at him with those icy eyes of hers. "I want a moving target," she replied, nocking another arrow to the string. "If it's dead, it doesn't move." Valyn had little trouble believing that Annick would destroy a tavern and the people inside it just to accomplish her objective. But then she, like Yurl, was no leach.

"How about a tall guy, ink on the arms, feathers in the hair?" Lin asked.

"Nah," Juren replied, waving away the suggestion. "Nobody like that."

"He's always got a couple of wolfhounds with him," she added.

"I *told* you. There wasn't no one like that there."

Valyn was about to ask what Annick was doing at Manker's when the door burst open. He dropped a hand to his belt knife. People who slammed open doors weren't usually looking for a quiet evening of cards, and he readied himself for some drunken sailor, half-dead on rum and swinging a busted bottle. Instead, a young woman stumbled into the room. She wore a grimy, red, low-cut dress a few sizes too big for her small frame, and a cheap ribbon in her mousy hair. Tears streamed like rain down her white cheeks, and her baffled brown eyes shone in the meager lamplight.

"Amie's dead," she sobbed. "They took 'er, and they sliced 'er up, and now she's dead!"

Valyn scanned the room. He had no idea who the girl was, who Amie was, or what in 'Shael's name was going on, but it didn't sound pretty. Usually the locals had enough sense to leave the Kettral out of their vendettas and turf wars, but if he'd learned one thing on the Islands, it was that fear and rage made people unpredictable. Whatever the girl was talking about, it sounded bad. He glanced over at Lin. It didn't seem like they were going to get much more out of Juren. There were a few more survivors that he wanted to hunt up, and he had neither the time nor the inclination to get caught up in some asinine local brawl at the Black Boat.

His friend, however, hadn't moved. She was just staring at the girl, lips parted, but silent.

"You know her?" Valyn asked.

She nodded. "Rianne. She's a whore. Works down by the docks, mostly, but she and her sister have a little garden on the hill above town. I used to buy firefruit from her in the spring."

"Who's Amie?" Valyn asked warily, keeping an eye on the seated patrons. Everyone was watching Rianne. No one had risen, but whispered conversations were starting up at a few of the tables, and men were easing back in their seats, freeing up the knives and cutlasses tucked in their belts, eyeing one another cautiously. None of the other patrons were Kettral, but evidently they, too, had learned the hard way to distrust surprises. Valyn measured the distance to the door, the gap between him and the other tables, running through a half dozen tactical responses if things went ugly.

"Amie was her sister," Lin replied. Her eyes remained fixed on Rianne. She seemed oblivious of the tension in the room.

Rianne took a couple of steps forward, her bony hands beggared before her as though she were holding up an invisible body. The people at the nearest tables leaned back in their chairs, giving her space. She stared helplessly from one face to the next, as though searching for something, the nature of which she had long ago forgotten. Then she saw Lin.

"Ha Lin," she whispered, dropping to her knees on the rough wooden floor. "You have to help me." Valyn wasn't sure if the posture was part of the plea, or if she simply lacked the strength to stand. "You're a soldier. You're Kettral. You can find them! Please." She raked a hand through her tangled hair. Dark streaks lined her face, tears smeared with the charcoal she used to darken her eyes. "You *have* to help me."

All eyes swiveled to the two soldiers.

"Not our concern," Valyn murmured to his friend, tossing a couple of coins on the bar and getting ready to step past the kneeling woman.

Lin fixed him with an angry glare. "Whose concern *is* it?"

"Her father's," Valyn replied, trying to keep his voice low, trying to turn Lin away from the prying stares. "Her brother's."

"She doesn't *have* a father. Or a brother. She and Amie were alone."

"How in Hull did they end up on Hook?"

"Does it matter?" Lin snapped.

Valyn took a deep breath. "We can't do this now," he ground out. Rianne's situation sounded horrible, tragic, but there was no way they could chase down every killer on Hook, no way they could defend every dockyard whore. Besides, even if they found the man responsible, the Eyrie explicitly forbade unauthorized violence against civilians. There were a thousand reasons to step past the girl, offer a polite condolence, and return to Qarsh. "This isn't why we're *here*."

Lin stepped in close, close enough that he could smell the sea salt in her hair, opened her mouth to say something, and then looked over her shoulder, as though noticing the other patrons for the first time. Her lips tightened.

"So much for protecting the innocent people of Annur."

Valyn swallowed a curse. All eyes were on him now, furtive, feral glances over the rims of tankards, calculating stares from the far end of the room. The whole thing was horseshit. They'd come to the Boat to get answers out of Juren, to learn something about the conspiracy to kill Valyn, to try to thwart a plot to overthrow the entire fucking empire. Evidently all it took to knock them off the scent was a sailor's whore with a sob story. In fact, once you started thinking about plots, Rianne's sudden, unexpected appearance looked pretty suspicious. He opened his mouth to protest, then closed it again.

Quarrel if you must, Hendran wrote, *but do so out of sight. Open division emboldens a foe.*

Valyn had no idea what to make of the girl's sudden arrival, but arguing about it with Ha Lin in the middle of a crowded tavern seemed like a poor way to proceed. Juren wasn't going anywhere with his busted leg.

Any secrets about the collapse of Manker's would still be there to uncover a day later, a week later. *There's time,* he thought to himself.

Besides, Lin had a point. Assuming Rianne was telling the truth, she, like Valyn, had lost family. She, like Valyn, wanted answers. Unlike Valyn, however, she was no Kettral. She lacked the tools to solve her own mystery, lacked the training to rectify a wrong. The memory of the corpses from Manker's came back to him, bodies broken and bloated with water. Whatever else was going on, the Kettral were supposed to protect people, to guard citizens and defend the helpless. That, as much as the swords and the birds, was why Valyn had stepped onto the boat eight years earlier.

"What do you want us to do?" he asked warily.

✝

The room was a cramped garret on the fourth story of a tall, narrow building next to the harbor. A rickety staircase spiraled up tightly, the ceiling so low Valyn had to crouch, boards so warped and twisted that each time they groaned beneath his weight he wondered if the whole thing was going to crumble, dumping him into the cellar. *If someone wanted to kill me,* he thought grimly, *this is the place to do it.* The sun had set while they were still in the Black Boat, and inside the building the only light came from Rianne's small storm lantern, a weak, flickering flame that did little more than carve furtive, jerking shadows from the darkness.

Valyn didn't like the feel of that darkness. For all that Hull was the patron god of the Kettral, for all the midnight training missions, for all the blindfolded practice assembling and breaking down arbalests and munitions, the close, claustrophobic dark of the stairwell felt alien and unfriendly. Shadows were supposed to be allies of the soldier, but this inky black was menacing and palpable—a cloak for any would-be assassin.

He glanced over his shoulder at Rianne. The girl had practically dragged them down the dusty street, but as they approached the building she grew suddenly reluctant, as though overwhelmed with dread at the thought of what waited above.

"What is this place?" Valyn asked her, trying to be gentle, trying to dampen his own apprehension.

She scrubbed a tear away. "It's nothing."

"Who owns it?"

"No one. Used to be a boarding house, but it's been abandoned better'n four years now."

"And your sister was here?" he asked, confused. "What was she doing?"

Rianne dropped her red-rimmed eyes. "We took 'em here, sometimes," she mumbled. "The men."

Valyn frowned. "Why didn't you just take them home?"

Rianne stopped on the stairs ahead of him, and turned until the lantern was shining directly into his eyes. He could smell her cheap perfume, and underneath, a sharper, more desperate smell of fear, hunger, exhaustion. "Would you?" she asked dully.

They climbed the remainder of the stairs in silence. As they neared the garret, Valyn noticed a new smell. It was the same as on the ship, the same as on every battlefield he'd ever studied, only those bodies had all been outside, washed by the rain and bleached by the sun before he got a look at them. As Lin shoved open the rickety door, the cloying, pent-up scent of death and rot threatened to choke him, and he stopped for a second, forcing down the bile in his throat. Rianne had started sobbing again.

"It's fine," he said. "You don't need to come in with us. Why don't you wait downstairs?"

She nodded feebly, handed him the lantern, and turned back into the darkness.

Once Valyn stepped into the cramped, peeling attic, he was glad he'd sent her away. There was only one body, but the sight was as disturbing as any tableau of battlefield carnage. Someone had stripped the murdered girl of her clothes—they were tossed in an untidy heap in the corner—and then hung her by her wrists from the low rafters. The corpse had bloated and rot had set in badly, but Amie looked as though she had been even younger than her sister—maybe sixteen, blond, pale, probably pretty. Festering red gashes ran the length of her slender torso, her arms, her legs, all deep enough to paint her skin with runnels of blood, but none severe enough to kill quickly. Tightening flesh curled back from the wounds. The rope groaned as she twisted, moved by some slight, unseen breeze.

Valyn sucked in an angry breath, clenched his hand into a fist, and turned away. Outside the narrow window, the night was calm and cool. Across the harbor he could see the lights of the Black Boat and the other alehouses, as well as the dark gaping hole where Manker's had been. People were walking on the streets of Hook, laughing and arguing, going on about their lives, heedless of the girl who had been tied up, murdered, and left to rot in an abandoned attic.

"Sons of bitches," Lin breathed behind him. She was angry, Valyn could hear that clearly enough, but there was a faint current of something else behind the anger—fear, and confusion.

He turned back to the room, trying to find something concrete, some particular detail upon which he could focus his training. There wasn't much to look at. A thin tick mattress stuffed with reeds lay heaped in the corner, evidently kicked out of the way during the assault. A three-legged stool squatted beneath the window, and a wooden shelf along one wall supported a few candles that had burned down to the nubs, splattering the warped floor with tallow. He considered those for a while. Candles were relatively expensive—fat had to be cut, rendered, then cast around the wick. They were a necessity, of course, for those who worked by night, but the poor and thrifty would never waste the excess drippings. Rianne's lantern, like most of the lanterns on Hook, was fed by cheap fish oil, and gave off an inconstant light that was as smoky as it was rank. He wondered if the candles had belonged to Amie, if she had intended to scrape the tallow off the floor later, or if her murderer had brought them, planning ahead to ensure he had plenty of light by which to perform his grisly work.

Reluctantly, Valyn turned back to the corpse. Her ankles were tied, no doubt to keep her from kicking. His eyes settled on the knot: a peculiar double bowline with a couple of extra loops. He started to study it, then tore himself away. *You're looking at the knot to avoid looking at the girl,* he realized, forcing himself to shift his gaze from her wrists to her face.

"All right," he said brusquely, turning to the training he had spent so many years perfecting. "How did she die?"

Ha Lin didn't respond. She stood in the center of the room, arms slack at her sides, head shaking silently, slowly as she considered the revolving corpse.

"Lin," Valyn said, edging his voice with what he hoped was something of Adaman Fane's characteristic growl. "What killed this girl? How long has she been dead?"

Ha Lin turned to him blankly. For a moment he thought she wasn't going to respond at all, but after a long pause her eyes focused, and she shook herself, as though awakening from a deep sleep. Her lips hardened into a thin line and she nodded abruptly before crossing to the dangling corpse. She leaned in to sniff the wounds, then ran a finger along the major lacerations, probing the flesh.

"No scent of poison. No major arteries severed." She bit her lip. "It looks like blood loss, pure and simple."

"Painful," Valyn added grimly. "And slow." He reached above the girl's head and cut the rope holding her up before easing her body to the floor. "Take a look at this," he said, holding out the severed rope.

Lin squinted in the darkness. "The rope is from Li," she said, the surprise clear in her voice. Li was on the other side of the world, months distant by sail. They made the best rope and steel in the world there, but it wasn't the kind of thing that found itself into the hands of the sailors on Hook. The Kettral, on the other hand . . . the Kettral used Liran cord sometimes. It was too slick for the taste of most soldiers, but it was light and strong, and there were those who swore by it.

Valyn and Lin exchanged a bleak stare.

"When did she die?" he asked finally, breaking the silence.

Lin hunched over the body, sniffing the wounds once more.

"Hard to say. The rot looks almost two weeks advanced, but that could swing a few days in either direction, depending."

"Must get pretty hot up here during the day," Valyn agreed. "Body would decay faster."

Lin nodded, then drove her fingers into one of the gashes, searched around for a minute before pulling out something white and glistening. "The skin might lie, but the bugs won't." She held up the writhing creatures for Valyn to inspect.

"Blood worms, still larval."

Valyn took the worm, a sickening sluglike thing, and held it up to the fading light from the window. "It's got its eyes just in."

"But no segmentation yet. Which means less than eleven days."

He nodded. "Six days to incubate. One to hatch. Four to grow the eyes."

"She's been dead for ten days, for almost exactly ten days."

Valyn nodded. "Which means she died . . ." He counted back, then paused, turning first to the body, then to Lin.

She stared back at him, brown eyes huge in the lamplight. "Which means she died the same day Manker's collapsed into the harbor."

14

The soil of Hook, like that of all the Qirin chain, was rocky and unforgiving, and so it took Valyn and Lin the better part of two hours, working in shifts behind the pathetic shack in which Rianne and Amie had made their home, to hack a hole deep enough to bury the murdered girl. That was the easy part. Then they had to return to the horrible, reeking garret, wrap the corpse in a scrap of sailcloth they bought down by the docks, and carry her back to her grave. When the stones and thin soil were finally mounded up over the earth, then scattered with the few wretched petals Rianne had scrounged from the yellowweed behind the house, the moon had dipped toward the horizon, while the bright stars people called Pta's gems hung directly overhead, cold, distant, and unpitying.

Valyn ached when he put down the shovel. Kettral training had prepared him for just about any kind of physical suffering, but there was something about digging a grave, an extra weight, as though the dirt tossed out of the hole were not just dirt, but something harder, heavier. He had seen plenty of bodies, had trained for years to kill people, but the corpses of the battlefield and the grown men he had seen there, armored for war and cut down in fury and rage, were different from the pale, flaxen-haired figure they had found mutilated in the tiny garret.

As Lin wrestled a rough headstone into place, Rianne continued to cry, low and quiet, as she had all night. Valyn turned to the girl. He wanted to say something wise, something comforting, but there just wasn't a whole lot in the way of comfort to be had. The normal platitudes one offered in such situations seemed ridiculous and trite. *I'm sorry for your loss?* Rianne's sister hadn't been *lost;* she'd been strung up and hacked at like a slab of beef in a slaughterhouse, tortured horribly and left to die. *She's gone to a better world?* What world? If there *was* a world after death, no one had come back from it with stories to tell. No, there wasn't a 'Shael-spawned thing to say, and yet, he couldn't just stand there staring at her.

"How about a drink?" he asked awkwardly. It was a soldier's response to death, but it would have to do. "We'll toast your sister."

"A . . . a . . . alright," she managed between choked-off sobs. "I've got some peach wine inside. It's not very good, but Amie and I used to—" The memory of her sister strangled the end of the sentence, and as Valyn watched helplessly, Lin wrapped her arm around Rianne's narrow shoulders.

"Your sister's fine now," she said quietly. "What happened to her was horrible, but it's over." As Rianne whimpered into her shoulder, Ha Lin raised her eyes to Valyn. "Why don't you get that wine? We can share it in Amie's memory. Pour some on her grave."

Valyn nodded and turned toward the house, grateful for a momentary reprieve. The Kettral spent years training soldiers to get used to the dead; they didn't say much, though, about dealing with the living.

The chipped crock of peach wine wasn't hard to find. The sisters had only a few possessions: a single straw mattress, neatly covered with a tattered quilt, a trunk with one drawer missing. Two bowls and two spoons next to a wide tin washbasin. He imagined them sitting on the bed together, no more than children really, spooning up some kind of broth and telling each other stories to keep their lives at bay. He shook his head and pushed open the door, stepping back into the darkness.

They passed the bottle around, poured a swallow on the grave, then passed it around again. Lin asked Rianne if she wanted to say a few words about her sister.

"She took care of me," was all Rianne could manage. "She was younger than me, but she took care of me."

"It's all right now," Lin repeated quietly.

Valyn wanted to ask what, exactly, was all right about what had happened to Amie, but willed himself silent. Rianne's life had turned dark enough without him dousing whatever light was left.

"Do you think Ananshael is kind to the dead?" she whispered after a while.

Lin glanced over at Valyn. People didn't tend to think of the Lord of Bones as "kind." It was hard to conceive of a god who ripped souls from bodies of the living, who parted parents from children and youths from their lovers, as anything other than fickle and malevolent. Macabre stories of the Skullsworn, the bloody priests of Ananshael, abounded: men and women who drank blood from goblets and strangled infants in their cribs. The Skullsworn were trained assassins, ruthless killers, and aside from the Kettral, probably the deadliest group on the two continents. If his chosen priests were any indication, it certainly did not seem that Ananshael would be kind.

On the other hand, Hendran had written that the last gift you could give to a suffering soldier was death. Valyn thought back to the corpse of Amie, dangling from her wrists in the garret, eyes straining from her skull. Perhaps, in the end, Ananshael had been kind to her after all. Perhaps he was no more vicious than a gardener trimming his trees, a farmer about his autumn harvest.

" 'Only the dead,' " Valyn said quietly, quoting the passage, " 'are at peace.' "

Rianne nodded. It seemed unlikely that she'd had occasion to study Hendran, but the sentiment seemed to make sense to her. When he considered the life she'd led, it wasn't hard to see why. He hoisted the crock to his lips, took another swig, and passed it. For a while the three of them drank in silence, sitting on the cold earth, staring at the cold mound of stones that marked the termination of a life.

"Do you have any idea who did it?" Valyn asked finally. He hated to break the quiet, the illusion of tranquillity, but the question had been gnawing at his gut.

"No," Rianne responded, shaking her head despondently. "I didn't think anyone *could* . . ." She trailed off, but didn't start crying again.

Tough girl, Valyn thought, to pull herself together in the space of a single night. He'd seen Kettral cadets who took more time to get over their first battlefield examination.

"Did Amie say she was going to be meeting anyone?" Lin prompted. "Any . . . men?"

Rianne bit her lip and squinted into the darkness. "She said . . . Yes . . . She said she was going to see a soldier, but that was early in the day."

Valyn and Lin exchanged a look.

"Kettral?" Valyn asked slowly, although the answer was obvious. Marriage was forbidden to the Kettral; a husband or wife was a liability, a distraction, a lever an enemy might use to manipulate or blackmail. Henderson Jakes, the founder of the Eyrie, had envisioned a cadre of elite soldiers dedicated to celibacy, the empire, and the art of war. He had to settle for two out of three. Young men and women willing to leap off massive birds into burning buildings at a mere nod from a commanding officer grew violently rebellious when required to abstain from sex. After six or eight soldiers had been marched to the gallows for fucking on night watch, fucking on recon, fucking while harnessed into one of the 'Kent-kissing birds (Valyn always found that one both implausible and impressive), resentment among the troops boiled over and it looked like Jakes might come to a violent and untimely end, along with the order he sought to found. Like any good tactician, Jakes knew when he had to give ground. The ban against marriage remained, but the prohibition regarding sex was lifted.

Hundreds of years later, whores and whorehouses abounded on Hook—a simple solution to an ancient problem. Valyn had visited a few himself, usually dragged along by Laith or Gent when they were in their cups. He always felt a little dirty afterwards, always knew he would go again when pressed. It seemed harmless enough, and after all, no one was forcing the women. Amie's death, however . . .

"She was going to meet Kettral?" he asked again, his voice rougher than he'd intended.

Rianne nodded.

"Did she say who?"

"No," she replied heavily. "Just that they were meeting at Manker's. She seemed excited, which was strange. Being a whore—there are worse jobs—but it's not something Amie enjoyed. She didn't look forward to . . . seeing the men."

Valyn's heart thudded in his chest. It made a sick sort of sense; if anyone knew how to truss up a girl, how to silence her, murder her, and slip away without anyone the wiser, it was the Kettral. That's what the Eyrie trained them for. And then, of course, there was the cord from Li to consider. The next question rose unbidden to his lips, but before he could ask it, a racket from the lane outside the shack brought him up short. Someone, two men by the sound of it—two drunken men were approaching the house, crowing out slurred lyrics as they came.

> We wear the blacks when we attack,
> From the moment we wake till we hit the sack.
> Black as darkness, black as death,
> We'll wear the blacks to our final breath.

We march alongside Ananshael
And leave the widows to weep and wail.
You ask by whom this woe was sent?
The Lord of Pain and Cries: Meshkent.

"Kettral," Valyn said, eyeing Lin.

She nodded tightly, removing her arm from Rianne's shoulders to free up her right hand.

"Rianne!" someone bellowed merrily, pounding at the flimsy door out in front of the hut. "Amie! We come bearing coin and cock!"

"And flowers," urged the other, deeper voice.

"And *be-au-ti-ful* flowers!"

"I'll deal with this," Valyn said, stepping through the back door of the house. He crossed the small space in a few strides, checking his twin blades as he went, then flung open the front door into the faces of two fellow cadets. Laith carried a bottle of wine in each hand and had struck a grandiose pose outside the door, head thrown back, hips thrust forward, arms wide in greeting. Gent stood half a step behind him, tunic unlaced halfway down his chest, a scraggly bouquet of island flowers held in one huge fist.

Both cadets reeled backwards, eyebrows drawn down as they tried to make sense of Valyn's unexpected presence in the doorway. Then Laith burst into laughter.

"Well played, Valyn! Well played! And here we thought you spent all your evenings mooning over Lin!"

"What are you doing here?" Valyn demanded, feeling foolish even as the words left his lips. Amie and Rianne were whores. It didn't take much calculation to figure out what might have drawn the two cadets, pounding on their door in the middle of the night.

Gent beamed drunkenly while Laith leaned forward with a conspiratorial grin. "Sometimes we come for the outstanding library, sometimes for the learned discussion of political affairs, but tonight"—he winked—"I think we're more in the mood for a little tickle, if you know what I mean, provided you haven't tired them both out. Amie!" he bellowed—so loud, Valyn's ears rang. "Rianne! We come bearing coin and cock!"

"Shut it, you 'Kent-kissing idiots," Valyn hissed, snatching them both by the blacks and dragging them inside.

Laith regained his balance first and peered blearily about him. "What's wrong with you? Where's Amie? Where's Rianne?"

"Amie's dead," Valyn snapped, waiting to make sure the words had penetrated the haze of alcohol. "Someone hung her from a rafter and cut her to ribbons."

The two cadets had seemed impressively drunk, but they sobered quickly. Gent still wobbled some on his feet, and Laith's eyes still twitched, but by the time Valyn had finished speaking, Gent was tossing his bouquet aside and both were reaching for their knives.

"Where?" Laith demanded, rotating to put his back toward Valyn and Gent, scanning the small, dark space of the cottage.

"Not here," Valyn replied. "She was—" He stopped himself as Rianne's words hit him: *She was going to see a soldier.* He eyed Gent and Laith, suddenly wary. He'd known them both for half his life. Laith flew too fast and drank too much, and Gent tore into other soldiers like a rabid bull in training exercises, but neither of them seemed capable of the violence inflicted on the dead girl. Besides, Amie had been dead for more than a week. If they were the ones to have killed her, they wouldn't be likely to show up in the middle of the night, looking for a tumble.

"Not here," he said again.

"When?" Laith asked.

"What about Rianne?" Gent rumbled, his voice hard.

"Almost two weeks ago," Valyn replied. "But her sister just found the body tonight, tied up and cut up in a garret down by the harbor. Rianne's fine. Or as fine as you'd expect, after finding her sister's body. We just got finished burying Amie."

"Shit and 'Shael," Laith muttered, sheathing his belt knife and shaking his head. "Where is she?"

Valyn nodded through the back door.

Laith took a step toward it, then stopped to clumsily gather up the flowers Gent had dropped on the floor, rearranging them into a lopsided bouquet once more.

Rianne started crying once again when she saw the two cadets. Gent's eyes flitted to the grave; then he turned to her with an awkward formality.

"Valyn told us what happened. You find the bastard, and we'll kill him." He concluded with a brusque nod, as though that settled everything.

Laith gathered Rianne in his arms. She started to resist, then sagged against him, snuffling. Another man might have felt awkward, comforting the whore he'd crossed the sound to bed, but Laith didn't feel awkward about much. He kissed her hair as if she were his own sister and rocked her back and forth without saying a word.

Lin watched the two with hooded eyes. "What are you doing here?"

"Does it matter?" Laith responded quietly.

They locked gazes over Rianne's head. Then Lin shook her head. "I suppose not."

Over the next hour, the five of them drank the wine Laith had brought. As it turned out, the two cadets had been bedding the sisters off and on since they were old enough to fumble their pricks out of their pants. Valyn was surprised at the range of stories they remembered about the murdered girl, each one bawdier than the last. At first he thought the coarse tales would insult Rianne or set her on edge, but the truth was, she seemed strangely touched to find that someone else remembered something about her sister, and she laughed along with their jokes, her words more slurred as the night dragged on. The jugs went round and round and finally the poor girl lapsed into a drunken sleep, her head resting on Laith's thigh.

The cadet ran a finger down her cheek, said her name once, then again louder. When it was clear she wasn't waking up, he turned to Valyn.

"What in 'Kent's name happened?"

It didn't take long to recount the story, and no one seemed to feel like speaking when it was finished. Somewhere down the lane a dog was barking over and over, a trapped, desperate sound.

"Kettral, eh?" Laith asked finally, his voice uncharacteristically subdued.

"Not necessarily," Lin replied, an edge to her voice. "Rianne said that Amie was looking forward to meeting a soldier that morning, but that doesn't mean it was a soldier responsible for her death. Whores get slapped around all the time. When a man pays for a girl like cattle, you shouldn't be surprised when he treats her like cattle."

Valyn grimaced. "Getting her up all those stairs, tying her up the way we found her, keeping her quiet the whole time—"

"It's not like Hook is a 'Kent-kissing monastery," Lin said, cutting him off. "The place is a madhouse. Between sailors brawling down by the docks and the rest of the town getting drunk, you could slaughter an ox in the street at high noon and most people wouldn't notice."

"I'm just saying," Valyn replied, "it doesn't scream 'amateur'—"

"It screams fucked up," Gent rumbled.

"Of course it's fucked up," Lin snapped, her voice filled with venom. "The whole *thing* is fucked up. You've been . . . *patronizing* Amie for years? Since she was *thirteen*?"

"Leave it alone, Lin," Laith replied. "We didn't kill her. Besides, how old were *you* the first time you had a tumble? Twelve? Whores and soldiers both grow up fast."

"She's not grown up," Lin snarled. "She's dead."

"And we're trying to figure out who killed her," Valyn said, trying to calm the two before Rianne woke to a full-blown brawl.

"Some sick bastard who likes to cut up his whores before he has his way with them," Gent suggested.

Lin darted her eyes at the sleeping girl.

"She's out," Laith said, not ungently. "I've thought I had some good reasons to drink myself dark, but this . . ." He shook his head.

"So who?" Valyn persisted. "Lin and I were here on Hook the day she died. It was the day Manker's collapsed. Sami Yurl was here, too."

"Sounds like Yurl," Gent said. "Force a girl. Hurt her."

Lin looked like she was going to say something sharp, but she bit her lip. "No," she said almost reluctantly. "He'd force a girl. Maybe even kill her. He'd certainly enjoy it. But the scene we found . . . the candles . . . the rope . . . the wounds—it was too . . ."

"Too private," Valyn agreed after a moment's thought. "Yurl likes to hurt people, to embarrass them, but he likes an audience."

"Well," Laith said, frowning, "it's not like he's the only one of our esteemed brothers-in-arms who enjoys causing pain."

It was a casual remark, but it brought back Valyn's conversation from the evening before. It seemed a week rather than a single night since he'd threatened Juren for information over at the Black Boat.

"Annick was on Hook the day Amie was killed," he said abruptly. "The guy who looks after Manker's saw her there in the morning."

"She's certainly a murderous bitch," Laith replied speculatively.

"Manker's," Lin cut in, nodding. "Amie was going to Manker's that same morning. That's what Rianne said."

"For what?" Laith asked.

"To meet a soldier."

They exchanged a look.

"Well," Gent said, "I don't understand much about Annick, but she ain't a man."

Valyn waved the objection aside. "We don't know that it was a man who killed Amie—we know it was a soldier."

A light breeze had picked up off the harbor, heavy with salt and low tide. Somewhere close by, a man and woman were screaming at each other, either in the street or in one of the sad hovels like the one where Amie and Rianne lived. It went on for a few moments before the woman let out a sharp cry of pain, then fell silent.

"A woman wouldn't do that to another woman," Lin said finally.

"Kettral aren't like other people," Valyn said. "And Kettral women certainly aren't like other women." He tried to lighten the tone of the final comment, but there wasn't much levity to be had.

"But *why*?" Gent asked, his blunt features screwed tight in concentration. "Why would Annick want to kill her? To do . . . *that*?"

"Why does that bitch do anything?" Laith replied. "She's crazy as a blind fox in a locked henhouse."

Though Annick was only fifteen years old, the hardened Kettral trainers joked that she had a rock for a heart and steel for a stomach. She ate by herself in the mess hall, trained by herself on the archery range, and if the rumor was true, slept with her bow lying beside her in her bunk. The idea that she might visit Manker's for a cup of ale and some idle chatter seemed about as likely as a shark strolling out of the sea on its fins to ask for a bowl of soup.

"Annick might be crazy," Valyn said quietly, "but she's deliberate. She could do something like this."

"We still don't have any idea why," Lin pointed out. "Annick went to a tavern and so now she's a murderer?"

"Just because she's a woman, she can't be?" Laith demanded.

Lin opened her mouth, but before she could retort, Valyn interposed a hand.

" 'Assume nothing,' " he said. The first chapter of the *Tactics*. "If we figure everyone might be a murderer, we're less likely to be disappointed."

15

A true Kettral," Adaman Fane bellowed, his voice loud enough to be heard on shore a thousand paces distant, "is not afraid of the water."

A dozen cadets stood on the deck as the *Night's Edge* rocked gently with the waves. Gwenna scowled through the introductory lecture, grimy and irritated, no doubt, at having been yanked away from her bombs. Yurl smiled that sly, superior smile of his, as though Fane and the rest of them were just servants waiting on his pleasure. Balendin leaned against one of the rails, eyes hooded. He twisted one of the iron rings on his fingers as his hawk flew overhead. It was an odd exercise, and Valyn knew he should be paying attention to the instructor, but he couldn't help sneaking surreptitious glances at Annick.

The sniper was thin and gangly, tall for her age, but not so tall as Valyn. Her thin arms didn't look like they had the strength to draw a longbow, but cords of muscle shifted beneath the skin whenever she moved, and Valyn had watched her put an arrow through a lemon at three hundred paces. None of the other cadets on the Islands could manage that. Neither could most of the real Kettral snipers, for that matter. Blackfeather Finn claimed she was the best hand with a bow he'd ever seen, at least at her age.

She didn't look like a flint-hearted killer. At first glance, she actually looked more like a farmer's daughter than a soldier: dusty brown hair flopped over her forehead and flicked out behind her ears, all cut short enough to avoid tangling in her bowstring. She had a sharp nose and sharp chin, both a little too small for her sun-browned face, but not so much that you'd notice if you weren't paying attention. She looked normal, harmless. That is, until you caught a glimpse of her eyes. As Valyn studied her, she glanced over suddenly, as if she'd felt his gaze. Those blue eyes were cold as fish scale.

"A true Kettral," Fane continued, "*embraces* the water. It is his home, just as the air is his home. What we will discover today is whether *you* are at home in the water. Or whether you panic when the waves press down." He looked over the assembled group. "Who wants to embarrass himself first? You're all going to suffer. It's only a question of when."

Valyn broke away from Annick's stare, hesitated, then stepped forward. "I'll go."

"Ah, the Light of the Empire stepping up to lead his feeble subjects by his own bold example."

Valyn ignored the gibe. "What do you want me to do?"

"You?" Fane asked. "I don't want *you* to do anything." He scanned the cadets. "Annick, get over here."

As the sniper stepped forward, the trainer produced a lead weight twice the size of Valyn's head, and a length of stout rope. Fane dropped the weight on the deck with an audible thump, and handed the rope to Annick. Valyn felt his muscles tighten and willed himself calm. *It's just an exercise,* he told himself. *Whatever happened up in that garret, this is just training.*

"You idiots have done this drill before," Fane continued, "but always in shallow harbor water. Today we'll find out if you're ready to swim with the sharks. Go ahead," he said, turning to Annick, but she had already started.

With quick, confident motions, she looped the rope around Valyn's ankles once, twice, three times, cinching it so tight on each pass that he started to lose feeling in his feet before she was finished. She looked up as she worked, ice blue eyes drilling into him, but said nothing before returning to her task, threading the rope through the large eyelet in the anchor, then twisting it over and over and back on itself. Valyn tried to see what sort of knot she was tying out of the corner of his eye, but Fane cuffed him across the face.

"When I want you to cheat, I'll tell you," he said curtly.

Valyn raised his eyes to find Balendin watching him from a few paces away. "Good luck down there, O Noble Prince," the youth smirked. "I hope today's drill works out better for you than our little scuffle last week."

Valyn felt the blood rise to his head, and he started to take a step forward, before remembering that Annick had lashed his ankles together. He teetered, straining against the bonds, before the sniper drove a vicious fist into the back of his knees, dropping him to the deck.

"He's done," she said, turning to Fane as she straightened.

"That was quick," the trainer replied. "I hope you didn't go too easy on him."

"He's done," she repeated, then stepped away, evidently indifferent to the outcome.

Fane shrugged. "You heard her. Over the rail with him, then."

A dozen hands gripped Valyn, hoisting him into the air. He tried to turn himself upright, to get his bearings before they tossed him from the ship, but Sami Yurl had his head, and the blond youth grinned down at him before twisting it so sharply Valyn thought his neck would break. He ground out a low, angry curse and then, the next moment, he was free, free and falling, thrashing wildly before he slammed down into the water.

He managed to suck in a quick breath, catch a glimpse of the dark hull of the vessel, and then the leash on his ankle was pulling him beneath the chop. He clamped his lips shut. He'd hit at an odd angle, but the lead weight would straighten him out. Now it was time to avoid drowning.

The water, pleasantly cool on the ocean's surface, grew colder as he sank. He tilted his head back, straining to see the sun, but the dozens of feet of murk above him had dulled its blaze to a fickle, sullen glow. Even here, barely a quarter mile off the coast, the ocean was deep enough to swallow a whole sailing vessel, masts and all. The weight of it pressed down on him until he could feel the pain piercing his ears, the pressure against his eyes, the full tons of seawater piled on the heart laboring in his chest, slowly crushing it into submission. And still he sank.

The urge to free himself and stroke for the surface was strong, but he thrust it down. *Quit being an ass,* he told himself harshly. *You've been under less than a minute, and you're already starting to twitch.* He knew well enough what to expect from the shallow-water versions of the exercise. The knots binding the anchor to his ankles would be complex and difficult to untie under the best of circumstances; they would be impossible to loose with the weight of the metal still dragging on them. He had to wait until his feet touched the bottom, had to gain some purchase on the ocean floor that would allow him to put enough slack into the ropes to work the knots free. To struggle with them now would be a waste of air, and Valyn could not afford to waste air.

Instead, he counted his heartbeats, trying to slow them as he'd been trained. Higher heart rate meant less air, and if he could still that hammering in his chest, he might gain himself the extra seconds necessary to live through the ordeal. *Twenty-one, twenty-two, twenty-three . . .* If any-thing, they seemed to be coming faster, but Valyn kept counting. *Not much else to do down here,* he reflected grimly.

At twenty-nine, he felt the ropes binding his legs go slack, then tighten again more gently. That was it—the ocean floor. It didn't look like much—*nothing* looked like much this far below the surface, just a world of blue-black forms and murky shadows—but he could make out the jagged shapes of a few large rocks. In a practiced motion he folded at the waist, grasped the cord around his ankles, and, neatly inverted, pulled himself the last few feet to the silty bottom. It was easy enough to wedge his hip between the rocks, and then he went to work on the knots.

The rope was the thickness of his thumb, supple, the kind that coiled easily on a deck and felt good to work between the fingers. Annick had cinched the knots as tight as possible, however, and they had swollen with water during the long, slow plunge to the bottom. Valyn forced himself to go slowly, to test the rope with his fingers, to work through the various loops and twists. The mistake most people made was to just start tugging and pulling before they understood the knot. That was a good way to stay tied up, a good way to drown.

Double bowline, he realized, his heart beating a little faster with antici-pation. Bowlines were easy to loose, even when they'd been doused and pulled tight. Maybe Annick had gone easy on him. He should be able to just . . . no. Valyn gritted his teeth. Of *course* it wasn't easy. The damn thing was a bowline all right, but the bitter end was wrapped up in some bastard of a follow-through that Valyn didn't recognize. If he'd gone about trying to loose it in the standard way, he would have fouled the thing up past all hope of retrieval. *You're a lucky shit for noticing it,* he told himself, but he didn't feel lucky. He'd been under for more than a minute, the air was starting to burn in his lungs, and what he felt was the first prick of the sharp claws of fear. Annick's eyes, hard as chips of flint, filled his mind—those eyes and the memory of the slaughtered girl in the garret.

Slowly, he reminded himself as he traced the devious loop between his thumb and forefinger. *Do it once and do it right.* The coil looped back on itself once, twice, disappeared down through the loop until it came out. . . . He felt an icy sickness lurch in his gut. Even in the blackness, even beneath the tons of water, he knew what kind of knot he was facing now: a double bowline with the extra loops, just like the knot that had bound Amie as she died. It was another piece to the puzzle, but he forced it out of his mind. If he died here at the bottom of the bay, his discovery would die with him.

Fathoms of water pressed down on him like an anvil. The low burn in his lungs had become a fire. *There's still time,* he told himself, clamping down on the animal panic. *Think about what it means later. Just get it untied.*

His abdomen had started to spasm, the muscles of his chest and stomach trying to override his brain, to haul in more air where there was no air to be had. Valyn closed his eyes—they weren't doing him any good down here anyway—and tried to concentrate on the knot. The first loop came free with a reluctant lurch, but there were two more to go.

Stars started to fill his vision, stars that had no business on the bottom of the ocean. He felt his heart lunge again, like a panicked horse stabled in a burning barn. He was getting the knot, but too *slowly.* Once the stars started, there wasn't much time left, not more than a dozen or so heartbeats. It would take him that long to return to the surface. The thought of the icy water sliding into his lungs and strangling him filled his brain, and he lost the bitter end of the rope. Shapes swam around him, sinister shapes circling and drawing closer. *Sharks,* Valyn realized, and clawed frantically at the knot. It was the wrong response. Even if there had been time left, which there wasn't, that kind of desperate action would only tighten the bonds digging into his ankles. *You idiot,* he cursed himself, trying once more to find the loops, to make sense of them as his mind went dull and the blood blazed in his veins, in his heart. *You stupid, 'Kent-kissing* idiot.

Darkness closed around him, cold, and black, and limitless as the sea.

†

He awoke on the deck of the *Night's Edge,* heaving a vile mixture of salt water and hardtack into the scupper. Another spasm brought up a second lungful of the briny muck, and then another, and another. He felt like someone had been at his ribs with their bare knuckles. His head throbbed, and each breath dragged gravel through his lungs. So the black shapes circling down around the ocean floor hadn't been sharks; they were trainers. Someone had waited for him to pass out and then cut him loose. *They should have let me drown,* he thought to himself, curling into a ball on the dry deck. *I was through the hard part already.*

As he shuddered to catch his breath, Valyn realized that someone was looming over him, blocking out the light. *Fane.* Part of him had thought it might be Annick. The enormous trainer was shouting.

"What in 'Shael's sweet name is *wrong* with you, soldier? How long have you been on the Islands?"

Valyn struggled to respond, but only managed to retch more water out onto the deck.

"I'm sorry," Fane said, cupping a hand to his ear. "I couldn't *hear* you."

"Couldn't . . . couldn't untie the knot, sir."

Fane snorted. "I concluded *that* all on my own when you failed to rise to the surface. Couldn't untie a basic double bowline? Looks like the Light of the Empire has grown somewhat dim."

That earned an appreciative chuckle from Sami Yurl.

"It wasn't . . . wasn't a simple bowline, sir," Valyn managed. He didn't want to sound like he was making excuses, but didn't want Fane to think he was inept, either. The memory of that extra twist, of Amie's bound hands, blackened and clenched into claws, gouged at his mind. Had she struggled like him in her last moments, trying desperately to scrabble her way clear of her captivity, to rip apart the rope and escape?

"Oh, I'm sure it didn't *feel* like a basic bowline down there, not with water filling your mouth and shit loading down the seat of your pants, but I assure you," Fane said, holding up a severed section of dripping rope, the knot still in it, "that this looks just like any other bowline I've ever seen."

"There was more."

"Annick," Fane said, turning to the sniper. "Is this the knot you tied?"

She nodded, eyes like stones.

"This is the *entire* knot?" Fane pressed. "You didn't do anything fancy that might confuse His Most Radiant Highness? He is easily confused."

She shook her head.

Valyn tried to read the emotion in those unreadable eyes. Annick was lying. It was as plain as that.

"Not a good start to the morning," Fane concluded, dropping the knot to the deck in disgust. "Not a good start at all. Annick, you're next. Sharpe, Ainhoa, toss our fearless leader over the side and let him swim back to the island."

16

Kaden glanced out the narrow window of the pottery shed. Despite the damp chill inside the stone structure that his rough robe seemed powerless to defeat, the sun had climbed above Lion's Head to the east, illuminating Ashk'lan's paths and buildings. It would be a pleasant day outside, young buds vibrant green against the deep blue of the sky, a fresh spring breeze gusting down off the summits, the sharp scent of junipers mingling with the warm mud. Unfortunately, the slaughtered goats and strange tracks outside the monastery had led to a change in routine, and the upshot of Scial Nin's interdiction against acolytes working outside the central square was that Tan had moved Kaden from his outdoor labors and into the shed.

"You can finish taking your castle apart later," the older monk had said, dismissing with a wave the structure Kaden had labored senselessly to build. "For now, I want you to make pots, broad and deep."

"How many?" he asked.

"As many as it takes." Whatever that meant.

Kaden stifled a sigh as he looked around the shed, eyeing the silent rows of ewers, pots, mugs, bowls, urns, and cups set carefully on the wooden shelves. He would have preferred to be out with the monks who were trying to hunt down the mysterious creature, not cooped up making pots, but what he preferred didn't figure into the matter.

Kaden knew his way around pottery, of course. The Shin traded their earthenware along with honey and jam in the spring and fall to the nomadic Urghul, a barbaric people who lacked the skill or the interest to make such things for themselves. He usually enjoyed time spent in the shed, kneading the cool clay between his palms, conjuring the graceful shape of a cup or jar between his fingers as he worked the treadle with his foot. Given the events taking place, however, an assignment to work in the clay shed from dawn to dusk felt a little like imprisonment, and he found his mind wandering in ways that would have earned him a beating if Tan had been around to see. He even had to scrap several pieces for novice mistakes he hadn't made in half a dozen years.

He was just about to take a break to eat the heel of hard bread he had tucked into his robe at breakfast when something darkened the window above him. Before he could turn, his mind filled with the *saama'an* of the slaughtered goat, brain scooped from its skull, and he reached for his belt knife as he rose from his seat. It was a ridiculous weapon but . . . there was no need. Akiil perched in the window, black curls backlit by the sun, a smirk on his face.

"Fear is blindness," the youth intoned solemnly, wagging a finger. "Calmness is sight."

Kaden let out a deep breath. "Thank you for that wisdom, Master. Did you complete your acolyte's training in the two days I've been locked in here?"

Akiil shrugged, then dropped from the window ledge into the room. "It's amazing the progress I was able to make without you around to hold me back. The *vaniate*'s like picking pockets—seems hard until you catch the knack."

"And what is it like, O Enlightened One?"

"The *vaniate*?" Akiil frowned as though pondering. "A profound mystery," he said finally, waving a dismissive hand. "An undeveloped maggot like you could never understand."

"You know," Kaden said, settling back onto the stool where he had been working, "Tan told me that the Csestriim practiced the *vaniate*." He had had plenty of time to ponder this peculiar claim, but Akiil had been cooped up in the kitchen for days, boiling down bruiseberries in Yen Harval's heavy iron pots, and the two hadn't been able to talk. With all the confusion about whatever was killing the goats, Kaden had finally set the information about the *vaniate* to the side until he could share it with his friend.

Akiil furrowed his brow. "The Csestriim? I didn't figure Tan to be one for tall tales and kids' stories."

"There are records," Kaden said. "They were real enough." The two of them had been over this before. Kaden had seen the volumes in the impe-rial library—scrolls and tomes penned in some illegible script that his father's scribes claimed belonged to the long-dead race. There were entire rooms given over to the Csestriim texts, shelf upon shelf, codex upon codex, and scholars visited from the two continents and beyond—Li, even the Manjari Empire—to study the collection. Akiil, on the other hand, tended to believe only in what he could see or steal, and there were no Csestriim wandering around the Perfumed Quarter of Annur.

"Maybe the Csestriim are the ones killing the goats," Akiil suggested with mock solemnity. "Maybe they eat brains. I feel like I heard that in one of the stories."

Kaden ignored the sarcasm. "You can hear anything in the stories. They're not reliable."

"*You're* the one who *believes* the stories!" Akiil protested.

"I believe that the Csestriim existed," Kaden said. "I believe we fought a war against them that lasted decades, maybe centuries." He shook his head. "Beyond that, it's hard to know what to think."

"You believe the stories. You don't believe the stories." The youth waggled a finger. "Pretty sloppy thinking."

"Look at it this way," Kaden replied. "The fact that half your tales are lies doesn't mean the Perfumed Quarter of Annur doesn't exist."

"My stories!" Akiil sputtered. "Lies? I *protest!*"

"Is that part of the speech you practiced for the magistrate?"

Akiil shrugged, dropping the pretense. "Didn't work," he replied, gesturing to the brand—a rising sun—burned into the back of his right hand. All Annurian thieves were marked in such a way as punishment after their first offense. If half Akiil's stories of picking pockets and pilfering wealthy homes were true, he was extremely lucky. A second offense called for a similar brand to the forehead. Men with the second brand had a hard time finding work, scarred, as they were, with the emblem of their misdeeds. Most returned to crime. For the third offense, the magistrates of Annur meted out death.

"Forget what you think about the Csestriim," Kaden pressed, "you have to admit it's strange that the Shin are pushing an idea based on the language and minds of an ancient race. It would be even stranger, actually, if the Csestriim *weren't* real."

"I think just about *everything* about the Shin is strange," Akiil retorted, "but they put food on my plate two meals a day, a roof over my head, and no one has burned anything else into my flesh with a hot iron—which is more than I can say for your father."

"My father didn't—"

"Of course he didn't," Akiil snapped. "The Emperor of Annur is far too busy to see personally to the punishment of a minor thief."

The years at Ashk'lan had blunted Akiil's bitterness toward the social inequities of Annur, but once in a while Kaden would say something about slaves or taxes, justice or punishment, and Akiil would refuse to let it go.

"What's the word from outside?" Kaden asked, hoping to change the subject. "Any more dead goats?"

Akiil looked ready to ignore the question and continue the argument. Kaden waited. After a moment he saw his friend take half a breath, hold it, then another half breath. The pupils of his dark eyes dilated, then shrank. A calming exercise. Akiil was as adept at the Shin discipline as any of the other acolytes—more so than most, in fact—provided he chose to exercise it. "Two," he replied after a long pause. "Two more dead. Neither were the ones we staked out as bait."

Kaden nodded, disturbed at the news but relieved to have avoided a fight. "So whatever it is, it's smart."

"Smart or lucky."

"How are the rest of the monks dealing with it?"

"About the same way the Shin deal with everything else," Akiil replied, rolling his eyes. "After Nin's meeting, aside from the prohibition on acolytes and novices leaving the main buildings, people are still hauling water, still painting, still meditating. Honest to 'Shael, I swear that if a murderous horde of your Csestriim rode in on a cloud and started hacking off heads and mounting them on pikes, half the monks would try to paint them and the other half wouldn't pay any attention at all."

"None of the older monks are saying anything else about it? Nin, or Altaf, or Tan?"

Akiil scowled. "You know how it is. They tell us about as much as I'd tell a hog I was planning to slaughter for the pots. If you want to learn anything, you have to go look for yourself."

"But you, of course, have scrupulously obeyed the abbot's command to remain at the monastery. . . ."

Akiil's eyes sparkled. "Of *course*. I may have lost my way from time to time—Ashk'lan is such a vast and complicated place—but I would never willingly disobey our revered abbot!"

"And when you lost your way, did you find anything?"

"Nah," the youth replied, shaking his head in frustration. "If Altaf and

Nin can't track the 'Kent-kissing thing, I don't have a chance. Still, I thought . . . sometimes you get lucky."

"And sometimes you get unlucky," Kaden said, remembering the savaged carcass, the dripping blood. "We don't know what it *is,* Akiil. Be careful."

†

The following evening Tan returned to the shed. Kaden stopped his work and looked up expectantly, hoping to read some clue about outside events in his *umial*'s weathered face. Tan knew more than the other monks. Kaden was certain of that. Trying to ferret out *what* he knew, however, was impossible. The sudden appearance of gruesomely mutilated corpses seemed to affect him no more than the discovery of a new patch of mountain bluebells. He closed the door behind him and looked with a critical eye over the dozen or so pots Kaden had thrown and fired.

"Have you made any progress?" Kaden asked after letting the silence stretch.

"Progress," Tan said, pronouncing the word as though it were new to him.

"Yes. Have you found whatever killed the goats?"

Tan tapped against the outside of one of the pots with his fingernail, then ran a finger around the inside of the lip. "Would that be progress?" he asked without looking up from his inspection.

Kaden suppressed a sigh and, with an effort, stilled his breathing and lowered his heart rate. If Tan wanted to be cryptic, Kaden wasn't going to be goaded into pestering him like a wide-eyed novice. His *umial* progressed to the next pot, rapped the rim with his knuckles, then scrubbed at some imperfection on the surface of the vessel.

"What about you?" Tan asked after he'd looked over half the pots. "Have you made any progress?"

Kaden hesitated, trying to find the hook hidden in the question.

"I've made these," he replied guardedly, gesturing to the silent row of earthenware.

Tan nodded. "So you have." He hefted one of the vessels and sniffed at the inside of it. "What is this one made out of?"

Kaden held back a smile. If his *umial* expected to trip him up with questions about clay, he was going to be sorely disappointed. Kaden knew the various river clays better than any other acolyte at the monastery. "That one's black silt blended with beach red at a ratio of one to three."

"Anything else?"

"A little resin to give it that hue."

The monk moved on to the next pot. "What about this one?"

"White shallows clay," Kaden responded readily, "medium grain." *Pass this test,* he told himself silently, *and you may just get to see the sun again before winter.*

Tan went down the line of pots, all dozen of them, each time asking the same questions: *What is this made out of? Anything else?* At the end of the row he frowned, looked at Kaden for the first time, then shook his head.

"You have not made progress."

Kaden stared. He'd made no mistakes; he was sure of it.

"Do you know why I sent you here?"

"To make pots."

"A potter could teach you to make pots."

Kaden hesitated. Tan might whip him for his stupidity, but the beating he would receive for trying to bluff his way through the conversation would be even worse. "I don't know why you sent me here."

"Speculate."

"To keep me from going up into the mountains?"

The monk's eyes hardened. "Scial Nin's command is not bar enough?"

Kaden thought back to his conversation with Akiil and schooled his face to stillness. Most of the Shin *umials* could smell deception or omission the way a hound scented a fox. Kaden himself hadn't stepped foot out of the clay shed, but he wasn't eager to land his friend a hefty penance.

"'Obedience is a knife that cuts the cord of bondage,'" he responded, quoting the start of the ancient Shin maxim.

Tan considered him, silent, inscrutable. "Go on," he said at last.

Kaden hadn't been forced to recite the whole thing since he was a novice, but the words came back easily enough:

Obedience is a knife that cuts the cord of bondage.
Silence is a hammer that shatters the walls of speech.
Stillness is strength; pain a soft bed.
Put down your basin; emptiness is the only vessel.

As he uttered the final syllables, he realized his mistake. "The emptiness," he said quietly, gesturing back toward the silent row of earthenware.

"When you asked me what they were made out of, I was supposed to say 'emptiness.'"

Tan shook his head grimly. "You know the words, but no one has made you feel them. Today we will rectify that. Come with me."

Kaden rose reflexively from his stool, steeling himself for some new brutality, some hideous penance that would leave him battered or bleeding or bruised right down to the bone, all in the name of the *vaniate,* a concept no one had ever bothered to fully explain to him. He rose, then paused. For eight years he had run when the monks said run, painted when they told him to paint, labored when he was instructed to labor, and fasted when they refused him food. And for what? Akiil's words from the day before came back to him suddenly: *They tell us about as much as I'd tell a hog. . . .* Training and study were all well and good, but Kaden wasn't even sure what he was training *for.*

"Come," Tan said, his voice hard and unyielding.

Though Kaden's muscles ached to obey, he forced himself to remain still. "Why?"

The older monk's fist struck his cheek before he realized it was moving, splitting the skin and knocking him to the floor. Tan took a step forward, looming over him.

"Get up."

Kaden rose unsteadily to his feet. The pain was one thing—he could handle pain—but his mind was blurry, dizzy from the blow.

"Go," Tan said, pointing toward the door.

Kaden hesitated, then took a step back. The split skin of his cheek wept blood, but he forced himself to leave his hands at his side. He shook his head again. "I want to know why. I'll do what you tell me, but I want to understand the point. Why do I need to learn the *vaniate?*"

It was impossible to read any emotion in the older monk's eyes. He might have been staring at a carcass or a passing cloud. He might have been a hunter looming over his wounded prey, readying himself for the kill. Kaden wondered if the man would hit him again, would keep hitting him. He had never heard of an acolyte being murdered by his trainer before, but then, if Tan wanted to beat his pupil to death, who would stop him? Scial Nin? Chalmer Oleki? Ashk'lan lay more than a hundred leagues past the border of the Annurian Empire, past *any* civilized borders. There were no laws here, no magistrates, no courts of justice. Kaden watched his *umial* warily, trying to still the pounding of his heart against his ribs.

"Your ignorance is an impediment," the monk concluded finally. He stood for one more moment in stillness before turning toward the door. "Perhaps your training will be more effective once you understand the urgency behind it."

✝

Scial Nin's study hunched against the cliffs a few hundred paces from the main compound. The building looked like part of the mountain—dry stonework shaded by a gaunt, withered pine that shed its brown needles on the roof and ground alike. Kaden and Akiil tended to avoid the place—an acolyte or novice was usually called before the abbot only for an extreme infraction requiring an extreme penance—and, despite Rampuri Tan's suggestion that Scial Nin would provide answers to his questions, Kaden now approached with some trepidation, following in the footsteps of his *umial.* Tan shoved the wooden door open without preamble, and suddenly reluctant, Kaden stepped over the threshold after him.

The inside of the room was dim, and he didn't immediately notice Scial Nin seated behind a low desk, the surface of which was empty save for a single parchment—the painting, Kaden realized, of the tracks left by whatever was slaughtering the goats. If the abbot was surprised or irritated by the sudden entrance, he didn't show it. He looked up from the paper, and waited.

"The boy wants answers," Tan said brusquely, stepping to the side.

"Most people do," Nin replied, his voice smooth and solid as planed oak. He considered the older monk, then turned his attention to Kaden. "You may speak."

Now that he stood before the abbot, Kaden wasn't quite sure what to say. He felt suddenly foolish, like a small child making trouble for his elders. Still, Tan had relented enough to bring him before the abbot; it would be a shame to squander the opportunity.

"I'd like to know why I was sent here," he began slowly. "I understand the goal of the Shin: emptiness, *vaniate.* But why is that *my* goal? Why is it necessary in ruling an empire?"

"It's not," Nin replied. "The Manjari Emperors beyond the Ancaz Mountains pay no homage to the Blank God. The savages at the borders of your empire revere Meshkent. The Liran kings on the far side of the earth refuse to worship gods at all—they venerate their ancestors."

Kaden glanced over at his *umial,* but Tan stood silent, his face like stone.

"Then why am I here?" he asked, turning his attention back to the abbot. "My father told me, just before I left, that the Shin could teach me things he could not."

"Your father was a talented student," Nin replied, nodding at the recollection, "but he had no experience as a *umial*. He would have had great difficulty with your training, even were there not an empire requiring his attention."

"What training?" Kaden asked, trying to keep the edge out of his voice. "Painting? Running?"

The abbot cocked his head to the side, looking at Kaden the way a robin might consider a spring earthworm.

"The Emperor has many titles," he said at last. "One of the oldest and least understood is 'Keeper of the Gates.' Do you know what it means?"

Kaden shrugged. "There are four gates to Annur: the Water Gate, the Steel Gate, the Gate of Strangers, and the False Gate. The Emperor keeps them, guards them. He protects the city from her foes."

"So most people believe," Nin replied, "in part because it's true: the Emperor *does* guard the gates of Annur and has for hundreds of years, ever since Olannon hui'Malkeenian built the first rough walls of the city from wood and wattle. There are other gates, however. Older. More dangerous. It is these to which the title refers."

Kaden felt a flame of excitement kindle inside him. He doused it. If the abbot saw a flicker of emotion, he was just as likely to send Kaden back to the clay shed as to continue his tale.

"Four thousand years ago," Nin continued, "perhaps longer, perhaps not so long—the archives are murky on the point—a new creature appeared on the earth. It was not Csestriim or Nevariim, god or goddess—those had all lived for millennia. The new creature was human.

"Scholars and priests still debate our origins. Some say Ouma, the first mother, hatched from a giant egg and bore nine hundred sons and daughters, and from these we are descended. Others hold that Bedisa created us, an infinite supply of toys for her great love, Ananshael, to destroy. The Kindred of the Dark believe we arrived from the stars, borne through the blackness in ships with sails of flame. The theories are endless.

"My predecessor in this post, however, thought that our parents were Csestriim. He believed that after thousands of years ruling the earth, the Csestriim, for reasons unknown, began to bear children who were . . . strange."

Kaden glanced over at his *umial,* but Tan's face was an inscrutable mask.

"Strange?" he asked. He'd always heard that the Csestriim and humans were implacable foes. The idea that they might be related, that the humans were *descended* from their enemies—it was bizarre beyond comprehension.

"The Csestriim were immortal," the abbot replied. "Their children were not. The Csestriim, for all their logical brilliance, felt no more emotion than beetles or snakes. The children they bore, the *human* children, were more fully in the grip of Meshkent and Ciena. Csestriim felt pain and pleasure, but humans *cared* about their own suffering and their bliss. Perhaps as a result, they were the first to feel emotion: love and hatred, fear, bravery. Alternatively, it could have been the birth of the young gods that led to human emotion. In either case, the Csestriim viewed this emotion as a curse, an affliction. There is a story claiming that when they saw the love that the first human twins bore each other, they tried to strangle them in their crib. My predecessor believed that Eira, the goddess of that love, hid the twins from their parents and spirited them away, west of the Great Rift, where they bore a race of humans."

"It sounds implausible," Kaden said. For years the Shin had trained him to believe only what he could observe, to trust only what he could see, or smell, or hear. And now, contrary to all prior habit, the abbot was spinning stories like a masker back on one of the great stages in Annur. "How do you know this happened?"

Scial Nin shrugged. "I don't. It's impossible to untangle myth from memory, history from hagiography, but one thing is certain: Before us, the Csestriim ruled this world, undisputed masters of a domain stretching from pole to pole."

"What about the Nevariim?" Kaden asked, drawn in to the saga in spite of himself. In all the old tales, the Nevariim were the heroic foes of the Csestriim, beings of impossible, tragic beauty who had warred against the evil race for hundreds of years before succumbing, finally, to Csestriim ruthlessness and guile. In the elaborate paintings of the storybooks Kaden and Valyn had pored over as children, the Nevariim always looked like princesses and princes, eyes flashing as they wielded their blades against the crabbed gray shapes of the Csestriim. *If Nin thinks the storybooks are real,* Kaden thought to himself, *I might as well get the full story.*

It was not Nin, however, who replied. Instead, Tan shook his head slightly. "The Nevariim are a myth. Tales told by the humans to comfort themselves as they died."

The abbot shrugged once more. "If they *did* live, the Csestriim destroyed them long before *our* arrival. The records that remain of the Nevariim are few, scant, and contradictory. By contrast, your Dawn Palace is filled with annals that tell the story of our own fight with the Csestriim. They tell the tales of the long years of imprisonment, when we were held and bred like beasts in the stables of Ai. They tell of Arim Hua, the sun leach, who hid his power for forty seasons, waiting for the sun storms that only he could feel before bursting asunder the locked gates and leading our people to freedom. There are heart-wrenching lays of the lean years, when the snow fell deeper than the highest pines in the mountain passes and children ate the flesh of their parents to survive. Those were the years of the Hagonine Purges, when our foes hunted us like beasts through the snow."

"Behind the abbot's poetry there is one hard fact," Tan said. "The Csestriim sought to annihilate us. We fought to survive."

Scial Nin nodded. "Men and women prayed then to gods both real and imagined."

"To the Blank God?" Kaden asked.

The abbot shook his head. "The Blank God has no interest in humans or Csestriim, war or peace. His domain is much wider. Our ancestors prayed to more practical gods, desperate not for victory, but for respite, even a moment's shelter. And then an amazing thing occurred: The gods heard our prayers. Not the old gods, of course; they walked their inscrutable ways as always, breaking and remaking worlds according to their ancient games, weaving webs of light and darkness, madness and law.

"But there were new gods, unknown to the Csestriim, and they left their home to come here in human form, despite the risks, to fight at our side. You know their names, naturally: Heqet and Kaveraa, Orella and Orilon, Eira and Maat. Even Ciena and Meshkent came. They fought, and slowly our flight became our holding, our holding became battle, battles became war."

"It was not so easy as that," Tan interjected. "We were overmatched, even with the help of the gods. The Csestriim were old past thought, immortal, implacable. Because they lived inside the *vaniate,* they felt no mercy, no fatigue, no fear of pain or death."

"In their own way," Nin added, "they were more powerful than the gods. The gods could not be killed, of course, but a Csestriim blade could shatter their human form, cropping their power for eons to come, and so they kept to the shadows, weaving their power in secret, subtle ways, and aside from Heqet, none would take the field."

Kaden tried to make sense of it. He had heard versions of all the stories, of course, about how the young gods of courage and fear, love and hate, hope and despair had taken the part of the humans, but he had always assumed they were simply stories. Hearing them now, from the mouths of his abbot and his *umial,* filled him with an unexpected fascination. "But we survived," he said. "We rallied and destroyed the Csestriim."

"No," Tan said. "We died. Died by the thousands and the tens of thousands."

Nin nodded. "It was not our cunning or our courage, but our numbers that saved us, Kaden. As the strength of the young gods waxed, the Csestriim, who had borne few children to begin with, could bear no more. Oh, their women grew heavy and brought babes into the world, but they were *human* babes, born fully in the grip of Ciena, Meshkent, and the young gods descended from them, sharing our fears and our passions, our hatreds and our hope.

"Our lives were short, no more than a blink to the foes we fought, but we were fertile. Fathers fought our battles, but it was our mothers who won the war. As the numbers of the Csestriim dwindled and ours grew, victory seemed certain."

"And then," Tan said, "the *kenta.*"

Kaden looked from his *umial* to the abbot and back again. He had never heard the word.

"It means 'gift' in the Csestriim tongue," Nin added, "but the *kenta* were no gift to the humans. The Csestriim leaches struggled for a thousand days and a thousand nights with powers even the old gods feared to confront, and they died in their efforts, but they created what our ancestors knew as the Death Gates.

"War as men had known it, as we know it today, disintegrated. With the gates, the Csestriim could appear anywhere at any time, ranging thousands of leagues in the blink of an eye. We still outnumbered them, but our numbers were useless without a front. Time and again, human armies believed they had trapped a Csestriim force only for their foes to evaporate through one of the hidden gates. While the human legions hunted them in the mountains, hundreds of leagues from family and home, the Csestriim arrived in the hearts of their cities. They killed without mercy.

"Crops were put to the torch, towns razed. Women and children thought safe, hundreds of miles from danger, were herded into temples and burned alive. What little restraint the Csestriim had to begin with vanished, for now they knew without a doubt that they fought for the very survival of their race."

"Why didn't we destroy the gates?" Kaden asked.

"We tried. Nothing availed. Eventually, men built fortresses around all those they could find, encasing many in stone and brick. Even those had to be guarded, lest the Csestriim break through to work their slaughter."

"Why didn't we just use the gates ourselves? Strike back at them with their own weapon?"

"Foolishness like that," Tan replied, "led to the deaths of thousands."

"People tried," Nin continued. "Men, whole legions, stepped through the *kenta* and simply vanished. Because the openings of the gates were opaque, no one realized the loss. When exploratory parties failed to report, it was assumed that the Csestriim had ambushed them. Human generals sent more and still more men through to the rescue. It was weeks before we understood our error."

"Where did they go?" Kaden asked, aghast. "People don't just vanish."

"This certainty of yours," Tan replied, "it could kill thousands someday."

"It was only later," Nin said, "that men learned the gates belonged to a power older than the Csestriim. They belong to the Blank God. He took the men."

Kaden shivered. Unlike Ananshael or Meshkent, the older gods didn't involve themselves in the human world, and the Blank God was the oldest of the old. Despite the fact that Kaden had spent the last eight years in service of the ancient deity, he hadn't really considered his power. Most of the monks seemed to think of and refer to him as an abstract principle rather than a supernatural force with desire and agency. The thought that the Blank God could touch the world, could swallow whole legions, was unsettling, to say the least.

The abbot continued. "It's not so surprising. When one uses the gates, the space separating here from, say, Annur, is not just shortened; it becomes nonexistent. One passes, quite literally, through nothing, and nothing is the province of our lord. Evidently, he resents the incursion on his territory."

The abbot broke off and for a long time the two older monks simply stared at Kaden, as though expecting him to finish the story.

"There's a way," he said finally, testing the idea as he spoke it. "The Csestriim used the gates, so there is clearly a way."

Neither responded. Kaden stilled his heart and ordered his mind.

"The *vaniate*," he concluded. "It has something to do with the *vaniate*. If we master it, we become like the Csestriim, and the Csestriim could use the gates."

Nin nodded at last. "A person cannot become nothing, not completely. He can, however, cultivate a nothingness inside himself. It seems that the god will allow someone carrying the void to pass through his gates."

"The Keeper of the Gates," Kaden said, thinking back to the start of the conversation. "That's why I was sent here. Something to do with these gates."

Nin nodded, but it was Tan who spoke.

"The Csestriim did not always slaughter their prisoners. Intrigued by our emotions, they kept a small number of us for study."

The words sounded strange coming from Rampuri Tan's lips. Of all the monks at Ashk'lan, he seemed just about the least likely to have any appreciation of human feeling.

"Some of those imprisoned," Tan continued grimly, "did clandestine studies of their own—they watched, they listened, they learned about their captors. They were the first to discover the secret of the gates and, in so doing, the *vaniate*. They vowed to one another that they would escape, develop their new knowledge, and use it to destroy the Csestriim."

"They were the first Shin," Kaden said slowly, the ramifications dawning on him.

Tan nodded. "Ishien, in the old tongue: 'those who avenge.'"

"But what does this have to do with the empire, or with me?"

The abbot sighed. "Patience, Kaden. We are coming to that. When the humans finally defeated the Csestriim, a large part of that final victory was attributed to the Ishien. Although the war was over, the Ishein continued to watch the gates, convinced that their enemies were not vanquished, only dormant."

"There were reasons," Tan interjected, his voice hard. "Our people hunted down Csestriim for hundreds of years after the close of the war. Then we started to forget."

Nin acknowledged the point with a slight nod of his head. "As the years turned to centuries, the charge lost its urgency. Some began to forget the Csestriim altogether. Meanwhile, generations of Ishien had discovered the quiet joy of a life lived in pursuit of the *vaniate*. They began to venerate the Blank God for his own sake, not for revenge on a long-dead foe. They put aside their armor, their blades, and took up less . . . agonistic pursuits."

"Not all of us," Tan said.

"Even you, old friend, arrived here in the end. One cannot hunt ghosts forever."

Tan's lips tightened, but he remained silent.

"Our way is not easy," the abbot continued, "and as the imperatives of the mission slipped, fewer and fewer young men joined the order. There were some, however, who had not forgotten our desperate fight for survival, and as the Shin diminished, as gate after gate was abandoned, these monks feared lest the Csestriim return.

"It was at this point that your ancestor, Terial, took the throne of a teetering kingdom torn with civil war—"

"—and at this point that the Shin abandoned their charge," Tan added.

"We did not abandon it. We passed it on. The Annurian state had grown too large for one man to control. Rebels and rival claimants rent the land. Terial had heard of the gates and realized the power they held for his own political ends. An Emperor who could instantly visit any corner of his empire need not fear rebellions of distant commanders or the misleading reports of provincial ministers. An Emperor able to use the gates could bring unity and stability to entire continents."

"He made a deal with the Shin," Kaden said, the pieces falling into place.

Scial Nin nodded. "If they would teach him the secret of the gates, the *vaniate,* he would commit his imperial resources to keeping those gates against the return of the Csestriim. The Shin, who had long ago lost both the ability and the will to carry out their original task, agreed. From that time on, all heirs to the Malkeenian line have trained here, with us. It is no coincidence that they have also enjoyed an unbroken line of succession."

"Keeper of the Gates," Kaden said, repeating the old title, understanding it for the first time. "We're guarding against the Csestriim."

"You should be," Tan replied curtly. "But memory is short."

"There are those," Nin said, nodding toward Kaden's *umial,* "who believe the Shin should never have given over their charge, who believe that the Emperors neglect their responsibility."

Kaden turned back to Rampuri Tan. The man stood in the shadow, arms crossed over his chest, eyes dark in the dim light of the study. He didn't move, or speak, or shift his gaze from his pupil.

"You don't believe they're gone, do you?" Kaden asked quietly. "You're not training me to be a monk or to rule an empire. You're training me to fight the Csestriim."

For several heartbeats, Tan didn't respond. That implacable stare bored into Kaden as though seeking out the hidden secrets of his heart.

"It seems the Csestriim are dead," the monk said at last.

"Then why are you telling me this?"

"In case they are not."

17

S he lied," Valyn insisted, slamming his fist down onto the table. "The
'Kent-kissing bitch *lied.*"

"Fine," Lin responded. "She lied. Saying it over and over again
isn't going to help."

"Although it *is* nice to get a firm grip on the facts," Laith added, his
voice too serious for the jest.

It was late—most of the soldiers were racked in their bunks or out on
night training somewhere—and the three of them had the long, empty mess
hall to themselves. Most of the place lay shrouded in darkness—no point
in wasting good oil lighting a room with no one in it—but down at the far
end of the space, through the open door leading into the kitchens, Valyn
could make out flickering lamps and the humming of Jared, the old night
cook, as he went about his business grilling pork for the next day's lunch
and keeping the kettle of tea boiling for soldiers returning late from their
training. Laith had kindled the lamp above their own table, although he
kept the wick barely long enough for Valyn to see the features of his friends.
The flier sat balanced on the back legs of his chair, gazing up into the rafters.
Lin's hair glistened in the lamplight, still damp from her long swim.

She held up her hands in conciliation. "I'm not saying you're wrong
about Annick, but are you *sure?* You told me Fane held up the knot afterwards, that it was a normal bowline."

Valyn tensed, then forced himself to take a deep breath. She was just
trying to help, trying to sort through the facts with him.

"I managed to untie part of it before I blacked out," he explained. "I
panicked at the end, but I remember the knot clearly enough. It *felt* like a
basic bowline, but it wasn't. It had those two extra loops—the kind we
found in the knot that was holding up Amie."

"Well," Laith pointed out, lowering the front feet of his chair to the ground and pursing his lips, "there's no *rule* that she has to give you an easy knot. It would be just like Annick to try to drown you on principle."

"It would," Lin admitted. "But why would she *lie* about it?"

Lin still wasn't convinced that Annick was behind Amie's death, and her refusal to accept the reality of the situation was starting to grate on Valyn. Normally Lin was objective and clear-sighted, but there was something about Amie's murder that she couldn't see past, as though, because of the nature of the violence, it had to have been committed by a man.

"Because she knows," he snapped. "That's the only explanation. She knows we found Amie—everyone on Hook probably knows that by now. And if she's got a brain in her head, she can figure out we were asking questions at the Black Boat."

"So . . . what?" Lin asked. "She decides to kill all four of us? And Rianne, too, for good measure? Even if she *did* kill Amie, that's an insane way to cover it up."

"From Annick?" Laith asked, raising an eyebrow. "That actually sounds like a somewhat measured response."

"I don't claim to have it all figured out," Valyn went on. "All I'm saying is there's too much coincidence here to ignore. She might even have something to do with—"

Lin shot him a sharp glance and he cut himself off. He'd been about to say the sniper might have something to do with the plot against his own life, which meant she might know something about the death of his father, about threats to Kaden. Only he had told no one aside from Lin about the words of the dying Aedolian. It was a measure of his fatigue that he almost slipped in front of Laith.

"Have something to do with what?" the youth asked.

"My bow," Lin supplied smoothly. "Cracked in the middle of my last sniper test. Valyn thinks someone sabotaged it."

Laith eyed one, then the other, then shrugged. "Trial's coming up. It's going to be people rather than bows cracking before the whole thing's finished."

"Provided we make it to the 'Kent-kissing Trial," Valyn added, turning to Lin. "All I'm saying is to go to the list. Then tell me if you don't think Annick looks bloody as a slaughterhouse floor."

"All right," Lin said, her eyes bright in the lamplight. "Let's go to the list."

The Kettral were great believers in lists. The soldiers had lists for everything—checking over a bird before flight, setting a demolitions charge, boarding a ship—*everything.* Valyn could hear old Georg the Tanner's voice droning on in the lecture hall: *People make mistakes. Soldiers make mistakes. Everyone else on this 'Shael-spawned island is filling your tiny little heads with ideas about spontaneity, adaptation, thinking on the fly.* He spat. *Thinking on the fly is a good way to make mistakes. Lists do not make mistakes.* Georg's voice could put a roomful of cadets to sleep in a matter of heartbeats, but the man had flown missions well into his sixties, and Valyn tried to listen to what he had to say. *You fools want to know how something gets added to the list? A soldier dies. Then we figure out why. Then we change the list. So learn the fucking list.*

Unfortunately, there was no list, no set of steps for ferreting out a traitor and a murderer, but a jolt of logical thinking couldn't hurt.

"First," Valyn began, raising a finger, "we know that Amie was going to meet a Kettral the morning she was murdered. Second, she was meeting that person in Manker's. Third, according to Juren, the only Kettral in Manker's that morning was Annick. Fourth, Annick is a cold-blooded bitch."

"Your fourth observation seems more emotional than analytical," Lin pointed out.

"*Fifth,* the way Amie was killed suggests both Kettral professionalism and a complete absence of moral sentiment. Sixth, that strange bowline shows up in both the garret where Amie was killed and the boat where I was thrown overboard today. And seventh, Annick tries to drown me a day and a half after we find the body and start asking questions."

Oh, Valyn thought to himself, *and finally, there's a plot to kill my entire family and take over the throne.*

"When you put it like that, she doesn't exactly come out looking like a priestess of Eira," Laith observed.

"All right," Lin said, nodding her head wearily. "I agree. It looks bad for Annick. But it still doesn't make any sense. Why would she want to kill Amie? And why in such a horrible way?"

"That's the one I can't answer."

"I suppose sheer unbuckled cruelty isn't reason enough?" Laith asked.

Valyn frowned. Maybe he was overthinking it. Even if Annick had killed Amie, maybe the murder had nothing to do with the plot against him. It seemed plausible that the sniper might just truss up someone and kill her for the practice. Only killing a whore who wasn't much more than a girl wouldn't be much practice. And it still didn't explain the knot that had almost drowned him earlier in the day.

"I just think we need more information," Lin said.

Valyn nodded slowly. "And I know one place to start looking."

✝

In theory, rummaging through someone's trunk was easy. Each of the five barracks was simply one long room, and the cadets weren't permitted locks. The problem was, someone was always *in* the barracks, just back from a night run or catching a quick nap before Blood Time. Lin would have raised eyes and turned heads if she just started rifling through the sniper's belongings, and so for a few days Valyn let the worry eat at his gut, tried to focus on his training, on his studies, and the upcoming Trial. Late each night, he would meet up with Laith, Gent, and Lin in their corner of the mess hall and exchange pointless observations and suspicions, marking time until Lin could find a way into Annick's trunk.

On this particular night, however, Lin was late. Valyn noted the moon through the window, measured it against the horizon, and shook his head.

"Calm down," Laith said. "Lin'll be fine."

"I know," Valyn replied, but he couldn't stop drumming his fingers on the tabletop. Ha Lin outweighed Annick and she was the better fighter if it came to fists and knives. On the other hand, most confrontations were decided by one simple rule: The person to strike first was the one to walk away, and Valyn worried that, in the crucial moment, Lin might hesitate. Annick would not.

"You ought to be concerned about *yourself,*" Laith added, gesturing with his glass. It was filled with water, but he waved it around as if it were a tankard and he were seated in an alehouse. "*You're* the one slated to go against Annick in the sniper test tomorrow."

"Thanks for the cheerful reminder," Valyn said.

"You're fucked."

"And for the optimism."

"Just trying to bring a healthy realism to the discussion."

Once more, Valyn shook his head. It didn't help matters that he more or less agreed with Laith's assessment. Valyn was a capable sniper and a reasonable hand with a flatbow, even by Kettral standards, but Annick was a 'Shael-spawned *ghost.* She'd lost only one sniper contest, to Balendin of all people, and Valyn was pretty sure the leach had found some way to cheat.

To make matters worse, if you went up against Annick, you usually ended the morning with a black eye, busted jaw, or chipped tooth. None of that was part of the contest—you were supposed to sneak close enough to shoot a bell before your opponent, and that was that—but Annick made it a point of pride to shoot the bell, then the trainers scouring the field with their long lenses, and then her opponent. She used blunt training arrows—stunners, the Kettral called them—but they could still break a tooth or knock you stone cold. A year earlier some of the cadets had complained to command. If Annick was good enough to pick her shots, they argued, she was good enough to shoot for the chest rather than the face. Annick's response, which the trainers had accepted with a sort of sadistic pleasure, was that if the people lodging the complaint didn't want to get shot in the face, then they should learn to keep their faces out of sight.

"This close to the Trial," Laith said. "I'd find a way to beg off."

"There's no way to beg off."

"There's always a way. I've spent the past five years dodging the worst of the shit. It's why I became a flier."

"You became a flier because you like to go fast and you hate running."

"As I said—dodging the shit." Laith's smile faded. "In earnest, though, Val. If Annick really *is* trying to kill you because of what you know about Amie, you don't want to be within a mile of the sniper field with her."

Valyn had thought much the same thing, but he'd be shipped to 'Shael before he let another cadet, murderer or no, scare him out of his training. "There'll be two trainers watching the test with long lenses," he reminded his friend. "She'd be crazy to take a shot at me then."

"Suit yourself," Laith said with a shrug. "I'll pour some ale on your grave."

It was supposed to be a joke, but it struck too close to the memory of the night they had buried Amie. Laith took a long swig of his water, scowled as though wishing it were something stronger, and the two fell into a gloomy silence. Lin found them in much the same position when she finally burst into the hall.

"I found something," she began, eyes fierce.

Valyn motioned her to a seat, then glanced over his shoulder to make sure they had the hall to themselves.

"You know what the girl uses her 'Kent-kissing trunk for?" Lin asked as she slid onto the bench next to Laith.

"Epistles of unrequited love?" the flier suggested.

Lin coughed out a laugh. "Guess again."

"A small orphaned infant that she has been secretly but tenderly nursing back to health?"

"Arrows," Lin said.

"Just arrows?" Valyn asked, confused. It hardly sounded like a revelation.

"Must be more than a thousand of them in there," Lin went on. "She makes her own. Strips the shafts, hammers out her own heads at the forge, even fletches the things with some kind of strange feather—northern black goose, or some shit. She's got enough to kill everyone on the Islands a few times over. I almost didn't bother to dig through them all."

"Well, it's hardly surprising that the best sniper in the cadets has a fondness for arrows," Laith observed.

"But there was something else," Valyn said, reading the truth in Lin's eyes.

She nodded grimly while she rummaged in the pocket of her blacks, then drew out something golden. She tossed it across the table to Valyn.

He caught it and stared. It was a lock of hair, light, soft, and flaxen, tied with a ribbon. "Is this—," he began, but he already knew the answer. By the time they found Amie, her body was a horrible rotting ruin. The flesh had started to sag on her bones, flies had picked over her tongue, and her eyes were already moldering in their sockets. The girl's hair, however— that soft, flaxen hair—had practically glowed in the pale moonlight.

"Well, holy Hull," Laith breathed. "I'll be buggered blind."

It was a tantalizing discovery, but they realized, as they bandied about possible explanations, that it didn't actually tell them anything conclusive. Annick had known Amie. So what?

"Could be a trophy," Laith said.

"Does Annick seem like the type to take trophies?" Lin countered.

"Maybe it's proof of some sort," Valyn suggested. "Proof that she killed Amie."

"Pretty shitty proof," Laith replied. "*Heads* are good proof. If you ship someone a head, chances are you killed the owner. Hands are pretty good proof. But hair?" He spread his hands.

"Besides," Lin added, picking up the lock and inspecting it once more, "what's it proving to anyone when it's stuffed in the bottom of her trunk?"

The more they talked over the possibilities, the more frustrated Valyn became. As Lin pointed out, Annick didn't even necessarily take the hair from Amie herself; someone could have given it to her to mark the target. Aside from Juren's suggestion, they couldn't be sure that the sniper had even been *on* Hook the day Amie died. By the time the wick in the lamp burned down to a charred stump, Valyn was ready to barge into Annick's barrack, confront her with the hair, and demand answers.

"That sounds like a good plan," Laith said dryly. "I'm sure she'll be happy to cooperate."

Valyn waved him off, weary and irritated at the same time. "You're right. You're right. 'Shael bugger me bloody, you're right."

"It's a step," Lin said, laying a hand on Valyn's shoulder, her grip at once strong and soothing through the fabric. She met his eyes with her own. " 'No one can run a thousand leagues,' " she said, quoting Hendran, " 'but anyone can take one step, then another step.' "

"The next step I'm going to take is toward my rack," Laith groaned, stretching in his seat like a cat. "I've got predawn flight drills in a couple of bells."

Valyn nodded toward the flier. "We'll put out the lamp and follow you out."

Laith glanced from Lin to Valyn with a sly smirk. "Never too late for a tickle under the trousers."

"Go fuck yourself, Laith," Lin replied tartly. They were all exhausted, but the tension in Lin's voice surprised Valyn.

"No other option, I suppose," the flier replied, glancing down at his right hand with a shrug.

"Now that your whore is dead, you mean?" she demanded.

The smile froze on Laith's face. "She wasn't *my* whore."

"Of course not. That's the nice thing about borrowed gear—if it gets busted, it's no skin off your nose. If Amie *had* been yours, maybe you would have taken better care of her."

Valyn raised a hand to stop the words, but Laith stepped in close before he could speak. The flier's normal genial humor had burned off like the oil from the sputtering lamp.

"I don't know how I became the villain in this little tale," he said, eyes bright, voice soft, "but don't drag me into your guilt."

"*My* guilt?" Lin sputtered.

"Oh, right," the flier shot back. "I forgot. You only bought fruit from her. You never bought sex." He held up his palms in mock surrender. "What'd you pay her? A few copper flames? Enough to put a decent meal on her table? Enough so she could stop whoring?"

Lin refused to respond, her face closed like a book.

"Before you come pointing your finger at me, why don't you ask yourself what *you* did to make Amie's life any better," Laith demanded, eyes ablaze. Before Valyn could say anything to calm things down, the flier turned on his heel and stalked out.

For a long time after the door slammed, Valyn and Lin sat in the flickering shadows cast by the dying lamp. After a while she reached across the table, twining her fingers in his. He couldn't see her face in the darkness, but he tightened his grip on her hand.

"I just can't . . . ," she began, then fell silent.

Valyn wasn't sure what she was going to say, but he felt the emotion, the deep, sick helplessness behind the words. It seemed impossible that someone could murder an innocent girl, could truss her up like a slaughtered pig for the bleeding, all within sight of the Eyrie. Not only had the Kettral failed to save her, it looked like one of Valyn's brothers or sisters in black was responsible for the killing.

"We'll figure it out," he said softly, trying to convince himself as much as Ha Lin. "We will."

She slid over onto the bench beside him, and for a while the two sat side by side, hands entwined, bodies separate. Valyn could feel the warmth of her, but she kept apart, rigid in the darkness.

"There's something else," she said finally. "I found Balendin outside the barracks. Or . . . he found me."

Valyn tensed, but Lin went on before he could respond.

"It was strange. He seemed nervous, almost frightened. Said he wanted to tell me something about Sami Yurl."

"Yurl?" Valyn asked, baffled. "What was it?"

"That's the thing. He wouldn't say. Told me it was something I had to *see,* but that it was important."

Valyn frowned. "I don't like it."

"What's to like? Still, if he knows something about Yurl, something incriminating . . . Whoever killed Amie didn't necessarily do it alone."

"Yurl and Annick?" Valyn tried to make sense of the unlikely pair. Sami Yurl had his own cadre of nasty followers among the cadets, but the sniper had never been among them.

"If Balendin discovered something like that," Lin pressed, "a murder—"

"He'd go straight to command."

"Unless there's a reason he can't."

Valyn puffed out a deep breath. He was weary, he realized, weary beyond the simple, honest exhaustion that came with a long month of training. The constant searching, guessing, and second-guessing, the glancing over the shoulder, the doubting and distrust were wearing him to a blunt edge. If one apple was rotten, you had to assume they all were, but that was a good way to starve.

"All right," he said, knuckling his eyes, "but why would he come to you?"

"Maybe he knows we found Amie's body. And he knows I'm more likely to listen than you are."

Valyn snorted. "That's debatable. You've got a shorter wick than I do when it comes to that temper of yours."

"Maybe he just hates me a little bit less. You have a way of attracting . . . resentment."

"So after all these years as Yurl's minion, he wants to make nice? Wants to quit the atrep's son and make friends with us?"

"Maybe," Lin replied. "Pounding cadets in the ring is one thing. Hunting a whore and cutting her to pieces in an attic is something else. Maybe Balendin *does* have some decency." Her tone suggested she didn't find that very likely.

Decency. It was a tricky word for men and women trained to stab people in the back.

"Then we'll *both* go see what he's got to show you," Valyn concluded. "If he can show it to one person, he can show it to two. I'll promise to listen."

"No," Lin said. "It's tomorrow morning. During your sniper test."

Valyn cursed. "Well, tell him we can't see it in the morning."

"I don't think it's a *thing,*" Lin replied. "I think it's an event. He wants me to see Yurl *do* something."

Valyn clenched, then unclenched his fist.

"Where?" he asked, the question bitter in his mouth. He didn't trust Balendin, didn't trust this sudden crisis of conscience. For eight years, the leach had baited and battered just about every cadet on the Islands aside from Sami Yurl and his coterie. Where there was room to cheat, he cheated. Where there was space to lie, he lied. The idea of Lin going off with him somewhere in order to watch some secret event made Valyn's stomach tighten. Of course, the blade cut both ways. If Balendin was treacherous, he could betray Yurl as easily as anyone else.

"Where?" he asked again.

"The West Bluffs."

The West Bluffs comprised the sere, broken terrain toward the northwest corner of the island: some scrub, some thorns, and a good view out over the center of Qarsh. There were a few nesting seabirds on the ocean side, and a handful of interesting shells dropped by the gulls up on the cliffs. That was about it.

"What could he possibly want to show you up there?"

"That," Lin replied, exasperation creeping into her voice, "is what I'm going to find out. Don't worry, Val," she added, softening her tone and squeezing his hand. "I'll bring my real blades, and I'll be careful."

Valyn blew out a slow breath. "You're just about a mile from the sniper test, up there," he said. The thought calmed him somewhat, and he realized he'd half-expected Lin to tell him the meeting was in an abandoned house over on Hook. It didn't make any real difference, of course. Something could go wrong up on the bluffs as well as in a cramped garret, but somehow the fact that Lin would still be on Qarsh, that she would be, in fact, only a few minutes' hard run from the sniper range itself, helped his stomach to relax.

"All right," he said finally. " 'Shael knows I don't trust that bastard, but it's not like you're a child." She hadn't moved her hand from his, and he found himself suddenly aware of its weight, of the gentle pressure of her callused fingers. They were alone in the hall, had been since Laith left, and for the first time since she had joined him on the bench he looked over at her, trying to make out the slender lines of her face in the darkness. "I'm just frightened for you," he concluded quietly. There was more to say, a lot more, but he didn't have the words.

Lin considered him for what seemed like a long time. Then, with no warning, she leaned over to press her lips against his. Her kiss was warm, and rough, and soft all at the same time. Valyn had bedded women before, but only whores over on Hook, and the experience had been somewhat uninspiring. This . . . this was something altogether different. After what seemed like a very long time, Lin pulled away.

"I'm sorry, I . . . I shouldn't have done that."

"You shouldn't have had to," Valyn replied, baffled but suddenly happy, his weariness stripped away, at least for the moment. "I should have done it a long time ago."

Lin grinned, then stood and cuffed him lightly on the cheek. "I'll see what Balendin has to show me. You just try not to let Annick mess up that fine face of yours too badly in tomorrow's test."

Before Valyn could respond, she turned on her heel. He was still smiling when the door closed behind her. She couldn't be his, of course, not in any of the traditional ways. Kettral never married, and the few clandestine relationships that took place on the Islands were carefully concealed, buried deep enough that they would never interfere with training or war. Still, there was a possible life, a future, in which they flew on the same Wing, worked with each other every day, even grew old alongside each other, provided neither of them took an arrow in the back. It wasn't much, but for a little while, Valyn let himself drift with the fantasy.

Then the bell rang for third watch, jolting him from his thoughts, and the darkness and silence settled down again, heavy as the water that had almost drowned him just days earlier.

18

The sun hung high and bright in the sky, which was bad. It gave the spotters the best chance of finding him. The day was still, which was bad; a light ocean breeze would have obscured any errant sound, any clatter of small rocks as his body scraped over the earth. The day was hotter than normal for the spring, which was also bad. Sweat dripped from his brow, stinging his eyes and blurring his vision. He longed to wipe it away, but wasted motion was anathema to a sniper. Instead, he blinked twice, squinted, and inched ahead along the small furrow. The furrow, too, was bad.

Sniper contests could take place anywhere on the Islands, but the trainers tended to favor a section near the northern coast of Qarsh, where the land sloped abruptly upward to terminate in limestone bluffs that plunged down into the waves. Hundreds of fractures rent the ground into tiny fissures and ravines, as though Pta, the Lord of Chaos, had hefted the entire island in a massive hand and then shattered it on the surface of the sea.

Atop the bluffs themselves perched the spotters' platform, a raised wooden construction sporting a bronze bell the size of a man's head. The goal of the exercise was straightforward: sneak close enough to shoot the bell, then sneak out. In practice, it was nearly impossible. Eyrie trainers manned the platform, sweeping the surrounding ground with their long lenses, waiting for the cadets to make a mistake, to slip into the open for a moment.

The hearty native scrub and broken folds of earth provided the only cover, and for Valyn's first three years, he hadn't come within a half mile of the platform, let alone close enough to take a shot at the bell. Recently, however, he'd found more success.

Of course, success was a double-edged blade with the Kettral. Success meant that the drills were getting too easy, which meant, in turn, that the drills were about to get a whole lot harder. It was one thing to skulk through the scrub alone, taking as much time as was necessary to work up close to the bell. It was another thing entirely to do so at the same time as someone else, taking care to avoid their eyes as well as those of the spotters, and always trying to eke out a little more speed to try to get to the bell first. Worst of all was squaring off against Annick. The young sniper was so good that for the past year, she'd been going against older cadets. Now, though, as Valyn's cohort approached Hull's Trial themselves, there *were* no older cadets.

Bad luck trumps a lifetime of training, Valyn thought, twisting his head without raising it from the rough ground to try to get a view to the west.

Rocks dug into his shoulder and chest, sharp stones tore at his blacks, and the miserable drainage along which he was dragging himself proved too narrow for the bent bow of the arbalest, which caught on a corner and gouged at his stomach. Kettral were trained in all manner of ranged weapons, but nothing could beat an arbalest for sniping. Unlike a normal bow, you could fire it from a prone position, and the only movement necessary, once you'd cranked it all up, was a twitch of the finger. Of course, it meant you had to haul the 'Kent-kissing thing around.

Compounding his problems, Valyn had no idea where Annick was. He hadn't expected to, of course. It was more than enough work trying to stay low and keep out of sight of the spotters without expecting to hunt down his competition as well. In any other contest, he wouldn't have given half a toad's turd for the location of the other sniper, but this wasn't any other contest. Annick was out there, and she was hunting him as surely as she was hunting the bell. Despite what he'd told Laith the night before, Valyn's shoulder blades itched at the thought. His only consolation was that the sun, the heat, and the ground would be as tough on her as they were on him.

Best get on with it, then.

He'd been counting on the meager ravine to carry him within shooting distance, had been following it half the morning, making reasonably good time—a pace or two every few minutes. Unfortunately, the groove had grown shallower and shallower as he moved uphill, until it provided no real cover at all. He had only to raise his head the barest fraction of an inch to see the wooden structure of the spotters' tower and the bright smudge of the bell hanging from it five hundred paces distant. Still too far off to make the shot, too far by a good stretch.

He considered doubling back. It was the right call, all other factors be-ing equal, but all other factors were definitely *not* equal. It wasn't enough to move silently into position; he needed to move quickly, too. In front of him stretched about eight paces of sparse cover—some loose scrub and a patch of dune grass—but if he could make it through those without being spotted, he could hunker down behind a line of boulders, maybe even fol-low them close enough. It was risky, but then, everything the Kettral did was risky, just *being* Kettral in the first place was risky. No one taught you to avoid risk on the Islands; they taught you how to assess it, how to gauge probabilities, how to deal with uncertainty.

At the moment, Valyn didn't feel much like assessing and gauging. An-nick was out there, and unless he was very lucky indeed, she wasn't spend-ing her time hemming and hawing over probabilities.

" 'Shael on a stick," he muttered, pushing himself up to his elbows and knees, then lunging forward in a mad scramble over the stone, trying to stay as low as possible and move quickly at the same time. It took him about fifteen heartbeats to worm through the dirt and gravel, and although his heart was pounding, each beat seemed to stretch on forever. He col-lapsed, finally, up against the back of a hefty limestone boulder, then rolled to his right, putting a leafy spray of firespike between him and the southern expanse of the area. Only once he'd managed to set up a reason-able amount of cover did he pause to catch his breath. The spotters hadn't blown the whistle. Annick hadn't shot him. He grinned to himself. Some-times gambling paid off.

Over the course of the next hour, he wound his way closer and closer to the observation platform, maneuvering from shrub to low grass, from broken ground to gravelly berm. The bell was clearly visible when he raised his head far enough to get a look at it, as were the two instructors flanking it, scanning the terrain with their long lenses. *Come on, Hull,* he prayed, inching forward through the grit. *Just a little closer.* The arbalest he car-ried was bulky but powerful. If the wind died, he could hit the target from a little over a hundred paces. *Just keep Annick busy for a little longer.*

He was moving forward behind the cover of a slanted shoulder when someone let out a sharp curse from the spotting platform. He risked a quick look. One of the two trainers, Anders Saan by the sound of the voice, was holding a hand to his chest and swearing like a sailor.

" 'Shael take it," Valyn snarled, scrambling forward. Annick had the range and had already gone to work. A few moments later, the other trainer on the platform doubled over, black silhouette jerking as though stabbed. Stunner arrows wouldn't kill you, and Annick was showing her respect for the trainers by aiming for their torsos rather than their heads. Still, the dull bolts packed a painful punch.

Valyn gritted his teeth. Annick would need to reload her arbalest before going after the bell. That meant cranking back the bow, fitting another bolt to the channel, and resuming her firing stance. There was a slim to vanishing chance that he could use the intervening time to get off a shot, especially now that the spotters were technically out of the exercise. It should take her at least forty seconds to—

An arrow shattered the stone inches from his head, then fell like a broken bird to the gravel. Valyn stared. Annick couldn't have reloaded the arbalest that fast. There were cords to notch and ratchets to twist. *No one* could reload an arbalest that fast.

"Well, she did, you 'Kent-kissing fool," he growled at himself, rolling hard to his left, trying to put some cover between himself and the general direction of the shooter. He tumbled into a small ravine just as another arrow clattered in the dirt above him.

An arrow.

An arbalest didn't fire arrows; it fired bolts. Annick was able to reload so fast because she was using a regular bow, although how she managed that lying down, Valyn had no idea. It didn't matter. She had him pinned, was undoubtedly moving to a new line of sight as he lay there, and would take another shot within the minute. The logical thing to do at this point was surrender. The sniper had clearly won the trial, could ring the 'Kent-kissing bell whenever she wanted, but something in Valyn kicked against the thought of giving up. For Annick, the game wasn't over until she'd shot everyone on the field, and if the game wasn't over, he could still win. He scrambled up the ravine on his hands and knees. He just had to reach the—

Another arrow scudded through the dirt right beside him. The girl was *fast,* but her normal accuracy was failing her. Valyn started to smile—it seemed even Annick had her off days—but as he crawled past the spent shot, his breath froze in his chest. A razor's edge glinted, bright and vicious in the dust. The arrow was unblunted. A head like that would rip right through his chest and out the other side if Annick found her target.

With a bellow of rage and fear, he lurched to his feet. There was no playing now. No hiding. No ducking behind rocks and skulking through the brush. He had no idea how it was possible, not with both trainers watching the whole thing, but Annick was trying to kill him, had the range and angle already, could probably choose her shot.

He lunged ahead, darting back and forth over the jagged path. If he could reach the low gravel berm fifteen paces distant, he could make a reasonable stand, but fifteen paces was an eternity to a well-trained sniper. His heart hammered at his ribs, his lungs heaved, and he wrestled with the fear as he ran, forced it down into his legs, into his lungs, used it to drive him on. Five more paces. If he could just reach the berm—

The blow caught him high in the shoulder, right above the lung, driving him forward onto the gravel slope. First it was just the shock of the impact that hit him. Then the pain came, a savage tearing fire. He rolled to the side and looked down at the front of his jerkin. The arrow had punched directly through his body, tearing out the front of his chest. Blood coated the head and shaft. *Son of a bitch, a real 'Kent-kissing arrow,* he thought vaguely.

He tried to move his hands, tried to push himself to his knees, but failed. Fog filled his vision, but he could just make out a slender shape rising from the ground some hundred paces distant. Annick held the short-bow casually in one hand, another arrow nocked to the string. *They saw her,* Valyn thought groggily. *Doesn't she know that the trainers are looking at her?* She raised the bow easily, almost casually, drawing and releasing in the same motion. A moment later, the clang of the bronze bell reached Valyn, dim and tinny, as though heard underwater.

Only after she had lowered the bow did Annick glance toward him, turning her head with the curt, acute movement of a bird. Through the bloody haze that filled his vision, Valyn saw her eyes widen, but there was no joy, no celebration on that hard, child's face.

19

Uinian IV did not look capable of murder, certainly not the murder of an old soldier like Sanlitun hui'Malkeenian. Where Adare's father had been tall and strong, with powerful arms and hands, the Chief Priest of Intarra was nearly an albino, short and pale, thin-lipped and stoop-shouldered, with a head like a misshapen gourd. That her father lay dead in his cold tomb was pain enough, but that he should have been delivered to Ananshael by *this* pathetic wretch made Adare want to scream and sob at the same time. If Sanlitun had to die, he should have been cut down in battle, or swallowed by the raging sea. The chaos of war, the wrath of the depths: those were foes worthy of her father. Despite his post, Uinian struck her as a small, mean creature.

So why doesn't he look afraid? she wondered nervously.

The Dawn Palace was calibrated to overawe even the most jaded potentates. At its heart, Intarra's Spear loomed over the entire city, an impossibly tall tower of clear stone driven deep into the bedrock by some hand older than history. At the base of the Spear stood the Hall of a Thousand Trees. The longest and highest hall in the Palace was also one of the first, an echoing edifice of redwood and cedar, the huge pillars of which had taken ten thousand slaves a dozen years to haul across Eridroa from the slopes of the Ancaz. Polished and oiled golden trunks stretched upward in row after row, branches ramifying as they had in life to support the ceiling. The space had been built on a scale to humble even the Emperor who ruled it from his seat on the Unhewn Throne, and yet Uinian appeared unconcerned, bored, even smug.

His small dark eyes flitted from the Aedolians lining the walls to the benches where the Sitters would hear the charges and evidence against him followed by his own defense. He licked his lips, although the movement struck Adare as anticipatory rather than nervous; then he turned his eyes to her. She knew the power of her own gaze, the unnerving effect her burning irises had on those who tried to meet them, and yet the Chief Priest seemed no more unsettled by these than he did by the hall itself. He considered her cooly as she walked past him to take her seat, the faintest hint of a smirk playing at the corner of his mouth, then nodded.

"My lady," he said. "Or should I say, Minister? Can one be both a lady and a Minister?"

"Can one be both a murderer and a priest?" she replied, rage like fire running under her skin.

"My Lady Minister," he replied, raising a fluttering hand to his chest in mock horror, "I fear you refer to me."

Adare clamped down on her response. They had not spoken loudly, and yet already some of those gathered for the trial had turned to watch the exchange. There was a legal process to be followed, and it did not involve sparring with the accused. Such sparring was beneath the dignity of an imperial minister and besides, in moments her father's murderer would face a justice far more implacable than any of Adare's barbs. She bit into a fingernail, then remembered her post, the hundreds watching, and returned the hand forcefully to her lap. That Uinian *should* pay for his crimes before the day's end was clear to her, and yet Adare spent enough time studying history to know that Annurian justice, for all its glory, could sometimes fail.

The selection of the Sitters was the most important thing. They were chosen at random every day by bureaucrats trained specially for the task, dozens of groups of seven to sit on the dozens of trials that would take place, each group composed, as decreed by Terial himself, of the Seven: a mother, a merchant, a pauper, a prelate, a soldier, a son, and a dying man. Terial had believed that a group so comprised was fit to pass justice on even the empire's most august citizens, and yet it was possible, through fraud and bribery, to meddle with the composition of the group.

I went over all the potential Sitters myself, she thought. *What did I miss? What does he know?*

The reverberation of two great gongs broke the silence, echoing right down into Adare's teeth. It was the first time she had heard that sound, the presage to an imperial entrance, since the death of her father, and for a moment, she expected Sanlitun himself to stride through the twenty-foot doors and into the chamber in his simple robes of state. When Ran il

Tornja appeared instead, she felt the sharp twist of loss all over again. It seemed impossible that her father was truly gone, that she would never again sit across the stones board from him or ride at his side. The philosophers and priests dickered over what happened when Ananshael took a soul, but all their theological and doctrinal hairsplitting didn't make a thimble of difference. Her father was gone, and the *kenarang,* decked out in a riding cloak worth its weight in gold, ruled Annur now, at least until Kaden returned.

In cases of high treason, the Emperor himself played the role of accusing magistrate, and so, with Sanlitun dead, the role fell to the regent. That worried Adare. Il Tornja was clearly a brilliant general, and yet, by his own admission, he had no interest in or aptitude for the subtler maneuverings of politics. Of course, this was a legal rather than a political affair, and il Tornja had seemed genuinely interested in seeing Uinian's head parted from his shoulders, but having someone more shrewd, more deeply versed in the nuances of the Annurian legal code, would have been a comfort.

"I know you're worried," he had said to her the night before as they met over cups of *ta* in the Iris Pavilion to discuss the trial.

"You're a soldier," she replied bluntly, "not a legal scholar."

He nodded. "And one thing I've learned as a soldier is when to listen to the people I command. I've been over this thing a dozen times with Jesser and that finicky bastard, Yuel. What in 'Shael's name is his job, anyway?"

"Chronicler of Justice. It's the highest legal post in the empire."

"Well, he's been going at me hammer and tongs for days now. I can repeat my speech to the Sitters forward and backwards, could probably translate it into Urghul if you wanted. I didn't realize my first days as regent would be spent drilling like a grass-green recruit."

It should have been a comfort. Annur knew no finer legal minds than Jesser and Yuel, and the case against Uinian appeared relatively straightforward—an Emperor murdered in the heart of the Temple of Light during a secret meeting with the Chief Priest. If Ran il Tornja had the good sense to follow their counsel to the letter, she would see Uinian divested of his office, blinded, and put to death before the sun set.

Before il Tornja settled into his own wooden seat, he knelt respectfully to the Unhewn Throne looming in the shadows behind him. The throne would remain vacant until Kaden's return, but even empty it drew eyes and hushed voices, as though it were a sleeping and dangerous beast. It was older than the hall that had been built around it, older than the Dawn

Palace itself, older than memory, a mass of black stone jutting from the bedrock, thrice the height of the tallest man. Near the very top, eons of wind and weather had carved a seat perfectly fitted to the human form. The rock itself afforded no simple way to reach that seat, and one of Adare's forebears had commissioned a gilded staircase to aid the Emperor in his ascent. Before the staircase, however, if the writings of Ussleton the Bald were to be believed, before Emperors, before Annur itself, the primitive tribes of the Neck had once chosen their chiefs through a bloody melee, hundreds of men struggling to climb the stone and ensconce themselves while cutting down their foes with bright bronze blades. In the flickering torchlight Adare could see red beneath the lapidary black, a reminder of the generations of blood that had seeped into the indifferent stone.

If il Tornja was intimidated, he didn't show it. After paying his respect, he turned to cast an eye over the assembled crowd—hundreds of ministers and bureaucrats, curious merchants and aristocrats come to see justice served and one of the city's mighty brought low—then sat in his own wooden chair before waving a hand to silence the tolling of the gongs.

"We gather," he began, his voice carrying through the hall, "to find truth. In this we call upon the gods, and most especially Astar'ren, Mother of Order, and Intarra, whose divine light illuminates the darkest shadows, to guide us and gird our strength." The formula was rote, the opening to every judicial proceeding from the Waist to the Bend, but il Tornja delivered it clearly and forcefully.

He has the voice of a battlefield commander, Adare realized, hope swelling inside her for the first time. The man seemed, if not precisely regal, then capable and confident, equal to the day's work. She allowed herself to skip past the present for a moment, to consider the future. The conviction and execution of the Chief Priest would throw the Temple of Light into disarray. Not only would she have revenge for her father's death, she could use the chaos to see the rival order gutted and brought low. *Not that we'll eliminate them, of course. The people need their religion, but those legions will have to go—*

"Uinian," il Tornja continued, cutting into her thoughts, "fourth of that name, Chief Priest of Intarra, Keeper of the Temple of Light, stands accused before this assembly on two counts: Treason in the Highest Degree and Murder of a Government Official, both capital offenses. As regent, I will present the facts as they are known, while Uinian himself will speak in his defense. The Seven Sitters, guided by their own reason and the illumination of the gods, will speak to the man's guilt or innocence."

He turned to Uinian. "Do you have questions at this time?"

Uinian smiled a thin-lipped smile. "None. You may proceed."

Adare bit nervously at the corner of her lip. It was hardly the priest's position to tell the governing magistrate when he could or could not proceed.

Il Tornja, for his part, simply shrugged. If he was unsettled or put out by Uinian's posture, he didn't show it.

"You may choose your Sitters."

This, too, was standard. Dozens of panels of Seven waited in chambers below, each sealed with a number. Uinian, now, would choose any number from one to twenty, and the Sitters associated with that number would be summoned to the room to judge him.

Only, he did not speak a number. Instead, his tongue flicking between his lips, he glanced over at Adare, then up into the shadowy space of the rafters.

"As this trial has already shown," he said, his voice quieter than the regent's, but sly, snaking throughout the hall, "men and women are much given to folly. I will not be judged by them."

For the first time, il Tornja frowned and Adare's stomach clenched.

"If he will not be judged," Adare began, half-rising to her feet, "then let us send for the headsman at once. Annur is nothing if not an empire of *law*. It is this law that separates us from the savages offering blood sacrifice in the jungles and on the steppe. If this so-called priest would flout that law, let us be done with him."

Hundreds of eyes turned to her. Il Tornja, too, met her gaze, raising a placating hand and nodding that he already understood the nature of her objection. Adare let the words trail off, retaking her seat with as much dignity as she could muster. The ministers flanking the regent looked on like buzzards in their black robes. The men had no sympathy for Uinian, but they had not stopped looking for weakness in Adare, either. *It is no slight to you,* Baxter Pane had argued, staring at her with those rheumy eyes of his, *but women are not suited to the Ministry. They are too . . . fickle, too easily transported by their emotions.*

Adare swallowed a curse. *And here I am, allowing myself to be transported by my emotions.*

The priest paused, allowing the sudden buzz that had attended her outburst to subside, clearly enjoying the confusion of the crowd and Adare's own discomfort. Her father had tried to teach her to control her emotions, but it was a skill for which she had little talent.

"If you refuse the trial—," il Tornja began, but Uinian cut him off.

"I do not refuse the trial. I refuse *this* trial. The Chief Priest of Intarra, the chosen of the goddess on earth, is not subject to the petty minds and manifest error of men and women." He spread his arms wide, as though inviting all assembled to consider the very contents of his soul. "I refuse the judgment of the Seven Sitters and call instead upon the goddess herself to render her verdict. I demand, as is my ancient right, Trial by Flame."

Adare half rose to her feet once more.

Around her, the hall exploded into shouts and exclamations, dozens of arguments and questions kindled like fire. She had known, from the look on his face, that Uinian hoped to subvert the trial in some way, and yet this . . . The Trial by Flame *was* every citizen's prerogative, had been ever since Anlatun the Pious walked into his brother's funeral pyre to prove his innocence and emerged unscathed to take the Unhewn Throne. The fire had not burned him, Anlatun insisted, because Intarra herself had decreed his innocence. In the years that followed, there had been a spate of criminals demanding Intarra's justice. Without exception, they had burned. Screamed and burned. The Trial by Flame quickly lost its appeal, fading from practice and memory until it existed only as a scribal note in manuals of jurisprudence.

Until now.

"Let the goddess judge," Uinian continued, pitching his defiant voice to carry over the turmoil of the crowd. "Let the goddess judge," he said again, raising a hand to draw all eyes to himself. "The Lady of Light and Goddess of Fire. *My* goddess."

Adare drove her fingernails into her palms, but she refused to speak again, turning her gaze instead toward il Tornja to see how he would meet this new challenge.

The *kenarang* had risen to his feet, looking half-prepared to draw the long sword at his side. Instead, he gestured once to the slave at the gong, and in moments the deep reverberation silenced the chamber. With the crowd stilled, the regent reseated himself, then looked over to where Jesser and Yuel sat—one tall, one short, both skeletal in their ministerial robes, arguing heatedly but inaudibly, gesturing in the air with their ink-stained hands. The two debated a moment more; then Yuel rose to murmur something in il Tornja's ear. He listened, nodded impatiently, then waved the man away.

"Well, this should cut down considerably on the time," he announced at last, his voice too jocular for Adare's comfort. "There will be no Seven Sitters, no reading of the facts, no disputation by the accused. Instead, according to the law, the Chief Priest will thrust his bare arm into the flame up to the elbow for fifty strikes of the gong. If his flesh remains unburned through all this time, it will be decreed that Intarra, who watches over all Annur, has judged him free of guilt. He will walk free.

"If," he continued, a vulpine smile on his face, "the flesh or the hair upon the flesh singes or burns—" He shrugged. "—then the whole body will be consecrated to Intarra's sacred flame and fire."

He turned to Uinian. "You understand this, priest?"

Uinian smiled his own smile. "Better, perhaps, than any assembled here."

"It seems, then, that we will need a flame. This brazier," he continued, indicating a metal grate large enough to roast a goat, "should do the job nicely."

"No," Uinian replied, raising his chin.

You got your 'Shael-spawned Trial by Flame, Adare thought angrily. *You don't get to pick the brazier.* Blood hammered in her ears, but she kept her face still and refused to speak.

Il Tornja raised an eyebrow. "No?" Clearly he was unaccustomed to hearing the word.

"I will not be tested over some petty flame like a common criminal. I am the Chief Priest of Intarra, her officer here in this benighted world, and I will be tested in a manner and location worthy of my sacred trust."

Adare held her breath.

"I will be tested," Uinian continued, eyeing Adare, "in the Temple of Light."

She was on her feet again without realizing it. "No," she said, turning to il Tornja and the assembled ministers. "Absolutely not. This vermin has the right to due process under Annurian Law, which unfortunately includes this antiquated sideshow, but he does not dictate his terms. He has *armed men* in the Temple, if you don't recall. He has practically an army!"

Uinian smiled at Adare. "A sideshow? I would make a sacred appeal to the goddess you profess to worship, and you term it a *sideshow?*"

"It's a ruse," Adare snapped. "A trick. You can't survive the flame, and you know it."

"Then there is no harm in allowing me the Trial," Uinian replied. He turned to the assembled crowd, extending his arms. "All here are welcome. All who walk beneath the light of Intarra, all who see by her flames and cook by her fires, all who love beneath her lambent moon, all those who work the earth or ply the waves beneath her noonday sun. Come. Come! I have nothing to hide before my fellow men or my goddess. Watch as I allow the Flame to test me, and judge for yourselves who is pure in heart and truthful, and who is filled with deceit."

That sealed it. With a few words, the priest had appealed above the court, above the throne itself, directly to the religious sentiments of the people. Not every citizen of Annur was a devoted follower of Intarra, of course—other gods had their temples and clergy, some quite wealthy and popular—but the people of the city were pious enough to allow the man his test. Sanlitun had been a well-liked Emperor, and many no doubt wished to see Uinian burn, but they would give him his time and place. Il Tornja could refuse, but the thing had already gone too far. For the regent to balk now would bring accusations of tyranny and impiety both, accusations the Unhewn Throne could ill afford during a delicate transition of power. The priest wasn't offering a defense, he was making an *attack,* a more subtle attack than that which had killed her father, but one aimed at the heart of the entire Malkeenian line.

He knew it all along, Adare thought, sick to her stomach. *I should have stabbed him in his cell as he slept.* She scrambled to think of some third course, some alternative to this parade down the Godsway in the sight of all Annur. *Father would have seen a way. . . .* But her father had not seen a way. Uinian had lied to Sanlitun, tricked him, and murdered him, and now he seemed prepared to do the same to Adare. She wanted to scream, but screaming would do no good. *Think,* she spat at herself, but thought failed her. All she could do was follow and watch, as in a nightmare.

✝

No structure in the city stood far enough from Intarra's Spear to escape the sight of the impossible monolith, but Uinian IV's predecessors had been shrewd enough to move the locus of religious power outside the Dawn Palace, distancing themselves from the imperial family and consolidating their hold on the ecclesiastical rule of the city. The Temple of

Light, a soaring structure of stone and colored glass, stood halfway down the Godsway, close enough to the center of Annur for easy commerce with the Palace, but not so close that it fell under the shadow of those looming red walls.

Unlike the Spear, the Temple of Light was clearly a human creation, but *what* a creation. Tiers of arches, one above the other, climbed toward the sky, each filled with a huge window. Adare knew something of the glass trade. A single one of those panes cost more than a year's salary for a thriving merchant—not including the price of cutting and transportation—and there were *thousands* of them, so many that it seemed as though the temple were more glass than stone, a massive, glittering, multifaceted gem humbling the edifices surrounding it.

As a child, Adare had marveled at the scope and the color, but now, as she dismounted from her palanquin with what seemed like half of Annur crowded about, it was the armed soldiers ringing the walls and flanking the tall doors that drew her eye and stoked her fears. Il Tornja had insisted that a thousand guardsmen accompany the odd procession from the Palace to the temple, more than twice the number of the waiting Sons of Flame, probably enough to overwhelm them if it came to an open battle. Of course, if it came to blood, there was also the mob to consider. In addition to the hundreds formally attached to the trial, thousands more had gathered—some from curiosity, others indignation—and already rumors and anger had grown ripe in the restive crowd.

A battle on the Godsway, Adare thought. *Sweet 'Shael, my father's barely cold in his tomb and already the empire is pulling apart at the seams.*

If il Tornja was concerned, he didn't show it. The *kenarang* sat his horse in a casual half slouch, clearly more comfortable there than he had been back in the Palace. He might have been out for a ride in the country, only there was something in his eyes Adare had not noticed before, something alert and predatory, as he surveyed the crowd.

Uinian, for his part, looked triumphant. He raised his manacled hands to the mob in a gesture of blessing or defiance. *With the wrong words, he could start a riot right now.* And yet, after what seemed like an eternity, he turned to enter the temple.

The inside of the Temple of Light was, if anything, more impressive than the exterior. The light flooding through those tall windows danced on the surface of vast reflecting pools, scribbling bright shapes on the walls and pillars. Worshippers had dropped coins into those pools: copper flames, silver moons, even a few golden Annurian suns from the most wealthy. *Another source of revenue for Uinian,* Adare thought, only now fully realizing the extent of the priest's reach and influence, *and another one we do not tax.* Each of those suns could keep a soldier in armor for the better part of half a year, a soldier who might well choose to fight against the Unhewn Throne.

The Aedolians accompanying the party had ringed off a small space in the center of the temple, holding back the press of those eager to witness a death or a miracle, and it was into this space that Adare stepped along with il Tornja, the other ministers, and Uinian himself.

"Here," the Chief Priest said, casting a defiant smile to the crowd, "I will face my Trial."

Of course. The entire vault of the temple was a glass and crystal hymn to light—panes and facets reflecting and refracting a thousand hues—but the most striking sight of all was the enormous lens set into the ceiling directly above the nave.

Old Semptis Hodd had explained the principles of lenses to Adare when she was only a child, showing her how she could use a circle of carefully ground glass to ignite a small fire in the Palace courtyard. Adare had wanted to see how some ants would stand up to the treatment, but her tutor refused, assuring her that they would burn as readily as the grass but insisting that a princess should not sully herself with such crass pursuits. Adare was glad now that she had spared the ants, but she wished she'd paid more attention to Hodd's lectures on lenses.

There, on the floor at the center of the nave, a square foot of stone glowed a sullen red, shivering the air above it where the lens began to focus the noon rays of the sun. The effect would not last long; the sun would peak, then start her slow descent, and the stone would cool. For about ten minutes, however, that beam of liquid light could boil water, char wood, or blacken flesh in an instant, and it was there that for centuries priests had made offerings to Intarra.

"This," Uinian said, gesturing to the smoldering stone, "is where I will face my goddess."

A collective gasp went through the crowd.

He can't survive it, Adare told herself. *It's impossible.*

Il Tornja looked skeptical. "It's not a flame."

Uinian shook his head in scorn. "This is the pure kiss of Intarra. If you doubt her power," he continued, stripping the amice from his shoulders in one fluid motion and hurling it into the light, "observe!" The cloth caught flame in midair before landing in an ashen heap on the stone. A stir of excitement ran through the mob. Adare thought she might be sick.

"No!" she shouted, stepping forward. "The regent is right. This is *not* a flame. The man has demanded Trial by Flame. Let there be a *flame*."

"How little the princess understands," Uinian sneered, "of the nature of the goddess. Of the many forms she may take. When I step into her burning sight and do not burn, the world will know who is the *true* servant of Intarra. Your family claims descent from the goddess, but her ways are ineffable. Her favor has shifted. And without her favor, you are what? Not divinely ordained protectors, but simple tyrants!"

The heat lapped at Adare's face, and sweat slicked the flesh beneath her robes.

"You dare call us tyrants," she spat back. "You? Who murdered the rightful Emperor?"

Uinian smiled. "The test will tell."

He will fail, Adare said, repeating the inner mantra again and again. *He will fail.* But the man had mocked and manipulated the entire process thus far. That searing heat was not a flame, and the smile had not left his lips.

"I will not accept this," Adare insisted, raising her voice over the growing noise of the crowd. "I do not accept this trial."

"You may forget, woman," Uinian replied, his own voice vicious, scornful, "that *you* are not the goddess. Your family has ruled for so long that you demand too much."

"I demand obedience to the law," Adare raged, but someone was already taking her by the shoulder gently but firmly, drawing her back. She struggled to escape, but she was no match for the hands that held her. In a fit of fury, she rounded on the person. "Release me! I am a Malkeenian princess and the Chief Minister of Finance—"

"—and a fool if you think you can change anything here," il Tornja murmured, voice low but hard. His grip felt like steel as he held her back. "This is not the time, Adare."

"There is no *other* time," she spat. "It has to be *now*." She writhed in the *kenarang*'s grasp, unable to free herself but turning back toward the priest nonetheless. A thousand eyes fixed on her; people were shouting and yelling, but she ignored them. "I demand your life!" she screamed at Uinian. "I demand your life in return for the life of my father."

"Your demands mean nothing," he replied. "You do not rule here." And then he turned and stepped into the light.

Uinian IV, the Chief Priest of Intarra, the man who had murdered the Emperor and taken her father, did not burn. The very air ran liquid with luminous heat, and yet the priest himself merely spread his arms, raised his face to the radiance as he might to a warm rain, letting it wash over him. For an eternity he stood there, then stepped, finally, from the rays.

Impossible, Adare thought, slackening in il Tornja's grip. *It's not possible.*

"Someone killed Sanlitun hui'Malkeenian," Uinian declared, triumph writ large across his face, "but it was not I. The Goddess Intarra has declared me unsullied by sin, just as she once declared Anlatun the Pious, while those who thought to bring me low—" He stared pointedly from Ran il Tornja to Adare. "—have been checked, and humbled. I can only pray to the Lady of Light that they remember this humility in the dark days to come."

20

The morning sun blazed through the window, bright and unyielding. With a grunt, Valyn raised a hand to his eyes, shielding them from the glare. The entire room was white: white walls, white ceiling, even the wide pine boards of the floor had been scoured, sanded, and scrubbed so many times, they were bleached of all color. The place smelled of the strong alcohol the Kettral used to scrub out wounds and the herbal poultices they plastered on after the cleaning was done. Valyn would have preferred to move his bed into the cool shadow at the side of the room, but Wilton Ren, the medic on duty, had given him strict instructions about staying still and calm, instructions he would have happily ignored save for the lance of pain that drove through his chest every time he so much as shifted.

According to Ren, they'd dragged him in, pulled the arrow, stitched the wound, and bandaged it, all while he was unconscious. When he finally woke, after a day and a night, his first thought had not been for the puncture in his shoulder or the one who fired the arrow, but for Ha Lin. Whatever went wrong on the sniper field, he'd survived it. He had no such assurances about Lin's meeting with Balendin. Valyn tried to drag himself out of bed half a dozen times, reaching the door before he collapsed on his final effort. That was where Ren found him.

"Look," the man grumbled, hauling him up and depositing him back in the bunk, "I'm the medic here. People bust an arm, they come to me. Lose an eye, they come to me. Crack their fool heads on a barrel drop— they come to me. If there was something wrong with your friend, I'd have heard about it. Now," he said, eyeing Valyn appraisingly. "You can stay in that 'Shael-spawned bed on your own, or I can go get a nice length of stout rope and keep you there." Although Ren was well into his fifth decade and hadn't been out of the infirmary in half that time, he had a neck like a bull, arms thicker than Valyn's legs, and a scarred face that suggested he'd be just as happy to beat his patient into unconsciousness as to heal him. Despite the man's rough delivery, however, his words calmed Valyn. Qarsh was a small island. If Lin was hurt, the news would travel quickly.

He knew he ought to be thankful about his own injury. The arrow was a through-shot, missing all the main arteries and organs, missing his lung by the space of a finger. The medics had gotten to the wound quickly enough to clean it out with some sort of fluid that burned like acid, but that seemed to have stopped any infection. With a little bit of rest, Ren said, he'd make a full recovery. That kind of luck didn't come around too often, and a soldier was supposed to appreciate it when it did, but Valyn was in no mood to be appreciative. Once he got past his immediate concern for Ha Lin, the reality landed on him like a stone: Annick had *shot* him, had drawn a bow in broad daylight in front of two trainers and put an arrow through his chest.

When Ren came in with a bowl of broth, Valyn beckoned him over. His voice was too weak to do much more than whisper, but the words came out harsh and hard.

"Did they get her?"

"Get her?" Ren replied, setting the bowl on the bedside table. "Get who?"

"Annick!" he rasped. "The girl who fucking shot me!"

The medic shrugged. "Didn't take much getting. She seemed as surprised as anyone else that the arrow wasn't a stunner."

Valyn stared. "How could she be surprised? She's the one who shot it! She shot three of them!"

"But only the one that hit you had a chisel point. The other two were stunners."

"No," Valyn said, shaking his head at the memory of the arrow scudding through the dirt beside him. Seeing the point on the *second* arrow was what started him running in the first place. "No. At least two had live heads."

"You can tell it to Rallen," Ren replied with a shrug. "The Master of Cadets is holding an inquiry. Looks like she's going to be nailed for combat negligence. There'll be a review of her conduct, and she'll be suspended right up until Hull's Trial."

The words hit Valyn like a hammer.

"Combat negligence," he managed. "And in the meantime, she's walking around free?"

"Where d'you want her to be?"

Valyn's mouth hung open. "How did she explain the fact that she had even *one* live head in a training contest?"

"Said something happened to the head. Said the arrow that hit you was supposed to be a stunner, but that she must have got it wrong somehow."

"I'll say something happened to the 'Kent-kissing head," Valyn erupted. He tried to sit up, but pain blazed through his wound and he subsided weakly on the cot, exhaling between clenched teeth. "What happened to the head is that she switched a stunner for a razor."

"Look," Ren said, wagging the spoon at him. "I don't know all the details, but we're on the Islands. You're with the Kettral. This isn't a sewing circle. Give men and women bows and swords and tell them to start leaping off birds and blowing things up, and every so often someone catches an unhealthy bit of sharp steel somewhere it doesn't belong. I've been here a while and I've seen it before. A stunner and a chisel don't look all that different, especially when you're in the middle of a fight."

"And Rallen is buying this?" Valyn asked, amazed into something like acceptance.

"Rallen's seen it before, too. It's a training accident. Not worth sacrificing the best sniper in the class for."

Valyn shook his head, unable to respond.

Ren clapped him on the shoulder with a hard, callused hand. "Look, kid. I know how it feels. You took an arrow through the chest. You're angry. But there's such a thing as plain old shit luck. You may be the son of the Emperor, but not everything's a plot against you."

The medic stumped out the door, leaving Valyn with those words spinning in his head. *Not everything's a plot against you.* It was tempting to believe that, to believe that the whole thing was just a horrible mistake with a surprisingly fortunate outcome, but there was the Aedolian to consider. The ship was coming to take him away from the Islands. To keep him safe. According to the murdered man, anyone could be involved in the plot, anyone at all.

✝

Annick came just before the evening meal. Valyn was staring out the window, trying to decide if the boat in the middle distance was an imperial sloop or a trading vessel when the door swung open soundlessly. He looked over to find the sniper standing still and silent in the doorway, the ever-present bow in her hand. He realized, with a twist of fear, that it was strung.

"Valyn," she said, nodding curtly. Her eyes, blue as arctic ice, never left his face.

He tensed. Normally he'd have the advantage in close-quarters combat, but even sitting up took a major effort; he wasn't going to be wrestling her to the ground, not in his condition. He thought about calling for Ren, but the medic was over in the mess hall taking his dinner and filling yet another bowl of stew for Valyn. It would have to be the belt knife, then.

The knife lay beside the remains of an apple on the wooden table beside the bed. He figured the odds at about half that he could reach it and throw before Annick fished an arrow out of her quiver, and he counted himself lucky at that. It seemed like a long time since he'd had a chance at a fair fight.

"What do you want?" he asked, shifting slowly toward the table, freeing his right hand from the blankets in the process.

"I didn't try to kill you," she said simply.

Valyn barked a laugh that sent a stab of pain through his chest. "You're here to *apologize*?"

Annick tilted her head to one side, considering the question. "No," she responded after a moment. "I'm here to tell you I didn't try to kill you."

Valyn went for the knife. He was slower than he'd expected, slower than he hoped, but the 'Kent-kissing thing was only a few feet away. If he could just . . . Before he'd even extended his arm, Annick nocked, drew, and released. The blade went skittering away across the floor, while an arrow sprouted in its place, still quivering from the impact. Valyn watched it go still, then let his hand fall. That was it, then. The sniper had him pinned down and there wasn't a thing he could do.

She considered him calmly, another arrow already nocked to her string. It seemed like a poor way to die—murdered in an infirmary cot—but then, he supposed all the ways looked pretty poor to the person doing the dying.

"So you're part of it," he said wearily. It was a vague relief to put a face to the conspiracy at last, even if it wasn't the face he'd expected.

Annick paused before responding. "Part of what?"

"Whatever the fuck it is," he said, gesturing weakly with a hand. "My father. Me. Kaden." He closed his eyes at the thought of his brother, unwarned, unprepared, going about the strange, simple life that had been decreed for him right up until the moment someone put a blade in his back. It wouldn't be hard, all the way out there at the end of the empire.

Annick tapped at her bowstring with a finger. "You're not making sense. Has the medic given you something to dull the pain?"

Valyn started to respond, then checked himself. Maybe she was playing games, taunting him during his final moments. On the other hand, Annick didn't play games. She seemed to have only two goals—training or killing—and if she really wanted to kill him, she would have shot his neck a moment earlier, not his knife.

"Why did you come here?" he asked guardedly, a sick hope blooming inside him.

"To tell you I didn't try to kill you," she said for the third time, eyes hard as chips of glass. "If I wanted to kill you, there are better ways than the middle of the day in the middle of a contest."

"Well, it's a 'Kent-kissing good thing that you weren't shooting this well yesterday," Valyn said, gesturing to the arrow lodged in the table. "You would have put that chisel point right through the back of my head rather than my shoulder."

Annick narrowed her eyes. Were it not for the insanity of the notion, Valyn would have thought he'd insulted her professional pride. "The tips were wrong," she said finally. "They threw off the shots."

Valyn considered that. "You mean you thought you were firing stunners rather than chisel points." It made an unexpected sort of sense. The difference in the weight and shape of an arrowhead *could* account for the missed shots, especially over that sort of range.

"I mean," Annick corrected him, "the heads are wrong." She jerked her chin toward the one sticking from the side table. "That's what they ripped out of you. I found it in the other room when I came in. It's the other reason I came."

Valyn stared, first at her, then at the arrow. The brown stain on the shaft was blood, he realized, *his* blood. Awkwardly, he fumbled it free from the grain of the tabletop.

"It's a standard chisel point," he said, holding it up for her to see.

"Exactly," Annick responded, refusing to elaborate.

Valyn returned his attention to the arrow. There was nothing unusual aside from the stains. He'd probably fired thousands just like it in his training. Except . . . "You don't use the standard head," he said, realization dawning. "You hammer your own."

The sniper nodded.

"How did you shoot a standard chisel instead of your own stunner without knowing the difference?" Valyn asked, as confused as he was wary. "How did it even end up in your quiver?"

"I don't know," she replied, her voice flat, matter-of-fact, unreadable. Her whole 'Kent-kissing body was unreadable. Kettral trained from an early age to see a foe's intention in the way he stood, the way he carried his weapons, the angle of his eyes. There were a hundred things to look for—whitened knuckles on a sword hilt, raised shoulders, the flick of a tongue on dry lips. The tiniest twitch of an eye could signal imminent attack or the possibility of a bluff. Annick, however, might have been standing in line at a butcher's shop or considering a statue on the Annurian Godsway. If she was concerned at having nearly killed the brother of the Emperor, she didn't show it. She hadn't moved from the doorway, where she stood with her bow at her side, posture loose but ready, her thin, childlike face inscrutable as the blank white walls.

Valyn rolled wearily onto his side. His mind ached from trying to make sense of it all, and his body ached, too. In the course of his pathetic exertions, his wound had broken open, seeping blood down the front of his chest, stabbing him whenever he drew a breath. It no longer seemed quite so likely Annick was trying to kill him, at least not right away.

"What about the knot?" he asked wearily. "The one you tied during the drowning test?"

"Double bowline. Hard to untie in those circumstances, but not impossible."

Valyn watched her face. Still nothing. "You really believe that, don't you?" he asked after a long pause.

"It's the truth."

"The truth," Valyn said. "And what do you think I found, down there when I nearly drowned?"

"You found a double bowline," she replied. "When you failed to untie it, you wanted to make some sort of excuse in front of Fane. That's why you lied about the extra loops." Her voice was devoid of emotion, as though lying to a superior officer and accusing a fellow cadet were both just tactics like any other tactics, to be judged by their success or failure. Nothing rattled her. Nothing surprised her.

"What about Amie?" he demanded, gambling on a sudden impulse. "Did you kill her?"

That, finally, got a reaction. Something dark and horrible passed across Annick's eyes, a shadow of rage and destruction.

"We found her, you know," Valyn continued, pressing the attack. "She was a pretty girl, but not after whoever killed her got finished."

"She . . . ," Annick began, speechless for once, her slender features twisting. "She—"

"She what? She begged you to stop? She wasn't supposed to die? She had it coming?" The words were an effort, each syllable tearing at the wound in his chest, but he kept at them, thrusting them at the sniper like knives, trying to keep her on the defensive, trying to force the retreat that would lead to the stumble. "I know you were seeing her that morning," he continued. "Did you spend all day killing her?"

Annick half raised her bow, and Valyn thought for a moment that she was going to murder him after all. She was breathing hard suddenly, her fingers almost trembling. He stared, fear all but forgotten in his fascination, as she shuddered herself still. Then, without a word of explanation, she turned on her heel and disappeared through the door. For a long time, he just watched the empty doorway, trying in vain to recall the expression on her face.

When Ha Lin finally arrived hours later, she found him in the same position.

Valyn hadn't bothered to light the small lamp by his side, and in the gathering dusk, all he saw was her silhouette at first, the tight curve of her hip, the swell of her breast as she stood against the bleached wall. He could smell her, the light scent of salt and sweat he'd come to recognize over a hundred training missions.

"Lin," he began, shaking the memory of Annick clear from his mind, "you'll never believe what—"

The words died in his throat as she stepped over to the bed, into the fading light from the window. Her lip had been split open and a cruel gash sliced across her forehead. The wounds were a day old, but they were brutal nonetheless.

"What in 'Shael's name—," he began, reaching out for her.

She recoiled violently, jerking back. "Don't touch me," she said, voice hard but abstracted, as though she were speaking from the depth of sleep.

Valyn fell back against the pillow, eyes burning, heart hammering in his chest. "I asked Ren," he said. "He told me you were fine."

"Fine?" she asked, glancing down at her hands as though seeing them for the first time. "Yeah, I suppose I'm fine."

"What *happened* to you?" Valyn demanded, reaching out a hand once more.

She turned to the window, ripped a scab off her knuckle, and flicked it out into the night.

"Got careless," she said finally.

"Bull*shit,* Lin," Valyn snapped. "You didn't get those bruises tripping on the trail. Now, what in Hull's name happened up there?"

The fire in his voice burned away her lassitude at last, and she met his anger with her own. "Sami Yurl and Balendin Ainhoa happened," she replied grimly, her mouth twisting into a scowl or a sob. "They were *both* up on the West Bluffs."

"And they did—" He waved a hand weakly toward her face. "—this?" His hand curled into a hard fist. "Those bastards. Those 'Shael-spawned, 'Kent-kissing bastards. I knew I shouldn't have let—"

She started laughing then, a low, ugly laugh. "Let me *what? Let* me walk around the Islands by myself? *Let* me go out after dark?" She shook her head. "Maybe you shouldn't *let* me play with sharp things?"

"I didn't mean it that way—," he began, then stopped, a sickening thought boiling up inside him. "They didn't—" He wasn't sure how to say the words. "Did they—?"

"Rape me?" she said, raising a bruised eyebrow. "Is that what you want to ask? If they raped me?"

He nodded silently, dumb before the possibility.

She turned and spat out the narrow window. "No, Valyn," she said. "They didn't fucking rape me."

Relief washed through him. "Well, that's—"

"That's *what?*" she snarled. "Good? It's *good* that they didn't rip my blacks off and fuck me? What a *solace!*" Lamplight flickered in her eyes as though they had caught fire. "They shoved my face in the dirt, slashed me across the ribs, broke my nose and probably a rib, but at least my precious *cunt* is intact."

"Lin—," he began.

"Oh, fuck *you,* Valyn, you *idiot,*" she spat. She was crying, he realized, but the words came out fast and sharp. "The point is they *could* have done whatever they wanted. They *could* have raped me, or killed me, tossed my body in the ocean. Whatever. There was nothing I could do to stop them."

She took a long, shuddering breath, then scrubbed away the tears with the back of her hand.

"Why?" Valyn asked. "Why did they do it?"

"They said it was payback," she said, the sobs and the fury suddenly gone, replaced by a flat monotone. "Said it was to remind me what happens when someone steps into the ring against them."

"But they *won* the fight," Valyn said, his mind spinning.

"They won, all right," Lin replied, nodding wearily. "They won, and they won, and they won."

"I should have been there," Valyn said, struggling to sit up.

"What is wrong with you?" she demanded. "Are you listening to me at all?" She turned slowly to face him. "Honest to Hull, in some ways you're just as bad as those two bastards."

The words stabbed him more viciously than the wound in his shoulder. "What? I'm saying I wanted to *help* you, to have your back."

She took another deep breath, then spoke to him slowly, as though to a stupid child. "They attacked me because I stepped outside the boundaries they set up for me, because I wouldn't *behave.*" She shook her head again wearily. "And now you're doing the same thing, telling me I shouldn't go here or there, telling me that I should check with you before I lace up my 'Kent-kissing breeches."

"All right," Valyn said. "Fine. I get it. I'm sorry."

"No," she replied. "You do not get it. You cannot follow me everywhere. You cannot watch me every night while I sleep."

"I can help," he said stubbornly.

"Fuck. That. I'm a soldier, same as you. Same as Sami Yurl." She had worried off another scab as she talked and stared down at it, trembling. One by one, she flexed her fingers, watching the blood well up. "I got careless is all," she said finally. "It won't happen again."

Valyn felt a cold stone settle in his gut. His shoulder throbbed, but he didn't care a shit for his shoulder.

"Whatever you want," he said. "Whatever you need. You just tell me."

"I don't . . . I thought I needed to talk to you. I thought it would help." She flicked the blood from her fingers. "Stupid of me. How could it help? The thing's all over, all done. You might be an Emperor's son, but you can't stuff the sand back in the hourglass." She turned her head and met his eyes at last. "There's no going back—just forward. What I need is some time."

"No," he replied reflexively. "Lin . . ."

He reached out toward her one more time, but she slipped past his grip.

"I need to be alone for a while, Valyn. For now, that's what you can do. Stop thinking you have to protect me because we kissed once in the mess hall. I don't belong to those bastards, and I certainly don't belong to you."

21

One could be forgiven, Kaden thought, for believing that Tan might go easier on him now that the whole mystery of the *kenta* had been revealed. After all, the older monks had finally taken him into their confidence, had explained to him secrets to which only a few people in the empire, only a few people in the whole *world* were privy. One could be forgiven for thinking that the conversation in the abbot's study constituted a graduation of sorts, an acknowledgment that he had moved from being an acolyte to . . . something more. One could be forgiven, he thought unsmilingly, but one would be wrong.

As they departed from the small stone hut, Tan turned, blocking the narrow path. Kaden was tall, but the older monk overtopped him by half a head, and it took an effort of will not to retreat a step.

"The *vaniate* is not something you can learn like mathematics or the names of trees," he began, voice barely more than a growl. "You cannot study it. You cannot commit it to memory. You cannot pray that a god will deliver the wisdom to you in your sleep."

Kaden nodded, uncertain where the conversation was leading.

His *umial* smiled bleakly. "You are quick to agree. You fail to understand that the emptiness does not simply grow inside you like a plant. Think of the hollow of the bowls you just completed. You had to drive your fingers into the clay. You had to force the hollowness upon it."

"It feels more like guiding than forcing," Kaden ventured, made bold by the abbot's confidence and his newfound knowledge. "If you push too hard, the bowl is ruined."

Tan regarded him for a long, uncomfortable moment, his stare pointed as a nail. "If you learn one thing under my tutelage," the older monk said slowly, "it will be this: Emptiness exists only when something else has been gouged away."

And so it was that Kaden found himself on a bare patch of ground sandwiched between the rear wall of the refectory and a low band of cliff, shovel in one hand, a half-dug hole in front of him. A few feet away Tan sat cross-legged in the shade of a juniper. His eyes were closed, his breathing steady, as though he slept, but Kaden knew better. He wouldn't have bet money that his *umial ever* really slept.

The monk had instructed him to dig a hole straight down, two feet wide and as deep as Kaden was tall. The scent of stewed onions and hearty brown bread hung on the breeze, and through the refectory windows Kaden could hear the murmured conversation of the other monks, the scraping of benches, the clink of wood on clay as they filled their bowls. His stomach grumbled, but he forced hunger from his mind and turned his attention to the task once more. Whatever was in store, it would only go worse if Tan thought his pupil was shying away from the work.

The ground was hard and rocky, desiccated as stale bread, more gravel than earth. Time and again Kaden had to lower himself into the hole to claw at a large stone with his bare hands, scraping away at the outline until he could drive a couple of fingers beneath and pry the thing from its socket. The going was slow. He ripped two fingernails out of their beds, and his hands were cut and bleeding, but by the evening bell Kaden had hacked a hole out of the earth to roughly the right dimensions.

Tan stood when the work was complete, walked to the edge of the small pit, nodded once, and gestured toward the hole. "Get in."

Kaden hesitated.

"Get in," the older monk said again.

Kaden lowered himself gingerly into the hole. Once he'd found his footing on the uneven bottom, he could just peer over the lip. The faces of a few of the younger monks peered out the open windows of the refectory. Penance was a commonplace at Ashk'lan, but Tan had never had a pupil before, and evidently they took some sort of interest in Kaden's fate. They didn't have to wait long to satisfy their curiosity. The monk hefted the shovel and, without regard for Kaden's eyes or ears, started tossing earth back into the hole.

It took him a tenth of the time to fill the hole that it had taken Kaden to dig it. When Kaden lifted a hand to brush the dirt from his eyes Tan shook his head.

"Keep your arms at your sides," he said without breaking the steady rhythm of pitching and shoveling.

As the dirt inched above Kaden's chin, he started to object. A fresh shovelful caught him square in the open mouth, and before he could finish coughing or spitting, Tan had packed the earth up to just below his nose. Jagged stones gouged into his flesh in a dozen places. The heavy dirt might have been lead, and he felt the panic rise inside him. He couldn't move his arms or legs, couldn't even take a full breath. He might die here, he realized. If his *umial* threw just a few more shovels of earth over his head, he would suffocate beneath the gravelly soil, unable to breathe, to move, to scream.

He closed his eyes and let his mind float. *Fear is a dream,* he told himself. *Pain is a dream.* The rising flood of panic inside him subsided. He took a shallow breath through his nose, concentrating on the feel of the air in his lungs. With his eyes still closed, he held the breath for seven heartbeats, then exhaled slowly, relaxing his body as the air escaped. The fear drained out through his feet, through his fingertips, leaching into the soil around him until he was calm once more. The mind learned from the body, and if he kept his body still, if he refused to struggle, he could keep his mind still as well.

He opened his eyes to find Tan regarding him with a steady, low-lidded gaze. Kaden thought his *umial* might speak, if only to taunt him or make some final, gnomic command. Instead, the monk hefted the shovel over his shoulder and turned away without a word, leaving his pupil buried to his upper lip in the hard and unyielding soil.

For a while Kaden was alone. The sounds of the refectory rose, then fell as the monks departed from the evening meal, bound for the meditation hall or the solitude of their own cells. The large stone building blocked any view of the setting sun, but gradually the sky darkened from blue to bruised, and the night wind came, cold and biting, down off the mountains to blow grit and dirt in his face.

For a long time, all Kaden could think about was the pressure, the constant, enveloping sense of *weight* against his flesh, constricting his chest whenever he tried to take a breath. It was impossible to move, even to shift, and the muscles of his legs and lower back soon began to spasm, protesting against the confinement. As the air and the earth chilled, he found himself shivering uncontrollably.

Calm, he told himself, taking a shallow breath. *This is not a knife in the gut or a noose around the neck. It is not torture. It is only earth. Valyn probably endures far worse every day of his training.*

When he finally managed to still the quivering of his body, the fear came. He had not really thought about the mangled goat for some time. Whatever was killing the flock had yet to venture within miles of the monastery, and yet . . . the *saama'an* of the shattered skull grew unbidden in his mind. Here, immobile, buried to the lip in earth, Kaden would make easier prey than the most decrepit goat. The thing had not attacked a man, but Tan and Scial Nin had insisted it might be dangerous, insisted the acolytes and novices travel in pairs.

It was almost full dark when Kaden heard the quiet crunch of gravel behind him. It was impossible to turn. He could barely shift his head at all, and the effort sent a stabbing pain down his neck and into his back. *It could be Tan,* he told himself, trying to believe that his *umial* had returned to dig him out, and yet, it seemed unlikely that the older monk would release him before the night bell. Kaden opened his mouth to shout, to demand to know who was approaching, but dirt poured in, thick on his tongue, threatening to gag him. His heart strained against the weight of the earth, heedless of his attempts to slow it.

The steps drew closer, then halted behind him. Kaden managed to cough, clearing the grit from his throat, but he still couldn't speak. A hand came down on his scalp, pulling his head back, back, until he was staring at the night sky. Someone was crouching over him, a shock of curling hair—

Akiil.

Kaden felt his limbs go slack and watery with relief. Of course. His friend would have heard about the penance. He would be here to gloat.

"You look terrible," the boy announced after considering Kaden briefly.

Kaden tried to reply and got another mouthful of dirt for his trouble.

Akiil let go of his head and came around in front of Kaden, lowering himself to the dirt. "I'd dig you out a bit," he said, gesturing toward the brimming earth, "but Tan told me if I moved so much as a pebble, he'd bury me right beside you and leave me for longer. The heroic thing would probably be to dig you out anyway—loyalty between friends, and all that." He shrugged in the moonlight. "I've learned to be wary of heroism."

He squinted, as though trying to make out Kaden's expression. "Are you glaring at me?" he asked. "It looks like you're glaring, but with those burning eyes of yours, it's hard to tell glaring from just looking. Maybe you have to piss. Speaking of which, how *do* you piss while you're in there?"

Kaden silently cursed his friend for reminding him of the growing pressure in his bladder. It appeared that one of the parts of his pupil that Tan intended to carve away was his dignity.

"Sorry I brought it up," Akiil said. "And don't be angry. I'm sure there's a good reason for this. Just think—with such a concerned *umial,* you're getting a real jump on your training." He nodded encouragingly. "Anyway, you'll be happy to know that our fates are tied. As long as you're buried there, Tan wants me sitting behind you—in case a bird tries to shit on your head or some such." He frowned. "Actually, there were no specific instructions about what to do if a bird shits on your head, but Tan wants me here, watching over you."

He patted Kaden on the head as he rose. "I'm sure you'll find that a comfort. Just remember—whatever you're going through, I'm right here with you."

"Akiil," Tan said, his voice cutting through the darkness. "You are there to watch, not to talk. If you speak another word to my pupil, you will join him in the earth."

Akiil didn't speak another word.

For seven days, Kaden remained in the hole, baking in the noontime heat, shivering in his coffin of earth as the sun dropped beneath the steppe to the west and the stars swung up in a wheeling canopy of cold, distant light. He had been relieved to learn that he would not be left alone, but Akiil's companionship, if it could be called that, provided scant comfort. At Tan's insistence, he sat silently outside Kaden's field of vision, and after the first day Kaden almost forgot he was there.

Instead, a thousand tiny trials filled his mind, minuscule problems he could not address that grew to maddening proportions. An itch on his thigh, for instance, that he once would have scratched absently and been done with, dogged him for two days. A cramp in his immobilized arm drove a spike of pain up his shoulder and into his neck. Tan's digging had disturbed a nearby anthill, and the insects crawled over his face, into his ears and nose, into his eyes until he felt as though the creatures were everywhere, burrowing through the soil and swarming over his skin.

Every two days, someone brushed aside the earth covering his mouth and poured a cup of water onto his lips. Kaden lapped at it greedily, even going so far as to suck at the moist soil when the water was gone, a decision he always bitterly regretted when, hours later, he found his mouth plagued with grit that he could not spit out. He managed to tumble into a few hours of sleep late each night, when the monks had retired to their cells and the central square was still, but even his sleep was dogged by dreams of captivity and crushing confinement, and he woke haggard and exhausted each morning to find his nightmares real.

By the end of the first day, he thought he might go insane. By the fourth, he found himself hallucinating about water and freedom—vivid waking visions in which he splashed and danced in one of the cool mountain streams, whirling his arms and kicking his legs like a madman, slurping up great gulps of water, and sucking in endless breaths of clean, uncluttered air. When the monks came with his water, he found it difficult to tell if they were real or not, and stared the way one might at an apparition or a ghost.

On the eighth day, he woke to a cold dawn, the sky gray as slate, the light of the sun faint and watery over the eastern peaks. Several monks were up and about their morning ablutions, moving across the square, the only sound their bare feet crunching on the gravel of the paths. For a few heartbeats Kaden's mind moved with a clean clarity he thought he had lost days before. *Tan will leave me here,* he realized. *He will leave me here forever if I don't learn what he wants me to learn.* The thought should have filled him with desperation, but thoughts had lost all urgency. He felt as though reality was slipping from his grasp, and since his reality was a coffin of hard rock and unyielding soil, he was happy to let it go. After all, Kaden could suffer, but if Kaden wasn't there, there was no suffering.

For a while he watched a thin white cloud, light as air and impossibly far away. When it scudded beyond the range of his vision, he looked instead into the wide gray blank of the sky. *The empty sky,* he thought idly to himself. *A heaven of nothingness.* Without that space, the cloud could not sail past. Without it, the stars could not turn in their orbits. Without that great emptiness, the trees would wither, the light dim, while the men and beasts walking and crawling over the earth, moving effortlessly through the great void of the heavens, suffocated under an unfathomable weight, just as he, now, was slowly suffocating. Kaden stared into the sky until he felt he might fall upward, plummeting away from the earth into the bottomless gray, dwindling to a thin point, then to nothing.

Two days later, Tan broke him from his daze. Kaden hadn't seen his *umial* since the penance began, and he raised his eyes in perplexity, trying to make some sense of the robed figure above him.

"How do you feel?" the monk asked after a long silence, squatting down to scoop away the dirt covering Kaden's mouth.

Kaden considered the question, revolving it in his mind like a strange, smooth stone. *Feel.* He knew what the word meant, but had forgotten how to connect it to himself. "I don't know," he replied.

"Are you angry?"

Kaden moved his head slightly in the negative. It occurred to him that he had reason to be angry, but his imprisonment was a fact. The earth around him was a fact. Thirst was a fact. It made no sense to be angry at facts.

"I could leave you here until the new moon."

The new moon. Kaden had watched the moon each night, watched as the passage of time pared away sliver after lucent sliver. It was gibbous now, just fuller than half. The new moon was still a week off. Days earlier, the thought would have filled him with dread, but he could no longer muster the strength for dread. He could not even muster the strength to respond.

"Are you ready for me to dig you out?" Tan pressed.

Kaden stared at the man, at the puckered scars running down the sides of his scalp. *Where did he get those scars?* he wondered idly. Everything about the monk was a mystery. There was no point trying to guess the right answer to the question. Tan would release him or he would not, according to whatever arcane thoughts governed his mood.

"I don't know," Kaden replied, his voice raw and ragged in his throat.

The older monk considered him for a while longer, then nodded.

"Good," he said, then gestured to Akiil. "Dig," he added, gesturing to the earth around Kaden.

The sensation was strange and unsettling at first. As the pressing weight that had held him, had crushed him, for so many days began to disappear, he felt as though he were falling, endlessly falling. As the gravel crunched beneath the steel, Kaden felt something trickle back into him: thoughts, he realized. Emotions.

"You're letting me out?"

"It would have been better to leave you in another week," Tan replied, "but circumstances have changed."

Kaden squinted, trying to make sense of the words. "Circumstances?" The earth was packed around him. The sky spread above him. The sun carved its ineluctable arc through the blue. Those were the circumstances. What could have changed?

A cloud passed in front of the sun, casting the monk's face into deep shadow.

"I'd leave you here longer, but it's no longer safe."

22

The morning of the start of Hull's Trial dawned clear and cool. Valyn was relieved when the watery light finally leaked over the horizon. He had tossed and turned half the night, alternating between the worry about Ha Lin that had plagued him for the past week, and the more nebulous fear of the grueling test that lay ahead, the test that would determine the course of his life. It was all well and good to be selected as a child by the Kettral, all well and good to spend half a life training on the Islands. If you failed Hull's Trial, it was all finished, the years of work gone like yesterday's breeze.

Just get through the week, he kept telling himself. *You can't help anyone—not Lin, not Kaden,* no one—*if you don't make it through the week.*

The day was chilly for the Qirins, and as the cadets assembled on the rocky headland beneath the wide tenebral oak, a menacing black front was moving in swiftly from the north, darkening the waves beneath it and whipping their crests to a foamy chop. The storm, if it broke, would make for a dismal start to the Trial, not that the Eyrie commanders would take any more notice of the storm than they did of the inevitable injuries to come. When you signed on to be Kettral, you knew what you were getting into: sometimes it rained; sometimes people got hurt. You bandaged your wounds, buckled your slicks, and got on with it.

He looked through the group for Lin, but she stood on the far side, as far from him as it was possible to get, and met his stare only briefly, her eyes flat and unreadable. Balendin and Yurl were another matter. Yurl stood only a few feet away, chuckling under his breath with one of his minions. He caught Valyn's gaze and winked. Valyn forced himself to breathe, to keep his hands still at his sides, to ride out the tide of blood boiling behind his eyes. He'd almost gone after the two of them right after Lin left his room in the infirmary a week earlier, had almost hauled himself out of bed, busted shoulder or no, dragged himself to wherever they were, and broken their 'Kent-kissing knees.

Oddly, it was Yurl and Balendin themselves who convinced him not to. As he was hoisting himself out of the infirmary bed, cursing to keep back the burning sickness in his gut, he remembered the fight in the ring, remembered Balendin baiting Lin until she bit, then Yurl falling upon her, goading Valyn into his own error. The two were using the same strategy now, he realized, although on a larger, more horrible scale. They knew he'd come after them. How could he *not* go after them, after what they did to Lin? And, as in the ring, they were planning for it. They were ready.

Valyn had no idea what sort of sick game they were playing, had no conception of the rules or the goal, but one thing was certain: Playing into their hands was the quickest way to lose, and he had no intention of losing, not this time. As the storm cloud broke overhead, he met Yurl's eye and winked back. A shiver of unease passed over the youth's face, and he scowled, then looked away.

The first drops were pelting the ground as Daveen Shaleel, commander of operations for northeastern Vash, stepped onto a small rostrum. She began without preamble.

"Today you will begin your Trial. *If* you so choose." She paused there, shifting her eyes slowly from one cadet to the next. Shaleel was a slender woman, and well into her sixth decade, but Valyn had to force himself to meet that unbending gaze. "I am here," she continued finally, "to convince you to forgo the ordeal."

The words drew a surprised murmur from the assembled cadets, who glanced at one another in confusion. Eight years they had prepared for this moment, and now this woman was urging them to quit? Valyn scanned the faces. Talal looked cautious, careful. Laith seemed to think the whole thing was one more joke. Annick might have been considering the troublesome rigging of a smallboat she'd been ordered to sail around the point. Gwenna was picking something off her blacks and scowling. Only Lin showed no emotion. Her eyes were hollow, blank. Those eyes frightened Valyn more than the upcoming ordeal.

"The Trial," Shaleel continued, once the effect of her words had subsided, "is named, as you well know, for Hull, the Lord of Darkness, the Owl King, Lord of the Night. While the various soldiers here worship as they please, it is Hull who smothers the flame, Hull who hangs darkness over the heavens like a cloak, and Hull who spins the shade and shadows that allow you to slip close enough to slide your blade between the ribs."

Valyn was surprised to hear the long, graceful cadences from the woman. Most commanders tended to speak in the same clipped periods they had learned to rely on as soldiers in the field. Shaleel was no exception, but today, for some reason, she orated rather than spoke, as though she were leading a religious service rather than briefing her troops. Perhaps she was—the Trial, like other services, would hinge on sacrifice.

"Above all other gods, the Kettral worship Hull," the woman continued, gesturing to the tree behind her. The hanging bats swayed from the branches, susurrating quietly with each gust of wind. "But make no mistake, soldiers. Hull has no love for you."

Valyn looked over the crowd. Ha Lin stood almost directly across from him. He caught her eye, but she refused to hold his gaze.

"You have heard rumors about the Trial," the woman went on, "but you have not heard the truth. The truth is, the rigors of the week ahead will bleed you, crush you, maybe even break you, but they are only a prelude. The Trial, the *real* Trial, begins one week from now, for those of you foolish enough to persist."

This was news to Valyn. Everything he'd ever heard about Hull's Trial suggested it was just one long training exercise, far more brutal, to be sure, but fundamentally no different from anything else he'd encountered. A few paces away, Gwenna muttered something about "mysterious horseshit" and spat onto the stone. The other cadets seemed equally surprised, although they handled it differently. Annick held her bow, strung and ready, as if she expected to shoot something right away, staring down the commander the way a hawk might a mouse. Sami Yurl made some sort of crack that Valyn couldn't hear, and Balendin nodded. Unease filled the heavy air.

"The details of the Trial," Shaleel continued, "are reserved for those who successfully navigate this first week, but I can tell you one thing: It will break some of you, break you horribly, and for life." She paused to let her words sink in. "After eight years, no one doubts your valor. Step forward now and your labors are over. Arin awaits, just a day's sail distant."

Arin. The island of failures. The Eyrie had no intention of allowing

Kettral-trained soldiers to return to the world to find work as mercenaries or spies, and so those unable or unwilling to complete Hull's Trial were relocated to Arin, near the northwest end of the Qirin chain. It was the most luxurious of the Islands, more temperate and lush than the others, rising from the sea in a riot of green and blue. The empire took good care of those men and women who bowed out of the Trial, providing them with fine houses and food in perpetuity, all compliments of the good, tax-paying citizens of Annur. It was a life of leisure, a life that tens of thousands of people the continents over would have killed for, and yet, the failed soldiers paid for it with their freedom. They lived on Arin, in that tropical paradise, until they died.

No one stepped forward.

Shaleel nodded as if she had expected as much. "The offer stands," she said. "Remember that in the days ahead. Remember it as you labor in the surf, as you struggle through the sands, as you come near to drowning in the open sea. Remember, too, that this coming week is the easy part, a gentle prelude. At any point, right through the end, you can step away from all this, you can decide that the life of the Kettral is not a life you want to live."

The cadets stood still as stones, unwilling to risk one another's eyes.

"All right," Shaleel said, shaking her head as though in resignation. "The prelude to the Trial begins." She turned to her left. "Fane. Sigrid. They're yours for the next week."

Adaman Fane stepped to the fore. "One thing you maggots ought to realize," he began, a vicious smile stretching across his face, "is that I don't think a man's ready to be Kettral until he's puked up his own blood."

"What about a woman?" Gwenna shot back.

Fane grinned. "Well, you women have the higher pain tolerance, so we need to go even harder on you."

✝

The next six days passed in a fog of agony and exhaustion. Along with the rest of the cadets, Valyn ran until the promised blood wept from blisters and open wounds, swam until he thought he would sink to the bottom of the sound, then dragged his aching body out of the water to run some more. He crawled on his belly for miles over firespike and broken rock, carried an entire tree trunk across the island, then carried it back, wrestled Talal until both of them collapsed into the dirt of the ring, panting for a few hopeless breaths before a boot kicked him in the ribs and a voice told him to run some more. He navigated the coastline in a leaking smallboat with a plank of wood for a paddle. Then they took the plank away and told him to do it again; for half the night he clawed at the surf with his hands, trying to drag the tiny vessel forward.

Each day around noon the cooks slopped a few dozen dead rats, still slick and glistening from the drowning pots, onto the ground outside the ring. That was the only food. Valyn tried to force the meat down, ripping out the liver and heart, cracking the slender bones for the marrow while blood and viscera coated his already filthy fingers. The first day, he vomited it all back up. He cursed himself all night as his gut gnawed at itself angrily, impotently. The next day, he ate everything, even the eyes and soft putty of the brain, and he kept it down.

Like ghosts or apparitions, the trainers were everywhere, looming above the groveling cadets, alternately ridiculing their efforts and extending the soft, treacherous hand of relief.

"You don't have to do this," the Flea murmured to Valyn at some point on the fourth day, leaning over him as he tried to haul a huge barrel of sand up out of the surf. "I'll tell you, kid—you think this is bad? It only gets worse."

Valyn growled something cross and incomprehensible, even to himself, and kept pushing the barrel.

"Son of an Emperor," the man mused. "Lot of options for you. Maybe you don't even need to go to Arin. We could make an exception. Why don't you call it a day? We'll get you cleaned up. Set you up on a fast ship home. No shame in it."

"Piss. Off," Valyn snarled, yanking the recalcitrant barrel furiously, freeing it from the wet, sucking sand, then throwing his weight behind it as he struggled up the dunes. The Flea chuckled, but he went away.

Not all of the cadets resisted. The pain and exhaustion mounted every day, every hour, every minute, until it seemed that the sun had ground to a halt in its course through the heavens and the unbearable suffering would go on forever, longer than forever, an eternity of misery devised by Meshkent himself. The verdant shore of Arin beckoned, a paradise of leisure and ease to be had just by . . . stopping, by giving up. Valyn finally understood the true genius of the offer. Put a man's back to the wall, and he's got no choice but to fight; offer him a comfortable retirement before the age of twenty, and you learn who's committed to the cause. Valyn watched with a pang of exhausted envy as one, then two, then six cadets abandoned the Trial, gave themselves up to the quiet blandishments of the trainers.

Don't even think about it, he muttered to himself, straining to lug yet another sand-filled barrel out of the sea. Whatever the Flea claimed, failure meant Arin, Arin meant never leaving the Islands, and that meant leaving Kaden and Adare vulnerable, Amie and Ha Lin unavenged. *Don't even* dream *about it.*

On the fifth day, he found himself next to Gwenna, both of them harnessed like oxen to a large cart filled with small boulders. Jakob Rallen, the Master of Cadets, sat perched atop the pile, a whip in his right hand.

"Onward, mules!" he shouted in that shrill voice of his, cracking the whip close enough to Valyn's ear that it drew blood. "Onward."

Gwenna glanced over. Half her face had purpled with a vicious bruise, but there was no surrender in those green eyes. "On three?" she gasped, leaning forward to brace herself against the halter.

"What if we just strangled him with the whip and called it a day?" Valyn asked, forcing his weight against the collar, driving with his legs until the whole wagon creaked reluctantly into motion. The whip came down again, this time nicking Gwenna's cheek.

"Strangling's not my style," she replied. She was a head shorter than Valyn, but she was strong, and with the two of them hauling the cart, it slowly gained speed, jolting over the rocky ground.

"How 'bout a flickwick in his bed?" Valyn gasped, heaving air into his ragged lungs as he strained against the traces.

"Too quick. Plus, a slob like him—we'd be scraping gobbets of fat off the ceiling."

Valyn grinned in spite of the pain. "What if we toss him out of the cart and drag the thing over him?"

"I'll follow your lead, oh my prince," Gwenna replied before another crack of the whip silenced both of them.

He caught occasional glimpses of Ha Lin. On the third day, he managed to watch her briefly as she swam the harbor, dragging a barge behind her, her face a rictus of determination. He wanted to call out, to offer some encouragement, but it was all he could do to stand, and she was clearly past hearing anything but the salt waves sloshing in her ears. He tried to linger, to wait for her to reach the breakwater, but one of the trainers drove a hard fist into his kidney and sent him stumbling off down the rocks for yet another torturous circuit of the coast.

Each evening, the grinding midday sun bled into the horizon, and Valyn struggled on in darkness, shivering and chattering in the waves, his mind worn to a dull nub, his body depleted past pain, past suffering, into dead, leaden numbness.

At some point on what he thought was the sixth day, he found himself side by side in the surf with Laith, the two of them wrestling a swamped smallboat up out of the waves.

"Pull," Valyn urged him, straining at the ropes himself until he thought his tendons would tear. *"Pull!"*

"If you tell me to pull one more time," Laith responded breathlessly, hauling for all he was worth, "I am going to put down these ropes and bash the nose into your royal face."

Valyn had no idea if it was a joke or not. The other cadet certainly sounded serious, but after six days of dead rat and endless agony, he didn't care. "Pull!" he shouted again, bursting into helpless laughter. Some dim, lost part of him recognized the insanity in the sound, but it was powerless to stop it. *"Pull, you fucker!"* he screamed.

Laith bellowed right back at him, words as crazed and desperate as his own, and together they dragged that boat up onto the shingle only to be told to dump it, right it, and then swim it out to the ship swinging at anchor a mile offshore.

Valyn was convinced during that swim that he was going to die. His heart had never hammered so hard inside his chest. He felt like every breath was bringing up blood and lung, and when he spat into the waves, he saw pink flecking the foam. It was possible, he knew, for the body to simply quit. Cadets had died of burst hearts before, their bodies battered, then broken under the physical strain. *Fine,* he panted to himself, towing the recalcitrant boat through the waves toward that ship that never seemed to grow any closer. *This is a fine place to die.*

When he heaved himself onto the deck at last, the Flea and Adaman Fane were there, scowling and shouting something Valyn couldn't understand. What were the words? He peered around blearily for something to haul, to hit, to hurt, but there was nothing, just the wide expanse of scrubbed deck. As he stared in stupefaction, the words started to penetrate, like water dripping through a poorly thatched roof.

". . . you hear me, you idiot?" Fane was shouting, waving a thick finger at him from a few feet away. "You're done, at least for now. I suggest you hit the deck and get a few hours' sleep."

Valyn stared, his jaw slack. Then his legs collapsed beneath him and he fell into stunned, desperate darkness.

23

Three hours wasn't much sleep, not even by Kettral standards, but after seven unrelenting days and nights, each more brutal than the one before, Valyn fell to the hard deck of the ship that would take them to Irsk, the most remote of the Qirin chain, as if the planks were a feather mattress, slept a blank sleep with no dreams, and woke only when an ungentle boot gouged into his ribs. He rolled to his feet, baffled and disoriented, but groping for his belt knife all the same, trying desperately to remember where he was, to find his footing on the rolling deck, to ready himself for a continuation of the suffering that had become his life.

"You've got an hour before we make land." It was Chent Rall, a short veteran built like a bulldog with a personality to match. "I suggest you use it to get below and stuff down some chow."

"Chow?" Valyn repeated dumbly, trying to shake the fog from his head. All around him, the other trainers were rousting their charges from where they had dropped like dead men to the deck. The ship was rolling softly with the swells, her masts creaking as the boat heeled to port, running before a decent southerly wind.

"Yeah, chow," Rall repeated. "The stuff you put in your mouth. The good news is: you're done eating rat. The bad news is, after this you might be done eating, period. Not a lot to munch on down in the Hole."

Valyn didn't know what the man was talking about, but there was a gravity to that last word, a menace.

"What's the hole?"

"You'll find out soon enough. You want to eat, or you want to chat?"

Valyn's stomach rumbled angrily and he nodded. He had no idea what lay ahead, but, as Hendran wrote, *A choice between tactics and food is no choice at all. A soldier cannot live on tactics. He cannot improvise food.*

The vessel's tiny galley was a madness of clutching hands, raised voices, and the stench of unwashed bodies as twenty-one starving cadets jostled one another to shove the steaming food into their mouths. It wasn't much—bean stew, a couple trenchers of diced meat—but it was warm and, more important, it wasn't rat. Along with everyone else, Valyn shoveled up great handfuls and stuffed it into his mouth, wary that this apparent kindness, like so many others during the week, would prove a trap.

Someone touched his shoulder and he spun around, raising his fists, to find himself looking into Ha Lin's eyes. She had always been slender, but the exertions of the past days had rendered her positively skeletal. One of her eyes had swollen shut, and the skin surrounding it faded from purple to a jaundiced yellow. Someone or something had opened a new gash across her forehead, one deep enough to leave a nasty scar.

"Eira's mercy, Lin," he gasped, choking on the water he had been gulping down.

She grimaced. "Save it. We're all beaten up."

That was true enough. Just in the course of grubbing his meager share of food, Valyn had seen broken fingers, busted noses, and newly missing teeth. His own third rib stabbed into him at every breath, and he had a suspicion he'd snapped it, but no idea when, or how. He'd always thought the veterans acquired their scars flying actual missions, but he was starting to wonder if they took the worst of their beatings during the Trial.

"How was it?" he asked, struggling to find the right words. "The last week, I mean."

"Terrible," she responded flatly, "just the way they planned it."

"Are you all right?"

"I'm here, aren't I? You don't see me on a ship to Arin." There was something of the old steel back in her voice.

"Of course not. But you look—" He put a hand on her arm. It was thin as a stick. "How are you holding up?"

"I'm fine."

"Listen . . . ," he began, leaning closer, trying to achieve some kind of privacy in the hopeless tangle of bodies and voices.

"Not now, Valyn. I didn't come over here to be fussed over and mothered. I wanted to tell you to watch yourself in whatever's coming next. Watch Yurl."

"I'll do more than watch him, if I have the chance." The words came out sounding like bluster, but Valyn meant every one of them. Training was dangerous by its very nature, and the Trial even more so. Accidents could happen, could be *made* to happen.

Lin stared at him, a smile haunting her lips, then gone. "That cuts both ways," she hissed. "He'll be out there looking for you, too, and he's got a lot fewer scruples." She lowered her voice and glanced back over her shoulder before continuing. "There's something I need to tell you. Back on the bluffs, when they beat the living shit out of me, I got in a few shots of my own. If you *do* come up against Yurl, his left ankle—" She shook her head, suddenly hesitant. "I can't be sure—he seemed all right this past week—but I think I felt something pull, one of the tendons. You remember when Gent busted his ankle in the arena four years back? No one noticed. He could run and fight, but then in that swamp extract, he twisted it the wrong way and . . . snap."

Valyn nodded. Gent had been furious with the injury, refusing for months to give it the requisite rest, insisting to everyone that it was "fucking fine."

"Yurl might have some weakness there," Lin continued, grimacing with uncertainty. "I don't know. Diminished lateral motion, maybe. Maybe weakness at certain angles . . . something you could work with, anyway, if you find yourself in a tight spot."

Valyn considered his friend. As Hendran wrote in his chapter on morale, *There's a big gap between beaten, and broken.* Yurl and Balendin had taken something from Ha Lin up on the West Bluffs—her pride, her confidence—but the fight was still there. It would take a lot more to wash away her grit.

"He's not going to get away with it, Lin," Valyn said, putting a hand on her shoulder.

"No," she agreed, squeezing his arm, smile widening. "He isn't." Then, before he could manage another word, she turned back, and he lost her in the press of bodies.

┼

Valyn had never set foot on Irsk; the island was off-limits to cadets. He'd seen it from ships, however, and from the air during flight training, barrel drops, and the like. Unlike the other islands in the chain, all of which could boast some vegetation and fresh running water, Irsk was a grim place, all black limestone cliffs and jagged coast, rising abruptly from the water like a fist of hard stone. It was barely half a mile across, too small to support any life aside from the gulls and terns that nested all over the crags. Valyn had never realized that the island played any role in the Trial, and once he'd stepped out of the smallboat and onto a rocky promontory that served as a natural wharf, he looked around, a nagging splinter of worry gouging at him as he followed the others inland.

A narrow path threaded through the jutting rock, pressing ever higher until it spilled into a rough bowl, maybe thirty paces across, at what Valyn took to be the island's center. Cliffs rose in a circle around them, steep as the walls of an amphitheater. Above them, the gulls circled, shrieking in anger at having been driven from their nests. Valyn, however, like the rest of the cadets, had eyes only for the stout steel cage in the center of the bowl, its iron footings sunk into the rock itself. Beside it stood an old man, hair thin and gray, body trembling with fatigue or exertion. Or fear. There was plenty for him to be frightened of. The cage, not four feet from where he stood, contained two creatures that Valyn could only describe as monsters.

"These are slarn," Daveen Shaleel began, stepping forward once everyone had assembled and gesturing to the beasts inside the cage. "Both maidens. About six years old and a third their mature weight."

Valyn stared. So did everyone else.

Referring to the creatures as *maidens* seemed like some sort of grotesque joke. They looked more like nightmares, five feet of sinuous, reptilian flesh and scale ending in a mouth filled with razor teeth. Their skin glistened the sickening, translucent white of shattered eggs or rotted fish bellies, a web of blue and purple veins snaking beneath the surface. He was reminded of the flayed corpses he had studied on the Islands years before, only these creatures were very much alive, prowling around the small cage on short, powerful legs tipped with savage-looking claws.

"I must have misheard you," Laith began. He was standing a few feet from Valyn and tilted an ear toward Shaleel as though to catch her words more carefully. "I thought you said these were only the kids."

"They are," the woman replied. "Much easier to handle than the full wives and concubines."

"They look about as easy to handle," Laith said, eyeing the cage with a dismayed frown, "as a pile of greased eel shit on a marble floor."

"They'll die like anything else," Gwenna said, hefting a short blade, "just as long as you hit 'em hard enough."

"Maidens," Annick said flatly, fingering her bow as she spoke. "Concubines. Wives. What about the males?"

Shaleel shook her head. "There are no males. Or, to be more precise, there's only one. Just as there are thousands of soldier ants to a single queen, there are thousands of wives, maidens, and concubines to a single slarn king."

"Makes me rethink my positive opinion of harems," Laith said, eyeing the circling creatures with a mixture of interest and distaste. "The king must be a big, old ugly bastard to keep this lot in line."

"We don't know," Shaleel replied. "We've never come across the king."

"Where are they from?" Valyn asked, glancing around him. The island didn't look like it could support *one* slarn, let alone thousands.

"Here," Shaleel said, extending a hand down, toward the earth. "There's a network of caves beneath Irsk, dozens of miles of caves. The slarn live there. That's where Hull's Trial takes place."

The cadets drew in a collective breath. They'd all seen caves—Kettral training covered just about every type of terrain conceivable. The vast majority of their time, however, had been spent on the ocean, in the air, struggling through the mangroves or laboring around the beaches of Qarsh. The thought of descending into a maze of passageways buried beneath hundreds of thousands of tons of stone and sea, passageways stocked with monsters like the slarn, was more than a little unsettling.

"They don't have eyes," Annick said.

Valyn peered closer. The creatures had been turned away from him when he first stepped into the bowl, but now he saw that the sniper was right. At the front of the face, where the eyes should have been, there was only a swath of translucent skin, white as curdled milk.

"No need for eyes in the darkness," Valyn realized, speaking the words aloud as they came to him.

"I notice that they more than make up for it in teeth," Laith quipped, baring his own incisors. "Those things are as long as my belt knife."

"They're also poison," Shaleel put in. "Paralytic."

"Deadly?" Annick asked without taking her eyes from the slarn.

"Not for humans. The slarn mostly hunt smaller game, seafowl that wander into the cave, other subterranean creatures."

"What's the recovery time?"

Shaleel shook her head grimly. "Never.

"Carl," the woman continued, gesturing to the gray-haired man trembling beside the cage, largely forgotten in the flurry of questions about the slarn. "Please step forward."

The man shuffled a pace forward and stood unsteadily, his limbs racked with spasms.

"Carl once stood where you stand today."

It was hard to tell if Carl nodded or not, his head was twitching so badly. Yellow, watery eyes rolled from side to side in their sockets. The skin around his mouth hung slack, revealing loose, decaying teeth. His lips turned up in something that might have been a grin, but the expression seemed forced and unwilling, as though his face had rebelled against his mind.

"Do you remember the day, Carl?" Shaleel asked, not ungently.

"I d-d-do . . . ," the man stammered, biting down on the end of the word as though to keep the unruly syllables clamped inside his mouth.

"Carl was a good cadet. Fast. Strong. Smart. Just like all of you." She fixed them with that low, steady stare.

"He doesn't look so smart," Yurl cracked. He stepped forward, feinting a punch toward the shaking man's stomach. Carl took an uncertain step back, stumbled, and almost fell.

As Yurl shook his head in disgust, he turned to find himself looking at the Flea, who had slid up silently through the crowd. The trainer was shorter than Yurl by a head and older by at least twenty years, gnarled and pockmarked where the youth was clean-limbed and handsome. None of that seemed to bother him in the slightest. He took Yurl by the elbow with one hand and guided him back toward the assembled cadets.

"You will show respect," he said quietly, but not so quietly that the others failed to hear, "or you will spend your life envying Carl."

Yurl jerked his arm away. The Flea, for his part, just watched him the way a weary peasant might watch his own hearth, face flat and unreadable. He didn't look like much, didn't look like any iron-cold killer of men, but on the Islands, where everyone was hard as nails and awe was about as common as ineptitude, all the soldiers, even veterans, seemed to stand in something like awe of the Flea. After a tense moment Yurl shut his mouth, turned on his heel, and stepped back.

Shaleel watched the scene unfold with a small frown on her face, then nodded. "I was just about to ask Carl how old he is." She turned back to the former cadet. "How old are you, Carl?"

"Thir-thir-thirty-eight," the man managed, nodding convulsively as he spoke.

Valyn considered the man more closely. Carl was a human husk, all tendon and peeling skin. Wrinkles creased his face, and his thin gray hair barely covered his scalp. He looked closer to eighty than forty.

"Thirty-eight years old," Shaleel repeated, her voice clear and hard where the man's had quavered. "At thirty-eight, any Kettral still on Qarsh could run the perimeter of the island a half dozen times and then spend the night swimming it. Most of your trainers are older than thirty-eight. Carl, however, has trouble walking up a flight of stairs. We take care of him, of course. He has a beautiful house on Arin, overlooking the bay, and a slave to look after him, day and night. What he doesn't have is his health. That was taken from him years ago, and that's why he's here today. We don't *ask* him to come here to warn you; *he* asks *us*." She returned her attention to Carl. "Go ahead. Tell the cadets what happened to you."

The man gaped at the small crowd as though baffled, his jaw working futilely, a small string of spittle oozing from the side of his mouth. Valyn wondered if he had even heard Shaleel, but then he turned and lifted a wavering hand, pointing one crooked finger directly through the bars of the cage.

"S-s-slarn hap-hap-happened."

A chill silence descended over the group.

"So we're going down into the cave," Annick said finally. "We have to fight these things. If they bite us, we end up like him."

"Just a matter of not getting bitten," Yurl said, brushing his blond hair back from his eyes ostentatiously. "Shouldn't be too tough for anyone competent."

Shaleel chuckled mirthlessly. "Oh, they're *going* to bite you," she replied. "That's why Fane and the Flea went to all the trouble to haul these two out of Hull's Hole. We make *sure* they bite you. You're poisoned before you even go into the Hole. It's *why* you go into the Hole."

For a long while the cadets just stared.

"An antidote," Valyn said at last. There must be something in the caves that would serve as an antidote to the poison.

Shaleel nodded. "The slarn wives have nests scattered all through the caves. In some of those nests are eggs, milk-white things about the size of my fist. Whatever's in the egg guards the hatchlings against the toxins of their mothers. You find an egg, eat it, and get out—you're all cured; you're Kettral."

"And if not," Laith concluded, jerking a finger at the gray-haired wreck of a man, "we're Carl."

"That's right. Some of you will end up on Arin either way. It's your choice whether you go now, get right back on that ship, and leave with your mind and body intact, or if you go down there, into the Hole, and maybe come out shattered."

She paused and stared out over the group. A few cadets shuffled their feet. Balendin opened his mouth, as though to ask a question, then shook his head and shut it once more. Annick was all business, stringing her bow, although what use that would be in the winding passages of the cavern Valyn had no idea. Talal seemed to be praying quietly. No one stepped forward. Evidently the rigors of the previous week had weeded out all those whose determination fell short of the necessary mark.

Shaleel nodded. "You will have about a day once you've been bitten before the damage becomes incurable. Find an egg in that time and find your way back to the surface. There should be enough for all of you, but some will be easier to find than others. You may work in pairs, teams, or alone. You may even work against each other, although given the nature of the Hole, I don't recommend it. Fane will give each of you a torch. It will provide about ten hours of light."

"Ten hours is less than a day," Yurl protested.

"You're very astute. This is, after all, known as Hull's Trial."

The cadets took a moment to digest that piece of information.

"Anything else we ought to know about this 'Kent-kissing cave?" Gwenna demanded at last. She sounded angry rather than scared.

The very corner of Shaleel's mouth turned up. "It's dark."

24

Dark" was an understatement. Nights were dark. Cellars were dark. The holds of ships were dark. The cave beneath Irsk, on the other hand, plunged everything into an inky blackness so perfect, so absolute, that Valyn could well believe the world itself had vanished and that he crept forward in a vast, unending void with no up or down, no beginning or end. It was no wonder that Hull's Trial took place here. If the Lord of Darkness himself had chosen a palace, a seat for his empire of blindness, the tortuous twists and turns of the Hole would be entirely appropriate.

In addition to the darkness, there was pain. A hundred scrapes, cuts, and lacerations from the previous week burned with their tiny, invisible fires, while the ache of muscles beaten past exhaustion harried him at each step. There was pain behind his eyes, pain in his ribs when he breathed, and beneath it all, the ache of the slarn wound, a cold acid gnawing at the flesh of his forearm, singeing the skin and eating into the tissue beneath. The trainers had summoned their charges one by one, barking a name, then gesturing curtly toward the cage. It was up to each cadet to thrust his arm through the bars, to hold it there while the slarn gaped wide its jaws, and then to extricate himself while the creature tore at his limb, thrashing its horrible eyeless head back and forth. According to Shaleel, the fire coursing beneath his skin would grow, would spread, would burn brighter and brighter, hotter and hotter, until it reached his heart. By then, it would be too late.

He'd lost track of the labyrinthine twists and turns within the first hour. Aboveground he had a good sense of direction, but then, aboveground there were dozens of miniscule cues: the sun in your eyes, the breeze in your hair, the feel of the turf beneath your feet. Here there was nothing but sharp corners, slick rock, and darkness. He'd considered lighting his torch a hundred times and a hundred times had thrust down the urge. He was lost already and besides, he would need the light to find the eggs. The slarn nested far beneath the surface, and it seemed better to keep pressing deeper without the torch and to use the light later, when he really needed it.

Of course, "later" was a baffling term in the Hole. With no sun or stars, no bell, no ebb of the tides, it was impossible to gauge the passage of time. He tried counting his footsteps, but exhaustion from the previous week had claimed him once more; it was all he could do to get to a hundred without losing track, and he quickly abandoned count of the hundreds. The only progress he could follow was the ache of the slarn bite as it crept up his arm past his elbow, ice and acid swamping his veins. That was appropriate, he realized. After all, the sun didn't matter anymore. The tide didn't matter. The human habits and rituals upon which he had structured his life were distant and useless as the invisible stars. What mattered was the pain and the spread of that pain. The ache was the only hourglass.

Maybe this is what they want us to learn, he thought to himself blearily. *There are two worlds, one of life and one of darkness, and you cannot inhabit both.* It seemed like a good lesson for a Kettral, a lesson that could never be learned on the earth itself, not in a thousand days of swordplay and barrel drops, the kind of lesson that had to be bleached into the bone.

"A world of life and a world of darkness," Valyn muttered to himself, dimly aware that he was growing delirious. There was nothing to do about it, nothing but press on into the very belly of the earth, down, down, endlessly down, past forks and branches, wading waist deep in subterranean rivers, clambering over ledges and shelves, walking sometimes, sometimes crawling until his knees and his palms were sticky with blood.

He waited for the pain of the slarn wound to creep toward his shoulder, deadening the entire arm, before he paused, struggled briefly with flint and tinder, then lit the torch. The dancing flame seared his eyes and he squeezed them shut tight for a long time, then opened them slowly, peering carefully through slitted lids.

He stood in a narrow passageway, the floor uneven, the ceiling low and jagged. Tunnels snaked away on either side, gaping mouths down into the earth. He had thought the slickness on the walls was water dripping from the roof of the cavern, but he realized with a shudder of revulsion that it seemed to be some sort of slime, white as an uncooked egg, pale and stringy. The darkness had been frightening, but actually looking at the place was like waking to find the walls of a prison built around you while you slept. *Who'd have thought,* he wondered wearily, *that the darkness was the fucking* good *part?*

There was no sign of the other cadets. With all the branches and forks, it seemed entirely possible that he could wander in the catacombs for days without seeing another human being. That was fine, as long as he could find the nests.

"You're not going to do that standing here staring at the wall," he mumbled to himself, forcing his legs into motion once more.

He almost stepped over the first nest without realizing it. The twisted mess of slime and shattered stone didn't look like any sort of nest one would find in the outside world, but then, the slarn had nothing to work with but the rock around them. There was some kind of bird, Valyn remembered vaguely, a bird that built nests out of its own spit or vomit. He couldn't remember which. It seemed appropriate, somehow, for a creature to cough up its own being to protect its young. Appropriate and awful.

He thrust the torch into the nest, trembling with a combination of eagerness, exhaustion, and the poison that scraped at his veins. He thought, at first, that he'd found an egg, and he laughed out loud until he realized he was looking at a shattered shell. Someone had been here before him. That, or the creature had hatched, was even now crawling through the darkness with a thousand others, growing, hunting, prowling the tunnels for food.

He swung the torch behind him in a broad, blazing arc. He hadn't seen any slarn, but that didn't mean they weren't out there. He had no idea how the creatures hunted. Were they like wolves, harrying their prey until it dropped? Or like the great cats of the Ancaz Mountains, silent, invisible, waiting for their moment before the final strike? He held the light high above him and, with his free hand, loosed a blade from its sheath across his back. As Gwenna said, everything dies if you hit it hard enough.

The next four nests were all the same: empty, or littered with shards of pale white shell. At each one, Valyn felt his hopes flare up only to be doused by a wave of bitter disappointment, thick with the inky taste of fear. The burn from the poison had crept into his shoulder blade, and he tried to calculate what that meant. Shaleel had said a day for the toxin to migrate from the wound in his forearm to his heart. Assuming it moved at a steady pace, that meant he'd been beneath the earth around three quarters of a day. It seemed like no more than an hour. It felt like years.

The slarn found him after the fifth nest. He was so busy checking that they almost caught him unaware, three of them, swarming out of the darkness, sinuous and silent. Valyn glimpsed them out of the corner of his eye and spun, his body dropping instinctively into a low slicing attack that caught the leading creature across the head. The thing let out a piercing shriek, twisting in on itself like a salted slug, gnashing blindly at the air with those awful teeth and recoiling into the shadow. The other two drew back, cocked their heads to the side, and seemed to hesitate. Then they drifted apart, creeping around to come at him from two different directions at once.

Valyn didn't know a 'Kent-kissing thing about slarn, but he'd spent enough hours in the ring to dislike what was happening. They looked like brutal, mindless beasts, but they were working in concert, coordinating their angles of attack. He leveled the torch at one and his short blade at the other. He knew how to handle two assailants, but he didn't have to like it. With small, careful steps, he backed toward the wall of the low cavern. As long as he could keep them both in—

The left-hand slarn came at him in a flash of jaws and raking talons, and the second followed a quarter heartbeat after, the motion of both almost too fast to follow. With a roar, Valyn abandoned himself to his years of training, gave up all effort at thought or planning, and let his body move through the forms hammered into it over a thousand dusty hours in the ring. He dived to the right, rolled beneath the leaping creature while slashing upward blindly. The blade hacked deep into the flesh of the belly, lodged there, and twisted free of his grip. He let it go and doubled his grip on the torch as he regained his feet, holding it out in front of him like a broadblade.

The wounded slarn was shrieking a terrible, keening cry, dragging itself in aimless circles while loops of intestine sagged from the long, deep wound. The other creature turned on it and, with a savage snap of its jaws, bit straight through the neck, cutting off the movement and the sound at once. It shook the blood and venom free of its jaws with a flick of its head, then turned that awful eyeless face back to Valyn.

"So you're the smart one," he said quietly. "You're the survivor."

The slarn's head weaved to the right on its unnaturally long neck, then back to the left, serpentine and predatory all at once. A human foe would have broken and run after finding two of its companions cut down in as many minutes, but it was hard to imagine anything less human than the slarn. Its tongue flicked out, tasting the air, and it shifted slowly to its left. It was waiting for something, choosing its moment. Valyn didn't care for that one bit.

"You're not the only one knows how to attack," he spat, and hurled his torch directly at the beast's head. He had no idea how a blind creature could even see the thing coming, let alone react so fast, but it snapped the wood out of the air with a smooth movement, and tossed it to the side. He hadn't expected that, but then, the Kettral held a somewhat bleak notion of expectations. *Planning for what you want,* the Flea used to say, *is a good way to end up dead.* In the space of time it took the slarn to fling aside the torch, Valyn had charged forward and snatched his fallen sword from the belly of the felled beast. As the remaining creature turned to face him, he was already driving the bright blade down in a hard Manjari thrust, straight through the skull, pinning the jaw shut and slamming the whole head to the rock.

The slarn spasmed for a few heartbeats, so powerfully that Valyn thought it was still alive, then went abruptly slack. With a shudder of exhaustion, he wrenched his blade from the thing's skull, then wiped it carefully across the milky white carcass. As always after a fight, the blood pounded in his ears and his lungs felt as though someone had scoured them with sand. He had no idea how long the skirmish had lasted, but his chest was aching with the toxin now, and even once he picked up the torch, the cavern seemed dim. He had won the battle, he realized grimly, but he was losing the Trial. It didn't matter how many slarn he killed if he failed to find their eggs. How much time left? An hour? Maybe two? Torch high above him, sword held out in front, he forged deeper into the tunnels.

The full hunting pack caught up with him in a huge chamber bordered by a deep, swift river. He'd been searching behind a sharp tooth of rock and turned to find them flowing into the space, three, five, a full dozen at least, jaws hanging open, pale, eyeless faces bright in the shadow. Valyn's stomach turned to lead even as he raised his blade. Three had been hard enough, but twelve . . . even at his best, it was too many, and he was far from at his best. His hand had begun to tremble and his legs felt too weak to keep him up. He'd be lucky to fight one of the 'Kent-kissing things in this condition.

With uneven steps, he backed toward the dark, rushing water. There was nowhere to make a stand, nowhere to run. He risked a glance over his shoulder. The stream was flowing fast and hard, skirting the cavern for a hundred paces before plunging into a dark maw of stone. There was nothing that way but darkness and death, but the slarn were filling the room. *When faced with certain annihilation,* Hendran wrote, *delay. To the doomed man, any future is a friend.*

"All right, Hull," Valyn said, sliding his blade back into his sheath and readying his grip on the torch. "Let's make a real Trial out of it." He filled his lungs with air and leapt for the river.

The current caught him in strong, icy fingers and dragged him under, snuffing the light, plunging him into watery blackness. He struggled to right himself, then realized it didn't matter, and brought the doused torch up with two hands to protect his face. The river was even stronger than it had appeared. It roared in his ears, dragged him along over smoothed stone, threatened to dash him against hidden rocks, all the while plunging him deeper, deeper into the belly of the earth.

Stars began to fill his vision, light where there should be no light. Valyn realized with a strange sort of quiescence that he had chosen wrong, had embraced a cold, dark death miles from anyone he knew. The thought should have both angered and terrified him, but the water on his skin cooled the burning in his lungs, and the darkness wrapped itself around him almost gently. He wanted to see Ha Lin one last time, to tell her he was sorry, to tell her just how much her constant presence had buttressed and steadied him, but she had taken a different passage. *I should have taken a different passage, too,* he thought idly to himself.

Just as his breath was about to give out, the ceiling of the tunnel relented. He burst to the surface, heaving in deep, labored lungfuls of air. The shock of life hit him like a slap, and after a mindless moment when all he could do was thrash and gulp in the sweet damp air, he fell back into an exhausted float, staring up into darkness. He could see no more here than he had on the other side of the underwater passage, but the current had vanished, and he realized as he groped for the walls on either side that he was in a channel no longer. He took several strokes, then several more, then struck his knee against an underwater shelf. With the weight of his waterlogged blacks pulling him down, back toward the death he had so recently escaped, he pulled himself from the pool and onto a wide stone ledge.

As soon as he regained his breath, he realized something was wrong. He could feel it—the poison—raking at his heart, talons of thin, invisible fire.

"No," he groaned, rolling onto his side, clutching his torch with trembling hands. "Not yet."

It took him a dozen tries to light it. His arms felt like lead weights, his lungs wheezed against his chest, and he couldn't concentrate on the simple striking action of flint against steel. The torch was pitch-soaked, and the flint would make a spark, even wet, but he couldn't seem to focus on the task.

"Come on, Hull," he begged as the torch finally caught fire, tossing its flickering light onto dull stone and glinting quartz. "Just a few minutes more."

With a staggering effort he dragged himself to his knees, panting desperately, then to his feet. The cavern was huge, twice again the size of anything he'd yet encountered, as high as the Temple of Light, back in Annur. Great teeth of stone thrust up from the floor, hung from the ceiling, some joining into huge pillars wider than his arms could span. The place felt like the gullet of some massive beast, heavy, not just with the unfathomable weight of stone, but with a cold, brooding malice.

Valyn stared blearily about him, took a few steps toward a low ledge, stumbled, then forced himself up again. There was something there, something . . . a nest! It was larger than the rest, much larger, but the combination of stone and calcified slime was the same as everywhere else. Stomach heaving, hands shaking, mind reeling, he staggered forward, tossed the torch onto the bare stone, and dropped to his knees before it. *Please, Hull,* he thought, with the part of him that could still think, *let it not be too late.*

He groped blindly into the nest, felt his hands close around an egg, a *huge* egg, and lifted it out. He stared. Unlike the other slarn spawn, it was black, black as pitch, and almost the size of his head.

"What?" he mumbled, clutching it before him as a starving man might hold a rotten shank of meat. "It's not white. . . ."

Was it slarn? The walls of the cavern seemed to be flexing around him. A low grating rasped at his ears. From what seemed like another world, another *life* in which he had lived under the sun, and his body had obeyed, a life in which other people had cared for him, had tried to help him, the Flea's voice filled his head: *When you've only got one choice, you can bitch and moan, or you can draw your blade and start swinging.*

"All right, Hull," Valyn snarled, fumbling his belt knife free of its sheath and plunging it into the shell. The albumen of the egg spurted forth, thick as tar between his fingers and stinking of stone and bile. "I guess it's time for a drink now, just you and me."

He raised the shell in both hands above his head like a chalice, then brought it to his lips and tilted it back, his gorge rising even as he gulped down the slick, stinking liquid, gulped it and swallowed, tilting the egg until the black ooze ran down his chin, down the front of his shirt, down his throat, heavy as oil as it filled his stomach. He paused, gasping, savagely wrestled down the urge to vomit, to pour his guts out on the floor, then forced the shell to his lips once more, sobbing mindlessly as he did, slurping and struggling, the slime thick as marrow in his throat.

When there was no more to be had, he collapsed backward, his head against the nest, heart struggling to leap from his chest, skin ablaze, mind a bright spike of pain. Moaning filled his ears, a terrible, wounded sound. He tried to shut it out before he realized that it was coming from his own lips. He curled into a ball, his knees to his chest, while his stomach rolled and seized. This was death, he realized, this was what death felt like, and he squeezed his eyes closed and wished it would hurry up.

After a time—he had no idea how long—he realized the moaning had stopped. His stomach still kicked, but he could straighten out, could sit up. He eased himself back against the wall, then raised a hand, stained splotchy black with the remnants of the egg. He had dropped his torch. It lay on the cold stone a few feet away, still burning. He tried to remember what Shaleel said before she sent them down into the Hole, tried to guess how long he had stumbled in darkness before finding the egg. Pain still gouged at his forearm, but it was the bright pain of an honest wound, not the sick, gnawing burning from before. He took a tentative breath, then a deeper one. His heart seemed to have calmed itself. Once again he considered his black and sticky hand. The feeble torchlight danced across his outstretched arm and fingers, flickering and enigmatic. The light moved, but the hand was steady. For what seemed like the first time in his life, he smiled.

"Hull," he said, saluting the shadows of the hall. "If you're listening—next round's on me."

And then, as though the darkness itself had heard him, the cavern roared.

Valyn stumbled to his feet, snatched up the rapidly dwindling torch, and wrenched a short blade from its sheath. Slarn didn't make that sort of sound, at least not the slarn he'd encountered. *Nothing* made that sort of sound. The bellow came again, a hideous roar of rage and hunger that echoed off the hard stone walls, filling Valyn's brain, reverberating inside his skull. He forced his legs into motion, lurched toward the nearest passageway a dozen paces distant. Again the roar. Closer this time. Valyn risked a glance over his shoulder and glimpsed, in the distant recess of the cavern, in the fickle penumbra of the torch, a monster carved straight from the bloody dark of nightmare: scales, talons, teeth, all black as smoke steel, a dozen unnatural joints flexing in the shadow. And the *size* of it . . . It made the slarn he'd fought in the tunnels above look like puppies.

The king, he realized, dread lurching in his stomach. The underground river had dragged him to the lair of the 'Kent-kissing king. Without another thought, he turned toward the tunnel, praying desperately it was too small for the monster to follow, and fled blindly into the labyrinth.

†

By the time the torch guttered, flickered, then failed, Valyn knew he was getting close to the surface. He'd been climbing for what seemed like hours, always following the upward path whenever there was a choice. Also there was a tang to the air, the faintest hint of sea salt. He hadn't noticed it when he descended, but now, as he approached the sun, and sky, and freedom, he flicked out his tongue, tasting it.

Without the torch, the blackness swallowed him once more, just as he had been dreading. To his surprise, however, the absolute pitch no longer seemed quite so terrifying. Rather than an infinite void in which he was destined to wander forever, it felt more like a blanket, still, and soft, and familiar. He paused, trying to get his bearings, and realized he could feel faint hints of movement in the still air, echoes of hints of breezes, the memory of a dream of wind, tickling the hairs on his neck and arms. As he worked his way down the passage, he found that he could anticipate the side corridors, could almost see them in his mind, invisible tunnels of draft snaking away into the blankness.

"Stay down here long enough," he muttered to himself, "and you might come to like the place."

As he climbed, the scent of salt grew stronger in his nose. He thought he could even hear the reverberating crash of waves at points, although that was impossible. *Holy Hull,* he realized, a smile creasing his face, *you made it. You're* Kettral *now.* Of course, he'd have to avoid the other slarn. Avoid them or kill them. The prospect seemed less daunting, however, now that he had purged his veins of the throbbing toxin, now that he was moving steadily toward the surface of the Hole, rather than deeper into the blackness. Hadn't he already killed three of the bastards? *And half-crazed while I was about it.*

A slight flicker in the draft brought him up short. There was something toppled across the tunnel, he realized, something impeding the natural flow of air. He knelt carefully and reached out. So close to the end, so close to victory, he didn't want to break his arm crashing over a pile of rubble. He imagined Lin grinning at him, and Laith, and Gent. Shit, after what he'd been through, he'd even be happy to see Gwenna. Surely they'd made it through as well. Surely they'd found a way to survive.

His fingers came up against something soft, something giving. *Cloth,* he realized, running his hand along it. Then, with growing unease: *A body.*

In a few moments he'd found the neck and fitted his fingers to the artery. The skin was cold and clammy. No pulse. Fear mounting inside him, Valyn found the mouth, put his cheek right to the lips and waited, his heart thudding. He could feel the main draft from the sea on his skin, could feel the faint crosscurrent from a fork in the passage a dozen paces ahead, but from the lips, nothing.

"Shit," he swore, scrambling over the body, trying to get into a position where he could press an ear to the heart. " 'Shael take it!"

But Ananshael had been there already, he realized with a wash of cold sorrow. While he'd been struggling for his life in the catacombs below, the Lord of Bones had come and carried off the soul of one of the other cadets, here, so close to the surface. It seemed cruel beyond cruel, but then, neither Ananshael nor Hull promised kindness, not even to their adherents.

With tender, trembling hands, he felt along the body, trying to coax a name from the sprawl of limbs, from the texture of the skin. The blacks were the same, of course, everyone wore blacks, but the body beneath the fabric was a woman's. Annick? Gwenna? The cloth was rent in dozens of places and sodden with blood. She had died fighting, whoever she was. She had died fighting hard. He felt for the head. Gwenna's hair was curly, but the hair of the corpse was straight, fine. Black hair, he realized, though the darkness was absolute as ever. He had seen it a thousand times, a hundred thousand times, had seen it wet with salt water, had seen it tossed by the wind as they flew along strapped to a bird's talons.

He was crying, sobbing in great, silent gulps. He moved his fingers to her face, traced the soft curve of her cheek.

"Hull have mercy," he choked, pulling her to him, but Hull had no mercy. The gods of mercy would have offered meager trials.

"I'm sorry," he moaned, gathering her up in his arms. "I'm sorry, Lin. I'm sorry. I'm sorry."

They told him later that when he emerged from the Hole, the first thing people noticed was Ha Lin's body, limp and lifeless, sliced and bleeding, draped in his trembling arms. He was crying, they said, sobbing uncontrollably, his entire body shuddering with the tears. But the Kettral had seen death before; they had seen sorrow. It was his eyes that everyone remembered, eyes that had always been the dark brown of charred wood, but that somehow—fathoms beneath the earth and the ocean, buried in the Owl King's own temple—had burned past char, past ash, past the blackest hue of pitch or tar until they were simple holes into darkness, perfect circles bored into the night itself.

25

So, it didn't go quite as we'd hoped," il Tornja said, leaning back in the chair to prop his gleaming boots on the desk before him.

Weeks had passed since Uinian's trial, but the *kenarang*'s new duties had not afforded a chance to meet until now. Adare sat across the desk in what had been her father's personal library, a high-ceilinged room ten floors up inside Intarra's Spear. The space was as strange as it was spectacular—the transparent exterior wall, the very crystal of the Spear itself, giving an overview of the rest of the Dawn Palace—the Floating Hall; the twin towers, Yvonne's and the Crane; the massive central courtyard leading to the Gods' Gate, and beyond the gate, the Godsway, plunging like a great river into the chaos of the city beyond. It was a space in which a man might feel himself master of the world, aloof from the trials of mortals toiling in the shops and shipyards, alehouses and temples below.

Adare felt anything but aloof.

"It was a disaster," she said flatly. "Worse than a disaster. Not only does Uinian go unpunished for my father's murder, but the rumors of his miracle are probably halfway to the Bend by now." The memory of the serried ranks of the Sons of Flame marching in Sanlitun's funeral procession suddenly seemed more dangerous than ever. "Intarra has always been a popular goddess, Uinian has his own private army, and now, in a single day, he's managed to command the awe and imagination of every citizen in Annur. Anlatun the Pious come again, people are calling him, never mind the fact that Anlatun was a Malkeenian."

"It *was* a pretty good trick," the *kenarang* replied, pursing his lips.

"That *trick* may have spelled the end of the Malkeenian line," Adare snapped, amazed and irritated at the man's nonchalance.

Il Tornja made a casual flicking motion with his hand. "I wouldn't go that far. There have been birds in and out from the Eyrie every week since Sanlitun's murder, and they assure me that Valyn's hale and whole."

"Valyn isn't the heir."

"There's no reason to suppose anything has befallen Kaden, either."

"There's no reason to suppose it *hasn't*. Ashk'lan is at the far end of the empire, practically in Anthera. Uinian might have sent someone to murder Kaden. Kaden could have fallen off a 'Kent-kissing *cliff* and we wouldn't know about it. We haven't heard a thing from the delegation sent to collect him."

"Travel takes time. Meanwhile, you're here."

"I'm a woman, in case you hadn't noticed."

Il Tornja glanced down at her chest, then raised his eyebrows provocatively. "So you are."

Adare colored, though whether the flush came from anger or embarrassment she couldn't be sure.

"The point is, I can't sit the Unhewn Throne. You're regent, but you're not a Malkeenian. Uinian has an opening now, a gap in which he can assert himself as the inheritor to my family's tradition."

"So kill him."

Adare opened her mouth, then shut it, unsure how to respond. Il Tornja said the words the way another man might suggest purchasing more plums. Life, of course, was cheaper on the frontiers, and he'd spent a career watching men die, his own and those of the enemy. Unfortunately, they were not on the frontier.

"There are laws," she replied, "legal codes to be followed."

"The same legal codes that worked so well for us during the trial?" he asked. "Legal codes are all well and good, but there's a certain clarity to just lopping off a head. I don't know about you, but I take that trial as a personal affront. That weasel of a priest won, which means I lost. And I don't like losing."

"I can't just go around killing people!"

"You can't?"

"I'm the Minister of Finance, not the headsman."

"You're the Emperor's daughter. There's five hundred Aedolians whose only job is to fight for you."

"Their job is to *protect* me."

"Tell them they can protect you by sticking Uinian full of steel."

She shook her head. He was missing the whole point. "The Malkeenians are not despots."

He laughed at that, a long merry laugh. "Of course you are. You're just particularly good despots. You're enlightened. You try to do what's good for the people. All that sort of thing."

"Exactly."

"But you're still despots. Or tyrants. Do you prefer tyrants? The point is, no one chose you to rule over Annur."

"I *don't* rule over Annur," she protested, but the man waved her objection aside.

"You're the princess and a minister, your father's daughter and your brother's sister, and right now the only Malkeenian on the continent, let alone in the city."

"And yet the Council of Ministers chose *you* to be regent," she replied, trying to keep the irritation out of her voice.

"And I'm deferring to you. That should tell you just how much power you have." He dropped his feet to the floor and leaned forward in his chair, nailing her to the spot with his eyes, fully engaged for the first time in the conversation. "You're a remarkable woman, Adare. I've had the displeasure, as *kenarang,* to spend time with some of the men who like to think they hold Annur together, and I can tell you you're smarter than the lot of them combined. You see situations clearly and quickly and you're not afraid to speak your mind." She colored at the unexpected praise, but he wasn't finished. "The question is, are you able to *act?*

"I've known a dozen men with good enough military minds to rise to my rank. They understood strategy. They could see their way out of impossible tactical positions. They knew the importance of the boring stuff: logistics, transport, and all the rest. Their weakness was their inability to act. There comes a time in every battle when the necessary course of action is clear, at least to someone who understands battle in the first place. What thwarts most men is the nagging doubts. What if I'm seeing it wrong? What if there's something I haven't considered? Maybe I should wait another minute, another hour."

He smiled, a hard predatory smile. "I fight against men like this all the time, and I kill them."

"Kill Uinian?" she said, trying to feel the full implications of the idea. The whole situation was overwhelming, not just the problem of Uinian, but il Tornja's praise and criticism as well. No one had ever spoken to her like this, not even her father, who trusted enough in her judgment to raise her to the rank of Finance Minister. That post was more than she had expected from her life, and yet il Tornja, for all his criticism, spoke to her as though she had the potential for something more, something great.

"Why not? He murdered your father, he flouted your family, and he looks ready to make a major play for imperial power."

Adare considered this man who sat across from her. When they first met, she had thought him ostentatious and vain, a pompous fool who cared more for his wardrobe than for important affairs of state. She had been wrong; she could admit that to herself now. What was harder to admit was the fact that she wanted to impress him. It was a ridiculous thought, a girlish thought. *But why not?* she demanded of herself angrily. Here was a man who had risen to the highest military office, upon whose command hung the lives of hundreds of thousands, and who spoke to her not as a simpering girl or a sheltered princess, but as an equal. As she looked at him, she caught a glimpse of a pairing that might be—the princess who was a minister, the *kenarang* who became a regent—but she forced it down. The man eyed her calmly from across the table, his eyes deep as wells.

"Why are you helping me?" she asked.

"I'm helping the empire."

"That, too," she acknowledged, "but you're also helping me."

Il Tornja smiled, and this time the smile was warm, human. "Is it so wrong for a man to want to ally himself with a brilliant, beautiful woman? There is a thrill in campaigning, sure, but the bombast and endless posturing of military men grow old after a year or ten."

Adare dropped her eyes, tried unsuccessfully to slow her pulse. *Uinian,* she snapped at herself. *You're here to figure out how to deal with Uinian.*

"Killing the Chief Priest won't be as easy as you make it out," she said, forcing her mind to the matter at hand.

Il Tornja watched her for a moment longer with that same intensity, then leaned back in his chair. Adare felt relief and longing at the same time as he moved away.

"Men tend to die when you slide steel beneath their skin and wiggle it around. Even priests."

Adare shook her head. "He needs to die, you've convinced me of that, but you're still thinking like a soldier. Soldiers may not blink when their comrades fall on the Urghul frontier, but Annur is not a battlefield. The empire has outlawed blood sacrifice. The entire city will sit up and take notice if someone murders Uinian, especially after the trial. The man was popular before. . . . Now, if anyone knows, if anyone *suspects* that I ordered the killing, there will be riots in the street." She considered the matter for the first time from the perspective of the Chief Priest. "If I were Uinian, I'd be *hoping* we would try for something like this."

"So we're back to caution and waiting for Kaden?" he asked.

"No," Adare replied firmly. "We're thinking of a third path. Let's go back to the trial. How did Uinian avoid burning?"

"I hope you're not going to tell me that he really is the consort of some mythical goddess."

Adare frowned. "You don't believe in Intarra?"

"Do you?" Il Tornja spread his hands. "I believe what I can see with my eyes and hear with my ears. Men have won and lost battles for a thousand reasons, but never because a god came down to take part in the fray."

"That's not what the histories say. During the Csestriim wars—"

"The Csestriim are a child's tale, as are the gods. Think about the look on Uinian's face going into the trial."

Adare nodded slowly. "He *knew* he was going to survive. He didn't have a moment of doubt."

"And if you were counting on the favor of a goddess no one has seen or heard from in a thousand years, even if you thought she was going to bail you out, don't you think you'd be at least a little nervous?"

Adare stood up, her agitation demanding some form of physical expression. She paced to the far wall of the library, trying to sort and sift the facts and suspicions. Beyond the clear stone, the sun was setting over the city, and she could feel its rays warm on her cheeks and lips. When she turned, Ran was standing by her side, though she had not heard him approach.

"He's a leach," she said. It was the only explanation.

The *kenarang* considered the suggestion with pursed lips.

"I've read all the histories," Adare pressed on. "Linnae and Varren, even that endless commentary by Hengel. This is the sort of thing a leach can do, if his well is strong and close."

"It makes sense," Ran agreed finally, nodding slowly at the idea. "If you could get the people to believe that, they would tear him apart themselves."

"But how?" Adare said, fingernails biting into her palms. "The people believe that Intarra loves him. How do you distinguish between divine favor and some leach's kenning?"

"It's *all* kenning. There *is* no divine favor."

"*You* believe that, but they don't. The man has become practically a hero overnight. We can't kill him without disgracing him first, without revealing his secret in a way that no one can doubt or deny. When we've shown him for a liar and a leach, then it won't even matter what we do. He'll be finished."

"As you've already pointed out," Ran replied, putting a hand on her shoulder as though to slow down the flood of her words, "Intarra's rewards are irritatingly difficult to distinguish from a leach's kenning."

"I know," Adare said, biting her lip. "I know."

The sun had dipped under the horizon, bloodying the sky, but her cheeks still burned with the last rays or their own inner heat. There had to be a way. Her father would have seen it. If she could just come at the matter from the right angle, attack it from the proper direction. Every problem had a solution, if she could just . . .

"Leave it," Ran said, trying to guide her back toward the room. "Sleep on it. Sometimes the ideas come only when the mind is gone. You have to give them space."

Adare turned to stare at him, at that fine chiseled face, those deep eyes. There was something in what he'd said, something—

"Yes," she said, a thrill running through her, the shape of plan suggesting itself. "Yes! That's exactly how we'll do it." She smiled wide. "But I'll need someone good with poisons."

Ran frowned, "You just got done telling me that we can't just kill him."

"Oh," she said, hopeful for the first time since her father's death, "I'm going to do so much more than just kill him."

And then, to the *kenrang*'s evident surprise, she leaned close to kiss him full and thoroughly on the mouth, the fire inside burning hotter still, and spreading.

26

Valyn rose early, bathed in the cold water from the sluice outside his barracks, shaved with his belt knife, then donned his best Kettral blacks. A stiffness had settled into his joints overnight, the rigid ache of muscles used past the limit of endurance, then left to tighten, and his legs protested as he limped between the buildings, past the mess hall, past command, across the great empty muster ground at the center of the compound, and up the trail toward the small rise overlooking the harbor. On a knoll a few hundred paces to the east, the spreading tenebral oak clawed at the sky with its gnarled limbs, but today the Kettral would pass by the shrine of their patron and pay homage to a different god. The soldiers referred to the stone ledge at the top of this small rise as Ananshael's Table, and it was here that they commemorated their dead.

Others joined Valyn as he went, all Kettral now, a small stream of black flowing uphill. Gent walked a few paces ahead, favoring his left leg heavily. Gwenna followed half a dozen yards behind, her right arm in a sling. No one spoke. After the strain of the Trial, the weight of words was too great, their purpose too feeble.

For eight years, when Valyn had imagined this day, he had imagined celebration, laughter, backslapping, and, capping it all off, tankards upon tankards of beer over on Hook. This was the day they were finally Kettral; after eight years, *this* was the day they had proved themselves worthy successors to the line of iron men and women.

More recently—since the mysterious warning from the dying Aedolian—he had felt an even greater urgency to be done with the test. Those who survived the Trial were assigned to Wings in the roles for which they had trained, which meant, after a brief probational period, he would be commanding his own small group of soldiers and free, finally, to leave the Islands. Provided he was able to secure permission, he would be allowed to go after Kaden, to warn him. He'd thought about little else, over the preceding five weeks; certainly he had worried more for Kaden than he had for Ha Lin. Never in his worst foreboding had he imagined the Trial would prove her end.

Oh, she would be battered, maybe. He would be battered, too. That was all part of the fantasy—conjuring up the vicious but impotent wounds they would flash and flaunt, trading the stories of tests overcome, trials met, foes defeated. As it turned out, life with the Kettral didn't line up very well with the stories. In the stories the soldiers traded gibes and offhand jests while dispatching the enemy with casual grace. In the stories the soldiers fucking *lived*.

He crested the low hill and stared at the bier. The gravelly limestone of the Qirins wasn't suitable for burial, and although the Kettral spent countless hours in underwater training and missions, no one wanted to be laid to rest in the icy blue black of the ocean depths. They burned their dead, those whose bodies returned, here on this headland, on the sharp scrap of limestone thrust up through the earth like a bone tearing through flesh.

Someone must have built the bier in the night, while he and the rest of his cohort slept their own deathlike sleep, hammering the planks together with a carpenter's care, although the whole thing was fashioned only for the flame. *Like us,* Valyn thought to himself. *Trained, honed, drilled, and then . . . destroyed.*

He forced himself to raise his eyes from the woodwork to the body atop it. Someone had taken the same care with Ha Lin that they had with the bier itself. She lay in her dress blacks, hands folded neatly across her chest, eyes closed, as though sleeping. The vicious gouges that marred her body, that had killed her in the end, were invisible now, hidden beneath the dark fabric. Her hair was combed back from her forehead in the way she used to wear it after climbing out of the waves after a long swim, and Valyn ached to step forward, to touch her face.

That was not, however, the way. Even in this, there was protocol to be observed, and he stood stiffly toward the side of the assembled group, his eyes fixed on Ha Lin's smooth face, waiting for Daveen Shaleel to get on with it and make her speech. As he watched, a hand touched him lightly on the shoulder: Talal, another who had emerged from the Hole more battered than he had entered, his dark face somber.

"She would have made a good soldier," he said quietly.

The anger came over Valyn all at once, hot and bright and unexpected. "She *was* a good soldier," he snapped. "Better than the rest of this fucking lot," he said, gesturing with a vague arm to the cadets who surrounded them.

Talal nodded, opened his mouth, then shut it again.

"What?" Valyn demanded, rounding on the leach. "*What? You have* some more insipid consolation to offer?" Despite the Eyrie's tolerance, Ha Lin had never been able to bring herself to trust a leach, even Talal, and the fact that the youth stood before him now with no more than a few slashes and gouges while she lay dead on the hard wooden bier struck Valyn as some sort of crude final insult. "You went down into the Hole with your well and your *kennings,*" Valyn went on, gathering both speed and volume. "Protected by your secret, fucked-up powers. You might as well have had a dozen guards. We might as well have given you the egg right there on the island and skipped the 'Kent-kissing *act.* She went in there with nothing. With *nothing.*"

Talal's face closed.

Gwenna laid a hand on Valyn's arm, but he shook her off. "Get off me! All of you. Just get the fuck away from me." He stepped away before he hit someone, giving himself space from the group and some air of his own, which he drank in deep gulps. His pulse raced, and it took him a moment to unclench his fist.

A few squalls chased along the southern horizon, dark smudges against the humid air. Now and again, a fork of lightning would lance down into the waves, followed long heartbeats later by the muffled thunder. Finally, Shaleel stepped in front of the bier. She considered Ha Lin for a long time, then turned to the assembled Kettral.

"Today we mark the loss of three of our number."

Valyn had to keep reminding himself that Ha Lin wasn't the only casualty. Nemmet and Quinn, a leach and a would-be flier, simply disappeared into the cavernous darkness. There were mutters that Fane, Sigrid, and the Flea had gone in looking for them once the Trial was over, but something— slarn, or rock fall, or the endless winding darkness itself—had simply swallowed the two cadets whole. Others had been luckier, but not lucky enough. Ferron found an egg, but lost his arm fighting free of a pack of slarn. Ennel had fallen from a ledge in the darkness and shattered his knee. The Eyrie would find jobs for them, of course, but neither would ever fly missions.

"When we arrive on these Islands," Shaleel continued, "we give up the lives we might have led. We give up the comforts of home, the pleasures of peace and prosperity, the security of a life lived safely in the fold of the empire. In exchange we accept pain, and austerity, and, as this occasion reminds us, death. We give up our family, our fathers and mothers, brothers and sisters, blood of our blood, whom we may never see again. The men and women here become our family."

Valyn looked over the assembled soldiers. Annick, without her bow for once, was looking out over the harbor, evidently more interested in the approaching weather than the funeral. Gwenna picked angrily at a long, ruddy scab running from her elbow to her wrist. Balendin, who wore new slashes across his face and hands, was eyeing Lin's body with an inscrutable expression while Yurl managed to look smug and self-satisfied in spite of the bruise spreading across half his brow. *Some 'Kent-kissing family,* Valyn thought to himself grimly. Most of them he didn't trust, and there were two he wanted to kill. Avenging the assault on Lin seemed pointless now, but then, the whole 'Shael-spawned endeavor had started to look a little pointless. Despite all his efforts, he was no closer to discovering the identities of the Kettral conspirators than he had been when Manker's collapsed into the bay. One at a time he considered the various faces—Annick, Rallen, Yurl, Talal—each more unreadable than the last. He was *supposed* to be a warrior, a naked blade between the citizens of the empire and their foes, and yet all around him people kept dying, people he loved and those he barely knew. His stomach had twisted into a knot, torn between fury at his faceless enemy and disgust at his own failures.

The man still fighting last week's battle will always lose to the man already fighting tomorrow's, he reminded himself. He still had a couple weeks of training once they assigned him his new Wing, a couple weeks before he could go after Kaden. In the meantime, cutting down Yurl and Balendin was something concrete, something he could hold on to.

"Although we'll never know what happened to Nemmet Rantin and Quinn Leng, we know that Ha Lin Cha, who lies before us now, completed the Trial. She went down into the darkness and she found there what she sought. That makes her Kettral."

The words should have mattered. The *title* should have mattered. Even if only briefly, Ha Lin had achieved her goal, had completed her Trial. A month earlier, Valyn would have said it was better to die a Kettral than a mere cadet, but he wasn't so sure anymore. Dead was dead. Ananshael had her now, and the Lord of Bones wasn't likely to treat her any more gently because Daveen Shaleel had decided she earned a special title.

"We honor all three fallen soldiers as Kettral," Shaleel continued.

"*Ex*-Kettral," Yurl quipped with a grin. "Last time I checked, dead girls don't fly missions."

Valyn shifted his gaze to the youth. The hot rage blazed in his veins, his fingers curled into fists, but he forced himself to remain still, clenching those fists until his fingernails bit into his palms, tensing his muscles to still their trembling, forcing himself to draw even breaths as his heart clamored inside his ribs. For a long while he felt like he might explode just like one of Gwenna's starshatters, but then, as quickly as the fit had come upon him, it passed. The heat had burned away, leaving a cold, implacable hatred.

The rigors of the Trial had done nothing to smooth the smugness from Yurl's handsome face, but his smile soured when he found Valyn staring back at him. He tried to hold the gaze, then cursed under his breath and turned away. *My eyes,* Valyn realized. He'd seen them that morning in a mirror, but had been too wrung out to feel anything about the change. They had been brown; now they were black. It was a simple fact. Others, however, seemed to find them unsettling. He filed the observation away as something that could be useful at some point.

"Before we light the pyre," Shaleel said, "those of you who wish may approach the body."

Valyn waited for the line to form, then took his place at the end. Some of the soldiers took only a moment, touching Lin's hand or saying a few words, prayers or farewells that he couldn't hear. When Sami Yurl reached the bier, he grinned, then chucked Lin under the chin playfully. Valyn slowly unclenched his hand. Lin was dead. Yurl couldn't hurt her any longer. His time would come soon enough.

Gwenna pressed something into Lin's hands, Laith whispered a few phrases in her ear, a sad smile on his face, and Gent tucked his favorite knife into her belt. When Balendin stepped forward, wolfhounds at his heels, he just looked for a long time, silent as Lin herself, then turned away.

Valyn found himself before the bier. He glanced over his shoulder, as though someone watching might tell him what to say, but the assembled faces were cool and quiet, ghostlike above their black uniforms. He turned back to the body. The wounds that had killed his friend—a half dozen slashes across her stomach and chest—were covered now by a clean, black tunic. After he first carried her out of the cave, Valyn had run his finger's over those gashes, trying to understand how a life could have seeped away through a few slices. They were ugly, nasty rents, but surely they couldn't have killed her. Surely you had to rip a larger hole in the body, had to spill out more of the guts, had to crush more of the bone, in order to drive the life out of it.

He shook his head. *Evidently not.* Lin's face was sallow and waxen. *Dead a day and a half,* he thought, then cursed himself for the clinical calculation. This wasn't an exercise, wasn't a cadet's battlefield drill. It was supposed to be a chance at a final farewell, but there were no such chances. He should have said his farewells days ago, should have been saying them every day of every year. It struck him, as he looked down at the cold corpse, at his own body beside it, that the Kettral wore blacks, not to blend with the darkness, but to be ready, always, for the funeral.

There seemed little point in speaking, but he took her hand gently, closing his eyes as he held it between his own. This was the time to offer a prayer, but what god would he pray to? Hull, whose trial she had died trying to complete? Ananshael, who had killed her? Maybe Meshkent was most appropriate, but then, the Lord of Pain had already released her from his claws. Valyn opened his eyes, tracing the fingers one by one, the back of the knuckles, the wrist. . . .

He paused. Whoever had cleaned her up had done a good job—the blood had been scrubbed away, the wounds sutured with fine thread. On her wrist, however, just beneath the protruding bone, ran an angry red line of abrasions. He stared. Among all her other, more serious wounds, it would be easy to miss, the most insignificant scratch, but now that he'd seen it, he couldn't pull his eyes away: a faint line of herringbone impressions dug into the flesh, the kind of impression left by Liran cord, the kind of impression that had marred Amie's wrists when they cut her down from the rafter weeks before.

His breath stuck in his throat. Somewhere out over the harbor a gull cawed. He could hear the waves sucking at the sand, lisping the same malevolent syllable over and over. His eyes flicked back to her wrist, back to the faint abrasion, trying to make sense of it. He wanted to lean over, to look closer, but he was surrounded, all eyes upon him. How long had he been standing there, holding her hand? He had no idea. How much longer could he stay without raising eyebrows, raising suspicions? As subtly as he could, he pulled back the sleeve of her tunic. He had assumed her wounds came from the slarn, and in his grief he had not thought to examine them. Now, however, as he studied one of the rents in her flesh, he could see that the edges were clean, not jagged. His heart went cold inside him. Something that might have been fear or rage squirmed beneath his skin. Steel had parted Ha Lin's flesh, good steel. She may have fought the slarn in the darkness, but one of the newly minted Kettral had killed her.

And it wasn't easy for them, a part of him noted with grim satisfaction. Given the number and arrangement of wounds, it was clear that Lin had fought back, fought hard.

"You were a warrior," he murmured so quietly no one else could hear. The words sounded both right and meager.

With elaborate care, he returned her hand to her chest. Lin hadn't just died. Somewhere in the cave, somewhere so far beneath the earth the entire deed was blotted by darkness, someone had battled her to a standstill, then bound her wrists. The same person who had tortured Amie in the tiny garret and left her body hanging for the flies had got to Lin as well, had murdered her, a quarter mile from the end of the Trial.

He forced himself to turn, to walk a few steps from the pyre, and resume his place among the other soldiers. *One of you,* he thought, eyeing the faces. *It was one of you.* His eyes flickered to Annick. He hadn't spoken to her since the infirmary, but he hadn't forgotten the look of rage and death that flashed across her face when he asked about Amie. If she had been involved in the girl's death, then she was implicated in Ha Lin's as well.

The blaze caught quickly, the age-old scent of burning wood mingling with the sickening smell of charred flesh as the tongues of flame licked hungrily upward, gnawing through bier and body both. Valyn stared into the shifting flame and shadow, stared at the ruddy sparks, stared at the sudden gout of brilliant yellow flame that exploded from Lin's hand—the special starshatter that Gwenna had tucked there in her own bizarre tribute. He stared until his eyes watered with the smoke, until they burned, but he refused to close them or to back away from the flame.

27

D ead," Kaden said flatly, trying to make sense of the word.
"*Slaughtered*," Akiil amended, forcing a hand through his
dark hair. "Just like the goats."

Kaden turned the idea over in his mind. Serkhan Kundashi had
mostly kept to himself, spending his days on the trails beyond the monastery, studying trees. He always claimed he was preparing to write a trea-
tise on the flora of eastern Vash, but no one had ever seen him set brush to
parchment. Kaden hadn't known the man well, but the thought that he
could just *cease*, could go from a curious, quiet observer of the world to a
scattered heap of decaying meat, made him faintly queasy.

"I thought the monks guarding the goats were in groups," he said, putting down his spoon on the rough table. The bowl of turnip soup in front
of him no longer seemed so appetizing, and the large refectory hall, normally so welcoming, struck him as cold and austere. A chill spring wind
sliced through the open windows, rustling the sleeves of his robe, tugging
at the meager fire that flickered on the hearth, stealing away any warmth it
might have offered.

"They *were* in groups," Akiil responded.

"Then what happened?"

"No one knows. The monks were all hidden, remember? When it
came time to switch shifts, Allen found what was left of Serkhan scattered
over half the eastern slope."

"And the other monks didn't hear anything?"

Akiil squinted at him as if he'd lost his mind. "You know the spring
wind in the mountains. Half the time, you can't hear your own footsteps."

Kaden nodded, staring dully out one of the low, small windows. The sun
was falling down toward the west, and already Pta's gems, the brightest

stars in the northern sky, were visible, hanging in a glimmering necklace above the peaks. He pulled his robe tighter around him to guard against the gusts that blew through the chinks in the casement.

It had been more than a week since Tan had Akiil dig him out of the hole, and although his appetite had started to return, painful sores covered his elbows and hips, and it was still difficult to hobble from the refectory to the meditation hall to his bed and back. Worse, his mind felt . . . blinded somehow, as though he had looked too long at a bright light. He still wasn't sure what had happened to him inside that hole—the final days, in particular, seemed like a dream, or a story read from some musty tome—but he was glad to be free. He had a feeling that if Tan had left him buried much longer, his mind might have drifted away like one of those clouds. That, he suspected uneasily, might have been the point.

As it turned out, Tan hadn't cut short the penance out of concern for Kaden's mental state. It seemed as though, after Serkhan's death, he considered it too risky to leave his pupil buried to the neck in earth. Evidently, if Kaden was to be killed, Tan wanted the pleasure of doing it himself.

Akiil, for his part, was ready to leap out of his skin with excitement. He kept picking up and putting down his spoon, gesturing with it toward Kaden and then toward the world outside, thumping his finger on the table to emphasize his points, and generally ignoring his rapidly cooling bowl of stew. He was always complaining that nothing ever happened at Ashk'lan, and now that excitement had arrived, he seemed to accept Serkhan's death as the necessary price.

"Why now?" Kaden asked slowly. "I found the first goat over a month ago, and monks have been all over the trails since then. It could have attacked anyone."

Akiil nodded, as though he'd been anticipating this question. "The way I figure it, the thing never wanted to kill a person. It stuck to goats as long as we let it, but then we penned the goats, all of them except the ones we set out as bait. It couldn't get to those, and so it had no choice. Serkhan became dinner."

Kaden winced at the crack. "The man is *dead,* Akiil. Show some respect."

His friend waved off the remark. "You're a terrible monk, you know that? Don't you listen to *anything* you're taught? Serkhan stopped being Serkhan when whatever it is tore him apart. The statement, 'Serkhan is dead,' doesn't even make *sense.* Serkhan was. Now he is not. You can't respect something that's not."

Kaden shook his head. Leave it to Akiil to ignore Shin teaching until it suited him. The tough thing was that his friend was right. The monks weren't callous, exactly, but they didn't make any more allowance for grief than they did for the other emotions—it was clutter, all of it, an obstacle to the *vaniate.* When a brother died, there was no funeral, no procession of mourners, no eulogy or scattering of ashes. Several monks conveyed the corpse to one of the high peaks and left it there for the rain and the ravens.

Kaden had learned all that the hard way. He could recall the moment in excruciating detail, despite the passage of the years. He had spent the morning in the potting hall, seated on one of the three-legged stools in the back corner, his attention focused on the lip of the ewer he was turning. Four times he had bungled the vessel, earning sharp words and sharper strokes from his *umial.* In his determination, he didn't even notice the young monk, Mon Ada, until he stood directly before him, a narrow wooden cylinder in his hands, leather thongs dangling where they had been cut loose from the bird's leg. Pigeons couldn't carry any great weight and the letter was terse: *Your mother has died. Consumption. She went quickly. Be strong. Father.*

Kaden had kept his face still, set aside the note, and somehow finished the lip of the ewer. Only when Oleki dismissed him did he climb to the top of the Talon to weep in solitude. He had seen one of the monks at the monastery die of consumption and he remembered the fever and chills, the skin pale as milk, the bright red as the man coughed pieces of his own lung into the cloth. He did not go quickly.

After spending a night on the Talon, Kaden went directly to Scial Nin's quarters to ask permission to visit his mother's grave. The abbot refused. The next day Kaden turned eleven.

With an effort of will he hauled his mind back to the present. His mother was dead and so was Serkhan.

"Respect or no respect," he said, "you're acting like this is just all part of a game. Doesn't it make you even a little bit scared?"

"Fear is blindness," Akiil intoned, raising an admonitory finger and arching an eyebrow. "Calmness is sight."

"You can skip the sayings—I learned them the same year you did."

"Evidently not well enough."

"A man was *ripped apart*," Kaden insisted. He still felt dazed and a little detached from the world after his ordeal in the hole. The fact that Akiil refused to acknowledge the seriousness of Serkhan's death only made him feel more confused. "I'm not arguing we should be running around in a terror, but the situation seems to warrant more than . . . excitement."

Akiil stared at him for a while. "You know what the difference is between us?"

Kaden shook his head wearily. For the most part, years living with the monks had dulled his friend's bitterness about a childhood spent grubbing scraps in the Perfumed Quarter. For the most part.

"The difference," Akiil continued, leaning over the table, his stew forgotten, "is that I saw a dozen men torn to pieces every *month* back in the Quarter. The Tribes got some of them. Some of them wandered down the wrong alley on the wrong night. Some of them were whores, cut up and tossed out because that's what some men like to do, and some of them were men, lured in by whores, then strangled or stabbed, flung on the midden without their sack of coin, naturally."

"It doesn't make it right," Kaden said.

"It doesn't make it *anything*," Akill shot back. "It is what it is. People die. *Everyone* dies. Ananshael is always busy. You think the *Shin* taught me to scoff at death?" He scowled. "I learned that lesson on the streets of our beloved empire."

He eyed Kaden squarely. "I don't want to die. I don't want you to die. But I'm not going to start sobbing every time someone stumbles over a body."

"All right," Kaden said, "I understand. You watch my back, I'll watch yours, and let the crows feast on the rest. Still, something is out there killing monks and, in case you haven't been paying attention, *we* are monks."

"We'll be careful."

"Knowing you, that seems unlikely. What does Scial Nin plan to do?" It was frustrating getting all his news secondhand from Akiil, but he was too weak to move around the monastery on his own.

"No idea," his friend responded. "Nin's locked up in his study with Altaf and Tan again—worse than a bunch of elderly whores, those three."

Kaden ignored the aside. "What are the rest of the monks doing?" Despite the Shin reserve, he had noticed a vague disquiet hanging over the monastery.

"Nin's still allowing us outside the monastery, but only in groups of four now."

"Well that's not sustainable. How will the goats graze? Who's going to haul clay or water?"

"Look on the bright side," Akiil responded with a grin. "No running up Venart's, no carrying rocks down the mountainside for some *umial,* no hunting for squirrel tracks all over the 'Shael-spawned peaks. If we had a flagon of ale and a couple of girls to tickle, this would be almost as good as a week back in the Quarter."

"Except something out there is trying to *kill* us," Kaden pointed out, exasperated by his friend's levity.

"Were you not listening just a minute ago?" Akiil demanded, his face turning serious once more. "Something's always trying to kill you. And I'm not just talking about the Quarter. Ananshael is everywhere, even in that Dawn Palace of yours."

Kaden fell silent. The palace in which he had been raised was a fortified paradise: gardens of ailanthus, cherry blossom, and spreading cedar surrounded by impregnable golden walls. Even there, however, he had never scampered around without his Aedolian guardsmen a few paces behind. The men had seemed like friends or kindly uncles, but they were not uncles. They were there because they were needed, and they were needed because Akiil was right: Death walked even in the halls of the Dawn Palace.

A fresh gust of wind blew in as a robed figure opened the door, then closed it crisply behind him. It was Rampuri Tan, Kaden realized, and a jagged nail of apprehension scraped over his flesh. *Maybe he's just here for the evening meal,* he thought. Surely it was too early for another penance. Surely the man didn't mean to return him to that live burial. Tan ignored the nods from the other seated monks, striding across the flags of the floor with his broad, silent steps until he loomed over Kaden's table. He considered his pupil.

"How are you feeling?" he asked finally.

Kaden had heard that question enough times now not to fall into the trap. "This body is sore and weak, but it breathes and moves well enough."

Tan grunted. "Good. Tomorrow at dawn we resume your training. Find me at the trail to the lower meadow."

Kaden squinted, trying to make sense of the direction. "I thought the abbot was insisting on groups of four."

"Akiil will come as well," Tan replied flatly.

The fact that the man didn't even bother to glance over at Akiil as he

delivered the news seemed to rankle Kaden's friend, and with an ostentatious show of deference Akiil rose from his seat and spread his hands in
mock supplication.

"I would love to attend you, Brother Tan, but our abbot was quite clear
that *four* was the number, and I'm sure I couldn't possibly disobey—"

Tan's broad hand caught him flat across the face, knocking him backward into the table, where he upended the bowl of stew. A look of shock,
then rage raced across Akiil's face as the liquid spread across the table,
then began to patter into a small pool on the stone floor. The older monk
didn't blink. "Three will be adequate. I will see you both at dawn."

"He—," Akiil began after Tan had closed the door behind him. The
stew had splashed over his robe, and he wiped it away in short, angry
motions.

"He will tie you to a pitch pine and leave you for the ravens," Kaden
interjected. "You think Yen Harval is a tough *umial,* think again. Look at
this," he continued, gesturing to his sunken cheeks and skeletal arms. "This
is what happened to me, and I've been doing everything in Ae's power to
obey the man. Now, sit down and don't do anything to make it worse."

Akiil nodded and sat, but there was something new, and sharp, and
defiant in his gaze that worried Kaden.

28

The morning dawned bright and cold. Frost limned the needles of the junipers, and a thin pane of ice slicked the surface of the water in the bucket outside the refectory door. Kaden rapped at it, slicing the skin across his knuckles and dripping a thin line of scarlet as he reached in to scoop some over his hair and face. The icy water trickled down his back beneath his robe, but he was glad for the sensation—it woke him, and he wanted to be well awake for whatever Rampuri Tan had prepared.

"Why don't you ever remind me that 'early summer' up here doesn't necessarily mean 'warm'?" Akiil asked, joining him at the bucket. He dipped his hands, ran them through his scraggly black hair, then cupped them and blew into the palms.

The sun hadn't yet cleared the peaks to the east, but light filled the sky, limpid and spreading. Kaden and Akiil weren't the only ones up; a low hum emanated from the meditation hall—older monks about their morning devotions—while novices and acolytes lugged full pails of water across the paths of the courtyard.

"It'll be hot enough by noon," Kaden responded, although he could feel his skin rising in bumps beneath his robe. "Come on. Tan doesn't like to be kept waiting."

The two crossed the small square, sandaled feet crunching the gravel, breath feathering out in front of them. Normally Kaden liked this time of day, at least once he'd had a chance to come fully awake. Morning sounds were crisper somehow, morning light more gentle. Today, however, something tickled the hair on the back of his neck. As he and Akiil followed the rough path beyond the outskirts of the monastery, his eyes kept darting to corners and hollows where the low sun had not yet driven out the night's lingering shadow.

Tan waited in one of those shadows, standing silently beneath the large boulder marking the trail down to the lower meadow, his hood pulled up to shield his face from the morning chill. Akiil looked like he might walk right past until Kaden brought him up short with a discreet tug on the robe.

When the two had paused, the older monk stepped out from the shelter of the overhanging rock. Only then did Kaden notice the long staff he held at his side. *No,* he realized with a jolt of surprise, *not a staff, a spear.* The weapon looked a little like the polearms carried by the Palace Guard back in Annur, but unlike those, Tan's spear stiffened into leaf-shaped blades at either end. The entire thing looked as though it had been forged from a single piece of steel, although that much steel would be difficult for any man to wield effectively, even someone as strong as Tan. As the older monk joined the two acolytes, however, he swung the double-ended spear at his side casually, as though it weighed no more than a dry cedar branch. An unstrung longbow hung on his back, but bows were common enough around Ashk'lan. Someone had to put food in the refectory pots. The strange spear, on the other hand . . .

"What's that?" Akiil asked, excitement warring with caution in his voice. He didn't sound at all certain that Tan wouldn't spit him on the end of the weapon simply for asking, but he was willing to take the chance.

Kaden's *umial* examined the spear as though considering it for the first time.

"A *naczal,*" he said, pronouncing the strange word in a sibilant hiss.

Akiil looked at what should have been the butt end skeptically, eyeing the graceful blade where it gouged the dirt. "Looks pretty easy to chop off a toe. Do you know how to use it?"

"Not as well as those who made it," Tan replied.

"Who made it?" Kaden asked.

Tan considered the question. "It is a Csestriim weapon," he said finally.

Akiil's mouth dropped open. "You expect us to believe you're lugging around a three-thousand-year-old spear?"

"What you believe is a subject of indifference to me."

Kaden considered the *naczal.* As children, he and Valyn had marveled over the dark smoke steel of a Kettral blade, the grudging way it refused to reflect the light. At first glance, Tan's spear looked similar, but where the Kettral steel appeared to have been forged in a deep smoke, coated with the ashes and eddies, the *naczal* might have been made *from* smoke. It looked solid enough, hard as any steel, but somewhere deep in the shaft, drifting across the surface of the blades, it seemed to roil and smolder, as though heat and ash from an extinguished blaze had been frozen in the air, then hammered into shape.

"Where did you get it?" Kaden asked.

"I brought it with me."

"Why?" Akiil demanded. "Seems like overkill for slaughtering goats."

"If you wait until you need a weapon," Tan replied, "it is often too late to acquire one."

"What about us?" Akiil asked. "What do we get?"

"My protection."

"I'd rather have one of those."

"Then you are a fool," Tan replied. "We're going to the South Meadow. Now, run."

The South Meadow wasn't much of a meadow at all, at least not by the standards of the imperial heartlands, where rich farms stretched for unbroken acres over the soft earth. It was, however, one of the few places in the mountains where the haphazard tufts of grass were stitched into an unbroken blanket that was, if not exactly lush, at least softer than the dirt and gravel immediately surrounding Ashk'lan. The White River, which roared and leapt through the canyons above and below, grew sluggish here, dividing into a wet skein that was home to frogs, flowers, and buzzing flies. It would have made an altogether more inviting site for the monastery than the grim plateau carved out of the rocks miles above. Which was, Kaden supposed, why the first Shin had refused to build there.

At the north end of the meadow the mountains resumed their dominion, sweeping upward in ramparts and splinters of granite. The trail to the monastery wound through those rocks, climbing over a thousand feet in a little less than half a mile, a tortuous ascent over shattered boulders and the groping roots of junipers. It was one of the steepest sections, and Kaden had a pretty good feeling he knew what Tan intended.

"Today's study," his *umial* began once they had reached the soft grass, "is in *kinla'an*. The 'Flesh Mind.'"

Akiil's mouth quirked as though he were going to make some sort of crack.

Tan turned to face him, and the former thief schooled his face back to careful blankness. Akiil was rash, not stupid.

Over his years at the monastery, Kaden had spent countless days practicing *saama'an* and *beshra'an*. The latter—"Thrown Mind"—was what allowed him to track his goat to its demise all those weeks earlier. *Kinla'an,* however, he had never heard of.

"Do all the Shin study the Flesh Mind?" he asked carefully.

Tan shook his head. "The monks pick and choose the training that suits them. They have not entirely forgotten the importance of *kinla'an,* but few *umials* emphasize it."

"Let me guess," Akiil said. "You're one of the few."

"You will run the trail," Tan began, ignoring the crack and gesturing with the blade of his strange spear, "up to the sharp bend. Then you will return."

Kaden eyed the terrain. It was steep, but no more than a quarter of a mile. He'd been running more than that since his first day at the monastery. Even hobbled as he was after the week of immobility, the task sounded suspiciously sedate. That worried him. He glanced at Tan's face, but the older monk revealed nothing. Instead, he freed his bow, strung it, and nocked an arrow.

"You're going to shoot at us while we're running?" Akiil asked. It was supposed to be a joke, but Kaden wasn't so sure. His *umial* had come close to killing him enough times to take any threat seriously.

"I'll be halfway up the trail," Tan replied. "If anything . . . threatens you, the bow will be useful."

"I wonder," Kaden began hesitantly, "if we shouldn't be doing something . . . else. Whatever slaughtered those goats killed Serkhan, and it just seems strange for us to be training as though nothing happened."

Tan stared at him. "You're surprised that your training continues."

"Well," Kaden replied after a moment, unsure how to hedge, "yes."

"And instead of training, you think you should be doing what?"

Kaden spread his hands helplessly. "I'm not sure. It's just that no one seems to know what's happening. We're not sure of things."

Tan chuckled, a dry, barren sound. "We are not sure of things," he repeated slowly, as though tasting the words. "That much is clear. As for training . . . ," he continued, skewering Kaden with his gaze, "we use the time we have. There is no other."

The answer was cryptic at best, and Kaden waited for more. Instead of elaborating, the monk raised the spear and pointed to the trail with one of the blades. "Go."

They took the hill at a moderate pace, quick enough to avoid Tan's wrath, but not so fast that cold muscles would cramp or tear. There weren't many places around Ashk'lan where you could safely ignore your footing, but this particular stretch of trail demanded the utmost concentration, and Kaden found himself dropping into the kind of relaxed focus so common to his exercise in the high peaks. His knees, cold and stiff, protested at first, and his calves immediately caught fire, but halfway up the slope, his body found its rhythm and by the top of the prescribed pitch he felt warm and ready, better than he had since Tan stuck him in the hole, in fact, and he took a deep breath of the cool air, savoring it in his lungs.

"Well," Akiil said when they'd reached the bend, "you think we're done?"

While they ran, Tan climbed to the midpoint of the trail and settled himself atop a large boulder, spear at his side, bow in hand. Kaden supposed he should have found his *umial*'s presence reassuring, but the monk looked distant, distant and small. A longbow could cover the range, but whoever was shooting it would have to be pretty skilled in order to hit anything in particular. It was all well and good to make the most of training, but that training wouldn't be much use if the two acolytes ended up with their heads rent from their bodies.

"Where do you think he got that spear?" Akiil asked, squinting down toward the meadow.

"Good question," Kaden replied. His conversation in the abbot's study came back to him, and for what must have been the hundredth time, he wondered how much to share with Akiil. *Later,* he told himself. *Easier to recall a loosed falcon than a spoken word.* He could always talk with his friend about Nin's stories once he had them sorted out in his own mind. "It's not the first time Tan's mentioned the Csestriim," Kaden said. "I think he knows more about them than he lets on."

Akiil snorted. "I didn't figure him for a lover of legends."

"Maybe they're not legends."

"You see any Csestriim running around back in Annur?" the youth asked with a raised eyebrow. "If the Csestriim ever *were* real, they're dead as last week's dinner."

When Kaden didn't respond, he nodded, as though that settled the point. "Any rate, it's a nasty-looking piece of steel. Think he knows how to use it?"

Serkhan's bloody face loomed in Kaden's mind. "I hope so."

The two spent the next hour running up and down the quarter-mile pitch. What began as a light morning exercise gradually grew more strenuous. Tan allowed no rest, waving them on each time they passed him with a barely perceptible gesture. The steep grade seared Kaden's atrophied calves, and the descent ground away at his thighs until his legs wobbled when he stood still. The air, so cold when he first scrubbed his face in the bucket, had warmed as the sun rose, and now it burned in his lungs. He'd gone on longer runs, of course, much longer, but none with his *umial* watching.

"Watch your footing," Tan said each time they passed him. "Learn the trail."

Akiil wisely waited until they reached the upper or lower bends to complain, although he availed himself of each opportunity.

"I don't care what kind of fancy word Tan's got for this—it's running up and down a 'Kent-kissing mountain, pure and simple."

"That's something to be grateful for," Kaden responded. "Usually when Tan tries to teach me something new, it hurts a lot more."

"I don't know how I got roped into this," Akiil snapped. "He's *your umial*."

"Someone must have noticed your extraordinary potential."

Kaden was starting to think they'd go on all day like that: Tan urging them to watch the trail, Akiil griping, his own legs groaning and his lungs burning the entire way up and down. It was hard work, but preferable to freezing himself unconscious in Umber's Pool, or waiting for Tan to bury him alive. He'd begun to accept the soreness, to welcome it as he'd learned in his long years at Ashk'lan, when Tan brought the two of them up short.

"Now," the monk said curtly, "your study begins."

From somewhere in his robe he produced two lengths of black cloth—they might have been the hem of an old monk's habit torn into strips. With a fluid motion, he dropped down from his boulder, landing more lightly than Kaden would have expected, given his size.

"You will wear these," he said, looping the cloth over Kaden's eyes and a good portion of his nose as well, cinching the strip into a knot behind his head. There was a pause while he did the same for Akiil.

"Continue," he said when the blindfolds were affixed.

Kaden frowned.

"Continue *what*?" Akiil asked.

"Running," Tan replied flatly. "Up to the bend and back, as before."

It was impossible. Kaden had barely been able to keep his footing on the rough trail with his eyes open. With the blindfold on, he wasn't sure he could even *find* the trail, let alone follow it.

"You've got to be kidding," Akiil replied.

Kaden winced at the crisp sound of a hand striking flesh.

"I am not kidding."

The whole thing was absurd, but Kaden wasn't about to earn himself a bruise to match Akiil's. He could start, at least. It wouldn't take his *umial* long to see that the task was ludicrous.

The first ascent must have lasted the better part of an hour. Kaden couldn't be sure, as he had no way to track the sun in its arc across the sky. He fell about every third step, and by the time he reached the bend, he could feel the blood running down his shins from nasty gashes on both knees, sticky as sap between his toes. A dozen times he was convinced he had lost the path entirely, and Akiil insisted on following something that turned out to be a dry streambed for a dozen or so laborious paces before they came to a rough cliff and were forced to turn back.

Kaden tried to summon a *saama'an* of the trail, but found that he could recall only pieces and chunks: a root here, a sharp rock there, fragments of glances lodged in his mind from the morning's labor. The Carved Mind was a powerful tool, but always before he had used it to form a small and static image: a kestrel's wing, the leaf of a bloodwood. Trying to recall a quarter-mile of rocky path seen at a quick lope was like trying to hold five gallons of water in your arms.

"I can't see it," he said when they finally arrived back at Tan's rock, sweating, bruised, and bleeding. "I should have learned the terrain, but I didn't."

There was only silence, and Kaden wondered suddenly if Tan had left them, abandoned his post on the boulder and returned to the monastery. The thought that he and Akiil might have been stumbling around the trail for the past hour with blindfolds over their eyes while something capable of ripping out a monk's stomach roamed the peaks made him catch his breath, and for a moment he was tempted to remove the blindfold.

His *umial* responded finally. "If you didn't learn it earlier, then you will have to learn it now."

"How can we learn it if we can't *see* it?" Akiil asked.

"See with your feet," Tan responded. "Learn with your flesh."

"Kinla'an," Kaden concluded wearily. The Flesh Mind. The whole

thing was starting to make sense. At least, as much as anything else he'd learned.

"*Kinla'an,*" the older monk agreed, as though that concluded the matter.

The second ascent was, if anything, more laborious than the first. Rocks gouged into already bruised skin, the sun blared down, hot and invisible, and Kaden twice struck his toe so hard that he thought it might have broken. Learning by sight, he was used to. He had developed dozens of strategies and tricks over his years of practice in *saama'an.* This endless groping in the void, however, seemed designed to drive him mad.

At first he tried to make a sort of map, plotting each jutting corner, each winding root as though it were a figure inked on parchment. That seemed the sensible way to go about it, the method most in keeping with his earlier studies, but it proved almost impossible. Without the initial visual impression, the images simply wouldn't stick. They were like shadows, or dark clouds, shifting and mercurial. He would sketch a patch of ground in his mind only to find a certain rock missing, or twice as close as he'd expected. He couldn't keep track of whether he had covered ten paces or twenty. He couldn't tell one twisted root from the next. From time to time, he heard Akiil curse or mutter some imprecation, but the thief had fallen behind, and Kaden toiled on in his own floating void.

By the time he had descended to the meadow and then climbed to the boulder, he was on his hands and knees, palms bloody from pawing at the rocks, knees shredded by the gravel.

"What are you doing?" Tan asked.

Kaden stifled a laugh that he recognized as slightly insane. "Trying to learn the trail."

"With your hands?"

"I thought if I could get a sense of it with my hands, I could make a sort of map, something I could memorize for next time."

"Do you run on your hands?" Tan asked.

The question was clearly rhetorical, and Kaden didn't respond.

"Do you drink with your eyes? Do you breathe with your feet?" The older monk paused, and Kaden could picture him shaking his head. "Get up."

Kaden rose unsteadily to his feet.

"Walk the trail," the monk said flatly.

"But I can't *see* it," Kaden replied, "not even in my mind."

"Your *mind,*" Tan spat. "Still obsessed with that fine, elegant mind of yours. Forget your mind. Your mind is useless. Your body knows the trail. Listen to it."

Kaden started to object, then stopped abruptly when he felt the chill, sharp steel of the spear head nudging his mouth shut.

"Stop talking. Stop thinking. Follow the trail."

Kaden took a deep breath and turned from the darkness to the darkness, rotating in the blank void like a star turning in a starless night, and prepared to mount the path once more.

The next two dozen ascents passed in a strange sort of fugue. He continued to step, to stumble, to feel his ankles buckling under him when his foot came down on unexpected terrain, but here and there, for a few paces at a time, he found that he could walk almost normally. Then his thoughts would rise, like a hungry tide at the palace docks. *I'm at that short dogleg! I just need to turn left, step off the fallen cedar and*—and he would step off the trail, tumbling into a low ditch or cracking his head on a sharp, overhanging bough. Despite Tan's injunction, he had developed a rough map of the path, but it led him astray more often than not, and he certainly couldn't rely on it for the details of footing or the intricacies of minor directional changes. His body, however, *did* seem to know some of those things, and more often he found himself responding unconsciously: a patch of gravel led him to step a little higher over a small rock shelf. A slight declivity urged him to take a few unmeasured paces. It was a painful process still, and he shuddered to think what his face, hands, and knees would look like when Tan finally allowed him to take off the blindfold, but he felt as though he had developed some tenuous grasp on the concept of *kinla'an.*

"It's nighttime, you know," Akiil muttered when they ran into each other at the top of the trail.

Kaden stopped and raised his head. His friend was right, he realized. He was warm from the labor of climbing and falling, but the air was cool, and the daytime sounds of the birds had given way to the silent winging of bats.

"Your 'Kent-kissing *umial* has kept us here all day," Akiil continued.

"Are you getting the hang of it?" Kaden asked. It felt strange to talk to another person after so many hours of silent, blind groping, like meeting a ghost, or addressing a fragment of his own mind.

"Am I getting the *hang* of it?" Akiil responded, incredulity tingeing his voice. "The only thing I'm going to hang is you. Or maybe that sadist who calls himself a monk. Or maybe both."

Kaden grinned, but before long, he had turned back to the trail and was floating in that strange, vast landscape of shapeless forms in which his mind drifted while his body stumbled and fell. Climb and descend. Up and down.

When he reached the boulder for what must have been the hundredth time, Tan, who had been silent for hours, broke into the void.

"Stop. Take off your blindfolds."

It took Kaden a long time to work free the knot with his sliced and bloody fingers. When the cloth finally fell away, he squinted at the brightness, unable to make out much more than his *umial*'s dark form and the vague shapes of the cliffs and peaks.

"It's another day," he said dumbly.

"Morning," Tan replied. "The sun broke just an hour ago. You would have felt it, had you been paying attention."

Akiil had managed to free himself from his own blindfold, and he squinted about, as though trying to make sense of his surroundings.

"*Beshra'an,* I can understand," Kaden said. "And *saama'an.* It's useful to be able to track, to be able to remember."

Akiil grunted skeptically.

"What is the point," Kaden pressed, "of this? Of *kinla'an*?"

Tan studied him before responding. "There are three reasons," he said at last. "First, relying on the body allows you to let go of the mind—this brings you a step closer to the *vaniate.* Second, the Shin understand the *vaniate,* but they never put it to use. Our predecessors did not learn the emptiness simply in order to bask in it. They used it as a tool. Running or fighting—your body moves more quickly without the weight of thought pressing down upon it."

Akiil looked like he was going to object, then scowled and looked away. The bruise where Tan struck him earlier had purpled impressively, puffing out his cheek and partially closing one eye.

"What's the third reason?" Kaden asked cautiously.

Tan paused. "Bait."

"Bait?" Kaden responded, trying to make sense of the word. "You mean for—"

"You were alone. Blindfolded. Unarmed. I hoped that whatever killed Serkhan would come for you."

"Holy Hull!" Akiil exploded, rounding on the monk, his hands balled into fists. "What if it *had*?"

"I would have shot it," Tan replied.

"Well, I'm fucking glad it never showed up!"

"Don't be."

Kaden shook his head. "Why not?"

"I was standing motionless on that boulder. An animal would never have noticed me. It would have taken the opportunity to attack."

"Maybe the thing just isn't down here today. Maybe it's up in the high mountains."

"And maybe," Tan replied grimly, "it's smarter than we realized. Maybe it saw the bow and spear. Any beast can kill. Maybe this thing we face can plan."

29

W ing Selection felt like a twisted cross between a holiday ball and an execution. Most of the older Kettral certainly treated it like a holiday. Someone had rolled a couple of casks of ale into the main training arena—the Eyrie loosened the strict prohibition against alcohol on Qarsh for the event—and the grizzled veterans brought their own tankards. Most of them had been going at the liquor with a will since midmorning, staking out seats on the stone walls ringing the space, tossing back and forth taunts and insults with the careless cheer of men and women who narrowly avoided death day in and day out, but who, for the space of a few hours, could afford to let down their guard and enjoy the discomfort of others.

"Hey, Sharpe," one of the men bellowed down at Gwenna. It was Plenchen Zee—thick as a barrel but damned near impossible to kill, if the stories were true. Someone had sliced out one of his eyes, and he'd taken to filling the cavity with all sorts of unsettling things: stones, radishes, eggs. Today a ruby bulged jauntily from the socket. "I've got a spot on my Wing for a lady like you." He waggled his tongue while raising his eyebrows.

Gwenna turned on her bench to fix him with a glare. "If you're looking for a whore, I'd recommend Sami Yurl. I'm in demolitions."

"You might want to watch your tongue," Yurl snapped from a few rows away. He had no visible scars from the Trial, his blond hair was as carefully coiffed as ever, but his eyes were angry, sullen at the unexpected slight. "If you're assigned to my Wing, I just might have to cut it out."

Zee roared with laughter at the exchange, oblivious of or indifferent to the undercurrent of real hatred running beneath the words. This was the part of Wing Selection that felt like an execution. Sometime between the emergence of the cadets from Hull's Hole and now, two days later, a cabal of commanders and trainers had put their heads together to decide which cadets would go where. Their decisions were final and not open to appeal. Some of the newly minted Kettral would be assigned to veteran Wings, filling gaps left by those who had been killed flying missions; others would comprise original Wings of their own. Despite the barrels brimming with ale, the Annurian banners flapping against the sky, the tables around the edge of the arena piled with shanks of lamb, braised haddock, and a dozen kinds of fruit, some assignments today would turn out to be death sentences.

" 'Shael on a stick," Gent muttered, glancing over his shoulder, "I hope I don't get stuck with Zee."

"I think he's got eyes only for Gwenna," Laith replied with a shrug.

"Good. The soldiers on his Wing don't live that long."

"Could be worse," Laith said. "At least Zee's a vet. He's been out there. He's been tested. Valyn here's going to get four cadets, and he's green as the summer grass. You want to talk about a shitty draw—"

"I'm sitting right here, asshole," Valyn snapped. He felt both the excitement and the anxiety of his friends, but both were tempered by the angry ache lodged inside his chest. Lin should have been with them, swapping jests and gibes, her dark eyes bright as she waited for her assignment. Not long ago, he'd thought the chances were good that she might even end up on his Wing. It would be logical—

He cut the thought short. She was gone. Someone sitting in the arena had killed her, someone who had just been raised to the rank of full Kettral, someone who might end up assigned to his own Wing.

Laith, sensing the shift in mood, put a hand on Valyn's shoulder. "You can't have her back, Val," he said, his voice uncharacteristically sober. "But that doesn't mean you can't go on. We're all going to die at some point—at least she went quickly, still young and strong."

Valyn shook his head. He had to remind himself that he wasn't alone in his sorrow. Laith and Gent, half the 'Kent-kissing class, had liked and admired Lin. He didn't have a monopoly on his mourning. On the other hand, half the class hadn't kissed her just before the Trial. Half the class hadn't let her be beaten blue and bloody on the West Bluffs. Half the class didn't know that she'd been murdered down in the Hole. He carried that knowledge alone. He wasn't sure he would have felt any better if she had died honestly in the normal rigors of the test, but at least he wouldn't be nagged by guilt, by the crushing burden of knowledge. Laith and Gent had said their good-byes, shed their tears, and let Lin go. Valyn couldn't stop hashing and rehashing events, eyeing with suspicion everyone who crossed his path, plotting an inchoate revenge.

He scanned the faces. Yurl and Balendin were there, a dozen paces away, the leach's wolfhounds slavering in the morning heat. At some point, this week or this year, Valyn planned to hurt them, hurt them badly, for what they had done to Ha Lin up on the West Bluffs, regardless of whether they were involved in her death down in the Hole. It was the others he needed to worry about now, the ones he hadn't figured out. He shifted his gaze to Annick.

She sat on the far end of the benches, her bow across her slender knees. At this distance, without being able to see her eyes, he thought she looked almost like a child, lost and alone. Where most of the cadets had gathered in small knots, Annick held herself apart—no one had come within a few paces of her, although some of the veterans seemed to be considering the sniper from beneath hooded eyes. She was a good prospect to step up to one of the established Wings—she was as deadly as any soldier twice her age with that bow, and she certainly had no connections among her peers.

In retrospect, the fact that Annick had come out of the Hole alive was something of a mystery. Underground, in the dark, that bow of hers didn't count for much. Given the winding of the tunnels, it would take a miracle to even draw the thing before the slarn could attack. This would have been a problem for all the snipers, but most were more proficient with their blades. Valyn narrowed his eyes, but there was nothing to see—just a girl, her hair cut short, eyes fixed on the weapon in her hands.

He turned to look at Talal. The leach, too, sat a little apart, although he looked comfortable with his isolation. A slarn had raked its claws across his face, and while the wounds weren't immediately obvious on his dark skin, one of those claws had missed his eye by the barest whisker. Valyn eyed the bracelets racked on his wrists—bronze, steel, iron, jade—the hoops and stones, precious and ordinary, sunk in his ears. A leach could draw his power from any of those things, or none.

"I wonder what his well is," Valyn said, half to himself.

Laith raised an eyebrow. "You want to play *that* guessing game? Have fun. I'm sure the last eight years have narrowed it down to about a thousand possibilities . . . provided you were paying attention and taking notes."

"Doesn't seem fair, does it?" Gent chimed in.

"What?" Laith responded, grinning. "The fact that we got two blades and a torch when we went down in the Hole while Talal brought the ability to bend nature to his will?"

Valyn considered his next question carefully. He trusted Laith and Gent as much as anyone else on the Islands, but he wasn't ready to tip his hand, not yet.

"What *did* people bring with them?" he asked. "I was so wiped from the first week that I wandered in with just my blacks and the blades on my back."

Laith shrugged. "Most of the snipers had their bows. I think Gwenna carted along some demo—I could have sworn I heard an explosion down there. On the other hand, that might have been the poison pounding in my ears as my sanity slowly slipped away."

"Grub," Gent replied. "I stuffed my pockets before leaving the ship. Had enough of raw fucking rat." Of course. Even now, he held a massive turkey wing in his equally massive hand, waving it around the way a field marshal might gesture with his baton. Gent's favorite chapter of the *Tactics* was the eighth, the one that began, *On an extended mission, food is as important as fighting. . . .*

"Anything else?" Valyn pressed. "Did anyone bring . . . I don't know, packs or cord or anything like that?"

"What were you going to pack?" Laith asked skeptically. "A bottle of Raaltan red and an embroidered tunic for the ball?"

Valyn spread his hands in defeat. If his friends were anything like him, they'd been paying more attention to the slarn and the gaping hole in the rock than they had to the gear carried by those surrounding them. Anyone could have brought the Liran cord that had bound Lin's wrists. It was light and supple enough to pocket, cram in a small pack, or even thread through the belt loops that held up a cadet's pants.

The hooting and heckling from the soldiers crested for a moment, and Valyn looked over to see Jakob Rallen walking into the arena, leaning heavily on his cane to support his bulk. Although the Kettral were the only military branch to eschew formal uniforms, Rallen was dressed for the occasion in crisp blacks, his hair carefully combed across his sweating pate. As Master of Cadets, he would preside over the ceremony—Valyn remembered as much from past years—and he did all he could to invest the role with more pomp and grandeur than it deserved. A low table and a high-backed chair sat at the center of the arena, the focus of the assembled benches, and Rallen took his seat with obvious pleasure in front of a dangling Annurian flag, the sunburst bright against the white cloth.

"Flag," Gent grunted around a mouthful of meat. "First time I've seen one of those on the Islands."

"Rallen probably figures he'll cut a more imposing figure if he sits in front of something large and impressive," Laith pointed out.

"Let him," Valyn grumbled. "This is the last we'll have to hear from that miserable bastard."

After they were assigned to Wings, the cadets would no longer be cadets. Instead, they would report directly to their regional commanders. Rallen would turn his attention to the unfortunate classes below them, the young soldiers who had not yet passed the Trial. The fact should have made Valyn happy, but he eyed the master with a mixture of distrust and unease. Rallen had a satisfied smirk on his face as he eyed the crowd. Until the Wings were set, the man had not played his final card, and he had no love for the son of the Emperor.

"Today," he began after ponderously taking his seat, his voice pinched and imperious, "those of you who have spent the last eight years under my charge will move on, not to more important things, because there is nothing more important than the training a cadet receives, but to the next stage of your lives as Kettral."

The veterans had fallen quiet. They were willing to pay the man a measure of respect, although they looked anything but rapt. The Flea was trimming his nails with a long knife while Adaman Fane nodded impatiently, as though willing Rallen to get on with the preamble and reach the meat of the matter. Sigrid sa'Karnya, the Flea's stunningly beautiful leach, lay half-reclined on one of the stone walls, her closed eyes turned toward the sun, blond hair framing her ivory cheeks. Unlike the rest of the group, she wasn't wearing blacks. In fact, she wasn't wearing military clothing at all. Instead, a gorgeous red dress that emphasized the fullness of her breasts clung to her figure, draping her body and the stone beneath. Hull only knew where she'd come up with that, but Valyn tore his eyes away. The woman's reputation for cruelty exceeded that of most of the soldiers on Qarsh. She wouldn't appreciate him staring.

"In making these assignments," Rallen continued, "we have considered your strengths and your weaknesses as well as the needs of the various Wings. If you find yourself assigned to a group that is . . . not to your liking,

I would remind you that more careful and deliberate minds than yours have weighed variables of which you are entirely ignorant."

Valyn squinted. Had the man smirked at him when he mentioned undesirable assignments? The light wind had fallen, and the sun overhead was suddenly hot, boiling him in his blacks. He could hear the waves grating on the sand a quarter mile distant, the skirling of the terns as they soared, then plunged for fish. He longed for the coolness and solitude of the open bay, an escape from the mass of bodies pressed shoulder to shoulder, waiting for Rallen's pronouncements. Was it only his imagination, or could he hear the creaking of the hawsers down in the harbor?

"We'll begin with those Kettral assigned to established Wings," Rallen said.

"I wouldn't mind ending up with the Flea," Gent rumbled quietly.

"Someone on his Wing'll have to die first," Laith observed, "which is not all that likely."

Valyn glanced over his shoulder. The Flea was still trimming his nails. Sigrid was still basking in the sun. Newt, the small, ugly demolitions master, was leaning forward, picking absently at something in his ragged beard while waiting for the judgment. Chi Hoai Mi, the wing's flier, and Blackfeather Finn were nowhere to be seen. When you'd watched a couple dozen Wing Selections, they probably got a lot less interesting.

"Flying under Plenchen Zee," Rallen began, pausing dramatically, enjoying his moment onstage, "specializing in demolitions—"

"If it's me, Rallen, I swear I'll feed you your own nuts," Gwenna remarked in a voice loud enough for everyone to hear.

The Master of Cadets pursed his lips in an angry frown, but the crowd loved it.

"The girl has fire!" Zee boasted, standing and waving a fat finger. "She will come to love me in mere days!"

"Sorry to disappoint," Rallen said sourly. "Specializing in demolitions under Plenchen Zee . . . Gent Herren."

Valyn and Laith turned to stare at their friend. "Well, I'll be buggered blind," Gent muttered. He was probably the worst demolitions man in the class, but then, word on the Islands was that Zee didn't much care for subtle riggings and careful calculations. As long as there was a lot of smoke and more fire, the man was pretty much satisfied wading into the fray and finishing everything off with his blades. It was an honor to be chosen, but Gent didn't look so thrilled.

Zee, for his part, was already on his feet, arms spread in mock outrage, his ruby glinting bloodily from its socket. "You could have given me the Sharpe girl and instead I get this . . . this . . . ox creature? I told you I wanted tits!" He gestured vividly with his hands. *"Tits!"*

"A couple more years," Fane bellowed from a few seats away, "and you'll be fat enough to have tits of your own."

"Holy Hull," Gent said, holding his huge head in his hands. "Sweet holy Hull."

Laith clapped him merrily on the back. "Good news for us! At least Val and I know we won't have to lug your bulk around the better part of two continents. I swear, with you hanging from the talons, my bird flies at half speed."

Gent shrugged off the crack and rose unsteadily from his seat to meet his new Wing mates. They were already filling an absurdly large horn with ale, gesturing toward him eagerly.

Valyn watched him go with some trepidation. Laith's jesting aside, losing Gent to one of the veteran Wings was tough. He'd been one of the few cadets that Valyn trusted, one of the few he had hoped to serve with. Now the pool of soldiers remaining for his own Wing was that much smaller, the possibilities just a little more dangerous.

Rallen sent two more cadets off to the veterans—Jenna Lanner and Quick Hal—good soldiers, but unremarkable by Kettral standards. Then the real fun began. There were three Wing leaders in the class: Valyn, Sami Yurl, and Essa, a short young Raaltan woman with arms the size of her thighs. By the end of the morning, the three of them would be commanding the Kettral's newest soldiers.

"Sami Yurl," the Master of Cadets began, pointing imperiously to a spot just in front of his table.

Yurl rose, flashed a quick grin to the crowd, slapped a few of his cronies on the back, and crossed the intervening space. How he managed to look like royalty while dressed the same as everyone else, Valyn had no idea—probably something about the strut.

"Let's see who's lucky enough," Yurl began, raising his chin and eyeing the crowd coolly, "to serve under the next Kettral legend."

There was some hooting and heckling from the veterans at that, but Yurl only smirked.

"For those of you who might want to place a bribe with Master Rallen," he added, "I'm sure it's not too late."

"Enough out of you, Yurl," Rallen snapped. "You're here to listen, not to talk."

"I'm here to lead," the youth responded. He never even batted an eye while the names were called.

Valyn had no idea how the Eyrie drew up the various groups, but Yurl ended up with a Wing that was little different from his daily cabal of thugs: Remmel Star, the bearded demolitions master; Hern Emmandrake, a thin sniper who used the feral cats around the Eyrie as targets; Anna Renka, the only woman on the Wing, its flier, and probably Yurl's bedmate as well. Rumor had it that when he went whoring over on Hook, she liked to watch, liked to . . . encourage the girls. She was pretty enough—short blond hair, lithe limbs—but there was a cruel twist to her mouth that set Valyn's teeth on edge. And then, of course, there was Balendin Ainhoa, feathers and ivory hanging in his long braids, face a bored mask as he took his place alongside the other killers, hounds at his heels, falcon perched on his shoulder.

"Well," Laith said, drawing a sharp breath between his teeth, "that's about as nasty a crew as you could come up with."

Yurl had nodded at every name as though he expected it, and now, with his Wing assembled beside him, he shot Valyn a smug glance, then took a step forward.

"As I said, you've all just had the privilege of seeing the formation of what will be the Eyrie's best Wing. Fane, step aside. Flea, look out."

Adaman Fane snorted. The Flea didn't even look up from his nails.

"You're done here, the lot of you," Rallen said. Then his fleshy lips spread into a grin. "We need to make room for the Light of the Empire, Valyn hui'Malkeenian."

Valyn stood warily, then crossed to his place at the center of the arena. As he passed Sami Yurl, the youth elbowed him lightly in the ribs.

"Have fun up there. Too bad he won't be calling Ha Lin's name."

Valyn resisted the urge to seize the elbow and shatter it.

In a way, it was a blessing that Rallen had assigned the most sadistic soldiers to Yurl's Wing—it left a more manageable, if less deadly, lot for the next two commanders. Valyn scanned the faces. Peter the Black and Peter the Blond, the former as tall as the latter was short, were a solid combination. Or Aacha, the Hannan leach—Valyn would have preferred not to have a leach at all, but Aacha was more powerful than Talal, the weakest of the lot. There were capable soldiers still in the mix, if only Rallen would see fit to send them his way.

"Serving as flier under Valyn . . . Laith Atenkor."

Valyn found a smile creeping onto his face, the first, he realized, since Lin's death. Laith was a hothead, but he was a daring flier and a friend. Perhaps the selection wasn't rigged against him after all. The flier rose from his place, spread his arms to acknowledge the cheering and the heckling both, turned in a slow circle, then sauntered to the center of the arena.

"I hope you like to go fast," Laith murmured as he took his place at Valyn's side. "Fast and really, really low to the ground."

"Just remember that the rest of us have to ride *beneath* the 'Kent-kissing bird. I don't want to get scraped off by any treetops or chimneys."

"No promises," the flier replied, grinning.

"Serving as leach," Rallen continued, "Talal M'hirith."

So. It was Talal after all. Valyn met the youth's eyes as he approached, but it was hard to read anything in that somber brown gaze. *The fighters who frighten you are not the fighters to fear.* Hendran again. *The man you barely notice will be the one to bury a blade in your back.* Valyn extended a stiff hand.

"Welcome," he said. He would fly with a leach, but he didn't have to like it.

"As demolitions master," Rallen continued, his grin stretching into a leer, "Gwenna Sharpe."

Valyn stifled a groan. Gwenna *had* helped him out by diving into the wreck of Manker's, but if Laith could be a hothead, she was an open fire. She'd spent more hours on third watch than any cadet in the class, largely because of her inability to accept anything that sounded like an order.

"This should be fun," the flier murmured at his side.

"Shut it," Valyn hissed. The last thing he needed was a spat before his Wing was even fully formed. As long as he could corral Gwenna, get her to listen—

"Finally, assigned to a position as the Wing's sniper . . . Annick Frencha."

Valyn's stomach lurched. Annick, who had put an arrow through his chest, who had met Amie on the day that she died, who was concealing a secret dark enough that she might have been killing people for the last two months to keep it safe, who might have brought the Liran cord into the Hole and murdered Ha Lin. The sniper's eyes were blank as the sky when she joined the group, her face still. There was no telling if she was happy or sad, no telling if she even had the *capacity* for those emotions.

Valyn extended the hand again. "Welcome," he said, the word like sawdust on his tongue.

Annick considered Valyn's hand, shrugged, then took her place at the end of the line.

"On behalf of Eyrie command," Jakob Rallen said, intoning the phrase with obvious satisfaction, "may Hull guard your approaches and cover your flights."

The words sounded like a sentence rather than a blessing.

†

"You've got an hour," Fane said, tossing a map onto the bench where Valyn sat, still slightly stunned, with his newly formed Wing.

"An hour for *what*?" Gwenna demanded, raking her red hair back over her shoulder.

"Figure it out," Fane said as he walked away.

"All right, leader," Laith said, gesturing toward the map with a grin. "Lead."

Valyn scooped up the map. He'd hoped there'd be a chance to talk things over with the group, to establish some basic protocols, but evidently the Eyrie belief in preparing for the unexpected didn't end once you had your own Wing. In about a month, they would all pass probation and be sent out on missions of their own. Until then . . . he unfolded the paper, spinning it until the north end faced north.

"It's an island," he said, taking in the contours, searching along the bottom of the page for a scale marking out distances.

"He's going to be a good commander," Gwenna said, rolling her eyes. "He knows an island when he sees one."

"Save it," Valyn grumbled. "It's Sharn—about twelve leagues south of here."

"Means we'll want Suant'ra," Laith said, turning from the group, heading toward the massive rookery where the birds were tethered.

"Wait," Valyn shouted. He wasn't even sure what they were supposed to do yet, but the flier just waved.

"I'll be back by the time you've got it sorted."

" 'Shael can have him," Valyn said as he turned his attention back to the map. Gwenna was hovering over one shoulder, Talal over the other, and Annick seemed to be reading the entire thing upside down from her seat on the bench. "Everyone, just take a step back," he snapped. "I'll let you know when I've looked it over."

"Oh yes, Your Radiance," Gwenna said, recoiling with a look of mock horror on her face. "We didn't mean to crowd you, Your Excellency." She sketched a dubious curtsy. "I'm sorry, but I can't remember your proper honorific. Do you prefer Sir, Commander, or My Most Noble and Honored Lord?"

Valyn tried to keep his temper. Maybe Gwenna was testing him, and maybe she just didn't like the idea of taking orders from a Wing leader her own age. Either way, getting in a fight with his demolitions master on the day of Wing Selection wasn't likely to improve their chances of success at whatever 'Shael-spawned task Fane had thrown their way.

"Commander will do fine," he growled. "Do you have your kit? We don't know what we might need out there. Maybe some moles, or some starshatters."

Gwenna's green eyes blazed. "Of course. Maybe you'd forgotten that the new Wings always have a test right after selection."

Valyn silently cursed himself. Between trying to ferret out Lin's killer and recovering from his exhaustion in the Hole, he *had* forgotten. Not that he could afford to let the others know that.

"Good," he said gruffly. "Annick, you've got your bow."

"We're wasting time," the sniper said curtly. She gestured to the map.

Valyn bit off a sharp response and returned his attention to the inked lines.

"It's a grab-and-go," he said. "There's a target in the middle of the island—doesn't say what. We go in, we get it, we get out. Basic."

"What about the other Wings?" Talal asked. The leach wasn't paying as much attention to the paper in front of them as he was to the surrounding knots of soldiers. They had maps, too, Valyn realized. Sami Yurl was hunched over, gesturing to his people, then back to the paper. They had the *same* map, and they were already formulating a plan.

"Fine," he said, trying to slow down his thoughts and his pulse, failing at both. "We'll come in from the north—"

Annick shook her head, a curt, clipped gesture. "Not good."

"Why not?" Talal asked, turning to the parchment.

"Sharn is to the south," Valyn pointed out impatiently. "The interior is all jungle, too heavily forested to make a drop there, which means we need to put down on a beach. The closest is to the north, and the route overland to the target is shorter."

"Except it's overland," Annick said, her eyes locked on his. "If we come in from the east, we go a little farther, but we can take this ravine—" she pointed to a crooked line on the map"—all the way up. No getting lost. We walk in the water. No tripping over roots or hacking through brush."

Valyn eyed the ravine. He didn't like the thought of following the low ground, but the sniper was right—they *would* move faster out of the jungle. A good commander didn't just command; he listened as well. Valyn took a deep breath and swallowed his pride. "Thank you, Annick. I think you're right. Let's take the eastern approach.

"Talal," he went on, turning to the leach. "What's your well?"

The youth drew back, his dark eyes narrowing. "I don't . . . I don't tell anyone that."

Gwenna rolled her eyes. "This isn't just *anyone*. This is your *commander,* and he wants to know your well."

"Gwenna," Valyn said, raising a hand. "Please." He turned his attention back to Talal. "I need to know," he said, trying to sound reasonable. Yurl's Wing was already moving toward the harbor, and Essa was gesturing vigorously to her map and her soldiers, evidently putting together some sort of attack. "We're Wing mates now. You can share that sort of thing."

The leach shook his head. "I can tell you that I'll have access to it on the island, but it won't be very powerful."

"What *is* it?" Valyn demanded, more heatedly than he'd intended.

"I'm not telling you."

Annick looked from the leach to Valyn and back again. "You're acting like a fool," she said flatly. "You're hurting the Wing."

"I've told him what he needs to know," Talal insisted, his voice quiet but hard. "We can waste time arguing about it, or we can get on with the planning."

Valyn locked eyes with the leach. It was a direct challenge to his nascent authority, but the other Wings would be airborne shortly and bungling his first exercise as Wing commander might be even worse.

"We'll talk about it later," he said curtly, turning his attention back to the map. "Talal, you'll take point; hopefully whatever you *can* do will be enough if we're surprised. Gwenna will be a dozen paces back. I'll be moving through the trees to the right of the stream. We'll have Laith on the left bank. Annick, you'll be in the water, shallow enough that you can still shoot. If we flush out someone, hit 'em with a stunner."

The sniper nodded curtly.

"Here comes the bird," Gwenna said, gesturing over her shoulder, and then Suant'ra was upon them in a flurry of wings and wind.

†

The exercise did not go well. The river was deeper than anticipated, the current stronger. Valyn's Wing was forced out of the water into the thick brush along the banks, and even with their swords out hacking a path, they made horrible time and put up enough of a racket that anyone listening would have plenty of time to flee or attack, as they saw fit. Yurl's Wing chose to attack.

It was a standard rattrap ambush: three men high in the trees on the right bank, two in the water dead ahead. Laith went charging off before Valyn could give an order to consolidate, and one of Hern's stunners dropped him in his tracks. Valyn called for smokers to cover their retreat, but the wind was blowing the wrong way, as Gwenna pointed out in a fusillade of profanity. Whatever Talal's well was, he never made visible use of it, and after Annick had loosed her first arrow, something hard and invisible crunched into the side of her head, depositing her in the murky water. In the end, Valyn resorted to a pathetic, useless charge up the center channel, tripping a flash-and-bang, ending up on his back in the mud, staring up at Sami Yurl's grinning face while he tried to rub the stars from his eyes, to clear the ringing from his ears.

"Tough break, Malkeenian," the youth drawled, spitting a gob of phlegm into Valyn's face. "I have to say, I'm not surprised that you managed to bugger the attack, but I *am* impressed that you did so so adeptly.

"You know, all these years of you and Lin working together, I always thought *you* were the smart one." He chuckled. "Funny. Now it turns out that in addition to having the sweetest ass on the Islands, she was the brains as well." He shook his head in mock regret. "But you never managed to get into that, did you? And now she's dead. What a shame."

Rage burned in Valyn like acid, and he scrabbled to reach over his shoulder for the second of his two blades. Yurl's boot came down on his wrist, grinding until it felt like the bones would break. "Don't," he said, his face growing serious. "It's not that I *wouldn't* kill you, but it would be a blemish on my record. You *are* another Wing leader, after all, at least until you get yourself killed."

Valyn searched for something to say, for something to do that might buy him time, but Yurl never gave him the chance. The flat of his blade swung in a vicious arc, pain split Valyn's skull, and the sky went dark.

30

Kaden spent the lengthening days of late spring tracking, running—at night and during the day, blindfolded and not—throwing bowls in the pottery shed, and painting, all under the watchful eye of Rampuri Tan. There had been no more gruesome deaths since Serkhan's body was found, but the older monk insisted on accompanying his pupil whenever he left the central compound of the monastery, and it was some small comfort that Tan always carried that strange *naczal* spear. At least, it would have been a comfort if he didn't spend half his time beating Kaden black and blue with the flat of it.

The training, which had started out brutal, only got worse; the blows grew sharper, the labors longer, the respites ever more brief. Strangely, Kaden was starting to realize that in many ways his *umial* seemed to know him better than he knew himself—knew just how long he could be held under the mountain streams before drowning, how long he could run before falling, and how close he could hold his hand to the flame without burning away the flesh—and as the days passed, Kaden found that, though his body still recoiled from the physical torment, his mind accepted it with growing equanimity. Still, it was a relief when he had a few scant hours to himself.

The stone cell in which he slept was small, barely large enough for a thin reed mattress, a simple desk, and a few hooks on which he could hang his robes. The granite of the walls and floor was cold and rough. Still, it was his own, and when he closed the door to the hallway, he had the illusion of privacy and solitude. He seated himself at the desk, glanced out the narrow window into the courtyard, unstoppered his ink jar, and took up his quill. *Father*—he wrote at the top of the page. The letter would take months to reach the Dawn Palace, even if he was able to send it along with Blerim

Panno when he left for the Bend. From there it would have to go by boat to Annur. Whatever information Kaden cared to share would be hopelessly out of date by the time it arrived, and yet, it felt important to write, despite the fact that he didn't have anything to say. Maybe it was Tan's tutelage, or the deaths around the monastery, but Kaden felt as though some important part of himself, some human cord that tethered him to his past, to his family, to his home, was being stretched, that if he neglected it for too much longer, it might suddenly and unexpectedly snap. He paused before remembering to add his sister's name to the opening lines.

Father and Adare—
   I'm sorry it's been so long since last I wrote. We accomplish little here, but the days are full. Most recently

Before he could finish the sentence, the door crashed open. Kaden spun in his seat, searching for a weapon of some sort, but it was only Pater, sweaty and breathless in his robe. The small boy's face was flushed, his eyes wide with excitement.

"Kaden!" he shouted, trying to slow himself as he careened into the cell. "Kaden! There's people here, Kaden. *Strangers!*"

Kaden laid down his quill. Visitors to the monastery were rare, exceedingly so. There was a new crop of acolytes every year, of course, but they arrived together, on the same day, led by Blerim Panno, who guided them up into the mountains from the Bend. Sometimes Panno arrived from the west, but the way was long and arduous: barren steppe and intermittent desert with only the nomadic Urghul for company. Either way, the Footsore Monk wasn't scheduled to arrive for at least another month; Kaden had been getting an early start on his letter. "What kind of strangers?"

"Merchants!" the small boy chirped. "Two of them, and a pack mule, too!"

Kaden sat up. The Shin grew or made almost everything they needed, and for the rest they traded with the Urghul during the fall. Still, the occasional gullible trader, lured by rumors of fabulous hidden wealth in a monastery far to the north, would make the trek of hundreds of leagues. Their disappointment when they discovered the austerity of the Shin was so palpable that Kaden almost pitied them. It was unlikely that anyone would make the voyage so early in the year, but it sounded as though Pater had actually seen them.

"Where are they?" he asked.

"They're cleaning up now, but they're coming to the refectory for dinner. All the monks are going to be there, and we can ask questions! Nin even said so!"

The small boy was practically jumping out of his skin as Kaden rose to his feet.

"You run ahead," he said. "See if you can get a glimpse of them. I'll catch up with you in a few minutes."

Pater nodded and bolted out of the room all at once, leaving Kaden alone with his truncated letter. *Merchants.* The thought filled him with more excitement than he would have expected. It seemed he had almost forgotten what real excitement felt like. Still, these men would have news of the world, news of his family, Kaden realized as he doffed his mud-stained robe and started to pull a clean one over his head. It wasn't often that the monks had visitors, and Nin would want to make a favorable impression on whoever had taken the trouble to trek all the way across Vash.

"Don't bother," said Rampuri Tan. He had entered the room without knocking, and stood just inside the door, his dark eyes hard. The *naczal,* as always, was in his hand, although why he would carry it inside the dormitory was anyone's guess. Whatever had killed Serkhan surely wouldn't be bold enough to enter one of Ashk'lan's largest buildings.

Kaden hesitated.

"You won't be going to the evening meal," Tan continued. "You will not speak with the merchants. You will not approach the merchants. You will remain out of sight in the clay shed until they leave."

The words landed like a slap.

"They could be here a week," Kaden pointed out warily. "Longer."

"Then you will stay in the clay shed for a week. Or longer."

The older monk stared at him, then exited as abruptly as he had come, leaving Kaden with his rope belt halfway tied and a look of disbelief on his face.

Visitors to the monastery were such an unusual diversion that a large dinner was always prepared—two or three goats would be slaughtered, trenchers filled with turnips, potatoes, and carrots, and everyone would eat crusty loaves of warm bread. Even more enticing than the meal, however, would be the conversation. All the monks would have their chance to ask a question or two, to learn something of the world that continued to turn outside the walls of Ashk'lan. Bohumir Novalk would want to talk politics, of course, and so would Scial Nin. No doubt, fat Phirum Prumm would ask for news of Channary, which the merchants would have in abundance, and news of his mother, which they would not. Kaden couldn't remember an acolyte being forbidden to a meal when there were visitors present.

"Ae only knows what I did to deserve this," he muttered to himself, "but I hope Tan's got Akiil scrubbing out the privy."

He shrugged the clean robe back over his head and tossed it onto the bunk. No point sullying it with clay. He dressed quickly and then, just as he was leaving, walked directly into Pater's headlong rush.

"Kaden!" the boy shouted, trying to disentangle himself and pull Kaden down the hallway all at the same time. "Some of the monks are in the refectory already. We have to *hurry*!"

Kaden picked the boy up by his armpits, set him on his feet, and dusted him off.

"I know," he said, trying not to let his bitterness show. "But I can't go. You remember to tell me what they say, what they look like. You remember everything, all right?"

Pater stared at him, his mouth hanging open. "Can't go? Kaden, who even *knows* who they are? We *have* to go!"

It was just like Pater to shift from *I* to *we,* and Kaden smiled in spite of himself. "Tan sent me to the clay shed to polish bowls. He'll notice right away if I'm anywhere near the refectory. You go ahead."

Pater shook his head so vigorously it looked like it might rattle right off his shoulders. "We won't *go* to the refectory."

"But that's where the merchants are."

The boy beamed, obviously pleased with his chance to help. "We'll go to the *dovecote.*"

Kaden smiled slowly. The dovecote. Leave it to Pater to remember that old hideout.

The granite of the high peaks was cold and hard, impossible to cut or quarry. The Shin were forced to scavenge their building stone—exfoliated flakes and small, uneven boulders. Given the labor involved, the monks made the most of their existing structures and so, countless years back, when some brother long dead decided to build a dovecote, he built it up against the rear of the refectory, saving himself the labor of constructing a fourth wall. In their early years at the monastery, Kaden and Akiil had discovered the dovecote's true value: a hidden spot where they could escape the severe eyes of their *umials*. When they outgrew their childhood hideout, they had passed the secret on to Pater, and Kaden had to smile now at the idea of the younger boy reminding him of his own secret.

"Is there anyone out back?" he asked. "Anyone who might see us?"

Pater shook his head emphatically once more. "They're all out front, hoping to ask the merchants a few questions before the meal begins."

"And Tan?"

"He's there, too! Right next to Scial Nin!"

That settled it. As the two made their way toward the back of the refectory, Pater bounding ahead, Kaden pulled his hood up over his face, trying to look nondescript. He cast a glance over his shoulder before slipping through the narrow doorway, then climbed the ladder to the tiny second story, where the doves were housed in narrow cells. He could hear their soft cooing, the gentle, delicate sound they made deep in their hollow chests. Even the musty scent of hay and droppings was a comfort, a memory of a childhood when he and Akiil had hidden in the gloom, eluding their chores and their *umials*. That was before Rampuri Tan. Well before.

"Here," Pater whispered, tugging at the sleeve of his robe. The boy pointed to a place where the oakum chinking the cracks in the rock had long ago been gouged away by the fingers of novices. Feeling like a furtive child again, Kaden put his eye to the crack and grinned to himself as he peered down into the refectory.

The entirety of the long room, from the stone floor to the beams of the peaked ceiling, was given over to the broad, communal tables where the monks ate. Most of the monks were already seated, although none would take food until the visitors arrived. They spoke in low voices while some of the younger novices stole speculative glances toward the kitchen, clearly hungry, and clearly wary lest their *umials* notice the lapse in discipline. Kaden, however, had eyes only for the door, and so he saw the two strangers at the very moment that they entered.

A compact, blond man of middle years stepped through the doorway first. Despite the chill, he wore a sleeveless tunic of bright red leather, and even from his perch Kaden could see the muscle cording his arms and neck. He was far from handsome, his skin creased from long days in the sun, eyes hawkish and close together, but he moved with a brusque confidence. His companion entered a few steps behind, and Kaden was glad for the wall of stone to hide his stare. Pater had mentioned nothing about a woman.

The second visitor was lean and elegant in her carefully tailored riding cloak, rings flashing on half her fingers. At a quick glance she might have appeared young, but the years had left their subtle marks—a few faint lines creasing the corners of her eyes, a hint of gray streaking her long dark hair. She must have been a few years over forty, Kaden decided, and favored her right leg, as though some old injury still gnawed at the opposite hip or knee—the trail up to Ashk'lan would have been a trial for her.

Kaden started to look for Rampuri Tan, then went back to his scrutiny of the newcomers. He hadn't seen many merchants in the past eight years, but there was something strange about these two, something off, like ripples on a pool on a windless day.

"Let me see!" Pater whispered urgently. "Come on! It's *my* turn."

Kaden relinquished his post and as Pater clambered past him, closed his eyes, trying to work out what had struck him. He called the *saama'an* back to mind. It was imperfect, hazy around the edges since he hadn't had time to make a proper carving, but the details at the center were crisp enough—the man and the woman frozen in the act of entering the large hall. He studied the facial expressions, the posture, the clothes, trying to ferret out the source of his misgiving. Were they frowning? Frightened? Moving oddly? He shook his head. There was nothing to see.

"See Kaden? You don't have to worry," Pater whispered. "Tan's here. He's talking to the two of them."

The mention of his *umial*'s name hit Kaden like a bucket of frigid water, jolting him back to the scene in the man's cell nearly two months earlier, when he had whipped Kaden bloody over the painting of the slaughtered goat. *Any fool can see what's there. You need to see what is not there.* It was possible that whatever bothered him about the merchants wasn't something that he'd seen, but something that he *should* have seen. Kaden called the *saama'an* back and examined it once again.

"Now they're talking to the abbot," Pater narrated breathlessly. "I didn't even know they *made* clothes that color."

The abbot. Kaden stared at the image. The two merchants had traveled hundreds of leagues to sell *something,* and if they knew anything about monasteries, they knew that Scial Nin was the one man who would determine the success or failure of their venture. He was there, standing right inside the door, directly in front of them, and yet, in that first moment, just as they passed the threshold, neither was looking at him. The woman seemed to be peering above the heads of the monks as though searching the rafters, and the man's head was turned sharply to the left, checking the space occluded by the opened door. Kaden let the image snap into motion, and almost instantly the two turned their attention to the abbot, smiling as they approached.

"Let me have another look," Kaden said, elbowing Pater in the ribs.

The small boy glared at him, then moved a fraction to the left. "Here," he said, "we can *both* see." Kaden had to content himself with a knobby elbow digging into his ribs as he peered through the crack.

Scial Nin introduced himself with simple formality and the merchants followed suit, the man with a simple nod of his head, the woman eschewing a curtsy for a graceful bow. There was a bright glint in her blue eyes that mirrored the flashing gems on her fingers. Most people would be exhausted after the arduous trek up the mountains, but she looked curious about her surroundings, fully engaged with the people before her. Their names, Pyrre and Jakin Lakatur, sounded strange in Kaden's ears, and their accents, slow and sibilant, certainly weren't from Annur.

"It's a long hike up your little hill," Pyrre lamented wryly, rubbing her knee. "Perhaps you'd consider acquiring one of those kettral everyone is always telling tales about."

"We value our isolation here," Nin replied, not unkindly.

The merchant grinned and turned to her companion. "Meaning," she said with a rueful grin, "we should have saved ourselves the trip."

"Not at all," Nin said, gesturing to a long table. "You are here now. Although I can't promise we will offer you any custom, you are welcome to share our repast."

Frustratingly, the abbot made only small talk during the meal, polite comments about the weather and the state of the flocks, which allowed his guests to focus on their food. When Phirum cleared his throat to ask a question, Nin fixed him with that calm, implacable gaze of his, and the fat acolyte sagged back onto his bench. Only when the last crumbs had been wiped off the last plate did Scial Nin slide his chair back from the table and cross his hands in his lap. "So," he said finally, "what news from the world?"

Pyrre grinned; she seemed by far the more garrulous of the two. "Sailors fight pirates, soldiers fight Urghul, the Waist is still hot, and Freeport's still cold enough that you've got to fuck in your furs." She ran through the litany with the air of a woman who found something funny about the entire world, as though it were there for her amusement. "Mothers pray to

Bedisa, whores to Ciena, alemasters mix their malt with water, and an honest woman still goes poor to her grave."

"And you," the abbot asked with a genial nod. "Are you an honest woman?"

"My wife? Honest?" Jakin snorted, gesturing to the rings on her fingers, cabochons and cut gems glittering in the candlelight. "Her tastes are too expensive for honesty."

"Darling," the merchant replied, turning to her husband with a wounded look, "you would have the good brothers believe that a wolf has come among them to steal their sheep."

The words hit home, and Nin set down his teacup before asking the next question.

"You didn't come across anything unusual on the trail up to the monastery, did you?"

"Unusual?" Pyrre spun one of the rings on her fingers absently as she considered the question. "Not aside from more broken spokes than we normally see in a month. We were forced to leave our wagon halfway down that ludicrous goat track you call a trail." Her eyes narrowed appraisingly. "What did you mean by unusual?"

"A creature?" Nin responded. "Some kind of predator?"

Pyrre glanced at her husband, but he just shrugged.

"Nothing," she replied. "Should we be worried? I've heard that you raise crag cats the size of ponies in these mountains."

"Not a crag cat. We're sure enough of that. Whatever it is has been savaging our flocks recently. A few weeks ago, it killed one of our brothers."

A few of the monks shifted on their benches. A log on the long hearth collapsed in a shower of embers. Pyrre pushed back in her chair and took a deep breath. Kaden froze the image and looked closer. The woman should have been frightened by the news, confused and alarmed at the very least. After all, she and her husband had spent the better part of a day—longer, if they had a wagon with them—toiling up the very trails where Serkhan had been killed. Even if she was capable of protecting herself and her wares from brigands and highwaymen, a possibility that seemed unlikely, given her age and that hip, she should have registered some sort of worry at the realization that an unknown predator was stalking the mountains, killing men and beasts alike.

Certainly she had made an effort to mimic concern; her lips tightened, her brow furrowed. But here, too, something was missing. Where were the widened eyes, the involuntary glance at her husband that would have indicated true fear? Where was the surprise?

"How ghastly," Pyrre said. "I'm sorry for your loss."

"Those of us who live in the hollow of the Blank God's hand have no fear of Ananshael."

Pyrre pursed her lips, shot her husband a skeptical glance. "I guess that explains why I never became a monk."

"You never became a monk," Jakin replied, "because you have breasts and you like men to look at them."

"A thousand pardons," Pyrre interjected, turning back to the abbot with a horrified look on her face. "After months on the road with only me for company, my husband sometimes forgets his tongue."

"No apology needed," Nin replied, although his features had hardened somewhat.

"In truth," Pyrre continued, "I'm overly attached to this sad little life of mine. Hard to say why, really. It mostly consists of trudging, overcooked rice in the evening, sleeping in the rain, undercooked rice in the morning, and more trudging." She pursed her lips speculatively. "Occasionally my knee gives out. Sometimes there are gallstones."

"And yet you would not give it up," Nin concluded.

"Not for all the gold you've got hidden in your granary."

"A nice gambit," Nin replied. "But we have no granary, let alone gold."

Pyrre turned to her husband. "It's worse than we thought." She returned her attention to Scial Nin. "This thing that killed your brother. Are we in danger?"

Nin raised a reassuring hand. "You made it here—that is the crucial fact. You should be safe in the buildings and central square. We can give you an escort when you descend the path once more."

"We thank you," she responded. "And again, we're sorry for your loss. It's bad luck to lose a friend—even for stoic monks indifferent to death. Perhaps we can take your mind off it with news of the outside world. You're just a step or two off the main trade routes."

That opened the floodgates, and for a while the robed men lost some of their austerity in their eagerness. Nin did his best to maintain order, but more than once two or even three monks spoke at the same time, each trying to pitch his voice just a little louder than the others.

"How many ships of the line has O'Mara Havast taken this year?" asked Altaf the Smith. The man had plied his trade at the Bend before joining the Shin, and he retained a keen curiosity about the Annurian navy.

Chalmer Oleki wanted to know if the rebel Hannan tribes had stepped up attacks on the empire. Phirum Prumm, true to form, asked nervously if any plagues had swept Channary recently. "My mother," he added apologetically. "She lives there still, at least she did when I departed."

"I have no news of your mother," Pyrre responded, "much to my chagrin. I *can* tell you that the atrep of Channary has redoubled his efforts to keep the city streets clear of filth, and the plague has not visited the city since."

"How about the Urghul?" Rebbin wanted to know. "There were rumblings of war this year when we went down to trade with them in their winter pasturage. Something about a new chieftain unifying the tribes."

"The Urghul," she replied, turning her palms to the ceiling helplessly, "are the Urghul. One day they seem massed for an assault over the White River, following this new shaman or chief or whoever he is. The next, they're sacrificing captives or buggering elk or whatever it is they do for sport."

When the questions got around to Akiil, Kaden's friend had the temerity to ask the merchants to describe "with careful attention to detail" the body of Ciena's new high priestess. Pyrre laughed at that, a long melodious laugh, while the abbot shot the youth a look that promised penance on the morrow.

Kaden had been at Ashk'lan so long that he didn't know most of the names and places his brothers asked after. At best they were dimly recol-
childhood so far away, it might have been a different
pure fantasy, and he let the strange syllables
ile he forgot the questions pricking his mind,
spicions about the merchant and her husband.

uestions in long, literary cadences while Jakin
ed that someone named the Burned King was
ties of southeastern Vash. Tsavein Kar'amalan
, as ruthless and shadowy as ever. An odd ru-
the tribes of the Darvi Desert were trying to
caz, though how they could hope to establish a
tory held by Annurian legions was unclear. On
til at long last, Halva Sjold asked the question

Kaden had been waiting for: "And the Emperor? Sanlitun is still the strong, stubborn oak I remember from twenty years ago?"

Pyrre continued to smile as she had throughout most of the evening, an easy, casual grin that invited camaraderie and confidence. As she nodded, however, Kaden felt a pricking under his skin. "The books say Sanlitun means 'stone' in the old tongue. If so, the name suits the Emperor. It will take a hurricane to dislodge him."

The words should have been comforting. *It will take a hurricane to dislodge him.* They *should* have been comforting, but the woman was lying, Kaden was sure of it. At the very least, she was concealing something. He reached for the calm he had summoned at the start of the meal, tried desperately to empty his mind and fill it with the image of the merchant smiling and nodding. The *saama'an* eluded him. He could think only of his father grasping his small forearm. *I will teach you to make the cold, hard decisions through which a boy becomes a man. . . .*

The conversation dragged on, but Kaden moved away from his post, allowing Pater the full space. As the boy peered in fascination into the room below, Kaden leaned back against the rough stone wall of the dovecote. *Any fool can see what's there. You need to see what is not there.* As he stared into the darkness, he tried to imagine what Pyrre wasn't saying about the empire, what she wasn't saying about his father.

31

I want to know your well," Valyn began, trying to keep his voice reasonable and firm at the same time.

It had been over a week since the disaster in the swamp, and he'd made next to no progress in pulling together his Wing. Gwenna was still insubordinate, Laith was still reckless, Annick was still . . . Annick, and Talal still refused to share the secret source of what little arcane power he possessed. Worse, Valyn continued to harbor doubts about the sniper and the leach; they both had secrets, and he was learning quickly not to trust anyone with secrets. It was impossible to tackle everything at once, but learning Talal's well would help him in his command of the Wing and might just fit one more piece into the larger puzzle of Amie's and Lin's deaths.

Talal nodded guardedly. "I wondered when we would get to this."

The two of them sat face-to-face across a scarred wooden table. They had their own barrack now, a narrow wooden building with bunks in the back, a large room devoted to weapons and gear on the side, and out front, the "ready room"—a small space with a cast-iron stove, five chairs, and a large wooden table around which the whole Wing could gather to sort equipment, study maps, or plan for the next mission. It wasn't glamorous, but after the cavernous cadets' barracks, it felt private and secure. *Would feel even better,* Valyn thought bleakly, *if I shared it with anyone I trusted.*

The other three members of his Wing were off at the mess hall, but Valyn had asked Talal to stay behind.

"I'm the commander of this Wing," he began, careful to douse the heat in his voice. "I choose strategy and tactics based on our assets and liabilities. I've respected your privacy so far, but it's killing us out there."

For the first couple of days, he'd hoped he would be able to ferret out the leach's well with a little well-timed observation. It seemed like a straight-forward problem: Look around whenever Talal used a kenning, make a list of possible wells, then narrow that list at every future kenning until there was only one possibility left. The problem was, Talal didn't rely on his strange powers as much as Valyn had expected. Unlike a lot of leaches, he was more than proficient with a blade, better than anyone on the Wing except Valyn, in fact, and he seemed to prefer conventional tactics to more exotic solutions. Worse, even when he *did* use a kenning, there were just too many possible wells to narrow it down. Valyn might rule out firespike and blood one day, but that still left a legion of possibilities: sea, salt, stone, light, shade, iron . . . A clerk with a ledger and a year of study might manage it, but not Valyn, not while he was trying to keep his Wing from falling apart.

"If you want me to keep the secret from the rest of the group," Valyn urged, "I can do that."

Talal shook his head almost reluctantly. "I can tell you before the mission whether I'll have access to my well or not, can probably even tell you how strong it will be."

"Not good enough," Valyn snapped. "I need backup plans, contingencies. I need all the knowledge we've got in order to improvise on the fly." *And I need to know if you took down Manker's,* he thought grimly. *I need to know if you killed Amie and Ha Lin.* There was still nothing linking the destruction of the alehouse with the deaths of the two women, nothing but the timing of Amie's murder, but Valyn hadn't abandoned the suspicion that it was all part of a larger, more intricate plot.

"I'm not sure you realize what you're asking for," Talal said quietly.

"Information," Valyn said, spreading his hands. "That's all. Just information."

Talal shook his head once more. "You don't understand."

"Enlighten me."

The leach took a deep breath. "I grew up with the same fear of leaches that anyone felt. My uncle used to come over and frighten us with stories of the Atmani—bloodcurdling stuff. My father once walked three days just to see a leach hanged. He returned home with a smile on his face." Talal's eyes went distant as he spoke. "We—my brothers and I—were so *angry* we hadn't been allowed to go. We begged for all the details. Did he have a forked tongue? Did he cry blood? Did he piss himself when he died?

"A week later, I had my first delving." The leach's eyes were far away, his face blank as he continued. "I was working late in my father's shop. I'd mismeasured a tenon, ruined a whole evening's worth of effort. I was cursing the thing, cursing myself, cursing the chair, when suddenly, the chairback shattered. At first I was busy just picking the splinters out of my flesh. Then I realized what had happened. What it meant.

"No one had seen it—if they had, I'd have been hanged or burned or stoned in the street before the sun rose—but I still felt the guilt, the *disgust*. It didn't matter that I hadn't *tried* to use it. I knew the stories. When you had a well, it came to possess you, to twist you. It unmade everything good inside you until you would stop at nothing to bend the world to your will."

He paused, gazing at his palm as though searching for something written there, some explanation scrawled in the lines of his flesh. "I found a rope in the barn, tied a careful noose, pulled it tight around my neck, and stepped off the back of the wagon."

He stopped, and raised his eyes to the bruised sunset beyond the grimy window.

"And?" Valyn asked, drawn in to the story in spite of himself.

Talal shrugged. "My father found me. Cut me down. He never did know why I'd done it. A couple men from the Eyrie came three weeks later."

"How'd they know?"

"They've had time to learn what to look for," Talal replied. "Unexpected outbursts, children gone missing in safe towns, suicides that don't make sense." He fixed Valyn with a level gaze. "I wasn't unusual. No one wants to learn that they're an abomination."

"Your family?" Valyn asked cautiously.

"They think I'm just a soldier. It's a lie, but it makes them proud."

A silence hung between them, heavy and grim as lead. Valyn could hear laughter and roughhousing in the next barracks over and faintly, in the distance, the clink of spoons against bowls as the Kettral tucked into their meals over in the mess hall. The room in which he sat, however, was still and nearly dark.

"I'm not your family," Valyn said finally. "I've spent half my life here, on the Islands. I don't feel . . . that way about leaches."

Talal met his eye, then smiled bleakly. "You're a shitty liar, Valyn. You may make a good Wing leader someday, but you're a shitty liar."

Valyn took a deep breath. "It's hard, knowing that someone else can do things you can't, things you can't even *begin* to understand. I won't deny that, but we're on the same Wing now. That should be a bond stronger than blood. We need to start trusting each other."

Talal considered him soberly. "And when are you going to start trusting me?"

Valyn felt as though he'd been caught wrong-footed in a duel, attacking when he should have been looking to his defense.

"I do," he protested weakly. "I trust you."

"No," the leach replied evenly. "You trust Laith a little, Gwenna less, and Annick and me not at all."

Valyn leaned back in his chair. He thought he'd hidden his emotions, thought that he'd been distant and professional, the way a Wing commander was supposed to be. "Are you—?"

"Using a kenning?" Talal asked, his mouth quirked in a wry twist. "Looking into your mind?"

It sounded foolish, once the words were said aloud, but Valyn had no way to know what the leach could and could not do.

"No," Talal said. "I'm watching. Listening. It's pretty clear you'd rather bury a knife in my gut than work with me." He shook his head. "I'm not Balendin, you know. He's a lot stronger than I am. His well, whatever it is, runs incredibly deep, but that's not the only difference."

Valyn could only nod mutely.

"Let me ask *you* a question," the leach asked after a long silence, "since you're so intent on sharing secrets."

Valyn shrugged his acquiescence.

"What happened to you? During the Trial? What happened to your eyes?"

I should have known it wouldn't be easy to answer, Valyn thought to himself. Some of the cadets had emerged from the Hole gushing with stories, almost desperate to relate the minute details of their foray into the darkness. Talal was not one of them. Neither was Valyn. He had confided in no one about the black egg or his encounter with the slarn king. It was enough that he went into the cave poisoned and emerged cured. No one needed to know the details, certainly not a leach.

But then, he needed that leach to trust him. Much as Valyn hated to admit it, the youth had a point—there was no reason to share secrets with someone who refused to divulge his own. *To get ground,* Hendran wrote, *it is sometimes necessary to give ground.*

"I found a different egg."

"Different?"

"Larger. A lot larger. And black."

Talal's eyes widened in the lamplight. "Slarn?"

Valyn nodded hesitantly. He was committed to the truth now, for good or ill. "I think so. The nest was the same."

"A black slarn egg," the leach mused, pursing his lips. Then, after a long hesitation: "You know they changed us, right?"

"Changed?" Valyn asked. For the second time, he felt the conversation slipping from his control. "What do you mean 'changed'? Who?"

"The eggs. They cured the toxin, but there were . . . secondary effects."

Valyn stared. This was the first he'd heard of it.

"At first I thought I was just exhausted," the leach continued. "Thought I was imagining it."

"Imagining *what?*" Valyn demanded, trying to keep his voice level as the memory from the cave filled his mind, the feel of the black slime slipping down his gullet as he emptied the contents of the shattered shell into his mouth.

Talal shrugged. "The dizziness. That passed in the first day or so. Then the night vision. The hearing."

Valyn shook his head, lost.

"Listen," Talal said, holding up a finger.

Valyn listened. The noises from the neighboring barracks had fallen silent, but there were other sounds: waves washing over the rocky beach, waves farther out breaking on the Gray Shoals. Had he been able to hear those before? To sort the soft susurration of water on shingle from the sharper, more percussive striking of the long swells against the reef? He closed his eyes. He could hear the creak of rope against wood. Rigging, he realized, of the ships moored in the bay. And beneath that, the slow groaning of those ships' timbers as they flexed with the roll and wash of the sea.

He opened his eyes but found he had no words.

"Better?" Talal asked, his eyebrows raised. "More acute? More precise?"

Valyn nodded. "Holy Hull. You think it was the slarn eggs that did this?" He paused to listen again. A door crashed open far away and he heard a high voice—he thought it was Chi Hoai Mi—laughing at someone inside.

The leach nodded. "It makes sense. The egg provides the food for the slarn before they hatch. It's what makes them what they are—creatures that live in darkness, that *thrive* in darkness. They need better hearing, more sensitive touch. They may even have senses we're unaware of. It comes from somewhere. Why not their food?"

"And now we've eaten that food as well," Valyn concluded. *Some of us more than others,* he added silently, dread roiling in his stomach. If the eggs had permanent effects, there would be risks as well. There were always risks.

"They didn't just send us down there as a test," Valyn went on, amazed. "Even for the Kettral, a trial that could end in half the class dead and the other half crippled for life is a little severe. They *needed* to send us down into the Hole. Those eggs didn't just cure us."

"They changed us," Talal agreed. "Not in major ways, but slightly."

"That explains why our 'Kent-kissing instructors were always one step ahead," Valyn realized, a jolt of indignation riding up his spine. "They always knew we were coming. The Hull-buggered bastards could *hear* us half a mile away."

Talal nodded. He'd had more time to come to grips with the fact, and the corner of his mouth turned up in the tiniest grin. "They're bastards," he agreed, "but they're *clever* bastards."

"Who else knows about this?"

The leach shook his head. "Hard to say. Daveen Shaleel didn't exactly trumpet the fact. I would imagine that most Wings are like us . . . maybe a few have realized. Maybe more. It's possible some never will."

"But you figured it out."

Talal's face went wary once more. "Something about being a leach, I guess. When you've worked with a well as long as I have, you . . . notice things. You notice the little changes."

Abruptly, Valyn started to laugh. "Well, I'm glad you were able to explain it to *me.* Left to my own devices, I probably never would have thought beyond the foul taste of that 'Kent-kissing thing. . . ." The laughter shriveled in his throat. "But the egg I found—"

"—was different," Talal concluded, nodding.

"I wasn't supposed to eat that egg. No one in the Eyrie planned on it. No one knows what it does."

"Well, it didn't kill you."

"Yet."

"I'll bet my blades it was what changed your eyes."

Valyn nodded, comprehension and unease washing over him at once.

"And there are other things—," he murmured, breaking off as he remembered who he was talking to.

"—but you don't want to tell me about them," Talal finished, his expression unsurprised but sad.

Valyn took a deep breath. He was walking the narrowest of lines: Step too far to one side, and the leach would never lower his guard. Step too far to the other, and he'd give up more information than he gained.

"I can feel things," he admitted reluctantly.

Talal leaned in closer.

"When I found Ha Lin," Valyn continued, "I knew something was lying across the floor yards before I reached her." He closed his eyes and let the memory wash over him, the whispering currents of air eddying over his skin, the faintest scent of her hair in his nostrils. He hadn't noticed anything like that since leaving the cave, but then, since leaving the cave, he'd been overwhelmed with more ordinary sensations: a new Wing, training runs, arguments with Gwenna. Now, however, with his eyes shut, he let his breathing slow and just . . . waited.

There was a crack in the wall, he realized, a few feet above his head and to the left; the draft lifted the hairs along the back of his neck. He could hear the wick fizzling in the lamp. He could . . . he squeezed his eyes shut tighter . . . he wasn't sure if he was seeing or feeling, but he knew right where Talal was sitting, even something about his posture.

The leach remained silent, still.

"I knew it was her," Valyn went on, voice quiet, eyes still closed. "I didn't believe it at the time. I didn't want to believe it, *couldn't* believe it. Lin." He shook his head. "I knew. Even dead, even in the pitch-dark, I knew her."

There were tears in his eyes when he opened them, but he met the leach's gaze defiantly. *She was my friend,* he told himself. *There is no shame in weeping for her.* They were the first tears he had allowed himself since finding her, and for a long time they just streamed down his cheeks, puddling quietly in the table's ruts. After a while, they stopped. He wiped his cheeks roughly with a palm.

"If you speak a word of this," he said, his voice ragged, "to anyone on the Wing, I'll rip out your throat and we'll make do without a leach."

"Iron," Talal replied, voice quiet but sure.

"What the fuck are you talking about?"

"Iron," the leach said again, gesturing to the knife at his belt, the rough bracelets around both wrists. "That's my well. Of course, we don't carry much iron, but there's plenty of iron in steel, enough to do the job."

Valyn put his palms flat on the table, trying to stow his own emotions and make sense of the claim. There was every chance the leach was lying to him, and no way to know for sure. He considered those dark, still eyes.

"Why isn't it more powerful?"

Talal shrugged. "Not that much iron around most of the time—a few blades, a few arrowheads. Enough to work with, usually, but rarely enough to do anything impressive."

"If we were going in after a fortified position," Valyn asked warily, "could you bring it down?"

"Not a chance."

"What about something that wasn't built out of stone? Something less sturdy—like a wooden palisade?" *Or an alehouse on stilts,* he thought to himself. *What about Manker's?*

Talal considered the question. "If there was a great deal of steel present— as there would be on a densely packed battlefield—maybe. And if the structure was already flawed in some crucial way." He spread his hands. "Then I *might* be able to manage it. Or I might not." He shook his head ruefully. "I'm sorry, Valyn. I'm sure you were hoping for more out of your Wing's leach. Aacha could have knocked down a stone gatehouse when his well was running strong. Same with most of the leaches." He frowned. "Bad luck. I've got enough power to get me hanged, but not enough to protect myself. It's why I had to get so handy with the blades," he said, gesturing over his shoulder to the twin swords sheathed across his back.

That fact, more than anything else, carried the question for Valyn. Soldiers gravitated to their strengths, as much as their trainers tried to beat the tendency out of them. Annick carried that bow of hers everywhere, Laith preferred to be on the bird's back, and Gwenna never seemed happy unless she was blowing something up. Deception or no, it was hard to believe that Talal would have devoted so much time to his blades if he had a powerful, secret well to draw upon. Anything was possible, of course, but sometimes you had to play the odds.

"What about Balendin?" Valyn asked cautiously. "Could he knock down a building?"

Talal nodded slowly. "He hides his full strength pretty cleverly, but I've seen him manage some things. . . ." His eyes drifted with the memory, then snapped back. "He's dangerous, and not just because he's cruel."

"Any new ideas about his well?"

"Nothing."

"Do you have any *guesses*?" Valyn pressed, wary and impatient all at the same time.

"I've had about a thousand of them."

"He keeps those dogs of his close—"

"That's the obvious thing," Talal agreed, "but the obvious thing isn't usually the right one. We've all got our masks and disguises." He gestured to the stone amulet hanging around his neck, to the gold hoops in his ears. "And then there's the whole business of intentional deception. Before I started flying with you, I would avoid using my well on random days, even if it meant losing an exercise or contest, just to keep the others off my scent." He grimaced. "It's a bad way to live. Always lying. Always trying to lead people on. . . ."

Valyn had never considered it that way. In the stories, the leaches were always the villains, the nefarious meddlers behind the scenes, the ones pulling the strings, the ones making the world dance their own unnatural jig. He had never thought that their power might force *them* to dance.

"Thank you for telling me," he said finally, awkwardly.

"I always figured I'd tell someone eventually," Talal replied. "You keep something like that hidden for too long—" He shook his head slowly. "—there's no telling what it might do to you, no telling what you might become."

32

There were no locks on the door, but for three days, ever since the dinner for Pyrre and Jakin, Kaden had been a prisoner in the clay shed. He had sneaked back just in time, slipping out of the dovecote with Pater, sprinting down the path, and sliding inside with barely enough time to light a lantern, slow his heartbeat, cool his skin, and compose his face before Tan arrived to check up on him.

"How was the dinner?" Kaden had asked nonchalantly. He yearned to question his *umial* about Pyrre's strange behavior—if anyone else picked up on it, it would have been Tan—but, of course, if he let on that he'd been hiding in the dovecote, Ae only knew what sort of penance the monk would devise.

"Unremarkable," Tan replied, looking over Kaden's work. "You haven't made much progress."

"The process is the goal," Kaden responded innocently, trying not to feel smug. It was about time one of those Shin maxims worked in his favor.

"You will continue the process tomorrow."

"And tonight?" Kaden asked. "Should I return to the dormitory?"

Tan shook his head. "Sleep here. If you have to piss, use a pot. Someone will come for it in the morning."

Before Kaden could formulate another question that might lead back to Pyrre, Jakin, and the evening meal, Tan was gone, leaving him in the narrow stone room surrounded by the silent shapes of the bowls and jugs. Kaden worked awhile longer—busying his hands helped to still the worries in his mind—and then curled up in his robe on the hard stone floor to sleep. He woke in the night, shivering so badly, his teeth rattled against one another, and moved up to a hard wooden bench. It was narrow and uncomfortable, but at least the cold didn't radiate out of it.

He expected Akiil to come that night. Before the dinner had finished, while the monks were still nursing the dark dregs of their tea, Kaden had left Pater with a message for his friend: *Find me after the midnight bell.* The bell came and went, however, a somber tolling in the darkness, without a sign of the young monk.

He spent the next two days crafting pots and mugs that Tan never bothered to inspect, the following two nights huddled in awkward positions on the small bench, trying to shrink into his robe to avoid the night's chill. Nightmares filled his dreams—inchoate visions with no real narrative in which his father fought against a host of foes while Pyrre looked on as though nothing were amiss. It was a long time since he'd had nightmares—years, in fact. The Shin believed that disordered dreams were the product of a disordered mind. The oldest brothers claimed not to dream at all. Kaden would have been happy enough to join them, but the visions kept coming, night after night, as soon as he closed his eyes. Finally, on the third night, Akiil arrived, slipping through the wooden door just after the midnight bell.

"Nice jug," he said, glancing at Kaden's newest project—a large, two-handled ewer of red river clay. "Too bad we don't have any wine to go in it."

"'Shael can take the jug," Kaden responded more harshly than he'd intended. "It's been two days. What's happening out there? Did anyone find what's killing the goats? What's going on with those two merchants?"

Akiil flopped onto the bench wearily and spread his hands. He looked bored. Bored and frustrated. His robe, never very clean to begin with, had dirt ground into it, a sure sign that he, like Kaden, had been spending the bulk of his days performing some sort of menial labor rather than lounging around with the strangers. He raked a mop of hair out of his eyes.

"What has been happening with the merchants is what always happens with merchants. A lot of song. A lot of dance."

"Meaning *what?*"

Akiil shrugged. "Pyrre and Jakin try to sell us shit. Nin says we don't want it. Pyrre says, 'But surely you would enjoy a robe made of these fine silks.' The abbot says he prefers roughspun. You're not missing much."

Kaden shook his head in frustration. "There's something strange about those two, something . . . not right."

"They're shitty merchants, that's for sure." Akiil's eyes narrowed. "Wait. How do you know? Tan's had you locked in here the whole time."

"I was in the dovecote," Kaden confessed. Quickly, he ran through the whole story—the merchants' strange entrance, the overpowering sense that Pyrre was holding something back, despite her urbane geniality, that vague suspicion that Kaden felt so powerfully but could barely articulate. "There's something . . . something they're not saying about my father," he concluded weakly.

Akiil frowned. "Sounds like your imagination has flown the coop."

"I didn't imagine it."

"Halva's always lecturing me about how we see what we want to see. That could have happened to you. Of course, if I saw what I wanted to see, Pyrre's breasts would be a fair amount larger."

"Why would I *want* to see something troubling about my father?"

"Not that you want bad news, but it's only natural to worry about your parents—provided you know who they are. It's an affliction I've been spared."

"I'm looking at Pyrre's face now," Kaden replied, his mind filling with the *saama'an.* For the hundredth time, he tried to pinpoint what it was about the woman's expression that bothered him so. "There's . . . *something.*" He sighed. "There's something strange, but I can't see what it is."

"Sounds like you've been spending too much time buried up to your nose or running around with a blindfold on. That can do things to a man, can do things to his mind—"

"There's nothing wrong with my mind."

"That's up for debate," Akiil shot back. Then, seeing the blaze in Kaden's eyes, he raised his hands in surrender. "But let's assume you're right. Still, wouldn't Nin or Tan or one of our aged wards have noticed? I mean, you're good at the *saama'an,* but they've been going at it hammer and tongs for decades."

Kaden spread his hands helplessly.

"Of course," his friend went on, a sly grin creeping onto his face, "old Shin tricks are all well and good, but there's a way we can get some more . . . practical information."

Kaden looked at him. That grin suggested Akiil had devised a plan that would get them both beaten half to death if Nin or Tan found out. Which was all the more reason to make sure they didn't find out. "Go on."

Akiil leaned forward conspiratorially, rubbing his hands together, fully engaged for the first time since he entered. "I've been watching that woman, Pyrre." He pursed his lips appraisingly. "She's not much, compared to the whores I grew up around, but, up here in the mountains, I figure you have to take what you can get."

"You've been spying on her."

"Let's call it 'supervising.' At any rate, she's slipped away from the monastery a few times, usually at dusk, when Jakin's haggling with Nin."

"Maybe she's just taking a look around," Kaden responded. He wanted Akiil to have an idea, but this seemed pretty thin.

"She goes *east*. Away from the sunset. Away from all the pretty views. Besides, Nin told her the first night about whatever's been killing the goats. You know many women who enjoy taking midnight strolls around a strange mountain monastery perched on the edge of a cliff when they've just learned that an unknown predator is ripping the heads off goats and men alike and then eating the brains?"

Kaden nodded, warming to the idea. "That's strange. So where does she go?"

"No idea," Akiil replied. "I haven't had a chance to follow her—I've been shoveling out a new channel for a branch of the White River the past three days. *Tonight,* however . . ." He grinned. "I thought maybe we might put some of our Shin tracking skills to work."

Beshra'an, the "Thrown Mind," had originated as a way to trail lost livestock or to hunt down predators; it was, in fact, the way Kaden had tracked down the slaughtered goat two months earlier. Following prints in the earth was all well and good, but most of the land around Ashk'lan was rock, not earth. When the prints disappeared, as they inevitably did in the granite peaks, the monks needed another method.

The goal of *beshra'an* was to slip outside one's own head, to throw one's mind into another creature, to think, not like a man following a goat, but like the goat itself. The monks who were good at it could follow animals over blank stone with uncanny success, abandoning their own humanity to sniff out the scent of fresh grass, to tread the fine gravel that the goats favored, to move into the lee of a massive boulder when the storms came. Kaden had had some luck with it, even a few times where he felt as though he really *had* "thrown" his mind into the head of his quarry. Unfortunately, he'd never tried following a human.

"All right," he whispered to Akiil once they'd slipped from the monastery proper and out toward the broken land to the east. A gibbous moon hung low in the sky, and once his eyes adjusted, there was enough light to see by. Rock slabs and boulders leaned against one another, casting dark shadows beneath the argent glow of the moon. Crooked branches of the junipers, twisted by the wind, reached toward them, threatening to snatch a robe or scratch an eye. The evening sounds of the monastery were barely audible above the light breeze.

"This seemed like a better idea when we were inside," Akiil said. His voice was sarcastic, but his eyes flitted from rock to rock, quick and alert. Kaden didn't have to remind him that whatever killed Serkhan was still out there, still waiting. They had to hope that the staves they'd taken from the goats pens along with the knives at their belts would be enough to discourage it. *After all,* Kaden reasoned with himself, *Pyrre is sneaking around out here every night, and she hasn't been killed yet.*

"We'll be quick," he said, trying to reassure himself as much as his friend.

"That's what I told myself right before I cut that purse. The one that earned me this," Akiil replied, gesturing to his brand. "I don't suppose there's any way you can dim those eyes of yours. It's nice that a goddess fucked your great-great-grandad, but they're a little obvious."

"Maybe they'll scare away whatever needs scaring."

Akiil snorted.

"All right," Kaden said, shivering beneath his robe. "You're Pyrre, a merchant woman from the empire. You leave your perfectly nice monastic cell to skulk off into the rocks. Why?"

Akiil grinned. "I'm hoping to tickle one of these strapping young monks up under that robe of his."

Kaden considered this. Women never visited the monastery, and there probably *were* a couple of monks who wouldn't mind spending a few minutes alone with Pyrre, Akiil chief among them.

"Fine," he replied, "let's say it's a rendezvous. Where do you go?"

"I'm not from here. I go wherever I'm told."

"All right, then, let's get into the mind of this hypothetical monk. You want to meet up with Pyrre. Where do you tell her to go?"

"One of the abandoned buildings to the south. The lower meadow, although that's a little far. Maybe into the dovecote." Akiil winked. "Someplace with a little romantic character. You got to treat the lady right."

"I'm sure she'd be flattered to bed you while surrounded by shitting pigeons. What about east?" he asked, gesturing to the rocks in front of them. "That's the direction you said you saw her going. Would you tell her to meet you up there?"

Akiil hesitated, then shook his head. "Nothing but gullies and fissures. I don't want to be picking pebbles out of my ass."

"So she's on her own," Kaden concluded. "A monk would have sent her somewhere else."

"Seems reasonable," Akiil replied, "but not that helpful." He gestured to the forbidding labyrinth of rock before them. "You're her. Where do *you* go?"

Kaden considered his options by the meager moonlight. There were half a dozen goat tracks leading up into the broken mountain, any one of which the woman could have followed. Most of them were obvious—trails clear as highways to anyone who'd spent time in the mountains—but Pyrre wasn't from the mountains, at least not *these* mountains. He tried to look at the land with an unfamiliar eye.

"The streambed," he said finally. "She'd take the streambed."

Akiil waved a dismissive hand toward the channel. "What would she want to roll her ankles in the streambed for when there are plenty of good tracks to follow? Doesn't make any sense."

"Because," Kaden replied, "the streambed doesn't *look* like a stream-bed. It's dry this late in the spring. It's broad. It's relatively flat. For someone who didn't grow up here, it's the most obvious way through the rocks. She won't have realized that the rounded stones will make for impossible footing, and she probably didn't even *notice* the trails left by the goats. They don't look like much, if you've never tried to follow them."

Akiil shot him an appraising look. "Have you been tracking women without me all these years? Keeping secrets?"

"Why would I tell you my secrets? You're a thief."

"You wound me, brother. You wound me. I'm a humble monk, devoted to my god."

"Well, devote yourself to this for a few hours instead," Kaden replied, gesturing toward the stream.

A few dozen paces into the mountains, they came across the first sign of the woman—an overturned rock. Then there was a bootprint in the soft mud. And then another rock kicked out of its divot. They followed the signs for less than a quarter of a mile until Akiil spotted a low pile of stones. They didn't look like much, just a few cobbles in a world of rock, not something that would draw the untrained eye. But river stones didn't mound up like that. The spring flood would have washed them right down the drainage.

"Well, look at this," Akiil said, lifting one of the stones off the pile. "Let's see what the good merchants have to hide."

He was grinning, eyes bright in the moonlight. Kaden didn't share his enthusiasm. The streambed wasn't very wide, but he felt exposed beneath the lambent stare of the moon, and despite the cool night air, sweat poured down his back. He hefted the stave in his hand, reminded himself that Serkhan had been attacked when he was alone, tried to believe that two young men together, armed with sticks and knives, would be enough to scare it off. When reason failed, he worked through the Shin exercise to slow his pulse, and bent to the cairn of stones only when his breathing was slow and regular once more.

Pyrre had cached two oilcloth bundles under the pile, and Kaden lifted them out carefully, then handed one to Akiil. He fumbled briefly with the ties binding it shut, trying to calculate whether he could retie them if he heard the woman returning. His fingers were clumsy as though with long cold, and by the time he had opened his bag, Akiil had already spread out half the contents of his sack on a flat rock. Kaden paused to look over the things while his friend ticked them off in a whisper.

"Clean tunic. Clean socks. Disappointingly light purse," he said, tossing the small cloth pouch in the air so that it jingled when he caught it.

Kaden winced.

"Hat," Akiil continued. "About twenty yards of rope . . ." The process was nerve-racking, but the results were not. Nothing that a normal merchant wouldn't carry on a long trip. Nothing to lend heft to Kaden's vaguely adumbrated suspicions.

Then Akiil found the knives.

Everyone carried a knife, of course, and a merchant would have more need of one than most. There were harnesses to mend along the road, rocks to dig out of the mule's hoofs, frayed ropes to slice and retie, dried meat to cut for dinner. There were a thousand reasons Kaden could think of for a merchant to carry a good knife. A merchant would not, however, need a dozen of them. Akiil laid them on the stone one by one, six identical eight-inch blades, the kind men fought with in the killing pits of Annur, honed and polished edges glinting in the cold moonlight.

"Brought them along to trade?" he suggested. His voice had lost some of its boyish enthusiasm.

"To a monastery?" Kaden asked.

They gazed at the weapons for a moment before Akiil gestured to the oilcloth bundle that Kaden was still holding.

"What's in there?"

Kaden managed to untie the last knot, then reached into the sack. His fingers brushed over wood and steel. When he had finally wrestled the thing out of the bag, he found himself holding a crossbow.

"It could all be for protection," Akiil pointed out. "It's a dangerous road over the steppe. The Urghul don't usually molest traders, but you never know when you're going to end up on the wrong end of a human sacrifice."

"If it's all for protection," Kaden replied, "then what's it doing hidden in the rocks?"

They considered the weapons for a few more heartbeats and then, as though responding to some silent command, began packing everything back the way they had found it. The jovial, larking expression had left Akiil's face. He looked angry as he thrust the various items back into the satchel. Within moments they had returned the weapons to the bags and the bags to their hiding spot under the rocks. Akiil was replacing the final stones on the cairn when something clattered farther down the stream-bed, stone on stone.

Kaden spun to peer into the darkness.

"Did you hear that?" he murmured, trying to sort shadow from shape in the meager light.

Akiil nodded, hefting his stave in front of him. Kaden dropped a hand to his belt knife, then decided against it. He didn't know much about fighting, but he didn't like his odds if whatever it was got close enough for him to use a knife.

A cloud passed over the moon, plunging the ravine into even deeper shadow. Kaden could barely make out Akiil standing only a few feet away. Beyond him, the bare shapes of the cliffs and crenellations loomed, more felt than seen. He turned in a slow circle, leveling his staff, searching for light, movement, *anything* that might give him a warning of danger before it arrived.

"You see anything?" he hissed.

Akiil's only response was a low *umph,* like a cough that never made it out of the chest. Kaden spun just in time to watch his friend collapse onto the streambed. Before he could cry out, a strong, implacable hand clamped down on his mouth.

Kaden was not soft. Eight years of hard physical exercise high in the mountains had seen to that. He could carry a quarter of his weight in water up hundreds of steps from the stream or run all night over rocky paths. He should have been able to put up something of a fight, and yet the hand that held him might have been made of granite. As he struggled, his adversary's other arm closed around his neck, crushing his windpipe. *This is the result of bad decisions,* thought the part of him that could still think. In desperation, Kaden threw an elbow, hoping to dislodge his opponent. The man's stomach was as solid as his arm. Kaden screamed silently as his mind failed.

33

He woke in a hard wooden chair surrounded by stone walls. Someone had lit a few candles, and when he first tried to open his eyes, the light drove a spike of pain directly through his head. He closed them again with a slight groan. He didn't know where he was, but when the memory of the attack came back to him, he tensed himself to run or fight. No one had bound his hands or feet, and through slitted eyelids he tried to locate the door. They couldn't have carried him far. He was in Ashk'lan still—the rough granite walls were proof enough of that. If he could just . . .

"We took some pains to bring you here silently. Please do not ruin it with clamor."

He knew that voice, dry and tough as rawhide, although for half a heartbeat he couldn't place it.

"What is it in obedience that the young find so difficult?" the voice went on.

The abbot, he realized with a start, and in spite of the pain, forced his eyes open once more. He was seated in the center of Scial Nin's study, the humble, one-room structure where Nin and Tan had revealed the secret of the *kenta* a few weeks earlier. Nin slept in a dormitory cell like the rest of the monks, but he was known to stay late in his study when occupied with important business. Generally, a visit to the abbot's study did not augur well, and this episode was starting out far worse than usual, although Kaden's head still throbbed too badly for him to make much sense of what was going on.

A small fire burned in the hearth, but that was the only welcoming thing about the room. Nin sat behind his bare wooden desk, fingers steepled under his chin, dark eyes fixed on him intently, as though Kaden were some new species of squirrel that he had found in one of his dead-falls. A few feet from the desk, Rampuri Tan stood staring out the small window into the night. He hadn't said anything at all, hadn't even looked at his pupil, and Kaden felt his stomach tighten, an uncomfortable sensation, given that his head was still pounding and his legs felt like water. He started to groan, then suppressed the sound out of habit—it would earn him no sympathy from the older monks.

"Akiil?" he asked weakly, feeling like someone had scoured his mouth with coarse wool. His friend was not in the study. "Where is Akiil?"

"He is not here," the abbot replied evenly. Normally Kaden would have ground his teeth in silent frustration at the response, but the knives they had discovered leapt into his mind, along with the memory of the hand clamped over his mouth, cutting off his breath. . . .

"The merchants," he managed. "They're—" *What?* he asked himself. *Carrying knives?* How was he going to explain the fact that he and Akiil were rummaging through their private belongings? "Who tried to kill us?" he asked instead. "Did you capture them?"

The abbot looked away, gazing at an indeterminate point over Kaden's left shoulder. Rampuri Tan shook his head, not turning from the window. Kaden looked from one to the other, but neither seemed willing to speak.

"You *did* capture them, didn't you?" he asked. He tried to stand, but his legs would have none of it, and he dropped back into the chair. Silence stretched out before them, bleak and cold as the night sky.

When the abbot finally spoke, it was not to him. "You told me he was making progress."

Tan grunted.

"I don't see progress," Nin continued. "I see a blind, impulsive boy tied so tightly to himself that he can barely move."

Normally the insult would have stung, all the more so for the flat, care-less tone in which it was delivered. Memory of his assailants and worry for Akiil, however, left no space for wounded pride, and as Kaden lowered the pressure of the blood in his veins, he tried to make himself sound rational, unemotional.

"Abbot," he began quietly, amazed that his voice was so level—he felt like shaking and screaming all at the same time. "Clearly you know already, because you rescued me, but the merchants are not what they appear. One of them or both caught Akiil and me—"

"How long," the abbot interrupted with a raised hand, "has Tan been your *umial*?"

"What does Tan have to do—"

Without raising his voice, the abbot cut him off. "How long?"

"Two months," Kaden replied, mustering his patience.

"And after two months, you still don't recognize your own master when he is close enough to kill you?"

Kaden looked in confusion from the abbot to Tan, who turned from the window, eyes inscrutable as always. "I came to check on you at the shed," the monk began. "When you were not there, I tracked you and brought you here. Akiil is unharmed."

Kaden gaped.

"*You* brought me! How did you track me?"

"The *Beshra'an*. Your mind is a simple thing, although cramped to inhabit."

He ignored the insult. "What about the merchants? Why didn't you just *ask* me to come? Why did you attack me?"

"You would have argued," Tan replied simply. "And the woman was approaching. There was no time."

Kaden took a firm grip on his emotions. He had been conscious for several minutes now, but things weren't getting any clearer. Determined not to make a fool of himself again, he paused to consider this new information. Tan returned to his post at the window as if there were nothing left to discuss, but the abbot continued to look directly at him.

"You didn't send me to the clay shed as some kind of penance," Kaden concluded after a time.

"I might as well have," Tan responded, "considering how poorly you have performed."

"But you didn't," Kaden replied doggedly. "If you had, there would be no need to knock me out in the dark, no need for this late-night conference. When you found me in the streambed, you would have simply sent me to haul water all night, or to sit on the Talon until dawn. But then we would have run into the merchants.

"You weren't trying to keep me from seeing them," he went on, the realization seeping in slowly. "You wanted to keep *them* from seeing *me*."

He shivered beneath his robe. During his years at Ashk'lan, the maneuverings and machinations surrounding the imperial throne had faded to a distant memory. In fact, Kaden often wondered if he had been sent to the monastery, not for any particular education, but simply to keep him out of harm's way until he was older. Was it possible that Annurian politics had found him even here?

"This is about my father," he said, feeling the truth of the statement as it left his lips.

"Why," the abbot responded slowly, "do you think anything is wrong with your father? Pyrre Lakatur said that the Emperor was strong as ever. Jakin agreed."

"I know," Kaden replied. He took a slow breath. What he was about to reveal would earn him an even more severe penance, but the water around him was already boiling. He had to know the truth. "There's something not right about Pyrre, about both of them. You obviously already know about the knives and the crossbow, but that's not all. That first night, the night in the refectory, I was in the dovecote, watching."

Tan's face hardened, but he did not speak. The abbot raised an eyebrow.

"Pyrre wasn't looking at you when she came in the door," Kaden continued. "Then, when she answered the question about my father, something was . . ." He paused, the scene springing clearly into his mind once more. He examined the faces for the hundredth time: the woman's easy smile, the casual wave of her hand, the angle of her head as she looked down the table at the gathered monks. Everything *seemed* normal. Kaden let out the breath he'd been holding. "Something was . . . not right," he trailed off lamely.

The abbot looked at him hard for a moment or two, then addressed Tan. "I take it back, friend. The boy *has* come a long way."

"Not far enough," Tan responded without turning.

The abbot leveled a bony finger at Kaden. "How many people in the world could have seen what he saw, even without being able to identify it? A few dozen?"

"More than that," Tan replied dismissively. "Meshkent's high priests. Most emotion leaches. Any of the Csestriim—"

The abbot laughed gently. "I'm talking about *humans,* my friend. I know that you have once again begun honing that old blade of yours, but the fact of the matter is, Csestriim have not been seen on this earth in millennia." The abbot gave Tan a long, searching look that would have had Kaden squirming in his seat. His *umial,* however, simply shrugged. "There may be a handful of emotion leaches scattered around Annur," Nin continued, "but no more than a handful. I doubt that even some of them would have seen what the boy saw."

Tan opened his mouth, but the abbot continued, forestalling any protest. "The Shin are trained from the moment they arrive in close, careful observation, and yet, who here noticed Pyrre Lakatur's misstep? You and I. Maybe one or two of the older brothers." He looked at Kaden almost sadly. "The boy would have made a fine monk."

"Noticed what?" Kaden asked. "What did I notice?"

"There is more to being a monk than hunches and guesses," Tan responded.

"He did not guess. He observed."

"What did I observe?" Kaden asked again.

Tan shook his head brusquely. "He is in a dangerous place. He sees enough to question, but not enough to know when to hold those questions."

"I understand that you're telling me to stop asking," Kaden said, stifling his frustration, "but I'm not going to stop asking. What did I see?"

"A sliver of a pause," the abbot replied, ignoring the outburst. "A few blinks more than normal. A slight tightening at the corner of her mouth." He waved a dismissive hand. "Individually, those signs mean nothing."

"Taken together, they may also mean nothing," Tan added.

"But you don't think so," Kaden interrupted, a sick dread rising in his throat. "You think Pyrre is keeping something back. Why don't we *confront* them? Demand to know about the weapons. Demand to know about my father?"

He lapsed into silence as Tan turned from the window.

"If I hadn't found you, you might be dead now, instead of whining like a child in the abbot's study."

Kaden stared incredulously.

"Lies," his *umial* continued. "Deception. These are not remarkable in a man or woman. They are even less remarkable in one who makes her living buying and selling. What is remarkable about Pyrre Lakatur is how *well* she lies. How ably she deceives." The large monk approached until he loomed over his pupil. "The pricing of silk and the driving of wagons are the least of this woman's training. Somewhere she has learned to suppress the most basic imperatives of the flesh. You may want to ask yourself, when you finish playing the impetuous prince, why a woman with such impeccable training comes here, to the end of the earth, dressed as a merchant. While you spend the following days digging out the cellar of the meditation hall, you may want to consider the goals of such a woman. What has she come here for? *Who* has she come here for?"

34

Whatever wary trust Valyn managed to establish with Talal, nothing had changed in the course of daily training. The Wing was halfway through its probationary period, halfway to flying its first real mission, and they still hadn't managed to win a single contest. *I'd be surprised if Command lets us stand guard over a vegetable stand,* Valyn thought to himself grimly as he rolled over in his bunk, restless in the predawn darkness, *let alone fly to northeastern Vash to hunt for Kaden.*

It wasn't that the individual members of his Wing were incompetent. In fact, operating independently, each had shown moments of genius: Gwenna rigged and blew an entire bridge by moonlight in less than an hour; Talal swam the entire breadth of the Akeen Channel underwater; and Annick, of course, hadn't missed a single target, regardless of distance, weather, or time of day.

In spite of these successes, however, the Wing just could *not* manage to get out of its own way. Gwenna blew the bridge while Laith and Valyn were still crossing it, singeing half their clothes off and dumping them in the water; Talal emerged from the Channel only to take one of Annick's stunners to the back of the head; and Annick's perfect shooting only led her to grow more and more scornful of the Wing, as though she were the only professional in a group of children.

Valyn rolled onto his back. It was still pitch-black outside, and the early bell had yet to ring, but after a few hours of uneasy slumber, he had lain awake, staring at the bunk above him. He could analyze and condemn the mistakes of his Wing mates until he was blue in the face, but the real truth was that *he* was failing *them.* It was *his* responsibility to formulate each mission plan, *his* job to make sure his soldiers understood their roles, and *his* job to stave off personal problems before they became a threat to the integrity of the group. So far, he had done piss-poor work on all fronts.

His mind drifted to the memory of Ha Lin—the banter, shared jokes, and easy camaraderie; the quiet, solid comfort he had felt when she was at his side or seated across the table. All these years, he'd never realized how much strength he drew from her, how much he had always assumed that she would always be there to bolster him. When he pictured commanding his own Wing, he'd imagined Lin there, quibbling with his small decisions but never doubting him, not really. He'd been unconsciously counting on her to back him up. Of course, when it really mattered, *he* had failed *her*.

The low tolling of the morning bell broke into his bleak thoughts, and his feet hit the floor before the sound had faded from the air. If the past weeks were any indication, the day was bound to be another failure, but anything was better than lying in his bunk, gazing up into the incriminating darkness, worrying that he wasn't getting it right, worrying that while he bungled his command, danger, swift but unknowable, was drawing closer and closer to Kaden, his brother, the Emperor.

"Rise and shine," he said, stomping into his boots before plucking a glowing ember from the fire to light the lamp.

Gwenna cursed from the bunk above, but made no effort to rise, let alone shine.

Valyn shrugged into his tunic and shouldered aside the door into the front room only to find Annick already awake and seated at the large table. She was fully dressed and oiling her bow with long, smooth strokes. For the hundredth time, Valyn wondered what went on behind those ice-cold eyes. He hadn't had a chance to speak to her alone since before the Trial, since their encounter in the infirmary. Whenever he looked to have a word with her, there were others around or she had mysteriously melted away. She'd convinced him that she hadn't tried to kill him during the sniper contest, but she was a riddle, and any riddle was dangerous. He shivered at the realization that she had managed to rise, dress, and go to work on her bow mere feet from him without making a sound, all in complete darkness. *Why was Amie going to meet you?* he wondered for the hundredth time. *What are you hiding?*

Talal had rolled to his feet and slipped into his blacks while Gwenna grumbled herself halfway out of her bunk. Laith refused to budge.

"Briefing in ten," Valyn announced, stepping back through the door and kicking the pallet in an effort to jolt the flier into life.

" 'Shael's sweet suckling whores," Laith cursed, rolling away from the light. "Why don't you just beat me bloody and light my hair on fire here? Save another Wing the trouble?"

"I'm happy to light your hair on fire," Gwenna growled. She was perched on the edge of her bunk, raking fingers through her own tangled mane. The light shirt in which she slept did nothing to conceal the curves of her breasts beneath, and Valyn looked away awkwardly. There was no mystery around the female form, not with the Kettral. He'd been eating, sleeping, swimming, and shitting next to his peers for eight years. *Better get used to it,* Fane used to say. *You're not going to be much use in a fight if you're ogling the ass of the soldier next to you.* Valyn *was* used to it, but he'd been sharing a barracks with men ever since he arrived on the Islands, and there was something a little distracting about walking into the bunk-room to find Gwenna or Annick bare-assed or halfway into her blacks. He shut his eyes and put a hand to his forehead, hoping Gwenna wouldn't notice. Staring at her breasts wasn't going to help his Wing any, and besides, it felt like a betrayal of Ha Lin.

Idiot, he cursed himself. *You had nothing to speak of with Lin, and Gwenna would just as soon gut you as kiss you.* It was true, all of it, but he felt guilty just the same.

Gwenna was still harassing Laith. "Maybe our royal leader would like me to rig your bed tonight. I'm sure I could arrange a little something to wake you up in the morning."

"You are an evil bitch," Laith groaned, rolling over onto his back. "Why couldn't Rallen have assigned Gent to this Wing?"

"Because *Gent* is about as capable as a whore with the pox. At least if I blow you up, you'll know I *meant* to do it."

"What?" the flier shot back. "Like the other day?"

"You weren't supposed to *be* on the bridge, you idiot."

"None of this is helping," Talal said quietly. He sat on his own bunk, lacing up his boots.

"Helping what?" Laith demanded. "It's certainly helping to ruin my sleep."

"Good," Valyn interjected, before the argument could go any further. "We've got a lot to work through today, and not much time to do it." Technically, this was information for the briefing, but they hadn't been doing anything else by the book. *Why start now?* he thought to himself.

"What?" Annick asked. She had set aside her bow and was looking over the fletching of her arrows. She didn't bother to look up at Valyn when he turned.

"Barrel drops," he replied.

"Oh, for 'Shael's sake," Gwenna groaned. "Again?"

"Well, well," Laith said, rising for the first time, picking his teeth absently with a finger. "I might go an entire day without a bruise after all."

"Speak for yourself," Gwenna said. "It's not so easy when you're the one dropping instead of the one flying."

"The other Wings quit doing barrel drops a week ago," Annick pointed out flatly.

"Well," Valyn responded with more heat than he had intended, "we haven't."

"Who's in charge of the training?" Talal asked quietly.

"Not Fane," Laith groaned from the bunk. "Not Fane again."

"The Flea will be overseeing today's training," Valyn replied, trying to keep his voice level.

Silence reigned in the room as the soldiers eyed one another warily.

"Well," Gwenna snorted finally, dropping out of her bunk and fixing Valyn with those green eyes of hers. "Today, my illustrious lord commander, would be a good day to start getting things right."

†

At least it's sunny, Valyn thought to himself, closing his eyes and leaning back into his leather harness. Wind tugged at his hair and clothes, threatening to rip him from his perch on Suant'ra's talons while the back draft from the great bird's slow, powerful wing beats buffeted him from above.

After eight years on the Islands, Valyn still marveled at the power and grace of the kettral. Without the kettral, there would be no Kettral. The creatures could cover ground faster than any horse, faster than a three-hundred-oar galley, soar over impregnable walls as though they were thin lines drawn on the dirt, land on towers, and outdistance any pursuit in a matter of minutes. If necessary, the bird herself could even fight, tearing through flesh and armor with her claws and beak as if they were cloth.

In taverns all across Vash and Eridroa, men told tales of the birds, whispering that they fed on human flesh. Most people had never seen one, of course—there were only a few score in the entire world, and the empire guarded them closely—but a good look at Suant'ra wouldn't have done much to calm anyone's nerves. She was clearly a predator, with all the attributes of her tinier cousins writ large: the hooked razor beak and raking talons; the long, packed pinions of jet and white that allowed her to ride the thermals or swoop at speeds that would drive a rider's eyes into the back of his head. She was a bird of prey, all right, and a predator with a seventy-foot wingspan is a fearsome thing.

Flying around enjoying the breeze was all well and good, but it wasn't much use unless you could get on and off of the bird's talons quickly. The Kettral often landed in heavily patrolled areas, and a few extra seconds fiddling with straps and buckles could mean the difference between life and death. Barrel drops trained the Wing to disembark over water. It sounded easy enough: fly in low, unbuckle the safety straps, unhitch the barrel filled with weapons and gear (for which the exercise was named), and dive into the water. In practice, however, a barrel drop ranged somewhere between terrifying and deadly.

For one thing, a kettral could fly far faster than a galloping horse. When you hit the waves at that speed, they felt more like brick than water. For another, there were four bodies in play, along with a dozen or so straps and buckles; a collision with any of them could easily bruise a rib or slash a cheek. And then, of course, there was the barrel itself. Some situations didn't require extra gear, and the Wing could drop in with only the weapons and clothes on their backs. Plenty of more complicated missions, however, called for disguises, extra munitions (that had to be kept dry), even food if the team needed to stay in the field for more than a few days. All of that went into the barrel, which could weigh upward of fifty pounds and hit the waves like a boulder plummeting down a steep hillside. Soldiers had been killed in barrel drops before, and Valyn was starting to think that someone on his Wing was going to be next.

The main problem was Laith. Unlike the four other members of the Wing, who crouched on the bird's talons during flight, the flier sat in a modified harness on the kettral's back, just behind her head. The view was better from there, and Laith could control Suant'ra far more easily than from any position below. As a result, the flier felt much the same control as a man on horseback might. The rest of his Wing, on the other hand, felt like cargo. During his years as a cadet, Laith had built up a reputation as a fearless flier, pressing himself and his birds up to and beyond their physical limits. Suant'ra was his creature; he had raised her and trained her, and sometimes the two seemed to share one mind. It made for impressive aerobatics when watched from the ground—impossible-looking loops and rolls and twists. Unfortunately, the two weren't accommodating to passengers. The kettral were trained to fly with their talons down, and Suant'ra did this well enough, but Laith never seemed to care if anyone happened to be *on* those talons.

Valyn's stomach leapt into his chest as his flier dropped the bird into the start of a dive. He glanced over to see Gwenna scowling and tightening her grip on the leather loop tied high on the bird's talon. *Maybe today's the day we get it right,* he thought to himself as Suant'ra gained speed, angling into a stoop. The bright blue of the ocean rushed up at him, filling his vision. *Or,* he amended as the wind threatened to tear the clothes from his body, *maybe not.*

All fliers tried to go into a barrel drop fast—quick entry and exit gave the enemy a briefer target of opportunity—but as with everything else, there was a standard protocol, an angle of attack, refined over the years and passed down to the junior Wings, designed to optimize the trade-off between speed and security. Laith didn't much care for the protocol, and didn't give a horse's ass about optimization. In fact, he seemed determined to shatter his own Wing against the rapidly approaching waves. As the bird plummeted, Valyn felt his foot slip on the talon. Moments later, he was dangling in space, suspended by his harness and one hand on the safety loop. Whatever shout escaped from his throat was torn away by the screaming wind in his ears and 'Ra's own piercing shriek.

Talal noticed Valyn's predicament first and stretched out a hand to try to pull him in. At that speed, however, with the wind whipping around them and the blinding blue of the ocean rushing up, the gesture was futile.

"Unclip yourself!" Valyn screamed, gesturing furiously. The strain was wrenching his shoulder from its socket, but he couldn't do anything about that now. If the others could manage to execute their parts of the plan, Valyn might be able to extricate himself. "Make your own drop!"

Gwenna already had the barrel swinging free of 'Ra's talons and with a savage yank on the final hitch, she sent it plummeting directly into Valyn's shoulder. He bellowed as the muscles of his upper arm tore under the strain, then bit into his own tongue as Laith hauled the bird level just feet above the slapping chop.

Annick hit the water first, skidded once on the surface, then plowed into the waves. Talal dropped next and Gwenna, evidently flustered from her effort to free the barrel, followed him too closely. The two tangled on impact in a desperate flurry of limbs.

That left Valyn. Laith was flying so low that Valyn's boots slapped against the crests of the waves, each jolt sending a new flash of fire through his shoulder. Now that the bird had leveled out, he should have been able to regain his footing on the talon, but his left arm wasn't functioning correctly, and the sea kept tearing at his boots. With his free hand he tried to unclip the buckle to his waistbelt, but the 'Shael-spawned thing had cinched tight when he weighted it, and no amount of tugging would pull it free. Valyn gritted his teeth. The drop was already a disaster. Talal and Gwenna were probably black-and-blue from their collision on landing, Ae only knew where the barrel was, and Valyn himself, the Wing's commander, was being dragged farther from his Wing with every heartbeat. As he watched, the ocean started to pull away beneath him. Laith had guided the bird into a slow, steady climb, unaware that Valyn was still entangled in the straps beneath.

They had failed again. *He* had failed. There was nothing for it now but to let go of the wrist strap, take the agonizing weight off his shoulder, settle back into the harness, and wait for Laith to swing around to pick up the rest of the team. There wasn't any other reasonable course of action.

Except they were supposed to be training for real missions, and if he were flying a real mission, he'd need to rejoin his Wing, regardless of the circumstances. He glanced down between his legs and swallowed heavily. 'Ra didn't climb as fast as she stooped, but they were already a good forty paces up and gaining height with every breath. Valyn loosened the knife from his belt, then hesitated. He'd catch hell from Shar in the gear shop for slicing his harness, and without a controlled dive, he was going to hit that water like a stone. The impact might well tear his already battered shoulder right off.

" 'Shael take it," he muttered, severing the thick canvas with a single swipe of the blade and tumbling headlong toward the brutal waves below. "At least if it kills me, I won't have to do it again."

"Well, that was a goat fuck," the Flea said quietly.

Valyn nodded stiffly, the motion sending a spike of pain down his neck and into his arm. He had flown six more drops with his Wing, hanging on desperately despite the damage to his shoulder, and each had gone more poorly than the last. He tried to tell Laith to slow down, to take a shallower angle, but the flier didn't seem to understand the words *slower* or *careful.* For eight years, he'd been flying belly in the dirt, right at the limit, and two weeks of training failures hadn't done much to alter his old, reckless habits. On the final run-through, Valyn, Gwenna, Annick, and Talal had been scattered across so much water that it had been quicker to simply swim it in rather than waiting for Laith to pick them up.

The Flea had watched the whole morning's fiasco from a low headland overlooking the bay. When Valyn finally hauled himself out of the water, then made the short climb to the top of the cliff, soaked to the bone and bleeding from half a dozen scratches and abrasions, the older soldier didn't say a word at first, just looked at him with those flat, measuring eyes. *This,* Valyn thought to himself, *is not going to be good.*

The Flea didn't have problems with his own Wing. His Wing was a legend: Blackfeather Finn, the finest tournament archer in the world; Chi Hoai Mi, the fearless flier who carried with her a small silver cup from which she drank the blood of her slain foes; Newt the Aphorist; and Sigrid sa'Karnya, the demolitions master as ugly as the leach was beautiful, the two of them the only people ever to escape from the Spire and the cruel priests of Meshkent; and, of course, the Flea himself.

When Valyn first arrived on the Islands, eight years old with eyes wide as saucers, he had asked the short, broad, slightly hunched soldier why people called him "the Flea." The older man had cracked a crooked smile. "Because I'm small, black, and annoying," he had responded to Valyn's surprise and discomfort. It wasn't until a week or so later that Valyn learned the real story.

The empire's eastern frontier, the part that didn't disappear into the Urghul steppe, butted up against the Blood Cities—dozens of independent city-states dotting southeastern Vash. Normally those cities spent their time warring against and betraying one another, and as a result, posed little threat to Annur. That changed when Casimir Damek rose to power.

Damek was a brilliant general, a master politician, and a leach who claimed to be a god. The Annurians ridiculed the notion, but after a series of improbable victories, the citizens of the Blood Cities believed, and for the first time in several centuries, the empire found itself facing a unified army led by a man whose powers, admittedly, seemed godly—generals struck down by arrows shot from a mile distant, geysers of earth routing cavalry, entire rivers diverted to drown his foes as they thrashed in their armor. In a single season, he destroyed the eastern imperial army and marched on the Bend with fifty thousand troops.

The Kettral were called in.

The Kettral, shockingly, failed.

Damek captured three Wings in quick succession, captured, castrated, mutilated, and decapitated them. It was the worst string of defeats in the history of the Eyrie. In his camp east of the Bend, the general boasted that he gave no more thought to the Kettral than he did to the fleas on his great gray mastiffs.

Four days later, he was dead.

On the Qirins, mission assignments were confidential. No one asked questions and no one made boasts. Within days, however, Anjin Serrata, a quiet, capable Wing commander who was known for nothing more than keeping his head down and his eyes up, acquired a new nickname: the Flea.

And that was just the *beginning* of the legend, Valyn reminded himself as he prepared for the tongue-lashing.

The Flea, however, didn't say a word. He waited silently until the whole Wing assembled before dismissing them with a curt wave of his hand. Valyn hesitated, uncertain, then turned with the rest. The man's voice brought him up short.

"Not you."

So, Valyn realized. *Here it comes.* At least the commander wasn't going to ream him out in front of his own people.

"A solid and thorough goat fuck," the Flea said again once the others had left.

"Yes, sir," Valyn responded wearily. "It was a mess."

"What went wrong?" the man asked. He sounded curious rather than angry.

"What *didn't* go wrong?" Valyn exploded. He shook his head. "We couldn't get the 'Kent-kissing straps to release quickly enough, for one thing. And the angle of attack was all wrong—we kept slamming into each other, and the barrel almost took off Talal's head two drops in a row. As it is, he's going to need to get stitched up at the infirmary. You can see a little chunk of his skull when you pull the skin out of the way." He grimaced. "It's Laith's flying," he concluded reluctantly. "That's the root of all the problems."

The Flea picked absently at a new scar on his thumb, but didn't respond.

"I *know* I'm the commander," Valyn replied, raising his hands in surrender. "I know it's my responsibility and I *accept* that responsibility. I've explained the standard protocol to Laith a dozen times, and I've gone over the reasons for it. He just can't do it . . . won't do it . . . I don't know, but the bottom line is he comes in too fast and too hard. The rest of it all stems from that."

The Flea frowned out over the waves, as though considering some indiscernible shape in the distance.

"You're frustrated with your Wing," he said finally.

Valyn bit down on the temptation to agree. "They're my Wing, sir. We'll work things out."

The Flea nodded, but didn't take his eyes from the horizon. "You're commanding the wrong Wing," he said.

Valyn's eyes widened. He had no idea how the Wing selection process happened, but obviously the Flea did. "I didn't choose them," Valyn replied cautiously.

"That's not what I mean. You're trying to command the Wing you expected, the Wing you wanted."

"Sir?" Valyn asked, shaking his head.

The Flea snorted. "You wanted rule-abiding, book-crunching professionals. That's not what you got."

"You can say that again."

"Then stop commanding the Wing you wanted. Start commanding the Wing you have."

Valyn puzzled over this for a moment. He'd spent the entire day trying to get Laith to follow barrel drop protocol, and he had failed. If anything, the flier had come in faster and harder than ever on that last run, frustrated at the repeated failures. Everything hinged on the speed and the angle: the order of buckle release, the placement of the barrel, the timing of the jumps. If he just let Laith continue to fly by the seat of his pants, they'd have to change everything, have to rework the barrel drop from the ground up. There were *reasons* the Kettral had instituted the protocol in the first place.

"I was a part of the group that picked the Wings," the Flea said, breaking into Valyn's thoughts.

Valyn stared at the man, aghast. "*You* helped select that team?" he asked, trying to keep the bitterness out of his voice.

The Flea shrugged. His pockmarked face remained indifferent. "I didn't select 'em, but I approved the list."

"*Why?*"

"Thought they'd make a good Wing," the commander replied simply.

Valyn opened his mouth to snap a quick response, then shut it. Either the man was taunting him, or there was something to the lesson. *Command the Wing you have, not the Wing you want.* It would mean throwing out the whole protocol and reworking the barrel drop entirely.

"So what you're saying, sir—," Valyn began, trying to work through the implications.

The Flea cut him off. "Can't talk now. I gotta go."

Valyn looked around, confused. "Where are you going?"

"Barrel drops," the Flea grunted, gesturing over his shoulder toward the dim shape of a bird in the distance.

"Barrel drops like we did?"

"Hopefully a lot better than you did. Those were shittiest barrel drops I've seen since I was a cadet."

Valyn tried to wrap his weary mind around it. "Why are you still doing them? What's the twist?"

"No twist," the Flea replied, picking idly at a callus on his thumb, seemingly unaware of the rapidly approaching bird.

"But they're a novice exercise," Valyn protested. He'd heard fables of the training the veteran Wings went through: rose-and-thorn scenarios, impossible point landings, high-speed multiple casualty extracts . . . "None of the veteran Wings do barrel drops."

The Flea shrugged. "We do."

It didn't make sense. The Flea and his Wing were professionals. They were practically *gods.* It was like hearing that a master bladesman still practiced slicing vegetables for the dinner pot.

"How often?" Valyn asked, stepping back as the massive black bird swept in on close approach. Chi Hoai Mi, the Flea's flier, was coming in fast and hard, faster than Laith, even, and seemingly low enough to knock her Wing's commander from the cliff. The Flea didn't even look over his shoulder at the approaching bird. He just raised one hand and seemed to contemplate Valyn's question.

"Just about every day," he replied, eyes abstracted, as though tallying up the days and weeks, the *years.* "Yeah," he concluded, nodding as though that were settled. "Just about every day."

The bird was upon them in a rush of wind that knocked Valyn back onto his heels. The Flea, however, just leaned forward slightly, snagged a leather loop that had appeared at the last moment, seemingly out of no-where, and pulled himself effortlessly onto the talons. Before Valyn could make sense of the sight, Chi Hoai had put the bird into a steep bank and the whole Wing disappeared over the edge of the cliff.

35

For two days Kaden remained in the cellar of the meditation hall, toiling with a shovel and pickaxe in the rocky soil. Tan had said he wanted the cellar deeper, but he hadn't specified by how much. Kaden took the omission to mean he had a lot of work ahead of him. He had rolled the huge hogsheads of vinegar and weak beer out of the way, stacking them in the far corner, then set to work on the task. The ground was stony and unyielding. Often he would spend hours trying to find the edges of a boulder, then further hours levering it out of the earth with various picks and prybars. The solitary, monotonous work provided labor for his back and hands, but allowed his mind to wander over the events of the last week.

Pyrre and Jakin Lakatur weren't merchants; that much was clear, and their arrival had something to do with Kaden. It seemed as though, however improbably, the intrigue of the imperial court had found its way to Ashk'lan, a thought that made Kaden shiver despite his labors. The silk-hung corridors of the Dawn Palace had seen both spies and assassins over the centuries, and here, a thousand leagues from his father's court, Kaden had no Aedolian Guard to protect him.

What information a spy might hope to glean from Kaden, however, he had no idea. Despite the fact that he stood to inherit the Unhewn Throne, after eight years at Ashk'lan, he knew less about politics than the most incompetent footling. Pyrre and Jakin weren't likely to have undertaken a trek of a thousand leagues just to watch him run up and down Venart's Peak and turn bowls in the clay shed.

Assassination struck him as the more likely possibility, troubling though it was. *Something* was happening back in Annur, something with his father, and it wouldn't be the first time a rival faction had attempted to strike at the Emperor through his children. During their early childhood, Kaden and Valyn were abducted from the Dawn Palace by Armel Herve, the malcontent atrep of Breata. For weeks they shivered in one of the man's freezing tower chambers, each night terrified that they would be executed with the sunrise. Then the Kettral came.

Kaden, four years old at the time, had only scattered memories of the event: screaming, blood, fire, and, in the midst of the chaos, three men in black, shadows within shadows, smoke-steel blades flickering as they cut souls from bodies. Kaden could still feel the strong arm around his waist as the closest soldier gathered him up, holding him tight as the great bird took flight, lifting them into the air and away from the dark, fetid room.

From the moment they collected their wits, Kaden and Valyn both vowed that they would grow up to join the ranks of their heroes. They raced around the tapestry-hung halls of the palace swinging wooden replicas of the short Kettral swords, driving the poor palace staff to distraction. Valyn had made good on the dream, taking ship for the mysterious Qirin Islands on the same day that his brother was packed off to the monastery. After eight years training with the Kettral, Valyn would have nothing to fear from Pyrre and Jakin.

"But you're not Valyn, are you?" Kaden muttered to himself as he drove the shovel into the earth, squinting in the dim light of the lantern. "And you're not Kettral either." The realization of his own helplessness galled him, but there seemed no remedy for it. He had trained in painting and patience, the one he could see no use for, the other he needed far more than he had. There was no telling how long Tan intended him to skulk in the cellar—doubtless until any trace of danger had passed.

On the third morning, just as he was finally wrenching a stone the size of his torso out of the hole, Tan came for him.

"Leave it."

Kaden straightened, resisting the urge to knead the ache in his lower back. *If he sees that, he'll probably decide I need to spend the rest of the year hauling rocks and clearing out cellars.*

Tan, however, paid no attention to either the rock or the back. His eyes were on Kaden's face. "Let's go," he said after a long pause. "There are more than merchants here to see you."

The older monk led Kaden out the back door of the hall and into a narrow passageway between the buildings. After so many days in the cellar, Kaden had to squint against the afternoon brilliance, and it was only after his eyes adjusted that he could see the pail of water sitting on the stone step and the clean robe beside it. Tan gestured to them.

"You're going to want to get cleaned up," he said, his face blank as stone.

"Who's here?" Kaden asked.

Tan pointed at the pail once more. When Kaden realized he wasn't going to get any answers, he plunged his head into the cold water, then began scrubbing the grime from between his fingers. It took more than a few minutes to scour away the worst of the dirt, digging deep beneath his fingernails, scrubbing with rough gravel scooped from the ground until he thought he might end up taking off the flesh with the grime. Tan clearly had no intention of letting him go anywhere before he'd finished, so he went as fast as he could. When the worst of it had been scoured away, he pulled the clean robe over his head.

"All right," he said. "Where are we going?"

"Nowhere, yet," Tan replied. "We are going to take a look at these visitors of yours from the window of the hall."

"Why don't we just go out to meet them?" Kaden asked, curiosity overwhelming his deference.

There was iron in the monk's voice when he replied. "From the hall, we can look at them without them looking at us. It might be time you started thinking about more than pots and the *vaniate*."

Kaden almost fell over. Since becoming his *umial,* Tan had drilled him relentlessly in nothing *but* the *vaniate*. Everything Kaden had undertaken, from morning prayer to afternoon labor to the bare slab on stone on which he lay down at night, had been devoted to that goal. There were subsidiary challenges, of course—*saama'an, ivvate, beshra'an, kinla'an*— but they were all just rungs on the ladder. He stared at his *umial* in perplexity, but Tan steered him firmly back into the meditation hall to a window overlooking the central square.

Two men seemed to be arguing with the abbot while a small crowd of monks gathered around at a respectful distance. Kaden's breath caught at the splendid figures they cut. Eight years among the Shin had accustomed him to shaven heads and plain, brown robes. A leather belt was an extravagance; leather sandals, a preposterous luxury. These newcomers, however strode directly out of the pomp of his childhood.

The taller of the two wore full plate armor, burnished steel shining so brightly Kaden wanted to avert his eyes. The golden sun of the imperial

throne gleamed from his breastplate as well as from the massive shield
that rested at his feet. The grip and pommel of the largest broadblade
Kaden had ever seen extended up behind the man's head. He carried his
helmet beneath one arm, a single concession to the heat of the day. Even
from a distance, Kaden could make out deep blue eyes in a face that might
have been hammered out on an anvil, not a handsome face, but a familiar
one. Micijah Ut, he realized, a small smile creeping onto his face.

"Aedolian," Tan said softly.

Kaden looked over at the other monk, wondering for the thousandth
time about the life he had led before arriving at the monastery. The golden
knots on Ut's shoulders identified him clearly as a member of the Emper-
or's personal bodyguard, of course, but the Aedolian Guard rarely left the
capital. How would Tan recognize the insignia?

"The commander," Tan added.

Kaden glanced back to those knots. *Four,* he realized with a start.
When he left the Dawn Palace, Crenchan Xaw had been First Shield, and
though Xaw seemed almost as old as the empire itself, he had run the
guard with unerring competence since well before Kaden was born.
Whenever Kaden and Valyn tried to slip away on one of their childish
adventures, it was Xaw who caught them, Xaw who harangued them
about their responsibility to the empire, and Xaw who turned them over a
chair and caned them, heedless of their demands to be set free, of their
protestations that they were *princes,* that he had to *obey* them. Once, when
the brothers were still very young, they had foolishly complained to their
father about his First Shield's treatment. Sanlitun had only laughed and
resolved to pay Crenchan Xaw an extra stipend "for educating as well as
guarding his sons." The old man was dead now; the fact that Micijah Ut
wore the four golden knots of the First Shield could mean nothing else.
Although Kaden had spent almost all his young childhood at war with
the old commander, he felt a hollowness in the pit of his stomach, a dull
ache that the Shin would dismiss as illusion but that he still recognized
as sorrow.

When Kaden departed from the capital, Micijah Ut had been one of
four commanders directly beneath Crenchan Xaw. As leader of the Dark
Guard, he was charged with watching over the royal family between the
midnight bell and dawn. Kaden remembered him well, a stiff, formal man
who lacked the charm of many of the other Aedolians. He walked his
nightly rounds in full armor, even inside the Dawn Palace, his face turned

down in a perpetual frown, barely illuminated in the lamplight. Valyn and Kaden had always found him intimidating, despite the fact that he was there to protect them.

After eight years at Ashk'lan, however, Kaden was a child no longer, and in all that time, Micijah Ut was the first person he had seen from his old life. Despite Tan's admonition to wait and observe, Kaden felt an itching to step outside and batter the block of a man with his questions. In fact, he could hardly have asked for a better emissary than his father's own First Shield to clear up whatever was happening back in the Dawn Palace. Whatever secrets Pyrre Lakatur was keeping, they wouldn't last long now that Ut was here. Kaden turned toward the door of the hall, but Tan held him back, redirecting his attention to the scene outside.

With his free hand, the Aedolian was gesturing firmly at the abbot, almost poking him in the chest with his finger. When the wind fell, Kaden could hear his voice, an iron monotone that sounded more accustomed to command than negotiation. ". . . irrelevant. He is here because of the needs of the Unhewn Throne, and now the Unhewn Throne is . . ." A gust snatched away the end of the sentence.

Kaden frowned. The Ut he knew had been distant and difficult to know, hard as cast iron in his convictions, but never rude, never bullying. Whatever brought him here had both strained and hardened him.

The second man appeared content to let his companion do the talking. Kaden couldn't see his face, but long dark hair tied with red silk hung loosely down his back. Despite the rigors of travel and the unpredictable weather of the mountains, he wore a finely tailored red silk coat, buttoned up the center in the style of the highest-ranking imperial ministers, a low collar ringing his neck. Sunlight flashed on the man's golden cuffs, and Kaden blinked. Only the Mizran Councillor, the highest ranking nonmilitary minister, wore gold at both his cuffs and his collar. This man was one of a half dozen in the entire empire who outranked the Aedolian at his side.

Suddenly the councillor turned his head, and Kaden drew in his breath in surprise. The strip he had taken for a band to hold back hair was, in fact, a thick blindfold completely covering the man's eyes. In spite of it, he looked directly at the window where Kaden stood, then put a hand on the soldier's arm, as though to calm him. Unlike Ut, the Mizran was a complete stranger—he must have been extremely talented to have risen through the baffling ranks of the imperial bureaucracy in the eight short years since Kaden had left Annur. Once again the wind died, and this time Kaden could hear the councillor's voice, smooth as the silk he wore.

"Patience, my friend. He will come. Tell me," he said, addressing himself to the abbot, "how old is the monastery?"

"Almost three thousand years," Nin replied. If he was uncomfortable hosting two of the most powerful men in the world, he didn't show it. In fact, he spoke with the same measured patience that he used when addressing novices in his study.

"And yet," the man mused, "there are maps in the imperial library, recovered from the Csestriim, I believe, showing a fortress here long before that time. Of course, such maps are often the unreliable children of rumor and mythology."

"The place was chosen," the abbot replied, "for the preexisting foundations, among other reasons. Someone built here long before us. I cannot say if it was the Csestriim. It was not a large structure—as you can sense, perhaps, there is little space—but judging from the foundations the walls were thick and strong."

"Nevariim?" the councillor asked, tilting his head to the side speculatively.

The abbot shook his head. "In the stories I read, the Nevariim never built fortresses. They didn't build at all—it was one of the reasons the Csestriim were able to destroy them."

The man in silk waved a hand dismissively. "Ah well, stories, stories. Who's to say what to believe? There are plenty back in the capital who would claim the Nevariim didn't exist at all."

"I admit," Nin replied, "we have little knowledge of such things here."

As the wind picked up, carrying away the two voices, Tan looked over at Kaden. "Do you know them?"

"The Aedolian is named Micijah Ut," Kaden responded. "He once commanded the Dark Guard and now, evidently, has risen to the rank of First Shield." He returned his gaze to the other, sorting through his memories. "But the man in the silk . . . no. I don't know him."

In the few minutes they had paused to gaze down on the scene, Kaden's excitement had cooled, like bathwater left too long standing. Micijah Ut seemed different, transformed somehow, and the other man was a complete stranger. Moreover, he felt a growing unease as he considered the rank of the two. His father would not have sent the commander of his personal guard and his highest minister all the way across Vash for a social visit. Something was awry here, badly awry.

"All right," Tan said finally. "Let's go see what the First Shield of the Aedolian Guard and the empire's Mizran Councillor want with a boy who hasn't even learned to paint."

36

For the better part of three days, Valyn's Wing spent every spare hour in the gear shop trying to redesign the harness and buckle system for Suant'ra's talons. The work did not go smoothly. Although everyone seemed to accept the fundamental premise—that they needed a quicker and more efficient way to detach from the bird if they were going to make drops at Laith's speed—each member of the team had a different idea of the form that new system should take.

Gwenna was all for simple hand loops and no backup belts.

"And if you can't hold on to the 'Kent-kissing thing," she argued, stabbing a finger at Valyn, "maybe you *ought* to get dumped in the drink."

Talal shook his head. "That'd be fine for short runs, but do you want to be hanging from hand loops all day? And what if we need to retreat with someone wounded?"

Annick was even blunter. "No. I need two hands to shoot."

They had, strewn over the table in front of them, a baffling array of buckles, straps, hooks, catches, harnesses, rope, even an old leather saddle, although what they were supposed to do with that was anyone's guess. There was enough gear in the shop to rig a dozen systems—and yet, none of them could figure a way to make it all fit, to put the pieces together in a way that was actually useful. Gwenna kept her hands busy tying knots, lashing hook and eye pieces to lengths of leather, while Talal held up one piece at a time, gravely considering each in turn. None of it was getting them anywhere.

At first Laith just sat back in his chair, regarding the whole conversation with a faintly concealed grin. He'd brought a firefruit from the mess hall, and seemed more concerned with trying to spit the seeds into the rubbish bin than he was with their abortive engineering project.

"You're the one who's been flying this 'Shael-spawned bird the past decade," Valyn said. "You have anything to add?"

"Careful how you talk about my bird," Laith said, spitting another seed toward the bin. Missing. "Women come and go, but Suant'ra's been true to me for years."

"How romantic. Do you have any ideas that might help?"

The flier shrugged. "I'm up there on her back. I wish you all the best, but it seems like what happens down on the talons is your problem."

"It's our fucking *problem,*" Gwenna snapped, "because you never learned to fly your bird the right way."

"The right way?" Laith mused. "I prefer to think there's not just one right and wrong, but rather, a great palate of options, each—"

"Oh, for Hull's sake," Valyn broke in. "Leave off with the horseshit for half a second." He considered his friend carefully. Laith had a good mind, but as long as he considered the whole exercise irrelevant to his own role, he wasn't likely to use it. Of course, if something happened to make him care . . .

"What about," Valyn suggested innocently, "putting *two* soldiers on the bird's back? As Laith's pointed out, it's easier riding up there."

Talal opened his mouth to object, then, seeing what Valyn intended, shut it quietly.

"Two?" Laith spluttered, dropping all four feet of his chair onto the floor. "Where would the second one go?"

"Right behind you, I thought. They could hang on to your waist."

"Any idiot hanging on to my waist while we're flying maneuvers is just going to pull me off!"

"Luckily," Talal slipped in, "we're not idiots."

Annick rolled her eyes at that.

"All I'm saying," Valyn continued, pressing his success, "is that we need to keep all options on the table. If we can't figure a way to get all four of us below, maybe we need to put an extra person on top."

After that, Laith tossed the remainder of his firefruit in the trash and started confronting the problem in earnest.

At the heart of the matter was the trade-off between speed and security. It was easy to arrange a quick drop—it just meant you didn't have much holding you in place during the gut-wrenching maneuvers leading up to it. On the other hand, all the buckles and knots of the conventional system made for great security—you could fall fully asleep dangling from the bird's talons—but inefficient drops.

"What we *need*," Laith burst out after they'd been going around and around for the better part of an hour, "is to stop screwing around with buckles. Why can't the things just *explode* off?"

Gwenna pursed her lips, then nodded slowly.

"No," Valyn said, stopping her before she could get started. "We're not going to rig charges to ourselves *or* our buckles."

"A very *small* charge," Gwenna suggested, her green eyes bright, "if handled carefully, could do the job. We'd just need a slow-burn wick attached to—"

"No explosives," Valyn said, setting his fist firmly on the table. "We may be the worst 'Kent-kissing Wing on the Islands, but at least we still have all our fingers."

"For now," Laith added.

"I'm sorry, my most exquisite and sublime commander," Gwenna shot back. "I'll attempt not to speak out of turn in the future. Perhaps His Lordship would like to put a gag in my mouth?"

Valyn would have liked nothing better, but he was *trying* to bring the Wing together, not browbeat them into submission.

"I've got something I could put in your mouth," Laith suggested, managing to look innocent and depraved at the same time. "Might keep us both out of trouble."

Gwenna smiled back compliantly, but her words were barbed. "I'd like that," she said. "I've always enjoyed my meat soft and tender. It's easier to chew."

Annick snorted, whether with amusement or disgust Valyn had no idea.

"We *could* try going in slower," Talal suggested quietly. "It's what the other Wings do."

Laith rolled his eyes. "You sound like my grandmother, 'Shael rest her soul. We had horses, but she always insisted on walking, said that if Bedisa had intended us to gallop around the globe, Bedisa would have made us with four legs and hooves. Anyway, if I went in any slower, everyone with a bow could take a shot at you. We might as well just hang dead meat from 'Ra's talons."

"It's what the other Wings do," Annick pointed out. "It's the protocol."

"Aren't you the one who hammers her own arrowheads?" Laith demanded. "Since when do you give a whore's heart for protocol?"

"Wait," Valyn cut in, trying to focus on the words he'd just heard. "Hold on a second."

The rest of the group stared at him for several long moments.

"You have something to say?" Laith asked finally. "Or you just need to take a shit?"

"Hooks," Valyn replied, fixing on the idea. "Meat hooks."

As a child, he'd been morbidly fascinated with the larder deep in the cellars of the Dawn Palace, where rows on rows of slaughtered pigs, cows, and sheep had been dressed and hung from frightening steel hooks. He and Kaden used to sneak down there, daring each other to snuff the lantern and wander in the darkness, hands stretched out before them to fend off the carcasses. It was where he had first learned about hearts, and brains, and livers, where he first understood that if you cut a body and bled it dry, the creature died. It did not seem an auspicious place to be gleaning combat ideas, but then, they didn't have much else to work with.

"We use hooks instead of buckles."

Annick squinted, tilted her head to the side as though calculating, then nodded once. "Good." The sniper was a thorn in his side, but she was *fast*.

The rest of the Wing wasn't so quick. "Hooks *where*?" Gwenna demanded.

"High," Valyn responded, warming to his idea. "High on 'Ra's talons, a little above our heads. We toss a loop of rope from our belts over the hooks, and our weight holds us in place."

Laith shook his head. "You'll have the same problem you've got with the buckles—you can't release the loop from the hook with your weight on it."

Valyn smiled. "That *would* be a problem . . . if you bothered to follow standard drop protocol."

"Ah," Talal chimed in, understanding spreading across his face. "As the angle of our descent gets steeper and steeper, the loop will slip closer to the lip of the hook."

Valyn nodded. "When we're in a near-vertical dive, the loop will slide right off. We drop. We don't ever need to touch a thing."

"It's clever," Gwenna replied with a frown, "but it means we all drop at the same time."

"Not if we change the angles of the hooks slightly," Laith countered. "First to drop has the shallowest angle, the last, the most severe. As 'Ra stoops harder, you'll fall off one by one."

Talal nodded. "It makes so much sense," he marveled. "Why don't any of the veteran Wings do this?"

"Because *their* fliers follow orders," Valyn responded, eyeing Laith appraisingly. "The hooks wouldn't work at shallower attack angles. The attack angles we're *supposed* to adhere to."

"This mean we get to quit following orders?" Gwenna asked with a smirk.

For the first time, Valyn found himself smiling in return. It was a small step, really—smaller than small. They hadn't even built a mock-up of the system, hadn't come close to testing it, and yet, for the first time, he thought he understood the Flea's words: *Command the Wing you have, not the one you want.* For the first time, they'd demonstrated that they could work in concert to solve a common problem. *Who knows,* he thought to himself with a small smile, *we might turn out all right after all.*

Then the door to the shop slammed open.

Daveen Shaleel stepped into the room, followed immediately by Adaman Fane and the other four members of his Wing, all decked out in full combat kit.

"Don't tell me," Laith groaned. "You want us to swim around Qarsh underwater."

Valyn started to chuckle, but the sound died in his throat. The soldiers in the door weren't laughing. They weren't even smiling. In fact, Valyn realized, his stomach tightening suddenly, they'd taken up standard assault positions just inside the room, as though they were getting ready to clear an enemy compound. He took a step forward, toward Shaleel, trying to formulate the right question. Fane's blade brought him up short, whispering out of its sheath to point directly at Valyn's throat.

"Less moving," the man said grimly. "More listening."

Shaleel took in the scene at a glance, then turned to Valyn. She seemed as calm as a housewife going about her chores, but steel edged her voice when she spoke.

"Valyn hui'Malkeenian," she began, transfixing him with her gaze, "your Wing is hereby suspended from all training and combat missions. You will retain your freedom of movement on Qarsh itself, but you are forbidden to leave the island, forbidden to bear arms, and forbidden to have any substantive contact with other Wings, commanders, or cadets until the completion of our inquest."

Valyn had never heard the words before, but they carried the ring of legal formula.

"What inquest?" he demanded, angry despite Fane's blade in his face. "What are you talking about?"

"As you and your Wing are all aware," Shaleel continued, "Kettral code forbids unauthorized assault on civilians, imperial or otherwise. It has come to my attention in the past hour that a member of your Wing may be implicated in just such an assault."

"What?" Valyn asked, trying desperately to follow the conversation, to gain his footing. "*Who?* And how did this 'come to your attention'?"

"Sami Yurl," Shaleel replied. "According to him, a young woman over on Hook was murdered several weeks ago—a whore named Amie, no surname. Yurl presented us with compelling evidence that suggests your sniper—" She indicated Annick with a nod of her head. "—was involved."

"Sami Yurl? That vat of pickled pig's shit?" Gwenna burst out, rising from her chair. "Why would you listen to him about anything?"

"Take your people in hand, Commander," Shaleel said, never shifting her eyes from Valyn's face, "or they may get themselves hurt."

"You can talk to me, you know," Gwenna said, taking a step forward. "I'm right here."

"*Gwenna,*" Valyn snapped, surprised at the edge of command in his own voice. "*Not now.*"

For a moment, he thought she was going to defy him, but Talal put a hand on her shoulder and, after a final spasm of anger, Gwenna cursed and threw herself back into her chair.

A hole opened in Valyn's stomach. He wanted to scream that it was impossible, that Yurl had played him, played Shaleel, played the whole 'Kent-kissing lot of them. He wanted to bellow that Annick was innocent, but he couldn't. For all he knew, Yurl was right.

"Where is he?" Valyn managed. "I want to talk to him, personally."

Shaleel shook her head. "I sent Yurl's Wing out this morning—their first mission. Besides, the code forbids such contact until the inquest is finished."

"Why all of us?" Laith demanded. At least he had remained in his seat, but he was leaning forward hungrily, his hand on his belt knife. "If Annick's the one you're worried about, why don't you just lock *her* up and leave us out of it?"

"I will chalk up the impertinence of your question to your shock, soldier," Shaleel replied evenly. "The Eyrie has found it . . . prudent, to detain an entire Wing in the event of an inquiry into the conduct of one of its members. We don't want any ill-conceived 'rescues' or 'last stands.'"

Wing loyalty is a powerful thing." She eyed the lot of them up and down, "Although in your case, it doesn't appear to be a problem."

"Blades and bows," Fane said. "We'll take them all."

"Possession of any weapon aside from a belt knife between now and the end of the inquest," Shaleel added, "will be construed as treason. Until we sort this out, the five of you should consider yourselves civilians."

37

As they entered the quad, Micijah Ut fixed him with dark eyes, eyes that seemed somehow colder and darker than Kaden remembered. The man didn't smile or even nod. He simply turned to the abbot and said, "It is lucky for you the boy is unharmed." Whatever they had been arguing about, Kaden was impressed that Nin had managed to stand his ground. He knew the old monk was not weak, but Ut's gaze made ice seem warm and steel soft.

The abbot opened his mouth to reply, but Ut had already turned back to Kaden, dropping to one knee, mailed hand to his forehead. His companion mirrored the gesture and the two spoke together, their voices merging as though through long practice.

"All hail the Scion of Light, the Long Mind of the World, Holder of the Scales, and Keeper of the Gates." The words echoed down to Kaden from the formal halls of his childhood. They were old words, as old as the empire, hard and unchanging as the stones of the Dawn Palace. He had heard the formula a thousand times when his father took his seat on the Unhewn Throne, when his father left the palace to walk along the Godsway, when his father appeared for state dinners. As a child, he had been comforted by the litany but now, as he listened, the words dragged a cold, iron nail up his spine. He knew what was coming, knew how it had to end, and though he wanted to beg the two men to stop, they spoke on, relentlessly: "All hail he who holds back the darkness. All hail the Emperor."

Kaden felt he had been dropped from a great height. His mind tumbled over and over, trying to gain purchase on something solid, familiar. Outside this small circle comprising the abbot, the Annurians, himself, and Tan, the monks went about their quotidian business, heads bent beneath their cowls, hands drawn into the sleeves of their robes, their pace measured and deliberate, as though nothing in the world had changed. They were wrong; everything had changed. To speak the formula he had just heard in front of anyone but his father constituted the highest treason, punishable by the old and horrific rite of blinding and live burial. For the minister and the Aedolian to use them now could only mean one thing. His father was dead.

Images flooded unbidden into his mind. His father patiently drawing his bow over and over while Kaden and Valyn struggled to imitate the smooth motion with their own, much smaller weapons. His father's grim face as he watched the men hang who had abducted his sons. His father pulling on his splendid golden greaves before marching to meet the armies of the Federated Cities. It seemed impossible that Ananshael could take a man of such force and vigor before his fiftieth year. Impossible, except that Ut and the councillor were here, and they had spoken the irrevocable words.

He wasn't sure how long he stood there, but finally the abbot broke him from his daze.

"Kaden," he said quietly, gesturing to the two men. They continued to kneel, hands to foreheads. Kaden wondered why they remained there, then realized with a start that they were waiting for him as so many thousands had knelt, waiting for his father before him. They were waiting for their Emperor. He wanted to moan.

"Please," he said weakly. "Please get up."

They rose, Ut no more slowly for the weight of his armor. As Kaden tried to master his shock long enough to compose his thoughts into sensible questions, the door to the guests' quarters clattered open and Pyrre Lakatur sauntered into the courtyard, her husband a few steps behind.

The top three eyelets of the merchant's tunic were unlaced, as though she had spent the afternoon napping, and she scratched her ear absently, waiting for her husband to catch up. On seeing the group, however, she paused, seemed to take stock, then forged ahead, a broad smile on her face. She might have been sallying into a country fair, sizing up Ut and the minister as if they were blowsy farmwives or blacksmiths tipsy with ale, fishmongers or haberdashers upon whom she could foist her wares. Jakin hung back momentarily, patting the sides of his vest unconsciously, as though to smooth it. Pyrre addressed herself to the Aedolian, nodding her head in casual deference.

"All glory to Sanlitun, may he live forever."

The Aedolian fixed her with a blank stare, but it was the minister who responded.

"Sanlitun, bright were the days of his life, is dead. You stand where you should kneel, for you are in the presence of Kaden i'Sanlitun hui'Malkeenian, twenty-fourth of his line."

"This whelp?" Pyrre laughed skeptically, eyeing Kaden. It was the first the woman had laid eyes on him, and beneath the offhand jocularity, there was something careful and measuring in that momentary gaze.

Ut's broadblade was out of its sheath before Kaden could think to breathe, flashing in a savage arc. Pyrre didn't move so much as a whisker, not even to flinch, and Micijah Ut's cold sword came to rest on her neck, the pressure drawing a thin line of blood. The merchant's eyes widened in obvious shock. She began to raise a belated hand to the blade, then thought better of it.

Ut addressed Kaden without taking his eyes from Pyrre. "Should I take her head from her shoulders, Your Radiance, or just remove the tongue from her mouth?"

Kaden stared from one to the other. What had happened to the Micijah Ut that he knew, the captain of the Dark Guard, the man who had looked in on him and his brother countless midnights, careful to see that they were safe in their beds? Was his change the result of the Emperor's demise? The Aedolians had sworn to protect Kaden's father with their lives. If Ut considered himself somehow responsible for Sanlitun's death . . . that could alter a man, even a strong man like the soldier Kaden remembered.

The thoughts tumbled through his mind, blending in a turgid swell with grief for his father and confusion—confusion about everything. Only after a few breaths did he realize that Ut's blade was still at the merchant's neck. Pyrre had gone utterly still, her eyes blank. She looked as though she wanted to lift a hand to the broadblade, but didn't dare stir. Ten minutes earlier, Kaden had been an acolyte digging out a cellar, and now a woman's life hung on his next syllable. He shook his head unsteadily.

"No," he said. "No. Just let her go."

The Aedolian's sword slid back into its sheath with the hoarse whisper of steel on steel. Ut's face betrayed neither relief nor disappointment, and Kaden realized with deep unease that the man considered himself no more than an agent of the Emperor's will, of *his* will. If he gave the word, Pyrre's head would roll in the gravel before him. As if coming to the same conclusion, the merchant rubbed gingerly at the line of blood on her throat, then lowered herself unsteadily to her knees. A few steps behind her, Jakin did the same.

"You are unaccustomed to both the prerogatives and the dignity of imperial power," the minister put in smoothly, smiling thinly at Kaden from beneath his blindfold. "For that reason, I have been sent to you with this delegation. My name is Tarik Adiv. I served as your father's Mizran Councillor these past five years, and if you wish it so, I will serve you as well."

Kaden's mind was still reeling. He tried to focus on the man's words, on his face, but the whole world shimmered as though seen through rough water.

"This man," Adiv continued, gesturing to the Aedolian, "I believe you already know. Two years ago, Micijah Ut was raised from Captain of the Dark Guard to First Shield after the sad but not altogether unexpected death of Crenchan Xaw." Ut stood straight as a spear once more, eyes fixed forward, no visible hint of the violence suspended only moments before. Adiv might have been commenting on the price of beets, for all he seemed to care. "He commands your personal guard," the minister continued, "and is here to ensure your safety on the voyage back to Annur."

As Kaden stared dumbly, Adiv went on. "We are not alone, of course. Most of your retinue waits on the steppe below. It seemed . . . unwieldy to bring one hundred men and twice as many horses up this narrow path. A few more of your servants will be arriving shortly with gifts. We outstripped them in our haste.

"If I may, Your Radiance, I suggest we dine and rest here tonight. You can put your affairs in order and we can depart tomorrow morning. A ship swings at anchor for us back at the Bend, fully provisioned and ready to sail for Annur. The sooner we depart, the sooner we will be aboard. This is only a suggestion, Your Radiance, but prudence urges haste. The empire grows unruly when the Emperor is long away. Though it pains me to say it, there are those who would work you ill."

"Fine," Kaden said, not trusting himself to speak at more length. The silence stretched, and then he remembered Pyrre kneeling on the flagstones. "Please," he said awkwardly. "Rise." The woman got to her feet, favoring her good leg, but kept her eyes downcast. The casual swagger that had marked her attitude since her arrival at the monastery had vanished utterly.

"If I may, Your Radiance," she began hesitantly. Her fingers kept reaching for the scratch on her neck, as though drawn to the blood.

Kaden waited, but when the woman did not continue, he said, "Go on."

"Scial Nin has informed us of the danger here around the monastery—something killing your goats and even your brothers. If we might travel with your retinue as you head south, we would be forever grateful."

Kaden thought back to the woman's hesitation at the banquet, seeing it with new eyes. Pyrre claimed to be a merchant, and merchants trafficked in news as much as they did in goods. Word of a revolt in Ghan or an outbreak of diphtheria in Freeport affected their choice of goods as well as their direction of travel as surely as the fluctuating price of silver. She must have heard rumor of the Emperor's death and decided to keep it hidden. Kaden suddenly felt overwhelmed by the small courtyard audience. The sun overhead beat down, and rivulets of sweat ran down his back beneath his robe.

"I will . . . consider it," he said unsteadily, his head still spinning. "For now, I would like a time to mourn." Then, turning to the abbot, "May I meet you in your study?"

"Of course," the old monk replied.

"This is a sad time for us all, and for you more than any," Adiv put in smoothly. "Please don't hesitate to call upon either of us if we can be of service or consolation. The slaves will be arriving shortly to erect your pavilion and prepare dinner. Perhaps, while you put your affairs in order, the abbot would be kind enough to ask one of the brothers here to provide us with a tour of the monastery."

"Naturally," Scial Nin said. "I will have Chalmer Oleki meet you in your chambers. He knows more of Ashk'lan's history than any."

"We are grateful," Adiv replied with a nod. "Until tonight, then, Your Radiance." Once again he knelt, his head bowed, while Ut did the same at his side.

"Rise," Kaden said, feeling all at once just how wearying it would be to utter that simple word again and again to men and women of all stations for the rest of his life.

Only as they withdrew to their quarters and silence descended on the courtyard once again did Kaden realize he did not know how his father had died. Oddly, he had not thought to ask.

38

I'm not ready.

The thought plagued Kaden like the fragment of an inane tune reeling about in his head. *I'm not ready.* He sat in the same chair from three nights before, and as on that night, the abbot sat silently behind his desk. A small fire burned on the hearth, filling the room with the scent of smoke and juniper while keeping the mountain chill at bay. Outside the windows, Kaden could hear the bleating of goats as Phirum Prumm and Henter Leng shepherded them toward the pens for milking. Nothing was different, but everything had changed. The old monk hadn't begun falling to his knees or calling him *Your Radiance,* a fact for which Kaden was profoundly grateful, but there was a new distance in Nin's steady blue gaze, as though the old abbot had already let him go.

"I guess I won't make a good monk after all," Kaden began at last, laughing weakly.

"Life is long," the abbot replied, "and the paths through it are many."

Kaden shook his head at the absurdity of the past hour. "I'm not ready."

There. He had said it, and having said it, the other words came out in a rush, as though the stopper had been pulled from the base of a large cask. "I haven't learned anything. I don't know anything. You've trained me to be a monk, not an Emperor."

The old man raised an eyebrow at the outburst, but that was all. A week prior, the rant would have earned Kaden five laps on the Circuit of Ravens or a night on the Talon, and he found himself wishing the abbot would snap at him as he had in the past, tell him to stop being a child, to master his emotions, then send him out to haul water from the black pool. *But you don't send an Emperor to haul water,* Kaden thought, and indeed, Nin's response was calm and measured.

"As I have already explained, you were not sent here to become a monk."

Kaden opened his mouth to respond, then closed it when he found he had nothing to say.

"I'm doubly sorry for your loss," the old monk began after a time. "First, because every son should have a chance to know his father, not as a child knows his protector, but as a man knows another man. More pressingly, however, I worry for the empire. As you have observed, Sanlitun died before he could complete your education. He would have taught you the intricacies of politics, intricacies of which we know nothing here. Annur is the most powerful empire since the fall of the Atmani. The fates of thousands, millions, depend on your knowledge."

"And the gates," Kaden added, glancing out the window as though there were some escape in the serrated mountains beyond. "I still haven't learned the *vaniate*. I can't use the gates."

The abbot nodded somberly. "You're close, very close, but close is irrelevant. If you tried to pass the *kenta* without achieving the *vaniate*—" He shook his head, gestured to the air around them with one mottled hand.

"The Blank God," Kaden concluded.

"The Blank God."

Kaden hesitated before his next question. "Is there one here?" He asked finally. "A *kenta*? Could I see it?"

The abbot shook his head. "The Ishien used to build their fortresses by the gates in order to guard them, but Ashk'lan . . . we don't know who laid the foundations, but there is no *kenta*. If there were, your father could have visited you whenever he pleased. Many have been lost, but to the best of my knowledge, there is not a Csestriim gate within a hundred leagues of here."

"So . . . what?" Kaden asked. "I have to return to Annur—it'll take months, even if we travel by ship from the Bend—and Adiv says I don't have months."

"It's unusual," Nin replied. "Both your father and his father completed their training here. Perhaps we could convince Rampuri Tan to accompany you."

Kaden stifled a desperate laugh, but Scial Nin caught the expression.

"You find the idea troublesome?" he asked.

"I'm just trying to imagine holding court while buried up to my nose in gravel," Kaden replied. "My subjects might have difficulty looking up to me if I'm constantly scouring the privy."

"It will be difficult," the abbot agreed, nodding his bald head, "and yet, I can see no other way."

"What about Akiil?" Kaden asked, remembering his friend for the first time.

Nin raised an eyebrow. "What about him?"

"Can he . . ." Kaden trailed off. It was one thing for Rampuri Tan to accompany the delegation. It was quite another to expect Akiil to simply leave the monastery. Monks were free to come and go as they chose, but Akiil was still an acolyte. Until he completed his training, he was bound to the Bone Mountains. "Never mind."

"Do not grasp things so tightly," the abbot suggested, his voice a shade more gentle than normal. "You must be prepared to let go of homes, friends, family, even yourself. Only then will you be free."

"The *vaniate*," Kaden said wearily.

The abbot nodded.

"Tell me something," Kaden continued after a long silence. "Do you really believe that there are Csestriim out there, lurking somewhere, plotting?"

"I believe," the abbot replied, "what I can observe. What I observe is that the world is ruled by men—good men and bad, desperate men and those with principles. I may be wrong—Ae knows it would not be the first time— but I see no Csestriim."

"But Tan—"

Before Kaden could finish the sentence, the door burst open, and as though summoned by the mention of his name, Rampuri Tan strode into the room, a parchment in one hand, the strange *naczal* spear in the other. Sweat beaded his forehead, and his jaw was tight.

The abbot looked over. "Kaden and I were speaking in private, brother," he began, voice severe.

"It will have to wait," Tan replied curtly. "Altaf caught a glimpse of what's been killing the goats. Down in the lower meadow. He painted it."

The monk slapped the parchment down on the table and spread it open. Kaden struggled to make sense of the image—black lines slashed across the page in a jumble of limbs and claws. The smith had drawn something like a spider—eight legs, heavy carapace, segmented body—except whatever killed the goats was too big to be a spider.

"What's the scale on this?" the abbot asked.

"It's the size of a large dog."

And the size was the least of it. The creature looked like something out of the depths of nightmare, with legs like blades or shears, savage hacking members designed by some cruel god to cut and to crush. Worse, dozens of eyes, glassy orbs the color of spilled blood, protruded from it everywhere, even from the limbs, as though they had been grafted on by some unholy kenning. Kaden had studied a thousand species during his time at Ashk'lan, creatures as strange as the albino stream crab and the flame moth, plants he couldn't have dreamed up in a year of dreaming. They had been bizarre, but not unnatural. If Altaf's painting was anything to go by, there was something *wrong* about this creature. Something twisted.

"I've never come across anything like it," the abbot said after a long silence, steepling his fingers and turning his gaze to the other monk.

"That's because it should have been extinct thousands of years ago," Tan replied.

"I gather you know what it is?" Nin asked.

"If I'm right," the monk said grimly, "and I hope I am not, it is an abomination. An abomination and an impossibility."

Kaden frowned. The word *abomination* wasn't part of the Shin lexicon. It implied hatred, emotion.

Tan grimaced at the painting, as though trying to accept what he saw, then went on. "What Altaf has drawn looks like an *ak'hanath.*" He indicated the serrated legs, the claws. "A creature of the Csestriim."

Kaden drew in a sharp breath.

"So they *are* still around," he said. Then, when no one responded, "But we won. Remmick Ironheart killed the last of the Csestriim on the fields of Ai."

"Maybe," Tan said.

"Maybe," Nin acknowledged with a weary nod.

"And now that Altaf has seen this thing," Kaden interjected, "this *ak'hanath,* you think the Csestriim have returned." It was impossible, like hearing that the young gods had come to walk the earth once again.

"It's hard to say," Nin said. For once, he almost looked his age, his eyes weary beneath his weathered brow. "I believe what I can observe, and I have not observed everything. Perhaps your *umial* is mistaken. Perhaps he is correct, but even so, a Csestriim creature does not mean that the Csestriim themselves still walk the earth. Certainty is hard to come by."

"Certainty is impossible," Tan added, a flat, hard light in his eyes. "The world is a shifting, dangerous place. Those who wait for certitude before they act almost always wait too long."

"But what *is* it?" Kaden asked, returning his gaze to the painting with horrified fascination.

"The Csestriim made them," Tan replied. "No one is quite sure how. Bedisa weaves the souls of all living things, spinning them into existence at their birth, but the *ak'hanath* were not born. They were *made*." He paused. "It should not have been possible."

"Made?" Kaden asked. "Made for what?"

"To sniff out," Tan said, his eyes hardening, "to track. To harry, and to hunt."

39

Kaden almost hadn't recognized the refectory when he entered. Adiv described the meal as "a small, informal dinner," and the Mizran Councillor had brought only a half dozen slaves up the mountain, but they must have been run off their feet all afternoon. Long ivory banners hung from the rafters, stitched in gold thread with the rising sun of the Malkeenian line. Someone had lugged in a huge Si'ite carpet, all swirls and patterns, spreading it over the uneven flagstone floor. The rough sconces on the wall were replaced with silver lanterns, and ornate silver candlesticks graced a lacy tablecloth ringed by six settings of Basc porcelain.

Kaden glanced warily at the empty chair to his left, wondering who would occupy it. A day ago the question would have filled him with excitement, but the odd string of visitors to the monastery had not proved auspicious, and he was reluctant to meet another unfamiliar face. The world beyond Ashk'lan, which only a few days before had beckoned so brightly, now seemed a dark place, filled with treachery and confusion, death and disappointment.

Tarik Adiv sat just around the corner of the table to his right, leaning forward slightly in his straight-backed wooden chair. The Mizran Councillor still wore the bloodred blindfold around his eyes, although at the moment he seemed to be staring directly at Kaden, as though he could see right through the cloth. Micijah Ut occupied one of the two seats across the table, his back straight as his broadblade, which leaned against the wooden chair within easy reach. As far as Kaden knew, Nin and Tan had told no one about the *ak'hanath,* but then, it was the Aedolian's job to be vigilant, regardless of the situation.

Scial Nin joined them, of course; Adiv could scarcely leave the abbot out of his invitation, although the old monk in his old robe looked small and poor beside the massive Aedolian at his side. Kaden had insisted on Rampuri Tan's presence as well, an insistence to which Adiv had acquiesced with far greater grace than Tan himself. "You should be studying," the monk had said, "not feasting."

The rest of the Shin had been politely asked to spend the evening fasting, a request that Kaden was sure would mean some kind of retribution from Akiil. Kaden hadn't seen his friend so prickly for years; clearly the arrival of the imperial delegation had dragged to the surface all the old animosity that their time at Ashk'lan had done so much to bury. It was hard to know how to talk to Akiil about this sudden elevation, and Kaden worried about it almost as much as he worried about leaving the monastery and returning to Annur.

Now, however, he had to concentrate on playing the Emperor without making an ass of himself, a task he was not at all sure he was ready for. He looked over at the empty seat again.

"Will someone else be joining us?" he asked, trying to keep his tone light.

Adiv smiled a sly smile beneath his blindfold. "As I said, Your Radiance, we come bearing gifts."

Kaden had to remind himself that, while news of his father's death was fresh as an open wound for him, Adiv and Ut, everyone from Annur, in fact, had had months to accustom themselves to the fact. Doubtless they had done their mourning long ago, and yet still, it was hard to sit down to a festive dinner with others while his own grief—or what meager grief his years of training had not effaced—was still so fresh.

One servant stood behind each seat, and the man behind Kaden's chair had kept his eyes downcast as he pulled it back. Kaden had taken his place somewhat uncomfortably. After eight years sitting on hard benches and fetching his own stew and bread from the kitchen, he found the habits of the imperial court alien and unnecessary. He was Emperor now, though, and certain things were expected of the Emperor.

Despite his blindfold, Adiv seemed to miss little, and a small smile played around the corners of his mouth. Kaden was beginning to think the man not only noticed his awkwardness, but enjoyed it as well. As the silence stretched out, the minister's smile widened.

"It would be inappropriate for the Emperor to dine alone," he said finally, spreading his hands in invitation before bringing them together in a crisp clap. The twin wooden doors at the end of the refectory swung open.

Kaden's eyes widened. Alone in the doorway, half in darkness, half illuminated by the lanterns inside the hall, stood a young woman. That would have been reason enough to take notice. After all, Ashk'lan was a monastic community and Kaden had not left it for eight years; Pyrre had already occasioned a good deal of glancing and chatter among the acolytes, but if Akiil had seen this . . .

While the merchant had a certain rough elegance, the woman in the doorway looked as though she had stepped straight from a vision of opulence, a dream of beauty made flesh. She wore a long gown of Si'ite silk, the fabric red as arterial blood and supple as water. The dressmaker had known his art, cutting the cloth to emphasize the fullness of her breasts, the curve of her hip, while a separate loop of fabric ringed her neck, tied below her chin in an elaborate bow.

Even more striking than the presentation was the girl herself: the Dawn Palace had been filled with attractive women—the wives of atreps, well-known courtesans, priestesses and princesses by the dozen—but Kaden was certain he had never seen one so beautiful. Night-black hair cascaded past her shoulders, framing a pale face with full lips and high cheekbones. She might have been one of the Nevariim he read about as a child—an impossibly beautiful, infinitely graceful creature from the tales told at his bedside. Of course, the Nevariim were long dead, if they had ever lived at all, and this woman was very real. Kaden put the children's stories out his mind.

Adiv had cocked his ear to one side, as though listening to the stunned silence. After a moment he grinned, evidently satisfied with the reaction, then spoke: "She is called Triste, and the bow around her neck is yours to untie. Although," he added, turning to face Kaden with that disconcertingly blank blindfold, "I would leave her at least partly packaged until after the meal. The Shin are famed for their asceticism, but I fear our dinner conversation might suffer if she sat here just as Bedisa made her. Triste," he said, beckoning imperiously, "come closer that the Emperor might admire you."

The young woman kept her eyes fixed on the rough stone floor as she approached, but there was nothing bashful about her stride, a languorous swaying of the hips that arrested Kaden's gaze. He stood hastily, almost knocking over his chair in the process, grabbing at it with his hand to keep it from falling and cursing himself silently for an idiot as he did so. From the length of the hall, the ripeness of Triste's body had led him to believe she was older than him, a woman grown. This close, he could see how young she was—sixteen at the most. He wondered absently if someone had lit a fire in the hearth. He was sweating beneath his robe as though he had been running for hours.

"You should greet the Emperor, Triste," Adiv urged. "Be thankful you have been given to a great man."

She raised her head slowly, and Kaden saw that her round violet eyes were full of fear.

"It is an honor, Your Radiance," she said, the hint of a quaver in her voice, and suddenly he felt shame mixed with his desire, shame for drinking in the sight of her so fully and shame for thinking that she might be his, packaged up and delivered like a new suit. He bent to free her from the bow at her throat, and her perfume, a concoction of sandalwood and jasmine, made his head reel.

He fumbled with the simple knot for what seemed like minutes, uncomfortably aware of his knuckles pressing into the girl's firm flesh and the eyes of the small dinner party on his back. He didn't dare look at her face again, fixing his gaze instead on the tiny, intricate tattoo of a necklace that circled her neck.

"Go on," Adiv urged. Even the man with that infernal blindfold could sense his awkwardness! Ae only knew what Tan and Nin were thinking. "She won't thank you for keeping her standing much longer."

Kaden's face burned, and all the exercises he had studied over the past eight years to still the mind and slow the pulse fled. Pain was one thing, but this . . . this was something else altogether. He thought he might never be able to look Tan in the eye again. Finally the silk fell away.

He went to pull out her seat and found that one of the slaves had already done so. Awkwardly, he gestured for her to sit down. Adiv clapped his hands together again in good humor.

"I understand from his silence that the Emperor is not used to such . . . luscious gifts. You will soon become accustomed to the trifles that befit your exalted station, Your Radiance."

Kaden risked a glance at the other guests. Micijah Ut sat ramrod straight in his chair, arms folded across his chest. The two monks watched Kaden with blank expressions. He looked away, turning to Triste in desperation, casting about in his mind for something to say. The normal monastic subjects of conversation, the things he had talked about day after day, night after night for years, seemed suddenly drab and pointless. This woman didn't care about the level of snowmelt from the Triuri glacier or the sighting of a crag cat on the Circuit of Ravens. He tried to imagine his father or mother entertaining guests in the comfortable opulence of the Pearl Hall, their easy manner as the servants poured the wine and arranged the plates.

"Triste, where are you from?" he asked at last. The words had sounded all right in his head, but as soon as they were out of his mouth, he felt ridiculous. The question was at once pedestrian and awkward, the kind of thing you might ask a merchant or a sailor, not something you put to a beautiful woman moments after she had joined you at the table. Triste's eyes widened and she opened her mouth to respond, but before she could speak, Adiv interceded.

"Where is she from?" The councillor seemed to find the question amusing. "Maybe she'll tell you tonight, over the pillow. Now, however, it is time to eat."

Triste closed her perfect lips and for a sliver of a moment Kaden saw something flash through her eyes. Terror, he thought at first, but it was not terror. Whatever it was felt harder, older. He wanted to look closer, but the girl had dropped her eyes, while at Adiv's command the servants, who had left the table after everyone was seated, glided in through the side door, carrying delicate plates of artfully arranged food.

After setting up the refectory, the Mizran's men had taken over the kitchen, going to work with a stock of ingredients carried all the way from the markets of Annur. Kaden couldn't begin to recognize all the flavors and smells. There were battered locusts and duck with plum sauce, some kind of delicate cream soup that reminded him of summer in the south, and noodles mixed with sausage so hot, it made him sweat. Each course came with a different kind of bread or cracker, and between plates the servants produced tiny silver bowls filled with mint or lemon ice or essence of pine drizzled over rice to cleanse the palate.

Each plate arrived with an accompanying wine, delicate whites from the Freeport hinterland, and rich, heady reds from the plains just north of the Neck. Kaden tried to take only a sip or two of each, but he had spent years drinking only tea and water from the mountain streams, and he quickly found the alcohol dizzying. Triste, on the other hand, drained every glass the slaves set in front of her until Kaden worried she might be sick. After a while, Adiv directed the man to stop pouring for her with a curt motion of his hand.

When the whirlwind of the first few courses had finished, a silence settled over the table and Kaden took a deep breath, steadying himself to ask the question that had been tugging at his mind since the men first fell to their knees before him and recited the ancient formula, the question he had somehow forgotten to ask.

"Councillor," he began slowly, then threw himself into it, "how did my father die?"

Adiv put his fork down, lifted his head, but did not speak. As the silence stretched, Kaden felt himself growing dizzy with a sort of vertigo, as though he stood at the lip of a great cliff and stared down countless fathoms at the surf pounding the rocks below. He dropped his eyes from Adiv's face, focusing on the plate in front of him, and only then did the minister answer.

"Treachery," he said at last, his voice edged with anger.

Kaden nodded, his eyes still fixed on the table in front of him, suddenly fascinated by the grain of the wood, its intricate twistings and unravelings. It had been possible, of course, that Sanlitun had choked on his food, or fallen from his horse, or simply died in his bed, but somehow Kaden had known—maybe it was Ut's grim transformation, or the alacrity with which Adiv wanted the retinue to depart for Annur—he had known that his father did not die a natural death.

"A priest," Adiv continued, "Intarra's High Priest, in fact. Uinian the Fourth, he styles himself. We departed before his trial, but no doubt his head has been taken from his shoulders by now."

Kaden picked up the pigeon wing before him then set it down again, untouched. He had a vague memory of Intarra's splendid temple, but knew nothing of this priest.

"Why?" he managed after a long pause.

Adiv shrugged. "Who can know the heart of a murderer? Most likely he resented your family's ancient connection to the goddess. The man was an upjumped peasant with delusions of his own importance. He preached openly that Annur should be guided, if not ruled outright, by priests rather than Emperors. Your father agreed to meet with him in secret, leaving the scum an opening for his treachery."

Kaden's head ached with the thought; he wanted to hide his face behind his hands. This was not a time, however, for boyish weakness. It occurred to him, in a bleak flash, that there might never again be a time for either boyishness or weakness.

"How did the empire take his death?"

"Uneasily," Adiv replied. "As long as you remain away from the Unhewn Throne, there will be worry over the succession. Meanwhile, the Urghul take this opportunity to press our northeastern frontier."

That last comment brought Ut into the conversation for the first time. "Nomadic waste," he grated. "We will sweep them aside like chaff."

"Annur is at war with the Urghul, then?" Nin asked, his brow furrowing.

"It comes," Adiv replied. He spread his hands. "It is regrettable, but it comes. Something has stirred them up. Some chieftain or shaman who has begun to unify the tribes. There are tales of his power. He may be a leach."

"Leaches die just like other men," Ut interjected, his jaw set. "We will put the Urghul down as quickly as they rose."

"You speak as though they will be easy to defeat," Tan said. They were the first words Kaden's *umial* had offered all night, and as he turned to face the Aedolian, Kaden was struck by the similarity between the two men, the similarity and the difference. Both were hard, but Ut's was the hardness of worked metal, hammered and annealed to its purpose. Tan, on the other hand, reminded him of stone, of the emotionless, unyielding firmness of the cliffs and the peaks themselves.

"The Army of the North will deal with them quickly enough," Ut replied.

Tan's eyes narrowed, and he looked at the soldier thoughtfully. If he was intimidated by Ut's bulk or manner, he didn't show it. "I have met the Urghul," the monk began. "The children are taught to ride before they can walk, and the most inept among them can hit a man in the heart with an arrow at fifty paces from the back of a galloping horse."

Ut dismissed the objection with a snort and a wave of his hand. "Individually they are strong, but they have no discipline. The Annurian soldier, on the other hand, is trained from the day he enlists to fight as part of a unit. He drills with the other men, eats with them, sleeps with them. If he takes a shit, his brother holds his spear. If he wants a woman, the others guard the door. You have not seen Annurian infantry take the field. They move, thousands of them, tens of thousands, as though controlled by a single hand. The Urghul," he shrugged, "they are dogs. Vicious dogs, bloody dogs, but dogs."

Adiv nodded regretfully. "Sanlitun, bright were the days of his life, never wanted to engage them. In fact, he planned to sign a treaty. There is nothing on the steppe to justify the expense of a major military expedition. The Urghul have no cities, no wealth, no arable land to tax. They are a nomadic, horse-herding rabble."

"And yet, it is said the Emperor planned to move in force across the White River," Scial Nin responded in his quiet voice.

The Aedolian looked at the abbot, a hard, searching look. "You are well informed here, on top of your mountain at the end of the world."

Nin shrugged. "The Urghul are the closest group to us. When they are in their winter pasturage, they come to trade from time to time."

Adiv's voice was smooth as the silk he wore. "As I said, the empire would have preferred to leave these people alone. And yet, for the last ten years, they have persisted in attacking our border forts."

"Forts you built on their side of the river," Tan countered.

Adiv spread his hands in a conciliatory gesture. "More than Annurian forts are at issue. Their people are taken with some strange prophecy, the usual inanity about saviors rising and yokes being thrown off. Every conquered people has such stories and legends—the Annurians themselves did, during the tyranny of the Kreshkan kings. Normally such tales are harmless, but this new chief has galvanized the Urghul, breathed fresh life onto old tired coals, and suddenly they are mad for war.

"Unfortunately, they must be put down. This is rebellion—even if they are not a part of the empire—and rebellion encourages rebellion. Sporadic raids on the frontier a thousand leagues from Annur, we could tolerate. But what if Freeport is reminded of its ancient history and the Vested get it into their heads to look south of the Romsdal Mountains, to Aergad or Erensa? What if Basc decides the Iron Sea can protect it from Annurian navies once again? That would not do, not when we fight an ongoing war with the ever elusive Tsa'vein Karamalan and the jungle tribes of the Waist. No," the councillor said, shaking his head, "resistance must be put down, even if we would prefer otherwise." He turned to Kaden. "It is partly for this reason that we must make such haste to return you to Annur to take your father's place on the Unhewn Throne."

Kaden's mind swam, partly with wine, partly with the staggering scope of the responsibility so recently laid in his lap. Tsa'vein Karamalan? The Vested? Half the things Adiv talked about he knew only from vague childhood stories, and the other half he didn't know at all. It would take him months, *years,* to catch up, to learn the barest fraction of what he needed to govern the empire effectively.

"And now?" he asked. "Who has governed Annur since my father's death? Who is taking care of my sister and of the needs of the empire?"

Adiv nodded as though he had been anticipating the questions. "Your sister needs no taking care of. She is a shrewd young woman, and your father's last testament elevated her to the head of the Ministry of Finance. As for the governance of Annur, it falls to Ran il Tornja," the councillor replied. Kaden shook his head. Another name he had never heard.

"Il Tornja had only just become the provincial commander of the garrison in Raalte when you left. That's why his name is unfamiliar," Adiv said. "I first met him when he was raised to Commander of the Army of the North, and then worked closely with him when your father raised him to *kenarang* and recalled him to Annur."

Kenarang. It was an ancient title, dating all the way back to the golden age, when the Atmani ruled Eridroa from their capital far to the south, before they went mad and destroyed it all. The Annurians had borrowed some of the old Atmani terminology, hoping the hoary names and titles might lend their rule an air of antiquity that it had lacked when Terial hui'Malkeenian first cobbled together the empire out of the shambles of the republic using only his sword and the strength of his will. The *kenarang* was the highest military rank in the empire, overseeing the four field generals. It was strange, Kaden thought, that two men he had never known, Tarik Adiv and this Ran il Tornja, occupied the two highest posts below the Emperor himself.

"How did the provincial commander of Raalte come to be *kenarang* in less than eight years?" he asked. His mind was still aching, trying to make sense of it all, and he stared at his palms as though he might find some answer there.

"Micijah can answer that question better than I," Adiv responded. "I have no more than a bureaucrat's understanding of the military."

At first Kaden thought Ut might not say anything at all. Then he shifted in his seat, the steel plates of his armor grinding against one another in a way that made Kaden wince.

"While soldiers from Nish to Channary played politics, il Tornja won battles, and important ones," he said finally. "The Urghul dogs were getting restless, and it didn't take long for Sanlitun, bright were the days of his life, to realize what he had in his provincial commander. He raised il Tornja to command the Army of the North, and only barely soon enough. A month after the appointment, the rabble came at us in waves, crossing the White River in force for the first time. The cohorts from Breata and Nish were still a thousand miles to the west, whimpering about defending us from an emboldened Freeport." Ut's mouth twisted in a snarl. "If your father had let me have my way, I would have put every captain's head on a spike." For a moment the large soldier was speechless, trapped inside his rage. After years with the monks, Kaden had almost forgotten just how disfiguring anger could be; Ut's emotion was even uglier than he remembered. Finally the Aedolian spoke again, his voice tight and clipped.

"Raalte can't field more than five thousand foot and no horse. Il Tornja's company was tired and undermanned when the rabble came. Most generals would have crumbled, but the *kenarang* isn't most generals. He split his force in four, *four,* and slaughtered them, nailed the head of every tenth Urghul—man or woman—to a post along the west bank of the river." Ut chuckled grimly, as though satisfied with the memory. "The eastern tribes won't trouble us again for some time.

"After the victory, your father named il Tornja *kenarang.* Even Ewart Falk couldn't object. He had the good sense to kill himself, at least."

It was by far the longest speech Kaden had heard from Ut since the Aedolian arrived in Ashk'lan.

"Ran il Tornja is a good man," Adiv appended after a moment. "Your father trusted him and so should you. He is serving as regent presently and will look after your sister and your empire both until you arrive."

Suddenly Kaden felt extremely weary, as though he had raced the Circuit of Ravens a dozen times with Pater on his back. Men he didn't know were running his father's empire—*his* empire now, he reminded himself—making decisions and giving orders he could only barely begin to understand. He had eight years of history and politics to catch up on in what would be a trip of little more than two months, and hundreds, maybe thousands of new names to learn: atreps and ministers, envoys and captains on the frontier. If Ut and Adiv were to be believed, the empire had come to a dire pass and, Intarra help him, it would be his hands on the reins as soon as he sat down on that cold stone throne.

He reached for the empty calm that the Shin had spent eight years trying to teach him, reached for the tranquillity that would allow him to see the world with clear eyes, to judge it truly. It eluded him. He could feel his heart thudding dully in his chest, could trace the thoughts chasing one another like feral cats in his mind, and for the moment, he could control none of it. Scial Nin had said he was close to reaching the *vaniate,* and yet, as he sat there, trying to make sense of the past, trying to comprehend the future, he felt almost like that small lost boy who had left Annur for some unknown monastery in the mountains all those years ago.

40

W hat," Gwenna demanded, squaring up across the table from Annick, one hand on her belt knife, the other thrusting out an accusatory finger, "the fuck?"

The fact that she'd waited until the entire Wing was back in their bunkhouse with the door firmly closed was something of a minor miracle, and Valyn had little hope of controlling the outburst now. In fact, he wasn't sure he wanted to. After weeks of lurking, pondering, guessing, and second-guessing, he just wanted the 'Kent-kissing truth. If Annick really *had* murdered Amie, then she was almost certainly implicated in Lin's death as well. If she hadn't—well, then, maybe she could at least tell him what she was doing over on Hook the day the girl died. He was enraged over Yurl's maneuvering—there was no telling how long they might be confined to the Islands—and yet, there was a strange sort of relief in the fact that everything was coming to a head.

"Slow down," he growled. "Everyone just slow down." He gestured to the chairs around the low table. "Take a seat. Yurl's out to screw with us somehow—we all know him well enough to realize that. There are some hard questions we need to ask ourselves, questions *I* want answered, but we're not going to start ripping each other apart with our bare teeth like dogs."

"Teeth's about all they left us," Laith observed sourly, jerking his head to the empty scabbards on his back.

"Teeth is all I'll need if I find out he's lying," Gwenna said, her mouth twisting into a snarl as though she were preparing to make good on her threat.

"Yurl can wait," Talal interjected. "We need to have our own conversation first."

"Agreed," Valyn said. "We've all got questions, and we're going to ask them one by one. And we're going to get to the bottom of the answers." That last comment was intended for Annick, and he fixed her with a stare. Before the Trial, her eyes had made him nervous, but now, after a long silence, the sniper was the one to look away. She was smaller than he remembered, sitting slumped in her seat, as though without her bow she was just a child once more, angry but lost.

"First," Valyn said, "and most important—"

"Did you kill the fucking girl?" Gwenna cut in, rounding on Annick, leaning in so close that the sniper must have been able to feel her breath on her cheek. "That's all we need to know."

Annick's fingers twitched, but she did not look up. "No," she replied curtly. "I didn't."

If only it were as easy as that, Valyn thought to himself bleakly. *If only you asked honest questions and people gave you honest answers.*

"But you met her," Laith said, his usual good humor evaporated. He leaned forward angrily, hungrily. *Perhaps,* Valyn thought, *Amie was more than just a dockyard whore to him after all.* Laith had patronized a dozen girls over on Hook over the years, but that didn't mean he didn't have some sort of feeling for any of them. "Rianne told us her sister was meeting a soldier at Manker's the morning it collapsed," the flier continued. "The morning she was murdered. You were the only Kettral there."

"I met her," Annick replied with obvious reluctance, "but I didn't kill her."

"Why?" Valyn demanded, reining in his impatience and anger. "Why did you meet her?"

The sniper looked to the window, as though there were some escape beyond the thin pane of glass. Emotions flitted across her face as quickly as clouds before a storm. She was trapped, Valyn realized, and trapped creatures were dangerous, unpredictable. His hand drifted to his belt knife, and out of the corner of his eye, he caught Talal shifting to put the table between himself and the girl. Annick was a terror with her bow, but now she seemed vulnerable, almost naked. Her eyes flicked from one face to the next, as though looking for support. When she found none, her lips tightened.

"Why?" Valyn demanded again.

She opened her mouth to speak, shut it, then returned her gaze to the window. "For the same reason anyone else met her. For the same reason Laith did."

"But . . . ," Gwenna said, shaking her head in confusion. "You're . . . Oh."

The sniper's chin was set in a rigid line. She refused to respond.

Talal spread his hands. "All right," he said matter-of-factly. "She was a whore. You paid her for her services."

Valyn turned to Laith. "You . . . knew Amie. You ever hear anything about this? About her going with women?"

The flier shook his head slowly. "She always seemed happy enough with the cock—"

Annick rounded on him in a flash, drawing her knife and putting it to his throat before the rest of them could so much as twitch. The flier held up his hands slowly. *Idiot,* Valyn cursed himself. Fast was fast, regardless of the weapon.

"All right," he said warily. "All right. Annick—just relax."

"She *wasn't* happy with it," the sniper hissed into Laith's stunned face. "Not with your coin, not with your 'Kent-kissing cock. But she was poor, and so she took both and put a brave face on it." It was more words together than Valyn had ever heard Annick utter. Her face was flushed with anger, the tendons of her neck straining beneath the skin.

"All right," Laith said slowly, nodding. "I'm sorry. I didn't realize—"

"You didn't realize, because you didn't *care.* Whenever you got drunk and needed a hole to stick it in, you'd take the ferry over. It didn't matter who. You fucked her *sister* as many times as you fucked Amie."

The flier took a deep breath, then shook his head slowly, deliberately, careful not to slice his flesh on the knife. "I did care," he said, "but maybe not in the right ways. There are a lot of kinds of caring. I didn't love her, but that doesn't mean I didn't like her. I paid her for sex, but that doesn't mean I wasn't gentle with her. You cared about her more; I can see that. Believe me, though, when I tell you I want to find whoever killed her as badly as you do."

The sniper stared at him for another tense moment, then nodded, slid the belt knife back into her sheath, and sagged back into her seat. Talal let out a long, ragged breath.

" 'Shael on a stick," Gwenna muttered. "The whole fucking lot of you are insane."

For a while they just sat there, Annick staring blankly out the window, Gwenna lost, now that her fury had no direction, Valyn struggling to make sense of the new information, to fit it in with everything else he knew or suspected. For the hundredth time, he wished he could talk things over with Lin, but Lin was dead. The four soldiers in the room were his Wing now. He wasn't sure he could trust them, but he was certain he couldn't trust anyone else.

The leach was the first to pick up the thread of the rapidly unraveling conversation. "I have some experience keeping secrets, and I, for one, believe Annick. She couldn't have predicted Shaleel's arrival or Yurl's accusation. The emotion we just saw is difficult to fake."

"What are you?" Gwenna asked, "a professional masker?" For once, there was more weariness than challenge in her voice.

"I'm a leach, and a leach learns to lie early on. He learns it, or he dies. I may be wrong, but I believe what Annick tells us." He eyed the others, as though welcoming them to disagree. When no one spoke, he pushed ahead, his voice quiet but firm. "But we still need to sort this out, and we'll sort it out quicker if we work together."

The sniper hesitated, then turned back to the room. "Fine," she replied brusquely. "Let's work."

Valyn caught Talal's eye, nodded his thanks, then turned back to Annick.

"Did you see Amie that morning?"

"For about an hour," she responded. "We took our normal room in a boarding house a few doors down from Manker's." The confusion and desperation she had shown moments ago were gone, like strong currents frozen under the winter ice. *She may not have killed Amie,* Valyn thought to himself, *but she's still dangerous.*

"Not the building where Lin and I found her?" he asked carefully.

"No. That's all the way across the harbor."

"Did she say what she was going to do when you left her?" he pressed.

"Make money," Annick replied grimly. "Down at the docks."

"Whoring."

"Yes, whoring. That was the last I saw of her."

"Well," Laith said after a long pause. "We've ruled out one person that *didn't* kill her, but that still leaves a few hundred more who might have. Now that we know it wasn't Annick, we're not even sure it was a soldier."

Valyn ground his teeth silently. There was more to the story—the marks on Amie's wrists, the same impressions on Ha Lin's corpse. His Wing didn't know any of that, but he wasn't sure he was ready to share it.

After Lin's death, he had trusted no one, nursing his suspicions in guarded silence, vowing to work alone until he had ferreted out both Lin's killers and his father's. Working alone, keeping his own council, he was unlikely to be betrayed. *And just as unlikely to learn anything new.* He'd been fighting his private war since Ha Lin's death. Fighting it, and losing it.

The final chapter of Hendran's *Tactics* sprang to mind: *Plan all you like, but remember: war is chaos, and at some point every soldier has to throw the dice.* The old Wing commander must have had something figured out—he had supposedly died in his bed at the age of eighty-four. *Of course, no one was trying to scrub his whole 'Shael-spawned family off the face of the earth.* It didn't matter. If Valyn didn't solve some of the mysteries confronting him, he would live and die a prisoner on the island where he had trained for life as a soldier, sitting impotently by as some shadowy cabal killed first his brother, then his sister, and then, if they still thought he was important enough to bother with, Valyn himself. His Wing would probably die with him—a thought that had not crossed his mind before. Anyone thorough enough to plan the assassination of the Malkeenian line wouldn't flinch at a few extra bodies, especially if those bodies might have known things they shouldn't have. Talal and Annick, Gwenna and Laith, they were all in danger just because Eyrie Command had assigned them to his Wing. They were in mortal danger, and they didn't even know the facts.

"I think Amie's murderer *was* Kettral," Valyn said at last. "And I think the same person captured Lin in the middle of the Trial—captured her, then killed her."

For a while they just stared at him, Laith and Gwenna incredulous, Talal confused, Annick unreadable.

"It was the slarn," Laith said. "You saw her wounds yourself. After you carried her out."

"Something's got all twisted here," Gwenna agreed, "but Ha Lin died an honest death down there, a soldier's death."

"The slarn may have landed some of those blows," Valyn agreed, trying to keep a rein on his anger, "but most of the slashes were made by good steel. Not just that: there were marks on her wrists, impressions from a rope."

"A rope?" Talal asked. "Like she'd been bound?"

Valyn nodded grimly. "With Liran cord—you know that tight pattern. It's different from what you find in any other kind of rope."

"What does it have to do with Amie?" Annick asked, her voice tight.

"Amie was strung up with the same sort of cord. Ha Lin and I found her. We cut her down. It was one of the things that made us think her killer was Kettral."

The conversation faltered as everyone tried to make sense of the new information, staring into the lantern on the table as though the flicker of the inconstant light held some sort of answer.

"Other people have access to Liran cord," Laith pointed out after a while.

"Not that many," Gwenna said. "Your standard dockyard thug isn't going to waste something like that just to tie up a whore." As the word left her lips, she seemed to realize her audience. She glanced over at Annick, and a flush rose to her cheeks. "I'm just saying," she bulled ahead, "that Valyn's right. It's strange."

"About Lin," Talal pressed, shaking his head in dismay. "Are you sure about the marks? We were all so beat up after the Trial—" He gestured to his arms, his face. "I had dozens of cuts, scrapes, gashes."

"Not to mention a slarn bite to the arm," Laith agreed. "It was brutal down there. Lin was good, better than good, but any one of us, with a little bad luck . . ." He grimaced. "It could have happened, Val. It could have been just the slarn."

"It could have," Valyn replied, keeping his voice level, "but it wasn't. I saw plenty of slarn wounds after the Trial, and I saw the slices on Lin's body. They were different. I looked at her wrists just before they burned her, both wrists. Maybe it's just a freak coincidence that Amie had the same marks, but we know one thing for sure: Only cadets went down in the Hole. One of the cadets killed Ha Lin, and I'd wager both my blades against a bucket of piss that whoever killed her killed Amie as well."

"Holy Hull," Laith muttered. "One of our own fucking cadets. Who?"

"I don't know," Valyn replied, "but there's more."

Once he'd told them the truth about Lin's death, it only made sense to plunge into the whole thing, the Aedolian on the boat, the plot against him, everything. They stared, eyes filled with the lamplight, features fading in and out of the shadows as he spun the tale. It was impossible to believe, even as he told it. He half expected them to laugh when it was through. They didn't laugh. Even Laith didn't crack a joke.

"And that's why you wanted me to look at Manker's," Gwenna said, slapping the table with her palm. "You weren't just playing the paranoid prince. Someone actually was trying to kill you."

"Manker's?" Talal asked. Valyn had never seen the leach over on Hook. It was possible he never even heard about the collapse.

"An alehouse," Annick replied.

"A shithole," Laith amended, "but one I was fond of."

"The Aedolian's warning is what made me wonder about Manker's," Valyn agreed. "It was also what made me suspect Annick of trying to drown me during the sinking test, that and the strange knot she tied."

"A double bowline," the sniper said. "I told you before." Her blue eyes bored into him, cold and defiant.

"So let's get this straight," Gwenna said, shaking her head. "Some poor bastard on a ship tells you the Kettral are trying to kill you. Then Manker's collapses. Then it seems like Annick tries to drown you. Then Annick shoots you in the shoulder."

"Annick shows up a lot in this story," Laith added. "I'll bet you were thrilled to have her on your Wing."

"I didn't try to kill him," she said flatly.

"I'm not saying you did," Laith replied, holding up both hands. "But someone's doing a 'Kent-kissing good job of making it look that way."

"Yurl," Valyn growled. "It's got to be Yurl. Let's not forget he's the reason we're boxed up in here without a blade or a bow between us."

"Yurl's a pox-ridden asshole," Laith replied, "but this seems a little over that pretty boy head of his."

Talal frowned. "He *is* the one who told Shaleel about Annick and Amie. Maybe he wants to take us out of play for a while."

"We're out of play, all right," Valyn agreed. "But it still doesn't make sense. What do Ha Lin and Amie have to do with everything else, with the Aedolian, with the whole 'Kent-kissing plot?"

"Manker's," Annick replied flatly. "That's the link."

Valyn blew out a long, frustrated breath. "The place collapsed at the same time Amie was murdered, but that's not much of a link. You said it already—the garret where we found her was on the other side of the bay."

"You've almost died how many times now?" Gwenna asked irritably.

Valyn considered. "Manker's. Drowning. Sniper contest." He shrugged. "Four if you count the Trial itself."

"All right," Talal began, picking up the thread. "There's the connection—

two of the times women were attacked and killed. The first time, Amie. The last, Ha Lin."

"The problem with fifty percent," Laith observed, "is that it's fifty percent."

A shiver run up Valyn's spine. "Seventy-five," he said grimly.

Even after revealing everything else, he had planned to keep Lin's beating a secret. It was foolish, irrational. She was dead and burned; telling the tale wasn't a betrayal and the revelation couldn't injure her pride any further. Still, the attack on the bluffs had shamed her, shamed her to the core, and he felt as though sharing the story would somehow violate a trust they had shared, would strip her secrets bare for everyone to stare at. Besides, it hadn't seemed relevant until they started hashing through the connections.

"Yurl and Balendin attacked Ha Lin during the sniper trial, the one where Annick shot me. They lied to her, tricked her, then held her down, beat her bloody, tried to break her. That's where she got those wounds before the Trial—not in some training exercise the way she claimed. They said it was payback for her willingness to take them on in the arena."

Four pairs of eyes swiveled to him. "Those whoreson shit-licking *bastards*," Gwenna swore, flexing and unflexing her hand as though itching for a sword.

"Where?" Annick asked, her voice calm, hard.

"The West Bluffs."

"Overlooking the sniper test," Talal concluded quietly.

"It's something," Valyn said, shaking his head in frustration. He felt like the truth was *there,* but just out of range, like a familiar tune at the very edge of one's hearing. "I just don't know what."

"But how would beating Lin a mile away get Annick to shoot chisel points?" Laith asked.

"I didn't shoot chisel points," the sniper responded. "Those were my arrows, but the heads had been changed."

Talal started. "Changed?"

"Changed," Annick said. "This is the fourth time I've explained it to Valyn. Those weren't my points. They weren't the arrows I fired."

"Maybe you made a mistake," Laith suggested.

The sniper fixed him with a frosty stare. "I did not make a mistake."

"Well, how in Hull's name did they change midflight?"

"I don't know."

The leach took a deep breath, then let it out slowly. "Maybe I do." He considered the table in front of him, gathering his thoughts. "Holy Hull, I think I understand."

"Some kind of kenning?" Valyn asked, trying to catch up.

Talal nodded grimly. "It's not Yurl. It's Balendin."

"You all want to keep chatting in code?" Gwenna demanded. "Or you going to fill the rest of us in? Try using complete sentences."

"My well is iron," Talal said, raising his eyes, looking from one to the next. "I told Valyn several days ago, but we're a Wing, and you all deserve to know. Iron and steel."

"Iron?" Laith asked, tapping his chin with a finger. "Not very exciting, is it? I thought the wells were all babies' blood or boiled piss or something suitably vile."

Talal shrugged. "If you have to be a leach, iron is a mediocre well to have. On the one hand, there's never that much of it around. On the other, my power almost never runs dry. Especially if you're a soldier, there's usually something." He took a deep breath. "Other leaches have more . . . complicated wells."

"I knew it," Laith said, sitting back in his chair and looking pleased. "Babies' blood."

Talal ignored him.

"Like Arim Hua?" Valyn asked. "The Sun Lord in all those stories?"

Talal nodded. "If the legends are true, Arim Hua's well was sunlight. In the tales, he was fearsome during the day—he could raze cities, destroy armies—but nearly powerless at night. That's how he was killed."

"What does this have to do with the arrows?" Gwenna demanded. "With Manker's?"

"It's not all about cities and armies," Talal replied. "For years, I've puzzled over Balendin's well. I've seen him do some things . . . frightening things. Things I could never manage, not without an ocean of iron surrounding me. Other times—" He shook his head. "—nothing."

"Could he change an arrowhead?" Valyn asked. "An arrow in flight? From a mile away?"

The leach nodded. "He has the skill and, if his well is running deep enough, the power, too."

"The skill is different from the power?" Gwenna asked, her face puzzled.

"Of course. A leach's strength is like physical strength, a gift—or a curse—from Bedisa. Having a deep well is like being large and well-muscled. Imagine Gent."

"I'd rather not," Gwenna shot back.

"The point is, Gent's strength is only useful to a certain degree if he doesn't train, doesn't study how to *use* that strength. A smaller man—or a woman—could take him down through superior skill. There are leaches with enormous power who never understand what to do with that power. They're just as likely to hurt themselves as they are to achieve anything useful."

"And you don't have enormous power," Valyn put in.

Talal nodded. "All the Kettral leaches study and practice, but I've had to work harder than most. I've certainly had to work harder than Balendin."

"And when are we going to get to the part," Laith asked with exaggerated patience, "where you tell us what the 'Shael-spawned asshole's well *is*?"

Talal paused, then spread his hands ruefully. "I didn't realize it, because some people claim they don't even exist. I'm almost certain the Eyrie's never had one before, but I think Balendin is an emotion leach."

The statement sounded dramatic, but Valyn just shook his head in perplexity.

"Meaning what, exactly?" Annick asked.

"He doesn't draw his power from iron or water or sunlight, or anything like that. His well is emotion, human emotion."

For a while the five of them sat in silence, trying to make sense of the idea.

"That sounds," Gwenna said finally, her face screwed into a frown, "like bullshit."

"Unfortunately not," Talal said. "Emotion leaches are horribly powerful, and horribly unpredictable. I've read some of the old codices, the ones cataloging the known leaches in Annurian history and earlier. The trouble is, an emotion leach doesn't simply draw from an existing well, he needs to *create* his well. He has to manipulate people in order to have any power at all."

"But how do Amie and Ha Lin figure into this?" Valyn asked.

"It's not just them," Talal replied. "It's everyone Balendin has ever come in contact with. He leaches his power from emotion, other people's emotion. Specifically, emotion that's directed at *him*."

"And that's why," Gwenna concluded, punctuating her syllables with a finger stabbed repeatedly into the table, "he was such a 'Kent-kissing *bastard* all the time."

Talal nodded. "A leach's well shapes who he is to a frightening degree. Once you get used to the power, you start to *need* that power, and you'll do more and more to get it. When I'm without iron, I feel . . . nervous, naked. I can only imagine how Balendin feels without emotion."

"Why not take a more amiable approach?" Laith asked, pursing his lips. "Make a lot of really good friends? Maybe fall in love a few times—a girl in every port, that sort of thing. . . ."

"A lot easier to evoke hatred than love," Annick said. "Quicker. More reliable."

They turned to look at her, but she averted her face from the lantern and seemed to have no more to say.

"Annick's right," Talal continued after a moment. "You can't evoke love on command the way you can hatred, and a leach without a well is vulnerable."

Valyn shook his head in amazement. "That time in the ring, when he and Yurl beat up on Lin and me—he was taunting her the whole time, making her hate him."

Talal nodded grimly. "He needed her hatred if they were going to win."

The horror of it all socked Valyn in the gut like a fist. "That's why he tortured Amie," he said slowly. "He needed her fear, her terror, to knock down Manker's. That's why they were in that garret—there was a clear line of sight from across the bay."

"Could you even *do* that?" Gwenna demanded. "Take down a big building like that?"

"Think about Amie's fear," the leach replied leadenly. "He set up the whole thing—the dark room, the ropes hanging from the ceiling, the long slices of the knife beneath her skin—to dredge just about every ounce of her terror."

"And the attack on Lin," Laith said, recoiling. "While Yurl was beating her, taunting her, Balendin could have leached off the residual rage, could have used it to change the arrowhead."

"The tampering would explain why the first two shots flew wide," Annick confirmed, lips tight. "Those are not shots I would have missed, but a change in arrowhead requires a change in aim."

"And the knots," Valyn said, his mind spinning. "Balendin was on the ship. He was one of the people who tossed me over, taunting me the whole time."

"It would be enough," Talal replied. "To tangle a basic knot, a quick burst of anger would be enough."

For a while they just looked at each other, aghast and amazed.

"What about the Trial?" Valyn asked finally. "What about Ha Lin?" He could hear his own voice freighted down with anger and pain. "Why did she have to die?"

Talal spread his hands helplessly. "I'll bet she didn't even have anything to do with you. You remember what it was like down there. I was pressed to the limit, and I'm better with my blades than Balendin. I *had* my well, even if it was only shallow. If he was going to survive, he needed power, which meant he needed emotion. He may have been planning it as far back as the attack on the bluffs—capture Ha Lin, goad her, leach off her, and then kill her."

"Holy Hull," Gwenna muttered. "Meshkent, Ananshael, and sweet, holy Hull. And now he's off the Islands."

The realization hit Valyn like a bucket of ice. He'd been so busy looking backward, trying to make sense of the past months, that he'd nearly forgotten what started them down the path in the first place. Balendin was not only free; he was also *away*.

"Who did Shaleel say assigned them their mission?" he demanded, slamming a hand down on the table.

"What does that matter?" Laith asked.

"*Who?*"

"She assigned it herself," Annick replied, voice hard.

Valyn's skin prickled, waves of cold and nausea rolling over him in great, heady swells. "We've got to go," he said. "We've got to gear up, get the bird, and go."

Talal raised a hand to slow him down. "You heard what she said. We're grounded. We can't leave the Islands. We so much as touch a flatbow, we're all traitors."

"That's the point!" Valyn erupted. "That's exactly what Balendin *wanted*. Shaleel is the commander for operations in northeastern Vash."

"So?" Laith said, trying to catch up. "What's in northeastern Vash?"

"Ashk'lan," Valyn growled. "My brother. Kaden. The Emperor."

41

It was all well and good for Adiv to joke about the talks that Kaden could have with Triste "over the pillow," but now that dinner was over, he found himself suddenly and acutely nervous. It didn't help that his head was muddled with wine, and it *certainly* didn't help that once they stepped out of the refectory door, all four men had looked at him expectantly.

"Your pavilion awaits," Adiv said with a generous sweep of his arm, as though Kaden couldn't see the 'Kent-kissed thing perfectly well from where he stood. The fact that the servants had erected it smack-dab in the middle of the main square made him cringe. If it wasn't enough that his special dinner had deprived the monks of their own meal, now they couldn't look out the windows of their own sober cells without staring at the palatial opulence of his overgrown tent. White canvas walls, immaculate as if they had been woven the day before, practically glowed in the light of the setting sun. Pennons fluttering from the central pole overtopped even the roof of the dormitory, Ashk'lan's largest building.

Akiil is never *going to let me live this down,* Kaden thought ruefully.

"A fitting pavilion for the Emperor and his lovely consort," Adiv said, the shadow of that mocking grin lurking around his lips.

Kaden knew how this was supposed to work, of course. Despite his eight years away from the Dawn Palace, he still remembered his father's concubines, a dozen or so quiet, graceful women who slipped through the marble halls in silent satin shoes, eyes demure and downcast. When still very young, he had asked his mother about those women. She had put down her carefully buttered bread and looked at him for a while, lips pursed tight.

"They are concubines," she said finally.

"What's concubines?" he had asked, perplexed.

"Women who . . . comfort a man when his wife cannot."

Kaden had rolled that idea around in his head for a while. It didn't sound like a bad thing, although something in his mother's bearing had him on edge.

"Do *you* have concubines," he had asked, "to comfort you when father is away?"

She had laughed then, a short bitter laugh. "It is a man's prerogative."

Kaden considered that. "Will *I* have concubines someday?" he asked.

His mother never took her eyes from him. "Yes. I suppose you will, Kaden."

Well, he thought, glancing over at Triste, *evidently this is the day.* Whatever education his mother had neglected, Akiil had more than made up for, regaling Kaden almost nightly with tales of the delicious, foul-mouthed whores from the Perfumed Quarter. Triste, however, was no whore, and Akiil's stories had neglected the finer points of romantic etiquette.

The abbot, as though sensing Kaden's discomfort, said softly, "You are welcome, of course, to spend your last night in your own cell, putting your things in order."

Adiv laughed good-naturedly. "What things? A few robes? He would shame the servants not to sleep in the pavilion they have labored to set up." He turned to Kaden with a more deferential tone. "Your Radiance, you are the Emperor. Today or tomorrow, you must accept the trappings as well as the title."

Kaden looked from the two monks wrapped in their coarse robes to the councillor who would be his right hand in the months to come. He wished that Nin could accompany him to the capital—despite the old monk's lack of "practical" knowledge or political training, Kaden would have welcomed his steady, familiar wisdom—but the wish was a childish one, and he put it out of his mind. There was nothing to do but to take a deep breath and nod. Adiv and Ut evidently understood this as a dismissal, bowing low, fingers to their foreheads.

"Until the morning then, Your Radiance," Adiv said. "Micijah will keep guard here, in the square."

Kaden shook his head dubiously. "I've lived here for eight years without protection."

Adiv's tone stiffened. "You are the Emperor now, Your Radiance, and the Aedolian Guard does not take chances with the Emperor." Kaden found himself wondering if the man actually had eyes underneath the blindfold, or if they had been plucked out. The thought of the raw red sockets seeping blood beneath the cloth made him shiver.

Kaden acquiesced with a nod. There *was* the matter of Pyrre and Jakin Lakatur. Tan had insisted that the two were not merchants, that they had come for some sinister purpose. Now that they knew who Kaden was and where he was sleeping, perhaps it wouldn't be a bad idea to have someone watching the pavilion after all. He realized, with a sickening lurch, that his days as an anonymous acolyte were over. The sooner he accepted the burdens of his new office, the easier it would be for everyone.

And then, of course, there was the *ak'hanath*. The surprise he had felt at the arrival of the Annurians, the grief at the news of his father's death, the glasses of wine at dinner had pushed the creature to the back of his mind. It was hard to worry about a monster he'd never seen, a thing that, by Tan's own admission, should have been wiped out thousands of years earlier. And yet, as the cold night wind picked at his skin, he felt a shiver of dread. There was *something* out there, something capable of killing a man. It hadn't attacked inside the walls of the monastery, but that didn't mean it couldn't. Perhaps he *would* sleep better with the Aedolian outside.

As Adiv bowed his way out of the square, the abbot approached. "We will speak in the morning, Kaden. Until then, rest, and try to clear your mind."

Tan looked at Triste swaying slightly on her feet, then turned away without a word.

"Until the morning," the abbot repeated, not unkindly, and the two monks turned down the gravel path to the dormitory.

Eager to put off entering his new lodgings, Kaden stared out over the shapes of the mountains, dark and slumbering in the moonlight. He could hear the rushing of the White River in the canyon below, the distant crack and rumble of rocks, loosened from the icy grip of winter, crumbling from the cliffs to smash themselves to pieces on the ground below. The Bone Mountains were a hard place, and for the past eight years he had thought longingly of Annur, wishing something would happen to end his exile and bring him home. The low, drafty buildings of the monastery were just a world he had to endure—and endure it he had, although not without a constant spark of resentment. Now that the time had come to leave, however, he found that he had developed more of a connection to Ashk'lan than he could have known. When he thought about the crowded, vibrant chaos of Annur, the squares filled with vendors, the streets packed with thousands of people, he realized that he would miss the cold, clear nights, the sight of the sun rising over Lion's Head to the east. He laughed softly to himself. He might even miss running the Circuit of Ravens, although he wasn't about to bet on that.

He turned around to face the central square of the monastery. A few monks went about their business with heads bowed, silent as shadows in their dark robes. They paid no more mind to the enormous tent that had abruptly sprouted in their midst than they might to a stone wren scratching at the gravel. He had come to admire these men, Kaden realized, had come to appreciate their calm and unflappable resolve.

A flickering light in the deepening darkness drew his eye. Ut was walking a circuit around the pavilion, one hand resting on the pommel of his sword, the other holding a torch aloft. A sudden gust of wind blew the light to a blaze, illuminating the southern buildings of the quad, and Kaden realized with a start that Pyrre Lakatur stood in the window of the guest quarters, looking down at him. The woman's eyes held neither the jocularity of her first arrival nor the deference that had marked her behavior since the Aedolian almost took off her head. They were the eyes of a cat, still and focused, as it crouches by the pond. Yes, perhaps it was good after all that Ut would be standing guard. Kaden wondered if the Aedolian ever slept, then decided that was for him to figure out. He glanced over at Triste shivering silently beside him. He had his own problems to attend to.

42

As he pushed back the canvas flap that served as a door to the tent, the delicate scent of incense wafted over him. The servants had been as busy with the interior of the pavilion as they had with the outside, and now it glowed like something out of his childhood memories. Dozens of paper lanterns—red, gold, green—cast playful shadows onto the floor. Delicate tapestries from Mo'ir hung from the walls while intricate woven rugs covered the packed earth.

His eyes barely flickered over them, fixing instead on the wide bed that dominated the space, a bed decked in silk and strewn with plump pillows. He cast about for a chair or bench, but the servants who had carted the entire kit up the mountain evidently considered lamplight more important than seating. There was nowhere to go, nothing to turn to except that enormous bed. Triste froze just inside the door, but he did his best to appear casual, approaching the mattress, running his hands over the cashmere blankets gingerly.

"Well," he said, "at least it's big. . . ."

Triste did not respond.

Kaden turned, casting about for one of Heng's jokes to ease the tension, but all thought of joking vanished when his eyes fell on her.

She stood trembling just inside the door, her dress pooled on the carpet at her feet. She wore nothing beneath. Involuntarily, almost instinctively, Kaden drank in the sight of her: slender legs, satin skin, the full curve of her breasts. In Annur, outside the temple of Ciena, stood a marble statue of the goddess herself, the incarnation of physical perfection, the apogee of human pleasure. He had overheard men joking about that statue, about what they'd like to do with the goddess if they could get her alone, and on one outing, Kaden and Valyn had spent some time furtively staring at the idol, intrigued by a beauty they could only just apprehend. Compared to Triste, however, the marmoreal curves and elegant proportions seemed awkward, almost misshapen.

He groped for the Shin exercises he had spent so many years mastering, exercises that would cool the heat and bring reason to the chaos cluttering his mind. It was no good. Triste was slender, fragile even, but that fragility drew him with more force than knotted cord, and for the space of a few heartbeats, he was frightened of himself, frightened of what he might do to her. He tried to avert his eyes, but he could no more look away than he could stop his own heart.

Suddenly, with a small cry in the back of her throat, Triste threw herself at him, propelled, he realized, by wine and fear rather than lust. She crashed awkwardly into his chest, knocking him backward, and they collapsed on the bed in a tangle of limbs. Kaden tried to pull away, but she clung to him, desperately ripping at his robe.

"Wait," he pleaded, trying to calm the girl without drawing attention from beyond the insubstantial canvas walls of the pavilion. "Stop!"

The words only spurred her frenzy. Each year, Kaden helped to tie goats for shearing and slaughter—and each year, he found himself shocked by the strength in the body of an animal driven to panic. That same panic had seized Triste, and for several heartbeats she overpowered him, driving him down and backward despite his greater height and weight. Her hands around his wrists might have been manacles, for all his ability to break her grip. *She's stronger than I am,* he thought, amazed even in the midst of the contest. Then something seemed to snap in the girl. She fought still, but the impossible power had gone, and Kaden was able to subdue her at last. When he finally managed to extricate himself, he looked down to see her violet eyes welling with tears.

"We must," she sobbed. "We must. We *must!*"

"Must what?" Kaden asked, although he had a pretty good idea already. "We don't have to do anything," he added quickly.

Triste shook her head so violently, he thought she might hurt herself. "They *told* me," she cried. "They told me we must."

Kaden stood quickly, straightening his robe about him and turning to examine one of the priceless tapestries hanging from the wall. It depicted a battle, he realized gradually, some sort of conflict between gorgeous men and women, half naked but wielding long spears against ranks of foes in drab, gray armor. He bent all his energy to the study of the weave, the alternation of color and pattern, using the focus to still his pulse, slow his breath, relax . . . everything, and after a long, awkward minute he was able to look back at Triste. She was crying softly.

"They may have said we must," he began, trying to put more resolve into his voice than he felt, "but they also told me that I'm the Emperor, and as your Emperor, I command you to put on some clothes."

It was a ridiculous commencement of his imperial prerogatives, but he had to start somewhere. He risked a glance over his shoulder and saw that she had ignored him, wrapping her naked body tightly into a ball instead. *So much for the irresistible heft of the Emperor's decree,* he thought to himself.

"He said that you would want to," she moaned, hugging her knees to her chest in a way that covered her breasts but accentuated . . . other things. Kaden quickly looked away again. "He said if you didn't want to, that it was my fault. Now they'll kill her," she choked. "They'll turn her out of the temple and she'll die."

In spite of himself, Kaden turned back to her, curious and disturbed.

"They'll kill who?" he asked carefully. "Who is threatening to kill whom?" As he spoke, he picked up one of the blankets folded at the foot of the bed and hastily draped it over her shivering form. Huddled under the fabric, cheeks streaked with tears, she suddenly looked like the frightened girl that she was. "You can tell me," he added gently.

Triste shook her head miserably, but met his eyes for the first time, her face filled with blank resignation. "My mother," she responded when the sobs had subsided enough to allow her to speak. "Tarik said if I didn't lie with you, he would see that my mother was turned out of the temple and forced to earn her living as a common whore."

"What temple?" Kaden asked, anger slowly replacing the confusion inside him. "Who is your mother?" He remembered Adiv's mocking smile at dinner, the smugness with which he had presented Triste as Kaden's "gift." Sanlitun may have promoted the man to the Mizran rank, but Kaden didn't intend for him to stay there long if this was how he treated innocent girls.

"Louette," Triste responded. The shuddering fear had gone out of her, replaced by a deep, unplumbed grief. "That's my mother's name. She's a *leina.*"

Kaden stared. The *leina* were the high priestesses of Ciena, women trained since childhood in the arts of pleasure, *all* the arts of pleasure.

"Stuck-up, too-good whores," Akiil called them, but he was only half right. The *leina did* trade their skills for money, but they had no more in common with the whores of Akiil's Perfumed Quarter than a two-penny fishmonger did with the Vested merchants of Freeport.

The *leina* were a religious order. Like the Shin, they spent their time in study, exercise, and prayer, but unlike the monks, they would have scoffed at the never-ending rigor of the *vaniate*. Ciena's priestesses were devotees of pleasure. They spent their days and nights studying dancing, fine wines . . . and other, more alluring arts. The richest men spent princely sums to share the company of a *leina,* even for a single night, such princely sums, in fact, that Ciena's temple in Annur boasted nearly as much gold, marble, and silk as the Dawn Palace itself.

Regardless of the wealth lavished upon them, however, the women owed their devotion to the goddess they served rather than to the men who paid so richly for their attentions. There were rules governing the behavior of the *leina,* observances to be paid, holidays to be observed, tradition to be respected. A man could not simply arrive at the temple, toss a jingling sack of Annurian suns on the counter, and demand to be served. It didn't work like that, at least not in the stories Kaden had heard. Even Emperors owed respect to the handmaids of a goddess.

"Adiv can't do that," he said. "He might be the Mizran Councillor, but he's not in charge of Ciena's temple."

"He can," Triste insisted, nodding vigorously. "You don't know him. He *can*." She sat up on the bed, hugging the blanket tightly to her chest.

"Well, I'll see that he doesn't," Kaden replied firmly. "It's as simple as that. I'll just see that Louette, that your mother isn't harmed." The words sounded confident as they left his lips, and he dearly hoped they were true.

For the first time, Triste regarded him with what might have been hope. It was buried deep beneath fear, suspicion, and doubt, but it was there. Kaden's heart warmed at the sight.

"How did Adiv . . . find you?" he asked slowly.

A cloud passed over Triste's face, but she answered readily enough. "I grew up in the temple. My whole life, I lived there." With a sweep of her fingers she brushed back her black hair, revealing the necklace tattoo. At least, it *looked* like a tattoo, but Kaden had never seen work so delicate.

"What is it?" he asked.

"Goddessborn," she replied.

Kaden shook his head at the unfamiliar word.

Triste continued, "My mother always says, 'Men want the bliss without the burden.' The ones who come to the temple are always rich, and they pay well, but they have names and estates. They have their own *proper* children to think of."

Kaden thought he heard a note of bitterness there, but she continued without dropping her eyes.

"The *leina* are careful—my mother taught me all the herbs and potions—" She colored, then rushed ahead. "Even though I haven't needed them, she taught them to me, just to be sure. Anyway, even if you're careful, sometimes things happen, sometimes a man gets one of the *leina* with child. Then the woman has a choice—she can kill the baby or mark it as goddessborn." She touched the tattoo at the base of her neck again, as though assuring herself it was still there.

Kaden had some idea where this was going; it made perfect sense when you thought about it.

"The goddessborn belong to Ciena. We can never own anything, never inherit anything, never lay claim to our fathers' names. Most of us don't even know who our fathers *are*."

She shrugged, a frustrated, girlish gesture that seemed somehow incongruous after her matter-of-fact description of the political realities underlying her station.

"So," Kaden pressed gently, "Adiv came to the temple looking for a—" He was about to say "gift" but changed his mind at the last moment. "—for a *leina,* and you were the one he chose."

"No. Well, yes." Triste bit her lip. "But I'm not a *leina*. My mother never wanted me to enter the service of the goddess."

"But you were raised in the temple," Kaden replied, confused.

"She raised me in the temple because there was nowhere else, but she always said that if I studied hard and made myself into a proper lady—" She paused and looked down at the blanket wrapped around her, as though remembering her nakedness for the first time. "If I made myself into a proper lady," she persisted, her voice cracking just slightly, "my father might take me in. Not as his daughter," she rushed on, as though frightened Kaden might reprimand her for the thought. "He wouldn't have to acknowledge me ever, but as one of the ladies of his court, maybe a handmaid or something."

It seemed an unlikely proposition to Kaden. Bastards were dangerous business, even if they were girls, even if they were tattooed girls. A young woman as beautiful as Triste would have dozens of suitors, and if one of them married her and then realized she was the daughter to some sort of potentate . . .

"I studied the low arts at the temple," she continued, oblivious of his thoughts, "but my mother refused to have me inducted into the high mysteries."

"The high mysteries?" Kaden asked, intrigued.

Triste colored once more. "The arts of bodily pleasure," she responded, eyes downcast. "All girls in the temple learn the low arts—dancing, singing, all of that—but you can't be a *leina* without years studying the high mysteries. My mother says you can sing yourself hoarse—that's not what the men pay for."

"So you haven't done . . . this . . . before?" Kaden asked, cursing himself silently for his clumsiness.

Triste shook her head. "No. My mother never wanted . . ." She trailed off, staring at her hands as though she had never seen them before. "No."

A rustling at the back of the tent interrupted her before she could say more. Eyes wide, she put her finger to her lips. Kaden nodded. Perhaps it was only wind, but the memory of Pyrre Lakatur and the *ak'hanath* remained fresh in his mind. Ut was an Aedolian, but he was only one man—he couldn't watch all the walls of the pavilion at once.

Kaden gestured toward Triste's fallen dress urgently—her nakedness seemed to make both of them more vulnerable—and as she struggled to pull it on, he cast about for something that could serve as a weapon. He still carried the short knife on the belt of his robe, but that seemed a feeble defense. The supporting poles holding up the pavilion might stave off an intruder, but they were inextricable from the canvas. A heavy gilded candlestick caught his eye—twice as thick as his thumb and two feet long. The rustling came again, punctuated by a short ripping. Kaden hastily snuffed the wick, yanked the taper out of its sconce, and hefted the makeshift weapon tentatively. It wasn't a sword, but a solid blow would knock a man unconscious. He forced himself to move toward the sound.

43

A glint of steel poked through the canvas, then the body of a belt knife, flashing in the lamplight as it sawed back and forth slowly, carving down through the heavy fabric. Kaden's mind darted immediately to the long blades he had discovered inside Pyrre's pack, and he tightened his hold on the candlestick, trying to get a good grip with his sweaty palms. Whoever it was would have to come through headfirst, and as soon as they were partway inside the tent, he could smash the candlestick down on the nape of their neck. He moved cautiously to the side of the growing rent and raised his weapon.

A small shaved head poked inside, pulled back a moment, then reappeared, followed immediately by a wriggling body.

Kaden started to swing, then checked himself.

"Kaden," the intruder whispered urgently. "Kaden, you've got to listen!"

"Pater," he exhaled heavily. "What are you doing here?" The small boy looked over at Triste, and for a moment it seemed all thought had gone out of his head, but when he turned back to Kaden his urgency returned in a rush.

"There's men, Kaden, with *armor.*"

Kaden let out a long breath and Triste slowly relaxed. He noticed she had picked up the other candlestick, but lowered it now, unsure what to make of their diminutive intruder. "Those are probably just a few of the Aedolian Guards. They're here to protect me, Pater."

"*No!*" Pater insisted. "They're in the mountains. All *over* the mountains. I was on the Talon. Heng caught me eating a carrot when I should have been fasting, but we only had to fast because you took over the refectory—" He glared at Kaden accusingly, then remembered his purpose.

"But I was on the Talon and I heard them and I knew that you're

Emperor now and I thought like you thought, that they were soldiers, but then I listened to them and they *are* soldiers, but I listened to what they were saying, listened to it and remembered it exactly, just like those boring exercises we always have to do. One of them said, 'Make sure the perimeter is secure before you move.' Then another one said, 'I don't see why we don't just kill the boy and have done with it.' And I got scared then, because I didn't know who *the boy* was, but I kept listening, and the first one called the second one an idiot, he said, 'If those were our only orders, we could have taken off his head in the square.' "

Kaden felt the hairs on the back of his neck begin to prickle. He glanced over at Triste. Her pale face had gone white in the candlelight and she shook her head in confusion, hugging her arms around her chest. "What did they say next?" Kaden asked, his voice a hoarse whisper.

"He said, the first one did, that if they didn't secure the perimeter before the attack, some of the monks would get away. 'Once you've nailed down the perimeter, make sure they're all dead, but do *not* begin until they've finished with the boy.' " Kaden could feel his heart thundering in his chest and he took a moment to slow his pulse. He had to *think*. Triste was staring at Pater and tugging her gossamer dress tighter about her.

"He said they brought that pavilion all the way up the mountain just so they'd know right where *he* was and they didn't want *him* slipping away when things got messy," Pater tumbled on, still breathless from his run down from the Talon and the urgency of his message. "That's when I figured out that *he* was *you*! I almost fell off the Talon, I was so scared. I climbed down and I ran all the way here, but there's a huge man with a sword in front of the door, and so I had to sneak in the back. You have to *leave,* Kaden!" he finished with a rush. "You have to leave right *now*!"

"We have to tell Ut," Kaden responded, heading for the door.

Pater dived for him, grasping him around the legs while shaking his head furiously. "No, Kaden," he begged. "He's on their side! They said his name, the men in the mountains, and I made sure to remember it. 'Ut wants this. . . .' 'Report to Ut. . . .' He's on *their* side," Pater repeated. "That's why I had to sneak in the back of the tent."

Kaden tried to gather his wits. The sudden arrival of the imperial delegation combined with the shock of his father's death had left him disconcerted and raw, but he had done his best to tamp down his emotions, to smother them and play the young Emperor. Micijah Ut, even changed as

he was, had been one familiar spar in a baffling flood, something to cling
to as Kaden made his way back toward the capital. And now, it seemed,
the man had been sent to kill him. The discipline he spent years cultivat-
ing threatened to evaporate as quickly as a late spring snow, and with
desperation he reached for the novice exercises he had mastered in his
first years among the Shin.

Each breath is a wave, he told himself, visualizing the long, lapping
breakers of the bay outside Annur as he inhaled. *The fear is sand.* As the
breath escaped, he let the sand and the fear slip from his mind, sliding
down the long shingle into the bottomless belly of the sea. Slowly, he
brought his breathing and then his pulse under control.

"All right," he began finally. "All right. We have to warn the other
monks. We'll tell the abbot first—"

Triste cut him off. "We have to get out of this tent. Listen to him—
they're coming *here* first!" Fear filled her voice, but beneath the fear there
was something else, something surprisingly hard. *Resolve,* Kaden realized.
Readiness. Triste had shown neither quality all night, not at dinner, nor
when he brought her back to the pavilion. The realization gave him pause,
but Pater was nodding vigorously in agreement, tugging at Kaden's robe,
leading him to the hole he had sliced in the back of the canvas. The boy
started for the small tear, but Kaden held him back.

"Let me go first. Once I know it's safe, I'll motion you through."

The hole Pater had torn in the canvas wasn't quite big enough for
Kaden's larger shoulders. He set the candlestick down and tugged gingerly at the fabric. It tore easily, but the harsh ripping sound made him
wince. Pater had said Ut was out front—how much could he hear?

Kaden waited, straining his ears for the crunch of boots on gravel or
the dull clank of armor. He could hear nothing but the sound of blood in
his ears. Slowly, he eased his head through the rip.

The courtyard was empty and the night calm, the moon climbing her
quiet path through the stars overhead, casting shadows beneath the junipers. Kaden listened again and then, with a gulp, levered himself out
through the gap. For a horrible moment the canvas tightened around his
torso and he thought he was stuck, but a strong tug freed him and he
stood up in the cool night air, trembling.

Shame filled him. Pater had run all the way back here without a thought
for his own safety and all he, Kaden i'Sanlitun hui'Malkeenian, twenty-

fourth of his line and Emperor of Annur, could do was peer uselessly into the night. Ruthlessly, methodically, he identified his fear, compartmentalized it, and put it to the side. *Fear is sand,* he reminded himself. *Nothing more.* Steadied slightly, he put his head back in through the flap.

Triste and Pater crouched just inside the canvas, staring at him wide-eyed. Kaden nodded urgently and Triste grabbed the boy by the back of his robe, thrusting him at the opening with surprising strength. Pater squirmed through in a flash and crouched beside him in the dark. Kaden put his hand through to motion the girl to follow, then froze. Across from the pavilion, pressed close to the wall of the dormitory, something moved in the shadow.

He shoved his hand back through the canvas, frantically trying to keep Triste inside. His fingers met with the smooth skin of her chest, and she paused. He could feel her heart pounding beneath her rib cage, a frenzied counterpoint to his own, but she kept still as Kaden peered into the darkness.

A thin strip of shadow hemmed the back of the pavilion, and he tried to will himself into it more deeply. Pater crouched motionless at his side. They could run. He and Pater had run these paths every day for years—no armored soldier would be able to keep pace with them. But running would mean leaving Triste, and in a flash, he understood the subtlety of the plot. Triste was the bait and the distraction all rolled into one. She was the excuse to separate Kaden from the rest of the monks, the trump card that would ensure he left the dormitory, and the guarantee that when the men came to kill him, he would be distracted.

She could even be part of the plot, Kaden realized after a moment. He hastily recalled the *saama'an* of her face as she told her story. There was terror there, and regret, and even anger, but no halting or deception. Unless he had badly miscalculated, she was as much a victim of Adiv's schemes as he was, and he didn't want to contemplate what would become of her if they left her behind.

As he racked his brain for another option, the figure in the shadows across from him took form. Kaden's body tightened, then sagged in relief as he recognized Tan's solid shape. His *umial* stepped into the moonlight, beckoned to them urgently, then stepped back. Kaden closed his hand around the front of Triste's dress and hauled her through. As soon as she gained her feet, they raced across the moonlit space, hunched over as though cringing from the blow of some great hammer. They reached the shadow of the dormitory just as a cry went up from inside the stone building—a befuddled yell twisted abruptly into a scream of terror, then silence.

Kaden looked back for Pater, but the boy, already tired from his sprint from the Talon and slowed by his shorter legs, hadn't even made it halfway across the square. At the bloody shout from above, he had dropped to the ground, a dark huddled mound in the vast expanse of silvery moonlight. Kaden silently cursed himself for not taking the boy in his other hand when he ran.

Immediately, other cries inside the dormitory filled the terrible silence left by the first, followed shortly by the sounds of flight and struggle. The rough voices of soldiers called out to one another, cursing their victims, and then the men poured into the square, making for the front of the tent, the steel of their drawn swords flickering with cold menace.

As the men disappeared, Pater stared longingly at the gulf separating him from the others, then back at the shadow of the tent. A deep hole opened in Kaden's stomach.

"No," he hissed, "over here!" but Pater was already scurrying back to the dubious safety of the pavilion. Kaden could hear Ut curse inside the tent, then begin barking orders. "Pater!" he called again, letting go of Triste for the first time in order to run back for the boy. Tan stopped him with an iron grasp on his wrist just as Ut's broadsword swept a long gash in the canvas, and the man stepped through.

The Aedolian peered right then left. Kaden prayed he might not see the small boy huddled almost at his feet. *It works for fawns,* he told himself, years of useless accumulated knowledge bubbling to the top of his mind. *The fawn has no scent. So long as it remains motionless, the crag cat passes by.* He had almost managed to convince himself when the Aedolian glanced down, snorted, then hoisted his squirming quarry into the air with one arm, the action terribly effortless. Pater stopped wriggling when Ut brought the point of his sword to the boy's belly.

"Where is the Emperor?" he ground out.

Pater shook his head defiantly.

"I'm here to protect him, you fool," the man insisted, lowering without softening his voice.

"No, you're *not!*" Pater insisted. "You want to hurt him. I *heard!*"

Kaden tried to wrest his arm free of Tan's viselike grip, to step into the moonlight. Whatever these men wanted with him, whoever they were, it had nothing to do with Pater. Before he could move, however, the Aedolian slid his sword smoothly into the boy's body, driving it all the way through until it emerged, slick and dripping, just below his shoulder blades. Kaden stared, transfixed.

"Run, Kaden," Pater tried to yell, but his voice was terribly weak, the strangled wheeze of a dying creature. No sooner were the words out than he slumped forward against the blade.

For what felt like an eternity, Kaden couldn't move. His mind played and replayed the horror of the scene until he thought the vision might have scoured all other thought from his mind.

Casually, almost dismissively, Ut let his sword drop, sliding the limp body onto the ground. The tiny heap of bloodied rags was no larger than a dog. Was it possible Pater had been so slight, so insubstantial? *It was his voice that made him seem bigger,* Kaden realized. *He was always talking.*

The thought snapped something inside him, some bundle of caution, fear, and restraint, and with a roar he leapt into the square. He could hear Tan trying to follow him, but he had always been faster than his *umial,* and half a step was all the lead he needed.

Ut turned toward the sound, and Kaden could see a cold, cruel smile spread across the Aedolian's face.

"We would have stabbed the kid anyway," he said, slinging the blood off his sword in a slow arc. "We're not leaving anyone alive."

I don't need to kill him, Kaden thought. *I just need to distract him, and Tan will finish the job.* A small part of his mind told him that the idea was incoherent. He had no idea if the older monk was following him, no idea if he had his *naczal,* no idea if he even knew how to fight.

Kaden was beyond caring. He felt only a hint of dismay when two soldiers burst through the tear in the canvas while a half dozen more appeared around the side of the pavilion. When they saw the figure rushing at them across the flagstones of the courtyard, they hesitated, then spread out, flanking their commander. Whichever one he attacked, the others would cut him down from the side. Even now, the closest was readying his blade as Kaden clumsily raised his candlestick in defense.

Then, with the moist sound of metal tearing through flesh, the man collapsed, a crossbow quarrel jutting from his neck.

Kaden didn't have time to gape before two more fell, blood gurgling at their throats. The others paused, then took a tentative step back. With a curse, Ut turned his attention from Kaden to the darkness surrounding them, searching for their invisible assailant. They both stared as Pyrre Lakatur strode into the square.

Kaden recognized the knives first, the same knives he had seen in the merchant's pack three nights before, the long, oiled killing knives. Lakatur held one in either hand, loosely, as though she could scarcely be bothered to keep her grip on them. Gone was the brash merchant's swagger, the easy grin and expansive manner. Gone, too, were the cringing and doubt she had shown when Ut put the sword to her neck the day before. If Pyrre was concerned about the Aedolian's huge broadblade, or the soldiers massed before her, or the whistling crossbow bolts that struck like hail all around, she didn't show it. She walked into the killing with all the concern of an atrep entering her own ballroom, nodding to the baffled soldiers as though they were young gallants, sweaty-palmed and twitchy at the thought of their first dance.

"Ananshael will be pleased," she said, surveying the carnage with a sober eye.

Tan's words of caution shoved into Kaden's mind: *Somewhere this woman has learned to suppress the most basic imperatives of the flesh.* Overhead the moon still shone, but the night seemed to have grown darker, heavier.

Ut gestured curtly, and two of the Aedolians took a step forward, tentative now. The first collapsed with a bolt through the eye. Seeing his companion fall, the second roared, raised his sword to strike, and charged. Though the man stood half a head taller than her and wore steel to her leather, Pyrre Lakatur didn't break stride. She stepped easily into the space beneath his raised arms, driving, as she moved, one of her knives up into the soldier's armpit. As her foe crumpled with a sickly, rattling cough, Pyrre rotated past him, eyes locked on Ut. The other soldiers rushing to intercept her might as well have been wheat for all the attention she paid them.

In the explosion of activity, Tan had caught up with Kaden, seizing him by the forearm.

"We go *now*," he barked, "if I have to knock you over the head and carry you." Adrift in his own shock and confusion, Kaden allowed himself to be led, looking back over his shoulder at Pyrre as he went.

The other soldiers were down, either fallen beneath the merchant's blades or the quarrels of their invisible assailant. With a growl, Ut swung his sword in that wide terrible arc that had almost taken off Pyrre's head the day before. Kaden stared, unable to tear his eyes from the inevitable. This strange woman had defended him, saved him, and now she was going to die. The sword sliced through the air and Pyrre simply . . . wasn't there. Even as Ut tensed for the blow, the merchant rolled beneath the attack while the Aedolian's blade swung harmlessly into the night. Then it was Ut's turn to look shocked, and a moment was all Pyrre gave him.

The merchant's knives flashed, first high, then low, probing, pressing—so fast, it seemed she must have five or six spinning between her fingers rather than the two Kaden had seen when she walked so calmly into the slaughter. Ut was quicker than his men, however, and wearing heavier armor.

As the two circled each other in the center of the yard, a man's voice hissed from the shadows. Kaden turned to see Jakin, a crossbow in his right hand, Triste's arm clasped roughly in his left. He was dressed in his customary tunic and breeches, as though he never went to bed, as though he had expected the sudden outburst of violence.

"Worry about yourselves," he snapped. "Pyrre Lakatur has lived long in the shadow of Ananshael. She will meet us later, if the god wills."

Kaden felt Tan stiffen at his side. He looked over at the monk, surprised to see his mouth twisting with some sort of emotion. Tan started to speak, but more soldiers were already flooding into the square, slowed for the moment by the sight of their commander locked in a duel.

"I need to find Akiil," Kaden insisted. "He's in the dormitory."

"The dormitory is crawling with Aedolians," the man shot back.

"Then kill them!" he replied, gesturing to Jakin's crossbow.

"This is useless indoors," he spat. "Your friend's dead, or he will be dead. I've been paid well not to let you join him."

Kaden hesitated, but Tan took him by the arm with that implacable grip.

"Now!" he said. With a wordless shout of rage, Kaden turned, and the four of them rushed past the stone dormitory, past the screaming and bellowed commands, past the flames licking from the meditation hall, and into the night.

They raced up the trail to the Circuit of Ravens, Tan keeping pace despite his bulk, Triste and Jakin stumbling every so often on the unfamiliar stones. Kaden tried to shut out the sounds echoing at his back: harsh orders barked in the darkness, the clash of steel on steel, screaming. The scene of Pater's death kept running through his mind, and he realized sickly that the boy would not be the only one murdered that night. Kaden thought back to his words—*I heard them, Kaden, "Make sure they're all dead. . . ."* Jakin had insisted that the monks in the dormitory were already dead, but Akiil was no ordinary monk. He was fast and smart. He'd learned to stay alive in the alleys of Annur before he was ever carted off to Ashk'lan. He would have been sleeping in the dormitory with the rest of the monks, but surely he'd heard something. If he could win free of the immediate carnage, he could lose himself in the rocks for days. Had he escaped? Or had Kaden already heard his dying scream? Nausea filled him.

Near the top of the ridgeline, just below the notch that would lead over the saddle and into the shallow defile beyond, Jakin pulled up sharply. Kaden started to ask what was wrong, but the man glared him into silence, then inched his head up over the rise. After only a moment, he pulled back with a low curse.

"What is it?" Kaden whispered, his throat tight.

"Men."

"With you?"

"There *is* no one with us," he hissed. "When they sent us to protect you from assassins, they forgot to mention that the assassins were an entire regiment of the Emperor's own 'Kent-kissed Aedolian Guard."

"What about that?" Triste asked, gesturing to the crossbow.

Jakin hefted it with disgust. "Only one quarrel left. I didn't count on having to use so many down below." As they spoke, Kaden realized with a sickening lurch that the sounds of slaughter behind them had ceased. Sooty red tongues of flame licked against the night sky, casting shifting shadows on the rocks around them. So they were finished with the monks, and presumably their own slaves as well. *It doesn't take long to kill two hundred people,* Kaden thought hollowly, staring back over his shoulder until Tan broke into his daze.

"They're coming up the trail behind us. How many ahead?"

"Four," Jakin replied.

"The crossbow will make it three," Tan said. "And if you're anything like your friend with a knife—"

"I'm not," he spat, glaring at him. "There's a reason we work as a team. She does the close work; I deal with unexpected problems from the roof."

Tan cursed, then hefted his *naczal*. "Ahead there are four. Behind, looks like a hundred. You shoot, we go. Kaden, hold the girl. Stay back."

Jakin looked hard at the monk, then nodded.

Their attack seemed to last only moments. Jakin shot one soldier through the eye, and then he and Tan were on the remaining three. The monk's spear flickered out to catch the closest man in the neck, while Jakin cut down one of the others, finding with his knife the weak joint where helmet met gorget.

So he can *use that spear,* Kaden thought to himself absently. He didn't know much about combat—his father's guardsmen had taught him and Valyn only the rudiments before they were shipped away—but Tan moved with a confidence and deadly speed that couldn't be faked.

Rather than pressing the attack, the remaining Aedolian stepped back, unnerved by the death of his companions. He seemed to have no relish for a heroic duel, and turned his head to glance down the trail behind him. That's when Jakin leapt.

He was fast, almost as fast as Pyrre, fast enough to close the distance and thrust his knife through the gap in the helmet and into the brain, but not, Kaden realized with horror, before the soldier could raise his blade. The two fell to the ground, the Aedolian dead where he lay, the sword he still clutched buried in Jakin's stomach. Kaden started to run to him, but Tan stopped him with a hand on the arm.

The monk wasted no time catching his breath. "He'll be dead in minutes," he said, as though that settled the matter.

Kaden tugged his arm free and turned to the fallen man.

He had pulled the sword from his body and rolled onto his back, blood welling from the deep puncture. Pain creased his face, and when he spoke, his words were weak, his lips flecked with blood and spittle. "The base of the Talon," he managed weakly. "Pyrre will meet you at the base—" He broke off as coughing racked his body, squeezing his eyes shut with agony. Kaden made to cradle his head, but Triste stopped him.

The girl's gown was badly ripped, her jaw trembling, her breathing heavy, but she hadn't panicked. If she didn't have Tan's stony resolve, she did, at least, seem in control of herself, and she pushed Kaden out of the way gently but firmly, then took the dying man's hand in her own and pressed her other palm to his brow. "Thank you for saving our lives," she said simply. The two remained motionless, like a statue carved from the mountain. Then, for the first time since the two merchants had arrived at the monastery, Kaden saw Jakin smile, the spasms that had racked his body subsiding.

"Go," he said weakly, then closed his eyes. "I will wait here for the god." With a final squeeze of his hand, Triste nodded, then stood, unshed tears in her eyes.

"There is nothing more we can do for him," Tan said. "Come."

They had just started to run once more when Kaden remembered his candlestick—the only weapon he had. It was just a few paces behind, and heart hammering in his chest, he turned back for it. The unlikely weapon had yet to prove its value, but it would be foolish to leave it behind for the sake of a few more seconds, seconds that couldn't possibly make a difference. He was bending to pick up the bloodied silver shaft when he heard the panting and scrambling. Someone was coming, climbing the far side of the small rise just a short stone's throw away. Cursing himself for a fool, Kaden snatched the candlestick and spun about to chase after his companions. The voice stopped him cold.

"Kaden! Help me!"

He stared as Phirum Prumm hauled his bulk up over the rise. The monk was sweating and shaking, his robe ripped away from one shoulder, blood from a gash on his forehead running down over his quivering jowls. His chest heaved with the effort of running up the path. How he, of all people, had escaped the carnage below, Kaden had no idea. All he could think was that Phirum was in danger because of *him,* because of the soldiers he had somehow brought down on them all, and he had to find some way to help.

"Can you keep running?" Kaden asked.

Phirum's eyes widened still further, as though the question terrified him, but then he looked behind him to where the ruddy flames from the burning monastery flickered against the clouds, the roar of the fire punctuated by curses and screams. He turned back to Kaden and nodded.

"All right," Kaden said, taking a deep breath. "Keep a hand on the belt to my robe. You're still going to have to run, but I can help pull you some, especially on the uphills."

"Thank you, Kaden," the youth replied.

Kaden just nodded.

"Let's *go*," Tan said. The older monk started to double back, but Kaden waved him on.

"We're coming," he replied.

Without another word, the four of them turned from the ghosts of the dead and the cries of the living to race into the emptiness of the night.

44

Dawn will come.

All night Kaden had repeated the mantra to himself as they fled through the darkness beneath a moon pale as the belly of a fish. Tan led the small party up treacherous streambeds, through narrow defiles, and along ledges a pace wide where the cliff face threatened to shoulder them into the abyss. Pyrre appeared a few miles from the monastery, as promised, at the base of the towering granite spire known as the Talon. The entire side of her once-fashionable coat had burned away, and splattered gore, black and glistening in the moonlight, coated her left arm to the elbow.

"You monks really know how to move," she gasped, falling in beside them.

Kaden wondered how the woman could still walk, let alone run, until he realized that much of the blood belonged to soldiers dead on the slopes below. When three Aedolians burst from the shadow, threatening to block their path, Pyrre killed two without breaking stride while Tan knocked the third screaming from the ledge with his *naczal*. The old monk seemed strong as a bull, and the merchant—*she's not really a merchant*, Kaden reminded himself—moved smoothly and silently as a shadow cast by the moon.

Dawn will come, Kaden told himself as he labored up the steep grade, Phirum tugging at his belt and wheezing with exhaustion and terror the entire time. The monk was slowing him down, there was no question about it, but leaving him behind was unthinkable. Too many people had already died. Ruthlessly, Kaden thrust the visions of Pater from his mind, forced down the thoughts of the Shin lying slaughtered in their cells, of Akiil hiding somewhere or bleeding slowly to death, shoved away everything until there was only the steady heave of his chest, the burn in his legs, and the gray blur of the rock beneath his feet.

Dawn will come.

And yet, when the sun *did* finally rise, wan fingers of rose and russet coloring the sky, the nightmare persisted.

Tan led them east, always east and upward, stabbing deep into the heart of the peaks. The decision made sense—without the burden of weapons and armor, Kaden's group would move more quickly than the Aedolians. The problem was, Phirum was having trouble keeping up, just hauling his own bulk along the broken path. Tan and Kaden had taken turns towing him through the night. (Triste was too small to help, and Pyrre just laughed at the suggestion.) The fat acolyte had stumbled countless times already, twice dragging Kaden down with him. The whole situation was untenable, but there was no other choice, and so Kaden gritted his teeth and ran on.

The sun climbed and the air warmed. He started to sweat beneath his robes. All at once, the defile opened out in a small bowl, where Pyrre pulled up short. Kaden thought briefly that the Aedolians had somehow managed to get ahead of them, to cut them off, and he craned his neck, steeling himself for the sight of helmed men with drawn swords. Only there were no soldiers—just a sparkling mountain lake, small enough that he could throw a stone across it, and a few patches of crag grass. The trail, if it could be called a trail, circled the lake, then knifed up a horribly steep ravine.

"Up again?" Kaden asked wearily.

"Just a second," Pyrre replied. "They left most of the soldiers to mop up at the monastery, but I want to know just how many are following. I think from here I can see part of our backtrail."

"You can't," Tan said curtly, but Kaden and Phirum were already turning to look.

As Kaden tried to see past a stand of priest pines in the middle distance, the fat monk at his side let out a quiet sigh and dropped to his knees. Kaden suppressed a moan. If Phirum couldn't even stand, it was going to be almost impossible to drag him up the steep climbs that awaited.

"Come on," he said, reaching down to grasp him by the robe. "It'll only be harder to start again if you sit down now."

The monk didn't respond.

Kaden turned to him, sharp words on his lips, but as he tugged at the robe, Phirum's head lolled to one side, and Kaden realized with shock that blood was trickling from his lips, pouring down his fleshy chin in a crimson stream.

"Tan!" he shouted. "Something's—"

The words died on his lips as he found Pyrre wiping her blade calmly on the leg of her trousers, then slipping it back into its sheath.

For a moment, no one did anything. Kaden stared at Pyrre, Triste stared at Phirum, and the fat monk stared at nothing as his eyes glazed over. Then Tan was sliding between Kaden and the merchant, hefting the *naczal* in both hands.

"Get back," the older monk said, his voice flat, hard.

Pyrre spread her hands inquisitively. "Aren't you Shin supposed to be great observers? I've saved Kaden's life four times in the last half a day—I would think my goodwill would be clear by now."

"Goodwill?" Triste demanded, her voice quivering with anger and disbelief. "You murdered Kaden's friend and you want to talk about *goodwill*?"

Pyrre shook her head as though she'd had this conversation a hundred times before, and to no effect.

"Why did you kill him?" Kaden asked finally, hearing the hollowness in his own voice.

"He was killing you," Pyrre replied. "He was slowing you down, sapping your strength, making it ever more likely the Aedolians would catch up." She sighed extensively. "I know I've been making this look easy, but saving your life has already proved more . . . interesting than I anticipated."

"We haven't heard the Aedolians in *hours*," Kaden replied. "They could have given up already."

Pyrre widened her eyes in amazement. "You think Ut and Adiv crossed a thousand leagues only to give up after one night? They are still chasing you, and Phirum, may Ananshael look over his fat soul, was slowing you down enough that they would catch you. Then they would have killed him *and* you." She frowned speculatively. "And incidentally, the rest of us. I gave him a quick death—no pain, no fear. We should all be so lucky."

"Who *are* you?" Triste demanded, shouldering past Tan and advancing on the woman until she stood inches away from her, glaring up into her face. Pyrre was older and taller, Pyrre held the knives, but Triste appeared undeterred. "Who are you to decide which people get to live and die?"

Pyrre looked like she was considering the question, but it was Tan who responded.

"She is Skullsworn," the older monk said. Kaden felt the muscles of his back and shoulders tighten at the word. "She is a priestess of Ananshael," the monk continued, voice like a file rasping over stone. "Her god is the God of Death."

Triste took an abrupt step back, and Kaden shook his head. "No," he said slowly, trying to work the thing through the way he had been trained. "No. It doesn't make sense. The Skullsworn only kill. She saved my life."

"If she saved you," the monk ground out, "she was well paid to do so." He rounded on the woman. "Tell me I'm wrong, assassin."

"No," Pyrre replied calmly. "You're not wrong. And at any other point, I'd be delighted to spend a sun-filled spring morning learning about my fellow travelers on the path, but Ut is still alive." She grimaced, as though the fact galled her. "It's been a long time since I killed men in full armor, and I'm afraid my skills have softened. Unless you want to end up like Phirum, I suggest we move."

"You're not coming with us," Tan responded, his voice flat, hard.

Pyrre raised an eyebrow. "The only question," she responded, "is whether *you* are coming with *us*. I was paid to rescue the Emperor. No money changed hands for the life of a middle-aged monk or an under-dressed whore." She glanced at Triste, then added, "Begging your pardon, of course."

"Who paid you?" Kaden demanded.

"No idea," she replied with a shrug. "Clients pay Rassambur, and Rassambur sends someone. Neater that way. Now, who's coming and who's dying?"

Tan flexed his fingers on the *naczal,* and though Pyrre didn't even seem to notice, Kaden had the sudden, overwhelming premonition that violence was about to erupt, brutal, fatal violence.

"We all go together," Kaden said firmly, looking Pyrre in the eye, then Tan. "She may be a priest of Ananshael, but she's on our side." He forced himself not to look at Phirum's crumpled form, not to think about that dark steel parting the boy's soft flesh. His stomach was churning with guilt and fear, but if he failed to convince his *umial* to go along, someone else was going to get killed. *Maybe* all *of us are going to get killed.*

"A few hours ago, the imperial embassy was on your side as well," Tan growled. "Don't be so eager to count a man your friend."

"Or a woman," Pyrre added.

"I'm not saying she's my friend," Kaden responded, trying to keep his voice level. "I'm just saying we can go with her for now. Once we're free, we can decide what to do."

"I'm not going anywhere with her," Triste said. Since Tan had uncovered Pyrre's real identity, Triste had been staring at her as if she were a viper poised to strike, and now Kaden noticed that her knuckles were white where she gripped the shaft of the candlestick. "I'll go on alone before I go with one of the *Skullsworn*!"

Pyrre waggled a knife at her. "Evidently, I was not as clear as I had hoped. Your continuing on alone is not one of the options. If you leave us, they will take you and you will tell them who I am, which will diminish our chances of escape. I'll go over it again. Please try to follow along this time: You come with us, or I deliver you to the god."

Kaden snatched Triste by the wrist, worried that she might try to dart away. "And if we all come with you," he asked guardedly, "you won't hurt them?"

The assassin spread her arms guilelessly. "I've said as much, have I not? Besides, I never hurt people; I only kill them."

Tan shook his head. "You can't barter with her. You can't negotiate. The priests of Ananshael have no loyalty to anyone but their blood-spattered god. This savior of yours has no pity, no compassion."

"It sounds like you're describing an obscure sect of monks I recently had the misfortunate to come across," the assassin replied, an eyebrow arched.

"The question is not one of emotion," Tan replied, "but of loyalty." He turned to Kaden. "Did you see this woman hesitate when we told her her husband had fallen?"

Pyrre said, "Jakin was not my husband—that was only a story—but we worked together many times. He was honest, kind in his rough way, and deadly with that crossbow. I will miss him, monk, but I will not weep for him. The god comes for us all."

Kaden took a deep breath. "Your contract instructed you to save me. So you won't kill Tan or Triste if I tell you not to."

Pyrre seemed amused by the idea. "I was paid to keep you *alive,* not take your orders. Emperor, butcher, peddler: all men die in much the same way, and the god's ministers tend to them all equally." She paused. "However, the monk seems to know these mountains, and the girl . . . the girl may have her uses yet. I have no quarrel if they join us, at least for now."

Kaden turned to Tan. "What is it Nin was always saying? 'Truth is just the straightest line between two points.' Right now the straightest line is all of us together, straight up that ravine."

Tan considered this, dark eyes hard and impossible to read. "Up," he said finally, turning toward the path.

"Up," Pyrre said, shaking her head in bemusement. "Why does it always have to be up?"

45

Valyn had seen some forbidding terrain during the course of his training—the icy Romsdal peaks south of Freeport, the blistering sands of the Seghir Desert, Hannan jungles north of the Waist—but nothing so vast and daunting as the Bone Mountains. The peaks were aptly named: white shards of granite stabbed into the clouds like the bones of the earth itself, shattered and thrust up through the thin soil. Where the white of the rock ended, the white of snow and ice began, glaciers and seracs, sharp cornices edging the highest ridgelines, bowls of dirty snow leaking into frothing white rivers. They went on forever, these peaks, rank after serrated rank, etching the frigid blue sky.

It had taken them four days, stopping only an hour at a time to rest the bird, to reach the southern foothills. Aside from the fatigue, which was standard Kettral fare, the flight was easier than anything they'd done in training. If Valyn could have forgotten what precipitated the journey, forgotten what lurked ahead, it could have been a pleasant training exercise in a remote corner of the world. Except it wasn't an exercise. After what they'd done, there would *be* no more exercises.

Traitors. That's what they were now. That's what they'd been since the moment they raided the armory and loosed Suant'ra from the roost. Valyn had been shocked at his Wing's willingness to follow him north into lawlessness and disgrace. After all, if they'd remained on Qarsh, if they'd obeyed Shaleel's orders and submitted themselves meekly to Kettral justice, the chances were good that they could have exonerated Annick. At the very least, the other four members could have cleared their names and, after finding a new sniper, gotten on with their duties.

On the other hand, *meek* and *obedient* were not the first words he would have chosen to describe his Wing. He realized with a grim smile that the same stubbornness that made them question his authority day in and day out had probably caused them to kick back against the injustice of Shaleel's inquest. The Flea's words came back to him, calm and confident: *Thought they'd make a good Wing.*

Only, they were the Flea's enemies now. That was a sobering thought, one that scrubbed the smile right off Valyn's face. In the history of the Eyrie, only two Wings had ever turned their coats—all cadets learned the stories—and they were both hunted ruthlessly into the ground. The commander of the Silent Stoop ended up slitting his own throat, while the Wing leader of Darkness was captured, tortured, then executed on the Qarsh muster grounds. Even as Valyn and his Wing flew north in pursuit of Yurl, others would be following, veterans, professionals. Maybe Fane. Maybe the Flea. It didn't much matter. If any of them caught up to Valyn before he reached Kaden, the fight was likely to be quick and horribly one-sided.

Almost there, Valyn reminded himself, scanning the peaks to the north. *Almost to Ashk'lan, wherever that is.*

The Eyrie had the most comprehensive maps in Annur, maps detailed enough to show the alleys and sewers of a dozen cities on two different continents. Unfortunately, there was no reason to chart a sprawling mountain range at the northeastern perimeter of the empire. Aside from a few mining camps and a smattering of hardy goat herders, the Bones were too high for settlement. In terms of military strategy, they might as well have been an impregnable wall or a vast ocean—an army wouldn't make it through the lowest of the passes, and from what Valyn could see from the bird's back, even well-equipped men on foot would have trouble crossing between the highest peaks. The range was far too wide and rugged for anyone—Annurians, Antherans, Urghul—to think about crossing, and so, aside from a few impressionistic scratches on the parchment and a blotch indicating the approximate position of Ashk'lan, he didn't have much to go on when it came to finding his brother.

As Suant'ra approached the peaks, Laith brought her down to within a few hundred paces of the jagged summits, just below the building cumulus clouds, into the systematic flight plan they'd agreed upon at the last stop. He'd climb a thermal in a low, lazy spiral to gain height, sparing 'Ra the effort, circle a few times to scout the mountains below, then glide down the far side in a rush of frigid wind that numbed the fingers and threatened to rip Valyn off the bird's talons.

The land comprised a maze of defiles, ravines, box canyons, and frothing white rivers as bleak and desolate as anything he'd seen. They quartered it for the better part of the morning, sketching out the standard grid
search pattern one painstaking square at a time, finding nothing larger
than a fairly impressive crag cat. According to Kaden's few letters, Ashk'lan
wasn't much of a compound—no more than a few stone buildings nestled
against the cliffs—and Valyn was starting to worry they'd fly right over it
without noticing. *It's just one 'Kent-kissing stone piled on another down there.*
Some of the piles of scree and rubble looked so much like dilapidated
buildings that he had no trouble believing he might mistake an actual
building for a rockslide. His eyes stung from the strain of scanning the
ground below, but he refused to look away.

Gwenna was sharing a talon with him, her bright hair whipping in her
face as she studied the ground below. After a while she leaned over to
shout in his ear. "How high up the peaks?"

Valyn shook his head.

"How many buildings?"

He shook his head again, and Gwenna rolled her eyes.

For the hundredth time, he found himself wishing his brother had
written in more depth about his life with the Shin. There had been
letters—brief notes arriving via ship from Annur, sometimes years out of
date—but the little "training" Kaden described sounded as bizarre as it
was pointless. Evidently, the monks spent their days crafting pots or
painting or just sitting around, admiring the mountains. As his eyes flickered over another rock-strewn valley, Valyn realized that, for all his anxiety, he didn't really *know* his brother anymore. They had been constant
childhood companions, but as their father used to say, different soil
yielded different fruit, and it was hard to think of any soil more different
from the Qirins than these hard, unforgiving peaks. Kaden the boy had
been quick to laugh, eager to explore, but Kaden the boy was nearly a decade gone. For all Valyn knew, he could have thrown away his training,
maybe even his life, in order to rescue an imbecile or a tyrant.

Gwenna's elbow jarred him from his thoughts. Dusk was gathering,
the sun sagging toward the western steppe, but his demolitions master was
pointing off to the northeast at what looked like one more notch in another file of peaks. Valyn couldn't make out much of anything at that distance, certainly not the indistinct hue of stone huts against a stone
background, but then, just as he was about to look away, a bright flash

caught his eye. *Setting sun on steel,* he realized, then tugged a quick code on the signal straps leading to the flier's perch above.

Laith pulled the bird up above the highest peaks, above the low, scudding clouds—so high, the thin air scraped at Valyn's lungs, and he thought his fingers might freeze to the rigging loops on 'Ra's talons. Kettral had no protocol for fighting other Kettral, but Valyn's Wing had discussed this ahead of time. Yurl would be flying low, scanning the ground just as they had been. Valyn calculated the angles. They were south of the flash and quite a few miles to the west—it was possible that the other Wing had glimpsed a similar reflection of light, but it didn't seem likely, especially if they were focused on the terrain below.

Men are like deer, Hendran wrote. *They never look up.*

Laith was urging the bird higher and higher still, until they soared through the darkening air thousands of paces higher than the highest mountains. If he was able to bring 'Ra down from above, it seemed possible to destroy Yurl's entire Wing with one of Gwenna's arrow-mounted starshatters—Annick had only to bury the thing in the bird's tailfeathers and let the wick burn out. He glanced over at the sniper and saw that she'd already nocked an arrow to the string of her bow, leaning far out in her harness over the edge of the talon, searching the sky below for her quarry.

There's even a chance that we got here first, Valyn realized, hope rising within him. *The thing Gwenna saw could have been Ashk'lan itself, some monk returning from the fields with a hoe slung over his shoulder.*

As they drew closer to the flashing light, however, Valyn realized that whatever they were looking at, it wasn't Ashk'lan. The light seemed to have come from a saddle in the distant ridgeline. There were no buildings, not even small ones. *No one would build that high, not even these 'Shael-spawned monks. You'd have to spend all your time hauling water.* But then, what was it Gwenna had seen? His pulse quickened as they passed overhead.

There were troops, he realized, maybe a dozen of them, scurrying over what seemed to be a makeshift camp. *Yurl,* he thought at first. Only Yurl didn't command nearly as many men. *Did Shaleel send more than one Wing?*

Gwenna was gesturing vigorously, and he waved her off before she felt the need to drive that elbow into his ribs once more.

"I see them!"

Now that he had something specific to focus on, he fished the long lens out of his pack and trained it on the group. The figures, antlike to the natural eye, leapt into startling detail and precision, the rising sun on their armor sharp enough to touch. *Aedolians,* he realized with a fierce smile. Sanlitun must have dispatched two groups when he learned of the plot. The ones who had come to rescue Valyn had been slaughtered on their ship before they arrived, but it looked as though the contingent to protect Kaden had won through. Valyn had no idea what in Ae's name was going on down there, no idea where Ashk'lan was, where Kaden was, but one thing was clear—he wouldn't be alone in his fight against Yurl's Wing. The delegation was sure to know the location of Ashk'lan—it was probably quite close by. Valyn and his Wing could fly ahead, secure Kaden, and wait for the guardsmen to arrive.

Then he caught sight of the bird—Yurl's bird. The creature had settled down to roost in a small alpine meadow a quarter mile from the main body of men.

"That 'Kent-kissing bastard's here already!" Gwenna shouted into his ear, pointing.

Valyn nodded grimly.

Yurl must have spotted the Aedolians from the air, or they spotted him. Either way, he would have thought fast enough to realize the game was up, and come in for an easy landing. After all, the Aedolians slaughtered on the boat to Qarsh all those months ago hadn't known exactly who was behind the plot. These were likely no better informed. They probably thought Yurl was flying a lawful mission from the Eyrie, probably thought the son of a whore was there to *help.* The youth could have fed them any one of a number of plausible lies, could even now be helping to arrange a "rescue," one that would end, undoubtedly, in a tragic accident and Kaden's death.

Except, of course, that Yurl believed Valyn's Wing was back on the Islands. As Hendran had written: *There's no blade as keen as surprise.*

The saddle stretched between two jagged peaks, offering a passage between them and a momentary respite from the unrelenting steepness of the surrounding terrain. Deep banks of snow piled in the shadows of the most jagged escarpments, but the center of the broad notch was clear. There were even a few patches of stunted grass thrusting up between the rocks. To the east, the ground fell off abruptly—so abruptly, Valyn wondered if it was possible to descend in that direction at all—but westward, the declivity was more gradual, and a quarter mile distant, the land leveled off again for a hundred paces. There, out of the worst of the wind, the grass grew more evenly, and it was there that Yurl had tethered his bird.

The Aedolians had taken up a rough defensive position in the pass, groups of three marking out the perimeter of an uneven square. A few of the men clustered at the center of the pass hunched over a cook fire, although where they found the wood to burn, Valyn couldn't say. Others were erecting a handful of low canvas tents, tucking them behind shoulders of rock or up small ravines—anywhere to get out of the wind. It was a messy camp, but the Aedolians couldn't have been expecting an attack out here in the middle of the wilds, and even if a foe *did* materialize, the position, sloping away as it did on either side, was nearly impregnable. The men wouldn't even need weapons; they could just trundle a few of those medium-sized boulders down the escarpment and be done with it.

Yurl, likewise, had taken minimal precautions. It took Valyn a moment to pick the Wing leader out from among armed men, but once he spotted him, there was no mistaking that yellow hair whipping in the mountain wind. Even the way he *stood* was arrogant. Balendin had joined him at the center of the camp. The leach had been forced to leave his dogs behind on Qarsh, but that hawk perched on his shoulder. *Not his well, though,* Valyn reminded himself. *Just a bird.*

The leach and the Wing leader were locked in conversation with a group of Aedolians. Yurl was making broad, expansive gestures with both hands while Balendin stood stock-still at his side. Valyn wondered what kind of lies the bastard was spinning. Anna was down by the bird, and Remmel Star and Hern Emmandrake had taken up positions on opposite sides of the pass. They looked a little more vigilant than their Aedolian counterparts. Emmandrake even had an arrow notched to the string of his bow. The youth wasn't as good as Annick, but he could hit his targets. None of it mattered. *They're looking into the valleys. Every single one of the 'Shael-spawned sons of whores is looking* down.

Valyn grinned savagely, then looked over at Gwenna.

"It's time to settle some scores."

†

Laith landed the bird in a flurry of wings and wind, and Valyn rolled up from his dismount to find himself facing a stern Aedolian in nearly full armor. It took him a moment to place the man. He knew the face, but it had aged, of course, hardened. . . . Micijah Ut, he realized, a smile tugging at the corners of his mouth. Better and better. As a small child, he had always admired the commander of the Dark Guard, and Ut, for his part, had been kind to Valyn in return. Valyn stood up a little straighter, aware that the Aedolian was seeing him as a man now for the first time.

"Commander Ut," he said, stepping forward and extending a hand.

Instead of accepting his greeting, the huge Aedolian took a step backward, preserving the distance between them while he drew a massive broadblade from the sheath across his back. If he was shocked to find Valyn here, a continent and a half away from either Annur or the Qirins, he didn't show it. Nor did he seem pleased.

"No closer, Malkeenian. Keep your hands in front of you, and tell your people to stand down."

Valyn frowned. He'd known that Yurl would see them coming in the final seconds—there wasn't much avoiding that. He'd even expected the other Wing commander to have sown a few desperate lies. He had not, however, expected those lies to bear fruit so quickly. Laith, who had started to dismount from the bird, squinted warily, then swung back into his harness. The Aedolians who had been setting up the tents and watching the perimeter drifted toward their commander, hands on their weapons. Annick and Talal drifted out to either side to avoid being flanked.

"Stand down?" Valyn asked, conscious of the chill in his own voice but making no effort to hide it. "No one on my Wing has so much as bared a blade. It's you holding the naked steel. Hardly a way for an Aedolian to greet the Emperor's brother."

"I serve the Emperor."

"Last I checked, you were sworn to serve the entire imperial family."

"Only those who remain loyal."

Valyn snorted. "So Sami Yurl has been at you already. The Micijah Ut I remember wouldn't have been duped so easily by a traitor's lies."

"Throw down your blades," the man growled, "and we will determine who is lying."

Before the conversation could continue, Gwenna shouldered forward, pushing past Valyn, her face twisted with anger.

"I've got no idea who you are, Aedolian," she said, jabbing a finger at him, "but wearing that heavy helmet all day must have stewed your brains. Where's Sami Yurl and that pet leach of his? We know they're here—saw them just before we landed. We know they've been filling that stone head of yours with perfect idiocy while you let them run around unguarded. Wait a little bit longer, and they'll have time to jump on their bird and fly off."

She looked ready to draw her blades and hack her way straight through the Aedolian, but Ut lowered the point of his broadblade directly at her neck. "Take another step," he said angrily, "and I will cut you down."

Gwenna scowled, but she didn't back off. One problem with Kettral training, Valyn realized suddenly, was that his soldiers didn't have the healthy respect for bared steel and superior numbers that one would expect from a green Wing with an average age of seventeen. To the Kettral, everyone else, everyone including Aedolians, were just amateurs. It was an attitude Valyn understood, but it was also an attitude that could get them all killed. In addition to Ut and the two soldiers flanking him, there were a half dozen archers scattered through the rocks, arrows already nocked to their bowstrings. They were all on the same side—given time, he'd be able to make Ut see that—but everyone was exhausted and tense. There was no telling what lies Yurl had spread just before their arrival. It would be all too easy for someone to make a mistake, and any mistake here would turn fatal quickly.

"Back off, Gwenna," Valyn growled.

"But—"

"Back. Off."

She bared her teeth, but obeyed.

"Your weapons," Ut said. "All of them, on the ground."

Valyn hesitated. A soldier never willingly sacrificed his weapon, but this was an unusual situation. As long as the two sides remained in a standoff, they weren't finding Kaden or hunting down Yurl. Someone needed to make a gesture of trust, and Valyn didn't see any compromise in Ut's hard, dark eyes.

"Let's get this charade over with quickly and cleanly," he said finally, glancing over his shoulder at the rest of his Wing. "Do as the man says."

"I don't like it," Annick said. She might have been talking about too much salt in the soup.

"Neither do I," Valyn said, "but this is Ut's command. The sooner we do what he says, the sooner we can start doing what we came for—finding and securing Kaden. Besides," he continued, trying to force some levity into his voice, "we don't have much choice, do we?"

"I could kill him," Annick replied. She hadn't so much as raised her bow, but the soldiers in the rocks shifted warily. Several went so far as to half draw their bowstrings—a mistake, given she could draw and fire while they were still finding the range. Annick didn't seem to notice. "One arrow through the eye. Your call."

"Your sniper seems to have a little trouble with obedience," Ut said.

"Yeah," Valyn replied, glancing over his shoulder at her. "But she grows on you."

"Tell her to drop the bow or she'll be the one sprouting arrows."

Annick looked unimpressed. "Still your call, Commander."

"Just put down the 'Kent-kissing bow," Valyn snapped. "All of you, get rid of your weapons. All we're doing here is wasting time."

The sniper shrugged, then set her bow on the ground. The others followed suit, but Valyn noticed that they kept their belt knives.

"The flier, too," Ut ground out. "Get him off the bird, then we'll talk."

"I don't know," Laith replied. "You all don't seem to be getting off to such a great start down there on the ground."

"Off the bird, Laith," Valyn snapped. "Now."

He wasn't angry at his Wing. They were playing by the book, playing it safe, but there was no benefit to a pointless standoff with a dozen Aedolians. At best, they'd end up wasting valuable time. At worst, someone was going to get killed. If Annick killed Ut, there was no telling how the men under him might respond. The last thing they needed was a pitched battle here at the ass-end of the world while Yurl and Balendin and the rest of their ilk looked on grinning from the rocks.

"There," he said, after a few of Ut's men had scuttled in to remove the discarded weapons. "Now that you don't have to worry about Annick putting a chisel point through your armor, maybe you can listen to me." It wasn't the most diplomatic opening, but Ut hadn't been exactly welcoming.

"Speak," the Aedolian said.

Valyn searched for the words. "Sami Yurl and his Wing have colluded against my life, and Kaden's as well. Whatever they told you, they're here to kill him."

"That's what they told me," Ut replied. "I wasn't sure whether to believe them, but now you've confirmed it."

Valyn stared. "They *told* you?"

A rich, sardonic laughter filled the evening air as Yurl himself stepped from behind a low boulder.

"I guess I gave you too much credit, Malkeenian," the Wing commander chuckled. "I never thought you were all *that* intelligent, of course, but I didn't expect you to actually *help* me."

Gwenna growled something deep in her throat. Without taking his eyes from Yurl, Valyn clamped down on her wrist. He had no idea what was going on, but he wasn't about to let her get herself killed over it. He turned his attention to Ut.

"If he told you he's here to kill Kaden," he ground out, "then what is he walking free for?"

He had to ask the question, although the sick feeling in his gut told him he already knew the answer.

"Because he's going to help us," Ut replied. "*We* came to kill your brother. I oversaw the destruction of the monastery. Most of my men are there now, cleaning up, hunting down the remaining monks. And tomorrow, at first light, we're going to find the 'Emperor' and remove his head from his shoulders."

46

The ground before the Temple of Light looked more like a muster field than a holy space. *The bastard must have added another five hundred soldiers,* Adare thought to herself, eyeing the Sons of Flame as they stood at their posts. None challenged her palanquin, none so much as glanced in her direction, and yet the message sent by all that glittering mail, those twelve-foot polearms, was clear: The Church of Intarra felt as though it had enemies inside the city of Annur, and it intended to defend itself.

Aside from the soldiers, a middling crowd had assembled before the temple, filing in for the noon service. As Adare stepped down, an angry stir passed through the group. Her role in Uinian's trial had spread as quickly as his "miracle"—the jealous princess who had tried to see an innocent man, a *holy* man, condemned—and the Aedolians were forced to shoulder a path through the throng. A few of those closest dropped to one knee, knuckling their foreheads, but for many the gesture was slow, almost resentful, and a few rows back, people were mocking her or shouting open defiance.

There were many ways that her plan could fail, but the thought that she might not even make it to the door had not occurred to her. *I should have taken Ran up on his offer to provide more troops.*

The *kenarang* had been adamant.

"I don't want to see you cut down by an angry mob," he insisted, "especially now that I know how well you kiss."

She had pushed him away, flattered and irritated at the same time.

"You can't be part of this."

"I'm the regent. You can't stop me. Besides, against my better judgment, I find myself smitten."

"Listen," she said, "this can't be about you. First of all, it can't look like we're forcing the issue or overwhelming the temple with an Annurian legion. That will just breed more resentment of the Dawn Palace and more support for Uinian. More *importantly,* though," she pressed on, putting a finger to the *kenarang*'s lips to stifle the objection, "this is between Uinian and me. He's made a personal attack on Malkeenian power, and if my family is going to hold on to the throne, I have to humble him personally, not through some overbearing show of force."

The argument had made sense at the time, but as the grumbling mob pressed close around her knot of Aedolians, Adare found herself wishing for just a little more support. Sanlitun had once explained to her that men were most fickle in the grip of emotion, and that mobs magnified emotion. If the crowd were to turn ugly, the dozen Aedolians surrounding her would crumple before they could even draw their steel.

Just keep walking. Hide the fear. Hide the doubt.

She managed to keep her head high and her eyes level, but heaved a sigh of relief nonetheless when they passed, finally, beneath the gate.

†

Thankfully, the imperial family kept a small booth inside the temple, from which the Malkeenians could observe the ceremony without rubbing elbows with the common folk. The wooden walls of the box wouldn't restrain an angry mob, but they gave her some breathing space, especially after the Aedolians had taken up their posts around the perimeter, and she sat on one of the plush chairs to hide the trembling in her legs. Some of the parishioners looked her way and pointed with angry mutters and scowls. She ignored them, keeping her eyes on the charred stone beneath the lens. The sun had risen almost to its noonday height, and a column of air beneath the lens had begun to shimmer already with that blistering heat.

Only when the crowd had settled did Uinian IV make his entrance from a gilded door halfway down the southern aisle. *If you stripped off that overwrought amice and alb,* Adare thought, *you might mistake him for a carpetmonger or a wheelwright.* The priest's entourage ensured that there was no danger of that. Before and behind him walked two columns of novices, boys and girls both, each dressed in the gold and white of Intarra, each swinging a crystal from a golden chain. The stones caught the light and scattered it dizzyingly across the walls and floor, but Adare kept her eyes on Uinian.

The man's defiance and ambition had only grown in the weeks since the Trial. In addition to augmenting the Sons of Flame, he was preaching openly on the distinction between human and divine rule, turning what had been an abstract theological issue into a contention that could overturn an empire. According to il Tornja, people were arguing about the difference between Divine Mandate and Divine Right in the Graymarket and the dockyards, arguing, that was, about the very legitimacy of Malkeenian rule. Worse, Uinian had taken to repeating his "miracle" every day in the noon service. To the men and women gathered in the pews, he was not simply the Chief Priest; he was the anointed of the goddess herself.

Which is why I have to be here, Adare reminded herself. *To do this.*

For a long time it appeared that Uinian had not noticed her, but as he drew abreast of the imperial booth, he halted the procession with a gesture, and turned to face her. When he spoke, he kept his eyes on hers, but his voice was meant for the congregation.

"How unusual. The princess graces us with her presence." A hiss and murmur rippled through the crowd, but Uinian raised his hand for silence, a sly smile on his face. "We have not seen you in this place of worship for a very long time, my lady."

Adare took a deep breath. She had broken the dam; it was time to see if the flood would carry her on its current or drown her. "My family worships the goddess who gave us life in the old place, atop Intarra's Spear each solstice."

"Of course," Uinian nodded, steepling his fingers before his lips. "Of course. An ancient place, and holy. And yet, the solstice services come but twice a year."

"It would be strange," Adare shot back, "if we had more solstice services than solstices."

As soon as the words left her lips, she knew she had made an error, conceded territory in the dangerous game they were playing. The parishioners who came to the daily noon service were pious folk, devoted to the goddess. Some, no doubt, made the visit every day from as far away as the dockyards, the Graymarket, or south of the Godsway. Her flippant tone grated against their faith.

Uinian's smile widened.

"Each of us serves the goddess in our own way," he acknowledged. "I'm sure there are more . . . bureaucratic tasks that demand your attention. But tell me, why have you joined us today? Might I be so bold as to inquire if you come in penitence for your recent . . . errors?"

The man was bold indeed, to insult her to her face before the assembled citizens of Annur. Ran's words came back to her: *There is a time in every battle when you must* act. There could be no half measures now.

"I come to illuminate my people, to bring them the truth."

Uinian narrowed his eyes. He was on his own ground here, surrounded by his own people, hard on the heels of his recent triumph. He had nothing to fear from her, and yet, clearly he had not expected this line of attack.

"Illumination? Those eyes of yours may smolder, but they fail to cast much light."

Adare ignored the gibe, turning instead to the congregation and raising her voice. "Your priest claims to be half divine himself."

"No," Uinian said firmly. "Just a faithful servant of the goddess."

"He claims," Adare continued, pressing on as though the man had not spoken, "that Intarra guards him from the flames. He lies."

An angry chorus exploded at her charge. Those who came for the noon service were the heart of the faith, the most devoted. She was treading on very dangerous ground here. Uinian himself, however, held up a hand to still the congregation.

"Those who have seen, know the truth," he said, "while those who have come now, questioning, will have it revealed." He turned to gesture to the lens above him. "The goddess has graced us with her light this noon, and I will undertake the Trial once more, as a gesture of my faith."

"Your faith is barren falsity."

He turned to the crowd once more. "You hear now the sad and desperate recriminations of a house that will lie, even kill, to retain its grip on power. You hear the empty mewling of a tyrant so far fallen in her faith that she would utter bald untruths here in this holiest sanctum."

Uinian leaned close then, pitching his voice for her ears alone. "Your father was a thorn in my side," he murmured. "I was delighted by his death. But it is you, yourself, who have sealed the fate of your family."

She almost vaulted over the wooden partition to claw out that smug smile. It was the memory of her father's voice that restrained her: *To rule over others, Adare, you must first learn to rule yourself.* She could almost hear him, as though he stood at her shoulder, his words staying and steadying her.

"You will fail," she replied simply.

The Chief Priest shook his head and turned to the altar.

"Behold," he said, raising his hands to the great lens as though inviting the heat, "the grace of the goddess."

Then, as the congregation drew in a great gasp, he stepped into the beam of molten light.

The stone beneath him smoldered as it had during the Trial, and, as during the Trial, he turned, triumphant, to the assembled multitude.

"Now," Adare murmured.

In that moment, the assassin il Tornja had found for her stepped forward, a man dressed like the other Aedolians but carrying a thin wooden tube, a blowgun he called it. He raised the weapon to his lips and a dart flicked out, quicker than sight, catching Uinian in the neck.

"I have paralyzed your priest," Adare announced, turning to the congregation, "to show you the truth." There was no going back. She had moments only before the crowd realized what had happened, before it fell on her and destroyed her, and yet she had to speak clearly, calmly, to make them understand. "To show you that he is *not* a priest at all, not the favorite of Intarra, but a charlatan, worse, an abomination. The man you know as Uinian is a filthy leach, who would have you take his kennings for divine grace."

Dozens of people were on their feet now, a few were shouting, and yet the crowd was confused, uncertain. *I have time,* she told herself. *I have time.*

"But how to tell a leach's kenning from the love of Intarra, a miracle from a monstrosity? For a long time I pondered this question in my heart. How to know which is true, and which is treacherous?"

She turned to consider Uinian. He stood in the blaze, his arms stretched out as before, as though accepting the impossible light and heat, but there was something different, a bead of sweat on his forehead, a glint of fear in his eyes.

"Yesterday," she pressed on, "I climbed to the top of Intarra's Spear, to the old sacrificial altar of my family, to sit as close to the sun as I could, to meditate on this question, and Intarra spoke in my heart. The goddess reminded me that there *is* a way."

She had stepped over the wooden balustrade and approached as closely as she dared to Uinian in his pillar of liquid light. Even at half a dozen paces, she felt the cloth of her cloak burning against her flesh, smelled the singeing silk. She turned her gaze to the Chief Priest. His face was twitching, his lips squirming with the effort of speech, but he would speak no more today—the paralytic had seen to that. Sheets of sweat poured off his brow. Adare favored him with a grim smile of her own.

"This is for my father," she murmured before turning back to the congregation.

"The difference between the miracle of the holy man and the kenning of the leach, is that the holy man relies on his *goddess,* while the leach trusts only himself. The leach, through his own foul machinations, twists the world around him, *he himself* does the work. The holy man need not raise a finger." Adare shifted to meet the eyes of those closest to her one by one, willing them to see the distinction, to understand. "This is what the goddess reminded me. She can rain down her favor, weave her protective shroud over one who is distracted. Even one who is asleep.

"At the moment he is simply immobilized, and so his kenning still holds."

A man in the foremost pew lurched to his feet, murder in his eyes, but one of the Aedolians brought him down with a quick blow to the head.

Quickly now. They're ready to break.

"Now," she pressed on, "I will prick him with a different dart, one that brings on a gentle, dreamless sleep. If Intarra loves this man, she will watch over him and you may do what you will with me for forsaking the sanctity of this place and the holiness of your priest. *If,* however, *if* he is a leach . . ." She trailed off, shaking her head. "If he is a leach, he cannot weave his kenning while asleep. The fire of the goddess will wash over him. It will consume him."

Uinian's hands, outstretched in benign acceptance, had stiffened into claws. The tendons of his neck strained beneath the skin, and his eyes bulged in their sockets. *He's terrified,* Adare realized, the satisfaction running through her veins like strong wine. *The man who murdered my father is terrified, and soon he will be dead.*

She raised a finger and the assassin's second dart hummed through the air, burying itself in the priest's neck.

With what must have been a desperate effort, Uinian forced his mouth open a crack, but instead of words, his tongue lolled out, frothing and red between his lips. A shudder ran through his chest, convulsing up through his neck, and his eyes rolled back in his head. As he dropped, slowly, to his knees, his garments, so white and pristine, began to smoke, then char. Then his entire body burst into flame as he toppled from the beam of light.

With a howl, the crowd closed around them like the sea.

47

For the rest of the day they had pressed east, past the Tower, past Buri's Leap and the Harpies, past the Black and Gold Knives, dropping into valleys and scrambling through passes no wider than their shoulders until they were in a region of peaks Kaden had never seen before. In the early morning, Pyrre pushed them hard, but as the day wore on, the assassin began to flag and the monks' long years in the mountains started to show their value. Tan kept the pace, never slowing, even when the others stumbled or paused for breath. How Triste managed to keep up, Kaden had no idea. On the steeper sections, he put a hand on her lower back, helping her up the scree and talus, but for the most part, she climbed and ran on her own, face drawn with the exertion, chest heaving as she gasped the thin air, but she ran. No one had forgotten what happened to Phirum when he began to fall behind.

They didn't stop until the sun hung just above the western peaks, a bleary red smudge on the darkening sky. They had just crested the steepest ridge yet, a great wall of granite running north and south as far as the eye could see, when Tan finally called the halt. Triste collapsed into a heap on the rocks, shuddering with exhaustion and falling asleep almost instantly. She had lost the second of her light shoes crossing a river, and her feet were an excruciating mess of slices, blisters, blood, and bruises that made Kaden wince just looking at them. It seemed a miracle that she could continue to stand, let alone run.

Wearily, he peered over the ridgeline to the east. The terrain made his heart sink: rank on rank of mountains and ridges stretching away toward the horizon. He started to say something, to point out that they couldn't possibly cross all of them, but Pyrre and Tan were looking west, studying a saddle they had passed through maybe an hour earlier. It had been a brutal climb and an even more brutal descent, interrupted by a few paces of level ground where Kaden had wanted nothing more than to sprawl out on the earth and surrender himself to slumber. He had suggested they stop there for the night, but Tan was having none of it.

"You were right, monk," Pyrre said, gesturing.

Kaden stared. There were men in that saddle, he realized, squinting until his eyes hurt. Aedolians.

"I have to admit, I'm impressed," the assassin continued, hunched forward to catch her breath, palms on her knees. "Dismayed, but impressed. I didn't think they'd be able to track us."

"*How* did they track us?" Kaden asked, incredulous. He was a fair hand at tracking himself, as were all the monks. It was possible to follow their path through the mountains—Pyrre's leather boots would scuff the stone and Triste had been bleeding since they fled Ashk'lan—but it would be laborious, time-consuming work, work that should have slowed their pursuers to a crawl. "They should not be able to move so fast."

It was a fatuous comment, an inane denial of empirical fact, but for once Tan let it go. The older monk's mouth was set in a grim line as he stared west. "The *ak'hanath*," he said finally.

The assassin raised an eyebrow. "Is that some kind of secret monk word?"

"It's what's been tracking us," Tan replied, then shifted his eyes to Kaden. "More than likely, it's been tracking *him*."

In the mad terror of the slaughter of the monastery and the exhaustion of their flight through the mountains, Kaden had forgotten all about the terrible creature Tan had shown him on the parchment nights before.

"Why?" he asked wearily. "What does the *ak'hanath* have to do with any of this?"

The monk shook his head. "Impossible to be sure, but it seems the Aedolians found it . . . or bred it. They used it to keep an eye on you while they were setting up their attack."

"I don't want to seem like the dunce," Pyrre said, "but what *is* it?"

"All these months," Kaden said slowly, "and it was there just to watch me?"

"Hard to be certain. If the annals are correct, the creatures are fearsome fighters, but they were not made to fight. The Csestriim created them to track, to hunt."

"It killed all those goats. It ripped out Serkhan's throat easily enough. Why didn't it come for me?"

"I don't know," Tan replied. "Perhaps it did, but failed to find an opening. Perhaps Ut and Adiv did not want to take a chance with your assassination, did not want to risk assigning the task to a creature of which they remained uncertain. This is all speculation, worthless as wind."

"I don't like to make frivolous offerings to my god," Pyrre said, raising a hand to slow the conversation, "but it is growing very tempting to stab one of you repeatedly in the neck until the other explains to me what you're talking about."

"A Csestriim creation," Tan replied, ignoring the assassin's skeptical look. "A creature built to hunt."

Pyrre laughed. "I'm no historian, but I think the last of the Csestriim died a few thousand years ago."

"The *ak'hanath* is not Csestriim," Tan responded, rounding on her. "It is a *creation* of the Csestriim."

"I've traveled two continents, from the Waist to Freeport and west beyond the Ancaz Mountains, and I've never heard of such a thing."

"Now you have."

The assassin pursed her lips and nodded. "All right. We'll use the assumption, for now. Why does the thing hate Kaden so much?" She turned to Kaden. "You piss in its nest or something?"

"The *ak'hanath* follows commands," Tan replied. "A dog set on a hare doesn't hate the hare, but it will harry it and tear it apart just the same."

"Then we'll have to make sure the hound doesn't find our rabbit," Pyrre said, clapping Kaden on the shoulder jocularly. "There are a dozen ways to cover his scent. The next time we cross one of those rushing streams—"

"It doesn't track by scent."

"Then what," Kaden asked, trying to make sense of that, "does it use?"

The monk shook his head. "There's not a word for it—not a modern one, anyway. The histories call it *atma*. 'Self' might be the best translation. The *ak'hanath* is tracking your sense of self."

Kaden stared.

"That," Pyrre said, raising an eyebrow, "is by turns fascinating, implausible, and horribly inconvenient."

"Take your pick," Tan replied grimly. "It's out there—one of the monks saw it back at Ashk'lan—and it has Kaden's *atma*. You put the thing on a boat to the Manjari Empire, and given enough time, it will find its way back to him."

Kaden shuddered at the thought of those awful, unnatural eyes, those skittering claws, bent to one single purpose—hunting him.

"I'm waiting for the good news," Pyrre said.

"There is no— Get down," Tan growled, hauling Kaden beneath an overhanging shelf of rock. "Get the girl and get under cover."

Pyrre, for once, didn't waste time bandying words, turning instead to gather Triste up and duck beneath the same shelf. Only when they were hidden away did the assassin turn to the monk.

"What are we doing under this rock?" she asked, her voice curious rather than annoyed.

Tan gestured toward the sky above the Aedolians. "We've got more than the *ak'hanath* to worry about. Now they've got a bird, as well."

Aside from once, as a child, Kaden had never seen a kettral, and he marveled at the sight of the majestic creature. *So that's what Valyn's been flying around on all these years,* he thought, envy, for the moment, threatening to overwhelm dismay as he studied the massive wingspan and huge, raking talons, each big enough to support two tiny figures in black. He watched as the bird circled once, then landed gracefully among the Aedolians. The assassin was not so excited.

"I don't know anything about your Csestriim horror," she said, "but this bird is really going to put a hitch in our plans. On foot, those troops are an hour away. By wing . . ." She spread her hands.

"Will they come for us immediately?" Triste asked. She had woken when the assassin dragged her under the overhang, and was propped on her elbows, staring off into the gathering gloom, fear and defiance warring in her voice.

Pyrre produced a long lens from her pack, peered through it for a while, then shook her head slowly. "It doesn't look like it," she replied. "The sun's just set, and Adiv's a crafty one. He knows that now that they have the bird, we can't possibly outdistance them. He'll wait for the morning, for full sunlight. Then they'll come."

Kaden looked from Tan to the Skullsworn, then back. "So we've got one night," he said finally. "What do we do?"

Pyrre shrugged. "We're not spoiled for choice. Normally, I'd recommend spending your last coins on a favorite meal or a good whore, but I don't think you monks tend to carry much coin, and you seem to be lacking in whores. Mostly lacking, anyway." She smiled at Triste with this last comment.

"I'm not a whore," the girl snapped.

The assassin raised her hands in surrender. "Me, I'm exhausted. There's just time to enjoy a good sound sleep."

Kaden stared as Pyrre Lakatur rolled onto her back, locked her fingers behind her head, and closed her eyes.

"That's it?" he asked, amazed. "You cross an entire continent to save me, and then just give up?"

"Everyone thinks that Rassambur is all about learning to knife people in the belly and poison their soup," the assassin responded without opening her eyes. "What you really learn there is a pretty basic lesson: Death is inevitable. The god comes for us all."

"What about back at Ashk'lan? When you fought Ut? You didn't seem so resigned then!"

"Then, there was a chance. Now . . ." Pyrre shrugged. "I've been running for a day and a night. We all have. The traitors behind us have five times our numbers as well as a Kettral Wing, not to mention, if your sour master here is to be believed, the evil pet creature of an ancient and immortal race that could track you across moving water by moonlight. Tomorrow, we'll fight, and I will give some of them to the god, but we will not win. And so, for now, I will enjoy a few hours of uninterrupted sleep."

Kaden turned his attention to his *umial*. "I assume you're not content to lie down and die, too?"

The older monk shook his head. "No, but the way is not clear. I must think."

And then, as if they were back on the ledges of Ashk'lan, Rampuri Tan shifted into a cross-legged position and gazed out across the valley toward the west, chest rising and falling so slowly, the movement was almost imperceptible. The monk's eyes remained open, but the sharp focus had left them, as though he were dreaming. *Or dead,* Kaden reflected grimly.

He considered Tan for a while longer, then took the long lens from where it lay beside Pyrre, training it on the enemy soldiers once more. "There's got to be *something,*" he muttered, studying the Kettral as they exchanged handshakes with the Aedolians. The leader was a blond youth, tall and well-built, dressed all in blacks like the rest of his Wing. The short Kettral swords crisscrossed his back. *Valyn and I used to play with wooden swords like that.* They had pretended to be great warriors, but when the men came for them on the morrow, when Pyrre "gave a few to the god," Kaden doubted he would manage to land a single blow. Bitterness welled up inside him, hot and sour. He allowed the emotion its flood, then shunted it aside. Bitterness would do him no more good than regret.

Look at the men, he told himself. *Find a solution.*

The newcomer commanded a standard five-man Wing, only . . . Kaden peered through the long lens once more. One of them—the flier, it looked like—was a woman, middling height with short blond hair. The only other Kettral he could get a good view of was a lanky soldier with feathers in his long hair and ink running up his arms. It was a strange look for a warrior, but after everything Kaden had seen in the past week, he was numb to strangeness.

As the two talked vigorously with Ut and Adiv, Kaden lowered the glass. Night already smudged the sky. Maybe the assassin was right. Maybe it *was* time to accept the inevitable. *Beshra'an, saama'an, kinla'an,* even the *vaniate*—they all seemed frivolous and inconsequential pursuits in the face of all that steel.

"What's that?" Triste asked, pointing at something in the distance.

Kaden squinted. A dark shape was moving across the gathering gloom high above the mountain peaks. He raised the lens to his eye once more, and a second bird burst into view, winging in hard and fast.

" 'Shael take it," he swore.

"Take care," Pyrre murmured without opening her eyes. "That's my god you're invoking." The woman rooted awkwardly beneath her back, tossed aside a sharp rock, then settled once more.

"They've got a second bird," Kaden said. "You want to see?"

"Not particularly."

"We don't know who these new ones are."

"We don't know who *any* of them are except for Adiv, who's a bastard, and Ut, who's a much bigger bastard with a very large sword. Their names don't matter. What matters is that they want to kill you and they are setting up to make a very thorough job of it."

"We might learn something."

"We will learn that there are five of them with two swords apiece. Making ten swords, if you're keeping count. They will also carry belt knives and at least two will have bows, maybe all five. By my count, that gives them roughly fifteen more weapons than we have, not counting, of course, whatever explosives they've brought."

"You've studied the Kettral."

"I've studied everyone I might have to kill," Pyrre replied, "and they will be harder to kill than most. I don't need to look at them to know that."

"Well, *I* want to see," Triste said, wriggling forward on her elbows, shouldering past the drowsing assassin.

She raised the glass, frowned, then slowly shifted it, following the bird as it approached. Kaden watched it with his naked eye, squinting as it landed. He could make out the dismounting soldiers, shadows in the gathering dusk, but nothing more.

"The new soldiers don't seem to be getting on as well as the first ones did," she said after few moments.

"Meaning what?" Kaden asked.

"I'm not sure. There seems to be some sort of standoff. Here."

Kaden took the long lens and trained it on the far pass. It took him a minute to sort out the new Kettral from those already there.

"This Wing has a woman, too," he said, "long red hair. And . . . two women, although the second one doesn't look like she's much older than you."

"Is she wearing blacks?" Pyrre asked.

Kaden nodded. "And she's carrying a bow. The thing is practically as big as she is."

"Don't let her size fool you," the assassin replied. "A killer doesn't always look like a killer. The girl may be young, but if she's flying missions for the Eyrie, she can probably put an arrow through your eye at three hundred paces. You know, the Kettral tried to clear out Rassambur once—one of your revered ancestors decided he didn't like the idea of a church of Ananshael up in the Ancaz. They sent ten Wings, ten veteran Wings . . ."

The assassin continued talking, but Kaden had ceased to hear the words. He had brought the long lens around to the commander of this second Wing—a tall, sun-darkened youth with short hair, a grim set to his mouth, and eyes dark as pools of pitch. At first he'd been paying more attention to the youth's altercation with Micijah Ut. The two were arguing about something, the Aedolian had his blade drawn, and other soldiers were drifting toward their commander as though sensing a fight. Kaden was about to take another look at the bird when something drew him back to that face. The sun had all but set and the light was poor, and at first he thought the shadows were playing tricks on him, but then the commander chopped downward with a hand, a curt, exasperated gesture, and Kaden knew. The eyes were darker, somehow, and bleaker. The mischievous boy had become a man grown, with a man's height and a soldier's build, but Kaden knew that gesture and he knew the face, even after eight years. He struggled to make sense of what was happening on the far pass, but even as he watched he felt the cold blade of betrayal take him through the gut. He lowered the glass.

"It's Valyn," he said, his voice hollow. "It's my brother." He set the long lens down wearily and lay back against the rough stone. It seemed, suddenly, that the assassin was right, that lying down and getting some rest before the end was all they could hope to do. "At least now we know who's behind this whole mess."

"Your brother?" Pyrre asked, suddenly interested, propping herself up on one elbow. "Are you sure?"

Kaden nodded wearily. "I spent half my life racing around the Dawn Palace with him. He's bigger now and there's something . . . more dangerous about him, but it's him."

The assassin picked up the long lens and peered through it for quite a while, pursing her lips as she watched.

"Well," she said finally, a grin spreading over her face. "If the reception he just received is any indication, it looks like he's on our side."

Kaden shook his head. "Why would you say that?"

"Once again, I find myself underwhelmed by the Shin powers of observation. Micijah Ut, may Ananshael gnaw the flesh from his overlarge bones, has just stripped your brother's Wing of their weapons. His men are currently trussing them up. The woman with the red hair and the beguiling figure just took a bite out of one of their ears, and, if your brother's face is anything to go by, he'd like to go quite a bit beyond ears."

A sudden, fierce hope leapt in Kaden's chest. "They're fighting?"

"Well, they tried, but it was a pretty one-sided fight. Teeth against steel doesn't make for a great matchup."

"But they're not *with* the rest of them," Kaden said. "They're not part of it."

"The good news is," Pyrre continued, as though she hadn't heard the question, "a bird like that should be able to fly us all out of here."

"The bird is there," Rampuri Tan said. His eyes were sharp, focused. He had left whatever trance he entered far behind. "We are here. A valley and over a dozen armed men separate us."

"Well," Pyrre said, "I was still on the good news. You've jumped ahead."

"That's the end of it?" Triste demanded, anger creasing her brow. "That's all you have to say?"

"Oh, no," the assassin replied, turning to her. "There's more good news: I have a plan."

Kaden narrowed his eyes. There was a barb in this bait—he just couldn't see it.

"Your plan?" Tan ground out.

"*Now* we come to bad news." Pyrre put down the glass, drew one of those long, cruel knives of hers, and turned to Triste. "The bad news is that the plan involves sacrifice, and in this unfair world, some of us will be called upon to sacrifice more than others."

Kaden lunged for the woman's wrist at the last moment, trying desperately to stop the knife, but he was only a monk, not *even* a monk, while Pyrre Lakatur was a priestess of Ananshael, assassin, Skullsworn, trained to follow the ways of her bloody god in the unholy halls of Rassambur, so quick, so precise, that Triste barely had time to scream before the blade bit down.

48

Valyn had rubbed his wrists bloody and just about torn his shoulder from its socket trying to wrench a hand free from the ropes binding his wrists behind his back. He knew all the tricks for escaping a slaughter-knot, but then, so did the people who trussed him up in the first place—that was the problem with fighting other Kettral.

His body ached from the strain, but the physical pain was nothing beside the searing, lacerating guilt. In his eagerness to save his brother, he had led his Wing directly into harm's way, had ignored the signs, spurned sensible caution, and now, unless he figured some way to cut them all loose, they were going to die here in the shadow of an unnamed mountain at the end of the world. It would have been bad enough to fall with a blade in each hand and a ready curse on the tongue, but this . . . trussed up like a pig for the butcher. The shame was far, far worse than the pain.

Keep working, he told himself. *Keep thinking. As long as you're alive, the fight isn't truly over.*

Escape, however, seemed unlikely. The Aedolians had halted for the night in the notch of a long, serrated ridge, hundreds of paces above the land before or behind. It was a good place with excellent lines of sight, easily defended from either direction, although difficult to retreat from if a fight went against them. That seemed unlikely. The only other people for a hundred leagues in any direction had been the monks, and, if Micijah Ut was to be believed, his men had killed all of them. Kaden was out there somewhere, scrambling through the darkness, but Kaden was *fleeing.* That left Valyn and his Wing, and they were thoroughly incapacitated, trussed up and then dumped in a rough jumble of scree right at the center of the notch. Even if they managed to cut their way loose, they were still trapped between the rock to the north and south, and the men guarding the pass to the east and west. A few boulders offered some meager cover, but they would be easy to flank, and . . .

And before you start thinking tactics you've got to get out of these 'Kentkissing ropes.

The task seemed next to impossible. Yurl and Ut both knew their business. They'd taken down Valyn's crew by the book, seeing to Talal first. None of them knew the leach's well, but they didn't take chances: Yurl put a knife to his throat, and then Hern Emmandrake, his master of demolitions, handed him a cloth soaked with adamanth. Talal tried to jerk away when they pressed the sodden material to his nose and mouth, but within moments he slumped into a limp heap, the cloth draped over his face, while Yurl looked on, grinning smugly.

"Now," he said, "we can see to making the rest of you comfortable."

It didn't take long for his Wing to truss them up like livestock for the slaughter, binding them hand and foot, with an extra loop around the throat to discourage struggling. Gwenna managed to take a chunk out of the ear of one of the Aedolians, but all it gained her was a cuff across the face that split open both lips and half closed one of her eyes. The hurt did nothing to tame her, but once they'd stuffed a dirty rag in her mouth, she could neither curse them nor snap off their faces, and after a few minutes of futile struggle, she sagged back against the ground, green eyes blazing with silent rage. Despite the bleakness of their situation, however, Valyn felt a moment of relief at being shoved to the sharp gravel of the pass rather than killed outright. *It's a mistake. Yurl's got no reason to keep us alive except to gloat.* Then, in a sickening surge of anger and disgust, he realized why they had been spared.

Balendin.

The leach approached, sauntering into the light of the fire as though he were a provincial nobleman strolling into his manicured grounds. He paused in mock surprise when he saw the prisoners, tsked at them disapprovingly while waggling a raised finger, then dropped into a squat a few paces away, satisfaction shining in his eyes. His dogs were nowhere to be seen, but that falcon rode on his shoulder; it cocked its head to one side and fixed Valyn with a hungry glare.

"So flattering," Balendin began, winking at Valyn as he spoke, "for all of you to care so very much about me."

"I'm going to kill you, leach," Annick said. It was an unlikely threat. Valyn's whole Wing was incapacitated, but Annick looked particularly vulnerable in the flickering firelight. The rough bonds emphasized the slenderness of her arms, her child's figure; she might have been some lost girl tied for a slaver's ship, except for her eyes, sharp and malevolent. "I'm going to put two arrows in your gut," she went on, ignoring the blood seeping from the gash on her forehead, "and another one in that filthy, lying mouth of yours." The threat shouldn't have been credible, coming from someone in her position, yet it made Balendin hesitate.

The leach actually seemed to consider the risk, then waved a dismissive hand. "I don't think so, although you have no idea how much I appreciate the sentiment." He closed his eyes and tilted back his head, as though letting a warm rain wash over his face. "All that hatred, that rage, that beautiful . . . feeling!" He licked his lips and smiled. "It's a gift, you know—this human capacity for feeling. Some animals have it, but only faintly, faintly. The shadow of a shadow. That delicious hatred of yours—" He licked his lips. "—as I said, you have no idea what it means to me."

We're helping him, Valyn realized grimly. *All our rage just makes him more powerful.* He took a deep breath, exhaled slowly, and tried to calm his feelings. Without a well, Balendin was just like them, just another Kettral-trained soldier, and considerably worse with either a bow or a blade than most. If Valyn could just find some sort of calm. . . .

"She tried not to squeal, you know," the leach continued, his tone casual, conversational, while the corners of his mouth twisted up in a slight grin as he turned to Valyn. "Your friend Ha Lin, I mean. The one with the whore's ass." He whistled a low appreciative whistle and shook his head. "Wish I could have done more with it, that day on the West Bluffs, but I was busy. Besides, you know Yurl," he added, jerking his head toward where the Wing commander stood, a dozen paces away, engrossed in conversation with Micijah Ut. "He wanted to do most of the beating himself. Spent a good half hour with his knee on her throat, prodding her with the tip of his belt knife. Barely let me get in a few punches." He shrugged. "Must be something about growing up the child of privilege."

"You 'Shael-spawned son of a whore," Valyn ground out, twisting helplessly against his bonds. "You fucking pig, you'd better hope Annick kills you before I get there."

"Aaah," Balendin said, closing his eyes in contentment. "That's more like it." He leaned closer to Valyn. "You know," he continued, "it's amazing. I think you feel more powerfully about your friend's suffering than she did."

"Balendin," Yurl barked, turning from the Aedolian and gesturing urgently. "Get over here, there's something—" He squinted into the darkness. "There's someone coming."

The leach straightened, a momentary look of irritation flashing across his face.

"Who?"

Yurl shook his head. "How the fuck do I know? The sun set an hour ago. Just one person, but I want you over here, ready."

Valyn tensed against his bonds. The makeshift camp was good, but it wasn't invulnerable: one Wing of Kettral, a score of Aedolians under Ut's command. A small force—fifty men, say—could probably overwhelm them. Fifty men or one veteran Wing of Kettral. Valyn's mind spun out a dozen scenarios—the Flea and Adaman Fane had caught up to them finally, a contingent of loyal Aedolians had tracked them through the mountains, a mob of monks from another local order . . . *Fool,* he hissed to himself. *Quit dreaming and focus on what's here, what's real.* The approaching figure was more likely to be one of Ut's men than anything else, a returning scout or a messenger from the main body of his force.

The Aedolian commander, however, didn't seem to think so. With a few barked orders, he set men on either side of the pass, bows trained on the darkness below, while Yurl and Balendin set themselves directly in the path of whoever approached. Yurl drew one of his two blades and dropped into a half guard. Balendin spun a dagger between his fingers, affecting calm. Valyn wasn't fooled—most of the soldiers were wound tight as bowstrings, ready for Ananshael himself to stride into their camp.

The person who walked out of the darkness, however, was not Ananshael, not an Aedolian, not a monk, not a Kettral with bared blades. She was a vision, a dream of perfection—some kind of goddess who had lost her way through the heavens to stride into the slender compass of the flickering fire. Her gossamer robe was torn to tatters, but even that served to accentuate her beauty, the rent cloth exposing the hint of a hip, the silken line of her thigh. Valyn stared. He should have been thinking about Balendin, about his Wing, about how to use the slight distraction to engineer an escape, and yet, for a few long breaths all he could do was marvel, caught up in the spell of those violet eyes, that cascading black hair, the scent of jasmine mingled with fresh blood.

She's been hurt, he realized, the thought stirring a deep, unexpected anger in him. Someone had carved a long, slender slice down her cheek, narrowly missing her eye. The wound would heal up fine—he'd seen worse in standard training—but there was something about this girl that made any injury seem like desecration, a sacrilege, as though someone had chiseled a gouge across a priceless statue.

Ut had his broadblade out of the sheath in a flash while Yurl drew his other sword. Why they needed them, Valyn had no idea. The young woman was a head shorter than the shortest of the Aedolians and slender as a willow. She was unarmed, her hands extended in supplication, and tears poured down her cheeks.

"Please," she sobbed. "Please. I'm sorry!"

"No closer," Ut said, scanning the darkness beyond her with wary eyes. She had come from the east, from the vast gulf into which Kaden had presumably disappeared earlier in the day. "On your knees."

She dropped, heedless of the rough stones. "I'm sorry!" she moaned. "They forced me to follow them. I didn't want to! I'm *sorry!*"

"Well," said a new voice, rich and almost amused. "Triste, Triste, Triste. My lost little girl returns at last." From behind a leaning boulder, a man with a bloodred blindfold wrapped around his eyes sauntered into the light.

"Adiv," she gasped. "I did it! I did what you said. I brought him to bed, I was touching him, undressing him, I was going to—" She shook her head helplessly. "—but then it all started, the killing and the fire, and he just dragged me along, he and that other monk."

The blindfolded man—some sort of Annurian councillor, if Valyn hadn't forgotten the rank—crossed to her and raised her chin almost tenderly.

"And you followed him for two days," he said, shaking his head. "You are a lovely creature, my dear. Nothing would delight me more than be-lieving this . . . tale of yours, but it strains credulity."

She cringed, as though he had struck her. She looked terrified, but Valyn caught a whiff of something . . . *defiance,* he realized, blinking in surprise. He had no idea how he knew—something to do with what had happened to him down in the Hole, he suspected, but he recognized the smell the way he would the scent of terror or lust. The girl was frightened, he smelled that even more clearly, but beneath her fear ran the cold current of resolve.

"I didn't know what to do," she sobbed, her words belying her scent. "I saw them kill soldiers, Aedolians. That horrible woman, the merchant, stuck her knives into them, and they died. She told me to run, and I ran. I'm sorry. I'm *sorry!*" She folded at his feet, grasping with feeble hands at the man's knees.

"And how is it," Adiv replied, "that you return to us now?"

"They were going to—" Her chest heaved with terror. "—she was going to kill me!"

"Who?"

"Pyrre! The merchant! She stabbed that poor, sweet fat monk when he couldn't keep up, and she said she had a plan, but she'd have to kill me, too." She gestured helplessly to her feet, which were, Valyn realized with shock, ripped and bloodied past belief. It was amazing that Triste could even stand on them, let alone run.

"We did find the body of the monk," Ut interjected curtly. "Single stab wound."

Adiv tapped a finger against his chin, pondering, as though oblivious of the supplicant clutching at his knees. "Who is this woman you're talking about?" he asked after a moment. "Her name is Pyrre?"

"Skullsworn," Triste gasped. "She said she was a priestess . . . a priestess of Ananshael."

Ut grunted. "That explains something."

"Like the fact that you failed to kill her?" Adiv asked.

"We'll take care of that tomorrow morning," Yurl said. He'd sheathed both his weapons now that he saw that Triste was no threat, and stepped into the circle with smug superiority. "We'll put the bird in the air at first light. Even if they spend the whole night running—this kind of terrain—there's nowhere to hide."

"No," Triste managed, gesturing wildly. "No, you can't wait! You have to go after them now!"

The Wing leader turned to her with a sly smile. "Don't you worry, darling. They won't get away. In the meantime, maybe I can do a little something to . . . cheer you up." He eyed her up and down appreciatively. "It's clear that the men you've been with just don't know how to treat a woman."

The minister cut him off with a curt chop of his hand. "Why do we have to go after them now?" he asked, his voice calm but measuring.

"The old monk," Triste explained, raising her eyes for the first time. "He knows this part of the mountains. There are caves, he said, *huge* caves. They're going there now."

Ut glanced over sharply at Adiv. "Is that true?"

The minister shook his head impatiently. "How should I know? We never expected to be out here. The maps we have don't even show the main peaks."

"What kind of caves?" Ut demanded, seizing the girl by the hair and dragging her to her feet.

"I don't *know*!" she cried, arching her back and rising onto her toes, face twisting in anguish. "I don't know! Just that they're big. The monk said once they were inside, they could walk for days, could come out in dozens of places."

" 'Shael take it," Ut cursed.

"My bird won't do much good if you let them skulk off into a cave," Yurl said, chuckling, as though amazed at the incompetence of those around him.

Valyn felt a sudden fierce hope. If Kaden could reach the caves, Yurl and the Aedolians could spend days searching for just the entrance, *weeks*! Of course, Triste stood to ruin everything. Evidently she was as treacherous as she was gorgeous.

"Always the unexpected," the minister said, shaking his head. "Where are these caves? How far away is Kaden?"

"I don't know," she replied. "A few miles? The monk said they could make it by dawn."

Adiv nodded slowly, then turned to Yurl. "All right, then. Can you find them by dawn?"

The gibbous moon gave ample light, but anyone searching would have to keep the bird low. If Kaden and his company could stick to the shadows, it would be hard to hunt them down. On the other hand, if they had to cover a few miles of extremely rough terrain by dawn, they wouldn't have the luxury of choosing the most sheltered route. There would be sections where their haste would force them into the open. Valyn ground his teeth. It wasn't a foregone conclusion, but he didn't like his brother's chances.

"I can have my people in the air in two minutes," Yurl replied, "but it's a big world out there, and it's dark. If he's changed course to break for these caves, we could spend half the night soaring around the wrong valley."

Ut glanced at Adiv, and the minister, as though he could feel the other man's gaze upon him, looked up, tightened the blindfold uneasily, tilted his head to one side, then nodded. "Kaden's not moving at the moment. If he does, I can tell you roughly what direction he's headed."

Yurl raised an eyebrow. "Seeing in the dark's an impressive trick for a blind man. You want to explain how you know all this?"

"Not especially," Adiv replied evenly.

"Well, if I'm going to put my Wing at risk by taking them into the air on your say-so, why don't you just go ahead and *try*."

"You're telling me you're not comfortable flying after an unarmed band, three exhausted people?"

"One of them's *Skullsworn*!"

Adiv waved a hand dismissively. "There are five of you. You are Kettral. You have a bird. Pyrre, Tan, and Kaden have been running for days. If you would have me believe you can't handle this tiny little chore, I will begin to wonder if we made a mistake involving you at all."

Yurl twisted away and spat, but the minister had him in a bind. "Once we're in the air, how does this *secret knowledge* of yours get to us?"

"Simple," Adiv replied, gesturing toward the fire. "Two flames means north, three means south, four means east. Just glance back here from time to time—you'll be able to see this pass from fifty miles out."

"Fine. Wait here, and I'll try to clean up your fucking mess," he snarled.

Ut turned toward him. The Aedolian had drawn his blade when Triste appeared, and he looked ready to use it now. Adiv, however, stepped between the two.

"If we're going to discuss messes," he said, nodding toward where Valyn and his Wing were bound, "it seems you've got some cleaning of your own to do."

Yurl grimaced. "One of my men thinks they could still be useful. We bag Kaden, then they're dead."

"In that case," Adiv replied, "it might behoove you to find the Emperor and kill him. I hate loose ends."

Yurl turned to gesture to his Wing, but Ut stepped forward. "I'm coming."

The Wing commander hesitated, then shook his head. "You've never been on a bird. You don't know the first thing about kettral."

"I'll learn," the Aedolian replied.

Yurl turned to Adiv, his hands outspread, but the minister just smiled a dry, serpentine smile. "It appears," he said, "that you and 'your people' are not entirely trusted. Ut will go with you and you will leave—" He scanned the Wing, then pointed a thin finger at Balendin. "—your second-in-command with us."

"Kettral Wings don't *have* a second-in-command," Yurl snapped.

Adiv shrugged. "Then he won't be missed." Yurl started to object, but the minister cut him off with a raised finger. "This is not negotiable. And you are wasting time."

The young woman, Triste, was trussed up despite her pleas and protestations, then slung to the ground along with Valyn and the rest of his Wing.

"I'll be back to entertain you later," Yurl quipped, eyeing her appraisingly. "I like the way you look with that rope around your neck." He grinned when she didn't respond, then motioned to his Wing and strode down the western slope into the darkness, toward the birds.

Triste lay in a heap, her dress hitched up around her thighs, whimpering and shuddering until Gwenna shifted to kick her ungently in the head.

"Knock it off," the demolitions master growled. "It's enough you just sold out your own Emperor. The least you can do is to quit that fucking whining."

Valyn was inclined to agree, but there was something about Triste . . . that defiance he'd smelled, and now . . . something like satisfaction. He needed to think. Yurl's sudden departure had left the Aedolians, the minister, and Balendin to guard him and his Wing. If they were going to make their escape, this was the time to do it, and the last thing he needed was the treacherous girl's sobs breaking into his thoughts. To his surprise, however, she raised her head, violet eyes blazing with anger rather than fear. She glanced past him, but Balendin and the rest were clustered around a small lantern a dozen paces distant, watching the great dark shape of Yurl's bird launch itself into the air.

"I didn't sell him out," she hissed. "There's a plan. This is all part of the plan."

†

"Well," Pyrre said, gazing across the narrow valley as the enormous silhouette of the bird floated noiselessly into the night sky, blotting the stars. "Normally I find elaborate plans just the slightest bit untenable, but I have to say, this one seems to be working out quite nicely. Of course, we're not yet to the point where an entire Kettral Wing chases me through a maze of razor-sharp rock."

"She did it," Kaden said, shaking his head. "I wasn't sure she could do it."

"It looks like we can add 'brains' to your paramour's list of impressive . . . assets," the assassin agreed.

Tan was in no mood for celebration. "The girl has done her part," he said, turning to Kaden. "Yours is considerably more difficult."

Kaden nodded, stilling his excitement and his apprehension both. His *umial* was right. If he failed, all Triste had managed was to expedite their capture and execution.

"I don't know how the *ak'hanath* communicates with its handlers," the older monk admitted, "but it does. During the day, they might have relied on the bird to hunt us down, but at night that Csestriim *thing* will be their guide. If we fail to elude it, the entire ruse is pointless."

"I'm still looking forward," Pyrre interjected, "to hearing how you elude a creature that tracks your sense of self."

"You destroy the self," Tan responded.

A long silence followed. The stars burned like silent sparks on the vast sheet of darkness.

"I take back what I said about liking the plan," Pyrre said finally.

"The *vaniate*," Kaden breathed.

Tan nodded. "The *vaniate*."

"It sounds very impressive," the assassin interjected. "And I hope it's equally fast, because that bird is half a mile off. If they're following the Csestriim critter, they'll be here before long."

Kaden felt his heart quicken, then forced it down. He had never summoned the emotionless Shin trance before, had no idea if he could do so now, but Tan had said he was ready. Besides, there was little choice, if he was to elude the *ak'hanath* and the men following.

"Clear your mind," the monk instructed. "Then bring up a *saama'an* of a bird, a heart thrush."

Kaden closed his eyes, then did as he was told, the image of the creature leaping bright and sharp into his mind as it had in a thousand painting tests.

"See the coverts," Tan continued, "the pinions, the flight feathers . . . see every detail . . . *feel* the rough scales of her leg, her smooth beak, the soft down of her breast."

Somewhere to the south, the kettral let out an ear-piercing shriek. Worry surged through Kaden's blood, and the image of the thrush wavered until he forced down the anxiety. *See the bird,* he told himself. *Just the bird.*

"Leave your hand on her breast," Tan said. "Can you feel her heart beating?"

Kaden paused. This was new. The *saama'an* was a visual exercise. No one had ever asked him to file away tactile sensation. He took a deep breath.

"She is frightened," Tan said, "trapped in your hand. You know her fear. Let yourself feel that fear."

Kaden nodded. This was like the *beshra'an,* he realized, throwing himself into the mind of a creature, only this creature lived inside his brain. He let himself sink deeper into the vision, laid a hand on the bird's heart and felt it beating.

"Can you *hear* her heart?" Tan asked.

Kaden waited. A mountain wind skirled in his ears. Something down the slope somewhere knocked free an avalanche of pebbles. Behind it, though, beneath it, the bird's heart beat, quick and light, thumping, thumping, until it filled his ears, his mind. He held the creature in his hand—so fragile, he could crush her with a squeeze of his fingers. She was terrified, he realized. He was terrifying her.

"Now let her go," Tan said. "Open your hand and let her fly away."

Slowly, Kaden opened his fingers, reluctant to let the thrush escape his grasp. It seemed important that he hold her, for some reason, that he clutch her to him . . . but Tan had said to let her go and so, ever so lightly, he let her slip from his fingers.

"She's flying now," he whispered.

"Watch," Tan replied.

Against closed lids, Kaden watched as the bird dwindled, smaller and smaller against the great blue of his mind's vast sky, smaller and smaller until she was a smudge, a speck, a pinprick on the great open emptiness of the heavens. And then she was gone. Blankness filled his mind.

He opened his eyes.

Almost overhead now, the kettral shrieked. *They're close,* he realized, *but they're too late.*

Then he saw the eyes. At first he wasn't sure what they were: glowing bloodred orbs, at least a dozen, some the size of apples, others no larger than Annurian copper coins, floating up the slope below. As they drew closer, he could make out the irises, pulsing with crooked veins, dilating and contracting, and then he understood. The *ak'hanath* had come.

He should have been terrified, and yet the realization carried no fear. The creature was a fact—no more, no less—like the fact that night had fallen, or that Pyrre stood, staring, at his side. Like the fact that people would die tonight. It was strange, he realized, this lack of feeling. He *used* to feel something. Only minutes ago, before he had freed the bird inside him, his mind had been a welter of emotions: fear and confusion and hope. Inside the *vaniate,* however, there was only a great, blank calm.

The *ak'hanath* was larger than he had expected, almost the size of a female black bear, but it skittered up the rocky slope more quickly than any bear, claws clicking over the stones, chitinous legs flexing and unflexing, causing the eyes at the joints to bulge under the strain. A dozen paces off it paused, turned back and forth in the darkness as though sniffing for something, then let out a thin but piercing wail just at the edge of hearing. Twice more the creature uttered its unnatural scream and then, from farther down the slope, an answering call.

"Two," Tan observed as the second horror approached.

As it drew near, the first *ak'hanath* raised wicked, slicing pincers, as though testing the air, clicking them open and shut spasmodically. One of those things could hack through the skull of a goat. They had killed Serkhan back at the monastery. Facts. Just more facts.

Kaden turned to Tan. "Is it too late?"

"Not if I kill them."

"About that," Pyrre interjected, hefting a small stone and hurling it at one of the creatures. It flew true, striking one of the eyes with a sick, popping sound. The *ak'hanath* spasmed a moment, let out another high-pitched shriek, then sidled farther up the slope. Kaden could make out the tiny limbs around its mouth twitching feverishly. "Any advice?" She might have been asking about the best local wine.

"Leave them to me," the monk replied. "You have your own part to play."

"You don't want help?"

"The *ak'hanath* are trackers, not killers, although these—" The monk frowned. "—they differ from those I have studied."

"They seemed like they were doing plenty of killing back there in Ashk'lan," the assassin pointed out, crushing two more eyes with two more thrown stones. The spiders were agitated now, thrashing violently, and they had resumed their approach.

"In Ashk'lan, they had not come up against someone who knew how to fight," the monk replied, stepping forward to meet the foe.

Even from inside the *vaniate,* everything seemed to happen at once. The closest creature, still a few paces distant, crunched itself into a ball, then sprang. Kaden had watched crag cats attack—they were the fastest animals in the mountains, quick enough to take down a deer in full flight, but even at its fastest there was something relaxed, almost languorous in the cat's motion. The *ak'hanath* moved with the violence of a mechanical device tightened past tolerance in an explosion of grasping claws and slicing arms.

Tan's *naczal,* somehow, was there to meet it, smashing the creature aside as the monk rolled with the blow, coming back to his feet in a fighting crouch the like of which Kaden had never seen. The strange Csestriim spear spun above his head in quick, looping arcs.

"Stay behind me," he said to Kaden, not taking his eyes from the creature.

Pyrre had kept up her assault with the rocks—she would have run out of knives long before the creatures ran out of eyes—but the effort of the attack didn't seem to wind her.

"I never expected to find a Shin monk fighting *dharasala* style," she said, a new note of respect in her voice. "And in the old forms, too."

"I wasn't always a monk," Tan replied, and then it was his turn to attack.

He darted between the two spiders, swinging the spear in a great overhead arc. For a moment Kaden thought the man had missed his target, then realized the true intention behind the blow as each end of the *naczal* connected with one of the *ak'hanath*. In the cool space of the *vaniate,* Kaden wondered how long Tan must have studied with the weapon, how carefully he must have trained. Had he learned those skills among the Ishien, or were they older still, a remnant of some prior life Kaden couldn't begin to imagine?

Tan stood almost between the spiders now, in what seemed an impossible position, too close to maneuver, surely too close to bring his long spear to bear. And yet, with short, savage motions, Tan was striking them, each blow counting double as it connected with the creature before and behind. More, when the spiders thrust back against his blade, metal scraping against shell and ichor, he was able to use the strength of one against the other, allowing the *naczal* to pivot in his hand. The creatures were landing their own blows, vicious cuts and snaps, but the monk was able to keep them away from his head and chest, driving his own attack harder, harder, until, with a great plunging motion he was able to force the spear between the flailing arms and into the gullet of the first *ak'hanath*. As the thing spasmed and screamed, he ripped the blade free, wrenching it over-head in a crushing arc that staggered his remaining foe, then stepped in close to finish it.

For a heartbeat, the mountainside was still and quiet save for the sound of the monk's breath rasping in his chest.

"You're hurt," Pyrre said, stepping forward, but Tan held up a hand to keep her back.

"Nothing fatal." He glanced down at his robes. "Though the creatures should not have been so large, nor so strong."

"When this is all finished," the woman said, giving the monk a hard, appraising look, "you're going to have to tell me where you learned to fight."

"No," Tan replied. "I won't."

Before the assassin could respond, a clicking and screeching broke the silence beyond their small circle. At first Kaden thought that Tan had failed to kill one of the creatures, but both spiders lay still, their horrid red eyes dimmed by death. Down the slope, however, fifty paces away and closing, more eyes floated through the night, dozens of eyes, scores.

"They brought more," Tan observed, a hint of weariness in his voice.

"How many?" Kaden asked, trying to sort through the glowing red orbs into individual spiders.

"Looks like ten, maybe a dozen. They weren't at the monastery all these months. We would have seen them. They must have come with the Aedolians."

"You can't fight a dozen of them," Pyrre said.

"Can, or cannot," Tan replied, "it is what needs to be done." He turned to Kaden. "You can both still escape them if you break free. They fol-lowed the others here; they cannot track you in the *vaniate*."

"You're going to die here, monk," Pyrre observed.

"Then your god will be glad," Tan replied. "Go now, both of you. The time has come to make good on our words."

And then the monk was moving forward, the *naczal* swinging above his head. A part of Kaden knew he should be frightened, horrified. But fear and horror—they were like distant lands he had heard of but never visited. Tan would live, or he would die. Either way, Kaden's own role was clear. He was to run. As his *umial* ducked and stabbed, sliced and hacked at the fetid tide rolling over him, as Rampuri Tan fought for his life against something dark and unnatural, something that should have been wiped from earth millennia earlier, as the old monk struggled for the very survival of his pupil, Kaden turned into the darkness and ran.

†

It wasn't good territory for a breakout. The wind and cold had scoured everything from the notch but a few erratic boulders, scattered about like the remnants of some dilapidated tower. The Aedolian lanterns didn't cast much light, but still, the moon was out. Valyn frowned. Whoever planned to cut them free had a good bit of open ground to cover, with only the treacherous shadows to shield them from prying eyes.

The good news was, Balendin, Adiv, and most of the remaining Aedolians had drifted to the eastern end of the notch, fifteen paces distant, staring out over the great gulf of night. There seemed to be some confusion over the signal fires, the ones intended to mark Kaden's direction of flight. Balendin was arguing with Adiv while stabbing his finger alternately at the flames and the night-shrouded peaks beyond. The wind whipped their voices away before Valyn could make out more than scraps of words, but it seemed as though something had gone awry with their plan, a supposition that kindled in him a little bit of hope. Two men still guarded Valyn and his Wing, but they looked distracted, ill at ease, as though they wished they were with the others, comfortably within the compass of the lamplight. They carried swords sheathed at their sides, but it wouldn't be too difficult for an experienced fighter to get close enough to fire a couple of shots, or, barring that, cut their throats. . . .

But Kaden's not an experienced fighter, Valyn reminded himself grimly. Aedolians might not have presented any great threat to a Kettral Wing, but they were nonetheless accounted among the most capable soldiers in the world. Any mistake, and they'd raise the alarm, and once that happened, there wouldn't be *time* to loose any of the captives. Valyn chafed at his helplessness. He had come to save his brother, and here he was, trussed like a yearling lamb. He had a dozen questions for Triste, but after Gwenna's brief outburst and the girl's whispered warnings, the two Aedolians had cuffed them all into silence. *Just get us out, Kaden,* he thought grimly. *Just get us out, and I can take it from there.*

He smelled his brother before he heard him: just the faintest whiff of sweat and goat wool off to the north. He twisted his head in time to see a shadow ghosting down the nearly sheer northern wall of the notch. It looked like a difficult climb even in daylight, but Kaden had spent half his life in these mountains. Maybe he'd learned more than painting and pottery. Valyn glanced over his shoulder, worried that the guards would catch sight of his brother, but they were oblivious. *They can't see,* Valyn realized. *They can't see into the darkness the way I can.*

Suddenly, a clatter of rockfall broke the silence on the eastern slope, over by Adiv and Balendin, a hundred paces from where Kaden finished his treacherous descent and started forward, flitting between the boulders like a ghost. The minister turned an ear to the darkness, his lips pursed in a slight frown.

"Eln, Tremmel," he said, gesturing to a couple of soldiers. "Take a quick look down the eastern slope."

"There's no one there," Balendin said, his voice calm, confident.

Adiv turned to face the leach, as though studying his face from behind that uncanny blindfold.

"How do you know that?"

The youth shrugged. "I'm on this Wing *because* I know things like that. Trust me. There's no one there."

He can feel the emotion, Valyn remembered with a sudden stab of fear. Talal had insisted that Balendin relied on emotion directed at *him,* but perhaps he could feel the residue of other feelings, too. There was no telling just what twisted well of power fed a creature like that, and if he could feel emotion, it meant he could feel Kaden. However brave Valyn's brother had been in trying to stage a rescue, fear and excitement must be coursing through his body like poisoned wine. If Balendin caught even an eddy of that, the game was up.

Hurry, Kaden, Valyn prayed silently. *Hurry.*

The minister considered the youth a moment longer, then gestured to his men once more. "Check it anyway."

The two guards watching the prisoners had drifted toward the rest of the group, curiosity sucking them a couple paces toward the light.

Now, Valyn thought. *This is the time.*

And then, as though summoned, a shadow broke away from the darkness. Valyn stared.

It had been eight years since he'd last seen his brother, since he and Kaden raced around the hallways and gardens of the Dawn Palace, playing at being Kettral. He recognized his brother instantly, their father's jaw, their mother's nose, the distinct line of his mouth, and yet the person standing before him was a boy no longer. He was lean almost to the point of gauntness, the bones of his cheeks, the thin striated muscles of his arms tight under sun-darkened skin. Kaden had grown taller, as well, a few inches taller than Valyn himself. Of course, the Bone Mountains were a far cry from the luxury of Annur, from those pampered childhood mornings sipping *ta* and slurping down porridge in the warm kitchens. During his quick search, Valyn had seen enough to know that the mountains were a hard place, and Kaden had hardened as well. He held his belt knife as though prepared to use it, but the knife was the least of it. Valyn's gaze was riveted on his brother's eyes.

Those eyes had always been startling, even frightening for some of the newer palace staff, but Valyn had grown used to them over the years. He remembered Kaden's eyes being bright and steady as the flame of a lamp on a winter's evening, as warm as candles set out for the nightly meal. Those eyes still burned, but Valyn no longer recognized the fire. The light was distant, like twin pyres seen from far off, cold, like the light of the stars on a moonless night, cold, and hard, and bright.

Even given the circumstances, Valyn might have expected some sort of smile, a nod, some mark of recognition. Kaden showed nothing. He raised his belt knife, and for a horrible moment, meeting those pitiless eyes, Valyn thought his brother meant to kill him. Then, before he realized what was happening, the ropes binding his wrists had fallen away and he was free. Without a pause, without a heartbeat of acknowledgment or celebration, Kaden moved down the line, cutting loose the rest of the Wing.

All of it took less than a dozen breaths. Valyn could tell his Wing was shocked and surprised, but then, they'd spent a long time on the Islands learning to deal with shock and surprise. Valyn waved Annick toward the pile of their weapons, blades and bows leaning against a rock a few paces away. He glanced over toward the two guards. They were still peering toward the brink of the precipice, but they could turn at any moment. As Gwenna and Annick rearmed, he crossed to Talal, lifted the adamanth cloth from the leach's mouth, and waved away the residue of the noxious fumes. His friend choked, gagged, and then, after what seemed like an age, blearily opened his eyes. He'd been knocked out with adamanth before—all the leaches in the Islands trained for this—and only time would bring him fully awake. In a minute or so, he might be able to run, but it would be a long while before he could reach his well again, by which time the fight would likely be over, one way or another.

Valyn's first thought was to race for the bird. Yurl's Wing had tethered Suant'ra in a small depression less than a quarter mile down the slope to the west. But that was a fool's errand. There was no telling what kind of chaos could break out in the darkness with the Annurians behind them and Balendin wielding that well of his. *It has to be now,* Valyn thought. *Quick and brutal, while we have the advantage.*

Annick already had her bow strung. Valyn glanced over at the soldiers. The argument over the signal fires had intensified, drawing in Balendin and a few more of the Aedolians. Laith, meanwhile, was busy distributing the blades to the rest of the Wing while Gwenna silently rifled through her munitions, setting aside a handful that Valyn didn't recognize, shaking her head in anger as she worked. He briefly considered having her rig a covering blast with smokers—that would give them an even chance of reaching Suant'ra—but even Gwenna would need a few minutes to set the charges, and the smart money said they didn't have a few minutes. Valyn gestured to Annick for her small flatbow. The sniper was better with it than anyone else in the group, but she couldn't fire two weapons at once, and Kaden had only his belt knife. Valyn doubted his brother had ever fired such a thing, but it wouldn't hurt to have some more steel in the air when the chaos broke, and Valyn himself was better with his blades. Kaden eyed the weapon briefly, watched while Valyn mimed the mechanism, then accepted it with that same icy calm. That ice troubled Valyn, as though he had come all this way to rescue a walking corpse, or a ghost, but there wasn't time to worry about it now.

Not time left to do anything but go, Valyn thought, gesturing to Annick.

One of the two guards was pointing at something to the east. He spat into the darkness, then started to turn back toward the prisoners. Annick's arrow took him clean through the throat. He crumpled without even a groan, but his armor clattered against the rocks, and the second man turned into a second arrow, this one straight through the eye and into the brain.

That was two down in as many heartbeats, two out of a dozen. *But it's not them we need to kill,* Valyn thought, pointing hard at Balendin.

Both Annick and Balendin seemed to have heard his thoughts at the same time. The leach turned, anger and fear warring on his face, just as Annick loosed one, then two, then three arrows, her arm moving so fast that for a split second they all hung in the air at the same time, one before the other, like geese on the wing, all hurtling toward the leach. It was over. No one could defend against that—there were just too many arrows, just too little time—but at the last moment, just as he expected to see the leach's face transfixed with a quivering wooden shaft, the arrows veered wide, knocked skittering into the darkness by some invisible palm. Balendin glanced over his shoulder, as though he, himself, were surprised at the result, then turned back to the group, a smile stretching across his face.

"So," he began slowly. "I see you've all decided to have one last go at vengeance." He shook his head as though marveling, but made no effort to reach for his blades. The falcon on his shoulder let out an ear-piercing shriek, and the remaining Aedolians turned toward the fight. Metal grated on metal as they slid their swords from their sheaths. Balendin didn't seem to notice them. "Who would believe that people could get so worked up about a little torture, the occasional brutal murder?"

The remaining Aedolians and Tarik Adiv had had plenty of time to realize what was happening, but Annick never hesitated, shifting her fire to the armored men, who dropped like stones before they could even start to cover the gap. *Four, five, six.* The sniper realized that Balendin was invulnerable, at least for the moment, and she'd adjusted her attack to deal with the rest of the field. *Seven, eight.* The leach, for his part, seemed amused to let them die. Valyn ground his teeth. With his well running deep and strong, Balendin could clearly handle an entire Wing all by himself.

At the last moment, Adiv fled into the darkness, Annick's arrow clattering into the rock where he had stood. If Balendin was concerned about the disappearance of his final remaining ally, he didn't show it. In fact, the leach was grinning.

"The problem with confederates," he said, gesturing at the fallen bodies, "is that you never quite know how far you can trust them." He nudged one of the dead Aedolians with a toe. "Although I hate to cast doubt on the noble Micijah Ut, I half suspect he intended to murder us when this whole business was wrapped up. He really doesn't seem to *relish* his job in quite the way we do."

Annick loosed another arrow, but Balendin flicked a contemptuous finger, and it flew wide into the night. Kaden still held the flatbow, his finger on the trigger, but its bolts would prove no more useful than the sniper's arrows. *Talal,* Valyn thought angrily. *We need Talal.* But the leach was only now recovering from the adamanth, rolling groggily on the ground, trying to stumble to his knees.

Balendin considered the sight for a moment. "I hope you realize," he said, addressing Talal, "that as a fellow leach, I hold you in the highest esteem. We happy few, so reviled by the world, yet so blessed by the gods—we should stick together. So you understand it pains me that I have to do this—"

A stone the size of Valyn's fist flew through the night, hurled by some invisible force, striking Talal squarely between his eyes and dropping him to the earth.

"And now," Balendin added, turning smugly to Annick, "just because I'm getting tired of swatting down your arrows." Another stone leapt from the ground, hovered, revolving in the air before the leach, then whistled through the night, striking Annick with an audible crack and cutting a ragged gash across her forehead. She dropped, knees unstrung.

"Balendin," Valyn ground out, fighting for time, "you can't win."

The leach laughed, the sound rich with acid and amusement.

"No one ever said you weren't bold," he replied, shaking his head, "just that you weren't too bright."

Three more stones dropped Laith, Gwenna, and Triste like beef at the slaughterhouse, eyes glazed, hands limp on their weapons. Valyn had no idea if any of them were still breathing, no idea if they were even alive.

"I just cannot tell you how much I regret losing such delectable emotion," Balendin said, then shrugged. "But they have to go sometime, and with the hate rolling off you, I still feel like I could rip the top off this mountain."

"What did you do to them?" Valyn demanded, sickened by the possibilities.

The leach shrugged. "Nothing permanent. Not yet. I like to give Yurl the illusion that he controls the Wing, and he sometimes has some . . . unusual ideas about military protocol. Especially when it comes to female captives. Hard to say which one will give him the most pleasure. This delightfully treacherous young bitch," he said, indicating Triste with a jerk of his head, "is clearly the best catch, but then, there's always something satisfying about fucking an angry woman into sobbing submission."

Kaden took half a step forward, the flatbow aimed directly at Balendin's chest.

"Who are you?" he asked. They were the first words he'd spoken all night.

Valyn stared. If his brother was frightened to be facing a Kettral-trained leach, he didn't show it. He looked at Balendin the way a butcher might consider a cut of meat, as though wondering how best to start carving. The veterans back on the Islands were cool, collected, but this . . . it was as though Kaden had never even *heard* of fear.

"I," the leach responded, evidently enjoying his moment, "am Balendin Ainhoa, Kettral leach serving on the Wing of one Sami Yurl, himself serving the Emperor of Annur, Kaden hui'Malkeenian." He winked. "I guess that's you. At least, for a little while longer. I imagine we'll have some trouble deciding whether you watch your brother die, or whether he watches you, but, as they say, it all works out in the end."

If the threat bothered Kaden, he didn't show it. Those bright, calm eyes just bored into the leach, and for the first time since the start of the showdown, Valyn saw Balendin's confidence falter.

"As I'm sure your brother will tell you," the leach continued, "I've developed something of a reputation for killing people slowly, strip by strip."

"We all have our hobbies," Kaden replied. He could have been discussing farming techniques.

Balendin grimaced.

It's not working, Valyn realized. *Kaden doesn't feel it. He doesn't feel the fear, the anger.* He had no idea how it was possible, but his brother didn't seem to feel *anything.*

Then, in a flash, he understood what had to happen. "Kaden!" he began, "you have to—," but his brother had already pivoted toward him, drawing that short knife of his, raising it in a quick motion as Balendin started to shout. Valyn met his brother's eyes, those icy, distant flames, as Kaden closed on him. *He doesn't feel love, either,* he realized as Kaden hammered the knife down with a savage thrust straight at Valyn's head, *or sorrow, or regret. . . .*

Kaden glanced down at his brother's body, bleeding and crumpled at his feet. Deep in the *vaniate,* everything the Shin taught him seemed so much easier, more natural, as though this final skill enabled all the rest. He had wanted to know the leach's well and so he had cast his mind into the youth's head, abandoning himself to the *beshra'an* as he listened to the conversation hum around him. It hadn't been difficult then, to determine that he drew his power from emotion. It almost seemed obvious. Then it was just a matter of knocking Valyn unconscious. Some distant part of his mind hoped he hadn't killed him, but that, too, would serve the purpose.

Kaden raised his eyes to the leach once again.

"I'm going to murder you," Balendin panted, eyes desperate, darting.

Kaden remembered what it felt like to be afraid, but only vaguely, the way you remember a story from your childhood, events so distant, they may not have really occurred.

"Unlikely," he replied, hefting his flatbow and leveling it at the youth's chest. He'd never used the weapon before, but the *saama'an* of Valyn's mimed instruction filled his head, and he released the catch and slid his finger onto the trigger.

"Even without my well, I'm still Kettral. You're just a fucking monk. You don't know shit about—"

Kaden squinted and pulled the trigger. The mechanism worked as he had anticipated. The bolt tore into the leach, and with a shriek of rage and pain, Balendin Ainhoa tumbled from the low ledge into the vast darkness of the night.

Kaden turned back to the crumpled form of his brother, knelt down, and pressed a finger firmly to his neck. He hadn't known how hard he had to strike—he'd never knocked someone out with the pommel of his knife before—and so he'd erred on the side of caution, hitting him as hard as he could.

"Valyn," he said, his own voice cold and distant in his ears. He slapped his brother roughly on the cheek. "Valyn, wake up."

It took longer than he would have expected, but after thirty breaths, Valyn's eyes flashed open. He lunged forward, snatched Kaden by the wrists, and hurled him backward onto the scree. Kaden went limp. He couldn't fight a Kettral, not hand to hand, and he could only hope that Valyn understood the situation before he killed him. His brother was snarling, forcing him down, reaching for his belt knife, his eyes inches from Kaden's own.

His eyes, Kaden realized, staring. *Someone burned away all the color in his eyes.* He hadn't noticed before, not in the darkness, not with his focus on Balendin and the approaching Aedolians, but Valyn's eyes, eyes that had always been oddly dark, had grown darker still. They looked like holes burned into nothingness.

"Balendin's gone," Kaden said, his voice calm despite the blade suddenly pressed up against his throat.

"Kaden," Valyn gasped, searching the surrounding darkness, groping in the dirt for one of his blades. "Where? *Where did he go?*"

Kaden gestured to the flatbow. "I shot him. He went over the cliff."

For a long time Valyn just stared, then he nodded, then laughed. "Holy Hull," he breathed, rocking back onto his heels, freeing Kaden. He let out a loud whoop. "Sweet 'Shael on a stick! How did you *do* it?"

"I aimed, then pulled the trigger."

Valyn shook his head. "No, the *emotion* thing. I've been training for battle for years, and I was drowning in anger, and fear, and *shit,* Kaden . . . even now you look like you've been reading a somewhat dull book."

"The Shin. They taught me . . . some skills."

"I guess they fucking *did*!" Valyn burst out, catching his brother in a huge hug. Kaden did not return the gesture.

"Don't we need to be moving?" he asked instead. "I'm not clear on the tactics here, but haste seems at a premium."

Valyn let him go. "Well, don't get all mushy on me now," he muttered.

The next few minutes were a whirlwind of activity: Valyn slapping the others awake, everyone clutching their heads, then searching desperately for lost weapons, shadows darting through the darkness.

"Kaden," Valyn gestured, "you're with me on the bird. It's the safest place for now, especially if Yurl doubles back. Talal, can you delve yet?"

The leach's eyes were still glazed, but he rose unsteadily to his feet. "I can go," he said. "I don't know . . . I don't know about a kenning. But I can go."

Valyn glanced from Talal to the darkness, then back again, as though wrestling with some decision. When he spoke, however, his voice was sure.

"You're staying here. And Triste. And Gwenna."

"Bull*shit*," the red-haired woman snapped, stepping forward.

"This is not the *time,* Gwenna," Valyn replied. "Talal is busted up worse than he knows, and I'm not leaving him alone. You're staying."

Gwenna opened her mouth to argue, then looked over at Talal, who was leaning unsteadily against a boulder. "If you get yourselves killed," she hissed, turning back to Valyn, "I will come down there and kick the shit out of your corpses."

"Agreed," Valyn said.

And then they were running down the short slope to the kettral.

"Step into this," Valyn shouted, gesturing at a harness. Kaden did as he was told, staring as the bird gathered itself in a great burst of power and leapt into the air. Under other circumstances, the flight would have been terrifying and exhilarating both, but deep inside the *vaniate,* Kaden felt only calm, distance, as though he were no more than the wind rifling his robes, no more than the snow on the peaks, or the silent clouds scrubbing the sky.

"Pyrre will be down there," he shouted, pointing toward the southeast. "She said she'd keep the others busy as long as she could."

"What are you doing with a Skullsworn?" Valyn shouted back.

Kaden spread his hands, at a loss about how to explain. "I'm not sure. She's on our side."

Valyn shot him a strange look, but nodded.

It didn't take long to find the assassin. The enemy Wing had her pinned down in a dead-end canyon about a mile and a half from the site of the Aedolian camp. One of the attacking Kettral had lit a couple of long tubes that looked like sticks, but that burned with a bright, incandescent light, illuminating the entire scene. The blond youth that Kaden took to be the Wing leader had Pyrre hemmed in, his people arranged in a loose semicircle, blocking off any escape. No one, however, had yet dared to step into the lethal circle of the woman's spinning steel.

"Why haven't they taken her yet?" Valyn bellowed in Kaden's ear. "I don't care how good she is—one arrow and she's down!"

Kaden shook his head. "They think Tan and I made it to the cave. They need to capture Pyrre alive, to question her."

Kaden had taken the assassin at her word when she insisted that it was a lot trickier to capture a foe than to kill her. After all, Pyrre was the one getting either captured or killed. Valyn nodded, as if it all made sense.

He flicked a few quick signs to the dark-skinned youth on the far talon, and moments later, the bird dipped into a steep approach. The girl with the bow, she couldn't have been much more than fifteen, was hanging out into the darkness—ever since Kaden first cut her loose, she seemed to have been aiming or shooting at something—and as they fell on the circle of soldiers from above, she drew and fired, drew and fired, three shots in quick succession, and three of the Kettral collapsed into the dust—dead so quickly, they never had time to clutch at their necks. *I never saw a man die before last night,* Kaden realized. *I didn't think it would be so easy.*

Ut turned at the last moment, just in time for the arrow to glance off his breastplate, falling away into the darkness. The other youth, the Wing leader, dived into the darkness, and then the bird was upon them, shrieking an earsplitting cry, and Valyn was leaping free of the talons, rolling as he hit the ground, a knife in one hand, short sword in the other.

†

There hadn't been much time for elaborate tactics, but the plan had seemed like a good one to Valyn: Take down the Wing's sniper, flier, and demolitions man first, and then they could deal with the more conventional threats of Ut and Yurl. Valyn's own Wing could have dropped, of course. It would be nice to have Laith and Annick at his back, but he liked having them in the air better; the altitude gave Annick a better range of attack. As his feet hit the ground, however, he realized the flaw: Ut and Yurl had fled outside the blazing light of the flares, into the darkness. The air support he had counted on was no good if the members of his Wing couldn't see what was going on. He was on his own.

"That," came a voice from behind, "is an exceptionally large bird you've got."

Valyn spun to find himself face-to-face with the knife-wielding woman—Pyrre, Kaden had called her. Skullsworn. Valyn eyed the assassin, gauging her quickly. She was breathing heavily, and her clothes were sliced open in a dozen places—whether from this fight or something earlier, it was hard to tell—but she seemed strangely relaxed. The fact that Yurl hadn't managed to take her spoke well for her abilities, that and the blood on her blades.

"They went that way," she said, pointing with one of her long knives. "I've got a score to settle with the unpleasant gentleman in all the armor, but you're welcome to kill the other one."

Valyn considered the offer. Pyrre had helped Kaden, but he didn't like the idea of relying on an assassin he'd never met before to guard his back. Of course, there wasn't much to like, and every moment he delayed was a moment Yurl could be slipping farther away or honing an ambush. "All right," Valyn replied, nodding warily. "Ut's yours. Yurl's mine. Just don't fuck up."

Pyrre smiled an easy smile. She didn't look like a murderer. "I could have used that advice a few days ago, before we got ourselves chased into these miserable mountains."

"Good luck," he said.

"And with you," Pyrre replied. "Be careful. That bastard is good."

Valyn nodded grimly. For weeks now, for *months,* he'd been biding his time, waiting for just this opportunity, a chance to face Yurl one on one. So much the better that they had flown beyond imperial borders, past the aegis of law and the ambit of Annurian justice, into these unnamed peaks, where there were no trainers or regulations, no blunted blades or codes of conduct, no one to cry foul or stop the fight. It was just what Valyn had longed for, and yet the stark fact remained: Yurl was better with his blades. He was faster and he was stronger. When it was all settled, any blood on the ground was likely to be Valyn's. It was folly to chase after him, and for a moment Valyn hesitated. He could go back for the rest of his Wing. The other man was alone now, on foot in hostile terrain with minimal provisions. It was pride and folly to pursue him alone. *There is wisdom,* Hendran wrote, *in waiting.*

But Valyn was through waiting. The man who had brutalized Ha Lin, who had tried to murder his Wing, to slaughter his brother, to end the Malkeenian line, was only a few paces away. Valyn had tried playing by the rules. For as long as he could remember, he'd tried to weigh his options, to think before acting, to make the wise choice. It had all ended in ashes: Lin dead, himself and his Wing traitors in exile. Yurl might kill him, but what did that matter? He would die eventually, either on the point of a blade or in his bed, and something inside him was stirring, a part of his mind older than conscious thought, quicker and more savage, whispering to him, rasping the same malevolent syllable over and over: *death, death, death.* Whether the death was his own or Sami Yurl's no longer seemed to matter.

✝

The sword came hard at his head—so fast, he barely had time to knock it aside. Were it not for the residual light of the flares flickering behind him,

Valyn would have missed it entirely, and as he stumbled backward, trying to regain his balance, Yurl stepped from behind an outcrop.

The other Wing leader's grin was gone. "You killed my men, Malkeenian."

"As if you cared," Valyn said, trying to gain time, to see a way through the other man's guard.

"It's an insult," Yurl replied, swords flashing out as he spoke, one high, one low, probing, pressing. Valyn parried and launched a quick riposte, but Yurl swatted it down contemptuously. "*You* are an insult," he continued, circling as he spoke. "Valyn hui'Malkeenian, son of the Emperor, Kettral Wing commander." He sneered. "And any day I chose, I could have cut you down like grass."

The swords whistled at Valyn again, a double-wing attack that folded into something else at the last minute. Valyn leaned back, tried to create space to parry just as the steel bit beneath his ribs. The wound wasn't deep, but the blood was flowing.

"This is my point," Yurl said, dropping his upper blade to gesture languidly at the wound.

Valyn started to lunge for the opening, then checked himself. It was a trap, just like in the arena, just like on the West Bluffs. Instead of pressing the weak guard, he took a step back, trying to ignore the blood sheeting down his side, trying to think. The blades might do the cutting, but as in all true swordplay, the real fight would be won or lost in the mind. Yurl's words were as much a part of the thing as his footwork, those taunts as tactical as each feint and false position. Back on the Islands, Valyn always gritted his teeth and tried to ignore the distractions, fighting on in stubborn silence, refusing to be drawn in. *Drawn in.* He almost laughed. It was a ridiculous notion. He had fled the Eyrie, abandoned his training and his life to come here, to find Yurl and to stop him, to fight this fight. He hadn't been drawn in; he had hurled himself.

"You're fucked, you know," he said, jerking his head over his shoulder toward the flares. "Your Wing's dead. The Aedolians are dead. Even if you kill me, you're fucked."

A grimace twisted Yurl's face. "Then I'll have to settle for the joy of gutting you," he said, sliding into a folding fan attack, the feint blade slicing up and across while the true thrust came from beneath. Valyn battered it aside, but Yurl moved into the space, pressing forward, forward, raining down blows from above, from the side, twisting through obscure

Manjari forms Valyn scarcely recognized and could barely block. The assault seemed to last hours, and when it was finished, Valyn could feel his breath tight in his chest. Another wound seeped blood down his shoulder.

"I'm going to kill you," Yurl said, spitting onto the ground, "just the way I killed your little bitch down in the Hole when Balendin was done with her."

"You," Valyn said, his heart a block of ice threatening to choke him.

Yurl shrugged. "Along with the leach."

It was just more talk, more tactics, but Valyn could feel the rage rabid inside him. His teeth were bared as though he planned to leap on the other man and tear out his throat. Hot blood slammed behind his eyes in a frantic, murderous tattoo.

"Too bad she's not here to help you now," Yurl continued with a shrug. "Might have made for a passably interesting fight."

Oh, Valyn realized, the memory striking him like a slap across the face. *Oh.*

As the pain flared in his shoulder and side, he shifted to his left. He was losing blood, and with it, speed. Yurl's next attack would come hard and fast, which meant Valyn had one play left, and suddenly, he knew what it had to be. A vision of Ha Lin's smile ghosted through his mind. He was only ten years old when she first saved his ass, dragging him through the end of a long swim after his legs cramped, keeping his head above the slapping chop, alternately cursing and encouraging him, her pinched child's face angry, stubborn, determined. That was the first time she'd bailed him out, but it wasn't the last. Even now, even dead, the girl wouldn't quit.

With a roar, he threw himself into a bull's horns lunge. It was a desperate gambit, an insane attack that left him open to all manner of riposte. Only, in order to riposte, Yurl would need to settle back, to set his leg, his left leg. As Valyn fell through the night, both blades outstretched, he could hear Ha Lin's voice soft in his ear: *I got in some shots of my own . . . the left ankle . . . maybe something you could work with.*

Yurl's face twisted in confusion at the unexpected lunge. His step back was basic reflex, the kind of thing drilled into every Kettral over thousands of days in the arena, the motion trained and trained and trained until it was threaded into muscle and bone alike. His body obeyed the training flawlessly, sliding fluidly down and away, dropping him into the standard off-guard crouch as he swept aside the horns of Valyn's attack, the horns that weren't the true attack at all.

Valyn rolled, ignoring the stone scraping over his wounds, lashing out with a foot at that flexed ankle. It was a feeble blow, off balance and poorly timed, but he connected just as Yurl was transferring his weight, loading the foot for the counterstrike. The ankle buckled. Yurl staggered, his own blade sliding just wide of Valyn's neck, his face twisted with rage, and fury, and, beneath it all, another emotion blossoming, something new: the sweet, hideous flower of fear.

"Lin told me you weren't the only one to land some blows up on the bluffs," Valyn said, dragging himself back to his feet.

Yurl snarled wordlessly, dropped to a knee, struggled unsteadily to his feet, raised his blades once more, hesitated, then turned and stumbled into the deeper darkness beyond the light of the flares.

The darkness, Valyn thought grimly, *is my territory. Ever since the Hole, the darkness is my home.*

He closed his eyes and let the scents and sounds of the chill night wash over him. Yurl was out there—not far. Valyn could smell him—the sweat, and blood, and steel, and beneath it all, the acrid animal odor of fear. A feral smile tugged at his lips. Hendran would never approve of racing into the dark, but then, Hendran hadn't gorged himself on the bilious tar of the black egg. He let out a low growl, turned away from the light, and slipped into the endless realm of shadow.

There were a hundred smells: stone, and dirty snow, and the whisper of rain from the clouds above. A thousand currents of air tugged at his skin, teased the hair on his arms, on his neck. With some sense he knew but failed to comprehend, he could make out dozens of faintly adumbrated forms, echoes of shapes. Beneath his feet he could feel the stones grating against his boots. Bared swords held before him, he turned silently in the night, slowly, slowly. . . . He could feel it radiating from a few paces away—heat, where there should be no heat. Breathing. That same sick fear lacing the hard scent of the mountains. *Yurl.*

He felt rather than heard the blade slicing through the darkness, felt the air eddy and part and, without a thought, flung himself into a rolling lunge as the steel hacked a huge arc out of the space above him, smashing sparks from the rock. Behind him, Yurl cursed, and Valyn turned silently to face his foe.

The Wing commander had both blades drawn, holding them in front of him in the defensive half guard the Kettral had studied for fighting blind. *He can't see me,* Valyn realized. *He knows I'm here, but he can't see me.* Evidently Talal had been right. All slarn eggs conferred a benefit, but none so great as the great black monstrosity from which Valyn had drunk.

A hundred paces off, the flares were still sputtering, and somewhere off to the left, Pyrre and Ut hacked at each other, the sharp sound of steel grinding against steel shattering the night again and again. Valyn could hear the Aedolian cursing and gasping, and beneath that the skullsworn's quieter, quick breaths. None of it mattered. Yurl was before him now, fumbling blindly.

"It's over," Valyn said.

The gravel beneath Yurl's feet crunched as he shifted. Again, there was a swirl of air, a whisper of breath, a hint of fear, and Valyn knocked his attacker's sword aside. He felt at home, he realized, here in the great darkness, and closed his eyes, allowing the sounds and scents of the world to wash over him. His tongue flicked out, tasting the night.

Hull, what did you do to me? he wondered, but it was too late for such questions. It had been too late for a long time now, he realized, for what seemed like forever. The strange alchemy in his blood wasn't the whole story, either. Something in his heart had withered when he found Ha Lin's body crumpled on the floor of the cave, some part of him that loved the light and hoped for the morning had broken. After all, when he carried his friend out into the sun, she was still dead. *Better to stay in the darkness.* Tears were running down his cheeks, blurring his vision, but then, he didn't need his vision.

"You can't win," Valyn said, following the echo of Yurl's heat. "Drop your blades now, tell me what you know, and I'll give you a clean death."

A clean death. Even as he said the words, he felt that they were a lie. He wanted to cut the youth down and tear him apart. He wanted Yurl to hurt, to cry out in the darkness and to have only his own agony for an answer.

"Go to 'Shael," the Wing leader snarled, lashing out with both swords at once in an attack the instructors back on Qarsh called the Windmill's Vanes. It was either a very arrogant move, or a very desperate one. Valyn rolled to the side easily, dodging the blow. Even from two paces away, he could feel the labored breath, the panicked heat rolling off his foe, could taste the terror.

It feels good, Valyn realized, some part of his brain recoiling at the thought even as he bared his teeth in a snarl and stepped forward.

"Who's behind the plot?" he demanded.

"If I tell you, you'll kill me," Yurl replied, retreating through the darkness, his voice tight and desperate.

With one quick, clean motion, Valyn lashed out. He felt the steel bite, severing flesh, then tendon, then bone, and half a heartbeat later, Yurl screamed and a sword clattered to the rocky ground. *His wrist,* Valyn thought, nodding to himself. There was blood on the air now, Valyn realized, inhaling deeply—sharp, coppery blood.

"I'm going to kill you anyway," he said, taking another step forward.

"All right," Yurl gasped. His other blade fell to the rock. "All right. You win. I surrender."

"I don't want you to surrender," Valyn replied. "I want you to tell me who's behind the plot."

He sniffed the air, turned his cheek to the darkness to feel the breeze waft over his skin, then lashed out with his own sword once more, slicing clean through the youth's other wrist. Somewhere far in the back of his mind, Hendran was arguing for tactical calm and useful prisoners, while even further back, other voices, his father, his mother, mouthed words like *mercy,* and *decency.* Valyn silenced them. His parents were dead now, and so was Hendran. Ha Lin had played by the rules, and she'd been humiliated, beaten, and murdered for her trouble. *Mercy* and *decency* were fine words, but they had no place here in the darkness, alone with his cornered quarry.

Yurl let out a long, agonized cry, the keening of a trapped and desperate animal.

"You can't kill me!" he sobbed. "You can't kill me. Not if you want to know who's behind what happened here. You have to keep me alive!"

"We'll keep Ut alive," Valyn growled, but as the words left his lips, he realized the sound of fighting behind him had disappeared. Where steel had echoed off steel, he could hear only the vast sweep of wind over snow and stone. Someone was dead. Valyn sniffed the air. Pyrre was moving toward him, the scent of her hair light on the night breeze. Balendin, Adiv, and now Ut, all gone. Yurl looked like the last prisoner available to them, but though Valyn knew it made sense, the blood coursed cold and dark through his veins. He didn't want a prisoner.

"No one else knows the whole thing," Yurl moaned. He was on his knees now, sobbing desperately. "Please. You have to keep me alive."

"Tell me what you know," Valyn said, "and I'll take you back to the Eyrie for justice." Another lie, tripping off his lips like song.

"All *right*. It's a plot . . . it's . . ."

"I know it's a plot," Valyn replied. "Who is behind it?"

"I don't know. Don't know his name. But he's Csestriim. I know that. He's Csestriim."

Valyn paused. The Csestriim were ancient history, the last of them slaughtered more than a thousand years earlier. Yurl's claim was insanity, and yet . . . groveling in the dirt, his hands lopped from his wrists, he couldn't be lying.

"What else?" Valyn pressed.

"I don't know anything else," Yurl moaned. "That's it. That's all I know. Please, Valyn. I'm begging you."

Eyes still closed, Valyn stepped closer, close enough to press the point of his dagger against Yurl's gut. The youth had pissed himself, and the scent of blood and urine mingled, sharp and acrid in the cool night air.

"You're begging me?" he asked, voice little more than a whisper.

"I'm begging you," Yurl sobbed.

"What about Ha Lin? Did she beg you?"

"I'm sorry about Lin. It's not what you think. It was never what you thought."

"Did she beg you?" Valyn demanded, pushing the knife forward until it just broke the skin.

"I don't know! I can't remember!" He pawed at Valyn with the bloody stumps, but Valyn brushed them away.

"Not good enough," he ground out, driving the knife a hair deeper. "Down in the Hole . . . did you help Balendin kill her?"

"I didn't," Yurl babbled. "I didn't mean to. It wasn't—"

Valyn shoved the knife a little more. "Still not good enough."

"Sweet Eira's mercy, Valyn," Yurl wailed, stretching out his lopped arms hopelessly, "what's good enough for you? What's fucking good enough?"

Valyn considered the question. *What's good enough?* Once, he would have known the answer. Before his father was murdered. Before he climbed the stairs to the airless attic where Amie's body hung. Before he carried Lin from the dark mouth of Hull's Hole. *Justice? Revenge?* He shook his head. *Now . . .*

"I don't know," he replied, burying the blade to its hilt in Yurl's guts, feeling the muscles clench helplessly around it, then twisting it free. "Maybe nothing's good enough anymore."

The youth let out a long, ragged moan, then sagged to the ground.

Valyn straightened, wiping the dagger on his blacks. In the cloud-draped pall of night, he couldn't see the corpse, couldn't see what he had done, but then, he didn't need to see. He slipped the blades back into their sheaths. It was all around him on the midnight air—blood and offal, desperation and death. He could smell it, he realized with a shudder, part fear, part satisfaction. He could taste it.

49

The midnight gong tolled once, twice, three times, shivering the cool spring night, rousing Adare from where she coiled sleepily against Ran.

"It's late," she murmured, wrapping an arm tighter around his waist.

"Or early," he replied, returning her embrace and adding a light kiss on her forehead. "The list of petitions that need reading before tomorrow's audience is as long as my arm, and your little affair over at the Temple of Light didn't make things any easier."

"Did I make your life difficult?" Adare asked with mock solicitude, propping herself up on one elbow. "I'm so *sorry*. How can I possibly atone?" She batted her lashes.

Ran grinned, pulling her closer. "I can think of one or two ways."

She plunged into the kiss with a fierce abandon while a tiny part of her mind marveled at the situation. She hadn't intended to sleep with il Tornja when she burst into his chambers with news of her success, hadn't even allowed herself to consider the thought. Adare hui'Malkeenian had spent her entire life knowing that the most crucial contribution she could make to the empire would be the giving of her hand in marriage. An imperial marriage could avert a war, seal a crucial trade agreement, or cement an alliance with a powerful aristocratic house. *The choice is not yours,* her father had told her gently but firmly time and time again, *any more than I choose when to go to war, or receive a delegation from the Manjari.*

She thought she had long ago accepted the constraints of her position and yet, as she had recounted the showdown with Uinian over a glass of Si'ite red, as she saw the admiration and then the hunger in Ran's eyes, it suddenly seemed a small thing, less than nothing to fall into his arms. Only after, when they lay together, bodies pressed close in the tangled sheets, did she pause to reflect on the spectacular folly of what she had done. It *had* been folly, that much was clear, and yet it didn't feel wrong. *He's not a stable boy,* she reminded herself. *He's the* kenarang, *the 'Kent-kissing* regent. Were they to marry, no one could accuse her of matching beneath her station.

And so she had stayed while the night wore on, until it seemed pointless to return to her own chambers.

"I will sleep here tonight," she murmured, nestling her face into the firm flesh of his shoulder, "with you."

"You're welcome to the bed," il Tornja replied, "but you'll be the only one sleeping."

He kissed her once more on the forehead, then groaned as he rolled upright.

"Where are you going?" she asked sleepily.

"The horseshit associated with regency is never-ending," he replied. "The sooner your brother gets back here, the better."

"You're doing work now?"

"I'm not going far," he said, nodding toward the heavy wooden desk across the room. "If you get frisky, I'll be right over there."

Adare grinned and fell back against the pillows, weariness and satisfaction washing over her in great soft waves. She felt good. Good to be in Ran's bed. Good to have avenged her father. Good to have eliminated a threat to the Malkeenian line. For the first time in her life, she felt as though she had been truly tested, and she had passed the test. *I'm sorry about Ran, Father,* she thought, *but you taught me well. I'm playing my part.*

The thought of her father brought back the memory of his final bequest, the gift that he mentioned in his testament: Yenten's *History of the Atmani.* She tossed in the bed for a while, but sleep had left her, and finally she sat up.

"Can you send one of your slaves to my chambers for a book?" she asked.

"Am I keeping you up?" He turned and gestured to the lamp. "I can dim this a little if you want. We can't have the Imperial Princess uncomfortable."

"The Imperial Princess is just fine, thank you. The Imperial Princess has a yen for some reading material. It's Yenten's *History.* My father left it to me."

He raised an eyebrow. "A little light reading."

"I'm not just a princess," she replied, sticking out her chin. "I'm also the Minister of Finance."

"You know," he said carefully, "that the gongs have already tolled midnight. Tongues will be wagging about how late you lingered with the *kenarang*. . . ."

She stiffened. "You want me gone?"

He raised a conciliatory hand. "I want you here. Tonight. Tomorrow night. And all the nights after that. I'm just asking if it's wise."

She relaxed back into the bed. "A certain general once told me," she said with a smile, "that you need to know when to plan, and when to act. Well, I'm acting finally, and realizing I have a taste for it."

"So be it," he replied before crossing the room, sticking his head out the door, and murmuring something to the slave just beyond.

A few minutes later, the man returned and passed a thick leather-bound codex through the gap in the door. Ran hefted it in his hand, flipped a couple of pages, then shrugged and tossed it onto the bed beside her. It landed with a thump.

"One chapter ought to put you right to sleep. Worse than these 'Shael-spawned petitions."

"Just because you're an ignorant soldier doesn't mean the rest of us don't appreciate some high-minded thought from time to time."

"I should have stayed an ignorant soldier," he replied, lowering himself back into the desk chair with a groan and turning to the stack of parchment. "Ut and that bastard Adiv had best hurry up with your brother or I'll have plunged the empire into darkness before they get back."

Adare ignored the complaint and wriggled up in the bed until she had her back against the wall and the great book propped up on her knees. For a while, she just considered the cover. Her father had taught her so much, and this book would be, in a way, his final lesson. She opened it, perused the first page, then flipped ahead, trying to get a sense of the scope. Some maps, some tables—the sort of reading a man like Ran couldn't stand but that she found fascinating. Another map, another inventory. She was about to flip back to the start to begin reading in earnest when she turned another page to find a loose leaf of paper tucked deep into the spine. Curious, she drew it out and unfolded it, then froze. It was her father's hand.

She glanced up furtively, but Ran was still at his desk, his back to her, scratching away with his quill at some page or other. She flipped the paper over, but there was writing on one side only.

> *Adare.*
>
>   *You are reading this, and so I am dead and my gambit has succeeded. I could not place this note in my testament, because our foes were certain to read that testament before you, to alter it if necessary.*
>
>   *Months ago, I learned of a conspiracy arrayed against me, against the Malkeenian line, most likely against Annur itself. As I write, there have already been four attempts on my life. They were all subtle, probing, and unsuccessful, but I have been unable to track the beasts to their lair and each day they are testing, learning. It will not be long before they succeed and I am dead.*
>
>   *Rather than allowing my attackers to dictate the time and place, I plan to use this life of mine as a stone to be played on the board, a stone that may turn the tide of this silent battle we wage. As yet I do not know our foes' identities, but I have theories and suspicions. I have arranged secret meetings with those I mistrust, meetings I will attend without the protection of my Aedolians or the knowledge of the councillors. I will give these schemers the opportunity to strike me down with impunity, and I will leave a record of these meetings to you, that you will know whom to fear and fight after I am gone.*

Adare reeled. A list followed, a dozen or so appointments with times, places. Her father had met with Baxter Pane and Tarik Adiv, Jennel Firth and D'Naera of Sia. He had met on ships in the harbor and in alehouses by the White Market, in secret chambers of the Dawn Palace, and beyond the boundaries of the city. There were more than a dozen names on his list, powerful men and even a few women, but her eyes fell down the page to the only one that mattered:

> *On the evening of the new moon, I will meet with the* kenarang, *Ran il Tornja, in our family's private chapel in the Temple of Light.*

The evening of the new moon. The Temple of Light. She had been certain Uinian was responsible for her father's death, had seen the man torn apart for his transgression, had reveled in his destruction. She stared, first at the page before her, then at the naked back of the *kenarang,* of her lover, as he sat toiling over his papers. *Sweet 'Shael,* she thought, shivers running over her naked flesh. *Sweet, holy Intarra, what have I done?*

When the most paralyzing horror had passed, she turned her eyes back to the page.

I do not intend to die without a fight, Adare. Perhaps I shall win, though I find it unlikely. The foe we face is both sly and strong, thwarting me at each pass. I will bring my sword to these meetings, but you are my last blade. You, and Kaden, and Valyn. If you feel, any of you, that you have been hammered hard, it has been that you might better hold an edge.

Heed what I write here, Adare. Heed it, though it may implicate someone you have known a long time, someone you trust. You cannot bargain with this foe, cannot reason with him, cannot find an accommodation. Whoever it is, you must stop at nothing to bring him down. I have dispatched people to warn and protect Kaden and Valyn, but you alone are privy to this final letter.

The final lines were not a declaration of love or an expression of sorrow in the face of imminent death. Neither would have been Sanlitun's way. His last words to her were hard and practical:

Resist faith. Resist trust. Believe only in what you touch with your hands. The rest is error and air.

Adare raised her eyes from the page. Blood pounded in her ears, burned beneath her skin. Her own breath sounded ragged in her chest. She folded the paper neatly along the creases and tucked it back into the book, flipping a few pages to conceal it. Ran sat at his desk still, grumbling over whatever work lay before him. She could still feel his seed warm against her thigh.

The man shifted in his chair, then turned.

She forced a smile onto her face.

"Bored of that book already?" he asked, raising an eyebrow. "Looking for something a little more . . . engaging?" He winked.

She wanted to scream, to run, to pull the blankets over her head, to bury herself in the bed, in the very earth. She wanted to flee the room, to race back to her chambers in the Crane where the Aedolians stood guard over her door. All at once, she felt like a girl again, lost, and frightened, and confused. But she was not a girl. She was a princess, a minister, and maybe the last living Malkeenian.

I am a blade, she told herself.

The man before her had murdered her father, manipulated her, and escaped justice. She forced herself to meet his eye and let the blanket slip from her shoulders, revealing her naked breasts.

"Only if you think you can handle it," she replied.

50

Kaden sat cross-legged on a jagged escarpment above the Aedolian camp, ignoring the bite of the wind and the exhausted ache of his feet and shoulders, following the two kettral with his eyes as they quartered the sky. At this distance, it was difficult to judge their scale—they might have been ravens or hawks wheeling on the thermals, the kind of birds he had spent countless hours observing from the ledges above Ashk'lan. In fact, if he didn't glance back over his shoulder at the piled corpses of the traitorous guardsmen, if he kept his mind from the bloody edges of his memory, he might have been back at the monastery, seated on one of the jagged ledges, waiting for Pater or Akiil to jar him from his thoughts and drag him back for the evening meal. It was a pleasant delusion, and he lingered in it awhile, luxuriating in the lie, until a flash of sun on steel caught his eye: the birds were returning, and as they drew closer, as he made out the small figures perched on the talons, it became impossible to believe that they were normal birds of prey.

Valyn had taken his own kettral—Suant'ra, Kaden reminded himself—and that of the defeated Wing to search for Balendin and Adiv, neither of whose bodies had been found. The birds had been in the air the better part of the day, circling farther and farther from the camp, until Kaden was certain their quarry had eluded them. It should have been impossible; both men were wounded, at least slightly, without food or water, and on foot in treacherous country. But, as the Shin would say: *There is no should; there is only what is.* The two traitors had already proved themselves as unpredictable as they were dangerous, and who was Kaden to say that they didn't have further powers at their disposal, powers as yet unrevealed? Neither the leach nor the councillor had frightened Kaden while he was inside the *vaniate,* but now that he had let the trance lapse, the thought that they were out there somewhere, wandering the mountains, filled him with unease.

He watched as the two birds approached the ridge, considered the black-clad figures as they leapt from the talons, dropping a dozen feet or so to the rubble and coming up unharmed. They were young, this Wing of Valyn's, younger than the Kettral Kaden remembered from his child-hood—or was that only a trick of memory? Despite their age, the four soldiers under Valyn's command moved with a confidence and economy that could only come from long years of training, checking weapons and gear unconsciously, touching hands to hilts, scanning the surrounding ter-rain, running through a hundred habits built up over the years. Even the youngest of the lot, the Wing's sniper, seemed steadier, deadlier, than some of the Aedolians around whom Kaden had grown up. And then there was Valyn.

After gesturing to Laith to tie up the bird, Valyn looked around the camp, spotted Kaden on the ledge, and turned up the slope toward him. He was not the boy Kaden remembered from their childhood duels in the Dawn Palace. He had grown up and out, filling his broad shoulders in a way that Kaden never would, wearing the blades on his back as though they were a part of him, keeping his jaw clenched tight most of the time, and fingering the scars on his hands and arms as though they were good luck. It was the eyes, however, that had changed most of all. Unlike Kaden, Sanlitun, or Adare, Valyn had always had dark eyes, but nothing like this. These were holes into some perfect darkness, wells from which no light escaped. It wasn't the scars or the swords that made Valyn seem dangerous; it was the depth of those eyes.

His boots crunched over the scree, and when he reached Kaden, he paused, gazed out at the peaks beyond, then grimaced.

"I've got no idea where those bastards went. There should have been something, some kind of track. . . ." He trailed off. A nasty gash on his lower lip had opened up, and he spat blood over the edge of the cliff. The wind whipped it out and away, flinging it into the gulf.

"Sit down," Kaden said, gesturing to the rock. "You've been flying all day."

"For all the 'Kent-kissing good it did us," Valyn replied. Still, after a moment, he lowered himself to the ledge with a groan.

"I feel like someone's been beating me with the blunt edge of a board for the past week," he said, twisting his head, stretching the muscles of his neck. He balled his hands into fists, cracked the knuckles, then frowned at the palms as though he'd never seen them before. "Every part of my body hurts."

Kaden smiled wearily. "I thought you Kettral lived for this sort of thing. Martial valor, godlike endurance, the daily cheating of Ananshael—"

"Nah," Valyn replied, plucking at his torn, sweat-stained blacks. "I mostly got into it for the clothes."

"You should have been a monk. It's hard to beat a wool robe."

Valyn chuckled, and the two stared out over the mountains and valleys, side by side, companions in the simplicity of silence. Kaden would have remained there all day if he could, all year, enjoying the low rush of water, the sound of the wind knifing between the passes, the sun warm on his cool skin. He knew these things, understood them in a way he had ceased to understand his own brother, ceased to understand himself.

"So," Valyn said after a long while, "what do I call you now?"

Kaden kept his eyes on the far mountains as he revolved the question. During the long flight from the monastery, he hadn't had a chance to grieve for his father or consider his new station in life. After eight years with the Shin, he wasn't even sure he knew *how* to grieve anymore. The fact that he was Emperor of Annur, sole sovereign over two continents, leader of millions, felt like just that, a fact; the truth had not penetrated to any organ that could actually feel it. A part of him wanted to make a joke, to laugh it off with a wry remark, but the impulse felt wrong, somehow, unfair to the monks who had died, to Valyn's Wing, who had flown all this way to rescue him, to his father, who also had spent long years as an acolyte in the Bone Mountains and now lay cold in his tomb.

"I suppose it's 'Your Radiance' now," Valyn continued, shaking his head. "That's the protocol, right?"

Kaden stared at the blazing orb of the lowering sun. He wondered if his eyes looked like that.

"It is," he replied finally. Then he turned to Valyn. "But when we're not around others . . . When there's just the two of us . . . I mean *someone's* got to use my name, right?"

Valyn shrugged. "It's up to you. Your Radiance."

Kaden closed his eyes against the honorific, then forced himself to open them once more. "What happened with the other Wing leader?" he asked. "With Yurl?"

He'd seen the body—a carcass, really—gutted, the hands hacked away, eyes bulging with an expression that could only have been terror. It was a savage killing, purposeless in its violence.

Valyn grimaced, met his eyes, looked away, and for a moment Kaden caught a glimpse of the child he had known a decade earlier—uncertain but unwilling to show it, trying to put a bold face on his confusion.

"There was a girl, Ha Lin . . . ," he began, then trailed off, fingering a nasty scab on the back of his hand, ripping it free in a wash of blood without even glancing down. When he looked back at Kaden, his eyes were hooded again, unreadable. He looked like a soldier. *More than a soldier,* Kaden thought, *a killer.*

"All I could think was, *Not again.* I wasn't going to let him hurt anyone else. Never again." He clenched his fists, and blood flowed from the wound, puddling on the stone.

"But his hands . . . ," Kaden said, slowly. "Was it necessary?"

"*Fuck* necessary," Valyn replied, voice hard and brittle as steel too long hammered.

Kaden considered his brother for a long time, trying to read the tight cords running beneath his skin, the unconscious grimace, the nicks and scars that marked his face and hands. It was like studying a scroll in some long-forgotten language. *Rage,* Kaden reminded himself. *This is rage, and pain, and confusion.* He recognized the emotions, but after so many years among the Shin, he had forgotten how raw they could be.

Finally, he reached out and placed a hand over Valyn's fist. The monks weren't much for physical contact, and the sensation was odd, something remembered from a childhood so distant, it might have been a dream. At first Kaden thought his brother would pull away, but after a dozen heartbeats he felt the fist relax.

"What happened?" Kaden asked. "What happened to you?"

Valyn snorted. "Got a week?"

"How about the short version?"

"I learned to kill people, saw some people killed, fought some nasty beasts, drank some nasty stuff, and came out with black eyes, powers I don't understand, and enough rage to burn a city to the bones.

"What about you?" he asked, the question more challenge than inquiry. "You're not exactly the bookish monk I'd been expecting. I thought you were going to murder me last night."

Kaden nodded slowly. If Valyn had changed in the years apart—well, then, so had he. "The short version?"

"We can delve into details later."

"I got hit, cut, frozen, and buried. Men I trusted killed everyone I knew, and then, for a few minutes, I figured out how to stop caring about any of it."

Valyn stared at him. Kaden met the gaze. The silence stretched on and on until, without warning, Valyn started laughing, slowly at first, almost morbidly, then with more abandon, his body shaking on the narrow ledge until he was wiping away tears. Kaden watched for a while, confused, detached, until some childish part of him, something buried deep inside his mind awoke and responded. Then he was laughing, too, gasping in great breaths of air until his stomach hurt.

"Holy Hull," Valyn choked, shaking his head. "Holy fucking Hull. We should have stayed in the palace and kept playing with sticks."

Kaden could only nod.

✝

"It's not over," Tan said.

Kaden turned to find the monk climbing the short steep slope to where they sat, Pyrre a foot or so behind him. For a few pleasant minutes, the brothers had sat side by side, laughing at horror, trying to recollect something of their past, but the past was gone, finished, and the future loomed. A hundred paces back, in the dubious shelter of the pass, the rest of the group was making preparations to move out; Laith checked over the bird while the sniper and the red-haired girl sorted through the weapons of the dead Aedolians. Triste was shoving something that might have been food into a large sack.

As Tan drew alongside, he reached into his robe, then flicked something out onto the ledge. It rolled toward Kaden, bumping up against his leg before coming to rest.

Valyn looked up at the monk, then picked up the small red orb, squeezing it between his fingers until it bulged like a grape.

"What is this?"

"An eye," Kaden said, the mirth gone out of him as quickly as it had come. The memory of the ring of *ak'hanath* circling tighter and tighter, bloody eyes flickering in the moonlight, chilled him. How Tan had emerged from that fight at all, he couldn't say, though the battle had taken its toll: the monk's robe was cut to tatters, his body bruised. A long gash ran from his scalp to his jaw, and Triste had spent the better part of the day washing out the long rents in his flesh, binding them with bandages made from the uniforms of the dead Aedolians.

"Must've been an ugly bastard," Valyn said, considering the eye a moment longer, then flicking it toward Kaden, "but at least it *had* eyes." Something dark and haggard passed across his gaze.

Kaden caught the sphere, turned it until he could consider the pupil in the fading light—a dark, ragged slash, like something hacked out of the iris with a knife.

"How are your wounds?" he asked, looking up at Tan.

The monk moved stiffly, but his face betrayed no pain, and he waved a hand as though the question didn't warrant an answer. Kaden wondered briefly if the man had found a way to *live* inside the *vaniate*.

"The Csestriim have returned," he said.

"Csestriim," Valyn replied, sucking air between his teeth. "That's what Yurl claimed. It's tough to believe."

"It is *necessary* to believe," Tan replied. "Some of them have survived this long precisely because people *failed* to believe."

"Adiv?" Kaden asked, voicing the question that had been on his mind all day as he watched the kettral circle and search. "You think he's Csestriim?"

Tan considered him with a flat, disapproving stare. "Speculation."

Valyn glanced from the older monk to his pupil and back. If he felt any deference toward Tan, Kaden couldn't see it.

"I'm not sure what's so wrong with speculation, and I have no 'Kentkissing idea where those two bastards ended up, but I'll tell you one thing—they're not our problem anymore."

Kaden frowned. "One of them might be Csestriim and the other is a Kettral-trained emotion leach who nearly destroyed your Wing."

"And now we have two birds," Valyn shot back. "Balendin and the minister are on foot with no food or water and no gear to speak of. We can be in the air by nightfall and out of this miserable maze of mountains you call home by morning. Of course," he added grimly, "that brings us to our real problem—the Flea."

Kaden looked over at Tan and Pyrre. The Skullsworn shrugged; Tan made no reply at all.

"What," Kaden asked finally, turning back to Valyn, "is a flea?"

"The Flea is the best Wing commander in the Eyrie. He makes Yurl and me look like children, and his Wing is just as good as he is."

"And he's part of the plot?" Pyrre asked. Ut had left her with a light slice across the shoulder, but otherwise she seemed none the worse for wear. "Why can't some of the really dangerous players be on *our* side for a while?"

"I have no idea if he's part of the plot," Valyn replied, his expression bleak, "but I'll tell you this—he's coming for us, sure as shit. He's probably one day back, sent up as soon as my Wing went rogue. Yurl and Balendin were part of it, and we don't know how far up the conspiracy goes."

Pyrre shrugged. "If he's not part of the plot, he's not part of the problem. Kaden," she said, making an exaggerated curtsy, "bright be the days of his life, rules the empire now, which means he waves his little finger and your Flea has to start bowing or kissing the dirt or whatever it is you Annurians do."

"You don't know much about the Flea," Valyn said, "or about Kettral. It's the *mission* that matters. My Wing disobeyed orders to come after you. As far as the Eyrie's concerned, we're traitors."

"The Kettral serve the empire," Pyrre replied, "which means they serve the Emperor, which means, they serve him." She poked a finger at Kaden. "Working for Kaden is, by definition, not treachery."

"It's not quite that simple," Kaden said, thinking through this angle for the first time. "Imperial history has been pretty messy at times: brother fighting brother, sons killing fathers. Atlatun the Unlucky murdered his own father out of impatience. What was it, Valyn, four hundred years ago?"

Valyn shook his head. "If there wasn't a battle involved, I didn't study it."

"There wasn't a battle. Atlatun wanted to rule, but his father looked a little too healthy for his taste, so he stabbed him in the eye over the dinner table. The point is, despite being Atlatun's heir and having Intarra's eyes, he was executed for treason. The Unhewn Throne went to his nephew."

"You didn't kill your father," Pyrre pointed out. She frowned. "You didn't, did you?"

"No," Kaden replied, "but no one in Annur knows that. Whoever is behind the conspiracy could be spreading whatever rumors they want. They could be claiming that Valyn and I cooked up a plot against our father together, that we paid that priest to kill him while we were out of the capital."

"Until we know conclusively otherwise," Valyn said, "we have to figure the Eyrie views us as traitors."

"And how does the Eyrie handle traitors?" Kaden asked.

"They send people," Valyn replied.

"The Flea."

"His Wing might be in the mountains already."

"The mountains are endless," Pyrre said. "I've been running around the 'Kent-kissing things for the past week. The nine of us could have a parade with pennons and drums, and no one would find us."

"You don't know what they can do," Valyn replied, eyeing the dusky sky as he spoke. "I trained with them, and *I* don't know what they can do." Kaden followed his brother's gaze, searching above the snowy peaks for a hint of movement, for any suggestion of a dark bird bearing death on her wings.

"All I know is that he's coming," Valyn said. "I don't know how he'll do it, I'm not sure when, but he's coming."

"Then we will have to handle him," Tan replied.

Kaden watched Valyn turn to his *umial*, incredulity playing across his face.

"*Handle* him? And just who in Hull's name *are* you, old man? You've got the robe, but I've never heard of monks running around with gear like that," he said, indicating the *naczal* in Tan's left hand.

The monk met the gaze but refused to answer the question.

"All right," Pyrre said, spreading her hands, "let's take these birds, fly back to Annur, and set things straight. It's not like they won't know who you are—those ridiculous eyes have got to be good for something."

"Who made you a part of this, assassin?" Tan asked grimly.

Pyrre cocked her head to the side. "After I saved the Emperor *and* killed that ox of an Aedolian, you expect me to *walk* out of here?"

"She's coming," Kaden said, surprised at the certainty in his own voice. "We've got two birds. That should be enough to take everyone." He glanced over at Valyn.

Valyn nodded. "We can be in Annur in a week if we fly hard. If we stay ahead of the Flea. Maybe a little more."

Kaden turned his gaze west, to where the sun had just sunk behind the icy peaks. *Annur. The Dawn Palace. Home.* It was tempting to think that they might simply mount the kettral, fly from the carnage, return to the capital, and avenge his father. It was tempting to think it might be so easy to set things right, but from somewhere, the old Shin aphorism came back to him: *Believe what you see with your eyes; trust what you hear with your ears; know what you feel with your flesh. The rest is dream and delusion.*

". . . and stay well north, over the empty steppe," Tan was saying.

"No."

Three pairs of eyes turned to Kaden, boring into him.

"You don't think the steppe is the best route?" Valyn asked. "It'll keep us clear of the Annurian territory south of the White River—"

"I'm not going west at all. Not yet."

Pyrre squinted. "Well, to the north, there's a whole heap of ice and frozen ocean, south takes us right back toward any pursuit from the Eyrie, so—"

"And we can't go east," Valyn cut in. "Not that we'd have any reason to. Past the mountains there's just Anthera, and we'd all be killed on sight if we landed there. Il Tornja authorized some pretty nasty operations over the border in the past few years. We've got to go west, got to get back to the capital."

Pyrre was nodding. "How far north of the White do you think we need to fly to avoid these unsavory friends of yours?"

Kaden shook his head slowly, something hardening inside him. He didn't know what was going on in Annur, and neither did anyone else. It was tempting to return, to believe that the people would hail his arrival, but that was the dream and the delusion. His foes had killed his father, had very nearly destroyed his entire family, and the only certainty remaining was that someone was hunting him, guessing at his movements, tracking.

He thought back to the early spring, to the long cold day he had spent tracking a lost goat through the peaks, inhabiting its mind, feeling for its actions, following its decisions until he ran it down. *I will not be that goat; I will not be hunted.* If the Shin had taught him anything, it was patience.

"The rest of you *should* fly west. Go to Annur to try to see what's happening there as quickly as possible."

"The rest of you?" Pyrre asked with a raised eyebrow.

Kaden took a deep breath. "I am going to visit the Ishien. Tan and I both."

The older monk's face hardened, but it was Valyn who spoke.

"And just who in 'Shael's name are the fucking Ishien?"

"A branch of the Shin," Kaden replied. "One that studies the Csestriim. One that hunts the Csestriim. If the Csestriim are involved in this, they might know something."

"No," Tan said finally. "The Ishien and the Shin parted ways long ago.

You are expecting quiet monks and hours of contemplation, but the Ishien are a harder order. A more dangerous order."

"More dangerous than the *ak'hanath*?" Kaden asked. "More dangerous than a contingent of Aedolian Guards come to kill me in my sleep?" He paused. "More dangerous than the Csestriim?"

"I don't know shit about the Ishien," Valyn interjected, "but I'm not letting you wander off without protection. You're tougher than I'd expected, but you still need my Wing for cover."

Tan shook his head. "You do not know what you ask for."

"I am not asking," Kaden replied, stiffening his voice. "Valyn, I need your Wing back in the capital and soon, to sort out what happened there before the trail goes cold."

"Then we'll go visit the Ishien first, and then we'll *all* go to the capital."

Kaden opened his mouth to try to explain it once more, then closed it. Perhaps he could convince his *umial* and the others, and perhaps he could not—that was beside the point. He never asked for his eyes, but they burned just the same.

"Tan and I are going," he said once more. "The rest of you are returning to Annur. There is no more to the matter unless you would disobey your Emperor."

Pyrre chuckled and opened her mouth to speak. For a moment Kaden thought he'd made a fool of himself. They were thousands of leagues from the Dawn Palace, lost in a labyrinth of mountains, fleeing from the people he had been born to command. Why should a Skullsworn, a renegade monk, and a Kettral Wing leader listen to him, a boy with one robe to his name?

Then, all in one motion, Valyn stood. Kaden rose stiffly to his feet as well, in time to see his brother touch a hand to his blades before kneeling and placing his knuckles to his forehead.

"It will be as you say, Your Radiance. I will make the birds ready at once."

When Valyn finally raised those black eyes, Kaden could see nothing in them, not even his own reflection.

GODS AND RACES, AS UNDERSTOOD BY THE CITIZENS OF ANNUR

RACES

Nevariim—Immortal, beautiful, bucolic. Foes of the Csestriim. Extinct thousands of years before the appearance of humans. Likely apocryphal.

Csestriim—Immortal, vicious, emotionless. Responsible for the creation of civilization and the study of science and medicine. Destroyed by humans. Extinct thousands of years.

Human—Identical in appearance to the Csestriim, but mortal, subject to emotion.

THE OLD GODS, IN ORDER OF ANTIQUITY

Blank God, the—The oldest, predating creation. Venerated by the Shin monks.

Ae—Consort to the Blank God, the Goddess of Creation, responsible for all that is.

Astar'ren—Goddess of Law, Mother of Order and Structure. Called the Spider by some, although the adherents of Kaveraa also claim that title for their own goddess.

Pta—Lord of Chaos, disorder, and randomness. Believed by some to be a simple trickster, by others, a destructive and indifferent force.

Intarra—Lady of Light, Goddess of Fire, starlight, and the sun. Also the patron of the Malkeenian Emperors of Annur, who claim her as a distant ancestor.

Hull—The Owl King, the Bat, Lord of the Darkness, Lord of the Night, aegis of the Kettral, patron of thieves.

Bedisa—Goddess of Birth, she who weaves the souls of all living creatures.

Ananshael—God of Death, the Lord of Bones, who unknits the weaving of his consort, Bedisa, consigning all living creatures to oblivion. Worshipped by the Skullsworn in Rassambur.

Ciena—Goddess of Pleasure, believed by some to be the mother of the young gods.

Meshkent—The Cat, the Lord of Pain and Cries, consort of Ciena, believed by some to be the father of the young gods. Worshipped by the Urghul, some Manjari, and the jungle tribes.

The Young Gods, all coeval with humanity

Eira—Goddess of Love and mercy.

Maat—Lord of Rage and hate.

Kaveraa—Lady of Terror, Mistress of Fear.

Heqet—God of Courage and battle.

Orella—Goddess of Hope.

Orilon—God of Despair.

Turn the page for a sneak peek at
Book II of the Chronicle of the Unhewn Throne

THE
PROVIDENCE
OF FIRE

Available January 2015

1

Kaden hui'Malkeenian did his best to ignore both the cold granite beneath him and the hot sun bearing down on his back as he slid forward, trying to get a better view of the scattered stone buildings below. A brisk wind, soaked with the cold of the lingering snows, scratched at his skin. He took a breath, drawing the heat from his core into his limbs, stilling the trembling before it could begin. His years of training with the monks was good for that much, at least. That much, and precious little else.

Valyn shifted at his side, glancing back the way they had come, then forward once more.

"Is this the path you took when you fled?" he asked.

Kaden shook his head. "We went that way," he replied, pointing north toward a great stone spire silhouetted against the sky, "beneath the Talon, then east past Buri's Leap and the Black and Gold Knives. It was night, and those trails are brutally steep. We hoped that soldiers in full armor wouldn't be able to keep up with us."

"I'm surprised they were."

"So was I," Kaden said.

He levered himself up on his elbows to peer over the spine of rock, but Valyn dragged him back.

"Keep your head down, Your Radiance," he growled.

Your Radiance. The title still sounded wrong, unstable and treacherous, like spring ice on a mountain tarn, the whole surface groaning even as it glittered, ready to crack beneath the weight of the first unwary foot. It was hard enough when others used the title, but from Valyn the words were almost unbearable. Though they'd spent half their lives apart, though both were now men in their own right, almost strangers, with their own secrets and scars, Valyn was still his brother, still his blood, and all the training, all the years, couldn't quite efface the reckless boy Kaden remembered from his childhood, the partner with whom he'd played blades and bandits, racing through the hallways and pavilions of the Dawn Palace. Hearing him use the official title was like hearing his own past erased, his childhood destroyed, replaced utterly by the brutal fact of the present.

The monks, of course, would have approved. *The past is a dream,* they used to say. *The future is a dream. There is only now.* Which meant those same monks, the men who had raised him, trained him, were not men at all, not any more. They were rotting meat, corpses strewn on the ledges below.

Valyn jerked a thumb toward over the rocks that shielded them, jarring Kaden from his thoughts. "We're still a good way off, but some of the bastards who killed your friends might have long lenses."

Kaden frowned, drawing his focus back to the present. He had never even considered the possibility of long lenses—another reminder, as if he needed another reminder, of how poorly his cloistered life at Ashk'lan had prepared him for this sudden immersion in the treacherous currents of the world. He could paint, sit in meditation, or run for days over rough trail, but painting, running, and meditation were meager skills when set against the machinations of the men who had murdered his father, slaughtered the Shin monks, and very nearly killed him as well. Not for the first time, he found himself envying Valyn's training.

For eight years he had struggled to quell his own desires and hopes, fears and sorrows, had fought what felt like an endless battle against himself. Over and over the Shin had intoned their mantras: *Hope's edge is sharper than steel. To want is to lack. To care is to die.* There was truth to the words, far more truth than Kaden had imagined when he first arrived in the mountains as a child, but if he had learned anything in the past few days, days filled with blood, death, and confusion, he had learned the limits to that truth. A steel edge, as it turned out, was plenty sharp. Clinging to the self might kill you, but not if someone put a knife in your heart first.

In the space of a few days, Kaden's foes had multiplied beyond his own persistent failings, and these new enemies wore polished armor, carried swords in their fists, wielded lies by the thousands. If he was going to survive, if he was to take his father's place on the Unhewn Throne, he needed to know about long lenses and swords, politics and people, about all the things the Shin had neglected in their single-minded effort to train him in the empty trance that was the *vaniate*. It would take years to fill in the gaps, and he did not have years. His father was dead, had been dead for months already, and that meant, prepared or not, Kaden hui'Malkeenian was the Emperor of Annur.

Until someone kills me, he added silently.

Given the events of the past few days, that possibility loomed suddenly, strikingly large. That armed men had arrived with orders to kill him and destroy the monastery was terrifying enough, but that they were comprised of his own Aedolian Guard—an order sworn to protect and defend him—that they were commanded by high-ranking Annurians, men at the very top of the pyramid of imperial politics, was almost beyond belief. In some ways, returning to the capital and sitting on the Unhewn Throne seemed like the surest way to help his enemies finish what they had started.

Of course, he thought grimly, *if I'm murdered in Annur, it will mean I made it* back *to Annur, which will be a success of sorts.*

Valyn gestured toward the lip of the rocky escarpment that shielded them. "When you look, look slowly, Your Radiance," he said. "The eye is attracted to motion."

That, at least, Kaden knew. He'd spent enough time tracking crag cats and lost goats to know how to remain hidden. He shifted his weight onto his elbows, inching up until his eyes cleared the low spine of rock that concealed him. Below and to the west, maybe a quarter mile distant, hunched precariously on a narrow ledge between the cliffs below and the vast, chiseled peaks above, stood Ashk'lan, sole monastery of the Shin monks, and Kaden's home.

Or what remained of it.

The Ashk'lan of Kaden's memory was a cold place but bright, scoured clean, an austere palate of pale stone, wide strokes of snow, vertiginous rivers shifting their glittering ribbons, and ice slicking the north-facing cliffs, all piled beneath a hard, blue slab of sky. The Aedolians had destroyed it. Wide sweeps of soot smudged the ledges and boulders, and fire had lashed the junipers to blackened stumps. The refectory, meditation hall, and dormitory stood in ruins. While the cold stone of the walls had refused to burn, the wooden rafters, the shingles, the casings of the windows, and broad pine doors had all succumbed to the flame, dragging sections of masonry with them as they fell. Even the sky was dark, smudged with oily smoke that still smoldered from the wreckage.

"There," Valyn said, pointing to movement near the northern end of the monastery. "The Aedolians. They've made camp, probably waiting for Micijah Ut."

"Gonna be a long wait," Laith said, sliding up beside them. The flyer grinned.

Before the arrival of Valyn's Wing, all Kaden's knowledge of the Kettral came from the stories he had lapped up as a child, tales that had led him to imagine grim, empty-eyed killers, men and women steeped in blood and destruction. The stories had been partly right: Valyn's black eyes were cold as last year's coals, and Laith—the Wing's flier—didn't seem at all concerned about the wreckage below or the carnage they had left behind. They were clearly soldiers, disciplined and well-trained, and yet, they seemed somehow young to Kaden. Laith's casual smile, his obvious delight in irritating Gwenna and provoking Annick, the way he drummed on his knee whenever he got bored, which was often—it was all behavior the Shin would have beaten out of him before his second year. That Valyn's Wing could fly and kill was clear enough, but Kaden found himself worrying, wondering if they were truly ready for the difficult road ahead. Not that he was ready himself, but it would have been nice to think that *someone* had the situation in hand.

Micijah Ut, at least, was one foe Kaden no longer needed to fear. That the massive Aedolian in all his armor had been killed by a middle-aged women wielding a pair of knives would have strained belief had Kaden not seen the body. The sight had brought him a muted measure of satisfaction, as though he could set the weight of steel and dead flesh in the scales to balance, in some small part, the rest of the slaughter.

"Anyone want to sneak into their camp with Ut's body?" Laith asked. "We could prop him up somewhere, make it look like he's drinking ale or taking a leak? See how long it takes them to notice the fucker's not breathing?" He looked from Valyn to Kaden, eyebrows raised. "No? That's not why we came back here?"

The group of them had returned to Ashk'lan that morning, flying west from their meager camp in the heart of the Bone Mountains, the same camp where they had fought and killed the men chasing them down, Aedolians and traitorous Kettral both. The journey had occasioned a heated debate: there was broad agreement that someone needed to go, both to check for survivors and to see if there was anything to be learned from the Annurian soldiers who had remained behind when Ut and Tarik Adiv chased Kaden into the peaks. The disagreement centered on just *who* ought to make the trip.

Valyn didn't want to risk bringing anyone outside his own Wing, but Kaden pointed out that if the Kettral wanted to make use of the snaking network of goat tracks surrounding the monastery, they needed a monk familiar with the land. Rampuri Tan, of course, was the obvious choice—he knew Ashk'lan better than Kaden, not to mention the fact that, unlike Kaden, he could actually *fight*—and the older monk, despite Valyn's misgivings, seemed to consider his participation a foregone conclusion. Pyrre, meanwhile, argued that it was stupid to return in the first place.

"The monks are dead," she pointed out, "may Ananshael unknit their celibate souls. You can't help them by poking at the bodies."

Kaden wondered what it felt like to be the assassin, to have lived so close to death for so long that it held no terror, no wonder. Still, it was not the bodies he wanted to go back for. There was a chance, however small, that the soldiers had captured some of the monks rather than killing them. It wasn't clear what Kaden could do if they had, but with the Kettral at his back it might be possible to rescue one or two. At the very least, he could look.

Tan had dismissed the notion as sentimental folly. The reason to go back was to observe the remaining Aedolians, to ferret out their intentions; Kaden's guilt was just further evidence of his failure to achieve true detachment. Maybe the older monk was right. A true Shin would have rooted out the coiling tightness that snaked about his heart, would have cut out, one by one, the barbs of emotion. But then, aside from Tan and Kaden himself, the Shin were dead: two hundred monks murdered in the night because of him, men and boys whose only goal was the empty calm of the *vaniate* burned and butchered where they slept to cover up an Annurian coup. Whatever waited at Ashk'lan, it had happened because of Kaden. He had to go back.

The rest was simple. Valyn commanded the Wing, Valyn obeyed the emperor, and so, in spite of Tan's objections and Pyrre's, in spite of his own concerns, Valyn had bowed his head and obeyed, flying Kaden along with the rest of the Wing to discover what was left of his mountain home. They landed the bird a little to the east, out of sight of the monastery, then covered the final miles on foot. The track was easy, mostly downhill, but the tension built in Kaden's chest as they drew closer.

The Aedolians hadn't bothered to hide their slaughter. There was no need. Ashk'lan lay well beyond the border of the empire, too high in the mountains for the Urghul, too far south for the Edish, too far from anywhere for merchants and traders, and so the brown-robed bodies had been left to litter the central courtyard, some burned, others cut down as they fled, dried blood staining the stones.

"Lots of monks," Laith pointed out, nodding toward the monastery. "All pretty dead."

"What about them?" Valyn asked, pointing toward a row of figures seated cross-legged on the far side of the ledge, staring out over the steppe. "Are they alive?"

Laith raised the long lens. "Nope. Stabbed. Right in the back." He shook his head. "Not sure why they're sitting there. No one tied them."

Kaden looked at the slumped men for a moment, then closed his eyes, imagining the scene.

"They didn't run," he said. "They sought refuge in the *vaniate*."

"Yeah . . ." the flyer said, drawing out the syllable skeptically. "Doesn't look like they found it."

Kaden stared at the corpses, remembering the awesome emotional vacancy of the trance, the absence of fear, or anger, or worry. He tried to imagine what they had felt sitting there, looking out over the wide green steppe while their home burned a few paces behind them, watching the circling ravens as they waited for the knife. "The *vaniate* might surprise you," he said quietly.

"Well, I'm tired of being surprised," Valyn growled. He rolled onto his side to look at Kaden, and once again Kaden found himself trying to see his brother—the brother he had once known—beneath the scars and lacerations, behind those unnaturally black eyes. Valyn the child had been quick to smile, to laugh, but Valyn the soldier looked harried, haunted, hunted, as though he distrusted the very sky above him, doubted his own battered hand and the naked sword it held.

Kaden knew the outlines of the story, how Valyn, too, had been stalked by those who wanted to bring down the Malkeenian line. In some ways, Valyn had had it worse than Kaden himself. While the Aedolians had struck suddenly and brutally into the heart of Ashk'lan itself, the soldiers had been strangers to Kaden, and the sense of injustice, of betrayal, remained abstract. Valyn, on the other hand, had seen his closest friend murdered by his fellow soldiers. He'd watched as the military order to which he'd devoted his life failed him, failed him or betrayed him. Kaden still worried about the possiblity that the Kettral command, the Eyrie itself, was somehow complicit in the plot. Valyn had reason enough to be tired and wary, and yet there was something else in that gaze, something that worried Kaden, a darkness deeper than suffering or sorrow.

"We wait here," Valyn went on, "out of sight, until Annick, Talal, and Gwenna get back. If they don't find any monks, *living* monks, we hump out the way we came in, and get back on the 'Kent-kissing bird."

Kaden nodded. The tension from the walk in had lodged deep in his stomach, a tight knot of loss, and sorrow, and anger. He set about loosening it. He had insisted on coming back for the survivors, but it looked as though there were no survivors. The residual emotion was doing him no good, was, in fact, obscuring his judgment. As he tried to focus on his breath, however, the images of Akiil's face, of Pater's, of Scial Nin's, kept floating into his mind, startling in their immediacy and detail. Somewhere down there, sprawled among those blasted buildings, lay everyone he knew, and everyone, aside from Rampuri Tan, who knew him.

Someone else, someone without the Shin training, might find relief in the knowledge that those faces would fade over time, that the memories would blur, the edges soften; but the monks had taught him not to forget. The memories of his slaughtered friends would remain forever vivid and immediate, the shape of their sprawled forms would remain, carved in all its awful detail. *Which is why*, he thought grimly, *you have to unhitch the feeling from the fact.* That skill, too, the Shin had taught him, as though to balance the other.

Behind him, soft cloth scraped over stone. He turned to find Annick and Talal, the Wing's sniper and leach, approaching, sliding over the wide slabs of rock on their bellies as though they'd been born to the motion. They pulled up just behind Valyn, the sniper immediately nocking an arrow to her bow, Talal just shaking his head.

"It's bad," he said quietly. "No prisoners."

Kaden considered the leach silently. It had come as a surprise to discover that men and women who would have been burned alive or stoned to death for their unnatural abilities anywhere else in Annur served openly with the Kettral. All Kaden's life he'd heard that they were dangerous and unstable, their minds warped by their strange powers. Like everyone else, he'd grown up on stories of leaches drinking blood, of leaches lying and stealing, of the horrifying leach-lords, the Atmani, who in their hubris shattered the very empire they had conspired to rule.

Another thing about which I know too little, Kaden reminded himself.

In the short, tense days since the slaughter and rescue, he had tried to talk with Talal, to learn something about the man, but the leach was quieter, more reserved than the rest of Valyn's Wing. He proved unfailingly polite, but Kaden's questions yielded little, and after the tenth or twelfth evasive response, Kaden gave up his talk in favor of quiet observation. Before they flew out, he had watched the leach smudge the bright hoops in his ears with coal from the fire, then his bracelets, then his rings, working the char into the metal until it was almost as dark as his skin.

"Why don't you just take them off?" Kaden had asked.

"You never know," Talal had replied, shaking his head slowly, "what might come in handy out there."

His well, Kaden realized. Every leach had one, a source from which he drew his power. The stories told of men who could pull strength from stone, women who twisted the sharp grip of terror to their own ends. The metal hoops looked innocuous enough, but Kaden found himself staring at them as though they were venomous stone spiders. It took an effort to stamp out the emotion, to look at the man as he was, not as the tales would paint him. In fact, of all the members of Valyn's Wing, Talal seemed the most steady, the most thoughtful. His abilities were unnerving, but Valyn seemed to trust him, and Kaden didn't have so many allies that he could afford the prejudice.

"We could spend all week hunting around the rocks," Talal went on, gesturing to the serrated cliffs. "A couple of monks might have slipped the cordon—they know the territory, it was night . . ." He glanced over at Kaden and trailed off, something that might have been compassion in his eyes.

"The whole southeastern quadrant is clear," Annick said. If Talal was worried about Kaden's feelings, the sniper seemed indifferent. She spoke in clipped periods, almost bored, while those icy blue eyes of hers scanned the rocks around them, never pausing. "No track. No blood. The attackers were good. For Aedolians."

It was a telling crack. The Aedolians were some of Annur's finest soldiers, hand-picked and exhaustively trained to guard the royal family and other important visitors. How this particular group had been incited to betrayal, Kaden had no idea, but Annick's obvious disdain spoke volumes about her own abilities.

"What are they doing down there?" Valyn asked.

Talal shrugged. "Eating. Sleeping. Cleaning weapons. They don't know

about Ut and Adiv yet. Don't know that we arrived, that we killed the soldiers chasing you."

"How long will they stay?" Kaden asked. The slaughter seemed absolute, but some part of him wanted to descend anyway, to walk among the
rubble, to look at the faces of the slain.

"No telling," Talal replied. "They've got no way to know that the smaller
group, the one that went after you, is dead."

"They must have a protocol," Annick said. "Two days, three days, before
searching or retreating."

Laith rolled his eyes. "It may shock you to discover, Annick, that some
people aren't slaves to protocol. They might not actually *have* a plan."

"Which is why we would kill them," the sniper replied, voice gelid, "if
it came to a fight."

Valyn shook his head. "It's not going to come to a fight. There've got to
be seventy, eighty men down there—"

A quiet but fierce cursing from behind them cut into Valyn's words.

"The 'Kent-kissing, Hull-buggering *bastard*," Gwenna spat, rolling
easily over a spine of rock into a low, ready crouch. "That whoreson, slit-
licking ass."

Valyn rounded on her. "Keep your voice down."

The red-haired woman waved off the objection. "They're a quarter-mile
off, Valyn, and the wind's blowing the wrong way. I could sing the 'Shael-
spawned Kettral attack anthem at the top of my voice and they wouldn't
notice."

This defiance, too, surprised Kaden. The soldiers he remembered from
back in the Dawn Palace were all rigid salutes and unquestioned obedience. While it seemed that Valyn had the final call on decisions regarding
his Wing, none of the others went out of their way to defer to him. Gwenna,
in particular, seemed determined to nudge her toe right up to the line of
insubordination. Kaden could see the irritation on his brother's face,
the strain around his eyes, tension in the jaw.

"*Which* bastard are we talking about now?" Laith asked. "There are
plenty to go around these days."

"That fancy prick, Adiv," Gwenna said, jerking her head towards
the northwest. "The one with the blindfold and the attitude."

"The Mizran Councillor," Kaden interjected quietly. It was one of
the highest posts in the Empire, and not a military position. Kaden had
been surprised, even before the betrayal, when the man arrived with the

contingent of Aedolians. Now it was just more evidence, as if he needed more, that the conspiracy had penetrated the most trusted quarters of the Dawn Palace.

"Whatever his job is," Gwenna replied, "he's over there, on foot, picking his miserable way out of the mountains. Couldn't have missed our bird by more than a few hundred paces."

Valyn sucked air between his teeth. "Well, we knew Tarik Adiv was alive when we didn't find the body. Now we know where he is. Any sign of Balendin?"

Gwenna shook her head.

"That's something, at least," Valyn replied.

"It is?" Laith asked. "No doubt Balendin's the more dangerous of the two."

"Why do you say that?" Kaden asked.

Laith stared. "He's *Kettral*," he replied finally, as if that explained everything. "And a leach."

"Adiv is a leach himself," Talal pointed out. "That's how they kept up with Kaden in the mountains, how they tracked him."

"I thought they used those 'Shael-spawned spider creatures for the tracking," Laith said.

Talal nodded. "But someone needed to control them, to handle them."

"It doesn't matter now," Valyn said. "Right now Balendin's missing and Adiv is here. Let's work with what we have."

"I've got eyes on him," Annick said.

While they were talking, the sniper had moved silently to a concealed spot between two boulders, half drawing her bowstring.

Kaden risked a glance over the ridge. At first he saw nothing, then noticed a figure limping down a shallow drainage three hundred paces off. He couldn't make out the Councillor's face at that distance but the red coat was unmistakable, the gold at the cuffs and collar badly tarnished but glinting in the midday light.

"He made good time," Talal observed.

"He's had a night, a day, another night, and a morning," Gwenna said scornfully. "It's not more than seventy miles from where we lost him."

"As I said," Talal replied. "Good time."

"Think he cheated?" Laith asked.

"I think he's a leach," Talal said.

"So . . . yes," the flyer concluded, grinning.

"Remind me not to 'cheat,'" Talal replied, fixing the flier with a steady stare, "the next time you're in a tight place."

"Take him down?" Annick asked. The bowstring was at her ear now, and though the strain must have been immense, she remained as still as stone.

Kaden glanced over the ridge again. At this distance he could barely make out the blindfold wrapping Adiv's eyes.

"Isn't he too far off?"

"No."

"Take the shot, Annick," Valyn said, turning to Kaden. "She'll make it. Don't ask me how."

"Stand by," the sniper responded after a pause. "He's passing behind some rock."

Kaden looked from Annick to Valyn, then to the small defile where Adiv had disappeared. After hours of lying on their bellies, waiting, and watching, things were abruptly going too fast. He had expected the long wait to be followed by conversation, deliberation, a review of the facts and exchange of ideas. Suddenly, though, with no discussion at all, a man was about to die, a traitor and a muderer, but a man all the same.

The Kettral didn't seem concerned. Gwenna and Valyn were staring over the rock, the demolitions master eagerly, Valyn silent and focused. Laith was trying to make a wager with Talal.

"I'll bet you a silver moon she kills him with the first shot."

"I'm not betting against Annick," the leach replied.

The flyer cursed. "What odds will you give me to take the other side? Ten to one for her to miss?"

"Make it fifty," Talal said, resting his bald head against the rock, considering the sky.

"Twenty."

"No," Kaden said.

"Fine. Twenty-five."

"Not the bet," Kaden said, putting a hand on Valyn's shoulder. "Don't kill him."

Valyn turned from the valley below to look at Kaden. "What?"

"Oh for the sweet love of 'Shael," Gwenna growled. "Who's running this Wing?"

Valyn ignored Gwenna. Instead, his black eyes bored into Kaden, drinking the light. "Adiv's behind all this, Your Radiance," he said. "He and Ut. They're the ones that killed the monks, that tried to kill you, not to mention the fact that they're clearly involved in our father's murder. With Ut gone, Adiv is the ranking commander down there. We kill him, we take a head off the beast."

"I have him again," Annick said.

"Don't shoot," Kaden insisted, shaking his head, trying to order his thoughts. Years earlier, while attempting to recapture a goat, he'd lost his footing above the White River, plunging down the rocks and into the current. It was all he could do to breathe, to keep his head above the roiling surface, to fend off the jagged boulders as they loomed up before him, all the time knowing that he had less than a quarter mile to pull himself clear of the torrent before it plunged him over a cliff. The immediacy of the moment, the inability to pause, to reflect, the absolute necessity of *action* had terrified him and, when he finally caught hold of a fallen limb, clawing his way up and out, the feeling left him shaking on the bank. The Shin had taught him much about patience, but almost nothing of haste. Now, with the eyes of the entire Wing upon him, with the coal-smudged point of Annick's arrow fixed on Adiv, he felt that awful, ineluctable forward rush all over again.

"A few more seconds," Annick said, "and he'll be in the camp. It'll be more difficult to take him then."

"*Why?*" Valyn demanded, staring at Kaden. "Why do you want him alive?"

Kaden forced his eddying thoughts into a channel, the channel into speech. There would be no second chance to say what he had to say. The arrow, once loosed, would not be called back.

"We know him," he began slowly. "We need him. Back in Annur we can observe who he talks to, who he trusts. He'll help us to unravel the conspiracy."

"Yeah," Gwenna snapped, "and maybe he'll murder a few dozen more people on the way."

"I'm losing him," Annick said. "Decide now."

"Oh for 'Shael's sake," Laith grumbled. "Just kill him already. We can sort out the details later."

"No," Kaden said quietly, willing his brother to see past to the present, to understand the logic. "Not yet."

Valyn held Kaden's gaze for a long time, jaw tight, eyes narrowed. Finally he nodded. "Stand down, Annick. We have our orders."